Masquerade

Masquerade

The Lives of Noël Coward

OLIVER SODEN

W&N
WEIDENFELD & NICOLSON

First published in Great Britain in 2023 by Weidenfeld & Nicolson
an imprint of The Orion Publishing Group Ltd
Carmelite House, 50 Victoria Embankment
London EC4Y 0DZ

An Hachette UK Company

3 5 7 9 10 8 6 4 2

A CIP catalogue record for this book is
available from the British Library.

ISBN (Hardback) 978 1 4746 1280 7
ISBN (Export Trade Paperback) 978 1 4746 1281 4
ISBN (eBook) 978 1 4746 1283 8
ISBN (Audio) 978 1 3996 0645 5

Typeset by Input Data Services Ltd, Somerset

Printed in Great Britain by Clays Ltd, Elcograf S.p.A.

FSC
www.fsc.org

MIX
Paper from
responsible sources
FSC® C104740

www.orionbooks.co.uk

Noël Coward's bookplate

For Eileen Atkins

Gaiety transfiguring all that dread . . .

W. B. Yeats, "Lapis Lazuli"

To be free is often to be lonely . . .

W. H. Auden, "In Memory of Sigmund Freud"

It's all a question of masks, really . . .

Noël Coward, *Design for Living*

CONTENTS

LIST OF ILLUSTRATIONS

Frontispiece
Noël Coward's bookplate, designed by Gladys Calthrop

FIRST PLATE SECTION

p. 548 Eleven-year-old Noël Coward (*right*), making his stage debut as Prince Mussel in Lila Field's *The Goldfish*, 1911.

PROLOGUE

Ladies and Gentleman.
A prologue to a play is out of date
A leisurely technique of masquerade
So please regard me as a friendly shade,
Returning down the years to indicate,
More by my presence than by what I say,
The atmosphere and setting of this play . . .

Noël Coward, *Conversation Piece*

Another biography of Noël Coward?! But in fact there have been only four cradle-to-grave accounts of his life, none published in the last three decades. Remove from that list books by those who knew him well or who were refused permission to quote from his work, and there has been only one. Philip Hoare's *Noël Coward*, a magnificent feat of research that vastly extended our knowledge and understanding of its subject, appeared in 1995, when gay marriage was illegal and a law prohibiting the "promotion" of homosexuality was still in force.

In the intervening years a great deal of new information has come to light. Hundreds of letters and notebooks have been made available from Coward's private archive; a memoir written by his first partner has been discovered; lost scripts turned out not to be lost at all. Directors and scholars have begun to treat him with increasing seriousness. Forgotten plays have found productions and stagings of even his most familiar comedies have revealed an intensity and mournfulness we had not known were there. Time and mortality permit a new biography a freer, more disinterested, hand. The attitudes of society towards Coward's alternative designs for living and loving have changed utterly. There are new things to say about him; he has new things to say about us.

He was born a Victorian, in 1899; he died in 1973, seventeen years – to the day, oddly enough – before I was born. The most pressing reason to write about him afresh, from a half-century's distance, is that no biography has been published in my adult lifetime. It is worth presenting Coward to a new generation with whom he has much in common. He was always at his peak, as both playwright and songwriter, during periods of frenzied social change and liberation achieved against a backdrop of potential destruction. A century on from his first productions, in what is said to be a second "roaring twenties", the young stagger out into the light after a global catastrophe and, fearful of the environmental crisis, rebel against the certainties of previous generations and search for new ways of life. Ours is a divided and serious-minded age and we may be in need of someone who once wrote the line: "Be flippant. Laugh at everything."

There is rarely a week when one or other of *Private Lives*, *Hay Fever*, and *Blithe Spirit* is not in production, somewhere in the world. Phrases from Coward's songs – "Mad About the Boy", "Mad Dogs and Englishmen" – are in the public consciousness. It is no longer necessary to persuade readers of his lasting worth and quality, but, fifty years after his death, the scope and complexity of his output are still underestimated. Coward roved further and wider than the public conception of the varnished wit, the cigarette holder, the dressing-gown. Some of his most striking and daring writing lies outside the central clump of classics and remains unfamiliar. It is a shock to stumble across T. S. Eliot arguing, in 1954, "there are things you can learn from Noël Coward that you won't learn from Shakespeare".[1]

Coward was protean and inconsistent and above all prolific. Quite apart from his acting and directing, he wrote some fifty plays and nine musicals, as well as revues, screenplays, short stories, poetry, and a novel. He was both composer and lyricist for approximately 675 songs. Ardent Coward completists must forgive inevitable absences, but I have tried to burrow in unexpected corners, aiming especially to recreate his interwar revues. Lost to modern audiences, they are among his most radical inventions, in which he caught,

with accurate and exhilarating daring, the spirit of his age. Even those who dislike Coward's work will perhaps concede that the story of his astonishing life is worth telling and re-telling. So central was he to his age's theatre that any account of his career is also a vicarious history of the British stage in the twentieth century.

The challenges Coward sets to a biographer are many. A jumble of contradictions, he has inspired hagiography (testifying to his radical modernity, his charm, his generosity, his astonishing array of talents) and hatchet-job (baulking at his ego, his ruthlessness, his need for fame, his increasingly reactionary politics). He was, above all, *witty*, but wit is an elusive thing to capture within the pages of a book. It relies on delivery; it can rarely be tracked to its source. It must be light as air, such that attempts to work out how it is done risk its collapse. It is much easier to make the case for tragedy than comedy — just try arguing that *The Code of the Woosters* is on a level with *Anna Karenina*. Numerous volumes compile Coward's epigrams and witticisms, which vary wildly from account to account . . . and then turn up somewhere else, attributed to Wilde or Churchill.

I have been able to use hitherto unpublished letters and diary entries to let Coward speak not through gossip and anecdote but in his most private and intimate words: witty, certainly, often riotously and outrageously so, but revealing a man of surprising gravity and bleakness. His was the gaiety of a man who knew grief, a comic self-creation grounded in suffering and taking refuge in perform- ance as an armour against a dangerous world. Only half-mockingly he told Cecil Beaton that he took "ruthless stock of myself in the mirror before going out. A polo jumper or unfortunate tie exposes one to danger."[2]

Edward Albee once wrote an essay titled "Notes for Noël about Coward". This book is about Noël, rather than Coward, and is least of all about "the Master", that self-invented and unhelpful nickname, which manages to be both fawning and, with its Jack- of-all-trades undertones, dismissive. Designed to deflect attention from the man to the legend, it has accidentally cordoned off Cow- ard's work from serious appreciation. I have tried above all to give a sense of being in his company, although the surest means of conjuring his presence would be to douse the pages in cigarette smoke and Guerlain's Vétiver. The composer Ned Rorem, briefly his lover, thought him "among the golden few who, though seen but rarely, are so giving, so volatile, so *there* (not looking beyond you at someone more important), that their brief presence is more memorable than certain dear friends enjoyed daily".[3]

This book is biography rather than literary criticism, and discussion of Coward's work is contained within the narrative. Nevertheless, I have lingered over his greatest plays with the aim of restoring them to their rightful place at the centre of any account of his life. Louis Mountbatten's famous tribute argued that, while there were greater comedians, greater novelists, greater composers, greater painters and so on, only "the Master" had combined fourteen talents in one. Coward's range cannot be ignored, but his versatility has distracted from his foremost achievement and lasting importance: he wrote some of the most imperishable plays of his century, and was a songwriter who could set words dancing with one another. (It is no surprise that the comedian Victoria Wood, one of his truest heirs, nominated him as among the few lyricists whose work she enjoyed.) I have tried to refresh familiar material by considering how it would have appeared when it was new, and by binding Coward into the literary context that he often affected to despise, be that the modernism of the 1920s, of which he increasingly seems an integral part, or the Angry Young Men of the 1950s, of whom he can be seen as a vital ancestor. The surest means of weakening Coward's reputation is to defend him on his own terms; the biggest risk when writing about him is any attempt to be Coward-esque. His plays have long since escaped his protestations that he intended merely to entertain and amuse an adoring public; they repay serious consideration. To miss Coward's seriousness is to miss his wit.

As the cliché has it, he was his own greatest creation. But as first-hand memories fade, his oeuvre has survived the absence of a creator to whom it was once indissolubly bound. Among Coward's contemporaries were any number of celebrated novelists or composers, from Michael Arlen to Lord Berners, legendary for living eccentric lives in the public eye. Wonderful characters of their own creation, they were more captivating than anything in their work: interest in their writing rests on interest in their life. Even Somerset Maugham is now better known through biographies than through his books and plays. With Coward it is the opposite. Our conception of him is a result of continued fascination with his work, which he created only partly as a means of presenting himself to the world.

He admitted that his output varied hugely in quality. It is impossible to argue that his post-war plays are on the level of his earlier successes. His biographies risk being top-heavy, his most interesting inventions clustering in early chapters. One option for a fresh account would be to eschew chronology. But, with an uncanny eye on posterity, Coward ensured his life had a built-in structure that it would be foolish to ignore. His last years were a time of renaissance, restoring his reputation and (arguably) his talent. My imperfect solution has been not to scramble the chronology but to vary the pace. When covering his life after 1945, this book moves with much greater speed, on the logic that his day-by-day activities during this period can be charted in his published diaries, and that few readers will be familiar with his later plays, most of which are rarely, if ever, revived.

By far the biggest obstacle to anyone who seeks to write about his character is that it was just that: a performance of a character called "Noël Coward". The biographer snags himself on those quotation marks. ("Camp," said Susan Sontag, "sees everything in quotation marks.") Much of his writing is about the pain of being always on show, of being trapped within his own masquerade; in this too, for a generation performing to a permanent (online) audience, his relevance has been reignited. His was an extravagant array of lives, in which he cast himself in different lead roles; a seemingly endless masked ball, to which disguise and façade were inherent. This was a solution to the dangers of his homosexuality, which was illegal for most of his life. But it was also a means of surviving a world about which he was consistently and wittily embittered. One of his childhood loves was for the masked characters of commedia dell'arte, and his work is patterned with masks and masques, both metaphorical and literal. His famous song "Dance, Little Lady" was first staged to a crowd of eerily masked figures. Masks were used in his play *Conversation Piece* and for a sketch in his 1932 revue *Words and Music*: "We're going to do a Midnight Matinee! | We're going to

do a Midnight Show! | A sort of 'Masque' | Where everyone will
ask | And nobody will ever know." In *Sigh No More*, another revue,
he wrote a pageant featuring "the spirit of masque".

In an attempt to capture the way in which he seemed so often to
be playing a role, living as if on a stage, I have split this book into nine
sections, its shape taken from his nine-play sequence, *Tonight at 8.30*.
Each section is loosely structured as one of the varied genres in which
he wrote: plays, musicals, revues, screenplays, short stories. Passages
written as dialogue use only verbatim quotations; nothing is made up.
The final part is fashioned entirely as a play-script. It seemed a natural
conclusion to an enacted life, which was conducted either side of a
disconcertingly permeable barrier between theatre and reality.

This biography is the first to be written since the formation of
two major archives, both of which collate thousands of documents
previously in private hands. After Coward died, a large number of
papers ended up at the London flat of his secretary Joan Hirst; upon
her death, in 2002, these became the Noël Coward Collection at the
Cadbury Research Library, University of Birmingham. The remainder
of Coward's archive was meanwhile in Switzerland, in the posses-
sion of his partner, Graham Payn, who died in 2005. This collection
led to the formation, in 2017, of the Noël Coward Archive Trust,
which holds over 20,000 items at the Noël Coward Room, and
its overflow storage facility, in London. To both these collections
I have had unrestricted access.* When quoting from manuscript, I
have included all of Coward's idiosyncrasies of spelling and grammar in his childhood writing, but otherwise have silently expanded
abbreviations, emended rare spelling mistakes, maintained emphatic
underlining, and added any punctuation that will aid the reader.
Cuts are indicated by an ellipsis in square brackets. I have used
the latest edition of the collected plays (Bloomsbury, 2nd revised

---

* At the time of writing, further information about the Noël Coward Archive
  Trust, and details as to access, can be found at www.noelcoward.com

edition, 9 vols, 1999–2018), but to keep references to a manageable number I have cited only extensive quotations.

The three main sources from which Noël Coward's life can be chronicled – memoirs, correspondence, diaries – were all a means by which he fashioned his own legend. The three volumes of memoirs are now published together as his *Autobiography*, in which the opening volume, *Present Indicative* (1937), covers the first three decades of his life. The book contains gaps and (according to his closest childhood friend) inaccuracies. While we know what brand of baby food his mother favoured (Allen and Hanburys), we do not know the address of one of the houses in which Coward grew up, nor the name of his first school. *Future Indefinite* (1954) recounted the years of the Second World War but revealed very little of Coward's undercover activities; critics agreed that it was not on the level of its predecessor. In the mid-1960s Coward began, but never finished, *Past Conditional*, an account of his professional success and global travel in the thirties; it was released posthumously. All three autobiographies, which could only hint at his private life, are essentially "ghost-written", which is to say written by Noël Coward's public, rather than private, self. In one of Coward's final plays, *A Song at Twilight*, an ageing writer publishes a memoir described as a "superlative example of sustained camouflage".

There are fewer surviving letters written *by* Noël Coward than might be supposed, and at the time of writing no collected or scholarly edition exists (a valuable selection was published in 2007). Little effort was made during his lifetime to keep copies of outgoing letters, of which – excluding telegrams – roughly a thousand survive in collections across the world. Of these, a great many are of the "Mr Coward regrets . . . ", "Darling, thank you so much for . . . " variety. Letter paper was for Coward an empty stage, leading to documents that are theatrical and amusing, extravagant in their protestations of love and gratitude, but revealing for what they do not reveal. Coward rarely bared his soul in correspondence. Wartime communications were written under the cloche of censorship; the illegality of his sexuality during a lifetime of intense fame and scrutiny led to secrecy. *A Song at Twilight* features a young biographer hoping to track down secret love letters; few such documents are to be found in Coward's archive.

For the last three decades of his life Coward was a dutiful diarist.
He began on 1 January 1940 and continued with some regularity
until January 1970. Even during the war he rarely skipped a week,
carrying the journals with him around the world. The entries chart
– as a biography of readable length cannot – the sheer energy
with which he lived, the least eventful of days still swarming with
social engagements, performances seen and given, books read,
words written. But they mainly chronicle the least acclaimed period
of his career, capturing him at his most reactionary and, often,
bitter. The reader can pinpoint with precision the moment (halfway
through 1953) when the entries begin to be made with a view
to publication. *The Noël Coward Diaries* appeared in 1982, nine years
after his death, and, generous as the 700-page selection was, its
editors were coy about just how much had been omitted. This is
the first book about Coward to be given unlimited access to, and
permission to quote freely from, the unexpurgated diaries. I have
worked from facsimiles, held by the Noël Coward Archive, of the
handwritten manuscripts (the originals are at Yale University).*
There are twenty-seven volumes in all; around 5,500 handwritten
pages. *The Noël Coward Diaries* included a large proportion of the
post-war material but only a handful of excerpts from the wartime
journals, which contain over 1,900 entries. Many of these, not least
the 1940 diary, entirely unpublished hitherto, reveal in more detail
than ever before the nature and extent of his clandestine wartime
employment: one of the chief aims of this book is to give the fullest
account yet of Coward's life during the Second World War.

Coward was always conscious of the mass of material he was
leaving behind. As he wrote in his diary on 31 December 1969: "I
can only suggest to any wretched future biographer that he gets my
daily engagement book and from that fills in anything he can find.
And good luck to him. Poor bugger."[4]

---

* The original 1940 diary is lost, although complete transcript copies survive.
  The original diaries for 1966 and 1967 are held by the Coward Archive in
  London.

THE RAINBOW

___

An Edwardian Comedy in Six Scenes

CAST

MASTER NOËL COWARD, *a stage-struck little boy*

MRS VIOLET COWARD, NÉE VEITCH, *his mother*

MR ARTHUR COWARD, *his father*

MASTER RUSSELL COWARD, *his older brother*

MASTER ERIC COWARD, *his younger brother*

MISS ESMÉ WYNNE, *a young actress*

MISS LILA FIELD, *a playwright*

MISS JUNE TRIPP, *a young actress*

MASTER ALFRED WILLMORE, *a young actor*

MR CHARLES HAWTREY, *an actor-manager*

MR PHILIP STREATFEILD, *an artist*

MRS EVANGELINA (EVA) ASTLEY COOPER, *a socialite*

ASSORTED AUNTS, ACTORS, TEACHERS

The action moves from suburban townhouses to the theatres of London's West End.

TIME: 1899–1914

SCENE ONE

The scene is the stage of the Duke of York's Theatre in London, Christmas 1913.

What you see is the Neverland. You have often half seen it before, or even three-quarters, after the night-lights were lit. The figure who has emerged from his tree is MASTER NOËL COWARD, *dressed as* SLIGHTLY *in a fur coat and top hat, his boots striped in pink and black.* SLIGHTLY *is conceited. He thinks he remembers the days before he was lost, with their manners and customs. It is impossible to tell whether he is thirteen or thirty or seventy.*

SLIGHTLY: My mother was fonder of me than your mothers were of you. Peter had to make up names for you, but my mother had wrote my name on the pinafore I was lost in. "Slightly Soiled"; that's my name.

A lady falls out of the sky. It is SLIGHTLY*'s idea that they shoot her: the Wendy-bird. She falls to earth to lie unconscious at their feet.*

SLIGHTLY: This is no bird. I think it must be a lady.

The lady stirs; the arrow has caught in a button. PETER PAN *thinks the button is a kiss.*

SLIGHTLY: I remember kisses; let me see it. [*He takes it in his hand.*] Ay, that is a kiss.

ALL THE LOST BOYS: Wendy lady, be our mother!

In the wings a stage manager crouches with mirrors and a lantern, shooting TINKERBELL*'s light around the theatre. The pirates lurk.*

SCENE TWO

Violet Coward doted on her son. He was blond-haired, blue-eyed, disarmingly bright, and he showed signs of being musical, reaching tiny fingers up to the piano in the parlour of the Cowards' semi-detached house, known as "Helmsdale", at 5 Waldegrave Road in Teddington.[1] Violet and her husband, Arthur, had befriended the local celebrity Robert "R. D." Blackmore, bestselling author of *Lorna Doone*, and he agreed to become godfather to their child, sending a carriage drawn by a white pony to trundle the boy, resplendent in his Victorian skirts, around the streets of the prosperous Middlesex suburb.

Life unspooled in a world of bustles and Empire. Queen Victoria grew fatter on her throne; the railway chugged the Cowards in and out of Teddington when needed. Then, five months before his seventh birthday, the little boy caught a strain of meningitis that infected the fluid around his brain and spinal cord, and it killed him within days. He was buried in Teddington cemetery, five minutes' walk from the house.

> In loving memory of Russell
> Arthur Blackmore Coward
> Who fell asleep March 17th 1898
> Aged 6 years & 7 months.
> There's a crown for little children
> Above the bright blue sky
> And a harp of sweetest music
> And palms of victory

"Life seemed to have come to an end for me" Violet wrote.

> I became very ill, and longed and longed to die. To think that I could ever feel great happiness again, with Noël! I could never have believed it. Russell was our only child, and our world for those happy six years. Everybody was overjoyed when it became

known that I was to have another baby, and though my own feelings were unsaid, I did so long to feel baby arms around my neck again, I missed Russell so – and yet felt as if I were being unfaithful to him to have another in his place. But time does heal, and one cannot always be sad, and so on the 15th of December [1899], I was looking forward with joy and longing for my little newcomer, little knowing the great joy and happiness and pride I was to have in him and how he was to alter our lives. As I looked at the snow, I felt it beginning and at 4.30 on the morning of the 16th, my precious Noël first saw the light. He was a fine big baby, and oh the joy of him![2]

Noël, named for his birth's proximity to Christmas, permitted a fortnight's glimpse of the dying century, and spending an unremembered year as a Victorian baby swaddled in skirts and love, became Violet's miracle child, and her second chance at motherhood, into which she threw herself with startling vigour.

SCENE THREE

Violet never forgot, and would never let her son forget, that her family had seen better days. Her family tree was a distinguished one, and she minded, badly, that she clung onto the faded leaves of its lower branches when names such as Field Marshal Haig (the son of a distant cousin) nestled at the top. Her ancestors had enjoyed a family seat in Scotland and a crest that she would become determined Noël might use. Her efforts to propel her son into the limelight stemmed in part from her sense that the family should be restored to its former glory. Noël Coward's childhood was suburban and impecunious, but his mother would have argued that his blood was always bluer than anyone let on.

Violet Agnes Veitch was born on 20 April 1863, the granddaughter of George III's consul-general to Madeira, and the daughter of an asthmatic naval officer who died three months before her arrival, leaving his second wife, Violet's mother, to bring up six children on the meagre funds of a naval widow's pension. Violet's childhood was a little wild, in the absence of a father, and lived in genteel poverty. The family flitted from house to house, moving ever further away from the expenses of London. There was money enough to send Violet to a "finishing school", actually a convent in Belgium, where she caught an infection that went untreated and left her slightly deaf. Noël would later attribute his distinctive consonants to the clarity with which it was necessary to communicate with her.

Above all, Violet Veitch loved the theatre. There survives a collection of handbills and souvenir programmes that she hoarded from her theatre-going youth, the pages spangled with the great performers of the day, from Ellen Terry to Henry Irving. The margins are carefully annotated with her views – often acerbic – on the actors, whose delivery she was thought to imitate perfectly. Deafness did nothing to alter her love of music, and when the family ended up in Teddington, a riverside Middlesex town to which Victorians flocked after the railway linked it to London, she joined the local choir at the parish church of St Alban's. Here she met a fellow chorister called Arthur Coward. He, born on 20 November 1856, was thirty-three; she, twenty-seven. They were married on 8 October 1890 and wasted no time: Russell was born exactly nine months later.

Perhaps Violet and Arthur bonded over their shared experience of a fatherless childhood. Arthur's father, James, had died of tuberculosis in 1880, leaving a large family and a young wife. But James's financial arrangements had been prudent, and the Coward brood were well provided for. It is Arthur's side of the family from whom Noël's musical talent appears to stem: James Coward had been a choirboy at Westminster Abbey, and became resident organist at the Crystal Palace. All ten of his children bolstered local choirs and amateur theatricals, and most of them made music their profession. Arthur inherited the family traits of music and alcoholism. He became first a clerk and then a travelling salesman for the music publisher and piano maker Metzler & Co., demonstrating harmoniums to prospective clients. But, commuting into London five days a week and often sent abroad for work, he became a rather absent figure in Noël's childhood.

One of Noël's friends "thought it easy to see how a combination of the genes of his parents might produce such a phenomenon as their son".[3] Height, charm, and bone structure from his father; wit, temper, and ambition from his mother. Not that Arthur couldn't come out with a sharp one-liner when roused, as of a short and irritating local verger: "his brains are too near his bottom".[4] But Violet gave rise to so many anecdotes as to sound like a character in her son's plays. On surveying her deceased sister in the coffin: "Doesn't she look pretty, like a little snowdrop. It's a pity she looked so disagreeable when she was alive."[5] Can she really have driven her motor car through a shop window, ploughing into a display of glass jars and spattering the bonnet with marmalade? Did she really, on hearing that Noël had been hit over the head with a tennis-racket by his older friend Doris, march angrily over to Doris's house, whip out a racket from behind her back, and smite poor Doris over the head, telling her to pick on someone her own size? Doris might well have noted the hypocrisy.

Noël's first decade, nomadic and melodramatic, already contained something of the actor's life. His patchy schooling was spread across a number of small private institutions, not one of which gave him a comprehensive education or left his biographers a searchable archive. He had little domestic consistency, his parents lacking a decent income (or Violet's idea of one) to the extent that they made numerous attempts at different lives, in the town and in the country, as landlords and as tenants. House would follow house, bedroom follow bedroom, the walls decorated with pictures of Edwardian theatre stars, carefully cut from magazines. The erectors of commemorative plaques would be kept busy, a century on.

The house in which Noël was born – red-brick, three-storey, end-of-terrace, a handful of years old – he would never remember, as he spent no more than eighteen months in it, looked after by his mother and by a nineteen-year-old maid called Eva Stevens.[6] The river was a fifteen-minute walk away, but it was a noisy life at Waldegrave Road, its precarious gentility coated in a film of dust: the railway ran directly behind the garden, steam trains roaring their regular way to and from Waterloo. Amid thick snow Noël was christened at the cathedral-sized St Alban's by the Bishop of Kingston, on 11 February 1900. It was one of his few early skirmishes with religion, which impinged as little on the family's life as did the fight for women's suffrage or the Relief of Mafeking. Violet and Arthur were political animals on only one issue. Vaccination against smallpox had been mandatory in Britain since 1853, but in late-Victorian England the anti-vaccine campaign, which argued against state intervention in personal affairs, was at its height, and the Cowards supported it passionately. The death of Russell did nothing to alter their views, and in February 1901 Arthur Coward was summoned to the local magistrates' court for neglecting to have Noël vaccinated. He stated his "conscientious objection", but was fined ten shillings.[7]

Conversely Violet, made paranoid by Russell's death, flew into panic at any hint of illness in Noël and at the slightest provocation summoned the doctor, who would invariably diagnose the large and healthy baby with a case of too much molly-coddling and note that he was too clever for his age. The doctor advised Violet, as she remembered, "to be very very careful of him – to cut off all his beautiful curls and never to let him go to children's parties or be much excited, for, he said, his brain is far in advance of his years. Well I did all this, refused all invitations, and kept him very quiet, and he grew big and strong."[8]

In the second half of 1901 the baby's adoring audience grew. The family left Waldegrave Road and moved to a larger house close by, living together in a big room on the top floor, with Violet's sister Vida and their mother, Mary, ensconced below. When Violet became pregnant again the family pondered emigrating to the Commonwealth of Australia, a federation of colonies just three years old and thought to be a land of opportunity. An alternative history beckoned for Noël Coward, perhaps as a progenitor of Barry Humphries, skewering the housewives of Melbourne suburbs. But no. Noël's skirts were exchanged for trousers, and Teddington exchanged for the town of Sutton, then part of Surrey and swelling with commuters. A house, known as "Helsdon", was found at 56 Lenham Road, where Noël's brother Eric was born on 13 July 1905. Noël showed the expected disgruntlement at being upstaged by a new cast member who would turn attention away from the star of the show, but, alas for Eric, he didn't, much.

There was parkland nearby; there was a stained-glass front door; there was a maid called Emma Adams. Noël was sent to school and life should have settled itself. Instead, a teacher refused to tie Noël's shoelaces and after a row of some kind, Violet transferred him to a local girls' school. Her motives may have been social: St Margaret's was housed in a grand building on Worcester Road, in the smarter part of town, and run by the puff-sleeved Miss Willington whose arm Noël later claimed to have bitten, in a fit of temper, "right through to the bone – an action which I have never for an instant regretted".[9] In his unpublished novel *Cherry Pan*, written when he was eighteen, he made no efforts to disguise his former headmistress, in whose care his heroine is placed: "Miss Willington grabbed hold of the little pink arm. Cherry by this time hysterical and entirely desperate turned quickly and bit the fat hand with all her might. Miss Willington let go with a howl of pain and Cherry flew on the wings of fear up the stone steps and along the garden path."[10]

At six years old Noël was, as he later admitted, a badly behaved child, brought up by his mother in alternate stripes of indulgence and temper, the former shown until she lost the latter. Once, she slapped the boy in the street, to the shock of passers-by. Walked to and from school by the maid, more often than not Noël slipped her hand and ran home. Tantrums became his speciality. His behaviour may be evidence of a fast-moving brain denied serious exercise in Miss Willington's establishment, combined with the frustration of being the only boy in a sea of girls, at once oddity and exoticism. Mothering him so devotedly, Violet half forgot to be a mother: they argued like lovers and misbehaved together like school friends.

In 1907 Noël left his parents to spend the summer with his prosperous Aunt Laura at Charlestown on the south coast of Cornwall. The house was of a grandeur he had not yet known, with a lake in the garden and, on the horizon, a sliver of sea. He adored the place, working out what was missing when it came to riches and what they bought. (Decades later he paid for a bell in the local church that is still affectionately known as Noël.) He wrote to his mother from the holiday, the first of his letters to survive:

Darling Mother

I hope you are well. Girlie has taught me to row with two oars and I row her along. I had some little boys over yesterday afternoon to tea and I dressed up in a short dress* and danced to them and sung to them and we all went round the lake and on it. XXXXXOOOOXO I am writing this in the kitchen with love from Noel Coward[11]

Noël doesn't seem to have countenanced that he, aged seven, was a "little boy" in the way his teatime companions were. The letter, as lavish with affection and embrace as he presumably was in life,

---

* A "short dress" would have been a standard outfit for an Edwardian seven-year-old, rather than a female costume. "Girlie" was his cousin, another Violet, whose company he preferred to her lofty older brother, Walter.

makes clear his early love of performing, no matter to whom. Amid the disruptions of his childhood the lifelines of music and theatre loomed large.

No child likes having a December birthday, Christmas gifts and birthday presents all too often sliding into one. But Noël Coward's annual treat was to be taken by his mother to the theatre. As young as three he had sat through a local pantomime, and the main delight of seaside holidays had been the minstrel troupes and brass bands and puppet shows on the beaches and promenades, or the large music halls on the pier. Toy theatres and dressing-up became staples of his childhood play. Edwardian theatre was exploding in popularity, in a world that had yet to be dominated by wireless or cinema. Huge auditoria, designed by Frank Matcham and others, sprang up all across London and the provinces throughout Noël's childhood. Shaftesbury Avenue was only ten years older than he was, the major road improvements during the late nineteenth century having shifted Theatreland's centre of gravity firmly westwards. Noël Coward and the modern theatre, with all its technological and architectural developments, were of an age. They grew up together.

Violet and Noël sat in the dark as the orchestra tuned and the curtain rose. The actors shone under the electric lights, a novelty of Violet's youth but now fitted in theatres across London. Stars such as Gabrielle Ray and Phyllis Dare became the most photographed women of the era, and their images were soon among the clippings stuck to Noël's bedroom wall. In the auditorium he watched entranced, presumably from the cheaper seats, which gave a bird's-eye-view to the scallop-shell footlights, the dusty drapery, the dots of black in the orchestra stalls that dissolved as the men collapsed their top hats. He delighted in theatrical ritual, from the donning of evening dress required by Edwardian etiquette, to the curtain calls that were taken at the end of each act (a tradition that would hold fast for decades). Noël would stand for hours at the stage door waiting for his beloved Gertie Millar to emerge, and once she presented him with a red rose that he kept for years between the pages of a comic book.[12]

British theatre was in an interim stage. The dominance of Gilbert and Sullivan was over but American musicals had yet to arrive.

Playwrights such as George Bernard Shaw and Harley Granville-Barker were leading a period of "New Drama", and scandalous European imports by Ibsen and others were the talk of London. Oscar Wilde's reputation was slowly reviving after the scandal of his imprisonment. But Noël Coward and his mother were most interested in Edwardian musical comedies. More tightly constructed than burlesque yet lighter than opera, these usually featured plucky heroines – shop girls, chorus girls – who break into high society. *The Blue Moon* was a favourite: a British major falls in love with a Burmese singer, whom he eventually marries, without scandal, owing to the fact that she turns out to be British. Or there was *The King of Cadonia*: Princess Marie falls in love with a mysterious stranger, whom she eventually marries, without scandal, owing to the fact that he turns out to be heir presumptive to the Cadonian throne. And so on. As dated as the fashion crazes they inspired, shows such as these took hold of Noël's boyish imagination and lie like a thinly traced sketch behind his mature plays. The predictable plots and happy outcomes offered comforting consistency amid his disordered childhood. Brazenly insubstantial, they were neatly and sometimes brilliantly constructed: in Robert Courtneidge's *The Dairymaids* a cat's cradle of amorous entanglements is unravelled into no fewer than five successfully paired-off couples. The lyrics creak and, occasionally, teeter on the edge of sparkle: "Dairymaids we of alluring rusticity | Beauties whose freshness is all unadorned, | Set in surroundings that smack of simplicity | Where ev'ry useless embellishment's scorned."

The music was skilfully undemanding, but this made it naggingly memorable. Noël had no formal music lessons, and he never learned to sight-read, but he was able, on coming in late from the theatre, to rush straight to the upright piano and accurately pick out tunes, adding rudimentary chords underneath. That he should have such a fine-tuned ear was not surprising, given almost all of his aunts and uncles played or sang to professional standard, and music was a staple of the family's entertainment as they tried to fill the long winter evenings. Singing came naturally to Noël, and enjoying the acclaim that followed came even more naturally. The lack of any organised teaching meant that music-making never shifted from pleasure to chore. Copyright had been introduced and sales of sheet music, which Arthur could bring home discounted or for free, were booming. A new middlebrow musical culture had been created, and the Cowards revelled in it.

Noël's was a childhood measured out in song: performed by his father in a noticeably beautiful tenor, or by his mother accompanying herself at the piano after she had carefully removed her rings and placed them on the lid. Even a prospective lodger, viewing a later Coward residence, treated the family to a piercing recital. Parlour songs and Gilbert and Sullivan (whom, as an adult, he came to dislike) were laced into the rituals of life. His mother's friend Gwen Kelly sang to the family on her visits in a husky contralto, and her artistry was an inspiration to the little boy. At local fetes most of the family were involved with the entertainment, and "Master Noël Coward" invariably provided a routine. One memorable appearance came at the local town hall on 23 July 1907, as part of a prize-giving concert for Miss Willington's school; he sang from Paul Rubens's 1902 musical *A Country Girl*. The audience called for an encore but Noël's name was not among the prize-winners. "I did not realize that he had expected a prize", remembered Violet, "till he flung himself on the sofa and yelled crying. I felt so sorry for him."[13]

Later in life he recognised that there had been something off-putting about the way in which, at eight years old, he had mimicked with innocent accuracy the saucy delivery of the theatre's leading ladies. Looking back, from a time when adulthood and professionalism had taught him nerves, he noted with envy that his boyhood performances had had, above all, confidence.

In 1908 the Cowards decamped to 70 Prince of Wales Mansions in Battersea, with the intention of taking lodgers. Happy as they were to move into central London, and to a reasonably genteel block of flats, they were downsizing considerably, and living in what was then a cheap and unfashionable area, with slum housing prevalent in the district. The flat overlooked Battersea Park, and beyond that was the river, and beyond that, best of all, lay the London theatres.

Lodgers duly arrived, two bachelors who lived side by side with the four Cowards and Emma the maid. Life was cramped and quarrelsome, but also took on a ceremony – group sing-songs and formal dinners – that Noël enjoyed. Communal living gave him the chance to observe, and he did so, with an almost adult eye, calmly scrutinising the way in which the lodgers would flirt outrageously with his mother's friends. Otherwise he played with children in the neighbouring flats, and became a ringleader of pranks both silly and, on occasion, dangerous. Residents communicated with the porter by a long speaking tube into which Noël poured boiling water that ran down the floors and into the porter's ear. Another favourite game was to tie perambulators kept in the corridors to the apartments' front doors, and he was said to have pushed a pram, with a baby in it, down a flight of stairs. Any repercussions were lost in these escapades' gleeful recounting.

He and his mother were now a tightly bound unit on which other relationships barely impinged. But separation from her became inevitable when he set his sights on joining the choir of the Chapel Royal in St James's Palace, in which his father's brother Walter was a tenor. It was a mark of Violet's confidence in her son's talent, or of her inability to deny him what he wanted, that this was considered a serious ambition and swiftly acted upon. She seems never to have doubted that Noël, who had had no music teaching of any kind, who did not read music or show any inclination to learn, would be capable of navigating the complex polyphony that was the choir's stock-in-trade.

The Children of the Chapel Royal, as they were known, were a group of trebles resplendent in their ornate costume of red and gold, doubtless an attraction for Noël. They lived and were educated in a tiny school in an imposing Georgian townhouse in Clapham, which also took on a handful of non-chorister pupils. Noël enrolled as a non-chorister. The boys were looked after by Claude Selfe, the "Master of the Children", whose passion for the theatre did nothing to endear him to the new arrival.[14] He encouraged manliness among his pupils and had little time for those such as Noël, who, small and theatrical, was promptly bullied. But acting came to the rescue: Noël could pretend to faint with enough conviction that his school friends quickly became anxious. The need constantly to make new friends in new places had instilled a certain courage. Acting also enlivened the miserable daily commute to the school, which he made, alone, on two trams, regaling fellow passengers with fantastical stories of his hideous life and abusive parents. So convincing could he be that one apparently alerted the police. The theatre of his mind was more real to him than the journey to Clapham through gaslit winter fogs.

The day of his choral audition finally came, and he was brought before the organist for the Chapel Royal, Walter Alcock, a distinguished and later knighted man, confident of his intimate acquaintance with both the Royal and the Holy family. Noël launched into a self-consciously cherubic performance of "There is a green hill far away", using the tune by Charles Gounod rather than the standard Anglican setting:

> *There is a green hill far away,*
> *Without a city wall,*
> *Where the dear Lord was crucified,*
> *Who died to save us all.*

Singing fashions change, and Noël's childhood performances should be imagined not as a hooty treble such as opens twenty-first-century carol services, but as a boy soprano, swooping and tremulous, replete with the precise diction of the era and delivered with simpering artifice: he had been weaned not on church music but on musical theatre. He reached an almost disturbing frenzy.

> *He died that we might be forgiven,*
> *He died to make us good,*
> *That we might go at last to heav'n . . .*

By the time Noël got to the Amens, Alcock was panting and mumbling excuses about the choir's not having a vacancy after all. Violet was outraged. She blamed Alcock. And anyway, the whole choir had looked so extremely common.

🎭

NEW STORY BOOK!: **THE MAGNET**
The Making of Harry Wharton
HE TORE HIMSELF FREE AND GLARED AROUND![15]

Living in his imagination gave Noël a shaky grasp on the rights and wrongs of real life, and he thought little of petty thievery to supplement his supply of books and comics. To the latter he was devoted, thriving on a hearty diet of *Chums* and *The Boy's Own Paper* (traditional Victorian fare) and of the newer and more colourful *The Gem* and *The Magnet*. Alongside the standard adventure and detective yarns, these featured schoolboy stories – Billy Bunter of Greyfriars or the pupils of "St Jim's" – and Noël devoured everything he could, vicariously experiencing carefree schooldays within the orange pages. Edith Nesbit was serialising her children's novels in the *Strand* or *London* magazines: *The Enchanted Castle* appeared in 1907 and *The Magic City* in 1910. Noël's childhood copy of the former survives, the flyleaf curtly inscribed with a curlicued "Coward", as if the boy were already conscious of building an image with that single word. It would be decades before children's literature catered for the stage-struck, but Nesbit's collision of realism and magic was quietly revolutionary, and her books became for Noël a series of talismans that accompanied him first through childhood, and then through life.

Stealing papers and comics was one thing; stealing the jewellery of his mother's friends in order to pawn the loot for money (an elaborate swindle for an eight-year-old) was quite another. The shoplifting may indicate unhappiness but seems not to have been the conventional cry for attention: attention was on plentiful demand, and from the person he cared about most. In his mother's eyes Noël could do no wrong, and so the notion of wrongdoing made little sense. When the family relocated to a cottage in the country, Violet was not above taking Noël to steal fruit from their landlord's orchard after dark.

For the lodgers had departed from the Battersea flat, and not long afterwards the Cowards had followed suit. It was not out of character for Violet to leave London in a temper as a reaction to Noël's failed Chapel Royal audition, but it made financial sense to rent out the flat entire, and live cheaply off the income in the countryside. In the summer of 1908 they settled in Meon, a hamlet in South Hampshire. It was an experiment in rural life, after years of making ends meet, or rather not meet, amid the financial pressures of the city and its surrounds. The family took to it happily, renting a cottage where they lived for six months, poor but content, their financial hardship less apparent in the countryside. The cottage was tiny and thatched; the garden contained a privy, carefully bolted against the attentions of a local goat. Cut loose from the pressures of lodgers and relations, and brought physically together in the small number of rooms, the Cowards finally became a family unit (for great portions of Noël's memoirs, the reader would be forgiven for assuming him the only child of a single parent).[16]

It was in Meon that Noël first turned his hand to writing plays, producing some tragic drama, the script now lost, that his landlady's daughters were coerced into performing in the garden. The cast refused to take their writer-director seriously, so he hit them with a wooden spade. Writing and performing were their own kind of school, but during the idyllic half-year in Hampshire nobody appears to have thought that Noël should resume any formal education. Late in 1908 his maternal grandmother died, but Violet's share of the inheritance did not transform the Cowards' fortunes.[17] Nevertheless, by early 1909, they were planning their return to Battersea, and Noël found himself once again a pupil at the Chapel Royal school, facing the difficult task of reintroducing himself to social groups from which he had been absent for half a year. He was sent back to London a week earlier than his parents, staying with an uncle and aunt in Pimlico, from where he made his own way to school. The misery of being plunged suddenly back into a world of gowned masters and teasing boys and corporal punishment, culminated in a fit of screaming that might today be called a panic attack. Separation from his mother, even for a short while, had become agony for him. He began to entertain nightmares of

immense detail about her death, aware of the great performance
he could give in reaction to the news, brave orphans being a vital
part of the children's fiction to which he escaped. He wrote to her
in despair:

> I am still very unhappy and I shant get over it till I see you again.
> I would rather see you than Alladin but I suppose I cant. I saw
> the Portsmouth train going off the other day and I longed to
> get on it. I wish you would let me come back to you please do,
> for I do want to so I could never be happy without you. I cry
> every night and day and are so miserable do let me come back.
> I am quite alright now but I wish you were here. The dinners
> are alright, at school there are six new boys. [. . .] oh mother do
> send me some money to come down to you please do I am not
> very happy here without you[18]

Violet decided that Noël would benefit from being taught to dance,
and thought nothing of removing her son from school for two days
a week so that he could attend a cheap dance academy. Miss Janet
Thomas advertised in the *Morning Post*: "Receives and visits pupils for
ball-room and society dancing. Four private lessons or 12 classes,
£1 1s., Valse, Boston, La Vague, Reels, &c. Fancy Dances for private
theatricals, stage, &c."[19] Noël went for twelve classes, fancy dances
and all. Miss Thomas taught in a since-demolished house in Hanover Square, and Noël retained vivid memories of the long and dank
room, with its wall of mirrors and its smell of furniture polish, and
the bobbing bottoms and black bloomers of the instructors. Slowly
his dancing improved, though he began with much enthusiasm and
little skill.

Nine years old, his hair slick with grease and his collar stiff
with starch, he spent his days criss-crossing London on his own,
from Clapham to Battersea, Battersea to Westminster, while Violet
sat at home tense with worry. He had become independent, and
even an outsider. But an outsider by definition needs a world from
which to be excluded, and Noël had instead been denied the usual
communities of childhood, making his volatile way through his
first decade in varying moods of despondency, temper, and delight.

He was solitary, but, he insisted, never lonely. He had little need for the company of other children, who had always been a disappointment anyway. School and discipline caused him misery, but he later pronounced himself to have been a happy child beneath the hot-blooded tantrums, cocooned in his mother's love for him, and his for her.

His had nevertheless been a boyhood studded with accident. On the promenade of an Edwardian seaside town, a horse had lunged from nowhere at his head, taking a chunk from his neck, behind his right ear; later, a bull terrier had gone for his leg, the skin of the calf flapping and blood spilling until the doctor burned the flesh away to seal the wound, scarring Noël for life. Paddling in the sea, he had stood on a broken bottle stuck unseen beneath the waves, and severed an artery, the blood blossoming in the water like jellyfish. Aged nine, walking along the street, he was knocked down and concussed by a cyclist, an injury that would find its way onto medical notes made in the First World War. Such accidents and near-misses were so frequent as to imply that an incautious little boy was happier living on the stage of his mind's imagination than in the world around him.

The belief has arisen that he was staggeringly precocious, but it has to be admitted that he was far from an infant prodigy. He was instead a strange mixture of precocity and naivety – unless the latter, in being assumed or heightened for the delectation of his audience, was actually an instance of premature sophistication. In an age that expected drab rectitude from its young men, he was making early, even flailing, stabs at panache, in a household that did not panic at the prospect of a flamboyant and sensitive son. Violet thought nothing of rounding up all her neighbours and sitting them down in front of Noël's puppet shows. The theatre was an enhancement and continuation of all that he enjoyed at home, and it was an easy leap, from his red-plush seat, to see himself on the other side of the proscenium arch at the curtain calls. His singing voice was apparently good but its days were numbered; photographs do not prove him to have been an especially beautiful child, his face yet to come into its paternal inheritance. His knowledge was as patchy as his self-belief was certain, and neither his reading nor his writing was advanced for a boy of his age (it is his childhood drawings that show skill and care beyond his years).

And so he turned ten years old, and King Edward VII died, and the Battersea life continued, and he and his mother began to plot for him a life on the stage with a confidence that seemed, truth to tell, entirely unfounded.

SCENE FOUR

One of the hinges on which Noël Coward's life opened was the fact that his mother read the *Daily Mirror*, or saw the issue of 7 September 1910. Her gentility may now seem an odd fit with the oldest British tabloid, but the *Mirror* was originally pitched to a middle-class, and specifically female, readership. Violet came across an article entitled: "London Theatre for Children – Juvenile Actors and Actresses in Adventure Plays. Miss Lila Field's plan."* Miss Field harboured grand dreams of creating a permanent "children's theatre" and was in need of actors. "My plays will begin in the middle of October, at one of the large West End theatres", Miss Field told the *Mirror*, with what proved to be groundless optimism. "I am badly in need of five or six boys. The plays for these children to act I am having specially written. They will be 'children's plays' all right [. . .] the love element will never be very much developed, for instance." If that was not enough for Violet, the project also had the support of the aristocracy: Princess Dolgorouki, Princess Hatzfeldt, the Duchess of Norfolk . . .[20]

Two hundred mothers wrote to Lila Field that very day, Violet among them. She and Noël were invited to a room on Baker Street, where not a princess or a duchess was to be seen. Miss Field watched from behind rouged cheeks, replete with beauty spot, while Noël performed "Liza Ann" from *The Orchid*: "There's a Yorkshire town, very bleak and brown . . . " Violet sang the accompaniment and afterwards insisted that Miss Field was so overwhelmed by the boy's talent she "passed out".[21] Evidently she regained consciousness to the extent that she could offer to employ Noël for a guinea and a half each week (about £150 in today's money). And after a moment's confusion, in which Violet thought the sum was not a salary but a fee, mother and son walked out into the street delirious with excitement, assured of Noël's future stardom.

---

* "Lila" was pronounced to rhyme with "miller".

Lila Field was thin and erect and foaming with lace. She spoke, one pupil remembered, with a "devastatingly refined accent [. . .] and ruled like a rather cadaverous queen".[22] She and her sister Bertha were German in origin, had spent time in Peru, and ran a dance academy in Hanover Square. She had a good eye, having spotted amid the hopefuls not only Noël Coward, but a girl called June Tripp, later a star of silent movies, and a boy called Alfred Willmore, who grew up to become – using the name Micheál Mac Liammóir – a legendary figure of Irish theatre. Tripp noticed Noël's "elfin ears" and "foul temper", and admitted that she expressed her aversion to his "black suits, horse-laughter, and fiendish grimaces", in a series of "haughty head-tossings".[23] Eventually he cracked and hit her over the head with a ballet slipper. Mac Liammóir came gallantly to her defence and punched him. He found Noël "in manner and bearing a young man", with eyes that were "amused and slightly incredulous", and a speaking voice that had already developed its trimly idiosyncratic adult style. Frightened and uncertain, he asked what Noël was going to be when he grew up. "An actor of course", was the reply. "Why, what do you want to be?" Mac Liammóir hesitated, but Noël was firm: "You'd better make up your mind, you know. People should always be quite clear about what they want to be."[24]

Lila Field's grand plans dwindled into the mounting of a single children's play of her own authorship called *The Goldfish,* which she published with Mills and Boon. This was a three-act "musical fantasy" about fairies, a childish parallel to Gilbert and Sullivan's "fairy opera", *Iolanthe.* The Victorians' obsession with fairies had yet to abate, and in 1917 a series of ostensibly genuine photographs depicting two girls dancing with fairies would become a national obsession. The first act of *The Goldfish* showed a group of children taking tea in a garden (Noël was Jack, in a bowler hat) under the supervision of a French governess acted by Miss Field. The juvenile cast was then transformed, for reasons best known to the author, into various fish, living in a place called Sunny Cove and disporting themselves as if in Arthurian romance. Mac Liammóir was the goldfish, June Tripp a starfish. Noël arrived for Act Three as "Prince Mussel, the Court Jester", unrequitedly and unhappily in love with said starfish, and given a lovelorn ballad to himself: "When love enters a jester's heart . . ."

There followed three months of patchy rehearsal, which progressed as spasmodically as might be expected, given Miss Field's precarious management, and only intermittent payment of the temperamental star-struck children, chaperoned by a parade of ambitious mothers. The play was first performed at the Knightsbridge home of Lady Llangattock, where Miss Field unwisely dressed the first-act tea party with real cake. The actors could not contain themselves. At least one was sick during the performance. June Tripp, "completely immobilised by a chocolate éclair", forgot a vital line, so Noël said it instead, to her chagrin and his triumph.[25] Finally *The Goldfish* opened to the public on 27 January 1911, at the year-old Little Theatre, a 300-seater tucked away behind the Strand. Noël Coward delivered his first ever line on a professional stage: "Any luck, Dolly?" The costumes were suitably fish-like, bouquets and sweets were handed out at the end, and the reviews were indulgent enough. "None of these [performers] were really prodigies" thought the *Westminster Gazette*.[26] Noël decided a stellar career on the boards was now inevitable.

Less than a week later he had earache and couldn't perform, which Violet ever afterwards insisted was the reason Miss Field pulled the show. Given Noël's small role and the poor ticket sales, the playwright's reasons may have lain elsewhere. But *The Goldfish* was soon revived, first at the Variety Theatre (the smallest auditorium of the Crystal Palace) and then at the Royal Court for a handful of performances in April. Rehearsals had made Noël's already patchy attendance at the Chapel Royal school even more intermittent, and the prospect of returning to its bullying horrors after a taste of a different life was almost impossible. (Allegations of bullying at the institution became so frequent that in 1912 there would be a police enquiry, and Claude Selfe took early retirement on a comfortable allowance from the Lord Chamberlain.)[27] Calmly Noël played truant, preferring to walk alone around London, sitting in stations watching the trains, or purchasing a wig and beard so as to wander the capital unnoticed. The disguise was surely as necessary as it was convincing, intended not to avoid detection but to make his own theatre.

Back at Miss Field's academy, a promising thirteen-year-old dancer named Edris Stannus did her barre exercises under a framed photograph of *The Goldfish*, and noticed the boy dressed as a jester. "I was told how clever he was; I asked his name and was informed that he was called Noël Coward." How, thought Stannus, could she ever catch up? Soon to change her name to Ninette de Valois and eventually to found The Royal Ballet, she went back to her exercises "with a sigh and my eyes on 'Noël' who was so much ahead of me [. . .] and was going to be a great actor".[28]

Life might soon have become ordinary once again. Arthur Coward sold his pianos; aunts Antoinette and Vida were now boarding permanently at the Battersea flat.[29] Eric was six and overlooked; Noël was eleven and indulged. On one memorable occasion Anna Pavlova appeared in state at Miss Field's academy on the hunt for child dancers, but Noël, tripping up Ninette de Valois in his eager display, was not selected.[30] No prospect of further employment seemed possible until the late summer, when he was invited by some theatrical agents to audition, in the first week of September, for the great actor-manager Charles Hawtrey (not the *Carry On* actor, but a star of light comedy who had created roles for Oscar Wilde).

Hawtrey was to be the lead in a farce called *The Great Name*, due to open in a matter of days. He was badly in need of a young actor to play a page boy named Cannard, and Noël was engaged on the spot, for £2.10 a week (£250 today). He was also paid to understudy an older child actor called Sidney Sherwood, who managed never to miss a performance. Noël delivered his tiny part with such gusto and variation that when Hawtrey heard him prising every ounce of meaning and subtext from the role he asked never to clap eyes on the boy again – but relented, especially when Noël proved that he could gabble his lines in an accurate Cockney. The boy developed a major infatuation with Hawtrey, who wafted backstage in expensive clothes and a cloud of scent and enjoyed being exasperated by the puppy-dog affection. Since 1904 the law had required child performers to obtain a licence prior to each and every stage appearance, subject to the discretion of a local magistrate. The one to whom Violet applied in advance of *The Great Name* (who looked, Noël thought, "like a macaw") was for some reason suspicious of the whole enterprise and dug in his heels.[31] Violet burst into tears and insisted, with her customary allergy to understatement, that Noël would have to go to a sanatorium if he could not act. The licence was granted.

The Great Name had been adapted by Hawtrey from a German play about a composer who, fed up of his success in the trivia of musical comedy, swaps identities with a master of great classical works. It dramatised a tussle between the popular and the good, the frothy and the serious, that would resonate throughout Noël Coward's career. The show opened on 7 September 1911, and closed again not long afterwards, the reviews having agreed that it was thin and sentimental. But within three months, Noël found himself cast in the premiere of a play produced by Hawtrey that soon became a fixture of Christmas theatre in London: *Where the Rainbow Ends*. Written by Clifford Mills and John Ramsey, and with a score by Roger Quilter, a leading composer of light music, it would be revived almost every year for the next half-century. It was a fantasy owing a great deal to the novels of E. Nesbit: a quartet of children go in search of their missing parents on a magic carpet, taking with them a pet lion cub and guarded from danger by Saint George.

Among Noël's fellow cast members were Philip Tonge, the leading child actor of the day; Sidney Sherwood, whom he had recently understudied; a teenage Hermione Gingold (later a star of films such as *Gigi*); and Esmé Wynne, whom he dismissed as a "podgy, brown-haired little girl with a bleating voice".[32] They were to be trained by an actress named Italia Conti, who when *Where the Rainbow Ends* became a juggernaut, the *Billy Elliot* of its day, founded a drama school in which to coach the children for each revival. Noël was cast as yet another Cockney page boy. "He only had five lines", remembered Gingold (not quite accurately), "but what he did with them was something quite fantastic. People used to stand and gape in astonishment [. . .] Charles Hawtrey was always threatening Noël with the sack but never carried out his threat because even Noël's scene-stealing had a ring of genius about it."[33]

Rehearsals were enjoyable, parties were put on for the children, and Violet had the time of her life chaperoning Noël, frizzing her hair and wearing evening dress, and sparring with Philip Tonge's mother as if to see who was the more devoted to her son's career. The play opened at the Savoy Theatre, on 21 December, and was, thought *The Sunday Times*, "the very thing for boys and girls who love the heroism of St. George and the prowess of the British lion".[34] For an impressionable and star-struck eleven-year-old, its message would run deep.

The London County Council had begun to enforce certain rules over the treatment of child actors – Hawtrey's London offices on the Haymarket had to be turned into schoolrooms – but it would be some time before they enjoyed the same legal rights as child workers in other trades, not least where working hours were concerned. Violet remembered sitting at the theatre until half past four in the morning as the final rehearsal dragged on.[35] Italia Conti herself argued that child actors were essentially playing, not working, and that the law should treat them accordingly.[36] The forty children cast in *Where the Rainbow Ends* often worked fourteen-hour days: they attended school in the morning, were dined handsomely in a restaurant every lunchtime, gave two performances each and every day either side of a mandatory nap, and were sent home at 11 p.m. after hot milk with bananas.[37]

Philip Tonge, two years older than Noël and cast as the lead, never became a close friend. But from Esmé Wynne, despite his initial suspicions, Noël soon became inseparable.[38] There was something in this clever and passionate girl, already interested in the spiritual and moral issues to which she would eventually devote her life, that deeply attracted him, and the feeling was mutual. Even her name (assumed for the stage) was slightly rakish, "Esmé" having only recently become unisex. This was her second professional job and her first speaking part, and Noël was by no means latching himself onto the biggest name in the company.[39] Her father was a stockbroker, and her large family house in the elegant suburb of Stockwell was a quick cycle from the Cowards' cramped residence in Battersea. Esmé, eighteen months his senior, was already beginning to feel intellectually confined by performing someone else's words, and had set her sights on being a writer. Noël, though certain that he wanted to be an actor, threw himself wholeheartedly into a jovial game of one-upmanship.

After seeing Louis Parker's *Drake of England* – a pageant about the life of Francis Drake – he promptly wrote a burlesque version of it that led Charles Hawtrey to weep with laughter.[40] On 2 February 1912 the juvenile cast staged a one-off matinee that was, according to Hermione Gingold, Noël's idea. "As far as I remember, he wrote it, directed it, and starred in it, even managing to persuade Charles Hawtrey to let him use the theatre."[41] Noël's contribution to the show does not survive; Esmé Wynne provided a drama called *The Prince's Bride*, which was presented alongside *The Daisy Chain* by eleven-year-old Dot Temple. Charles Hawtrey, at the children's invitation, took a box to watch them, unwittingly alerting the press, which led the Lord Chamberlain to protest that the entertainment had not been licensed. Meanwhile the London County Council forbade Noël to charge for entrance, an edict he flouted by taking money from the audience at the door, asking them to sit, then promptly ensuring that they left and re-entered as "free" guests.

As the run went on, he and Esmé began to collaborate on plays and poems. They shared readings lists, swapped gramophone records, even bathed together, so loath were they to interrupt the pleasure of one another's company and of the long conversations in which they set the world to rights. Eventually they would draw up their "Rules of Palship": "If one hits the other either in anger or fun, he must allow the other to hit back." "We must not talk RELIGION unless it is inevitable."[42] The rules would be broken when Esmé converted to Christian Science.

Soon she was given his customary baptism of a nickname. She was Stoj, he Poj, as if in contrition for thinking her chubby, which she wasn't. Noël would use nicknames for beloved friends all his life (his mother, to whom he was Snoop, was usually Snig). They were a strange combination of intimacy and distance, an affectionate gesture that holds the other at arm's length, depersonalising even while being personable. It was an early attempt at belonging, emulating societies that circumstance had denied him, from the schoolboy slang that he read about in comic books to the maze of sobriquets beloved by the upper classes. At twelve years old, he was already ensuring that his acquaintances appeared in a world of which he was unquestionably the casting director.

SCENE FIVE

"Dear Darling old Mother", he wrote. "Thank you very much for your letter. I could not send a card and this was scarcely odd because there were no cards to send." Nodding to "The Walrus and the Carpenter", it may have been Noël's first attempt at literary allusion. He was writing in the summer of 1912 from his Aunt Laura's Cornish home. "Yesterday Girlie took me round the lake", he continued, referring to his cousin, "a very nice lady asked me to go to tea with her I went and had a huge tea [. . .] I am afraid she did not impress me much [. . .] I had 3 little boys to tea yesterday each about the size of a flea. I had to amuse them and didn't enjoy it much."[43]

For the first half of that year Noël had learned the frustrations, as well as the glories, of acting, spending his time sitting dolefully outside audition rooms or playing truant from school. July found him back at the Savoy Theatre, dressed as a mushroom in a little curtain-raiser of a dance ("An Autumn Idyll" by Ruby Ginner) that preceded an operetta called *The Cicada*: "I wore grey silk skin tights, a large grey silk hat like a gargantuan muffin, and a diaphanous frill round my middle to conceal any unaesthetic protuberances."[44] For years afterwards a photograph of him resplendent in fungal couture was proudly displayed in whichever house they found themselves living in, and Violet usually had to be dissuaded from showing it to distinguished visitors. What Noël always neglected to mention, and the photograph didn't show, is that his brother Eric was also in the cast.

By 21 October Noël was in Manchester, performing in a twenty-minute farce called *A Little Fowl Play*, which came into London a week later. Another vehicle for Charles Hawtrey, the comedy was part of a whole evening of sketches, which Noël enjoyed watching from the wings. He was to be a poulterer's boy, described in the script as "seventeen"; already he was playing beyond his years. His dialogue consisted of various exclamations of "The chicking, sir!" But he was permitted to appear only at matinees, the evening performance beginning so late that the local magistrate would not issue his licence, and he watched heartbroken as the assistant stage manager went on instead, chicken in hand.

By the time of his thirteenth birthday, in December 1912, he was back in *Where the Rainbow Ends*. Italia Conti then suggested that Noël join the children's chorus she was preparing for a performance of Gerhart Hauptmann's symbolist play *Hannele*, produced by the Liverpool Repertory Company and due to open in the first week of April 1913. Noël appeared as one of a trio of angels during a dream sequence, dressed in a green petticoat with silver leaves in his hair. The director was a bespectacled and irascible man in his mid-twenties called Basil Dean, who thought him a "pimply, knobbly-kneed youngster with an assured manner".[45] And in the children's chorus was a girl, one year Noël's senior, who had ringlets, and a black satin coat, and a black velvet hat, and a way with a powder puff that Noël thought the height of sophistication. "She then gave me an orange and told me a few mildly dirty stories, and I loved her from then onwards."[46] She was using the assumed surname of Lawrence and asked this love-struck boy to call her Gert.

Gert was one of the bright spots of the production. The weeks in Liverpool were predictably horrible, in that Violet reluctantly remained back in London while the children lived together in digs, under the supervision of Italia Conti. Noël's homesickness was acute, unalleviated by the Epsom Salts with which Conti habitually dosed him. In Manchester, when the play went on tour, a magistrate decreed that the children had to attend school for the duration of the run, but Noël behaved so badly that the teacher left him alone. He and Gert overdosed on peppermints before one show and, mid-performance, spattered their green costumes with a distinctly unangelic stream of vomit.

That summer the Coward family left the Battersea flat and moved a little way south-east to a larger apartment at 50 Clapham Common, South Side. Clapham, a grand district in Violet's youth, had faded into an archetypal commuter suburb and Arthur, still gamely selling pianos for a small living, became "the man on the Clapham omnibus". The Common could be seen from the front windows, just the other side of a road ever busier with motorcars.

Perhaps the extra money that Noël brought home aided the move.
The new flat's proximity to his school cannot have been a deciding
factor, for he seems to have given up on formal education almost
entirely. His schooling, such as it was, now came from the theatre and from books. Unguided by any teacher who would press
upon him the classics, he graduated from comics and E. Nesbit to
historical romance, reading his indiscriminate and voracious way
through *The Scarlet Pimpernel* and the bestselling adventure stories
of Samuel Crockett, Edgar Jepson, and Louis Tracy. He also took
strange refuge in numerous volumes of "women's fiction", usually
featuring steamy love scenes in some foreign clime, from the novels
of Cynthia Stockley (which tended to revolve around adultery in
South Africa) to accounts of love affairs in the Pacific Islands by
Beatrice Grimshaw, and the amorous sagas of Betsey Riddle, whose
titles are today irresistibly reminiscent of Victoria Wood: *Pam*, *Pam
Decides*, *What Became of Pam*.[47]

He had hit his stride and was in almost constant work, going
straight away into rehearsals for *War in the Air*, by Frank Dupree,
which opened at the London Palladium on 23 June 1913. This was
a grand affair, about a man named Tommy Vincent who, when a
child, designed a model aeroplane found to be of utmost value to
the War Office. Noël played Vincent as a boy and, thought *The Era*,
proved himself "a young actor of exceptional ability".[48] The bulk
of the action took place in the future and showed with horrible
prophecy the country enmeshed in a fruitless war with an unnamed
enemy. But little Tommy saves the day with his aeroplane, a model
of which was brought onto the vast stage of the Palladium and
flown over the heads of the audience – on those nights when it
didn't get tangled in the lighting rig. It was another patriotic play
of morale-boosting heroism. The Edwardian frame of mind, in
which empire and duty were paramount, was parcelled up as a
coup de théâtre and instilled in Noël Coward when he was at his most
porous and stage-struck.

The Cowards spent the summer of 1913 with family on the
south coast, and on their return Noël was outraged to find that,
owing to his absence during auditions, the role of a precocious
American boy in Hawtrey's latest farce had gone not to him but

to a child actor called Reginald Sheffield. Hawtrey loyally asked
Noël to understudy, and Noël perfected his American accent while
plotting various ways in which the dismayingly healthy Sheffield
might be, at the very least, incapacitated. But disappointment was
forgotten on the arrival of the invitation for which every young
actor in the country secretly longed: to appear in *Peter Pan.*

He auditioned for the producer Dion Boucicault Jr (son of the
Victorian playwright) and was offered his pick of the Lost Boys.
Violet had perhaps read up on J. M. Barrie's stage directions, for
she suggested that Noël would best suit the role of Slightly, who is
described as "quite possibly a genius", with "a home-made whistle
to which he capers entrancingly". Caper entrancingly Noël could
do, and he was engaged as Slightly for the London run and ensuing
tour, accepting the princely sum of £4 a week: just under £400
today, and over three times the average wage in 1913. With a
single job in a two-month run, he could earn more than his father,
knocking yet further askew the Cowards' strange familial hierarchy,
and enhancing the thirteen-year-old's oddly adult role in domestic
affairs.

Peter Pan, only ten years old and already immortal, was a Christmas staple for London theatregoers, who knew when to boo and
when to clap their belief in fairies. Slightly was the only one of
the Lost Boys not played by a girl, a situation to which Noël was
entirely used and which allowed him to make even greater an
impression. Noël's old acquaintance from *The Goldfish*, Micheál Mac
Liammóir, was John Darling; Peter Pan was the American actress
Pauline Chase, who had been in the role on and off since 1906, and
who, on one memorable occasion, consented to visit the Cowards
for tea. On the verge of retiring from the stage, she was rumoured
to have had an affair with Captain Scott, whose ill-fated Antarctic
expedition had recently been all over the papers. She arrived at the
Cowards in a yellow sports car. The curtains of Clapham twitched.

Devotees of *Peter Pan* enjoyed the burst of energy Noël gave to
the well-worn proceedings, for the role of Slightly had traditionally
been given to the 33-year-old Archie Baskcomb. "The immortal
Slightly", wrote one reviewer, "is quite a young boy and his grave
pretence at wisdom is all the funnier."[49] The critic Kenneth Tynan

wrote of Noël, four decades later: "In 1913 he was Slightly in *Peter Pan*, and you might say that he has been wholly in *Peter Pan* ever since."[50] The implication is that Noël was frozen in the amber of boyhood, forever a Lost Boy. The name by which, when legendary, he became known – "the Master" – would not shake off the honorific by which his juvenile performances had been listed in Edwardian programmes: he was, perpetually, "Master Noël Coward". But Peter Pan, although he was the boy who never grew up, is also the boy never permitted a childhood. His crowing youthfulness is matched only by his ancient weariness. He and his Lost Boys spend much of their time playing at adulthood, caught in a strange half-life, their odd Neverland, between youth and age.

So it was for Noël. A jobbing actor since the age of eleven, he had little experience of a childish childhood. Not for nothing had his mother suggested he play Slightly, the little old man trapped in a boy's body. He had perfected the comedy that could be wrung from the mismatch between an adult demeanour and his actual age, taking on with careful nonchalance the actor's vocabulary, flamboyant with affection, and polishing to a high sheen his veneer of adult sophistication, presumably through mimicry. It was an impersonation of urban worldliness without the experience to put behind it: an artificiality at several removes, because the very mode of behaviour that he affected was affectation. The first act of *The Goldfish* had found the children gathered around the tea table, speaking to one another in a language of dandyish artifice. Noël had been required to call everyone "my own dear" or "my dear boy" and to deliver lines such as: "Mother comes here to recoup in the matter of complexion".[51] *The Times* had complained of Lila Field's play that "children ought to be children in the theatre no less than in the nursery, or else where is the charm that is their especial glory?"[52]

But beneath the veneer, Noël remained riddled with the insecurities of boyhood, and his teenage letters combine stabs at loucheness with the spelling and (occasional) tantrums of someone half his age. His career rested, as for any child actor of the day, on all that was rosy-cheeked, innocent, patriotic, and good. It also rested on all that was young. Before every revival of *Peter Pan* the regular juveniles were measured to see if they had got too tall; if they had, they were unceremoniously fired. "Measuring day", wrote Pauline Chase, "is one of the tragedies of *Peter Pan*."[53] The result was that a generation of hard-working child actors, as they ricocheted between *Peter Pan* and *Where the Rainbow Ends* and back again, were trying hard to be grown up, while trying not to grow up at all. Noël flourished his consonants as Gertrude Lawrence flourished her powder puff. All of them were attempting to work out who it was they were supposed to be. Noël was one of the few among his circle to keep his own name – Esmé Wynne had been born Dorothy Ripper; Gertrude Lawrence was originally Alexandra Klasen; and Ninette de Valois, back at Lila Field's academy, was still known as Edris Stannus.

The Times had thought that, in *The Goldfish*, Noël "was more at home in the first act as a natural boy than in his second character as the Court jester".[54] But a "natural boy" was precisely what Noël Coward was never allowed to be. Years later, Mac Liammóir met him as an adult and wondered "what had made me dislike him as a child, because here he was [. . .], so much more charming, more natural, more himself".[55] At fourteen, Noël was arrested in childhood after childhood was over, and groping at adulthood before adulthood had begun.

SCENE SIX

His mother aside, few would have singled out Noël Coward as one of the century's great talents. He had become a stalwart supporting player without ever graduating to the level of Philip Tonge, who had moved to America and was enjoying success on Broadway. Cannily he realised that the smaller parts suited him; it is impossible to steal a scene if it already belongs to you. But when the tour of *Peter Pan* finished early in 1914 he was out of work, and remained so for the rest of that momentous year.

He had stayed close to Esmé Wynne, and as they grew older, quarrelling, collaborating, playing, they had run wild. They traversed London on the railway, dodging the fare and the ticket officer, and running from the clutches of stationmasters. She later insisted that she had stood back, disapproving, while Noël exercised his old habit of stealing what he needed and wanted, and that Violet, called on to intervene, had turned a blind eye.[56] But Noël painted a believable picture of a giggling pair of theatrical and innovative petty thieves, picking the locks of slot machines, or running off from shops and stalls with chocolates and cakes and even scent. Play-acting was paramount, and they swapped clothes, parading around the streets as each other while smoking packets of stolen cigarettes. Noël's eventually blasé use of the cigarette as sophisticated prop was achieved only by battling initial nausea, but cigarettes were now to accompany him through life, onstage and off, and would eventually hasten his death. Beginning the habit in his early teens he was hardly unusual; smoking had become so popular among juveniles that the Children's Act of 1908 had had to forbid the sale of tobacco to those under sixteen.

Most of all they continued to write stories and scripts together, and Esmé produced reams of verse that Noël, taking his first steps as a songwriter, set to music that has not survived. Together they created a children's newspaper, containing poems, letters to the editor, and an agony aunt's column.[57] Their outpourings were, he later thought, "beastly little whimsies", featuring elves, mermaids, fawns and fauns – and, especially, Pan. Noël's poetry became "rife with whimsical pixie allusion", and he began to fancy himself "a half-wild creature", darting through trees and "crouching in the bracken in faun-like attitudes".[58] Noël and Esmé had learned to read in the era of *Peter Pan*, *The Wind in the Willows*, and *The Secret Garden*, in all of which the pipe-playing god is shorn of Bacchanalian wildness and depicted as a personification of rustic, even Arcadian, innocence. One of the most popular musical comedies from Noël's childhood had been *The Arcadians* (1909), chief among its songs "The Pipes of Pan are Calling". Esmé's *The Prince's Bride* was, like *The Goldfish*, set in fairyland and *Rainbow*'s star attraction, each year, was the return of Mavis Yorke as "Will o' the Wisp". A generation of Edwardian children would come of age as the Bright Young People and carry over into their strangely infantilised adulthood ironic remnants of their Arcadian youth. When Noël was older, friends would still note his "mischievous faun's eyes" or remark that he was "lithe as a fawn", that he "looked like a satyr".[59]

But if the Edwardian era had ideas about innocence, it also set strong store by sophistication, and in 1914 Esmé was sent away to be "finished" at a Belgian convent. Dutifully Noël wrote to her, the letters covered in doodles and sketches: "I don't know what I am going to do without my Stodge [. . .] Can't we arrange so that we can be together lots? Please go on with all your wicked ways at the Convent and get expelled and come home! DO!!!!! I am longing for you. [. . .] Goodbye now darling old Stodgekins from your ever loving Pal to all Eternity."[60] Later she admitted to him how "letters from you preserved me from near-suicide at that dreadful convent".[61] The enforced separation from Esmé made room for another friendship that kept him from solitude for the rest of that year, and did a great many more things besides. On the top of one of Noël's childhood letters, Violet has written simply "Philip S time", as if referring to an era in her son's life that she knew would be important.

Noël met James Streatfeild, who went by his middle name of Philip, some time in 1914, when Noël was fourteen and Streatfeild was thirty-four. It was a formative friendship for the boy, so formative that whatever its nature it can be dignified with the word "relationship". But little survives to narrate it. Streatfeild was a successful artist, a silver medallist at the Royal Academy. Closest among his student friends had been E. H. Shepard, who remembered him as a fine pianist, "always cheerful and, being endowed with a good voice, [he] often led us in song while we were cleaning up".[62] Streatfeild was a keen amateur performer, and gave his Chelsea studio over to meetings of the Poets' Club.[63] Best known as a painter of landscapes and portraits, he had sketched a number of child actors, and would eventually draw Noël in what may have been a formal commission for promotional material.[64] Family legend had it that Violet, in need of money, was working for Streatfeild as a char-lady and suggested that Noël could stand in as the aristocratic child whose portrait Streatfeild was painting.[65]

Only a handful of Streatfeild's canvases now survives, mostly formal portraits in the manner of John Singer Sargent, with whom he had studied; he claimed some of Sargent's commissions to be his own work. It has been written of him that "he painted boys, usually naked, and usually young", the implication being that his friendship with Noël was tinged with a paedophilic attraction.[66] Only one such painting has been discovered, a roundel of nude children from 1914 in which, it has been suggested, one of the figures bears some resemblance to Noël.[67] The boy's head is turned away from the viewer, and the likeness is not pronounced. The style is reminiscent of Henry Scott Tuke, who was elected an associate of the Royal Academy during Streatfeild's studies, and who is now infamous for his paintings of nude boys and for hovering on the fringes of a group – led by Oscar Wilde, J. A. Symonds, and others – known as the Uranians, who celebrated the adolescent male in a manner that, to twenty-first-century attitudes, appears clearly pederastic.

By May 1914 Streatfeild and Noël had become close enough for the former to suggest that they holidayed together, and they set off happily on a motoring trip through the West Country, trundling through Devon and into Cornwall (the maximum speed for motor cars of the day was 20 mph). Cornwall is almost always the backdrop for Tuke's Uranian paintings, which were made *en plein air* with the juvenile models posed against sea and rocks

close to Tuke's home in Falmouth. Strengthening the possibility
that Noël modelled for Streatfeild in Tukeian fashion is the fact
that they were joined on the holiday by Streatfeild's friend Sydney
Lomer.

Lomer was thirty-four, a military man, privately wealthy,
famously flamboyant, fond of fast cars and flashy parties. In 1912 a
nineteen-year-old soldier from his regiment, Robert Buchanan, had
been found dead in Lomer's home with a suicide note scrawled in
soap on a mirror, but rumours were rife of foul play and a *crime
passionnel*.[68] Lomer was not only a friend but a patron and sponsor of
Tuke, to whom he once complained that the boy models' genitals
were not painted with enough clarity. He wrote verse under the
pen name of Sydney Oswald, and in the year of the Cornish trip
he privately circulated his translation of the *Anthologia Palatina* (Book
12), a favourite text of the Uranians in that it contained verse by
the Ancient Greek poet Strato about the desire of an older man for
a boy. Lomer's translation was dedicated to an anonymous love:
"Here in this book I will not write thy name [. . .] Men deem it
shame that thou and I should love."[69]

But any portraitist of the relationship between Noël and Philip
Streatfeild should tread carefully before painting it as one between
a predatory pederast and a sexually precocious teenager. It is uncertain whether Streatfeild made an attempt either to mask or to enact
his erotic feelings, such as they existed at all. "Uranian" is a broad
and loosely defined umbrella term, covering relationships from
the lecherous to the innocent. Images of bathing children were a
conventional genre, and the Royal Academy would annually show
a number of pictures and sculptures on the theme.[70] (One painted
advertisement for *Where the Rainbow Ends* showed the pre-pubescent
actress Mavis Yorke nude beneath transparent chiffon).[71] Much
Uranian poetry was positively reviewed in the mainstream press,
innocence taken for granted, and paintings of the type practised by
Tuke, in which untainted boys are shown at one with a pastoral
landscape, were self-consciously offered as a rural corrective to the
urban and dandy-like desires of figures such as Wilde. The Uranian
culture of Tuke and Streatfeild propagated the unsexualised and
ostensibly wholesome homosocial world (thinking itself quietly

superior to the carnal desires of heterosexual love): genitals invisible, bodies hairless, physical contact scant. None of Tuke's models, many of whom he supported financially, complained of abuse or assault. Sydney Lomer's verse translations venerate innocence, despairing at the passing of youth and the sudden sad appearance of hair on a boy's upper lip. Philip Streatfeild's drawing of Noël, carefully stowed away by Violet, makes the boy look only half of his fourteen years.

Noël, his career preserving him in an aspic of pragmatic, which is to say employable, innocence, shared with Peter Pan a strange sexlessness, sex having been discarded with the other trappings of grown-up life. When Philip Tonge had casually revealed to him the mechanics of sex, Noël responded in melodramatic but clearly authentic panic, at the sudden rip of physicality through the world of rainbows and Neverlands and the passionless conventions of Edwardian romance. (The heroine of his song "Alice Is At It Again" takes a calmer view: "The curious secrets that nature revealed | She refused to allow to upset her | But she thought when observing the beasts of the field | That things might have been organised better.") It was his combination of innocence and sophistication, at once old and young for his age, fancying himself a faun from one of his stories and flitting through the trees of his Arcadian imagination, that Philip Streatfeild may have found irresistible. The god Pan had become a symbolic emblem for Uranian poets. A photograph of the pair together taken in 1914 shows Noël grimacing for the camera, his socks pulled to his knees, and emulating the older man's debonair attitude and the easy drape of his scarf. Streatfeild is deadpan, inscrutable. The impression is of a fourteen-year-old with a crush on a prefect or schoolmaster.

Violet seems to have tolerated the "Philip S time", and perhaps was unaware, or kept in the dark, about its intensity, such as it was (she omits Streatfeild entirely from her otherwise detailed memoir of Noël's childhood). But the era was unsuspicious of such relationships. J. M. Barrie's love for the boys of the Llewelyn Davies family had given rise to *Peter Pan* and to a consequent slew of mainstream Edwardian literature in which nostalgia for childhood seemed to merge with desire for the child. Philip was part of the historic Streatfeild family, with a family seat and crest. Noël was in low spirits, owing to unemployment and Esmé's departure, and the friendship was not only distraction but a means of social elevation. Violet's sister Charlotte, still living on Cornwall's south coast, was around to keep an eye on things and eventually, after a happy few weeks with Streatfeild and Lomer, Noël was left with her and his cousins.

The Cornish trip was such a success that a few weeks later it was repeated. Streatfeild took a house on the sea at Polperro, and Noël went too, arriving on 1 July; the two were there together for over a month. Violet may have approved the company the pair kept in Cornwall. Also staying in the small village was Mrs Eva Astley Cooper, privately wealthy and the daughter-in-law of a baronet, who had taken her son and a friend of his (both nearing thirty) on holiday. The five of them struck up a friendship, and although Noël was half the age of the young men, he was comfortable in such company, or tried to be. His letters home are full to bursting point with attempts at sophistication; they were hardly the writing of a man enjoying a romantic get-away. He was, still, a fourteen-year-old boy on a seaside holiday.

Then, early in August 1914, they suddenly saw a newspaper, and the strange Arcadian comedy of his childhood was over. Every one of the boys who had modelled for Henry Scott Tuke, and perhaps for Philip Streatfeild too, naked and spotless in the Cornish seas, would be called up to the war, and many would not return. Charles Frohman, the producer of *Peter Pan*, would be killed on board RMS *Lusitania*, sunk by a German U-boat in 1915, the same year in which George Llewelyn Davies, one of the boys who had inspired J. M. Barrie, was shot through the head. Charles Hawtrey, looking sadly over the various casts of *Where the Rainbow Ends*, would soon note how many alumni of the production had been killed. Noël had starred in the play alongside Sidney Sherwood, a child actor known as Fuzzy, whom he had understudied back in 1911, and who was one of the very first young men to enlist.

A rainbow fuzz of memories, the half-remembered images and sounds of childhood, like bright photographs, coloured by memory as they would not have been by the Edwardian camera. The green hat and feather boa of a lady lodger; the blue cornflower in ARTHUR COWARD*'s buttonhole; the red cover of* The Magnet *comic book, Billy Bunter lumbering through its pages: "The newcomer was a somewhat stout junior, with a broad, pleasant face and an enormous pair of spectacles." The smell of the mud of the Teddington river. "Darling Mother I hope you are well, I am writing this in the kitchen with love from Noel Coward." The goldfish. The mushroom. The macaw. "They were not railway children to begin with . . ." A crown for little children, above the bright blue sky. "Do you believe in fairies? Say quick that you believe . . ." Suddenly all fades into darkness and silence. The lights slowly come up and the stage fills with weeping women and uniformed men. It is* SIDNEY SHERWOOD*'s funeral. A poem is read:*

> The sun still shines,
> Although the rain descends
> You have but danced
> To where the rainbow ends.[72]

THE CURTAIN FALLS

SERVICES RENDERED

——

AN ACT OF WAR

CAST

MASTER NOËL COWARD, *a promising young actor and writer*
MRS VIOLET COWARD, *his mother*

MISS ESMÉ WYNNE, *a young actress*
MR JOHN EKINS, *a young actor*

MR PHILIP STREATFEILD, *a painter*
MRS ASTLEY COOPER, *a socialite*
MR IVOR NOVELLO, *a songwriter*

MR GEOFFREY HOLDSWORTH, *a military convalescent from New Zealand*
MISS GLADYS STERN, *a novelist*
MRS CATHERINE DAWSON SCOTT, *writer*

ASSORTED ACTORS, SOLDIERS, REVELLERS

The action mainly takes place in a number of theatres and army training camps.

TIME: 1914–1918

Enter NOËL COWARD, *aged fourteen.*

NOËL [*writing excitedly*]: Dear Darling old Mummy-snooks. I am enjoying myself so much it really is perfectly heavenly here. It's generally been a leetle beet too cold a wind to be really nice but we bathe from a sandy cove about a mile along the cliffs and then lie in the sun and dry. I am now the coulour of a boiled lobster with which these shores abound (not to say sharks! O-o-er-r Auntie!) This house is so perfectly ripping. Philip has bought me a net with which to catch le denizens de la deep (Bow-wow!) We have a boat in which we have been as far as the mouth (or gaping jaws) of the Harbour and then we came back because Philip said it was too rough. I received le sweater et le lettre all right and it fits me, Tres chic!!! (More Bow-wows!) I haven't been very homesick but I have been a little (bless you). I shall have to stoppp now as I am going to wallow in Bacon and eggs so goodbye and love to Daddy and Eric. Hope you are quite well as leaves me at pres. Your everevereverever loving NOËL.[1]

Philip Streatfeild instantly arranged, now that Britain was at war, for Noël to rejoin his family. He put him in the hands of his friend Hugh Walpole, already acclaimed as one of the finest young British novelists, and on holiday close by. Walpole was gay, but Streatfeild clearly felt it necessary to disguise the friendship with his teen-age companion. "Taking boy, Streatfeild's nephew, Noël Coward by name, with me", Walpole noted on 6 August. "The train was packed, but no unwonted signs of any kind. The boy most amusing. Tipped him."[2] Noël was dropped off in Hampshire, where the Coward family holidayed for the summer, before returning, in mid-September, to Clapham, just as the first British wounded arrived from France.

For a boy weaned on Edwardian notions of patriotism and empire, the war had potential for excitement and theatricality.

Support for it remained strong among the British public; over one million young men enlisted to join Kitchener's army. It would be almost a year before the bombing raids began on London, and Noël's father was now fifty-eight and in no danger of being called up when conscription was eventually introduced. Day-to-day life continued as normal, but with the added excitements of Philip Streatfeild's friendship. Streatfeild lived at 53 Glebe Place in Chelsea, just up from the river, which was now crowded with war traffic. Artists from Augustus John to Walter Sickert had had studios in the building, and Noël appears to have spent a great deal of his time there, socialising with Streatfeild, Sydney Lomer, and their circle. "Philip is now a Soldier! (cheers)" he wrote to his mother from the studio, as if already incorporating stage directions into his prose. "I am going to stay tonight with him as I shant see much of him when he is drilling all day."[3] Evidently he was now able to inform his mother of his movements, rather than ask her permission to make them, and he gives the impression of living an independent life, more in Chelsea than in Clapham: "Captain Lomer is going to take Philip and [. . .] yours truly to a box at a Music Hall tonight."[4]

Streatfeild had joined the Inns of Court Officers Training Corps on the declaration of war, but in September transferred to the 6th Battalion of Sherwood Foresters, a volunteer unit of the Territorial Army of which Lomer, who had presumably pulled strings, was permanent adjutant. The Foresters were assigned a role in the defences around London and began to undergo intensive training. Between August and November 1914 the 6th Battalion was billetted in Harpenden, a town in Hertfordshire, and Lomer organised for Noël to pay a visit. Still three years the junior of even the youngest soldier, his idiosyncratic voice beginning to crack, trailing all the mannerisms of the child actor and with his mind mainly focused on whether or not he would be cast in *Peter Pan* that Christmas, the fourteen-year-old Noël Coward found himself at the centre of, and warmly welcomed by, a volunteer unit of the Territorial Army.

Lomer and Streatfeild made him a military mascot. He was billeted with the soldiers at a private house nearby, and threw himself into the days with high spirits and surprising physical stamina, marching in step amid the uniformed men, some thousands of them, through the genteel streets of the Hertfordshire town to the sound of the regimental band and the crack of rifles on Harpenden Common. "Just a line to tell you I shall be back in time for Friday afternoon", he wrote to his mother, who was either unperturbed or powerless to intervene. "I am having the time of my life here I have just come back from a long day with Lomer's division and I've marched 10 miles! and I'm [so] tired all the officers are so nice to me and all wanted to share their lunch with me you've got a fascinating youth for your son my dear."[5]

Streatfeild was made a second lieutenant on 10 November. The previous week he had made a will, as so many young soldiers did, leaving "my friend Noël Coward [. . .] the sum of £50". It was a generous but not a life-changing sum, just short of £5000 today, and a fragment of the wealth Streatfeild had to leave.[6] That month the 6th Battalion marched forty-five miles east to Braintree in Essex, under orders to depart for France. But fear of invasion became so acute that the orders were remanded, and the unit instead stayed in Britain to dig defensive trenches on the Essex coast. Noël returned to London in the hopes of getting work in a Christmas production, but Archie Baskcomb had returned to the role of Slightly. The theatres showed no signs of closing; the declaration of war had been so unexpected that directors were taken by surprise when planning the autumn seasons of 1914. A number of wartime plays, promoting British pluck amid the evils of a German invasion, promptly took over the West End, but were quickly replaced with escapist entertainment, as the realities of the battlefield became more and more apparent. Public transport was unreliable, and young male actors were scarce, but audiences flocked, longing for an hour or two's respite from the fear of the telegram delivery.

Early in 1915, Baskcomb fell ill, and Noël took over as Slightly at short notice for a handful of performances, standing proud on the pirate ship as Wendy told the Lost Boys, on behalf of their real mothers: "We hope our sons will die like English gentlemen." But there was no other work on the horizon. He took solace in his relationship with Esmé Wynne, which was of more comfort than the confirmation classes he received from a local vicar who, not long before Noël's confirmation on 7 March 1915, made a pass at him, killing stone dead the boy's already distant relationship with the Church. Not long afterwards Noël began to cough badly and was diagnosed as having a tubercular gland in his chest. TB was a disease endemic in the population, and in 1913 the Medical Research Council had been formed especially to combat it.

It is hard now to imagine the daily barrage of smoke and unclean air to which Noël had been subjected. The Duke of York's Theatre prided itself on having fires for the actors in every dressing room, and smelled constantly of burning during *Peter Pan* (the "Indians" lit real fires in the second act). The outbreak of war interrupted the government's plans to lessen pollution, and the law forbidding smoking in theatre auditoriums was quickly scrapped: the risk of fire was thought secondary to the importance of permitting cigarettes to soldiers on leave. Plays were now performed to the scratch and click of matches and lighters, dots of flame glowing beneath an omnipresent fug.[7] Noël himself may already have been a heavy smoker, and his daily life was one of coal dust and gas and tobacco, of steam and smog. It was suggested that he go and stay with a doctor friend of the family – Frederick Etlinger – in his house on the grounds of a sanatorium.[8] The Pinewood Sanatorium was in a forest in Berkshire (pine trees were thought beneficial to the tubercular) and rapidly filling with gassed soldiers. Noël seems to have spent some months living with Etlinger, talking with the doctors and reading in the sanatorium's library. It was a strangely dead period of his childhood, shadowed by the possibility of his disease developing in severity, and shorn of all distraction bar the ghostly company of dying men.

Philip Streatfeild, despite being a second lieutenant, was essentially in charge of his battalion, as his captain was on sick leave. If he wrote to Noël, or if Noël wrote to him, the letters do not survive. He dug trenches in Essex all through the bitter winter of 1915, and soon contracted trench fever, a disease transmitted by body lice. In March that year he was removed to hospital, where the doctors operated unsuccessfully on his lungs. It became clear that there was nothing more to be done, and he was transferred to a nursing home in north-west Croydon. On 16 April, for reasons unknown, he added a codicil to his will revoking his £50 legacy to

Noël, still calling him "my friend". He may simply have been able to distribute the legacies from his sickbed, certain that he would die, which he did, with his father beside him, on 3 June.

He was buried with full military honours in Streatham Cemetery, and although his family believed he had died from complications of trench fever, and his entry on the Bond of Sacrifice mentions peritonitis, his death certificate gives pulmonary tuberculosis, which had killed his older brother not that long before.[9] He may have given the disease to Noël, or caught it from him; army recruits were screened for TB on being called up, but the tests were imprecise. Of Noël's sense of grief or bereavement nothing survives bar a line of quiet regret, written seventeen years later, that Streatfeild would never fully realise "the great kindness he had done me".[10] It is a cryptic phrase, singular and specific (and quite different to, say, "Philip had shown me great kindness"). Perhaps it was the kindness of friendship, or the kindness − realised only in hindsight − of refusing to act upon erotic feelings. It may simply have been the kindness of social introduction, as, for Noël, there could have been no greater gift. Lying in the nursing home, not long before he died, Philip was visited by Eva Astley Cooper, whom he and Noël had met in Cornwall. "Is there anything I can do for you?" she asked. "Will you take Noël Coward home with you?" came the reply. "He is delicate and wants taking care of."[11]

That summer zeppelins began to sail through the sky to drop their bombs. Charles Hawtrey never forgot his first sight of the airships: "It looked wonderful, like a great big silver cigar floating in the air."[12] The military effects were few, and attacks over London were mainly confined to the east of the city, at a safe distance from Clapham, to which Noël, his health restored, had finally returned. But the "baby-killers", as the zeppelins were known after an infant became one of the earliest fatalities, were objects of hatred and fear. An excuse to leave London and to breathe the cleaner air of the East Midlands was welcome. Eva Astley Cooper had taken Streatfeild's request seriously, and promptly invited Noël to her family home in Rutland, halfway between Leicester and Peterborough. An invitation to stay with a grand family in their grand home was not to be dismissed in the Coward household, and Violet was soon seeing her son off at St Pancras station, undaunted even when she left her purse on the underground and had to pawn a ring to buy Noël's fare.

Mrs Astley Cooper, now aged sixty-one, lived at Hambleton Hall, a grand Victorian pile built on the centre of the Hambleton Peninsula, overlooking Rutland Water. It had been left to her by her brother, whose fortune, far from being passed down through the generations, came from a brewery business (a fact Violet was evidently prepared to overlook). Casting herself as a kind of Ottoline Morrell of the Midlands, draping the mirrors with cloth so as not to catch sight of her ever-stouter reflection, she set up a salon at the Hall of which she was an indomitable matriarch, collecting artistic eccentrics and curios. Her husband, Clement, had retired from the military and provided the place with an aristocratic glaze by dint of being a baronet's son. He now seemed happy to live in his wife's considerable shadow: she, stoutly upholstered in tweed, could give any character in a Coward play a run for their money when it came to wit and caprice.

Later in the war the Hall became a military hospital, and not until the 1920s would Hambleton start to welcome its more distinguished guests, by which time Noël would visit as one of London theatre's brightest stars. For now he was an awkward teenager recently discharged from a sanatorium and hosted in the spirit of doing a friend a favour. Ever adaptable, he could perform the role of country-house gentleman as easily as he could the Cockney page boy or the adolescent muse to a Bohemian painter, and he spent much of his time out of doors at Mrs Astley Cooper's maternal insistence that he breathe the clean air (hunting ruled supreme). He delighted at the new luxuries, and was perhaps set to entertain the guests amid the mesh of cigarette holders and the clink of champagne saucers. He was able to drink in a way of life both foreign and fascinating, scrutinising the English upper classes on their home turf, in all their tweeds and traditions. One characteristic of his country-house plays, for which Hambleton was an early model, is his ability to exist affectionately and easily within his onstage world while simultaneously commenting on it from the outside. It was as if he had opened the front of the Hall on hinges, like a doll's house, to see the goings-on behind, from the servants' bedrooms in the attic to the steamy kitchen beneath, and, between the two, the corridors of spare bedrooms, fires lit in each, in which guests would sleep beneath luxurious linen and, who knows, perhaps pad from one to the other in the dead of night. In his play *The Young Idea* (1921), he would describe the "English hunting county, where immorality is conducted by rules and regulations".

It was at Hambleton Hall that he saw, lying on the table, a book published the previous year. On the dust jacket was a man in a blue suit, cuffs immaculate, shoes shiny, looking quizzically through an eyeglass at a wolf. *Beasts and Super-Beasts* by H. H. Munro: "Saki". Noël may have been attracted either by the unusual pen name or by the parody in the title (of Shaw's *Man and Superman*), and he read through the night until he had finished it. It was a collection of short stories, featuring animals and humans equally untameable, and wise young children who are able – as in Saki's most enduring tale, "The Open Window" – to trick their elders. The writing is varnished to a high shimmer, the wit epigrammatic, and the politics conservative. Figures from socialists to suffragettes are objects of scorn, and the Edwardian world is at once ridiculed and venerated. The country-house party often becomes the setting for some transplanted Bacchic play performed in frocks and tweeds.

Noël soon read widely in Saki; maybe he noticed with approval that, in *The Chronicles of Clovis*, a vicious hyena is called "Esmé", and delighted at the appearance of his childhood obsession, the god Pan, who appears giggling with mirth as an Edwardian bride is gored by a stag. Later, introducing a collected volume of Saki's stories, he praised the writer for evoking the "evanescent charm" of the Edwardian era.[13] The phrase is a curious one, for it seems to miss not only the fact that Saki's humour can be savage and surreal, but that the stories hold a mirror up to high society no less accurate for being distorting and exaggerating, their characters built from silk and acid. Then again, Noël's description may reveal his perception that an evanescent society was the perfect material for permanent art, and his awareness of the dark and lethal glint that can exist within charm, which can stab as easily as soothe. Either way, he would happily admit that Saki was one of the most significant influences on his own work, and from then on made sure to visit the publishers in person when a new collection of stories was announced, wanting to be the first among his social circle to have read it.[14] Lying in the comfortable bed of Hambleton Hall, the war far off, with the prospect of a grand breakfast in the morning followed by a deep bath filled from steaming water that emerged from the delicious novelty of a shiny brass can, Noël found that several aspects of his career were slotting, neatly, into place.

Back in London the casualty lists were lengthening. The list of glorious dead erected in Clapham's Holy Trinity Church would eventually number 138. On 13 October 1915 an airship got to London, sailed above the Strand, and by the time the performances in the West End had reached the interval, began to bomb the area around Charing Cross in what was known as the "Theatreland Raid". A bomb fell directly on the Lyceum Theatre, killing seventeen. The Charing Cross Hospital was then occupying a building just off the Strand; huge banners were hung in the area demanding "Quiet for the Wounded", and traffic was diverted to minimise noise. The West End was a changed place, sombre and quiet, and the massive boom of theatre-building that had been ongoing for forty years was brought permanently to an end.

That Christmas Noël and Esmé Wynne once again joined the cast of *Where the Rainbow Ends*, she back in the lead role as Rosamund, and he re-cast as the Slacker, a figure out of a morality play who appears as a warning of what happens to those who shirk their duties. Noël stuck green sequins to his eyelids, and perfected a pantomime-villain laugh that usually won him an exit round. It was, thought the *Observer*, with a proto-Coward-esque sneer, "a very clever little performance".[15] But the role, thought one newspaper, had taken on a serious hue, and "will mean more nowadays than in the peaceful times".[16] Protected by a dragon, the Slacker is eventually defeated by Rosamund's brother Crispian, who recites to him Nelson's line: "England expects that every man will do his duty." The play's amiable character known as "the German" had quietly become French.

Soon a long theatrical tour beckoned. It was Noël's first biographer who wrote, in 1933: "The war might destroy civilisation, it might smash up Christianity, but it could not annihilate *Charley's Aunt.*"[17] Brandon Thomas's comedy had been a hit on its premiere, in 1892, and had toured intermittently ever since. Noël was Charley, who, in need of a chaperone so as respectably to woo his inamorata (Esmé Wynne was inevitable casting), persuades a rich friend to pose as an aunt from Brazil, "where the nuts come from!" The character was twenty; he, sixteen – in the absence of young male actors, Noël found himself again acting in counterpoint to his true age. (Around this time, he and Esmé began to write, but left unfinished, a script called *What Next?* that borrowed heavily from *Charley's Aunt*; it featured a young man and woman who swap clothes to prevent their discovery by a difficult aunt.) The director, Noël thought, rehearsed the new recruits with all "the airy deftness of a rheumatic deacon producing *Macbeth* for a church social".[18] He was disdainful of the play and thought the role of Charley, a straight man who set up the jokes, deeply dull. The tour opened in London on 31 January 1916, and on it went for half a year, offering beleaguered and bereaved wartime audiences the escape they craved. Most of the actors had been in the show for years and could do it in their sleep.

It was a glum troupe that crossed the country on steam trains increasingly full of wounded soldiers. Ticket prices shot up after the introduction that year of an entertainment tax to fund the war (it would remain in place until 1960) and audiences were small. Auditoria became impossible to heat as supply problems increased; transport was erratic, and the actors hauled their cases from the various stations to whichever cold or grubby room had to be booked in the interchangeable towns. They crowded into the small number of chilly dressing rooms, husbanding their precious supply of stage make-up, ready to give performances at the strangest times so that audiences could return home on whatever train had decided to run. The actors wore their own clothes, and Noël's flannel suit shrank

steadily throughout the tour's progressive washings, not helped by
the fact that he had suddenly become tall, even gangly, and – as his
fellow actors took delight in pointing out – prone to spots.

Sharing digs with Esmé was thought improper, and he was paired
off with another young actor, Arnold Raynor, whom he so disliked
that by the end of the run they had come to blows. As the months
were ticked off tempers ran high, and there were quarrels and tears
and stormings off to bed. Noël and Esmé finally flouted company
rules and insisted on living together, whether in a house shared
with travelling acrobats who left "a rim of grey horror" round the
inside of the bath, or in a comfortable establishment that turned
out to be a brothel – a fact they caught on to only after the third
nocturnal arrival of a strange man in Esmé's bedroom.[19] Neither of
them thought the nature of the establishment any reason to leave,
but the production company had other ideas.

It was a grim half-year. Noël's two pounds a week didn't go that
far, and he lived off buns and milk, scoffing fish and chips after
the show in the novelty of late evening light (British Summer Time
was introduced that May). At Southampton the cast entertained
recuperating soldiers at a local hospital. Otherwise, he and Esmé
had to amuse each other during the long empty days, and went off
together to explore the war-blighted town centres, flirting with the
locals and getting lost on long walks before suddenly remembering
there was a matinee – "we had visions of *Charley's Aunt* Charleyless".[20]
They went skinny-dipping when near the sea, photographing one
another on the rocks, or went off to play in arcades and mill about
in whichever shops were open. Noël's penchant for shoplifting, to
Esmé's dismay, was getting more inventive and ambitious, as were
his means of avoiding punishment when caught. Detained by a
shop assistant, he wheeled round in a temper: "Really! Look how
badly this store is run. I could have made off with a dozen books
and nobody would have noticed."[21]

Weekly he wrote to his mother ("Darlingest of sweet Snigs"),
who carefully filed each letter, the calligraphy flamboyant and the
spelling poor, the writing paper lilac and often sealed in wax with
the extravagant "N" that, as he grew older, he would stretch to
inch-long width when signing his name. "We have both been

crying hard for the last hour", he wrote, "never again do I go on tour this feeling of being so far away is too dreadful for words, but I must try not to be melancholy."[22] Amid the requests for cakes and vests and clean collars, bursts of wartime reality briefly emerge: "When I heard about that zepp raid (they told us it was in London) I nearly went mad!" Or: "I haven't been particularly ~~saw~~ sore" – this after a period of sun burn – "but I am nearly black and peeling gracefully at all extremities such fun! We had an Air Raid the other night a few miles away <u>also</u> a thunderstorm there's excitement!" Crude Freudianism it may be to suggest that his relationship with his mother – described as "Oedipal" by one close friend – was pushing from his life any possibility of desire towards women, who would never live up to, or would risk competition with, his love for Violet. But his correspondence with her takes on a disconcerting aura of romance: "I am longing and longing for you"; "Au revoir now my own darling"; "Farewell now my lamb"; "Ever your own sweet Noël."[23]

In letters home he was learning to be a writer, creating sharp, spiteful, Saki-esque little character portraits: "he drank ale and made a noise like water running out of the bath and crammed his fork with food and shoved it into his great gullet". He wrote with all the hauteur that comes of social uncertainty, for on which rung of society's ladder did this travelling teenage actor, the son of a music salesman, shunting between flea-ridden digs, a room at Hambleton Hall, a Bohemian studio, and a flat at Clapham, know where to perch? "Those friends of Auntie Helen's turned up on Tuesday night at the Theatre and took us home to supper with them also last night, they are quaint souls, very <u>very</u> suburban! but homely withall!" Flashes of Noël Coward rise to the top of his letters and pop like champagne bubbles, as after a quarrel with a cast mate: "I hopped up and said that perhaps I had better live by myself for the rest of the tour as the sight of him every day with a face on him like [a] seasick flamingo was rather too much for me."[24] He was slowly starting to play himself, learning the role of Noël Coward. And, for him, playing a role was the surest means of being genuine.

Charley's Aunt arrived at its final location on 29 May: "Here I am in Woolly Wolverhampton and what I've seen of it, it looks perfectly awful".[25] By the end of that week the tour was over and Noël was free. He spent the summer preparing a one-man show that came to nothing, partly because it was formed of impressions and few could guess whom he was mimicking; partly because he refused bookings he thought were beneath him, which amounted to nearly all of them. Around this time he holidayed with an actor friend, nine months his senior, named John Ekins, whom he and Esmé had met in *Where the Rainbow Ends*. John lived with his uncle at Catford, and returned during the summer to his parents in Cornwall, where Noël joined him, staying in the little hamlet of Rame on the south-east coast, where John's father was the vicar. Each was as obsessed with theatre as the other, and they soon became close, going into Plymouth to see performances and reading together in the garden. The Ekins offered a period of quiet and intimate family life, one Noël perhaps missed back in Clapham. John's sister, Audrey, had tuberculosis and was confined to bed, and the boys would entertain her in her bedroom.

By the autumn he and John were in London and in work. Noël was cast in *The Light Blues*, a new musical comedy, for which there was now insatiable demand, about an actress caught up in undergraduate jollity at Cambridge. The attraction of the show was to work with the director, Robert Courtneidge, and his actress daughter Cicely, one of Noël's boyhood stage-heroines, who found the young actor unattractive, astute, and amazingly outspoken.[26] Her father had a temper, and made Noël a whipping boy. Matters came to a head when, during performances on the three-week tour that preceded their arrival in London, Noël did little to repress his giggles at the onstage comedy, and was given an almighty dressing-down in front of the entire cast. Reading Noël's account of the episode, two decades later, Courtneidge wrote to apologise: "I'm sorry I hit you so hard – rather that the recollection should so persist."[27] *The Light Blues* opened in the West End on 14 September 1916, just a fortnight after the largest zeppelin raid of the war. The nights were striped with searchlights and shook to the sound of guns firing uselessly into the sky. Cicely Courtneidge remembered the rumble in the theatre disrupting the first night to the extent that she and Noël had to sing one of the jollier numbers early, to calm nerves and raise spirits. The favourable reviews did not prevent the show from closing two weeks later.[28]

John Ekins meanwhile had been cast in a much more successful play, *The Best of Luck*, which opened in October. Noël, out of work, took to walking on during the crowd scenes, just for something to do. He spent the rest of his evenings earning money as a dancer at the Elysee Restaurant in Piccadilly (now the Café de Paris): "A New Innovation" a flyer proclaimed, "Miss Eileen Dennis and Master Noël Coward. First appearance in New Costume Dances."[29] The pair of them made their stately way around the subterranean dance floor, but it was long before the place became a go-to venue for even the dimmest of the young things, and wartime dining was a sombre experience. Master Coward and Miss Dennis were engaged not to dance into the drug-fuelled early hours but to provide entertainment during the drab gentility of afternoon tea.

In November came the death of Noël's literary hero, Saki, who was shot by a German sniper while sheltering in a crater. John Ekins was cast as the lead in that year's revival of *Where the Rainbow Ends*; Noël made do with another Christmas play for children called *The Happy Family*, woven around a series of animal drawings by Cecil Aldin that were popular from picture books and nursery wallpaper. Noël was one of the few humans in the production, as was a twelve-year-old girl called Ethel McGlinchy, performing under the stage name of Fabia Drake. The two struck up a friendship, although she frankly admitted that "nobody recognized that here was a fellow – albeit only sixteen years old – whose abundance of talents, whose extraordinary versatility had never before been equalled". What she did notice, even then, was Noël's "extraordinary powers of application".[30] *The Times*'s reviewer proclaimed, almost wistfully, that "Master Noël Coward [was] very nearly grown up nowadays".[31]

He and Esmé continued to fill their days by writing together; a notebook from 1917 forms a kind of magazine filled with essays, recipes, games, and stories adorned with mock praise from newspaper reviews. One of Noël's contributions is a short

play called *Pan's Daughter*, featuring "Pattie Pan" – offspring of
the eponymous god – wreaking havoc in a country house. Esmé
meanwhile provided titles such as "An Airy Fairy Fragment",
and they worked together – he setting her words to melodies
held in his head but never notated – on songs about harlequins,
monkeys, and mermaids.[32] The tone and style are still so quaint
and scattergun as to make it seem near impossible that, within
seven years, Noël would write *Hay Fever*. They began to submit
stories to John Lane, hoping to be accepted by his Bodley Head
imprint (which had published Saki). Lane took them to tea and
said that though publication was impossible he looked forward to
reading more.

Noël was also, by this time, inseparable from John Ekins, and
whatever the competition between the three ambitious performers,
they seem to have made a close-knit trio, "always together in their
spare time", Violet noticed, "and I think they had a happy time
of it".[33] Esmé and John were becoming romantically attached, and
John seems to have managed potential awkwardness by becoming
fraternal to Coward without resenting his closeness to Esmé. Conscription had been introduced the year before, and John was called
up on 28 March and appointed to the Royal Flying Corps in South
Farnborough.[34] Noël was presumably dreading his own coming of
age, and ticking off his last months of freedom.

Three weeks later, the post brought two letters. The first was
from John, suggesting that they go and see a matinee on one of his
forthcoming days of leave. The second was from John's mother,
saying that John had died. He had caught spinal meningitis, which
killed him at speed. Alone, Noël walked in a daze to the theatre, his
place of refuge, but left during the interval, in tears. It was a violent
shock, seemingly greater and more upsetting than the death of
Philip Streatfeild, although Noël may have been grieving for both
of them, having lost his two closest male friends in the space of two
years. Neither had been directly a war casualty, but training camps
were breeding grounds for disease, and both meningitis and tuberculosis were constant and often fatal threats. A small line was added
to the notebook of Noël's and Esmé's collaborations, appended to
an instruction on how "to remove blackheads permanently" from

the skin: "Dedicated to the memory of J. R. W. Ekins. Our dearest friend, who died April the 17th, 1917."[35]

A stained-glass window was installed at the church in Rame, showing John dressed as Saint George; it was emblazoned with the emblem of the Flying Corps and inscribed with the same phrase as the gravestone of Noël's brother, Russell, who had died from the same disease twenty years before: "In memory of John Robert Warre Ekins, Who Fell Asleep." Three years later John's sister Christine would die in childbirth, not long before his sister Audrey died of tuberculosis. His parents brought up their granddaughter alone, in the little vicarage at Rame. Long afterwards, a famous writer, Noël returned to Cornwall. "I called at Rame for five minutes. The Ekins were out, but I saw the grandchild. She is perfectly lovely, and a darling little thing."[36]

Nineteen-seventeen was the year of deadlock. The end of the conflict seemed out of reach, and the papers were thick with casualty lists. Noël and Esmé became industrious and ambitious, as if time were limited, and submitted stories without success to American literary magazines. Their work remained light and comic, but they had become aghast at the pointless waste of life that assailed them from all sides. The horrors of war crowd in the wings of Noël's letters and memories, which take refuge in humour even when life was traumatic. He never described the fierce pacifism which Esmé believed had taken them over; she, a devotee of George Bernard Shaw, presumably agreed with the then-infamous Shavian argument that warring nations were equally culpable. She was becoming politically aware, and increasingly interested in humanitarian campaigns. Noël's politics, such as they were, took second place to matters of career, even if his burial in work, or the attempts to acquire it, were a means of escape.

In the middle of this strange time, still grieving the death of John Ekins, he found work as a supernumerary in a silent film, *Hearts of the World*, directed by the famous David Wark Griffith, a pioneer of the full-length movie, and starring Lillian Gish, a major star. Subtitled "A Love Story of the Great War", the film was an attempt by the British government to change the American public's neutral stance towards the conflict. Noël's small appearance in it is uncanny, given that twenty-five years later he would be tasked with influencing American political opinion in a similar direction. Two minutes in, Gish is followed down the street by a gawky young man in a cap, pushing a wheelbarrow. Noël, slathered in the thick make-up demanded by cameras of the day, towers over the leading lady, who later claimed to have noticed his extraordinary talent. (Given little was required of him beyond wheelbarrow-pushing, hindsight may have aided her judgement.) When the film reached the public its startling footage of trenches and battle scenes, made all the more dramatic by the cinema pianist, set pulses racing and its exaggerated depiction of German brutality was said to have helped engender a hatred of the enemy that lasted long after the Armistice.

In the late summer Esmé was given a role in Cyril Harcourt's *A Pair of Silk Stockings* (which caused more of a sensation than its title might suggest, being about a divorce). The production opened in Aldershot on 21 August, touring to Cambridge and Derbyshire through September and October, and the play was preceded each night by a short curtain-raiser called *Ida Collaborates*, advertised as being by "Esnomel". Friends surely worked out the spliced and oddly Arthurian nom-de-plume. The manuscript does not reveal how the writing labour was divided, but the fact that there is no part for Noël, and a very good one for Esmé, may give a clue. Surprisingly, the drama ended unhappily, Ida being in love with a famous author, whose books she improves but whose heart she never captures.[37] It was the first play (at least partly) by Noël Coward to be given a professional production.

As *Ida Collaborates* opened he was up in Manchester, rehearsing Dorothy Brandon's *Wild Heather* (about a young woman's adventures on a cruise ship), which opened on 27 August. The part was small enough that he could bunk off early and amuse himself. Just down the road, at the Prince's Theatre, an operetta called *Arlette* had opened, with new songs written for its revival by Ivor Novello who, at twenty-four, was already acclaimed as one of the great wartime songwriters and theatre composers. It was not surprising that Noël should bump into him in the centre of Manchester, and had they been alone, the star-struck young actor might have waxed lyrical about "Keep the Home-Fires Burning", asked for an autograph, and gone away. But Novello was with his partner, the actor Bobbie Andrews, once a child performer with whom Noël had been friendly. Introductions were made and Noël was invited for dinner.

Unshaven and tired, Novello looked nothing like his matinee-idol headshots, but Noël was soon noting the intimacy with which he spoke about great stars, and his easy way as a host, made generous by the security of success. Noël returned to his lodgings tingling with envy. Novello was evidence that youth was no bar to productivity and success, but it is hard to know where precisely Noël thought his own talents lay — as a singer-songwriter, playwright, or actor. He had few models when it came to performers successful in as many disciplines as he was attempting to master. Novello had yet to make his acting debut and, alumnus of choirs in Gloucester and Oxford, he had a classical musical training that Noël made no efforts to emulate. The top playwrights of the day — Shaw, Somerset Maugham, John Galsworthy — did not, as a rule, perform their own material. Not since the likes of David Garrick, Dion Boucicault, and (in his early career) Harley Granville-Barker, had the numerous disciplines of theatre settled in one figure.

It was as if Noël didn't much mind which strand of his life would provide fame and fortune, as long as one of them did. If he threw everything at the wall, something might stick. The abstract notion of success as a thing in itself was more important to him than the means by which it was obtained. The result was an attempt at a kind of all-round professional brilliance, which took longer to achieve than he at first expected. Inspired by the meeting with Novello, that week he wrote both words and melody for a song called "When You Come Home on Leave": "I'd like you just to realise | That though we're far apart | Where'er you be on land or sea | You have with you my heart." It was a clumsy emulation of Novello's lovelorn stoicism: "The weeks for me are very sad | And happy days are few. | Remember when you're feeling bad | That I am lonely too."[38]

Somehow he persuaded Max Darewski, a composer of light opera who lived in Manchester, to listen to the song that very day. "Max leapt off the piano stool" Noël told his mother, "and danced for joy and said it was going to take London by storm!" (it didn't) "it is to be published next week" (it wasn't) "I shall probably make a lot of money out of it" (he wouldn't).[39] Not that Darewski wasn't as good as his word: he remained encouraging, and put in a good report with his composer brother Herman, who was branching out as a music publisher and who duly contracted Noël for a handsome annual retainer. Noël seems mainly to have considered himself a lyricist at this time and, perhaps at Darewski's introduction, provided words for settings by a young songwriter named Doris Joel. The majority of the submissions they made to Darewski remained unpublished, and the firm eventually went bust.

But during that exciting fortnight in Manchester, in the summer of 1917, Noël was riding on air, and the good fortune continued. Charles Hawtrey had not forgotten him, and sent a successful American producer called Gilbert Miller up to Manchester to assess him for a part in a new comedy. "He said I was really splendid", Noël told Violet in high excitement, "and that I hadn't half enough to do! [. . .] He is going back to Hawtrey today to say that he had perfect confidence in me and that I am thoroughly natural and unaffected etc . . . Oh, I am a star!"[40] Strictly speaking, he was too young for the part in Hawtrey's comedy (*The Saving Grace*, by the Australian dramatist Haddon Chambers). But seventeen-year-old actors were worth snatching up before they were conscripted. Hawtrey played an old buffer desperate to rejoin the army at the outbreak of war; his niece becomes engaged to a rich but unsuitable young man: Noël, for whom the topic perhaps struck home.

It was his highest-profile role yet, and the first in which he began to think seriously about his performance, partly thanks to Hawtrey, who instilled in him a new awareness of technique and precision. At the opening preview, in Manchester on 3 October, Hawtrey told the audience to look out for Noël in the future. The West End run was a success, and the play helped ease Noël's transition from child actor to reliable company member: a small profile of him was written in *Talk of the Town*. He had a dressing room to himself for the first time and was recognised in the street. In fact he soon became, he admitted later, rather grand and prone to tantrums, but Hawtrey threatened such behaviour with instant dismissal.

The raids over London had increased in frequency and severity. There were no air-raid sirens and the alarm was instead raised by whistles, often blown by boy scouts; policemen toured the roads on bicycles wearing a sign saying "Take Cover". During performances Hawtrey was made aware from the wings if the warning had been raised, and he would advance to the footlights and invite the audience to leave, if they so wished. Most stayed put, and the actors bravely continued, and when the attack was over the sound of bugles blown from motor cars would be heard in the streets. The trip home from the theatre late at night would be always imprinted on Noël's memory, "a sinister air-raid consciousness in the air", the streets darkened, the roads empty, prostitutes calling from dark doorways and the stations bustling with soldiers, military police, and nurses in white uniforms stamped with a red cross.[41] On 20 October the actors got to the theatre to find that Piccadilly Circus had been bombed overnight, leaving a vast crater. Dawn raids became more frequent and in the early hours of 6 December forty-seven bombs were dropped on south-west London, three on Clapham, and fires blazed just a little north-east of the Cowards, sleeping, or rather not sleeping, in their flat on the Common.

He dated the new notebook 13 December 1917, and began. "Stoj and Poj had practically grown up together if they could be called grown up! They both prided themselves on their originality on being really Platonic friends. Many people having a [deficiency] of intelligence refused flatly to believe that they were not what is commonly termed 'Sweet on one another'."[42]

To his many-stringed bow he had decided to add the art of writing novels, and the book, called *Cats and Dogs*, would occupy him for the next six months. His emphasis on the Platonic friendship between his semifictional teenagers was perhaps meant to hint at why there was no sexual attraction between them.

The autobiographical element was thinly veiled and sometimes not veiled at all: Mrs Astley Cooper appeared as Mrs Pastley Stooper. It was as if, for Noël, worlds real and fictional had become confused. The mischievous pair in *Cats and Dogs* (she obsessed with Shaw, he rereading Saki every month) make it their business to bring together a novelist called Patricia Carlyon with a louche young man named Bobby Draycott. Shunting from bathing scenes on the Cornish rocks to the drawing rooms of country houses, the novel is a strange combination of rural romance and urbane archness; of youthful mischief and a middle-aged bitterness about the sadness inherent in romantic love. It was a shocking combination from a writer who was to turn eighteen on 16 December.

Two days after this important and frightening birthday, bombs fell at Charing Cross, horribly close to the theatre, just as the curtain was going up, and London was heavily raided throughout the evening. The actors heard the rain of shrapnel on the roof of the Garrick. But *The Saving Grace* soldiered on through Christmas and into the following year. "Whatever else the war destroys" *The Times* had written in its first-night review, "the art of comedy always seems safe."[43] As if aware of this, Noël and Esmé had written another curtain-raiser to precede performances on her seemingly endless tour of *A Pair of Silk Stockings*. Titled *Woman and Whisky*, the play was first shown at the Wimbledon Theatre on 21 January 1918.[44] It was advertised under the writers' own names, although neither of them acted in it.* The plot owed a great deal to *The Importance of Being Earnest*: a bluff major escapes the advances of a middle-aged woman and the irritations of a younger one by fabricating an identical twin and a wife. Childish romance had not entirely dissipated. Norah, the foolish ingénue, is a "young maiden of some twenty winters". But there are glimpses of epigrammatic wit: "I hate tact. It always seems to belong to those women who have a lot to conceal in their lives." Critics damned it with the faintest praise: "a slight [. . .] little piece, brightly acted".[45]

---

* The ingénue role, of Norah, was taken by Nancy Bevill, to whom Coward remained loyal, giving her a small role in his operetta *Bitter Sweet* (1929).

As Noël inched closer to success, his family's fortunes fell. Few
people bought pianos during wartime. Arthur, now sixty-one, faded
into retirement and alcohol, spending his time building model
yachts. But married men could claim a state pension only from the
age of seventy. Eric was only twelve, and his school fees needed
paying. A sister of Arthur's had been running a boarding house, and
Violet, now fifty-four, decided to follow suit. A building opposite
her sister-in-law was going cheap, and Violet took the lease and
most of the furniture, intending to advertise for lodgers and keep
the place afloat with the help of her sister Vida, who joined the
family permanently. The six-storey house of white stucco, 111
Ebury Street, was on a treeless road in what some might have called
Pimlico, but which Mrs Coward surely considered Belgravia.[46] Even
with the help of two servants, one of whom was let go when
financial realities became apparent, setting up a boarding house in
the final year of the war will have been hard work. Rationing was
introduced just as they got up and running, but standards were
maintained, a niece of a lord made the place respectable by taking
up residence on the third floor, and everyone dressed for dinner.
Arthur wandered mistily around and entertained the guests. Violet
wore an expression of permanent fatigue.

The division in Noël's life between the faded glamour of the theatre and the crowded reality of Ebury Street, where he slept under
the sloping ceilings of a little attic bedroom, was acute. But he was
back near his childhood haunt of Battersea Park and the commute
to the West End was shorter. Vita Sackville-West and her husband
Harold Nicolson lived at number 182; next door, at 109, were a
Mr and Mrs Evans, whose twenty-nine-year-old daughter Edith was
an actress enjoying increasing success. She was acclaimed for her
performances in plays by George Moore, who, better known as a
novelist (he was Hardy's arch rival), lived just a few doors down
and soon invited Noël for tea. Moore tackled controversial subjects
in his writing, and lent a touch of literary glamour to the neigh-
bourhood. A warring couple in Noël's *The Young Idea*, begun four
years later, decide to make a list of subjects they "cannot discuss
calmly. Religion, George Moore, Democracy . . ."

The Saving Grace ended in the spring of 1918, and Noël had made enough of a mark that he was straight away cast in, and began to rehearse, A. G. Rhode's *The Morals of Vanda*, due to open in Croydon on 1 April.[47] The press releases were out, and his name had been printed in the programme, when in late March a grey card flopped through the letterbox of the house at Ebury Street, telling him to present himself at the Camberwell Public Baths, enclosing a railway warrant, and calling his attention to the fact that, should he fail to appear, he would be guilty of desertion.

It was the actress Fabia Drake who christened Noël with the predictable nickname "Cowardy Custard". During the First World War it was a charged appellation. Women with white feathers drifted through the streets, pinning them to men in civilian clothes as a symbol of cowardice. Theatre programmes carried the proclamation: "The gentlemen of this company who are of military age have either served with the Colours, been rejected as medically unfit, or passed for home service."[48] Noël will have been eager to show that name and nature were not one and the same, despite the fervour with which Esmé, and to some extent he, damned the war and its futility. Germany was making its spring offensives in an attempt to defeat the British and French armies on the Western Front, and Allied victory would not feel assured until midsummer. Noël was able to take comfort from a medical examination back in January 1918, which had concluded that his history of tuberculosis would prevent him from seeing active service. This pronouncement became doubly reassuring when, three months later, the government lowered to eighteen the age of the youngest recruits sent to the front.

He had been automatically enlisted on 20 March 1918, and was given regimental number 767872. His part in *The Morals of Vanda* had to be instantly relinquished, and was given to a young unknown, already discharged on medical grounds, called Leslie Howard. On 23 March Noël made his nervous way to the Camberwell Baths for the routine medical examination. There followed a ramshackle march three and a half miles north-west, probably to the recruiting office at Great Scotland Yard, where papers were signed, and Noël will have sworn an oath of allegiance on the Bible before being assigned to the East Surrey Regiment (to which, in his play *This Happy Breed*, a toast is drunk: "the finest regiment in the world!").[49] He was assigned into a labour corps of the regiment, formed of men who were graded unfit for fighting. The vast demand for labour had led to a number of such battalions being formed within each infantry division, trained and capable of combat, but normally engaged in manual work. Another march, back across the river, brought them to Waterloo Station, where they caught a train to the barracks in Kingston.

The oily cocoa, grey porridge, and chilly temperatures can't have been a million miles away from the atmosphere of theatrical digs, but with fifty men to a hut, all brushing their teeth over a long trough and squeezing themselves into too-small uniforms, the conditions were grim. A typical training day would start with reveille at 5.30 in the morning. The nature of the labour corps to which Noël had been assigned meant that the majority of his fellows had already been invalided home or pronounced unwell. In the bed next to his was a soldier whose body was covered in sores and who was soon transferred. As Noël embarked on the morning's drill he began to contemplate various means of escape. Managing to bribe a sergeant with a ten-shilling note, he obtained an audience with the commanding officer, to whom he complained that his call-up had been so sudden as to leave his private affairs in a mess. Quite how Noël got away with this, which could have been the complaint of most recruits, is uncertain, but he was a persuasive actor and was given the rest of the day as leave. He shot back into central London on the train, still in his uniform.

After an ecstatic reunion with his mother, he began to roam London in a taxi, searching out every army acquaintance he had ever come across from his days marching with Philip Streatfeild among the Sherwood Foresters. Captain Lomer, Streatfeild's friend, seems to have been overseas. Noël eventually found someone in the air force – probably Lionel Charlton, another in the Streatfeild–Lomer circle – who brokered a speedy introduction to a Lieutenant Boughey, in the War Office on Horse Guards Avenue. Boughey lent a sympathetic ear to the young actor's complaints and arranged for a transfer. This young man, he argued, was perfectly fit, and there was no need for him to be in a labour corps. So on 3 April Noël was formally transferred to the Artists Rifles Officer Training Corps.[50]

Noël was grateful to Lieutenant Boughey, but he had been tossed from frying pan to fire. To be declared fit and well by someone senior in the War Office only heightened his chances of seeing active service, and the training programme of the Artists Rifles, on which he would soon embark, was no more congenial than the regime he had just escaped. Perhaps, as was not uncommon, he had complained at the very fact of being deemed unfit, wanting to contribute more than manual labour, and disliking or even fearing the company of soldiers who were often severely unhealthy. But he was quick to concede that gallantry and sacrifice had not entered the head of an egocentric young actor bothered by the interruption to his career. This was not an admission of cowardice – "the prospect of going to the front didn't worry me" – so much as a description of how he was able to take each day as it came, safe in the knowledge that being sent overseas lay on the other side of several months' training.[51] He was soon given the medical category "B2": "able to walk to and from work, a distance not exceeding five miles, and see and hear sufficiently well for ordinary purposes". But this, by that late and desperate stage in the war, was rarely taken to mean that the soldier in question could not be sent abroad.[52]

The Artists Rifles, so called because it had initially consisted of volunteer painters and actors, lost much of its artistic bent with the influx of conscripted soldiers. Given a wartime role as an Officer Training Corps, it was split into three lines of which new recruits, Noël among them, were put in the second and given the rank of private. It was a path that Wilfred Owen, R. C. Sherriff, and Edward Thomas had travelled before him. The battalion saw some of the highest casualty rates of the war (Thomas had been shot dead in 1917) and by the time Noël was conscripted it had earned the nickname of "The Suicide Club".

He was sent to Hare Hall Camp in Gidea Park, Essex.[53] The camp was built in the grounds of a large private house in Romford of the kind where, not so long before, he had been used to spending leisurely weekends. Poor as his health record was, years of performing twelve times a week had ensured he did not lack physical stamina. But he had been intent on standing out in a crowd; disappearing into one was unnatural. And the days were gruelling. The camp, set into the Essex countryside, had space for nearly 1500 men, and there were forty long wooden huts set in rows, thirty soldiers living and sleeping in each. Everything was clean and tidy; outbreaks of disease early in the war had led to liberal use of disinfectant, and the rooms reeked of carbolic. The headquarters were at the centre, next to a canteen, a hospital, and a lecture room. The YMCA had set up a refuge, as was standard in such camps, with reading rooms and a refreshment area. Noël was given every second weekend as leave, and could go to the shops and pubs on the Colchester road at the camp's northern edge.

The training was predicated on fostering physical endurance. Noël had missed the winter months in which, during the coldest of route marches from camps such as these, several recruits had keeled over and died, suffering from heart failure. Each day began with a long dawn march before breakfast, which was followed by exercise, a lecture, and at least seven hours of physical training. Furnished with a bayonet, he was taught to stab bales of straw standing in for German soldiers, for whom the troops were taught to feel murderous hatred. "They're bellies, they're bellies," a corporal would bellow, "they're all German bellies!"[54] There was a lecture in the evening, and each week one of the huts had to put on a concert or entertainment, but Noël seems to have kept his theatrical proclivities to himself. The Artists Rifles was known for its high number of men recruited from public schools, only increasing his outsiderness. The food was plain, and the showers icy. Lights-out came early, especially for one whose profession had for years made him a night owl.

He lay, wakeful and panicky, beneath the low wooden roof of the hut, and slowly began to disintegrate. Clumsy with his uniform, he was racked with homesickness, dreaming of home even when he was awake, worrying especially about his mother's newly heavy workload and the family's straitened finances, now bereft of his own income. Tortured with headaches, which aspirin furtively purchased from a local chemist did little to alleviate, he stopped himself from yelling aloud at night by pulling string around and around his fingers until they bled. He seems to have withstood the training for about a fortnight. Finally, perhaps inevitably, he tripped during drill, hitting his head so hard that he was concussed. He awoke properly three hazy days later, in the First London General Hospital, his mother by his bedside. A medical report made many months afterwards would note the scar on his right eye.

The hospital was a temporary wartime institution that had taken over a school in Camberwell and which overlooked a park now covered in huts to accommodate the ever-growing number of casualties. Voluntary nurses in white headdresses (Vera Brittain had once been among them) patrolled the corridors. The ward was full of shell-shocked soldiers lying amid the carefully curated cheeriness, with vases of fresh flowers, crocheted blankets in bright colours, and gramophones kept spinning, perpetually blaring jollity. Noël's superficial wounds healed, but the psychological damage remained acute. His headaches and fever continued, and he sank into hypochondria, convincing himself he had a brain tumour. The doctors examining him were suspicious, and Esmé Wynne, one of his early visitors, was briskly certain that Noël was putting it on. But whether his headaches and fever were psychosomatic or staged, they were symptoms of what seems clearly to have been a prolonged nervous breakdown.

He was in hospital for six weeks, visited every day by his mother, who made sure to tell the doctors of his long and troubled medical history. He took refuge in work, returning to his novel *Cats and Dogs*, which spilled over into a second notebook, dated 25 April 1918.[54] Another book, begun on 15 May, includes "Forbidden Fruit", later pinpointed as his first complete song lyric but jotted down amid dozens of others.[56] He was promptly put to use on the ward, delivering meals in the blue hospital uniform. For recreation he played the hospital piano, and befriended a fellow convalescent called Geoffrey Holdsworth, who, twenty-five years old, had served in the New Zealand Rifle Brigade (British-born, he had grown up in Auckland). Holdsworth had been gassed at Passchendaele, never fully recovering from his injuries, and he would spend much of his life in sanatoria abroad. The two became friendly, and began to treat their time in hospital like a spell in boarding school, bribing one of the cooks to hold them back the best meals and finding ways to escape the grounds and run free in the surrounding countryside, dodging the formal hours of exercise and the various roll-calls. Holdsworth found that his new friend reminded him "of the late Saki's characters [. . .] there is something freakish, puck-like, about the narrow slant of his grey-green eyes, the angle of his eyebrows, the sleek backward rush of his hair".[57]

Discharged from the hospital, Noël was given a blissful week's leave, where he returned to the family home at Ebury Street and reacquainted himself with the London theatres, visiting Ivor Novello in his flat and letting the delicious dramatic gossip work on him more effectively than any aspirin. There was also the pleasure of Esmé Wynne's company, and they managed a brief holiday together in Devonshire. Esmé, her twentieth birthday fast approaching, had become engaged to and soon married a pilot called Lyndon Tyson. And a strange trio they made, not least when Lyndon was thrown into panic as Noël and Esmé blithely resumed their childhood routine of going to the bathroom together, talking and talking. The jealousies and recriminations took time to iron out.

But the leave came to an end and Noël had to return to Hare Hall Camp. His medical absence led to his being put on "light duties"; he had more free time and the regime was less arduous, although cleaning the communal latrines was an unpleasant business. Still the war dragged on and victory was unassured. The Germans were fifty miles from Paris, and General Haig was facing defeat in Flanders. There seemed little end in sight to Noël's time at the camp, and he withered into depression, tormented (he said afterwards) by a piercing self-recrimination at his own inability to contribute to the war or even to survive more than a few weeks of military training.

On 1 June a revue called *Tails Up!* had opened in the West End, presented by the legendary impresario André Charlot, who used in the show a song called "Peter Pan" that Noël had written with Doris Joel. But it is unlikely that Noël was able to attend. He began another novel, returning to his juvenile idea that the god Pan had

had a daughter, whom he now imagined as the heroine of a love story set partly in Cornwall, partly in Hambleton Hall. *Cherry Pan: A Fantasy*, which he started on 17 June, was a strange creation to embark upon in an army training camp during hours snatched from the torments of training. It was as if he wove around himself a protective cocoon of whimsy: "Pan sat alone on the green hill of the immortals, below him the trees of the forest were swathed in lilac mists, while high in the pale air of the sky . . ." And so on – though wit peeks through the floss: "She knew Norman, a pasty young man with all the moral stamina of a newt." Cherry soon strikes up a friendship with a precocious teenager "whose musical ability reached the heights of genius", and whose mother "was so utterly devoted to him that the danger of being thoroughly spoilt loomed excessively near".[58] A friend, possibly Esmé, suggested the title could more suitably be *Bedpan*.

But writing novels was no miracle cure. Noël's headaches returned, becoming gradually more severe, until on 24 June, the day before he was to have performed at a theatrical garden party during a day's leave, he awoke with a blinding migraine and could not stand. It was perhaps no coincidence that the prospect of a brief slice of his former life had whipped him into turmoil. The next day he was driven fifty miles east to the General Military Hospital in Colchester, certain that he had a brain tumour and sure that he would die.[59]

He would stay for the best part of two months in the hospital, a vast modern building that could accommodate 2000 patients. He was put in a ward for epileptics, which he discovered only on witnessing several of the patients have fits. Not a war casualty, he was once again set to work, and became adept at dealing with epileptics suffering seizures. Witnessing several patients totally unaware of their condition, he suspected himself of suffering from the same illness, and frequently kept himself awake for twenty-four hours to ensure he didn't lapse into unconsciousness. He cannot have been a priority in that crowded hospital, which on top of the war-wounded was starting to see the first cases of Spanish flu.

On 10 July he was formally diagnosed with "neurasthenia". By this stage in the war there was already a move among psychiatrists to replace the term "shell shock" and to concede that the stress of war caused damage to those who had not seen active service. Noël's formal medical report, made by a Captain L. Lane, noted that "when nine years old he was knocked down by a bicycle and concussed. Since then he has been suffering from headaches and vertigo and general nervous debility." The neurasthenia was not, thought Lane, attributable to or aggravated by military service; it was marked as hereditary, not constitutional. "Looks pale, shaky, and nervy", Lane wrote, "cannot stand any noises and complains of constant headache. N[ervous] System: Tremors of both hands [. . .] emotional + unstable. Family history bad." He recommended "discharge as permanently unfit".[60]

It took weeks for a second opinion to make everything formal, and these were spent mainly in bed, reading and writing, although Noël was occasionally permitted to leave the hospital for the afternoon and he was able to visit Sydney Lomer, who had a house nearby. On 3 August the officer in charge of the hospital formally approved the recommendation of discharge, and on 13 August the hospital's Medical Board agreed on the nature of Noël's disability, which was estimated at 30 per cent and thus "permanent". His military character was marked as "good, steady, and well conducted". He was discharged from the British Army on 24 August 1918 and given a weekly pension of eight shillings and threepence – £20 today – for thirteen weeks.[61] Esmé wrote to the publisher John Lane: "Poj has his total discharge from the army and returns to town at the end of the week so I am very happy."[62]

So he went home.

Noël had been in the army for five months and four days (rather less than the "nine months" still given in most accounts of his career). That he would have evaded the trenches regardless, given his age and medical history, is by no means assured. New recruits were put through only four months of training, on average, and come late summer, had things run their course, Noël would have been eligible for active service abroad. The Artists Rifles' Roll of

Honour lists nearly 200 fatalities in the last two and a half months of the war, six from Noël's battalion.[63] He had had a lucky escape.

It is impossible to unravel the complex and overlapping relationship between deliberate evasion and nervous breakdown. Noël made light of it all in his recollection, and pooh-poohed critics who detected war-tainted bitterness in his writing: "I was not in the least scarred by the war".[64] The plays themselves tell a different story, and his wounds, thought genuine by a number of doctors, were no less distressing for being psychological. In October the following year he would be awarded the Silver War Badge, which was issued to men and women honourably discharged due to illness or injury: "For King and Empire, Services Rendered." It was not given automatically and Noël will have had to apply to acquire it, but he filled in none of the forms to confirm its receipt, leading to a stern reprimand from the War Office.[65] His mother was a meticulous filer of his childhood letters but nothing sent from camps or hospitals survives, and the medal is nowhere to be found.

Noël had whiled away much of his time in a hospital bed by reading novels, especially those of the writer Gladys "G. B." Stern. The five autobiographical comedies she had published were guaranteed to appeal to him; two of them – *Twos and Threes* and *A Marrying Man* – feature his soon to be favourite device of the love triangle and, often set against a Cornish backdrop, are a clear influence on the style, a kind of urbane pastoral, that he was developing in *Cherry Pan*. Twenty-nine years old, she had yet to write *The Matriarch*, the first instalment of a family saga that would really make her name, and Noël's approaches were not entirely a ruthless climb up the ladder of literary celebrity. He wrote Stern a fan letter that led to a correspondence and on his discharge, in late summer 1918, invited himself to stay with her when she was holidaying with friends at St Merryn, a village close to Padstow on the north coast of Cornwall. It is not every eighteen-year-old who writes to a distinguished author and finds himself holidaying with her within six months, and, within a year, brokering her marriage: his friend from hospital, Geoffrey Holdsworth, would marry Stern a few months later. Stern was gay and Holdsworth troubled; the union would be short-lived. Off he went to gatecrash the holiday at St Merryn, telegraphing news of his arrival in advance: "ARRIVING

PADSTOW FIVE-THIRTY. TALL AND DIVINELY HANDSOME IN GREY."[66]

He was in good spirits, life having been returned to him. Stern was staying with the writer Catherine Dawson Scott and her family, who instantly took a dislike to the bumptious new arrival. Dawson Scott had created the Women's Defence Relief Corps and her husband had served in the Medical Corps in France; Noël's army record had perhaps preceded him. "Call me Noël", he gushed at dinner. "I think, Mr Coward," came the response, "we would rather wait a little."[67] He spent much of the holiday talking books and theatre with Stern, who cut quite a dash in her bright clothes, dark pigtail, and heavy make-up. He was evidently happier in the company of friends older than himself; his fast-moving brain, which managed to be both bright and unpolished, was bored by most of his contemporaries even as he cultivated their adulation. Stern remembered him standing on a headland, "bare legs, flannel bags rolled up, an old grey sweater splashed with ink, silk handkerchief knotted tightly round his head [. . .] swaggering and singing along the cliff path".[68] Dawson Scott's children, finding themselves ignored, looked on in dislike and awe. "We rapidly recognised his wit and brilliance" remembered the daughter, Marjorie, "and listened spellbound to the endless game of repartee [. . .] a marvel I have never forgotten."[69]

The real boon of the trip was invitations to meetings of the To-morrow Club (soon the PEN Club), which Dawson Scott had founded the previous year so as to connect established writers with literary stars of the future. Noël was in no doubt that he had a place in the latter group and the meetings would mean that he could soon boast of a nodding acquaintance with many famous authors, from Rebecca West to John Galsworthy. Collecting stars was important to him, at least until the day – its arrival not far off, he was certain – when they would want to collect him. At one meeting the writers were treated to a recital by the famous Wagnerian tenor Lauritz Melchior, after which Noël thought nothing of following things up, uninvited, with a performance of one of his own songs.[70]

On a walk across the sands of Treyarnon Bay with the Dawson Scott children, Noël had paused to write on the sand in big letters: "Read *Cats and Dogs* by Noël Coward." The conversation drifted to their futures – which of them would be lawyers, which doctors. "What are you going to be, Noël?" they asked him. "A success", he replied.[71]

It was as if the war – bringing guilt, grief, and illnesses mental and physical – had blown a void into the heart of life, which only success, of all and various kinds, could satisfactorily fill. But Noël seemed destined either to become a competent supporting actor, or to join the ranks of the amiably minor playwrights whose work he had performed. He had the self-confidence that can be born of deep insecurity, and a drive almost startling in its fervour. Acquaintanceship and feuds came easily to him; intimate friendships perhaps less so. He had a capacity for adoration and for bleakness, romping unchecked and neurotic through life, flicking from disaster to elation, always seeking an audience, as if to emulate the one provided at home and to leaven the solitude of which childhood had often consisted. Equanimity was not his forte; even his truest emotions were performed. At eighteen, he had already started to offer to the world a performance of a sensation called Noël Coward, in whom depths and shallows were so curiously intermingled. He was a shape-shifter, a blank canvas onto which he painted any number of identities, trying them on and discarding them again like any theatrical costume. If Wilde's Lady Bracknell was proof that true nobility can, through hard work, be contrived, then he seemed to carry such an attitude over into talent. His fierce aspiration towards brilliance, a quality arguably not innate in him, would soon enough lead him to mastery.

Not everyone found the dazzle of his company as irresistible as they would in later life, and Noël's autobiography honestly records his adolescent insufferability. True, the writer Ethel Mannin thought him, in 1918, "the most electric person I had ever met", entranced by the mischievous riffs of his conversation, fizzing and unstoppable: "he only stays still by force of will".[72] His ebullience was also noted by the actor Douglas Byng, who watched him "leap into the air with the gay exuberance of air [. . .] so full of animation and *joie de vivre* that it made me feel I would never be able to compete with all that vitality".[73] But others could find him impossible. Taken one evening in October 1918 to 40 Half Moon Street, a tall white house off Piccadilly lived in by Oscar Wilde's lover Robbie Ross, he was introduced to Siegfried Sassoon, around whom he batted like a sycophantic moth, failing to notice that the famous poet had a headache and showering him with stories and autograph requests. "His behaviour struck me as too gushing", Sassoon wrote of the "youthful stranger", who "rattled brightly on, making smart remarks, which I considered cheap." Noël also, Sassoon thought, "made an unfavourable impression on Robbie, who, for once, lacked his usual liveliness as host" – as well he might; just two days later Ross began to complain of chest pains, and he died that very afternoon.[74]

For an eighteen-year-old to visit an associate of Oscar Wilde would still, in 1918, have shocked a great many people. Ross's house, decorated with gold wallpaper, was the centre of a homosexual literary coterie, and his private secretary was serving time in Wormwood Scrubs for the seduction of a youth. The meeting with Ross came about through a friendship with the writer Charles Scott Moncrieff who, ten years Noël's senior, had introduced him to a predominantly homosexual social circle. Moncrieff was permanently lame from a wound sustained at the Battle of Arras, and the contrast with Noël's military service could not have been more marked. He would dedicate his life to the first English translation of Proust, but was then working in the War Office and as a journalist, and was exhilarated by Noël's theatrical ambitions. The two of them entwined their social circles to form "The Phoenix Society", which went on to revive Jacobean tragedies at a theatre in Hammersmith – but Noël seems promptly to have left the group to its own devices.[75]

To move in such circles was to risk persecution and ostracism. The group surrounding Robbie Ross was targeted by the weekly journal the *Vigilante*, which peddled various conspiracy theories, not least that the Germans held a Berlin Black Book inscribed with the names of nearly 50,000 prominent British homosexuals and paedophiles (which, to the *Vigilante*, amounted to the same thing), and that homosexuality was the means by which German spies were stripping the United Kingdom of its virility. That Noël's sexuality was already the stuff of theatrical gossip is confirmed by rumours that had reached the holidaymakers at St Merryn: an actor friend had told the family that "this strange young man was a pansy", sending Mrs Dawson Scott into a panic that Noël would seduce her sons. On being told about the rumours Noël simply "threw back his head and laughed", though Dawson Scott's daughter afterwards saw "how shattering" the experience must have been.[76]

Little survives to lift conjecture into certainty when it comes to charting Noël's teenage relationships, with their ambiguous and overlapping layers of filial adoration, adolescent experiment, fraternal companionship, and maturing sexuality. The examples of love offered him through childhood were narrow, from his parents' faded affection to the artifice of Edwardian romance. His early song "Forbidden Fruit" shows, at the least, a grasp of sexual innuendo − but innuendo is, by definition, a means of holding sex at arm's length. Esmé Wynne, with whom he apparently made some tentative and unsuccessful sexual investigation, described Noël's virginal recoil from penetrative sex of any kind.[77] Not until he was twenty-four would he pursue a relationship with another man that can definitely and evidentially be called a sexual love affair. At thirty he was asked by a confident young actress during a late-night game of Truth or Dare, "Which do you prefer sleeping with, Noël − a man or a woman?" To this he apparently replied: "What a good question, dear. With whom would I rather sleep? Let's see now. Well − for pleasure a man, for comfort a woman."[78] But, as so often, it is hard to know whether he had hidden himself yet further behind a clever rejoinder.

At eighteen, his mind was on his career, which had so far offered him a sterile collection of roles in a series of comfortingly passion-less romances. The love scenes in his novels are too highly wrought to be entirely true: "Passionate desire leapt out of the darkness and clutched his heart with flaming hands [. . .] the perfume of her mouth as he crushed it with kisses. . ."[79] Nor could the months of communal life in a single-sex army training camp, with its toxic combination of homoeroticism and homophobia, have been a healthy atmosphere for his sexuality to settle. The chief potential objects of his romantic attentions − Philip Streatfeild and John Ekins − had died. His physical world had been one of ill health, and his emotional one a place of nervous collapse.

The British troops had broken through the strongest German defences. The Kaiser abdicated on 9 November 1918, and three days later the Armistice was signed. London echoed to the noise of rockets, which were let off at eleven o'clock to announce peace. Guns boomed in celebration over the fog of the city.[80] Noël wandered through the London streets in a daze, alone in the crowd. The pavements swarmed with people, and the roads were a crush of carriages and automobiles and omnibuses, with soldiers and munition girls cheering and shouting, waving flags like fury as there was no wind that day to do it for them – Union Jacks drooped forlorn from the poles on top of official buildings. But the mood was as sombre as it was jubilatory, and mothers wept in the streets even as songs of victory were sung and people danced on the pavement out of sync with the brass bands. Noël would recreate the day in his 1931 spectacle *Cavalcade*, a bereaved woman threading her way through "dense crowds of [. . .] screaming humanity". He knew of what he wrote, having gone home in the late afternoon to change into evening dress. Already he had got himself onto distinguished guest lists, having been introduced by a military friend to a wealthy Chilean diplomat called Tony Gandarillas, who kept a Bohemian household on Cheyne Walk in Chelsea. His was an exotic salon, and Tony had a taste both for opium and for young men, which may have been the reason for Noël's invitation.

A dark red Rolls-Royce belonging to TONY GANDARILLAS *emerges from the crowds, where people dangle from lampposts, and Nelson's Column is hung with bunting that descends from the tip of the statue's hat to the ground, its plinth emblazoned with propaganda. The crowds are so thick that the car gets stuck, and revellers climb up onto the bonnet and dance on the roof.* NOËL COWARD, *dressed in a tailcoat, emerges from the car to shake hands with the crowds – somehow we are aware that his chief pleasure is at being seen in public in such a car and in such company. The car moves on; the backdrop changes to the Savoy Hotel on the Strand. Revellers in evening dress are being sick in Savoy Court. Inside the hotel a group of soldiers has attempted to set fire to a German flag. Champagne runs like water, and the French actress* ALICE DELYSIA *emerges and is hauled onto a table to sing the Marseillaise.* NOËL COWARD *gets lost amid the crowd as* . . .

THE CURTAIN FALLS

LES ANNÉES FOLLES!

——

A Revue

CAST

NOËL COWARD, *an increasingly famous young playwright*
ESMÉ WYNNE-TYSON, *a young actress losing patience with the theatre*
GLADYS CALTHROP, *an artist and stage designer*

STEWART FORSTER, *a lieutenant in the Coldstream Guards*
EDWARD "NED" WILLIAM BOOTLE-WILBRAHAM, *3rd Earl of Lathom*
JEFFERY AMHERST, *Viscount Holmesdale*
ANDRÉ CHARLOT, *an impresario*
EDITH SITWELL, *an irate poet*
GEORGE BERNARD SHAW, *a leading playwright*
NORMAN MACDERMOTT, *a theatre manager*
LILIAN BRAITHWAITE, *an actress*

The revue takes place variously in an Ebury Street boarding house; London's West End; on board ship; and in Manhattan.

TIME: 1918–1924

PART ONE

"THE VICTORY BALL"

BILLIE CARLETON *and* CHORUS

The scene is the Albert Hall, late in the evening of 27 November 1918, a fortnight after the Armistice. Sombre commemoration has given way to revelry and celebration: it is the Allied Victory Ball. As the clock strikes midnight a procession is led through the arena by LADY DIANA COOPER, *in full costume as* BRITANNIA. *Lights are hung from the dome in the shape of a red cross, and the boxes are draped in Allied flags. In one box can be seen the eighteen-year-old* NOËL COWARD *in full evening dress. Among his party is a young couple:* BILLIE CARLETON, *twenty-two, the youngest leading lady of the West End, and her lover, the married designer* REGINALD DE VEULLE, *dressed in a Pierrot outfit. The revelry continues; the party disbands.* CARLETON *and* DE VEULLE *leave together.*

The scene changes to a crowded Bow Street courtroom early the following year. REGINALD DE VEULLE *is in the dock,* DR FREDERICK STEWART *in the witness box.*

STEWART: I am a friend of Miss Carleton. I went to her flat at four o'clock in the afternoon of November 28th, in response to a telephone message, and found Miss Carleton dead. Blood was oozing from the mouth and the pupils of the eyes were dilated.

PROSECUTING COUNSEL: Would the dilation of the pupils indicate anything?

STEWART: It is consistent with cocaine.[1]

"The Notebooks"
Noël Coward

Noël Coward presumably awoke rather blearily in the first morning – or perhaps afternoon – of peacetime. But he was in a frenzy of productivity and energy, matched by the vivacity with which many in his generation decided to experience the ensuing decade. Days which had so recently seemed numbered were to be seized with vigour. Individuality, which over the last four years had been subsumed into expendable anonymity, was to return with a vengeance. The heightened emotional tenor of the post-war era was to imbue everything from travel to love affairs with a sense of infantile humour and adventure, stripping life of emotional authenticity, as if to bury misery in near-hysterical enjoyment, and to armour relationships against loss by rejoicing in fleeting dalliances and romantic theatrics. Nineteen-twenties high life was to be lived so much on show, was so essentially theatrical, that the stage would become the natural medium in which its excesses could be mirrored and explored. No popular book went for long unadapted, and writers such as Evelyn Waugh or Ivy Compton-Burnett would begin to publish novels so reliant on dialogue as often to read like play-scripts, in which a gilded and epigrammatic surface hides both pain and malice.

It was Noël Coward's luck to be young and energetic at the beginning of the century's age of youth. His was the first generation to create an individual culture, with its own slang, music, and fashion, all quite distinct from its untrustworthy elders, whose decisions had recently proved so calamitous. But the tragedy of Billie Carleton was one of the first hints to the wider world that beneath the high spirits and endless revelry of the youthful party-going set, from its leading actors to its wiry aristocrats, lurked addictions and tragedies. A decade was already beginning to spiral out of control, and Noël would manage to exist both within and outside of it. His industry was such that he would manage to chronicle a slice of society so speedily as to seem almost to create, rather than mirror, his age. "We strain every nerve to keep young" says a character in his play *The Vortex*, produced seven years later. "We're all so hectic and nervy . . ." "It doesn't matter – it probably only means we shan't live so long . . ."

Reginald De Veulle was acquitted of Billie Carleton's manslaughter but was found guilty of conspiracy to supply a drug that had become illegal only in 1916; he served eight months in prison. The case became a national scandal. Noël was among the last people to see Carleton alive, and it is surprising that he evaded having to give any kind of testimony or statement. More and more details emerged, not least that Carleton had been addicted to sex-fuelled, day-long opium parties. The case gave rise to a swathe of plays and novels that dealt with the vogue for drug-taking, of which *The Vortex* would become the most famous. Noël claimed that his own drug-taking extended only to a brief and unhappy encounter with cannabis that left him feeling so sick he swore off drugs ever afterwards. Better to stay on the sidelines, he insisted, alert, watchful. But as the Carleton case played out in the newspapers in the last months of 1918, Noël – long before he began *The Vortex* – wrote a play called *The Dope Cure*.[2]

Unusually, he worked with a collaborator, Aishie Pharall, a former child actress who had starred in the curtain-raisers co-written by Esmé and Noël. The division of labour is unclear (an early draft is entirely in Noël's hand) and it may be that the script's explicitness prevented any attempt at production. *The Dope Cure* is at times only a thinly fictionalised version of the Carleton case, and deals with a novelist called Kit Saville, who is mired in a fearsomely unhappy relationship with his wife, Iris; she is a cocaine addict with whom, in a foretaste of *Private Lives*, he quarrels viciously. She hurls a vase at him, to which he responds: "Try the blue one, it's more valuable". In the central act, a group gathers to take opium, which is prepared with technical finesse: "I've forgotten how one cooks the damned stuff." "Where did you put the pastilles?" "I've always heard, sir, that opium pellets is white."[3]

But Noël's characteristic reaction even to the dangers of drug-taking was amusement. The play's twist is that the opium has been substituted with pellets of scent from an Oxford Street parfumier, and the participants' vivid hallucinations are psychosomatic.

The third act goes haywire, as Kit holds everyone prisoner, they try to shoot their way out with a revolver, and the whole thing is revealed as a set-up to provide material for Kit's novel. By the end he has separated from his wife and nearly kills himself, but he begins instead to write his book as the curtain falls. *The Dope Cure* would never see the light of day and, now hidden away in Noël's archive, is omitted from all previous accounts of his life. It contains his first use of the name "Elvira", over twenty years before *Blithe Spirit.*

With no chance of staging *The Dope Cure* he returned to acting. He had imagined casting directors waiting eagerly for his release from the army in order to put his name in lights, where it belonged. The reality was that nobody seemed to have noticed he had gone away. A production of Jerome Kern's *Oh, Boy!* was soon to open at the Kingsway Theatre, and Noël had auditioned for its producers, George Grossmith Jr and Edward Laurillard. Feeling that nobody was paying his performance sufficient attention, Noël came to a halt and told them all he was wasting his time. There were gasps around the theatre at such insolence, but Grossmith seems rather to have admired Noël's pluck, inviting him to sing again and then offering him a part. But when Noël turned up at the first day of rehearsal, having battled through a bad attack of what was probably Spanish flu, he found himself anonymous in the chorus, with not a line to his name. He went straight to Laurillard's office and lost his temper; Laurillard offered to cast him instead in a production of Cosmo Hamilton's *Scandal.* The part turned out to be disappointingly small, a grievance aggravated by the fact that the play, a romance set in New York high society, opened late in 1918, was a big success, and settled in for a long run.

Noël filled the days at his desk in an ink-spotted jumper, writing, writing, to the drone of the traffic along Ebury Street, his spiky pencil longhand tripping over itself to keep up with the brain it followed. In later life he covered his tracks, the better to make his talent appear a virgin birth, making dismissive mention of just two early plays that were never produced. In truth, his unpublished juvenilia fills a collection of over forty notebooks. Within their dusty pages and marbled covers, he forced himself into brilliance by dint of sheer industry. In many ways his ambition created his talent, rather than the other way around. One book was begun just five days after his discharge from the army, as if his release had pushed him onto a new level of ambition and productivity.[4] His air of effortlessness hid months of discipline and a determined auto-didacticism that led him to learn not only French but a smattering of Ancient Greek. Verb tables and vocabulary lists pile up alongside hundreds of lyrics, poems, sketches, and short stories; the margins swarm with potential titles, names, rhymes, and word counts.

It was an era most of whose successful playwrights – Maugham, Galsworthy, Barrie – were also successful novelists, and on 1 January 1919 Noël began a novel called *Shandy-Gaff*, in which oil paintings come to life in a country house; this he soon turned into a play.[5] By 12 January he had completed a three-act comedy called *Humoresque*, closely followed by a "comedy of sentiment" called *Sheep's Clothing*.[6] Both of these were written in collaboration with Esmé Wynne – now Mrs Tyson. Evidently Poj and Stoj were still working together a great deal. She had only just survived a bad bout of flu herself, and afterwards told him he had done "your perhaps most marvellous work of raising the (very nearly) dead at Connaught Mansions when Aishie Pharall and I were stricken with that frightful 1918 flu; and you came in without a trace of fear and made me laugh".[7] Early in 1919 an announcement appeared in the newspapers: "Max Darewski" – the impresario who had supported Noël in Manchester the previous year – "has written an opera of two acts, of which the scene is laid in Sicily. His collaborators are Miss Doris Doris,* librettist, and Miss Esmé Wynne and Mr Noël Coward who have done the lyrics."[8] Noël produced dozens of lyrics for the opera, which was called *Crissa*, but the project sank without trace. Undaunted, he and Esmé worked on a full-length book of short stories, each one a parody written "with apologies" to a series of writers, from Maeterlinck to E. M. Delafield.

In this mass of early material, Noël Coward wrote, as far as

---

* The eccentric professional name of Coward's songwriting collaborator, Doris Joel.

his hazy dating will allow the calculation, around thirty individual plays within just over a year (and that is only to count those that have survived), from modern comedy to operetta to melodrama: *The Welcome Guest*, *The Impossible Wife*, *The Unattainable*, *Miriam*, *In the Picture*, *Nature's Nobleman*, *Family Matters* . . . He began with the title, then wrote up a detailed prose scenario of each act, before finally embarking on the dialogue (a method he retained throughout his career). These early plays are strange melting pots of emulation, usually disdaining rural romance or Victorian farce; they deal exclusively with a slice of life at the top of the class scale, and are clearly influenced by the modern comedies of Shaw and Maugham. To this he added the flamboyant sting of Saki spiced with the adverbial gush of the younger generation's lingo, a strange remnant of his childhood comic books, in that everything is either "utterly beastly" or "perfectly ripping".

Slowly the "Cowardesque" dialogue was forming, as he began to perfect a surface prattle that crusted over deeper emotions. Epigrams were jotted down to find their place in scripts later on: "She lives at Croydon and wants to see more of life." "I regret to inform you he keeps a small mistress in a large flat in Ebury Street and a large wife in a small house in Bayswater." "She married in haste and repented at Brixton."[9] Aphorisms begin to fly through the pages, a staccato rally of arch quips shot back and forth like bullets in the fast tempo in which his era beat its time. "I think we are on the verge of firing epigrams at each other" says a character in *The Dope Cure*. "Do let's stop."[10] Even his earliest characters know that they are funny, and travel with an armoury of wit that is employed in defence and attack. It was the beginning of his writing's trick of using polish as a stripper, not to buff but to peel away the surface shine of life.

Many of the plays feature "Mrs Aston Hooper" alongside what he always called the "Poj and Stoj part", a pair of meddling young things often known as Billy and Phyllis, and clear progenitors of the Bliss siblings in *Hay Fever*. A constant theme is a woman in middle-age, often an actress, torn between a spouse and a lover, or a first and second husband. *The Shadow Show* takes place backstage in a theatre: a famous actress is asked to choose between her rakish but glamorous first husband, and her stolid but reliable second. In choosing the latter, she does not choose for love. *Barriers Down* is about a woman living in poverty who rejects a proposal from the impecunious man she loves, and marries a wealthy young man who is bland and unfaithful. Such plays were written against a backdrop of shifting attitudes, legal and social, to marriage and fidelity. Not until 1923 would it be possible for either partner to seek divorce on the grounds of adultery, an option previously open only to men.

These were bitter topics for a writer of comedy in his late teens. In Noël's novel *Cats and Dogs* the character of Bobby Draycott finds himself unrequitedly in love: "She must love him, she must, or he would kill himself, kill himself! His aching brain seemed to catch hold of the phrase and play with it as a cat plays with a mouse, he looked down at the pebbled beach far below and shuddered, one jump and it would all be over, no more torment, no more misery, his mangled body would lie there, lifeless among the little heaps of dark green seaweed . . ."[11] It is hard to know whether the writing is intended as genuine or pastiche and, if the former, whether it is born of skilful mimicry or personal experience. At eighteen, Noël's attitude to love seems already to have been characterised by bitterness, and by a theme that would weave through his collected works: the impossibility of combining friendly domestic companionship and burning sexual passion in the same figure. "Let's be platonic, after all there is much more sterling comfort in friendship", says Poj to Stoj in the novel. It would become the attitude of a man who loved women but could not love them romantically; who loved men but could not love them legally.

A poem by Ernest Dowson tolls through the chapters of *Cats and Dogs* like a mournful refrain: "What is love | Is it a folly | Is it mirth or melancholy?"

"PASSING PEACEFULLY AWAY"
NOËL COWARD *and* ESMÉ WYNNE

It was a bore to abandon his writing and make for the theatre to give yet another performance of *Scandal*. Noël kept himself amused by behaving very badly, both on and off the stage. There was still a surprising gap between his ambition and his professionalism. His fellow actors put up with his antics for many months until, at the end of May 1919, it was suggested he resign before he was officially sacked. This he duly did, mustering as much dignity as he could in a letter to the producers that blamed his behaviour on his colleagues. Having turned up at the theatre thinking his resignation would not be accepted, he was startled to be given half an hour to clear his dressing room.[12] He left the theatre more in triumph than in shame.

But his dismissal did not prevent him quickly finding work in the Birmingham Repertory Company's autumn season, and he was given the lead role of Rafe in *The Knight of the Burning Pestle*, a five-act Jacobean comedy now considered solely the work of Francis Beaumont (in 1919 John Fletcher was believed to be a co-writer): a grocer and his wife, attending the theatre, insist that the action would be improved if their apprentice, Rafe, were allowed to perform. The production was given in the spirit of a contemporary revue, which may explain Noël's getting away with his performance, for he had, he later admitted, little sense of the necessary style. It would play for the first two weeks of September 1919 before being put on ice prior to a London revival the following year.

Just two days before the opening night in Birmingham, life took a great lurch forward. One of Noël's final collaborations with Esmé Wynne, completed in March 1919, was *The Last Trick*, in which Noël's arch comedy combined with Esmé's breathless romance to form an uncomfortable melodrama. (Cocotte is persuaded by a friend to give up her lover – Cocotte vows revenge and informs friend of his wife's infidelity – friend murders wife – curtain.) Noël claimed sole authorship, but the manuscript lists two writers.[13] The fallout from the war looms large. "One sees everything more plainly out there" says a solder discharged from active service. "To be blinded or maimed . . . or to have to stand by and see one's dearest pals butchered. [. . .] It's frightfully fashionable to be callous nowadays isn't it?"[14] Gilbert Miller, the American producer who had admired Noël's acting two years before, sent a cable to say that the script had been optioned by the impresario Albert Herman

Woods for the princely sum of $500.* Ecstatic, Noël cabled his mother, translating "optioned" into something more definite: "PLAY ACCEPTED FOR AMERICA ADVANCE OF FIVE HUNDRED DOLLARS PASSING PEACEFULLY AWAY LOVE NOËL."[15]

His confidence would prove unfounded, and *The Last Trick* was never produced. But Gilbert Miller, soon afterwards, came up with the basic plot for another play as a potential vehicle for Charles Hawtrey: a dying uncle promises to leave his fortune to whichever of his nephews and nieces becomes the most successful. He even had the punning title – *I'll Leave It to You* – and passed everything over for Noël to write up. Despite misgivings at taking over someone else's skeleton plot, the opportunity could not be turned down, and some time in the second half of 1919, over the course of three days, Noël wrote *I'll Leave It to You*. He fashioned a Nesbitian quintet of children and tailored one into a role for himself: Bobbie, a suavely knowing youth who is skilled at the piano and in love with a vapid young girl (a cameo for Esmé, in what would be her last performance on stage). The uncle, of course, is neither wealthy nor fatally ill, his legacy merely a ruse to stir some life into his lethargic family. The play is too light-hearted to preach but is, essentially, a morality tale: be industrious and earn your pleasures. In this it has a feminist undertow: "What are you going to do with yourself? Sit at home and wait for a nice husband with mediocre prospects and perhaps an over-developed Adam's apple?" The mature Coward would have lopped off the "perhaps", but the dialogue has a semiquaver sparkle, all consonants and monosyllables: "You've wounded me to the quick." "I don't believe you've got a quick."

A preview run in Manchester was arranged for the following spring, in the hope that Hawtrey would agree to play Uncle Daniel in a London transfer. Noël spent the rest of the year waiting. His mother had let him move from the attic room at Ebury Street to a larger one on a lower floor. Flush from the American option on *The Last Trick*, he bought a grand piano for the room (much to the neighbours' annoyance), purchased a good suit, and dined daily at

---

* Around £100 in 1919 (£5000 today).

The Ivy, as if he were sure that maintaining the lifestyle of a great and successful writer, even on a shoestring, would lead to greatness and success. He began to host parties from his rooms, although his attempts at a Bohemian salon were presumably less convincing than intended, not least because his father, trying to be helpful, used to pad in with pots of tea. Mr and Mrs Tyson came often, and Gertrude Lawrence, her friendship with Noël rejuvenated since their days on the child-actor circuit, became a frequent visitor, invariably accompanied by Grenadier Guardsmen, who stood handsome and puzzled amid the gossip. (Now twenty-one, Lawrence had left a brief and unhappy marriage and was raising her one-year-old daughter in her mother's flat at Clapham.) In October 1919 Charles Scott Moncrieff moved into 136 Ebury Street, just up the road, and became a permanent fixture at the gatherings; he was soon introduced by Noël to Mrs Astley Cooper, who became the dedicatee of his first translated volume of Proust.[16]

The notorious nightlife of the 1920s was just beginning, and Noël embraced it eagerly, usually with Gertrude Lawrence as companion, although both were so strapped for cash that they had to share a single dish between them. Some of the clubs had turned into hospitals during the war, and were starting to re-establish themselves as society rendezvous while the dance craze swept London. Off the two of them would go to Murray's, disappearing into its austere entrance on Beak Street and descending the stairway to the ballroom below, with its wood panelling and nightly music show, in which Lawrence would appear for the next two years; or to Ciro's, tucked behind the National Gallery on Orange Street, a former public baths converted into a pillared room with a sliding roof that opened in the summer.

It was perhaps through Gertrude Lawrence that Noël met Stewart Forster, a young man four months his senior who, at precisely the time Noël had been playing a Sandhurst cadet on the stage, had actually been at the Military College, before becoming a second lieutenant in the Coldstream Guards. He was moustachioed, innocent, and seemingly didn't hold Noël's lack of military honour against him. It was through Stewart that Noël made his peace with the military, partly owing to the fact that – although there is no evidence that he and Stewart, who would marry in 1935, were lovers – he clearly found the uniform attractive. Noël's was a maso-chistic attraction to soldiery, as if he had eroticised a painful episode of his life as a strange form of healing, reducing it to costume and theatre – he liked nothing better than to watch Stewart parade in full military dress. They dined together at the officers' mess at St James's, and Noël spent time at the Forsters' family home in Kent. In January 1920 the two of them set off on a holiday: Noël's first experience of foreign travel.

He and Stewart caught Paris on a cusp between depression and celebration, beset by rationing and unemployment, and paralysed by a general strike the year before. But the *années folles* were soon to begin, and it is a mark of Noël's determination to rise to society's higher echelons that they spent their first night at the Ritz before moving to a cheaper hotel. Mainly he and Stewart were wide-eyed tourists, visiting Versailles; wandering through the Louvre and Notre-Dame before moving on to the Moulin Rouge and Folies Bergère, and dancing in Montmartre with "metallic tarts".[17] Noël even avowed, perhaps to divert attention from where the true romance lay, that they quarrelled over an American lady who, flirt-ing outrageously, played them off against one another.

The trip gave him a taste for travel and the following month he went, at Mrs Astley Cooper's invitation and presumably expense, to Alassio, a town on the western coast of North Italy, halfway between Nice and Genoa. They travelled down by train through Switzerland, Noël pinned to the cold window of the *wagon-lit* and gaping at the snow-covered mountains. He delighted in the strange and uncomfortable romance of long-haul train travel: stopping at the freezing frontiers in the middle of the night, and swaying across carpeted corridors from restaurant car to compartment, where the bed was made up each evening. They stayed at the Grand Hotel, an edifice of Belle Époque luxury overlooking the Ligurian Sea, which sparkled in the winter sunshine. They were an odd couple: Mrs Astley Cooper, now in her late sixties, holidaying with the promising young actor-writer, who was half Ritz habitué, half fish-out-of-water, awaiting the production of his play and still, all the critics marvelled, just twenty years old.

"A TENDENCY TO SMARTNESS"
NOËL COWARD

"To tell you the truth", the twenty-year-old admitted to the *Globe* newspaper, "the success of it all is a little bit dazzling. This may be an age of youth, but it does not always happen that young people get their chance of success. [. . .] I always felt it would be a success, [but] it has been rather nerve-trying." He was, the interviewer thought, a "tall, good-looking boy of twenty, with plenty of optimism and self-confidence". And indeed: "I made up my mind I would have one of my plays produced in London by the time I was 21," he continued, "and I shall be 21 in December."[18]

I'll Leave It to You opened in Manchester on 3 May 1920 with, among its cast, the young actress Moya Nugent, once a Lost Boy in *Peter Pan* and now making the first of her twelve appearances in a Coward play: he would often cast friends through loyalty, but was equally conscious of creating a troupe that would give his work a distinct identity. Most local reviewers thought the writing so flimsy as to make the description "light comedy" inappropriately heavy.[19] When Charles Hawtrey's wife, Katherine, turned up in Noël's dressing room after the performance, having been despatched by her husband to see whether the role of Uncle Daniel would suit him, she was stony-faced. No, it would not suit him. A West End opening seemed impossible, until the theatre manager Lady Mary Wyndham offered the New Theatre,* with E. Holman Clark (a famous Captain Hook) in the role of the Uncle. The opening night was on 21 July. After the final curtain calls, and "amid enormous applause", the author "came before the curtain and very modestly thanked Lady Wyndham for having given him his chance".[20] Ivor Novello attended and claimed to have been bored stiff, but the London critics disagreed. The construction and writing were, according to *The Tatler*, "that of an experienced playwright". Only the *Observer* was optimistically uncertain. "If he can overcome a

---

* Later the Albery, and now the Noël Coward Theatre.

tendency to smartness", wrote its critic St. John Ervine, "he will probably produce a good play one of these days."[21]

Overnight, Noël Coward's youthful success had become a sensation. Theatrical columns across the country marvelled that, so young was this new writer, his contract had had to be signed by his father. One article used the phrase "bright young people" – and this four years before the *Daily Mail* supposedly coined the description to refer to the exuberant twenties set of youthful high society.[22] It was indeed the Age of Youth, and the writers Reginald Berkeley and William Darlington, both nine years Noël's senior, were already established as reputable farceurs.[23] But Noël's self-assurance, his nonchalant mentions of his play that was to be produced in America, of the others he had already written, of the three days it had taken him to write this one, of the novels and poems and songs that were stuffed in his desk drawers, of the fact that he himself had written the song that he performed in the show . . . all this gave him almost uncanny prolificness and poise.

Truth was not high on his list of priorities when giving interviews. "Three plays accepted before I'm 21 is not at all bad", he told the *Daily Mail*, "and I've only been writing seriously for just over a year. I finished a novel when I was in the army and it taught me [. . .] that I had the knack of bright dialogue."[24] In all his interviews he made sure to mention the army, and most of the papers reported his enthusiasm for sport and his daily practice at tennis and rowing. He also made sure to inform journalists of his celebrated ancestry: his organist grandfather James (which was true), his distant relative the Victorian novelist Harrison Ainsworth (which may have been true), and his godfather R. D. Blackmore (which wasn't true at all, Blackmore having rejected the offer to be Noël's godfather before dropping dead a month later).[25]

But despite all the publicity *I'll Leave It to You* failed to attract audiences during the dusty final weeks of the season. It closed on 21 August, having spent its last fortnight in gloom: Lady Wyndham's efforts to economise had led her to insist that only half of the stage lights could be used. But when Noël went back into *The Knight of the Burning Pestle*, which opened in London on 24 November, it was as an established figure. The actress Mrs Patrick Campbell, fresh from her success as Eliza Doolittle in the West End, came to see the play and fell sound asleep. Noël knew her well enough to send a reprimanding telegram and she got her own back by attending the following evening and loudly applauding his every appearance. He left the stage in hysterics.

Then he got mumps, and it spread through the company, and the *Burning Pestle* burned itself out several weeks earlier than intended. But by this time "all London" was talking of "the new 'boy dramatist', Mr Noël Coward, who at twenty years of age finds himself already one of our most successful playwrights".[26] This was hyperbole at which even his mother might have hesitated – but his name was now a fixture on the published guest lists of society parties and first nights, and of the sepulchrally lit balls at the Hyde Park Hotel, where the rooms were thronged with jazz bands and the partygoers moved like ghosts amid the smoke, dancing on until morning.[27]

"BLACKIE"

NOËL COWARD *and* GLADYS CALTHROP

The British aristocrats who spent the coldest months abroad, nonchalantly using "winter" as a verb, were hardly known for their efforts to assimilate. Early in 1921 Noël took himself off to Rapallo but quickly realised that to be stuck alone even in a glamorous hotel, and without a word of Italian, was hardly ideal. He promptly moved west along the Ligurian coast to the tried-and-tested hotel at Alassio where Mrs Astley Cooper was once again staying and was (he insisted) "delighted to see me".[28] She spent her time in the Anglophone libraries and at the English Club, with its tennis lawns, concert halls, and decidedly un-Italian restaurants. Noël was inevitably asked to perform at the Club, and battled on with his set despite the hysterical giggles of a girl on the front row, to whom he was afterwards introduced: Gladys Calthrop. It was an inauspicious beginning to one of the most important and enduring friendships of his life.

Twenty-six years old, Gladys was already separated from her

husband, an army captain she had married when she was eighteen and with whom she had had a son, now five and mainly entrusted to her mother's care. Her brittle character and fierce independence of spirit were instantly attractive to Noël. Here was a stylish, hot-tempered, passionate woman, who had defied a life of finishing schools and domesticity in order to train as an artist at the Slade. She had pursued a number of affairs with other women, would eventually learn to fly a plane, and became an eminent set designer, of Noël's plays not least. The pair struck up their firm friendship in Alassio, spending their time deep in conversation as they drove along the coast or painted the landscape together, Noël guided by Gladys's firm eye and by Mrs Astley Cooper, who was more than certain of her own artistic talent. Esmé Wynne had begun to drift from his life and from the theatre, and Gladys arrived to fill the gap. She and Noël, their friendship secured by its lack of sexual attraction, gleefully retained the wild behaviour that had characterised Noël's and Esmé's youthful roamings. High on the pleasures of a new friendship made abroad, and perhaps somewhat the worse for wear, they graffitied the walls of the English Club and were asked not to return. Gladys had a core of steel, unknowable and even cold, which may have been her attraction – Noël had little time for simpering. His inevitable nickname for her was telling: Blackheart, soon shortened to Blackie.

London beckoned, and by February Noël had gone into rehearsals for *Polly With a Past*, by George Middleton and Guy Bolton that, in featuring a servant who poses as a glamorous femme fatale, contained one of the plot devices of his play *Relative Values* (1951). It opened on 2 March and Noël was soon so bored that he started to improvise dialogue to amuse himself, while the rest of the cast – which included his neighbour Edith Evans – confusedly tried to keep up. Even on the first night *The Times* noted that Mr Noël Coward "unduly prolonged" his clowning.[29] Acting in other people's comedies was by now little more than a way to fund the writing of his own material. Polly may have had a past but Noël was determined to have a future, and anyone hoping to catch him in the last few weeks of the run would have been disappointed. The young actor had left the play early in order to catch the *Aquitania* at

Southampton before it sailed first to Cherbourg and then to New York, a city that had been dazzling him from afar with its noisy and glamorous siren call.

"I LIKE AMERICA"
NOËL COWARD,
JEFFERY AMHERST, *and* CHORUS

1.

Noël set sail on 4 June 1921, giving his profession as "actor" on the passenger lists, having booked one of two adjoining first-class cabins in the Royal Mail Ship. The four-funnelled vessel was the third, and the most beautiful, of the Cunard Line's ocean liners, six years old and only recently returned to transatlantic passenger service after a period as a floating hospital. Given he had only a month's run in the West End to his name, it is a mark of how carefully Noël had built his own image that the New York Times, surveying the 2,025 passengers, carried a special announcement of his trip. A great deal got lost amid Noël's exaggerations and the vagaries of London-to-Manhattan communications: "Noël Coward Young, the English playwright, who produced several successful plays here in the last year, is also sailing tomorrow. He is travelling with Viscount Holmesdale, who is visiting the United States on important business for his father."[30] Anyone idly hoping to follow Mr Young's career in America must have assumed he sank without trace.

Viscount Holmesdale, known as Jeffery Amherst, was three years and three days older than Noël (he would become the 5th Earl Amherst in 1927). They had cemented their friendship at Ivor Novello's parties, which were held in an enormous flat above the Strand Theatre and reached by a perilous ascent in a self-worked lift. Visitors who didn't crash into the ceiling on arrival or find themselves helplessly returning to the ground floor would discover a crush of actors and singers crowding around the two grand pianos, with partygoers playing charades and doing stunts, ever more devil-may-care. Jeffery, mad on theatre and openly star-struck, was everything Noël was not: blond, aristocratic, Etonian, his war record as distinguished as Noël's was erratic. His similarities to Stewart Forster were pronounced — both had gone from Sandhurst into the Coldstream Guards — and he was, it can be tentatively surmised, Noël's type. Forster fades from Noël's memories, to be replaced by Jeffery, though once again little survives to confirm the nature of the friendship. Recollection of mutual acquaintances described Noël's unreciprocated passion, a situation which was becoming sadly familiar. Many decades later, unmarried and in his nineties, Amherst made use of his seat in the House of Lords to speak against Section 28 but, even then, admitted to no kind of love affair, hinting only that "my youthful military appearance and experience [helped] to feed an emotion in Noël".[31]

Noël and Jeffery had decided quite quickly that they should go to America together, Jeffery representing an ancestor who had given his name to Amherst College in Massachusetts, Noël in search not only of a producer who would stage his work, but of an indefinable American dazzle, which colleagues who had acted on Broadway always recounted with infectious glee. It was a peaceful crossing in good weather, and Noël, furnished with scripts and introductory letters, found excitement overtaking his nerves and seasickness. He was soon cajoled into performing at concerts in one of the many restaurants and saloons. There was even a ballroom and gym and, on the top deck, a large skylight of stained glass through which the sun shone onto an ornate staircase. It was as if the Ritz had floated out to sea (and indeed, the interiors had been designed by the firm responsible for the London hotel). The ship broke a speed record that year and they were at sea for only six nights, arriving into the Upper New York Bay on the sunlit morning of 10 June.[32]

Noël never forgot his first sight of New York, glimmering in the afternoon sunshine, with Brooklyn to the right, and ahead the first glimpse of the Manhattan skyline. The Statue of Liberty, proud on Bedloe's Island (as it was then, and still under military jurisdiction) struck him as "insignificant", but the overall impression was of "stinging enchantment".[33] The Woolworth Tower, then the tallest building not only in Manhattan but in the world, loomed above all. They proceeded up the Hudson River, and not until the early evening did the ship finally dock at Pier 56 in Chelsea. Getting through customs was its own rigmarole, and the queues were enlivened when a passenger called Weatherby Allen was refused entry to the country because he owned a pair of opera glasses that did not bear the proper stamp, whereupon an onlooker called McCarver, attempting to help, whipped out a revolver and threatened to shoot the customs officer dead.[34] Hundreds of passengers ran screaming from the scene, while Noël made matters worse by deciding to quote Blake at an official: "Little lamb, who made thee?" As he wrote in the tongue-in-cheek diary that he kept intermittently for his mother's amusement and hoped to publish, "a fracas far exceeding my wildest dreams ensued, during which [the official] delved down with malice aforethought to the bottom of my trunk and discovered the oddest things in my sponge bag. I think I am going to like America".[35]

2.

It was no ordinary quartet that awaited him, nor an especially sober one, but then Noël didn't do things ordinarily, and had Jeffery Amherst's connections to help him along.

First there was Napier Sturt, 3rd Baron Alington, a bisexual aristocrat who lived on gin and made it a rule never to go to bed before three in the morning. With him was the Argentinian film actress Teddie Gerard, a "hard-drinking, promiscuous adventuress with a drug habit", married to a powerful theatrical agent but pursuing various tempestuous affairs with women.[36] And finally there was the playwright and theatre historian Gabrielle Enthoven (recently widowed, in her early fifties) who had come with her lover Cécile Sartoris (now separated from her diplomat husband). Noël was in his element in such company; off they all went together, and New York hit him.

In *Easy Virtue*, written three years later, Noël would describe Manhattan's "tall buildings and the champagne air". No Chrysler Building, as yet, no Empire State, but towers were crowding around Wall Street, and the foot-high letters on the illumined billboards of Times Square shone brighter than any in London. Whistles blew from tugboats on the Hudson, police sirens howled, and the streets vibrated to the bang of endless construction work as the city grew up into the sky. Jeffery and Noël made their way to the Algonquin Hotel in Midtown, having heard of the daily lunches at the Round Table in the dining room, and feeling sure that they would fit right in to the so-called "Vicious Circle", trading quips with Dorothy Parker. So focused was Noël on the theatre that he refused an invitation to dine with his companions and, that first evening, went straight to the "Great White Way", a new nickname that referred to the bright lightbulbs recently installed outside the Broadway theatres, of which there were eighty-six (twice the number in existence today).

Silent movies offered the theatre only limited competition; auditoria were springing up everywhere. It was the beginning of a decade of song-and-dance revues, musicals, and vaudeville. Noël, almost frightened by the brilliance of the place he had so long imagined, bought a ticket for *Nice People* at the Klaw Theatre, a building just three months old – everything was shiny and new, a far cry from the war-tired feel of the West End. The four-act comedy (by Rachel Crothers) meant little to him, but the way in which it was delivered, the speed with which even British actors performed in America, took him by surprise. It was ten minutes before he tuned in to what they were saying, for all that it was a genteel English comedy. *The Times* in London had already begun to complain that West End performances "were all too slow", that the actors allowed themselves "several bars rest".[37] This was a lesson in delivery and dialogue that Noël would carry back to England.

After the show he went to Teddie Gerard's house on Washington Square, where she lived with an elderly maid who was secretly thought to be her mother. A party was in full swing, the rooms full of smoke and noise and music and dance. Here he ran into an old neighbour from Ebury Street: the Belgian–British musician Irène Dean Paul,* who had separated from her husband and moved

---

* Born Irène Régine Wieniawski, she published music under the pseudonym "Poldowski", and became Lady Dean Paul on her marriage.

to America. She helped herself to different languages during the conversation as others might have done to an array of canapés. But Noël, who had spent the day on the ship and the evening at the theatre, found himself overwhelmed by the party, and escaped back to the Algonquin for a steamy night in the airless rooms. The next morning he transferred himself to the fashionable Brevoort Hotel on Fifth Avenue, close to Washington Square and the Bohemian enclave of Greenwich Village.

For the first week, parties took second place to tourism. He and Jeffery Amherst spent most of their time – and their money – ticking off the attractions. Noël had managed to charm a society grandee on board the *Aquitania* who overcame her suspicions of actorly types and lent them the use of her chauffeur. Otherwise they navigated the Subway, were introduced to the novelty of hot dogs, and climbed the Woolworth Building to see a bird's eye view of Manhattan laid out in checks of streets and avenues around the green oblong of Central Park, the high-rise buildings slowly giving out north of 14th Street. They attended the theatre almost nightly, and ended up as guests of the banker and future politician Averell Harriman, who took them to a polo match and turned out to own most of the horses. On Coney Island Noël was, as ever, accident prone, or perhaps just dare-devil: "We went on The Whip, the sudden convulsions of which drove the clasp of my braces sharply into my back, scarring me, I think, for life. [. . .] The Giant Dipper was comfortingly tame, as I only bruised my side and cut my cheek."[38] Exaggerated as these diary entries were, there was still something childlike about him, or perhaps faux-childlike. On meeting members of the New York Theatre Guild, his first reaction was to play "Hide and Seek with them in the park. Helen Westley fell into the pond – how we laughed."[39]

Manhattan offered other, less childish, pursuits. He visited the triangular Flat Iron building: its base, and the trendy Taverne Louis in the basement, were famous cruising spots for homosexuals, as were the Everard Baths in Chelsea, though all were subject to periodic police raids, supported by the New York Society for the Suppression of Vice. The city was torn between Jazz Age permissiveness and nationwide puritanism. Prohibition had been in force for six months. Speakeasies and illegal alcohol, police bribes, and a thriving Mafia were crowded in beside the flapper outfits of short skirts and even shorter hair. Not until 1926, and the election of a decidedly easy-living mayor, did New York become a true rival for Chicago as the Jazz Age city, and America was still hauling itself out of a sharp recession that had begun the previous year. But for Noël it was intoxicatingly unbuttoned and fast-paced. Migrants were flocking across the newly constructed bridges. In Harlem, where he flicked from cabaret to cabaret, the Renaissance was just beginning, the district already a cultural hub for jazz and blues, the speakeasies thick with smoke and the strange chemical odour of bad gin. In Greenwich Village, composers such as Edgard Varèse and Leon Theremin were experimenting with electronic music. Noël remembered "jigging to the alien rhythms, and listening to strange wailings and screechings".[40]

His professional ambitions had been romantically optimistic rather than carefully planned. He had meetings with a handful of Broadway impresarios who were encouraging, friendly, and soon made their excuses not to read his scripts. He went back to the hotel, and downgraded his room.

3.

Jeffery Amherst left New York for Massachusetts. Noël, his funds running low, moved in with two of his welcome party, Gabrielle Enthoven and Cécile Sartoris, who were living in an apartment at 47 Washington Square South that they offered rent-free until he could afford to pay: "Why should Noël spend money which he hasn't got on a hotel when he can stay with us?"[41] It was a small, white-walled, flower-filled studio flat in a shabby and since-demolished row of peeling brownstones overlooking the park. The household was hot-tempered but the atmosphere was less Bohemian than might have been expected. They spent much of their time eating meals together in their pyjamas, buying food from a little Italian deli round the corner and obtaining cheap red wine (alcohol could technically be consumed in private). All this was exotic produce for someone weaned on the Edwardian British diet, not that Noël ever developed a taste for fine dining.

Gabrielle, curator of a vast and famous collection of stage memorabilia, seemed to know every theatrical figure of the age. She and Cécile were in Manhattan as Red Cross representatives to raise funds for French schoolchildren orphaned by the war, and their translation of d'Annunzio's *The Honeysuckle* was being revived on Broadway.[42] They went with Noël to concerts given by Irène Dean Paul in wealthy living rooms, where Cécile read aloud in a blank monotone. Dean Paul was a frequent visitor back at the apartment, living on nervous energy and easily enraged; she was attempting to deal remotely with the increasingly serious drug addiction of her daughter, Brenda, an actress and socialite who became a fixture of London's youth culture. But Noël came to like Dean Paul and her music so much that he thought her temper worth tolerating. It is surprising how resistant he was to her musicianship: she seems to have had no effect at all on his innate and untrained musical talent, which much to her displeasure he continued to steer resolutely towards comic song.

By the summer, many of the theatres had closed, and his new friends had left him alone in New York with low funds and lower spirits. He had not sold a single play. Manhattan had still not heard of him. "Why did nobody tell me", he wrote dejectedly to his mother, "that the streets of New York are so hot in the summer that you could fry an egg on the pavement (sorry, sidewalk!)."[43] He sank into gloom, roaming the streets people-watching, and buying packets of cheap bacon from the Italian deli and cooking alone in the tiny kitchen. Invariably he wandered about the apartment in the nude, as relief from the heat, and on one occasion was spotted through the window by a policeman who turned up at the apartment, irate – and was soon assured of Noël's innocent lifestyle, even leaving a revolver behind lest Noël ever need it for protection.

Noël's clothes were as well tailored as his manner, and he made sure to charm the wealthy, who thought nothing of dining him at the Hotel Astor or sending tickets to glamorous first nights. But a veneer of riches covered depths of poverty and solitude and he returned, each night, to an apartment as empty as his purse, buying food on credit. He took refuge in industry. Chief among the plays he wrote in that miserable empty summer is *Sirocco*; about an Italian painter's affair with a married Englishwoman, it would not be produced until 1927. He had also embarked on a series of satirical portraits depicting fictional aristocrats from the past: "Sarah, Lady Tunnell-Penge", "Sophie, the Uncrowned Queen of Henry VIII", and – an especially Saki-esque title – "The Education of Rupert Plinge". The collection, titled *A Withered Nosegay*, had found a British publisher and while in New York he managed to sell the American rights to the influential firm Boni & Liveright. The book would appear on both sides of the Atlantic the following spring to little fanfare, a minor contribution to the collection of post-war works – reaching its peak with *1066 and All That* – that sought to debunk British grandiosity in the recounting of history.*

The introduction to such a distinguished publisher as Horace Liveright may have come about via a new friendship with the critic George Kaufman, whose wife, Beatrice, was the firm's most distinguished and influential editor. George, drama editor of the *New York Times*, was about to embark on an amazingly successful career as a playwright. Noël seemed to belong in trios, slotting happily into place as a third figure to an older couple, as he had done in childhood to Esmé Wynne and John Ekins. Eventually, he would harness the dramatic potential of the ménage à trois in his play *Design for Living*, although in reality his relationships with straight couples seemed to work because he was a sexual threat neither to the man nor the woman. As well as the Kaufmans, he befriended the playwright Hartley Manners and his actress wife Laurette Taylor, spending Sunday evenings in their huge and ornately furnished house on the Upper West Side.

Manners was originally British and, back in 1912, had written a successful comedy called *Peg o'My Heart* as a vehicle for his wife.

---

* The American edition was retitled *Terribly Intimate Portraits* and included Coward's New York diary.

It was enjoying a revival, with Taylor once again the lead (eventually she would reinvent herself as a serious performer). With their two children they had set up a theatrical household, full of flamboyant quarrel. The friendship was a lesson in self-creation (Manners was never seen in public without a cape and cane) and Taylor was delighted by Noël's swift retorts, as when, asked to admire her new and self-administered haircut, he told her she looked like a "lousy Shelley". He would spend his afternoons in their hallway at the piano, while each member of the family in turn would stop on the staircase, lean over the banister, and invite him to stay for dinner. He frankly admitted that he drew on such experiences when inventing the Bliss clan in *Hay Fever*. But this was something the family found hard to forgive. "None of us", Laurette told him after seeing the play, "is ever unintentionally rude."[44]

The final and most important couple to whom he became close in New York were the actors Alfred Lunt and Lynn Fontanne, soon to become the most famous husband-and-wife duo in American theatre. He was twenty-nine, she thirty-five (but so cagey about divulging her true age that Lunt went to his grave believing she was five years younger than she was). Neither was yet a star; they had acted together only once, and planned to get married the following year, more from Lynn's urging than Alfred's enthusiasm. They were lodging in rooms on the Upper West Side, which they had turned into a kind of salon for aspiring actors. Lynn was born in England and Noël half-remembered her from dancing clubs in London. The three-way attraction was instantaneous, although Lynn was jittery with nerves about an upcoming performance in a play called *Dulcy* (George Kaufman was co-author). On 20 August Noël sat with Alfred in the first-night audience, their tension evaporating as they realised that it was an evident hit.

What brought the trio together was an almost uncanny combination of ambition and determination. "They're going to be huge stars", Noël wrote to Violet, "and since we all know that yours truly is going to be one too, we've decided that, when that great day arrives, we shall act together in a play I shall write for us and the cosmos will have a new galaxy."[45] Which is exactly what eventually happened. Lynn and Alfred became famous for throwing away or even gabbling and interrupting their lines, rather than speaking them decorously in turn. Theirs was precisely the realistic delivery that Noël wanted to hone in his own writing and performance. They would soon act exclusively in vehicles written for them as a couple, *Design for Living* not least.

The temperature in Manhattan finally fell. Broadway wound itself back up into glamour and industry. The sharp recession in America had ended in July, and the economy began its near-decade of roaring prosperity. But still Noël felt, as he later put it, "vaguely bedraggled, as though my spirit hadn't been pressed properly and was shabby and creased".[46] Lynn Fontanne was earning enough money to keep him financially afloat, but he was able to pay her back when he sold two stories to the *Metropolitan Magazine*. The new funds were also useful when, in September, Gabrielle and Cécile had to give up the Washington Square apartment, which had succumbed to bedbugs and burglary. He was able to move back into the Brevoort Hotel, where the American concert pianist Lester Donahue, a friend from London, soon joined him after they stumbled across one another at the theatre. They spent Noël's final weeks in Manhattan together, until Noël secured a berth on RMS *Cedric*, which sailed for Liverpool on 29 October 1921.[47]

The skyline receded; the world shrank to ocean and seasickness. Noël made an unlikely friend on board in the form of Marie Stopes, the birth-control pioneer whose Mothers' Clinic, the first of its kind, had opened in London earlier that year. She had, Noël thought, the "eyes of a fanatic" (her progressive views on women's rights sat uneasily with her enthusiasm for eugenics).[48] But she was also devoted to the theatre, which they spent most of the voyage discussing. "He is a dear", she wrote to her husband on 4 November, "full of youth and enthusiasm and yet sanity. . . He is using his money successes to help his mother and family and he is hoping to use his power of laughter to help in social progress." Soon she was reading his manuscripts: "One very good and one very bad. I told him it was putrid and he took it ever so nicely."[49] They maintained an on-and-off friendship until the colossal success, only three years later, of *The Vortex*, and her eager suggestion that she should write her own play using the same characters. His coldly

formal reply — "Dear Dr Stopes" — made it plain that the acquaintance was at an end.

The ship docked at Liverpool in thick November snow. Noël's
American aspirations had not come to fruition, but the four months
in New York had changed him as a writer and as a musician, as he
had somehow known they would. Before most of his generation he
had caught a glimpse of the dangerous and exciting excesses of the
1920s, which roared earlier in America than in Britain. His songs
were soon to be imbued with the blues he had heard in the clubs
and parties of Harlem and Manhattan, his music a collision point,
sparks flying, between British light music and American jazz. And
the way in which he wrote and delivered dialogue was now flecked
with an American tempo. "This is something in a different world",
he had written in letters home. "The speed! Everybody seems to
say their lines at such a rate you'd think you wouldn't understand a
word — but you do! And then it suddenly struck me — that's the way
people actually talk. Wait till I get back to Shaftesbury Avenue!!"[50]

With little to his name, Noël had infiltrated the echelons of
Manhattan high society or high-society-to-be. Drawn like a magnet
to movers and shakers, he also had an eye for spotting potential
talent or wealth: almost none of his promising friends failed to live
up to their promise. To his address book he had added prominent
American critics; wealthy socialites; and anyone who had a seat at
the Algonquin's Round Table. But he had also spent many weeks
solitary and penniless in the Manhattan streets. Determinedly,
throughout his life, he would place himself at the centre of crowds
and bustle, from the quasi-salon of his rooms at Ebury Street, to
backstage corridors, riotous parties, and the "family" of friends with
which he made sure to surround himself. But had anyone walking
along the south side of Washington Square, in that hot summer of
1921, looked up the zig-zag of fire escapes to the higher windows,
they would have caught sight of Noël Coward, twenty-one years
old, frying bacon without his clothes on, quite alone.

INTERVAL

PART TWO

"TOWN MOUSE, COUNTRY MOUSE"

NOËL COWARD,
NED LATHOM, VIOLET COWARD, E. NESBIT, ELSA MAXWELL

A little girl, living in the village of Lathom in West Lancashire, and standing in the lane that led up to Blythe Hall, saw three grown men bouncing past her on pogo sticks.

The first two were Ivor Novello and Noël Coward, though the latter was not yet a star. She was more likely to have recognised the third figure, owner of Blythe Hall: Edward Bootle-Wilbraham, 3rd Earl of Lathom.[1] "Ned Lathom" to his friends, he was one of the bright suns – gay in all senses, aristocratic, mad on theatre – around whom orbited the set in which Noël made it his business to move. It was at Lathom's introduction that Noël had met Jeffery Amherst and funds for the American voyage had been provided by Lathom's purchasing two of his songs, more out of generosity than need. He was fabulously wealthy and fabulously generous, although his money led him to indulge a flamboyance that bordered on the mad. He had seen active service in the trenches, and like many in his generation he emerged frightened of solitude, throwing himself into life with an extravagance, even silliness, that served as distraction. Conveniently for Noël, he was star-struck to a fault, and would himself write a number of plays, some of which were considered too risqué for public performance.

Lathom's parties became the stuff of legend: servants were said to waft perfume from heated spoons through flower-stuffed rooms or be despatched on a whim to London to return laden with priceless luxuries. He moved into Blythe Hall in 1922, the year in which the word "party" first began to be used as a verb. Lathom spent a fortune on renovations that included a bowling alley and swimming pool. "Wild life of young Noël Coward at orgies of playboy earl" ran one newspaper headline in 2000, as details of Lathom's lifestyle emerged.[2] But it is hard to trace back rumours to any first-hand factual account, and Noël's role is difficult to discern; rumours of a love affair are inevitable but unproven. Lathom's was a lifestyle built on a metaphorical sinkhole, and neither his fortune nor his health would withstand it.

It was to Lathom that Noël turned when, as he settled back into London routines on his return from New York, life became worryingly impecunious. He was combining parties and penury. The family's funds had sunk so low that his piano had to be mortgaged; bailiffs and pawnbrokers became familiar figures. Matters came to a head when Noël noticed with increasing panic how strained and ill his mother was becoming. He plucked up courage to ask Lathom for a loan. Perhaps fancying himself as a benefactor to the promising young playwright, Lathom instantly offered £200 as a gift. Noël was jubilant with gratitude and relief. Most of the funds were spent paying off creditors, but there was enough left over to repeat one of his parents' money-saving methods during his childhood and decamp to the country. In the spring of 1922 he and his mother found a cottage and a dog in St Mary in the Marsh, a small village near New Romney in Kent, two miles from the sea. His father was left in charge of the increasingly empty boarding house, which contrary to expectations Arthur managed with efficiency and contentment, the building becalmed without Violet's neuroses.

There was little to do in Kent but walk and read and write. Violet's fatigue fell away; Noël commuted to London when needed and spent much of his time writing two romances, *The Queen Was in the Parlour* and *The Happy Harlot*, of which only the first would see production, and not for another four years.[3] Strange, almost backward, diversions in his early work, these plays found him trying his hand at the Ruritanian romances that had characterised his childhood theatre-going – an odd choice given the recent injection of up-tempo modernity he had received in New York. Life with his mother in the Kentish marshes had temporarily returned him to adolescent enthusiasms.

A figure of enchantment from his infancy came to life in the guise of E. Nesbit, whose books he had continued to reread with delight, as if to cultivate the peculiar brand of soigné childishness

that characterised the party-going generation. Nesbit had moved
to Romney Marsh that spring, setting up a domestic trio with her
second husband and the children's writer Olive Hill. Noël being
Noël, he promptly paid a visit. Nesbit was in her sixties, her reputation and health fading. There was no love lost between her and
Violet, but she enjoyed the admiration and promise of her young
visitor, who regaled her with stories about stealing jewellery from
his mother's friends in order to purchase Nesbit's books with the
proceeds. He remained intermittently in touch with her until her
death, two years later.

The trios of Nesbit's love life were unlikely mirrors of a three-
handed one-acter that he had completed in New York the previous
year and which suddenly found itself a staging in the spring of
1922. *The Better Half* was produced as part of a season by the Grand
Guignol theatre company, an experimental group attempting to
emulate European traditions of combining horror and comedy on
the same bill. In retrospect Noël thought it unwise to have competed
with the thriller that opened the evening, which was by an Oxford
undergraduate called Richard Hughes, later famous for his novel *A
High Wind in Jamaica*. Hughes was a year younger and rather stole
the youthful limelight. The season opened on 31 May at the Little
Theatre, venue of Noël's stage debut in *The Goldfish*, and ran for a
month. The critics were not persuaded to agree with Noël's title as
to which of the plays were superior, and damned *The Better Half* with
the faintest praise: "a quite clever skit"; "a very pretty wit"; "the
author will get past the petticoat stage".[4] One reviewer pounced on
the accusation that would dog Noël's career: "Mr Coward is cursed
with fatal facility, that failing of the young writer, seeming to think
all his geese are swans, and writing them down without waiting to
see if nothing better can be found in their place."[5]

The play was filmed live for Alistair Cooke's *Omnibus* television
series in 1956, with Jessica Tandy and Hume Cronyn, after which
the script, never published in Noël's lifetime, was ignored for
many decades. One copy was found in the papers of the Lord
Chamberlain who, reading the script for approval and potential
censorship (as, until 1968, he was legally obliged to do), noted its
"daring" sexual politics.[6] Tired of her husband's irritatingly bland

decency and implied sexual dullness, a woman invents for herself an entirely fictitious double life of promiscuous infidelity in order to inject some energy into the relationship, only to be greeted with an understanding and forgiveness that lead her to walk out: "I am going to find a lover and live in flaming sin – possibly at Claridge's." Beneath the wit of the dialogue lies a portrayal of women not as objects of a man's passion but as figures with their own sexual needs, camouflaging "desire for your body behind a transparently effusive admiration of your brain!" (The Lord Chamberlain underlined such dialogue furiously with his blue pencil, but eventually decided not to insist on cuts.) The play is a claustrophobic and even savage portrait of a marriage stirred into sexual excitement only by infidelity or violence: "I'm going to kill you!" "If you kill me remember one thing. You'll be hanged by the neck until you are dead!" Once again the attitude to the world of love and sex is queasy: "It gives one a warm comfortable feeling doesn't it? Being loved?" "I don't know – I suppose so –".

Whatever Noël's own affairs of the heart in his early twenties, he gives the impression of being a lone ranger, still peering from the outside onto relationships or social groups. Invited to Oxford so as to attend the Bullingdon Club Ball, he noticed the way in which undergraduates let their woollen socks runkle around their ankles, before looking down at his own socks, which were silk, and carefully attached to suspenders. Not yet twenty-three, he felt old, distant, wrongly dressed, and detached from revellers who seemed youthful in a way he had never been. It was Noël's first prolonged glimpse of a world that had never beckoned for him, his experience of university life having been relegated to its caricatured onstage impression while acting in *The Light Blues*.

The Bullingdon Club was already associated with riotous and sometimes destructive behaviour. The ball was held in Oxford's town hall, decorated with palms and hydrangeas and specially fitted with a spring floor for the four hundred guests. Noël was there at the invitation of the socialite Sibyl Colefax, who soon introduced him to Elsa Maxwell, another pillar of 1920s party-going. Later a gossip columnist and screenwriter, she was managing to make a living and reputation as a party organiser, and was an incongruously large figure amid the slender students (Noël uncharitably compared her to the Michelin man). But she bounced through the ball, as she did through life, with a fizz of energy and fun. Many of the themed parties of the era – from treasure hunts to "come as your opposite" fancy dress – are thought to have been her idea, and one hunt-themed ball was said to have spilled the bounds of its venue and disturbed all of Paris. Within weeks of meeting her, Noël found himself invited to Venice, where she and her partner, the singer Dorothy Fellowes-Gordon, were shortly to holiday: "I'm giving a party for His Royal Highness the Duke of Spoletta. It will be great fun."[7] Noël was by this time well used to holidaying at others' expense, knew how to earn his keep at the piano, and just a few days later, he was on the boat.

It is a brave twenty-two-year-old who holidays with such brand-new friends, unsure whether he is there as guest or entertainer. But that was a tightrope he knew how to walk. He was predictably entranced by a summer fortnight of gondolas and sunshine and Elsa and Dorothy were generous, if difficult, travel companions, who introduced him to yet more brand-new friends. But soon he had to return to London in August, to begin rehearsals for his first major acting engagement in nearly two years, and in a play of his own.

"Squaring the circle"

NOËL COWARD, GEORGE BERNARD SHAW

It is hard, in recounting Noël's steady social and professional climb through the decade and its cat's cradles of *laissez-faire* sexuality and carefree infidelity, not to let the account drift into a fast-moving parade of interchangeable partygoers, of friendships made with amazing speed, love affairs ended and begun with hasty abandon, amid waterfalls of champagne and money. To give just one example: Elsa Maxwell's partner, Dorothy Fellowes-Gordon, had had affairs with the writer Mercedes de Acosta (who would later fall in love with Gladys Calthrop) and with Napier Sturt (who had met Noël from the boat in New York and among whose other infidelities, with men and with women, was the actress Tallulah Bankhead).

Amid the tangle of affairs, actual marriages wobbled and frayed. That Noël's plays had begun to depict knots of spouses and lovers and ex-partners is unsurprising, his treatment swerving between the permissive and the puritan. The ending of Somerset Maugham's *The Circle* (1919), which Noël had seen in New York, had led to minor outrage by showing a married woman happily eloping with her lover. Noël's own plays, by contrast, often showed the reuniting of married couples after an unhappy skirmish with infidelity.

The Young Idea, a three-act comedy that he had completed back in summer 1920, was a case in point.[8] Noël's talent could develop at such speed that even a two-year delay between writing and production made his scripts look old-fashioned compared to his more recent work. The plot of *The Young Idea* is straight out of children's literature (it foreshadows Erich Kästner's 1949 novel *Lottie and Lisa*, filmed as *The Parent Trap*). Noël had created a pair of adolescent siblings, Gerda and Sholto — his archetypal "Poj and Stoj" pair — who get up to various machinations in order to reunite their divorced parents. Their innocence is too knowing to be believed, and the play was an arch descant on the rash of Edwardian dramas — chief among them *Where the Rainbow Ends* or Violet Pearn's *The Starlight Express* — that featured children curing, via their purity, the emotional woes of adults.

Anyone familiar with George Bernard Shaw's 1897 comedy *You Never Can Tell*, with its twins Dolly and Philip, would have recognised an influence, even a plagiarism, to which Noël cheerily owned up. At sixty-five, Shaw was on the verge of consolidating his reputation with *Back to Methusaleh* (1922) and *Saint Joan* (1923), and he would soon be awarded the Nobel Prize. Noël avoided Shavian social commentary, and the estranged parents of *You Never Can Tell* are reunited through mistaken identity rather than their children's conscious machinations. But Shaw's influence was inescapable. Noël had yet to use the exact phrase "Anyone for tennis?" — spoken in Shaw's *Misalliance* and a shorthand for the genre of drawing-room comedy — but he had got near enough. Later, he would advise young writers to read "all of Shaw", as he had once done.[9]

Noël had boldly sent the script of *The Young Idea* to Shaw's long-time producer J. E. Vedrenne, who sought blessing from the playwright himself. "I have on my desk", Shaw had written in March 1921, "a typed play by a clever young writer whose dialogue is very vivacious and is that of an educated man accustomed to converse with educated people. It bristles with mad hyphens á tort et á travers;* but there is not a stop in it from beginning to end except the full stops at the ends of the speeches."[10] Shaw annotated the unpunctuated script with flourishes of mock outrage and Vedrenne promptly turned it down. On 27 June, when Noël was in New York, Shaw had generously written to him: "I have no doubt you will succeed if you persevere, and take care never to fall into a breach of essential good manners, and, above all, never to see or read my plays. Unless you can get clean away from me you will begin as a back number, and be hopelessly out of it when you are forty."[11]

Finally Robert Courtneidge, with whom Noël had had such a difficult time as an unruly teenage actor, agreed to produce *The Young Idea* and a provincial tour was scheduled for the autumn of 1922 prior to a London transfer. Matters got off to a bad start when Courtneidge suggested that someone other than Noël should appear as Sholto, but he was overruled. Esmé Wynne turned down the role of Gerda in favour of married life and Christian Science; her son remembered her decision as "shattering news to Noël, as he made clear on almost every occasion we met or spoke through the rest of his life".[12] Although Poj and Stoj would keep in affectionate and fractious touch by letter, the irreplaceable intensity of their early friendship was over for good, and the nineteen-year-old Ann Trevor became the other half of the double act. Rehearsals were tricky, but Courtneidge, although he had not mellowed all that much since they had worked together in 1916, knew to soothe his leading actor with protestations that the performance was a good one – a judgement that Noël, in hindsight, thought to be untrue.

The opening night of the tour was in Bristol, on 25 September 1922.[13] By this time, Noël had written two more plays: *The Last Resource* was staged at the Shaftesbury Theatre in January 1923, and

---

* "Wrong and crosswise", i.e. without rhyme or reason.

Mild Oats was presented as a curtain-raiser to the tour of *The Young Idea*. The former (undiscovered until now) was a brief comedy about a rich young woman auditioning to be a chorus girl and expecting to be a star. "Would you like to see my legs?" she asks a casting director, who replies "I can, thank you." "Oh", she says. "I always thought managers insisted on seeing one's legs." *Mild Oats*, much darker in tone, was about an ostensibly sophisticated pair of young things come back late at night to a London apartment in the hopes of sex. In the course of their dialogue, it is revealed – as they swap their whiskies for a pot of tea – that both are naive and unworldly; by the end of the ten-minute drama they have fallen genuinely, passionlessly, in love. The play extends Noël's juxtaposition of modernity and moralism: young couples these days, the sketch seems to say, would be better off snuggling over tea than dancing the night away. The oats they are trying to sow are more mild than wild. In interviews Noël laid his cards on the table with surprising gravity: "In comedy you depend on characterisation and humorous ideas. There must, I think, be a serious notion behind it all."[14]

"L.S.D."

NOËL COWARD, NED LATHOM, ANDRÉ CHARLOT

Noël amused himself, in the gap between the tour and the London run of *The Young Idea*, by holidaying with Ned Lathom, who was recuperating from a bout of tuberculosis in Davos, a small Alpine town in south-eastern Switzerland that had become a haven for sufferers from TB. In fact, Noël had invited himself, something he had become rather adept at doing, certain that his friends would be delighted to see him, which, it seems, they usually were. Lathom's fortunes were already faltering and the following year he would be forced to sell his entire estate. But if Noël were disturbed by the sudden reminder of a disease that had confined him to a sanatorium and killed Philip Streatfeild, he didn't let it ruin an exciting holiday. Dwelling on past sadness was not his style, and he bubbled with manic determination to have a good time.

Davos had a strange atmosphere of plush mortality, and the party-going nightlife of its luxurious hotels rubbed against the day-time worlds of disease and treatment. The silk handkerchiefs into which residents coughed discreetly were often stained with blood. En route, Noël had stopped off in Paris to see Elsa Maxwell, who introduced him to anyone worth knowing in Parisian theatre. He arrived at the Grandhotel Belvédère in Davos on 2 December, agape at the sunlit snow-capped mountains. Lathom had set up glamorous residence in the hotel and encouraged Noël to perform at the piano. Seemingly on the very day of his guest's arrival, he decided on a whim that Noël had composed so many songs that they should be made into a full-length revue. He still had the kind of money that could make whims a reality, and he instantly telegrammed an invitation to the French impresario André Charlot.

By the end of 3 December, Noël's second day in Davos, Charlot had arrived, and Noël wrote to Violet: "I've just played all the music to Charlot and he's <u>delighted</u>. He sat without a smile and then took me aside and said they were <u>all</u> good – so that's that."[15] By 5 December, having been in Davos for just three days, his ears ringing in the mountainous altitude and his piano battling with the coughs of the tubercular, Noël was able to send his mother a detailed outline of all the revue's numbers and sketches, adding to his back catalogue many newly written since his arrival. He even had some idea of the cast list and contractual terms. Gertrude Lawrence was chief on the wishlist, having recently moved from understudy to star in Charlot's latest revue, *A to Z*. The speed with which things developed is so astonishing as to imply that, contrary to Noël's account, he and Lathom had been plotting the collaboration before the holiday. Either way, the revue that became *London Calling!* had been born, although for many months its working title was *L.S.D.* – not a nod to the culture of drug-taking, but an abbreviation of the currency that fuelled it: pounds, shillings, and pence.[16]

André Charlot had first brought a Parisian revue to Britain in 1912 and soon turned the genre into one of the most successful in British theatre. His revues were formed of unconnected sketches, songs, and dance numbers; their scattergun nature fitted the era's tempo and attention span. His first introduction to Noël, four years

earlier, had been inauspicious. As a favour to a friend he had listened to Noël performing and dismissed the song in question as
trivial rubbish. But egged on by Ned Lathom, he now greeted the
prospect of a Noël Coward revue with eagerness. Noël had been
writing sketches for years, but only a handful of them had been
performed.[17] Lathom's suggestion, that Noël should provide words
and music for the entire evening, was something different again,
and a chance to flex his musical, writerly, and actorly muscles.
As sole author, he could proclaim himself the leader of a new
generation wanting to sharpen and tighten the frothy jumble of
revue. He was spurred on by a self-confidence that ensured the
possibility of failure didn't occur. "It's going to be colossal", he
told Violet. "And when you consider that bright particular star
will be me!" (His quote from *All's Well That Ends Well** lets slip the
breadth of his reading.) "It's a bit breathless!"[18] And all this from
a young man who still felt the need to tell his mother that, in the
surprising warmth of Davos's sunny winter climate, "I never wear
a vest during the day".[19]

    In the second week of December he took himself off for a sojourn
in Berlin, where he celebrated his twenty-third birthday, renting an
apartment in Wilmersdorf, south-west of the capital. He admitted
that he "laughed a good lot at the people [. . .] German is a terribly
funny language to listen to – I get weak at moments and laugh in
people's faces!"[20] Uncontrollable mirth was always near the surface
– partly as a weapon with which to deflect having to be serious
about anything other than his own work. It was his first sight of
Weimar Germany, and he was delighted by the hyper-inflation that
made dinner at the Ritz so amazingly cheap. Viennese operetta was
enjoying its last decade of favour and Noël was delighted by Leo
Fall's *Madame Pompadour*, belying his insistence that he could not read
music, he went off and purchased the score. The era-defining first
night of *The Threepenny Opera* was still some years away, but the city's
nightclubs and casinos already thrummed to the cabaret songs of

---

* "It were all one | That I should love a bright particular star | And think to wed
  it . . ." (I.i)

composers such as Werner Heymann and Friedrich Hollaender. It was in a Berlin nightclub that Noël watched a cabaret entertainer performing with a Pierrot doll, a stock character of *commedia dell'arte* and one of Noël's childhood obsessions.[21] And so his first really enduring song, "Parisian Pierrot", soon earmarked for *London Calling!*, was born. The trips to Paris and Berlin had widened his sphere of musical influence and "Parisian Pierrot" could at a stretch belong to the jazz-inflected world of Satie and Poulenc, or to the bluesy melody and gallows humour of cabaret.

Noël returned to Davos on 18 December and was persuaded to stay on at the hotel for Christmas so as properly to make the acquaintance of the renowned fashion designer Edward Molyneux, whom he had met briefly in Paris and whom Ned Lathom invited for the festivities. Molyneux had opened a salon on the rue Royale and his style was thought devastatingly refined by anyone who mattered. He agreed to design the costumes for *London Calling!* and was to dress Noël's leading ladies for four decades. Lathom's Christmas guest list, which included Elsa Maxwell, took over Davos: they skated on frozen lakes, and shot noisily down mountains on sledges. Micheál Mac Liammóir, who had acted opposite Noël as King Goldfish all those years ago, was staying at the hotel, having moved to Europe to avoid conscription. He found Noël and his group insufferable.[22]

By January 1923 Noël was back in London and panicking, lest *London Calling!* prevent him from performing in the London run of *The Young Idea*. In the event the revue was delayed until September, and his play was able to open at the Savoy Theatre on 1 February. That Noël had accurately caught his own generation was confirmed by a clique of delighted young admirers who already recognised as "a Noëlism" lines such as: "She's got no go in her that girl. She borrowed the top of my Thermos, and never returned it. Shallow, very shallow." Meanwhile he had churned out an adaptation of a French play; this seems to have been a translation of Louis Verneuil's *Pour avoir Adrienne* that opened in the same week under the title *The Love Habit*.[23] For a while he had two productions running simultaneously in the West End, and he could write to his mother "send me any bills that need paying".[24] But he was given no public credit for the translation, and although reviews and business for *The Young Idea* were reasonable, it fizzled out after eight weeks. "London is outraged at the play coming off" he told Violet, "everyone is talking about it and it's doing me a <u>lot</u> of good – I haven't written before because I've been working hard at *The Vortex*."[25]

It was a nonchalant reference to the play that would change his life. The title had been swimming about in his notebooks for years (Shaw's *Back to Methusaleh*, published in 1921, included a long discourse on the word "vortex") and he set properly to work in the spring of 1923.[26] It is easy to chart – as any reader of his early notebooks can – a talent being forced into place; it is much harder to say why or how it suddenly coalesces, which in *The Vortex* it had begun to do. About an amorous relationship between a mother and her drug-addicted, possibly homosexual, son, the play is in a different key to all his previous work. That he now had something to say, about addiction and sexuality, and the escape that both could provide, gave his writing a new atmosphere of honesty and of sensation. Within a year he would write *Hay Fever*, one of his most enduring comedies; within six, he would write *Private Lives*.

Then again, between those two hardy perennials, there would appear several plays that would survive neither the test of time nor the bar of public and critical opinion. His skills were not developing in a clear upward trajectory, as if his talent were something separate from himself, which he was powerless to control or even judge. Inspiration could arrive and disappear, and when it did not strike his technique was by now so sure that he could rely on it to prevent scripts collapsing in on themselves. That he had a genuine vocational need to write is certain, but it was the abstract notion of "success", combined with the necessity of funding his family and his frenetic social life, that drove his productivity.

Nevertheless, relations could be a millstone and he had few illusions as to whether he had outgrown his family. On finishing *The Vortex* he escaped to Cornwall and made dutiful trips to his aunt in Charlestown, scene of idyllic childhood holidays: "Auntie Laura was very sweet but she <u>has</u> aged", he told Violet, "[Cousin] Alan was detestable – gauche and rude."[27] Work continued even on holiday, but he seems to have had little conception that *The Vortex* was especially individual in his output or of a maturity worth capitalising upon. He simply moved on, writing an adaptation of Geoffrey Moss's romantic novella *Sweet Pepper* (a bestseller of 1923 set in a world of British officers and Hungarian aristocrats). In this idea he lost faith, and so he began *Catherine*, a musical comedy. "*Catherine* opens July 30th at Birmingham", he told his mother excitedly, "then a seven-week tour before London, when it will probably open at Drury Lane – <u>double</u> the capacity and a much larger production!"[28] But these plans fell through, and *Catherine* was abandoned in favour of a play, written in October, called *Fallen Angels*, a short comedy about two married women who have once shared a lover.[29] But producers did not seem interested in that, either.

There was little to do but wait for *London Calling!* to grind into gear. His mother, in better health and spirits after a year in the countryside, returned to Ebury Street and found the boarding house in reasonable shape. In April he and Gladys Calthrop holidayed in the south of France, staying at Cap Ferrat on the invitation of Mrs Astley Cooper who was for some reason accompanied by a disapproving Dominican prior. Noël and Gladys escaped to Italy for a long weekend, where they rushed about with low funds but high spirits. On his return the preparations for *London Calling!* began in earnest. Charlot's revues were known for a simple elegance in polar opposition to American equivalents such as the Ziegfeld Follies, which Noël had seen, and disliked, in New York. Nevertheless, the visual spectacle had to give the audience its money's worth, and between them Noël, Lathom, and Charlot began to hatch extravagant plans.

It is a mark of Noël's careful self-invention that *London Calling!* is now remembered as a revue for which he had written all the words and music, "with one exception", according to the current printed edition.[30] In fact, of the two-dozen numbers that made up the evening, just over half were by Noël alone. Charlot, perhaps to cover his back (although it was Lathom who footed the bills), had quickly brought on collaborators. The composer Philip Braham took over some of the music, and there were to be songs by Ivor Novello and by the African-American vaudeville duo Sissle and Blake. Ronald Jeans, author of a successful revue called *Oh, Law!*, contributed a number of sketches and the programme, listing Jeans and Coward as co-authors, did not put the names in alphabetical order.

Noël's songs, meanwhile, were notated with the assistance of a pint-sized musician in a large-brimmed hat, known as Elsie April, who would take dictation as he played. Born Sarah Doyle, now in her late thirties, she had been a child prodigy, which helped her escape her upbringing in a Manchester slum. At fifteen she enrolled at the Royal Northern College of Music, funded by a wealthy sponsor, and began to make a living as a pianist and accompanist.[31] She was seemingly content (or so Noël thought) never to have composed in her own right, but her sharp musical ear made her indispensable to the great revue producers of the day. Noël was said to become touchy when discussing the extent to which April – who had a technical knowledge of music that far outstripped his own – was midwife to his songs, but he happily conceded the importance of her role, as also her modesty and tirelessness. Nowhere did he mention any awareness of her private life: she was quietly married to the tenor John Luxton, with whom she had four children.

Until now Noël's work as a songwriter had predominantly been as lyricist. His playing had developed completely by ear, and he admitted to being at home only in a handful of key signatures. Nor could he notate the melodies he was hearing in his head (not one musical note is written in his notebooks). He took one or two lessons with the distinguished musicologist Orlando Morgan, who called out Noël's habit of using parallel fifths. Noël put a swift end to proceedings by remarking that Debussy and Ravel were happy to use parallel fifths and so, therefore, was he. Here he admitted a technical knowledge of music at the forefront of modern composition, but he seems almost purposefully to have made his songs the work of an amateur musician. In this may lie the secret of his compositional versatility: hearing so many different styles simply as sound helped him slip between genres with an ease denied him had he needed to master the notation. He told Violet, as work continued: "I now quite definitely enter the ranks of British composers!"[32] Perhaps he meant that he had a place not with Elgar or Delius but among composers such as Philip Braham or Jack Hylton, both – as in Braham's "Limehouse Blues" – combining their British inheritance with American jazz.

Noël temporarily refused to perform in *London Calling!*, worried that his reputation as an actor would suffer if he appeared in a musical. But he enjoyed being persuaded to appear and eventually accepted a salary that would translate to over £2000 a week in today's money. He had to get his dancing up to scratch (his singing, he later said, was a lost cause) and he sought assistance from none other than Fred Astaire, whom he had seen in New York. Astaire was fast becoming a renowned dancer and with his sister Adele was dazzling the West End, among the first wave of American stars transforming British musical theatre with unparalleled speed and dexterity. Fred got Noël's tap dancing up to scratch in sessions at the Guildhall. (This was generous, given that the revue contained a number clearly sending up the Astaire siblings.)[33] The dress rehearsal was frantic. Ned Lathom had returned from Davos and sat in the stalls being unhelpful. The actors moaned about the material, the chorus girls moaned about Molyneux's costumes, and Molyneux moaned about the way the chorus girls looked in them. André Charlot maintained an oasis of calm at the centre of it all, and on 4 September 1923, at the Duke of York's Theatre on St Martin's Lane, the curtain rose on *London Calling!*.

An evening so stuffed with material made for rather too long a show, but there was no doubt that the continued quality of the content had set a new standard. *The Times* concluded that "the production has more real humour – and more subtle humour – in it that many much more pretentious productions, and some of the spectacles are beautiful in the extreme".[34] Picked out for praise was a monologue Noël had written for Gertrude Lawrence to deliver entirely on a telephone: hearing of her husband's death, she tells all her friends, and is then enraged to find that the news was intended for the flat above. The telephone was a developing technology, commonplace only in affluent homes, and the sketch predates by nearly a decade both Cocteau's telephonic monodrama *La Voix Humaine* and Dorothy Parker's story "A Telephone Call".

Noël had given the form of revue a flavour of modernity free of the dusty remnants of music hall. Even the eponymous number (by Ronald Jeans) took its name from a phrase that had entered common parlance just ten months before, when the first British Broadcasting Company transmitter, 2LO, had crackled into life: "this is 2LO, Marconi House, London calling. . ." The phrase was boomed around the theatre on loud-speakers, a spectacular effect, as was the use of projected film featuring a young couple eloping in an aeroplane.[35]

And then there was Hernia Whittlebot.

"SACKING AND RHUBARB"
NOËL COWARD, EDITH SITWELL

She entered (in the form of the actress Maisie Gay) wearing "dyed sacking, [. . .] a necklet of uncut amber beads in unconventional shapes", and "a little clump of Bacchanalian fruit below each ear". Then she began to declaim her views on life and on literature: "To me life is essentially a curve, and Art an oblong within that curve. Rhythm is fundamental in everything. My brothers and I have been brought up on Rhythm as other children are brought up on Glaxo."* The audience was then treated to a recital of Whittlebot's poetry: "Life is ephemeral before the majesty | Of Local Apophlegmatism | Melody semi-spheroidal | In all its innate rotundity | Rhubarb for purposes unknown."[36] Whittlebot was eventually dragged offstage, even as she continued to declaim through a large megaphone.

More than one critic thought the sketch was poking fun at the older generation's inability to speak youthful slang.[37] But to most the parody was clear and hilarious. Here were the high-born Edith Sitwell and her siblings Osbert and Sacheverell, who appeared in

---

* The line was unconsciously prophetic. In Edith Sitwell's autobiography, published forty years later and containing no mention of Noël Coward, she writes: "Rhythm is one of the principal translators between dream and reality. Rhythm might be described as, to the world of sound, what light is to the world of sight." Sitwell, *Taken Care Of*, p. 123.

the sketch as "Gob" and "Sago". Earlier that year Edith, still in her thirties, had created a scandal with the premiere of *Façade,* a collaboration with the composer William Walton. From behind a painted backcloth, and to the accompaniment of the twenty-one-year-old Walton's music, she had declaimed her verse through an enormous megaphone that poked through the drapery: ". . . and the sea's blue wooden gendarmerie | Took them in charge while Beelzebub roared for his rum . . ." In the audience had been Noël Coward who, according to at least one reviewer, had walked out – an accusation he fiercely denied, claiming he wouldn't have missed an instant of the hilarity for all the world.

The Whittlebot sketch was partly vengeance for Osbert's lofty suggestion that Noël might learn something from *Façade*. But Noël's dislike of the Sitwells stemmed from his friendship with Charles Scott Moncrieff, who had published infamous diatribes against their work and become their implacable enemy. He and Noël spent many an evening together improvising in Sitwellese.[38] One of Noël's party tricks had been to combine recitations of poetry by Whittlebot with verse by Sitwell herself, challenging friends to separate the genuine from the pastiche. Few of them could, and the implication was that the parodist could have written the real thing, had he been silly enough to try. Parody was one of the most popular genres of the 1920s, catching the decade's insolent youthful confidence, and honouring as much as lampooning the material it sent up. A figure called "Ethelberta Standstill" had already spouted cod modernism in a publication called *Cranks*, and correspondence raged in the *Spectator* as to whether a recent (genuine) Sitwell poem had been a hoax.

William Walton confessed to finding the Whittlebot sketch "really not unfunny" and the Sitwells might have been expected to take the whole thing in good part.[39] Not so. News of the sketch reached Osbert first, who bombarded Noël with angry letters. "Insulting my sister is a fine beginning for you. We look forward to other triumphs. Have you tried cheating at cards?"[40] On it would go, for years. Osbert gave speeches decrying Noël, "whose dirty lyrics I will not wash in public".[41] Edith shared with Noël a creative commitment to grudge-bearing; in the blacklists she compiled in her notebooks his name would be entered for decades to come. She never saw the Whittlebot sketch itself, which would have corrected her increasingly paranoid conviction that Noël had implied she was suffering from some unspecified illness, and was, to boot, a lesbian. She was seriously upset, to the extent that she fell badly ill with jaundice that autumn, and refused to perform *Façade* again at Oxford. "I cannot risk it, as probably little Coward's supporters (being far in excess of intelligent people in number) would flock to the performance to insult me."[42] At a Sitwell dinner party, a guest ingratiatingly suggested that he might "exterminate" Noël. "I wish you would", said Osbert. "Edith would be so obliged."[43]

News of the feud spread in the gossip columns, and Noël gleefully churned out ever more suggestive verse in Hernia's name, rushing out a pamphlet of her poetry within months of *London Calling!*, replete with an "appreciation by Nöel Coward" and a gummed-in errata note: "for 'Chimneys' read 'Communication Cord'". Nor did he tire of the joke, even as his parodies moved further and further away from anything that could remotely have been by Sitwell. Eventually he published another volume, *Chelsea Buns*, with an introduction in bad French by "Gaspard Pustontin" – in reality, Gladys Calthrop.[44] Although he never performed Whittlebot himself, and claimed to dislike drag acts, Noël's creation of these alter-egos, with their own entourage, writings, and backstory, was an innovative form of dramatic comedy, Whittlebot a progenitor of Edna Everage, who once claimed to be Edith Sitwell in a previous life.

A barrier had been erected between difficult modernism and accessible entertainment. But Noël's satire was not a specific skewering of modernist poetry, so much as the laying-down of a gauntlet that advertised his own brand of modernity: arguably conservative in form and structure, but innovative and contemporary in topic and treatment, a vital part of a movement aiming to restore order and purpose to a world fragmented by the new. He had been associated with the theatrical experiment of the Grand Guignol and had written a play with a title that seemed to declare an affinity with the recent arts movement Vorticism.* An interest in façade was to be one of

---

* Wyndham Lewis, co-founder of the Vorticist movement, would respond to

the defining facets of his career. His song "Parisian Pierrot" made use of a symbol of modernism employed by figures from Picasso to Schoenberg. The Sitwells themselves had published a collection called *Twentieth Century Harlequinade*, and in Edith's poem "Clowns' Houses", released in 1918, "Pierrot moon steals slyly in | His face more white than sin." She shared Noël's frivolity, subtitling *Façade* "an entertainment" and insisting that it was meant to be funny. Not long after *London Calling!* she and Walton extended *Façade* with a number of now-famous additions such as "Polka" and "Popular Song", even quoting a patter number by George Grossmith, which added a jauntier flavour of cabaret and revue. Noël would surely have found the revised version more appealing, more allied to his own work, than the drier and more overtly *moderne* version he heard, and ridiculed, at the premiere.

London Calling!, bolstered by the feud, settled in for a long run, which left Noël financially secure but artistically bored; he was performing in a three-hour show up to nine times a week. Some of the songs became so popular that he would hear them in restaurants, but the evening lost its sparkle as material and performers came and went. Eventually he would leave it to its own devices, at which point – as reported in the *Daily Herald* – "he sent the management a score of telegrams in the name of very famous people, deploring his secession in most extravagant terms".[45] His friends could have swapped stories about this characteristic habit.

Audiences and critics alike remained deaf to the evening's shadows, not least the sketch featuring a warring couple who have settled into a purposefully sexless relationship. "Passion is such a terribly destroying thing", says the man. "Once you let go it burns and burns until everything is consumed utterly, and then you have to grope among the dead ashes to find a little affection and comradeship, and it's generally too late."[46] The dialogue recalls a moment in *The Young Idea*: "I wonder if you realise what a grand

---

Coward's appreciation of his *The Art of Being Ruled* with a suggestion that they collaborate. "Don't you think that perhaps portions of a few of our respective talents might be suitably mixed, with advantage to ourselves?" 2 March 1927, Coward Archive, NPC-7620.

passion means?" "Yes, it means wanting a thing very badly until you've got it."[47] *The Times* singled out the sketch's "nastiness" as reason for its removal; *The Era* thought it "nauseating"; the Lord Chamberlain demanded alterations to its more explicit side. Most reviews had preferred to focus on Gertrude Lawrence, dressed in yellow and green pantaloons while singing "Parisian Pierrot" to a doll. "Boudoir dolls" were the must-have fashion accessory for young women of the Jazz Age, who bought and carried and doted on them in such numbers that the craze was condemned as having led to a decline in pregnancies.

Yet even the Pierrot, pining for love of Columbine, was a figure of gloom. Reginald de Veulle, walking with Billie Carleton to her death as they left the Victory Ball five years before, had been dressed in the loose white blouse and dunce's cap of the sad clown, who is described in Noël's song as "divinely forlorn". The haunting and paradoxical phrase encapsulated the topsy-turvy atmosphere of the 1920s, in which grown women owned dolls, and low spirits were chic, and the sadnesses of life something to be celebrated as too, too divine.

"Vortex of Beastliness"
NOËL COWARD, GLADYS CALTHROP, NORMAN MACDERMOTT *and* COMPANY

Manhattan was buzzing with the music of Gershwin as the mounds of dirty snow froze onto the sidewalks in the cold New York winter.

André Charlot had quickly programmed numbers from *London Calling!* in his *Revue of 1924* on Broadway, and Noël took himself off to America to attend the opening night, arriving on 27 February 1924.[48] Having taken a first-class berth on the RMS *Olympic* and booked himself a week at the Ritz-Carlton on Madison Avenue, he soon found out that a West End salary wouldn't stretch all that far. After bumping into the pianist Lester Donahue, whom he had befriended on his previous trip, he ended up sleeping on Lester's sofa in his apartment. *Rhapsody in Blue* had its premiere a fortnight before Noël's arrival and he heard Gershwin perform the piece privately a few weeks later.[49] The revue was an enormous success, and made Gertrude Lawrence a Broadway star. Noël just about managed not to wince as Jack Buchanan had a huge hit with a solo number that, in Noël's hands, had never quite come off. But it was nice to reacquaint himself with Manhattan. Jeffery Amherst was now working in New York as a journalist; Alfred Lunt and Lynn Fontanne were now married and in October would appear together in *The Guardsman* and become Broadway's pre-eminent acting partnership.

The trip to America was also an ambassadorial mission. Noël had been despatched on the producer George Grossmith's behalf to meet the composer Jerome Kern (his favourite of all songwriters), with a view to a West End collaboration on what would have been Noël's first musical. Noël had already laid out a detailed synopsis: his hero was Atlas Blubb, a London costumier intending to apply for the advertised position of king in a Balkan country called Tamaran. This was surprising fluff to be working on after completing the serious drama of *The Vortex*. Despite or maybe because of his ambitions for prolific theatrical stardom, Noël had few structural plans for his career. In March *The Times* announced a "new musical comedy, tentatively called *Tamaran*", and the *New York Times* put a notice on its front page, with Grossmith as author of the script, and Noël given as lyricist.[50] The Winter Garden theatre in Covent Garden was booked for April 1924, and Grossmith told the *Telegraph* that the piece was "modelled on true Gaiety lines, and Leslie Henson and I are to appear in it".[51] But *Tamaran*, for reasons unknown, never happened, and given Noël's lyrics for the Tamaranite locals – "Hooska bolly wolly . . . tishka toodle oodle . . . blasko wagger wagger woo" – this may have been no bad thing. The two songs that Kern composed for it soon appeared in a Broadway flop – and using someone else's lyrics. Noël then tried to use Tamaran as the setting for a musical comedy called *Dream a Little* but this was likewise abandoned and, not one to dwell on failure, he omitted these projects from all accounts of his early career.[52]

"Darling", he wrote to his mother, who was now living in a Surrey cottage that cost to rent in a year what Noël could now earn in a week. "I go to practically two theatres every day and two to three parties every night – I'm <u>very</u> popular. By the way there is a <u>dreadfully</u> dangerous lift in this apartment several people are killed daily just getting in and out – and as the drains are <u>notoriously</u>

bad Diphtheria and Typhoid are inevitable. But don't worry."[53] He sailed for London on 5 April, in the company of yet another glitzy couple to whom he had attached himself as a third party, thrilled to find they were all booked onto the same trip. Douglas Fairbanks had become a swashbuckling superstar of silent movies; he had married the equally famous Mary Pickford in 1920. Not long after they docked at Southampton, Noël was invited to a party thrown for the Fairbanks so that they could meet the Prince of Wales. He promptly managed to forget the song that the Prince asked him to perform.

London Calling! was still running but was in a bad state. Charlot had lost interest in it, and the performances were as rumpled as the costumes. It closed in May.[54] Noël found London gloomy and escaped to the cramped little cottage in Surrey where his mother was living with his Aunt Vida. Here he caught a cold, had an idea while standing in the garden, wedged himself and his notebook into one of the thin-walled rooms, and wrote a three-act comedy. This was called *Still Life*, and he thought it patchy. Eventually he would change the title to *Hay Fever* and ever afterwards insist that he wrote it with great fluency and "finished it in about three days".[55] The handwritten manuscript tells a different story. Almost every page contains a revision or correction (a dramatic finale, in which the actress Judith Bliss announces her return to the stage, was cut altogether).[56] The first act, begun on 21 May 1924, took over a month; he started the second on 29 June and the third on 3 July.[57] Marie Tempest courteously declined the leading role, so Noël simply wrote another play, beginning on 20 July and finishing on 1 August.[58] This was called *Easy Virtue*, and he thought it excellent. But after the poor returns of *The Young Idea*, theatre managers would not risk any work by the same writer.

At the end of August he made a dispiriting trip to the shallow glamour of Deauville, where Sir James Dunn, a steel magnate on holiday from Canada, offered to pay him an annual salary of £1200 in exchange for a percentage of his forthcoming earnings. The suggestion was tempting and the rate of return on Dunn's speculation would have proved sensational – but Gladys Calthrop persuaded Noël not to tie himself to a benefactor. Summer dribbled away.

Noël and Gladys took to motoring around the Surrey countryside, and they overheard a local couple muttering darkly that the pair were clearly lovers in secret. Then, in the autumn of 1924, Norman MacDermott, the enterprising young manager of the small Everyman Theatre in Hampstead, offered to produce both *The Vortex* and *Hay Fever*, and life changed for ever.

It was the actress Kate Cutler, star of *I'll Leave It to You* and *The Young Idea*, who had passed on Noël's manuscripts to MacDermott. Overworked, MacDermott had handed them to a stage manager, who promptly dumped them on a pile marked NO BLOODY GOOD. In need of reading matter on a business trip, MacDermott had grabbed both scripts on the off-chance. He read them on a Sunday evening and rang Noël within twenty-four hours, offering him a fee of £5 a week. Both afterwards took credit for opening the season with *The Vortex* and insisted that the other had wanted to begin with *Hay Fever*.[59]

The Vortex had had a much more complicated gestation than Noël ever afterwards let on, and began life as a short story (also called "Easy Virtue"): "In the old days whenever Flo Lancaster came into a room, there was a sudden hush, as though everyone's breath had been abruptly taken away."[60] He then began writing little scraps of dialogue that, heavily revised, and over at least three drafts, he had worked into the finished play: Florence Lancaster, a married middle-aged socialite (named ToTo in the earliest versions), takes for a lover a much younger man. Her indolent son, Nicky, is indifferently engaged to a dull young woman. Nicky's fiancée and Florence's lover fall for one another. The climax is a savage confrontation between mother and son in which Nicky reveals his serious drug habit, while upbraiding his mother for battling the onslaught of age with her embarrassing and oversexed pretence at youth. Implicit attractions shiver beneath the dialogue, forming the eponymous spiral of dubious attachments that meld the erotic and the familial.

Florence's lover, Tom Veryan, is fashioned from the same cloth as Noël's military friend Stewart Forster, whose striking mother, Grace, had partly inspired the play. Noël had watched her "swishing across shady lawns and night clubs, wrapped in gallant vanity, and smelling slyly of amber"; witnessing Grace being criticised for flirting with a much younger admirer, he had embraced her in sympathy.[61] Strauss's *Der Rosenkavalier* had not been performed in London since before the war, but there is something of that opera's central character, the Marschallin, in Florence Lancaster, who loses her younger lover to a younger woman, while mourning her youth and fading beauty. The depiction of a woman in middle-age taking a lover (the theme of Somerset Maugham's successful play *Our Betters*) was of increasing relevance to a generation of war widows, and the following year Elizabeth von Arnim's novel *Love* would cover the same theme.

Predating Evelyn Waugh's *Vile Bodies* by seven years, *The Vortex* was one of the earliest works to dig beneath the age's frenzy while simultaneously skating on its slippery surface. Its central act opens with a party of "hectic amusement and noise", the air "black with cigarette smoke and superlatives". The dialogue proceeds in a hallucinatory whirl of unconnected fragments as characters come and go, catching the tone and tempo of twenties life. The play's relation to its age is complex and contradictory, in that Noël was trying to have his generation and eat it, becoming the chief spokesman for a social group of which he appeared to disapprove. But *The Vortex* may be more sympathetic to its characters than they are to each other. The drug-taking is not an object of sneering disapproval but a means of escape from a buried inner life of self-loathing and spiritual lassitude. Beneath the argot of determined enjoyment (the word "divine" adorns the text like cheap glitter) Nicky exists in a nervy state of existential bleakness, sure he will never be happy: "I haven't got the knack"; "it's always agony being in love". The clash with his mother – nodding to *Hamlet* and to Ibsen's *Ghosts* – depicts a harsh scorn of middle-aged sexuality, and in this the play may be thought obtrusive and misogynist. But the showdown is between two figures living in comparable states of aimless and doomed self-deception: "our lives are built up of pretences all the time [. . .] We swirl about in a vortex of beastliness – this is a chance – don't you see – to realise the truth."

Plays and novels about addiction were now their own genre.[62] Well-publicised drug scandals were regular occurrences: a young nightclub dancer called Freda Kempton had died of an overdose in 1922, and Edgar Manning, a Black musician, was convicted for dealing the following year, leading to a change in the law that prosecuted drug-taking more severely. Nicky Lancaster's drug habit was acutely topical and, in his friend's discovery of a small box containing cocaine, mirrored precisely the reports of the Billie Carleton case (the papers had made much of a jewelled box found on her dressing table). Cocaine was a specifically fashionable choice, too, the chief recreational drug of the era and part of the craze for all things American. It is hard to discern, though, whether the drug-taking in *The Vortex* was understood by the more worldly of its first audiences as a metaphor for Nicky's homosexuality, and to what extent its early performances underscored its erotic ambiguities.

Playwrights were becoming more ingenious at dodging the strictures of the Lord Chamberlain, and reviewing Frederick Lonsdale's *Spring Cleaning*, which would open the following February, *The Stage* calmly described one of its characters as "a bi-sexual youth", "an epicene creature" who "is called 'Miss' [and] says that he 'hates girls'".[63] Overplaying Nicky's homosexuality can dilute the sexual frisson in his relationship with his mother. But the clues in the script are clear. The "effeminate" Nicky – "that type", "that sort of chap" – admits that he hasn't "really noticed" whether his fiancée, the blandly named and physically "boyish" Bunty, is beautiful or not. He responds to a description of Tom Veryan's physical attractions with an enthusiastic "Oh!" and, thought by others to create a "queer" atmosphere, archly describes himself as "gay* and witty and handsome". Self-reflexively he asks his mother about her sex drive: "It was something you couldn't help, wasn't it – something that's always been the same in you since you were quite, quite young—?" And later: "I've grown up all wrong."

Over the decades the text has been ingeniously pored over as if to crack a code. Nicky's closest friend is called John Bagot, and

---

* The word "gay" had yet to be equated with homosexual in common parlance, but the *Oxford English Dictionary*, citing Gertrude Stein, tentatively suggests that the word was used in its modern sense, at least within homosexual circles, as early as 1922.

the derogatory term for homosexuals was at the time often spelled "fagot" (Noël would rhyme the two words in a later lyric). But *The Vortex*, forced by its era into implications and ambiguity, is an obliging script, with a supple subtext of clandestine excess that will bend to the tune of differing performances. It can be understood variously as a critical depiction of 1920s excess and drug addiction; a coded commentary on homosexuality; a study in self-deception and the longing for escape; a depiction of generational clash; and a scolding portrait of those who refuse to age gracefully. Noël was pushing at the boundaries of what was possible in the theatre of the 1920s, tumbling together in one script a mixture of puritanism, melodrama, sharp-edged comedy, and daring Bohemianism — and he very nearly didn't get away with it.

Rehearsals, which began in the autumn, seemed cursed. Norman MacDermott had planned, given *The Vortex*'s relative brevity, to present it in a double bill with Oscar Wilde's incomplete verse drama *A Florentine Tragedy*. It would have made for quite the scandalous evening, but rewrites to the third act of *The Vortex* extended the play so much that the *Tragedy* was reluctantly shelved. Claude Rains (not yet the movie star he would become) had already been cast in the Wilde and received his full fee — perhaps one of the reasons that money for the whole endeavour soon ran out.[64] Noël knew how to extract funds from rich supporters; the question was whom to ask, given that Ned Lathom, whose generosity had already been deep, had spent the year auctioning off his holdings. Noël racked his brains and riffled his address book and eventually settled on Michael Arlen, an Armenian writer who, four months earlier, had made his name with his era-defining first novel, *The Green Hat*, about the brief life and violent death of an attractive widow. Arlen was soon charmed into writing out a cheque.

Less easy to solve was the behaviour of Kate Cutler, whom Noël had intended to play Florence. Having been the reason for the staging in the first place, she took violent objection to his rewrites, apparently because they expanded his own role. Cutler, who had just turned sixty, made her name in Victorian musicals. She was not one to be daunted by a challenge (on one occasion she had appeared in two productions simultaneously, taking a bus between

them) but the more explicit side of *The Vortex* was out of her comfort zone. Noël's professional demeanour was neither pacific nor
calm in such situations. Cutler left the production, and Norman
MacDermott later insisted the rewrites were a red herring: "she
could not continue to bear with Coward's studied rudeness".[65]

At twenty-four Noël was firm that his youth need not lead to
humble concession should he be challenged by his elders. Nor
was he above refusing to perform unless an argument were won,
a tactic that stood him in good stead over the following days.
Within twenty-four hours he was reading the play to the actress
Lilian Braithwaite who, a decade younger than Cutler, took it more
in her stride. She had recently starred in Clemence Dane's *A Bill of
Divorcement*, which had dealt with divorce and mental illness, and
Noël's portrayal of extramarital sex may have struck a chord, her
own marriage having ended in adultery and separation fifteen years
before. It was a brave actor-writer who tried to lure a star such as
Braithwaite to a small theatre in Hampstead at any time, let alone
so soon before opening night. But Braithwaite must have had a
nose for talent, or at least for a good part, and she learned the
role in two days. MacDermott first heard of the cast change on
receiving Noël's telegram – "LILIAN BRAITHWAITE WILL BE REHEARSING
TO-MORROW" – and relations between the two were stormy.[66]

Noël and Lilian Braithwaite worked on their third-act showdown
until late into the night, fraught with nerves that were exacerbated
by the hysteria of the dialogue. Gladys Calthrop had been appointed
as designer, the first professional job of her distinguished stage
career. The sets were painted on the freezing street outside and the
costumes put together in a damp basement. One scene included a
backdrop made entirely of brightly varnished newspapers pasted
onto canvas. MacDermott meanwhile suggested the addition of a
fireplace in the central act, which he thought reason enough to give
himself a credit in the programme as sole designer of Act Two.
Tempers were running so high that Gladys burst into tears. Noël
refused to perform. The fireplace was hacked out of the wall.

Then came some hacking to the script, at the request of the Lord
Chamberlain, Rowland Baring. His office thought little of the play
and MacDermott was summoned to St James's and taken through

the dialogue line by objectionable line. The drug-taking was no problem in itself (a film called *Cocaine* had been controversially passed by the censors in 1922) and the hints at Nicky's homo-sexuality went unnoticed. But a line about two women travelling together in Venice was thought unconscionable in its implication of lesbianism. Noël rocked with laughter when he heard – "If only I had thought of that myself!" – but objected to any cuts.[67] Baring was determined not to grant a licence: "the time has come to put a stop to the harmful influence of such pictures on the stage". He found the open depiction of an upper-class woman taking a lover in middle-age "revolting" and worried (eight years after the Russian Revolution) that it would "provoke public disorder" and "foster class hatred". A report was sent to the King, who thought the play sounded "disgusting" but could not support any ban on production.[68] With days to go, MacDermott despatched Noël to meet the Lord Chamberlain in person. Noël returned to the theatre triumphant, saying nonchalantly, "no bother at all".[69] Baring had finally been convinced by the author's argument that *The Vortex* was a moral tract against the behaviour it depicted, which in some ways was perfectly true. "I am afraid there is no doubt", Noël wrote to MacDermott, "I am a fiercely moral influence in the dear old Motherland."[70] The play was granted its licence on 21 November.

The weather had turned icy, and motor cars skidded on the roads outside the theatre. By the dress rehearsal Noël had still not signed the Everyman's contract agreeing to the staging of *The Vortex* and *Hay Fever*, at which point MacDermott said he would not send the cur-tain up on opening night. With just hours to go Noël despatched a signed contract for *The Vortex* in the post but, perhaps smelling the first hint of success, he held *Hay Fever* close to his chest, as if hoping for greater things. It was a manoeuvre MacDermott found hard to forgive: "there was no word of appreciation either written or spoken, [and] I like now to reflect that it was my theatre, my money, my judgement, that gave him that first chance. No con-tract for *Hay Fever* ever came."[71] Four years later MacDermott went bankrupt and asked to stage *The Vortex* as a money-making scheme. Noël refused.[72]

The first night of *The Vortex* fell on 25 November 1924. In the

West End, the celebrated playwright Sutton Vane, whose *Outward Bound* had been the runaway success of the previous season, was opening a new play the very same evening, and it was touch-and-go whether critics would make the journey to Hampstead at all. Gladys was at the theatre at the crack of dawn, installing the set, which was finished half an hour before curtain-up. Noël spent much of the afternoon knocking picture nails into the scenery walls. He burned his mouth on tomato soup at a nearby café, rushed back to the row of icy cubicles that passed for dressing rooms, and finally walked up the chill iron of the spiral staircase that led to the wings, where actors were already crowding as the audience took their seats, and then Claire Keep, playing the maid, walked onto the stage: "I'm expecting Mrs Lancaster in at any moment now ma'am . . ."

FINALE: "NOW WHAT?"
THE COMPANY

November and December 1924.
A whirling chorus of critics.

WESTMINSTER GAZETTE: Mr Sutton Vane's new play is an unconvincing affair . . .

THE TIMES: *The Vortex* is a study of rottenness, of extravagant misery . . . It is a study that has wit, observation, and a sincerity, leaping out between flippancies . . . That his work would have more strength if he had not sometimes an air of attempting against his instinct, to keep in with those whom he attacks, there is little doubt . . .

OBSERVER: He has a perception of people's failings far more acute than his perception of their virtues . . . There's a forced smartness in the dialogue, that Mr Coward will probably grow out of . . .

TIMES: That his last act is a loss of balance there is no doubt at all . . . He should choose quietness where cleverness tempts him, his satire is of a vintage that should mature . . .

TELEGRAPH: There is a touch of genius here. We can remember nothing quite like it in all our experience of the theatre. But its power is of a diseased kind.

DAILY GRAPHIC: He takes his place as a writer whose work has to be seriously taken – the play is one which will not die easily. It holds up the mirror to 1924.

DAILY MIRROR: It makes Mr Somerset Maugham's smart set look hopelessly old-fashioned. . . . The little Everyman Theatre at Hampstead is being crowded every evening with playgoers. Lady Louis Mountbatten and some of her smart friends have been . . . I noticed Lady du Maurier, and almost all the West End managers. One lady was sporting the new "Eton boy" coiffure. Hair almost shaved to the head and deliberately cut away behind the ears. Hideous!

WESTMINSTER GAZETTE: Coward has had no fewer than eight offers from West End Theatre managers . . .

THE GENTLEWOMAN: Mr Noël Coward is being widely and loudly discovered . . .

DAILY MIRROR: Mr Coward was wearing a "reefer" jacket, double collar and an enormous black tie – an American innovation . . .

NORTHAMPTON CHRONICLE: That remarkable young man, Noël Coward, will be sure to get a rousing welcome tonight . . . when his play *The Vortex* is to be transferred from the Everyman Theatre to the Royalty . . .

WESTERN MAIL: That remarkable young man, Noël Coward, had a rousing welcome tonight . . .

TELEGRAPH: On the final fall of the curtain there was an outburst of cheering that was only silenced by the author's acquiescence in the audience's desire for a speech . . . The play deals with a section of society for which no right-thinking man or woman can have the slightest pity or sympathy . . .

THE PEOPLE: The frankest London play for years and the most scathing indictment of the year 1924 that I could imagine . . .

GEORGE BERNARD SHAW [*passing through*]: Damnable, wonderful . . .

ABERDEEN PRESS: An even more descriptive title for Mr Noël Coward's play might be *The Cesspool* . . .

ALICE DELYSIA [*on speakers only, starting to sing Noël Coward's new song "Poor Little Rich Girl"*]: *The life you lead sets all your nerves a-jangle, Your love affairs are in a hopeless tangle, Though you're a child, dear, Your life's a wild typhoon!*

WESTMINSTER GAZETTE: The Prince of Wales was present at Mr Noël Coward's play *The Vortex* at the Royalty Theatre on Wednesday night, and the Queen of Norway attended last evening . . .

SUNDAY POST: The quaintly decorated 50–50 Club in Wardour Street looks like establishing itself . . . Noël Coward came on to dance after acting a leading part in his own play . . .

They begin to talk over one another as the music gets faster.

DELYSIA: *Cocktails and laughter, But what comes after? Nobody knows!*

DAILY MIRROR: I saw Noël Coward forgetting the cares of youth while fox-trotting with Constance Collier . . .

WESTERN DAILY PRESS: Mr Noël Coward the well-known playwright will give an appreciation of and some readings from Miss Hernia Whittlebot's poems on the wireless this afternoon . . .

COWARD [*entering, begins to declaim as Whittlebot*]: ROUND – OBLONG – LIKE JAM, TERSE AS VIRULENT HERMAPHRODITES . . .

WESTMINSTER GAZETTE: Mr Noël Coward has organised an All-Star Café Concert as one of the features of a Fan Ball, which is taking place on 15 December at the Carlton Hotel . . .

DAILY MIRROR: It is not merely that it is both witty and dramatic, but that it holds the mirror up to our own times, and gives a carefully observed reflection of our jazzing generation.

ETHEL MANNIN [*a leading young novelist, enters, reading from her book* Young in the Twenties]: But they were hard, these children of the Jazz Age; they had Jazz Souls . . .

DELYSIA: *You're weaving love into a mad jazz pattern . . .*

SUNDAY MIRROR: This play is the search of a syncopated soul for a more restful rhythm . . .

DELYSIA: *By dancing much faster, You're chancing disaster . . .*

COWARD [*still reading as Whittlebot*]: GUTTED LIKE A PRATCHFUL UNI-CORN . . . SOG, SOG, SOG – WHY IS MY MIND AMPHIBIOUS?

MANNIN: A malaise of unrest . . . working it off in jazz . . .

DELYSIA: *Poor little rich girl . . .*

Silence.

COWARD: I remember saying dolefully to Gladys: "And now what?"[73]

BLACKOUT

THE MASK OF FLIPPANCY

———

A Play in Three Acts

CAST

NOËL COWARD, *a famous playwright and actor*

VIOLET COWARD, ARTHUR COWARD, ERIK COWARD, *his immediate family*

LORN LORAINE, *Noël Coward's secretary*
JOHN "JACK" C. WILSON, *Noël Coward's partner and business manager*

GLADYS CALTHROP, *a stage designer*
EVA LE GALLIENNE, *a British-born American actress and writer*
MERCEDES DE ACOSTA, *an American poet*

SIR CHARLES COCHRAN, *a theatrical manager*
TALLULAH BANKHEAD, *an actress*
DAME MARIE TEMPEST, *an actress*
BASIL DEAN, *a theatre director*

IVOR NOVELLO, *a composer and actor*
COLE PORTER, *a lyricist and composer*
VIRGINIA WOOLF, *a novelist*

PROUST, *a cat*

The action takes place variously in London, Manhattan, Kent, and Hawaii.

TIME: 1925–1929

ACT ONE

SCENE ONE

London. A warm evening in the second week of June, 1925. Crowds of figures — almost all of them wearing hats — are flowing back and forth amid the vehicles, quite a number still horse-drawn. It is just over six months since the first night of The Vortex *in the small converted drill hall in Hampstead. The play has transferred to the Little Theatre on John Street, the third venue of its long West End run.* NOËL COWARD *is at the theatre already, applying his make-up in one of the dressing rooms, which, in that small building, are situated right beneath the stage.*

In Trafalgar Square there are flocks of pigeons amid the flow of buses and motorcars. Beneath Piccadilly Circus work has recently begun on expanding the tube station; the statue of Eros has been removed to Embankment Gardens. At the corner of Shaftesbury Avenue and Coventry Street is the London Pavilion Theatre, where a new revue, written and composed by NOËL COWARD *has been running successfully on its tiny stage since April:* On With the Dance. *The wings are so small that large hoop dresses are suspended from the flies, as there is nowhere else to put them. A little way along Shaftesbury Avenue is the Globe Theatre, where* Fallen Angels *by* NOËL COWARD *is in the middle of its successful and scandalous run. Five minutes' walk west, back up to Shaftesbury Avenue and right along to Cambridge Circus, past* No, No, Nanette *at the Palace and turning right onto West Street, is the Ambassador's Theatre, where* Hay Fever, *a comedy by* NOËL COWARD *has just opened.*

Later in the evening, and the theatres are tipping their crowds out onto the pavement in a swish of brightly coloured gowns and capes. Some of them are off to the Café de Paris, which has recently opened in the basement of the Rialto Cinema on Coventry Street. Six months ago, in its smoky and overcrowded rooms, the actress LOUISE BROOKS *introduced the Charleston to London. Others are off to Roman's on the Strand, or to the Savoy Hotel, where it is fashionable to dance between the courses of supper. Cabs are hailed to take audiences and actors to the Hammersmith Palais de Danse to hear Paul Whiteman's Band, and to dance on its sprung floor of Canadian maple amid*

*the chinoiserie of the décor. A model mountain looms at the centre replete
with a model Chinese village, and lanterns hang from the pagoda roof . . .
At the Florida Club off Berkeley Street revellers dance on a revolving pane of
glass, lit from beneath, and outside people queue for entry just as, earlier in
the day, the ever-increasing number of homeless and unemployed has queued
for the dole . . .*

SCENE TWO

The Vortex had become a sensation. And Noël had accrued such a
backlog of work that, when his name became one to conjure with,
he could offer producers enough material promptly to take over
the West End. Within the space of half a year he became one of
the most famous figures in London theatre, with, for an enchanted week in June 1925, four shows running simultaneously. *The
Vortex* had shot into the West End on Noël's twenty-fifth birthday,
16 December 1924, and would run in various theatres until 16
June. His new revue, *On With the Dance*, had opened in London
on 20 April; *Fallen Angels* followed the very next evening; and *Hay
Fever* arrived on 8 June. Newspapers made jokes of the new star's
prolificness, and one columnist became genuinely worried, with
accurate prophecy, that he was en route for a nervous breakdown.
Noël's dressing room became so thronged with admirers after each
performance that his rather dour dresser was instructed to create
various excuses for escape.

The success of *The Vortex* needs to be filtered through the outlook
of its time in order for what was described as its "excessive modernity" to be understood. The uproar was on a level with the scandal
created by the violence or sexual explicitness of plays by Sarah Kane
or Mark Ravenhill, sixty years later.[1] Some dismissed the topic as
cliché, arguing that any new play thought itself "incomplete without
a pinch of cocaine".[2] Younger theatregoers were often forbidden by
their parents to attend, which was the best way of ensuring they
stopped at nothing to lay their hands on a ticket. Marie Stopes was
so outraged by the play's ostensibly bleak view of society that she
wrote a rebuttal, *The Vortex Damned* (the Lord Chamberlain forbade it

a licence). Even the sound of the production was new. As Nicky, Noël performed snatches of Gershwin's *Rhapsody in Blue* at the piano (proof of his porous musical ear, for he had heard it only once and no recording or score had been issued). Gershwin's piece would not be premiered in London until the following summer, and Noël was introducing the city to one of the key compositions of the Jazz Age. He had written directly to Gershwin: "I sit down to listen to [the *Rhapsody*] a normal healthy Englishman and by the time the second half is over I could fling myself into the wildest ecstasies of emotional degeneracy. Please be careful what you write in future or I won't be answerable for the consequences!"[3]

The Vortex would not have survived without the intensity of its acting. Success rid Noël of enough nerves to polish his performance into something on a different level to anything he had yet given. He was developing a technique that had moved on from the brilliant bluster of Charles Hawtrey or the mellifluous ardour of matinee idols. In this he may have owed a great deal to the actor Gerald du Maurier, hailed for the unique speed and throwaway naturalism of his delivery, the understated lightness of his voice, and his use of an omnipresent cigarette. This was ironic, in that the two had a very public scrap over *The Vortex*, which the homophobic du Maurier detested.[4] James Agate praised Noël for living "the part [of Nicky] with his nerves", for being "so lifelike that you seemed to be in the same room with him".[5] Sybil Thorndike agreed: "Oh my goodness, what an actor! As an actor he was absolutely in the front. He could play these nervous strange people, hysterical people, which is very rare."[6] Understudying the part of Nicky was twenty-year-old John Gielgud, who found it all but impossible to deliver the dialogue without giving a poor impression of its author – a quandary that would hamper future generations.

The infamy of *The Vortex* rode most of all on Noël's careful manipulation of press interest. It was not new for a writer to control his public image, but it was rare for actors or writers to be given in-depth character profiles such that biography and performance merged in the public mind. Noël was among the first to harness the decade's vortex of publicity, which was fuelled by technological advance and by an explosion in advertising that travelled from

America to Britain. The word "media" as a form of mass communication had only entered the language in 1923. Noël and the press (for now) embraced one another: papers carried his quotations and epigrams, and he featured in cartoons and fashion columns. He quickly became a celebrity sponsor, the "face" of various brands, and would be emblazoned on theatre programmes advertising the novel glories of his Bulova watch, which did not go on a chain in the pocket but was bound about the wrist with a strap.[7]

Most of all, he played on the notion that his work was heavily autobiographical. In many ways this wasn't far from the truth: a bitter, wounded, homosexual young man embroiled in a maternal relationship of amorous intimacy was close to the bone. A press photograph was taken of the young author in his bedroom at Ebury Street: "as the flash went my eyes shut so the result was I looked like an advanced Chinese decadent in the last phases of dope".[8] The photo was widely disseminated. "I am never out of opium dens, cocaine dens and other evil places," Noël told the *Evening Standard*, "my mind is a mass of corruption."[9] No matter that, out of shot, Arthur Coward was probably lurking with a tea-tray; no matter that lodgers still came and went in the rooms below and that the vaguely Oriental furnishings owed more to Violet's taste in décor than to her older son's propensity for opium dens.

In truth Noël prioritised the discipline of the theatre over partying. The vast majority of his time was devoted not to hedonism but to industry. Between interviews, photo calls, rehearsals, writing, performing, there was barely a free moment. The novelist Arnold Bennett noted that the famous young playwright was actually a "serious young man, with a sense of humour. He would have nothing to drink at all, except water. And he left early – 10.35 – because he had an early rehearsal."[10] But Noël's louche image – bedressing-gowned, cigarette holder in hand, swishing from party to party in a haze of drugs and merriment – had been created and had stuck. Its raw materials were hardly novel: cigarette holders had been a popular accessory for men since his childhood, and a stylish dressing-gown was *de rigueur* for any fashionable upper-class man of leisure in the days before central heating. It was his taste for turtleneck jumpers that really began a fashion craze, and papers

could run an entire article on the "mild sensation" he caused by
appearing in a double-breasted dinner suit.[11] Later in life he would
even be said to have popularised the previously unfashionable sun
tan. Accounts were opened at the smartest tailors and he filled his
small dressing room with silk gowns and bottles of cologne. Judi
Dench's abiding memory of meeting Noël, many decades later, is
"the smell of his aftershave – I wouldn't wash it off for ages!"[12]

This was partly a question of fashioning a visual mystique that
replaced the Victorian ideals of wholesome and brawny masculine
attraction with an alternative version of masculinity favouring the
slim, the elegant, the androgynous. Movie cameras were said to add
twenty pounds in weight, and leading actors became ever thinner
to compensate, as exemplified by Ivor Novello, whose world-weary
glamour Noël openly emulated. Body weight was losing its visual
appeal; clothes now had to be trim and stylish to look good in
motion as well as in a static portrait. In a certain sector of society,
skinniness exemplified the Age of Youth, which had brought about
a revival of the hollow-cheeked Byronic hero. As early as *The Young
Idea*, in 1923, Noël had begun to perfect a look of wiry and rather
haunted slickness, as if he had stepped from a Diaghilev ballet, or
from the dustjacket of a volume by Saki or Oscar Wilde. Ironically,
his metabolism was unhelpful and he had to work hard to avoid
putting on weight, but he had caught the way in which fashion was
subverting or blurring conventional notions of gender, often with
a daring implication of homosexuality.

The twenties had spawned a generation of young writers who
wrote with such speed, and lived with such theatrical energy, that
they could immortalise themselves and each other as they went
along, adept in the art of myth-making. Michael Arlen was known
for his impeccable grooming, drove through London in a yellow
Rolls-Royce, and became famous for wearing an Astrakhan coat.
("What do you think of yourself as an artist?" he was asked, reply-
ing: "*Per ardua ad Astrakhan.*") It was an age of scandalous memoirs
and Noël was unusual in waiting until his thirties to begin his own.
A number of writers still in their twenties – Ethel Mannin, Beverley
Nichols – produced volumes of autobiography in all of which Noël
and Arlen took starring roles. Nichols, young, homosexual, prolific,

acidic, darkly funny, especially exemplified the age's whirlwind, and of Noël he produced some of the earliest and most perceptive reports. He was one of the few to foresee the permanence of so ostensibly ephemeral a writer: "One could, indeed, write a monthly article about Noël Coward. About nobody else. [. . .] He is the only true interpreter of this age which this age has yet produced."[13] But Noël's attitude to the torrent of publicity was conflicted. In being a construct, the character of Noël Coward that he offered to the press was a form of disguise that kept his personal life well hidden. In an unpublished essay written in the mid-1920s he castigated "those too teeming thousands who derive an unhealthy satisfaction from prying through the medium of the press into the private habits of contemporary celebrities. [. . .] My conviction [is] that it is the public achievements of artists, statesmen, or athletes which should concern the masses, rather than their personal peculiarities."[14]

A plethora of so-called "boudoir plays" imitating *The Vortex* soon hit the West End, and young playwrights such as Reginald Berkeley and Phyllis Morris were marketed as being in the Noël Coward vein. Papers spoke of the Noël Coward Era. In February 1926 Ned Latham's *Wet Paint* would be performed at the Prince of Wales Theatre, and was said to "out-Coward Noël Coward at his extremist".[15] Flappers became a very "Noël Coward" type of person in the press. His name both adjective and verb, Noël had become the leading figure of the theatre's younger generation, emblematic of a turning-away from the old guard. In truth, he maintained cordial relationships with figures such as Bennett and Galsworthy, and of *The Vortex* the former had written to him: "your performance was masterly. As regards the play, first act very good, as an American imitation of an English comedy. But for the rest – Christ!"[16] J. M. Barrie wrote to Noël that *The Vortex* was evidence of "a real live new dramatist appearing [. . .] you belong to your time".[17]

Critics were divided as to whether his intense celebrity occluded the fact that his plays were merely passing fripperies, but by the end of 1926 his name would, more than once, be linked "with Shakespeare and with Oscar Wilde".[18] All this might have been expected to settle Noël in an uncomfortable emotional position, somewhere between invincibility and panic. He felt, he later admitted, as if he were "flying faster and faster through a nervous dream".[19] His confidence and ambition had prepared him for success, and friends testified to the speedy disappearance of any adolescent swagger. Ivor Novello found him an "infinitely nicer, kinder person since he's had success".[20] But Noël's inner life disappears beneath a double layer of public persona: the image he cultivated at the time, and the portrait he drew in hindsight. Perhaps speed and activity left little time for reflection. He went almost nightly to the theatre when he was not performing, a familiarly eccentric figure in that he rarely bought a ticket or sat through a show entire, preferring instead to stroll from play to play and sit, in the days before anyone thought of fire hazards, on the stairs of the dress circle.[21] On top of the alarming arrival of wealth after many years of financial struggle, there was also the sudden need to "be" Noël Coward in public, to live up to his image, to deliver witticisms and flourish his cigarette, and always in the knowledge that his companions' ears would be half-cocked for an anecdote to remember, recount, embellish. Beneath the intense activity his nerves may already have been fraying, and within two years they would give way altogether.

Frequent attendance at parties was not only for enjoyment but to ensure a place in the gossip columns, and his social life became both acrobatic and indiscriminate. In February 1925 his presence had been advertised on a poster for the upcoming British Fascists Carnival Ball, to be held in Hammersmith on 6 March. He and several friends, Ivor Novello among them, agreed to judge the fancy-dress costumes. Whether Noël actually attended is not known; his name was not mentioned in a report that praised "the great success of the evening".[22] The British Fascists was a disorganised group, founded two years earlier in order to combat the rise of Communism (an aim which, along with its aristocratic membership, may have vaguely appealed to Noël). Unassociated with either racism or anti-Semitism, it had distanced itself from Mussolini and would protest against Oswald Mosley when he founded what became the British Union of Fascists. Both Noël and Ivor Novello were to produce work that decried far-right politics, which their sexuality gave them every reason to fear. But perhaps Noël simply couldn't resist a good party.

One practical necessity of this hectic schedule was the need for a secretary. Noël had known Edith "Lorn" Loraine since they had been introduced by a mutual friend at a party back in 1919. From a smart Scottish family fallen on hard times, Lorn MacNaughtan, as she was then, had tried her luck as a chorus girl and was recovering from the (illegal) termination of an unwanted pregnancy. Her quietness, in rooms crowded with theatricality, gave her great authority. Lorn had worked informally for him over the years, contributing the illustrations to his book of satirical portraits, *A Withered Nosegay*, and she was able to indulge his whim of communicating not in prose but in rhyming verse. In 1921 she had married a naval officer, Rupert Loraine, with whom she had two children but whose carer she soon became on his developing Parkinson's disease. The remainder of her life would be devoted to Noël, who was five years her junior: she would combine the roles of assistant, manager, and intimate, quasi-maternal, friend. It is a mark of Noël's slapdash way with the details of his inner circle's lives that her surname is misspelled in all three volumes of his memoirs; it is a mark of her quiet forbearance that she made no efforts to correct him. *The Vortex* provided money to pay for her full-time help, and early each morning, commuting from her house at Herne Hill, she would arrive at Ebury Street to deal with the day's business and file the towers of letters that had begun to arrive.

Her help became invaluable when, all through the rehearsals and run of *The Vortex*, he had worked on the revue *On With the Dance*, which was produced not by André Charlot but by Charlot's greatest rival, Sir Charles Cochran. Noël, presumably thinking it wise to have a foot in both camps, had consented to being lunched handsomely at the Berkeley by Cochran during *London Calling!* But any plans for a collaboration had been stymied by Cochran's certainty that Noël was better at sketches than songs, and should not be entrusted with the musical side of proceedings. By the end of 1924 Noël had nevertheless written enough material – sketches, songs, ballet scenarios – for another revue. At this stage, pre-*Vortex*, his name did not guarantee sales, but Cochran took a chance, little knowing that by opening night the fortunes of the young composer-author would be completely transformed. Where Charlot's revues were often simple and intimate, Cochran's were extravagant. He was someone for whom the notion of expense didn't occur; on being told that a set would not fit because the roof was so low, his immediate thought was not to shrink the set but to remove the roof.[23]

The scale of *On With the Dance* was immense. On top of Noël's familiar musical collaborators such as Elsie April and Philip Braham, the revue's programme lists an astonishing roll call, and each sketch was worked on by an individual design team (Gladys Calthrop among them, contributing Vorticist backdrops of jagged and fragmented urban imagery). Proceedings were marshalled by the director Frank Collins, but Noël rehearsed most of the comic sketches himself. His recent success led to his perfectionism being given free rein, although the actors found him both kind and inspiring and worked hard to please him. Each evening he would rush from rehearsals to perform in *The Vortex*, and John Gielgud would anxiously await his arrival, standing "at the stage-door looking down the street with a stick of greasepaint in my hand, ready to rush off to his dressing-room and make up if he should fail to appear".[24] Appear Noël invariably did, but cutting it finer each evening. Eventually Gielgud was asked to perform so that Noël could go up to Manchester for the preview run of *On With the Dance*.

To leave London for Manchester was to be reminded that outside the glittering metropolis lay a greyer wilderness, of slums, unemployment, and hunger marches. But it would take at least a decade for many in Noël's set to develop a social conscience, assuming they ever did. Noël was, anyway, all but living at the Palace Theatre. He arrived to be greeted by a playbill that did not give his own name enough prominence, leading him to track down Cochran to a hotel bathroom: "I'm not at all sure that I didn't deprive him of his towel while I shrieked at him over the noise of the water gurgling down the plug-hole".[25] There followed three days of fraying tempers, bitter quarrels, and exhausted dancers who lay in various states of collapse around the huge auditorium. The dress rehearsal lasted twenty-six hours. The Hungarian band from Budapest slept through the night on the stalls floor.[26] Cochran tried to cancel the first preview, on 17 March 1925, but the management wouldn't hear of it, and somehow everything went without a hitch. The critical acclaim led to a long run of over 200 performances in the West End, where ticket prices reached unheard-of sums.

On With the Dance contained its fair share of satirical and comedy sketches, some decidedly risqué, moving from the Moulin Rouge to a sleeper carriage in which two passengers are heavily implied to have slept together. Douglas Byng and Ernest Thesiger made a cross-dressing double act as two society ladies who give a pair of young men, mistakenly arrived in their hotel room, rather too hearty a welcome. But the revue was an angular, frenetic evening, the orchestra augmented by the wail of a saxophone quartet. The show opened with a vast panorama of overheard conversation outside the Café de la Paix in Paris, the single sketch featuring a cast of thirty, led by Alice Delysia. It was she who, playing a maid in another scene, would regale her party-going mistress with Noël's song "Poor Little Rich Girl", another admonitory depiction of the era's lack of control. Cochran found the scene so dull that he had fought for its removal, but Noël and Delysia stood firm, and the song became the most popular of the evening.

All the ballets were created and performed by Léonide Massine, lately principal choreographer of the Ballets Russes, among his recent collaborators figures from Satie to Picasso. Massine was "immediately attracted" by Noël's "charm and crackling wit" and found himself "inspired by his inventive mind and [. . .] instinctive, unsentimental grasp of the spirit of the 1920s".[27] "The Rake" – a ballet that found contemporary resonance in Hogarth – featured original music by Roger Quilter, its costumes and scenery designed by William Nicholson. "Crescendo" was performed to an orchestral medley of jazz tunes, including Irving Berlin's "Pack up your sins", and was advertised as something tantamount to a Stravinsky ballet, featuring living puppets whirling to "the insistent clamour of modernity". Massine and his dancers were said to "jig to the tune of cocktails and jazz, until, willy nilly, they are swept up to a frenzied climax of impressionistic movement".[28] The stage was thronged with archetypal twenties characters – The Film Star, The Manicure Girl, The Mannequin – all of whom donned driving goggles and cardboard cars for a section called "The Automobile Age".

Massine himself danced "The Spirit of the Age" and Noël afterwards wrote to him, with a lyrical seriousness that was uncharacteristic:

There is something elegantly vicious in the strange extremities of [your work]; a corruption half base, half spiritual, with the inevitable latent sorrowfulness of conscious, unreluctant sin. The ballet itself is more or less incoherent, and trivial, but it is enough that you have created that strange, half-lunar figure, reaching blindly out to a beauty beyond its own posturing, as though it mocked lightly at things hidden from and sacred to itself.[29]

The dances would become such a highlight of the show that *The Times* reviewer eventually devoted himself to them almost entirely, and did not mention Noël's name.[30] The painter Gluck made a number of canvases of the revue, and later identified one of them as the encapsulation of art deco, a term introduced to the world just three weeks after opening night, with the International Exhibition of "Arts decoratifs".

While writers such as Woolf and T. S. Eliot were grappling with the sudden explosion of city life, few playwrights or composers were following suit. "In the tube at Oxford Circus" (a movement of a 1921 chamber work by Arthur Bliss) was an exception in a musical world dominated by the pastoral. There were few British equivalents of the evocation of New York by Gershwin or Varèse, or of Paris by the musical group Les Six.[31] The urban soundscape of *On With the Dance* predated by some years the symphonic jazz of Constant Lambert's *The Rio Grande* and the revue's ballets were novel in their blast of metropolitan life and its newly hectic pace. The accompaniment to "Poor Little Rich Girl" was jangled with a quotation from *Rhapsody in Blue*, yet to receive its London premiere. The *Morning Post* acclaimed the whole evening as "more than modern, bizarre, grotesque, fantastic, unnatural: the speed of the change from scene to scene, of the performance of each number, is feverish, burlesquing the speed of our overheated life. At times the players seem mad, intoxicated with the desire to force their bodies to do something faster, faster."[32]

The ostensibly revelrous title of *On With the Dance* was not appended to the revue until it opened in London. The phrase was taken
from Byron, but any theatregoer who cared to look up "The Eve
of Waterloo" would find the poem's revellers interrupted by the
sounds of battle. "Poor Little Rich Girl" depicted the carousing life
as a "wild typhoon" – just as, five years later, Evelyn Waugh's *Vile
Bodies* would conclude with "the circling typhoon" of encroaching
war.

Scene Three

"I'm sorry if I've upset the critics", Noël told the *Westminster Gazette*.
"It does seem rather a shame." If *The Vortex* had caused a scandal, *Fallen
Angels* promised to outdo it. The play features two women, bored in
their marriages, who get progressively drunk and progressively quarrelsome at the prospect of their former lover's return. Each, by the
end, believes the other to have an assignation with him. The dialogue
openly discussed pre- and extramarital sex and the Lord Chamberlain
licensed its production only reluctantly. A drama that ran for just
two hours was of almost brazen brevity to the long attention spans
of 1920s theatregoers: "I was amused by this adroit, superficial,
weak and very short play, which began at about 9 o'clock and was
over by 11 o'clock."[33] Noël had considered *Fallen Angels* a comedic
trifle influenced by French farce and was genuinely surprised by the
resulting scandal, which led to huge box office success, a deluge of
hate mail, and a press furore. A young man taking cocaine on the
stage had shocked; two women getting drunk sent the press wild,
and there were reports of the production's drunken orgies. The
Daily Express was reduced to incoherent stuttering: "Drunkenness.
Drunken women. Drunken young women. Drunken young married
women."[34]

The roles of the two women had initially been given to Edna
Best and Margaret Bannerman, but the latter dropped out not long
before opening night, having had increasing difficulty with the lines
and, eventually, a nervous breakdown. Enter Tallulah Bankhead.
Noël had known her (and at least one of her lovers) from his trips

to New York, when she'd noted "a frustrated young Englishman, then living on herbs and wild berries".[35] A regular at the Algonquin Round Table, she was more than a match for his wit: "my father warned me about men and booze but he never said anything about women and cocaine"; "cocaine isn't habit forming and I should know – I've been using it for years". After a series of American flops, she moved to London and had great success. The offer of *Fallen Angels* came at an opportune moment. Somerset Maugham had insisted she could not be given the coveted lead role in *Rain*, adapted from one of his short stories, after which she swallowed twenty aspirin and sank not into oblivion but into a deep sleep from which (she maintained) Noël's telephone call awakened her: "Tallulah, can you learn one hundred sides in four days?" To which her characteristic, and truthful, answer was "I can get it up in four hours". This promise, she argued, would be easier to keep if she were paid £100 a week.[36] She was.

Bankhead was a shot in the arm to *Fallen Angels*, and she went for the part with all guns blazing. Noël's first-night bow was delayed by ten minutes as the leading ladies took ovation after ovation, and Winston Churchill was said to have found Bankhead so attractive that he saw the play five times.[37] As the run went on she became increasingly indulgent and Noël's patience frayed. But it did no harm that she made a success of *Fallen Angels* not long after her well-publicised fracas with Somerset Maugham, whom the press were already setting up, not inaccurately, as Noël's rival.* She helpfully defended him in press interviews: "If I thought people were shocked by my part I should be extremely sorry – we are not drunk." Adding: "just tipsy".[38]

Many critics, some in disapproval and others in admiration, had begun to link Noël's sexual frankness, and the cuckolding of foppish husbands in *Fallen Angels*, to the world of Restoration

---

* The famous story of Bankhead's bringing the house down by changing a line from *Fallen Angels* – "Oh dear, rain!" – to "My gawd, RAIN!" (alluding to her dismissal from Maugham's play) doesn't add up, sadly. The nearest line in *Fallen Angels* is "there's a dreadful gale blowing". Not that she wouldn't have been capable of improvising.

Comedy, which was enjoying a revival after more than two centuries of distaste for sexual impropriety. And while there was little in
Noël's work to mirror the labyrinthine plots and political commentary of plays by Congreve, say, his warring couples – even prior to
Private Lives – were already reminiscent of Millament and Mirabell in
The Way of the World; he prised humour from the juxtaposition of the
witty rake versus the dull-witted businessman. It was as if the 1920s
had become another period of restoration, not of monarchy but of
peace, and wit had again found its way onto the stage not solely
as good clean fun but with a sense of cleverness and playfulness,
toying with words and ideas. But the scandal of *Fallen Angels*, however
confected, is also a reminder that the age was as puritan as it was
gilded. The Conservatives had returned to power the previous year,
and the Home Secretary, William Joynson-Hicks, attempted to crack
down on night clubs and alcoholism, and on the supposed obscenit-
ies of works by D. H. Lawrence, James Joyce, or Radclyffe Hall. The
infamous and much-read theatre critic Hannen Swaffer combined
sartorial eccentricity (high collars, wide-brimmed hat, flowing cape)
with passionate socialism and virulent racism: he is thought to have
attempted to ban Black actors from the theatre. He believed Noël's
plays exemplified a hideous decadence, and published vituperative
criticism at any opportunity. But Noël was both stoic and confident:
"He doesn't worry me at all – the more frightful things he says the
more sympathy I get and it doesn't matter anyhow what the papers
say, good or bad, I'm far beyond being harmed in any way by
the Press."[39]

Noël's success was also a red rag to the genteel bulls of the
London Council for the Promotion of Public Morality, which had
been set up in 1899 to combat vice and indecency. It was opposed
to public protest, and one of its members – Mrs Charles Hornibrook
– had to tender her resignation so as to disrupt the final performance of *Fallen Angels*, on 29 August. She waited until the conclusion
to stand from her box: "Ladies and Gentleman – I wish to protest.
This play should not go unchallenged." She was soon drowned out
by cat calls and escorted from the theatre, but she enjoyed giving
interviews the following day. "I am a whole-hogger in the matter
of agitating for cleaner plays, and I don't mind going to prison!

I say to Noël Coward most emphatically that he must stop putting this sordid, horrible stuff before the public and pretending that his characters are moral. They are utterly abnormal."[40] It was a pointed word, apparently referring more to sexuality than to alcoholism. "I simply feel that [Coward's] play is degrading and injurious to young people of both sexes."[41]

It was in this hysterical atmosphere of success and censure that the final play of Noël's triumphant quartet had opened, on 8 June 1925. The change of title from *Still Life* to *Hay Fever* was reasonably last-minute and perhaps decided upon only when a summer opening was assured (while writing the script he had called it *Gardening*).[42] After its predecessors, *Hay Fever* was a damp squib, critically speaking, and nobody pinpointed, least of all the author, that this of all Noël's early work would best stand the test of time. Back in June 1923, Noël had put down yet another title – *Silk Purses* – and a cast of characters including Simon Bliss, before scrawling "idea to be developed".[43] A year later, he had created the Bliss family, week-ending in their Bohemian, or mock-Bohemian, country house: actress-mother Judith; writer-father David; and the two Poj-and-Stoj children, Sorrel* and her brother Simon. (The parts were surely conceived for Noël to perform with Esmé Wynne, but were taken in the first production by Ann Trevor and by Ivor Novello's partner, Bobbie Andrews.) Unbeknownst to the others, each has invited a guest for the weekend in the hopes of a fling. The guests then seduce, or are seduced by, a member of the family who was not their original host before, hungover and depressed the next morning, they leave the Blisses to their own devices.

Almost despite himself, as if without noticing, in *Hay Fever* Noël had found the fine-grained style – a matter of sound as well as semantics – that would lead to *Private Lives.* Set across a hot June weekend, essentially a midsummer night's sex comedy, *Hay Fever* provided its fair share of Noëlisms: "she goes about using sex as a

---

* Like "Esmé" or "Nicky", the name "Sorrel" was androgynous, and used more often for men in 1923 (it was Julian Huxley's middle name). Such names continued to feature in Coward's plays, as with the male characters Evelyn "Evie" Bathurst (in *This Was a Man*) and Beverly Ford (in *Semi-Monde*).

sort of shrimping net"; "he's not dead, he's upstairs!" Within the confines, even the disguise, of the country-house comedy Noël had fashioned a play that can descend into the surreal, a mad-hatter's tea party that, like all good midsummer farces, takes on a quality of nightmare, where love arrives and disappears like an enchantment squeezed into the eye from a magic flower: "Sandy was in love with me this afternoon". . ."Not real love." The dialogue of the "divine- ly mad" Bliss family becomes a juddering stuck-record of absurdity from which there often seems no escape. ("I am the injured party, am I not?" "Injured?" "Yes, extremely injured." "Injured!") They pick over one of David's manuscripts as if prefiguring an Absurdist play by Ionesco:

DAVID: . . . a vast pattern of sound which was Paris —
JUDITH: What was Paris, dear?
DAVID: *Which* was Paris.
JUDITH: What was Paris?
DAVID: You can't say a vast pattern of sound *what* was Paris.
JUDITH: Yes, but — What was Paris?
DAVID: A vast pattern of sound *which was Paris*.[44]

The script is a hall of mirrors. Words are knocked back and forth like ping-pong balls by sparring lovers, communication all but disintegrating amid the rallies of dialogue. This is partly an issue of question marks: swathes of *Hay Fever* read like the game of questions in Stoppard's *Rosencrantz and Guildenstern Are Dead*, in which one query may be answered only by another. This was a result of Noël's musical ear, and certain words bounce through the lines like a recurring note, the constant queries introducing a motif of rising inflection. In their repetition words are stripped of meaning and mined for sonic humour: "Haddock?" "Haddock." "I'll have had- dock too." The script is pared to tall columns of monosyllables in which the occasional extravagant exclamation stretches luxuriantly. A forty-line duet between David Bliss and the house-guest Myra Arundel borders on a verse play in couplets: over fifteen pairs of repeated words are studded through just a minute of dialogue, a constant echoing that enacts the union of the characters even as it prevents the conversation from advancing to the matter in hand (seduction).[45]

Between the writing and staging of *Hay Fever* success had arrived with a vengeance, and the actress Marie Tempest suddenly found she did want to perform it after all. Tempest had been the most famous soprano in the world of Victorian light opera and Edwardian musicals. Her reputation for imperiousness preceded her, but she and Noël, who directed, got along famously. Many of the critics thought the evening relied on Tempest's star quality: "she lends her eternal youthfulness to the rather prematurely wrinkled lines of her author's invention".[46] *Hay Fever* did excellent business nevertheless, but, so unlike *The Vortex*, lacking the scandal of *Fallen Angels*, and with no star part for its author, it did not give the public what they had come to expect. Noël marketed it as a panacea to those who complained of his immorality. On its transfer to the Criterion in September, it was paid a visit by George V, who remarked "I may be old fashioned, but I do like these clean plays."[47]

Hay Fever has grown in consequence with age and revival, partly because it is now possible to see, in its rear-view mirror, not only the dialogue of Pinter or Stoppard, but the structure and matter of Edward Albee's *Who's Afraid of Virginia Woolf?*, in which a couple toys with guests as a means of revitalising an unhappy marriage. Later productions would tease out the fact that the Bliss family have let theatrical high spirits scab over emotional wounds. Unless their admissions of melancholy are only so much posturing: "If you troubled to look below the surface, you'd find a very wistful and weary spirit. I've been battling with life for a long time." "Marriage is a hideous affair altogether, don't you think?" "Couldn't you see that all my flippancy was only a mask, hiding my real emotions – crushing them down desperately?"

To dismiss *Hay Fever* as artificial is to miss the fact that it is a commentary on artifice: a dangerous balancing act, for the play must become theatrical in order to depict theatricality, and risk insignificance to expose meaninglessness. The gossamer is achieved, and self-conscious; the script may be thin but is not threadbare. In many ways it precludes analysis and second-guesses accusations of vacuity: "everything is empty and hollow, like a broken shell";

"this house is a complete feather-bed of false emotions"; "we none of us ever mean *anything*". *Hay Fever* was a dramatic riff on all senses of the word "play" – one of its most used stage directions is "playing up". A quintessentially urban family, the Blisses play at Bohemian rusticity – "I've been pruning the calceolarias" – rather as they play at emotion. Like something out of Pirandello, they seem on the verge of being aware that they are on a stage. In this, *Hay Fever* is an affectionate critique of actors and the theatre, but also of the performative, dangerously histrionic, nature of 1920s life. Judith's "sense of the theatre", her daughter concludes, "is always fatal"; she is "artificial to the point of lunacy". Emotions are not something to feel, but a state to perform: "You were being beautiful and sad" Judith is told, and later she is proud to have emitted "quite a genuine laugh". Sex may be employed like a shrimping net, but there is very little of it in *Hay Fever*, as everyone is too busy acting – "the kisses" thought the *Manchester Guardian*, "mean no more than their parlour games".[48] The famous game of charades, in which each participant performs an adverb for the others to guess, places the characters in a metatheatrical tussle with their creator. Judith Bliss is acting out "winsomely" even as Noël's stage directions interject: "witheringly", "acidly", "dramatically".

In the central act, a screaming row is offset by Judith's son, who diverts proceedings into a performance from one of her greatest hits. The join between the genuine and the dramatic is smudged. Artifice and truth have melded. "What's happened?" somebody asks. "Is this a game?" Are the lines delivered by Noël's characters, or are Noël's characters themselves in character? "Is this true? Answer me – is this true?"

CURTAIN

ACT TWO

SCENE ONE

In 1925 the RMS *Majestic* was the largest ship in the world, and when it left Southampton for New York on 12 August, it had quite the first-class passenger list. At the top was Coward, Noël, a twenty-five-year-old actor-dramatist about to make his Broadway debut with *The Vortex*, *Hay Fever*, and *Easy Virtue*. Beneath him were "Coward, Violet Agnes", sixty-two years old, and "Calthrop, Gladys", a thirty-one-year-old scenic designer. Also on the list was Laura Hope Crews, the American actress who was to play Judith Bliss on Broadway; Lilian Braithwaite, star of *The Vortex*; and the director Basil Dean, who had taken over some of the production duties. He and Noël had last worked together during *Hannele*, when the latter had been a knobbly-kneed boy vomiting peppermints down his costume.

When the ship stopped off in Cherbourg, the merry crew was joined by the American poet Mercedes de Acosta and her lover, the actress Eva Le Gallienne. Noël had met them on his first visit to New York, when De Acosta had found him "touchingly poor, charmingly unsure of himself, refreshingly unknown and beguilingly insecure".[1] Now the tables had turned. Relations between the two women were already under strain, partly because of De Acosta's recent marriage, and partly because the premiere of her play *Jehanne d'Arc*, written as a vehicle for Le Gallienne, had been a financial disaster. The pair separated permanently when, probably on board the ship, Eva began an affair with Gladys Calthrop (leaving Mercedes in deep misery). In not too long, Gladys would transfer her affections to Mercedes (leaving Eva in deep misery).[2] With all these actors and writers living together in the close-walled floating world, bemoaning recent failures, anticipating forthcoming success, with love affairs fraying and others beginning amid the riotous on-board parties, the air positively crackled.

The ship docked on 18 August, and Violet took to New York

with gusto, sorting all the living arrangements and eventually securing and maintaining an apartment in Midtown East. Noël was used
to the city's clamour, and to the amazing summer heat, but both
seemed to have intensified in the sixteen months since his previous
visit, in which time New York had become the most populous
city in the world. He was able to spend time with Jeffery Amherst
and was quickly sucked into the rounds of New York party-going.
He had been in the city just a week when, on 27 August, he
was a guest of the film producer Edwin Knopf, performing "Poor
Little Rich Girl" before ceding the piano to George Gershwin, who
played highlights from his in-progress piano concerto. Five days
later he and Gershwin were entertaining at another party alongside
Charlie Chaplin, then one of the most famous men in the world.
The revelry broke up at three in the morning.[3]

It was amazing that *The Vortex* managed to be rehearsed at all,
especially when the American producer, the notoriously ruthless
A. L. Erlanger, insisted that the third act be completely rewritten to
his instruction, wary of upsetting American audiences for whom
the play's excess, given the illegality of alcohol, had an extra charge.
Noël calmly responded that if a word were changed he would
return to England, and banned Erlanger from rehearsals. In the
end, production duties were taken over by Sam Harris in partnership with the composer Irving Berlin. Less than three weeks after
Noël's arrival in America, *The Vortex* opened in a preview run at the
National Theatre in Washington, and the actors staggered through
the performances, their make-up running in the heat, their lines
unheard beneath daily thunderstorms. Everything seemed cursed.
Braithwaite managed to throw the box of cocaine clean through
the window of the set, at which point a passing member of stage
management caught it and helpfully threw it back. Braithwaite had
another go at ridding herself of the troublesome prop, and broke
the window.[4]

The mishap was one of the few occasions on which the Washington theatregoers had been stirred into life or laughter by the
play. Reviews were poor, and the cast arrived on Broadway braced
for disaster. Lilian Braithwaite tentatively booked a cabin for a
return trip to London. The actors' nerves were such that on the

first night (at the Henry Miller Theatre, on 16 September) they performed very well, encouraged by unexpected laughs and rounds of applause. Broadway, unlike the West End, had done away with the practice of ending each act with a round of bows, and so the tension of *The Vortex* went unreleased until the final curtain, at which point the audience erupted in what papers would describe as "the biggest ovation any visiting player has received on Broadway in years".[5] One running joke was that the cast of *Love's Call*, performing two blocks away, thought the cheering was in their own theatre and came out for another bow. Noël threw a party afterwards at the British Embassy, its official nature presumably requiring its guests to sip decorously at cordial, although he later admitted that for certain gatherings he had resorted to paying "over two thousand dollars for drink".[6]

The papers arrived a few hours after the party broke up. The *New York Times* had emblazoned its front page with a huge drawing of Noël. Its reviewer thought the characters were all "flowers of evil", that the play was thin and flawed, but that the power and relevance of the last act were remarkable. *The Vortex*, the article concluded, was "sensational".[7] The word was used pejoratively, but that didn't matter. Noël had had a huge success, egged on by the American press, which repeated the British debate about the morality – or otherwise – of Noël's work. "It was fascinating", Basil Dean thought, "to watch him grasping [success] by the throat to make it sing his tune."[8] Not that there was all that much time to enjoy it, as Noël moved straight into rehearsals of the American premiere of *Hay Fever*, which he co-directed with Laura Hope Crews. These were farcical from the off. A play called *Spring Fever* was already running, and the papers announced that Noël had reverted to his original title of *Still Life*. Then a play called *Still Waters* opened, and the press reported that the name had changed to *Just Ourselves*.[9]

Noël then found that the Shubert Brothers, producing, had already cast the show, including a gum-chewing blonde who refused to try a British accent – "Accent hell! I've got a contract" – and over twenty extras whose purpose Noël never managed to discern.[10] After endless haggling he managed to assemble a more suitable, not to say smaller, troupe. With days to go the title came back round to *Hay Fever*, but the play never really settled, either during its trial week in Brooklyn, or in its main run at the Maxine Elliot Theatre, which opened on 5 October. The audience was star-studded and lethargic; the actors overcompensated; the evening shrivelled and died. The all-important write-up in the *New York Times* thought Hope Crews as Judith was "iridescent" and "subtle", but complained that the author "does not scintillate in the use of words" and found the evening "colorless".[11] *Hay Fever* closed six weeks later.

But *The Vortex* was doing good business, and Violet wept with joy at Noël's first nights and at the glory of American produce (sliced bacon! In packets!). She and Noël moved to a luxurious apartment close to Lincoln Square, and Noël's name became a permanent feature on party lists. Columnists gawped that, on one occasion, he and Michael Arlen (whom they falsely set up as rivals and without whose money *The Vortex* would never have happened) visited no fewer than nineteen separate establishments.[12] An adaptation of Arlen's novel *The Green Hat* had opened successfully on Broadway the night before *The Vortex* and on both sides of the Atlantic he and Noël were paired together as the two most successful writers of their generation. "My dear Noël", Arlen wrote to him, "I am so very happy for you and so proud of you [. . . and I take] very real pride in your stormy achievements."[13]

The third and final play of Noël's which was to open in America was *Easy Virtue*, written in the summer of the previous year. Basil Dean was to direct the world premiere in New Jersey in November, before a Broadway run opening on 7 December. *Easy Virtue* was a trumpet blast, in which Noël announced himself as a modern writer by manipulating traditional material. As a character says: "being modern only means twisting things into different shapes". The script was in dialogue with Victoriana, a riff on the "woman-with-a-past" genre exemplified by Wilde's Mrs Erlynne, Shaw's Mrs Warren, and Pinero's Mrs Tanqueray or Mrs Ebbsmith: women with scandalous histories pitched into a disapproving society. Mrs Tanqueray kills herself; Mrs Ebbsmith is forced to give up libertarianism for prayer. Noël's woman-with-a-past, Larita Whittaker, refuses to buckle to societal disapproval. A middle-aged American divorcee whose promiscuity has caught the attentions of the press, she has convinced herself that she is in love with a boring British man, whose upright family she visits in their country house, having committed to the "hideously intimate relationship" that is marriage. She quietly leaves both the house and the relationship, the curtain falling on the closing door in an echo of Nora Helmer's departure in Ibsen's *A Doll's House*.

The country-house comedy is suddenly seen through the eyes of a Bohemian foreigner, its clichés refreshed. The ubiquitous tennis game is now a form of torture: "you play tennis eternally – tennis – tennis – tennis!" The family eccentricities are not the theatrics of *Hay Fever* but are woven from poisonous and hypocritical mock-virtue, in which Larita begins to drown. *Easy Virtue* was a stinging rebuke to anyone who thought *The Vortex* was merely a finger-wagging criticism of an older woman's loose morals. Larita's past, and the escape from her present, are celebrated as an example of an enlightened person being permitted to live and love as she wishes, outside society. "I don't live", she says, "according to your social system"; "I have a perfect right to say what I like and live how I choose."

These would be the cries of any homosexual in 1925. And in Larita, a woman taking control of her own destiny and sexual needs, Noël had written a character indicative of a generation of women who were making a conscious attempt to break with Victorian social convention. Rebecca West, a friend since their days at PEN meetings (she had praised and encouraged his earliest plays), was publicly raising an illegitimate child as an unmarried single mother. Gladys Calthrop, presumably at emotional cost and to intense familial and social outcry, had left her respectable and monied family in pursuit of a theatrical career. Her son was now nine years old and almost absent from her life; she was already making plans to stay on permanently in New York, living with and loving other women as openly as possible. Artists and writers were assuming pen names that ignored gender – such as Gluck (who had painted *On With the Dance*), and "Peter" (the nickname of Gladys Stern) – and were living in openly homosexual relationships, their hallways often free of the prams that, according to Cyril Connolly, were the enemy of good art.

Such new adventures in living are implicit in *Easy Virtue*. Larita's perceived promiscuity, depicted during a time in which contraception was emancipating women's sexuality, is not something to be criticised. Her marriages are far more unhappy and transactional than her fleeting love affairs: "I've never had an affair with a man I wasn't fond of. The only time I ever sold myself was [. . .] to my first husband." The play is scathing about its English upper-crust family who, bar the surprisingly sympathetic patriarch, are religious, hypocritical, frigid, and unthinkingly philoprogenitive. They dismiss sex as "tosh" and Larita as a "moral degenerate". She survives by truth-telling and wit: "repartee helps". But her "flippancy" is dismissed as "unpardonable". *Easy Virtue* concedes that the cost of sexual and intellectual freedom is high, and she ends the play alone, a woman not only with a past but with an uncertain future, her face "set in an expression of hopeless sadness". Her exit is not entirely an escape but a depiction of a woman in perpetual flight, ungifted in love: "I sometimes wonder why we're here at all – it seems such a waste of time. [. . .] Women of my type are so tiresome in love. We hammer at it, tooth and nail, until it's all bent and misshapen."

Easy Virtue had much potential for scandal. Aside from the open depiction of a woman who enjoys and discusses sex unashamedly, Larita spends much of the second act reading Proust's *Sodom and Gomorrah*, the fourth volume of *In Search of Lost Time* and the one that deals most explicitly with homosexual love; it was a heavy hint to those in the know (or perhaps just those in the front stalls).* But some critics thought the play was emulating, rather than battling with, Pinero and so found it old-fashioned, a perception that apparently disguised the fact that *Fallen Angels* had nothing on *Easy Virtue* when it came to sexual frankness. Jane Cowl made a huge success of the star part, although she had spent rehearsals quarrelling with Basil Dean, who had a fearsome temper and was becoming

---

* But few in the audience would have read it. Cosmopolitan Larita presumably reads French. Charles Scott Moncrieff was yet to publish its English translation, and had bemoaned to Noël the impossibility of retaining its original title, settling eventually for *Cities of the Plain*. (See Findlay, *Chasing Lost Time*, p. 211.)

known in the theatre as "Bastard Basil". (Noël thought her delivery tipped the production too far into the Victorian melodrama he had attempted to update.) Reviewers found it hard to sympathise with the emotional plight of a woman rich enough to escape an unhappy marriage by fleeing to the Ritz Hotel with suitcases of clothes and jewels; others thought Noël was protesting unnecessarily against an increasingly liberal society. The *New York Times* – quoting Sheridan – described the play as a "rivulet of text meandering through a meadow of margin".[14]

Even the characters of *Easy Virtue* are unsure how to read the tone of its dialogue. Larita, having dramatically smashed a statuette of the Venus de Milo, is seen shaking into the sofa cushions, but "whether with laughter or tears it is difficult to say". "You're laughing again" she is told, responding: "Not altogether." The "not altogether" quality of Noël's humour, and the complex emotional register of his scripts, were escaping critics English and American – perhaps because, in being presented with so varied a set of premieres in such a short space of time, they were still unsure how to categorise his largely unclassifiable work. It would take decades for productions to treat his dialogue with either Strindbergian intensity or Chekhovian mournfulness (although in 1928 the critic Ivor Brown would publish an essay comparing Coward with Ibsen, noting parallels with Hedda Gabler or Nora Helmer).[15] That the plays would take so long to settle as anything more than transient froth may give a clue as to how they were performed and directed, even by their author, as if they were later to reveal riches that even Noël did not know were there.

Jane Cowl's star power ensured the box office success of *Easy Virtue*, but only one of Noël's three Broadway openings had been an unequivocal hit. He and Violet began to pine for London. Noël was already beginning to perceive how tenuous was any hold on success, and how easily critical and public opinion could turn. His ambition had always been self-aware, and he could admit how emotionally dependent he was on praise and publicity. At the back of his mind lurked suspicion and foreboding as to what he could now go on to achieve. His mood did not improve when the Broadway run of *The Vortex* came to an end and the play embarked on a short tour of America early in 1926. Almost every evening for the past year he had been whipping himself into a frenzy as Nicky Lancaster, and although he reduced his social life to the bare minimum as the months in America went on, he was exhausted, and lines fled from his head with panic-inducing frequency. He had his mother for company on tour, but Gladys had stayed in Manhattan, working on and even acting in productions of Ibsen and Chekhov with Eva Le Gallienne's Civic Repertory Company, of which Noël was mightily disdainful. It was many years since the grim rigmarole of *Charley's Aunt* and although he was now touring in considerably more style — booking grand hotels and purchasing a Rolls-Royce which, always a bad driver, he commandeered waywardly — he disliked the return to a world of interchangeable auditoria and heavy suitcases. One pleasure was to be introduced to more of America as the company trekked nearly a thousand miles westwards, through Ohio and into Illinois.

Chicago should have been an apotheosis for Noël Coward. Ultimate city of the Jazz Age, it was thronged with gangsters, speakeasies, moonshine, and even had a homosexual rights organisation, founded the previous year. An advertisement was taken out in all the newspapers: "My divine, windy city — you have four words that spell 'genius' in Chicago: Noël Coward, *The Vortex*!"[16] The play arrived at the Selwyn Theatre in February and was a disaster. The more serious it became, the more the audience roared with laughter. Lilian Braithwaite resorted to holding Noël by the shoulders in the interval and telling him, "Remember you are English!" By the third act the theatregoers were beside themselves with hysteria, and he scrawled despondent graffiti on the wall of his dressing room: "Noël Coward died here". The disaster was front-page news: "Something went wrong [. . .] the calculated 'smash' of the piece went for nothing."[17] Having planned to stay in Chicago for a long run, the company couldn't wait to leave. Noël's final performance in *The Vortex* (the last of some 450) brought more relief than regret. The tour finished in Ohio; he had a brief holiday in Florida; in March he and Violet departed for Britain, arriving on 2 April.[18] Gladys Calthrop had stayed on with the Civic Repertory Company, but Rebecca West was on the ship for company: "a very pleasant time with Noël Coward", she wrote, "who is a really nice person".[19]

And with Noël on the boat was a young stockbroker called John C. Wilson, with whom he had fallen in love.

Scene Two

In May 1925 Jack Wilson had been travelling in Europe and he soon arrived in London. Unable to get a ticket for *No, No, Nanette* he was offered a front-row seat for something called *The Vortex*. "This was dismal news", he recalled, "as we had never heard of Noël Coward nor his play." Noël had noticed the intense concentration of the young man in the front row and, to break the monotony of the long run, acted that evening exclusively for him. Wilson thought it "one of the most exciting performances I had ever seen" and "applauded with an enthusiasm and zeal that could only be justified by its genuine honesty". A few days later Jack, wild for Coward, sat enraptured through *On With the Dance* and wangled an invitation to go over to the Little Theatre and meet the star of *The Vortex*, who, to Jack's delighted consternation, "walked around his dressing-room clad only in a pair of silk drawers".[20] Jack had had to return to New York and the two agreed to meet when Noël was next in America.

Four months older than Noël, born in New Jersey, Jack would eventually make his name (with Noël's help) as a theatre director and producer. In the three years since he had graduated from Yale, he had worked for a brokerage firm in New York while indulging his love of film and theatre, acting in San Francisco and working as an assistant at the Astoria film studio on Long Island. The relationship had an unpropitious beginning. Noël waited for nearly an hour at their first lunch date in America before departing in a rage, only to find that his letter accepting Jack's invitation had never been posted. But after that things moved swiftly, and the importance of discretion often gave way to sheer daring delight at the new relationship: "We are having a perfectly fizzing time", he wrote, doodling in the margins of a notebook.[21] "The car broke down and Jack kissed me in the tonneau."* Jack was handsome, clever, and rich, and with his Wall Street contacts soon opened, and then began to manage, Noël's American bank account. When Gladys Calthrop

---

* The part of an open car occupied by the back seats.

moved in with Eva Le Gallienne, Jack and Noël were brought closer together. They were a match for one another as far as humour was concerned, and Jack's wit had a wisecracking quality that was still a novelty to the English, who had yet to be introduced to American humour via the movies.

By the time Noël returned to London in spring 1926 he had Jack with him in the capacity of business manager, a role that Jack would undertake for decades but which was also a good professional excuse for them to be so often together. The newspapers would soon talk of "Noël Coward and his ultra-modern friend, Mr. Wilson, an American".[22] Even in the seeming permissiveness of the decade, Noël's newfound fame increased the importance of secrecy. He was already actively creating – and funding – an entourage with whom he could move through life. In this he placed himself at the centre of a ring of acolytes, which was where he liked to be, but he was also inserting a protective social blanket between himself and the world. What had been a trio – of Gladys Calthrop, Jeffery Amherst, and Lorn Loraine – became a quartet. Presumably Violet, who seemed to accept her son's sexuality, hovered on the sidelines, and Arthur (now seventy) and Eric (now twenty-one) were left to their own devices.

Opportunities for cross-currents of theatrical quarrel and bitter recrimination were rife, with everyone vying for a special place in Noël's affections, a situation it is hard to imagine he discouraged. Jack's arrival can only have complicated matters, and perhaps the others already noticed, with concern, the young man's heavy reliance on alcohol, and his slapdash way with Noël's money – both investing and spending it – to which Noël himself seemed blind, instantly giving Jack power of attorney. It is the first relationship in Noël's life that can conclusively be called a love affair, where sex and love met, yet charting it is a task made difficult by the lack of surviving diaries or letters. The recollections of friends, and the way in which the relationship would eventually decline into resentment and recrimination, may point to an affair that even in its earliest days was unhealthy, both eased and damaged by Noël's wealth and fame, and complicated by layers of possessiveness, indulgence, generosity, and cruelty. The nicknames by which they addressed one

1. Arthur Coward, Noël's father.

2. Violet Coward, Noël's mother, 1910.

3. Noël Coward, photographed on 8 October 1904, two months before his fifth birthday.

4. Performing as Slightly in J. M. Barrie's *Peter Pan*, 1913.

5. James "Philip" Sidney Streatfeild (1879–1915).

6. Streatfeild's drawing of Noël: "To my friend Noël, from P. S. S. 1914."

7. Noël with Philip Streatfeild in Cornwall, August 1914.

8. Noël (left) with friends and fellow actors Esmé Wynne and John Ekins in 1915, two years before Ekins's death from meningitis.

9. The designer Gladys Calthrop, beloved friend and important colleague for more than half a century.

10. Coward with his "secretary" Lorn Loraine, her job title belying the depth of his reliance and love; in the background is Coward's home at Gerald Road in London, with a theatrical "stage" erected at one end of the living space.

11. Clemence Dane (the pseudonym of Winifred Ashton), writer and artist, and a fixture of Coward's "family".

12. Maisie Gay as Hernia Whittlebot (a parody of poet Edith Sitwell) in Coward's 1923 revue *London Calling!*.

13. "I'm trying to control myself but you won't let me!" Coward as drug addict Nicky Lancaster confronting his mother (Lilian Braithwaite) in *The Vortex*, which began its scandalous and successful run at the small Everyman Theatre in Hampstead, London, in November 1924.

14. Coward with American producer Jack Wilson, his romantic and business partner.

15. Coward with Gertrude Lawrence in "Shadow Play", the most experimental of his nine-play sequence *Tonight at 8.30*, 1936.

16. His famous professional relationship with Lawrence began thirteen years earlier, in the revue *London Calling!*, when she sang "Parisian Pierrot" to a "boudoir doll".

17. "Dance, Little Lady", a haunting number from Coward's revue *This Year of Grace* in 1928.

18. Coward's 1930 play *Post Mortem* was given its world premiere by Allied prisoners of war at Oflag VII-B, a German camp in Eichstätt, Germany, in 1944. Third from left is Desmond Llewelyn, later famous as Q in the James Bond films.

19. *Private Lives* was written just three months before *Post Mortem*, and its London premiere, at the Phoenix Theatre, in September 1930, cemented the fame of Coward's double act with Gertrude Lawrence.

20. "Chaos", the "Expressionist" final scene from Coward's *Cavalcade*, a smash hit in October 1931. At the piano is Black pianist and former Olympic sprinter Jack London; at the bottom-left are "incurables" from the Great War in hospital uniform; parents grieving the loss of their children are spotlit among political rallies and nightclub dances: "the general effect is complete chaos".

21. Coward with Alfred Lunt and Lynn Fontanne (his close friends and the most famous husband-and-wife acting duo of the century) performing in his play *Design for Living* in 1933. The script's open depiction of a bisexual love triangle necessitated a premiere in America, to escape British censorship.

22. Jeffery Amherst

23. Ivor Novello

24. Erik Coward

25. Charles Cochran

26. Alan Webb

27. Binkie Beaumont

28. Elsie April

29. Louis Hayward

30. Keith Winter

another – Noël was "Pop" and Jack was alternately "Penny Eyes", "Dab", or "Baybay" (a mock-Cockney "baby") – bespeak a relationship more lopsided than reciprocal, and more enchanted than realistic. Nicknames were as ever a way by which Noël translated people into characters, swathing them in a humorous wrapping that could divert engagement with their inner life.

Cole Lesley (who in 1936 would take his own place in the entourage as Noël's valet) described the affair and Noël's attitude towards it:

> When not in love, [Noël] could write, "How idiotic people are when they are in love. What an age-old devastating disease." But when he himself caught this disease there arose a resentment in him, at himself, against the unexplainable fact that he had fallen physically in love. He hated this loss of control over himself just as deeply as he loathed the loss of control brought about by drunkenness, or by drug-addiction in others. [. . .] When he was passionately in love he was not himself, and with his command of language he could plunge many a barb into the loved one's heart. As for his possessiveness, it became total at these times; utterly untypical of him when he was not obsessed. [. . .] He, Noël of all people, was hopelessly out of control, yet retained enough detachment to regard himself with an examiner's eye, and what he saw he despised.[23]

In his writing Noël had alternated a bitterly comic portrayal of love with the comfort, even sentimentality, of romantic convention, as if to take control of love's complexities within the comfortingly predictable world that was confined so safely within the bounds of the proscenium arch. His plays had acted as a prism through which love had been split into layers of romance, sex, friendship, and domesticity – individual facets rarely combined in one relationship. In *The Vortex* love had been either a bitter sexless experiment or a dangerous drugged escape; in *Hay Fever* a parlour game or theatrical charade; in *Fallen Angels* a quarrelsome, nearly nightmarish, farce ("it's so uncomfortable – passion"). Any references to sex had of necessity to be implicit and were often swathed in his circle's baby-talk. The Lord Chamberlain found himself objecting to use of the word "byes" (as in "beddy-byes"). "Byes" meant bed, and bed meant sex. Most of all there was Larita in *Easy Virtue*, whose amorous travails, although written before the arrival of Jack Wilson in Noël's life, seem to be clearly autobiographical. Her sense of being "so tiresome in love" would be echoed, nearly forty years later, by a number written for his musical *Sail Away*: "I am no good at love."

Almost all the likely objects of Noël's love or attraction had been fleeting presences in his life, from Philip Streatfeild and John Ekins (both of whom had died within years of meeting him), to figures such as Esmé Wynne or Stewart Forster, who had all, as it were, abandoned Noël for marriage. As if wary of repeat rejection, he had taken refuge in the safety of intimate friendships uncomplicated by sexual attraction, leaving sex to become fleeting and transactional, an almost routine and necessarily secretive part of the twenties life-style. The supposedly precocious Coward seems to have been a late starter when it came to affairs of the heart, and perhaps purposely so, in that he pushed from his life anything that dented his almost manic work ethic, or which left him, like any drug, lacking control. There had been something sterile about his carefully refined image, the pale and bony face, dark-rimmed eyes, short hair slick with grease as if painted on a wooden puppet. Beverley Nichols, in a typically trenchant observation from 1925, thought that Noël "found it exceedingly difficult to fall in love. Love, in the accepted sense of the word, demands quite a great deal of stupidity on the part of both concerned. Most of us have it. Noel hasn't. [. . .] One day, I believe, he *will* fall in love, and the prospect is so intriguing."[24] It was Jack Wilson who unleashed Noël's almost dangerous capacity for loving, with him since childhood and intensified by being so long pent up. Yet Noël was as powerless to restrain his affections as he was self-aware enough to recognise and dislike them. "It's funny, isn't it", says a woman in *Shadow Play*, which he wrote ten years later, "to be so frightfully in love that you feel as if you were going mad?"

While on tour with *The Vortex* early in 1926, as the relationship with Jack was developing, Noël had written *Semi-Monde*, his first new script in two years, during which time his personal and professional life had changed utterly. Neither a drawing-room comedy nor the "well-made play" that had been his stock-in-trade, in form it is hardly a play at all. Essentially a dramatic frieze, *Semi-Monde* is set in various rooms of a grand Paris hotel (its working title was *Ritz Bar*). It is spread across two years, with nearly thirty named characters appearing and disappearing in a tangle of plots and snippets of overheard dialogue. The hotel provides an enclosed and allegorical world by which an entire slice of society could be observed and dissected, a luxurious refuge for a gallery of lost outsiders: writers, singers, homosexuals, a White Russian émigré. "To hell with society", says one, "and all its rotten little codes." Only slowly is a doomed world of painful vacuity and fracturing relationships glimpsed beneath the gauze of social chitchat.

More explicitly than anything Noël had written, *Semi-Monde* depicted bisexual love triangles and gay or lesbian partnerships. Meeting the actress Diana Cooper in Chicago, Noël had read her the entire thing, and she described its "mass of on-edge lesbians and another very happy group of buggers [. . .] I doubt very much it being allowed on an English or American stage."[25] (Her vocabulary, not unusual for the day, disguises the acceptance with which she and her husband greeted homosexuals in their circle.) An unhappy group of quarrelling lovers, all women, may be a portrait – not unstereotypical – of Gladys Calthrop's complex and often unhappy personal life. A young man shuttles between a male and a female lover, eventually to choose the female, although she is perfectly aware of his sexual past. He is "more wretched than I've ever been in my life", to which she replies: "You'll get over that – and anyhow you do *know* about yourself." Almost no relationship, gay or straight, survives unscathed in a depiction of societal moral decay: "I find it so hard not to cheat when everyone else is cheating all around me." The cruellest sketches are reserved for camp middle-aged men trailing slim and much younger lovers. "My dear", says one, eyeing a handsome young man, "where did you find that? It's divine!"

In daring to portray homosexuals at the very limits of what was possible on the 1920s stage, *Semi-Monde* is not above cruel jokes at their expense. The character with whose views Noël seems most to be in sympathy is Jerome Kennedy, a heterosexual writer, married, adulterous, and given to nervous breakdowns. He longs to escape the hotel's world of camp theatrics and retreat to "the great open spaces" where "men are men"; the guests, he decides, are "not even real of their kind". The play criticises any form of homosexuality associated with florid or effeminate display, perhaps evincing its author's attraction to conventional masculinity. Noël's sexuality, as he settled into his first serious relationship, sat uneasily alongside what amounted to a dislike of same-sex relations lived openly or promiscuously. He seemed so often to swim on an artificial surface of life, perfecting his theatrical manner; yet he could find the layer of artifice inherent in camp dangerously false. He who had made his life in the theatre could disapprove intensely of others' theatrics. A character in *Semi-Monde* describes in passing a ludicrous opera production: "They did the whole thing with masks."

The extravagant requirements of *Semi-Monde* appealed to the director Max Reinhardt, already renowned for his innovative productions of Vollmöller's *The Miracle* and his annual staging of *Jedermann* at the Salzburg Festival. He and Noël were to meet in San Francisco later in the year and Reinhardt made genuine but unsuccessful attempts to stage *Semi-Monde* in Germany. Basil Dean's efforts likewise came to nothing, and the script was, for its day, so explicit that the Lord Chamberlain stood firm in his refusal of any London production. (*Semi-Monde* would not reach a theatre until 1977, starring a young Pierce Brosnan, and updated to a fascist 1930s.) The first play written since beginning his relationship with Jack Wilson, it is steeped in Noël's dislike of his own possessive sexual desires: less a self-disgust at his homosexuality than an aversion to sexuality in general, the discovery of which, when a child, had led him to run screaming to his mother. Such feelings were complicated by the fact that the partnership with Jack was not sexually exclusive and, when fuelled by alcohol, Jack could make a pass at friends such as Beverley Nichols. He became forceful if rejected, much to Noël's misery.[26] In *Semi-Monde*, Jerome is bitter: "We're all silly animals, gratifying our own beastly desires, covering them with a veneer of decency and good behaviour. Lies – lies – complete rottenness."[27]

During their first years together Noël and Jack threw themselves into an almost manic need to travel, as if pausing to consider where they stood were a dangerous thing. On their return to England in April 1926, they stayed in London only a few weeks before taking off again, holidaying in France and Sicily. Wealth was increasingly allowing Noël to live in a gilded cocoon divorced from the realities of life. On 4 May 1926 the General Council of the Trades Union Congress called the General Strike, and the country ground to a standstill. That very day, Noël and Jack were leaving the Grand Hotel des Palmes in Palermo and sailing for a brief stay in Tunisia. By the time the strike was over, on 12 May, they were in Paris with Edward Molyneux. Preparations for a British production of *Easy Virtue*, which had brought Jane Cowl over from America to star once again as Larita, were going on while they were abroad, leading to much back-seat directing from Noël by telegram.

Noël returned to England for the opening of *Easy Virtue* in the West End on 11 June. (During the previews at Manchester the city's Watch Committee, which oversaw its police force, had objected to the title and forced its advertisement as *A New Play*.) The run did good business but the reviews were mainly poor or indifferent. Already there was a sense that Noël's success was a flash in the pan, his wit mere passing frippery that had momentarily caught the spirit of the age. "I don't imagine", wrote *The Bystander*, "that succeeding generations will concern themselves greatly with the works of Noël Coward."[28] The *Westminster Gazette* agreed, not long afterwards: "Mr Coward is now probably on the crest of his fame: the present boom is likely to rise no further."[29] Back in 1924 the critics thought he had diagnosed a real malaise in society; two years on, it could seem as if he had projected onto an entire generation a way of life that affected only a small number of wealthy people. Churchill had reintroduced the gold standard, which kept interest rates high. The coal reserves were depleting, the economy was depressing, and unemployment was at nearly two million. The affluence of Noël and his characters was now a harsh contrast with working-class poverty.

Early in August 1926 he and Jack spent a week of almost unfathomable luxury in Venice.[30] So-called Lido Mania had swept the Jazz Age and turned Venice into one of the summer's greatest attractions

for the beau monde. Elsa Maxwell bounced around staging balls
and parties and taking sole credit for the popularity of the floating
city. Noël and Jack stayed with Cole Porter and his wife, who had
rented the Palazzo Rezzonico, one of the most majestic on the
Grand Canal. Lyricist and composer in one, Porter was eight years
older than Noël, his health not yet shattered by his riding accident
the following decade. He had yet to enjoy real success and was
on the verge of giving up songwriting, although within a year he
would have a hit with his Broadway musical *Paris*, which introduced the first of his "list songs": "Let's Do It . . .". As devoted
to his wife Linda as he was to affairs with handsome young men,
classically trained where Noël was self-taught, Porter had come
into an astonishing inheritance from his grandfather and would
think nothing, when in Venice, of hiring crowds of gondoliers
and tightrope walkers to entertain his friends. The guest list was
star-spangled, and included Richard Rodgers and Lorenz Hart, just
embarking upon their run of hit musicals. Amid the Tiepolo and
Giordano frescoes of the Palazzo's ten drawing rooms, some of the
great songwriters of the age took turns at the grand piano.

But even as Noël danced on the Venice beaches, work was never
far from his mind. His notebooks accompanied him on boats and in
train carriages, and Jack marvelled that, while they were in Venice,
"Noël, of course, never stopped writing".[31] When they were in
Sicily Noël had written *This Was a Man*, which contained such an
open depiction of enthusiastic infidelity that the Lord Chamberlain
promptly refused it a licence. *This Was a Man* would not receive
its British premiere until 2014, but a Broadway production was
scheduled for late in 1926. "In our country", Noël told the press,
"writers want to depict life as they see it with their own eyes, not
as it was seen fifty years ago. But what can they do with this awful
leash round their necks? In America there is no leash, but freedom
of thought. [. . .] I want to stir intelligent people up to help me in
my fight."[32] Not that America was entirely the land of the free: in
1926 the cast of Edouard Bourdet's *The Captive*, which featured an
openly lesbian couple, were arrested and hauled off to the police
station after its first night on Broadway, among them Ann Trevor,
not long out of *Hay Fever*.

This Was a Man was about a successful painter who, hidden in his studio, witnesses his wife Carol's infidelity and decides to do nothing about it: "she's a human being, not an inanimate object over which I can assert legal rights". The painter's best friend, Evelyn Bathurst, attempts to read Carol the riot act and ends up being seduced by her, but this, like most of the declarations of love and repentance, turns out to have been a charade. Bathurst, enmeshed in the various love knots, claims to have attempted suicide; the play ends with the blackest humour as Carol "sweetly" sits beside him: "There's still time for you to shoot yourself!" Perhaps the most painful line, if this account of infidelity and unhappy relationships were to be read biographically, is the dedication: "To John C. Wilson." The farcical mesh of amusing affairs and mock-affairs is something in which the unhappy characters are entangled beyond their own control. "Stop being flippant", says one. "It's only a mask to cover your humiliation."

Scene Three

Noël's work in the final years of the decade would, according to one reviewer, "progress backwards".[33] If this brought critical disdain, it also brought audiences, and it may be that Noël could already smell a change in the political wind, predicting the need for escape that would arise from a new world of strike and depression. His most daring work had no chance of production in England, and he would not countenance even a momentary absence from the stage. Instead, he turned to his back catalogue and premieres of two, much earlier, works were planned. *The Queen Was in the Parlour* (his Ruritanian romance from 1922, four years and as many lifetimes ago) was to be followed by *The Rat Trap*, a play he had written in the final months of the war. It was a brave move to risk revival of two scripts by a less mature author, but although their old-fashioned quality led to surprise, they received largely good reviews and are evidence that Noël had, for now, correctly read the rapidly changing atmosphere.

The Queen Was in the Parlour opened in Basil Dean's production at the St Martin's Theatre on 14 August 1926, almost as soon as Noël returned to London from Venice. Ruritanian romance was out of fashion and a better candidate for parody than reconstruction. But underneath the Ruritanian wrapping – the plot is essentially based on Anthony Hope's novel *Rupert of Hentzau* – lay not only Noël's characteristic dialogue ("she's got sweetbreads instead of brains") but his archetypal construction: a woman torn between love and duty, between an affair of the heart and a socially acceptable marriage. Madge Titheradge was Princess Nadya of Krayia, who wants to reject her royal inheritance to live with her civilian lover. Her eventual marriage to a prince leads the lover to kill himself. Written five years after the Russian Revolution, and premiered a few months after the General Strike, the play has scant time for those who rejected "the existing order of things, trying to tear down kings and queens". It would have been ripe for revival during the Abdication crisis, but has not been staged at all since 1932.

The Rat Trap would follow at the Everyman Theatre in October, by which time Noël was in America (he never saw it staged). It deals with a failing marriage between a novelist and a playwright, and explores – with despairing honesty for an author of eighteen – the incompatibility of domesticity and creativity, concluding that marriage, an institution from which his own unions were barred, tarnishes both sexual drive and artistic production. Overwhelmed by the laundry, the novelist escapes to Cornwall where, in happy isolation, she writes a very good novel. The play shares a theme with Somerset Maugham's fictionalised life of Gauguin, *The Moon and Sixpence*, with which it is exactly contemporary; it may be a loose portrayal of his friends G. B. Stern and Geoffrey Holdsworth and their short-lived unhappy marriage. Noël made sure to tell the press that he thought *The Rat Trap* had clear weaknesses, which meant that some reviewers rushed to disagree with him. The run was not extended beyond its scheduled fortnight but one critic wrote that it was, "in the opinion of many, Noël Coward's best play".[34]

In between these two productions, Noël agreed, with misgivings, to act in a work by another author, which he had not done in five years. Margaret Kennedy's *The Constant Nymph*, published in 1924, is thought to have been the bestselling novel of its decade. With Basil Dean, Kennedy had adapted it for the stage and Noël was persuaded to add his star power to the cast in the role of composer Lewis Dodd. Noël agreed on condition that, after a month, he could hand the part to John Gielgud. Explicit for its day, the story was calculated to appeal to him: Dodd loves and is loved by a fourteen-year-old girl called Tessa, but marries someone else, coming to resent both his wife and the stultifying nature of marriage and London society. Like *Easy Virtue* or *The Rat Trap* the play contrasted a world of Bohemianism and creativity with the constraints of conventional living.

Basil Dean, whom everyone found perfectly amenable outside of the rehearsal room, directed with his usual short temper, and Noël frequently lost his own, at one point making a terrific scene and striding grandly to the emergency exit, only to find it padlocked. But Dean managed to get a real performance out of Noël, refusing him a cigarette to gesture with or a dressing-gown to hide within. He insisted on spectacles and loose-fitting suits, and asked Noël to grow his hair long; ungreased, it was frizzy and, apparently, flammable, so that sparks from a pipe were forever flying up and setting light to his fringe. It didn't help that the play ran for three hours, and ended with Noël staggering under the weight of his co-star Edna Best, not long out of *Fallen Angels* and trying hard, at twenty-four, to convince as the doomed teenager of the title: "Tessa's got away. She's safe. She's dead." During one performance, as Noël was meant to be sunk in grief, a window of the set would close abruptly on his fingers – "Tessa's got away. She's safe. She's OW!" – leading the dead Tessa to leap wildly into the air just as the curtain fell.[35]

The first night, on 15 September, was interrupted by Mrs Patrick Campbell's Pekinese, who yapped from his mistress's lap during the quieter scenes. "How bad Noël is!" Mrs Pat told Basil Dean afterwards. "I *must* go and tell him."[36] But *The Times* was not alone in acclaiming the "strength and brilliance" of his performance.[37] Noël's success shows that he could discard his polished sleekness and convince as the virile romantic lead, for which Ivor Novello (who took the role on film) was more conventional casting. But critical acclaim did not prevent Noël becoming first irritable, and then seriously depressed. He sank into a self-confessed "coma" of low spirits all through September, the first sparks of a serious breakdown beginning to smoulder in tandem with his scorched fringe.[38] High spirits had been his default mode since the war, but the "neurasthenia" that his doctors had diagnosed during his traumatic period in the army seemed to be returning, as if exacerbated by Jack's arrival. And no wonder: in under two years, he had acquired fame on a level, some said, with the prime minister; given over five hundred performances; and overseen nearly ten productions of his own work in two continents. To say nothing of parties. Or sleep.

Rehearsals and performances of *The Constant Nymph* also coincided with major domestic upheaval. There was no financial need for the Coward family to continue running a boarding house, but Violet remained adamant that they should all stay at Ebury Street. Noël had made little of his background in the press, beyond his emergence from the child-actor scene; evidently he did not think it worth risking his upper-crust demeanour with any suburbs-to-riches story. In September 1926 he renewed the lease on Ebury Street, and spent £1,600 on its renovation (nearly three times the average property price of the day). Journalists reported that he had purchased a new home: "his bathroom" wrote one, "is the last word".[39] Jack was rather shocked at the two floors of the house which Noël took over as a private apartment: "in this staid, old-fashioned routine boarding house, there suddenly appeared two floors of vermillion, orange, and pink".[40] A house-warming party was thrown, at which the Astaire siblings mingled uncomfortably with Noël's aunts and uncles, and Arthur Coward tried to serve sandwiches to a taciturn Jane Cowl. Noël, happiest of all in the company of animals, got a cat and christened it Proust.[41] "I adore animals", he told Beverley Nichols in an attempt to explain his inability to resist cradling any cat that crossed his path. "I cannot see a water-bison without bursting into tears."[42]

But he had been pining for the kind of country retreat that he wrote about in his plays. Rural solitude would be a way of sharing life with Jack while avoiding press interest. It did not help that the Ebury Street address was public knowledge, and the papers, casting him as an eligible bachelor, breathlessly reported the "constant stream of women admirers" arriving at his front door (which was now embellished with an enormous elephant-head knocker).[43] An old neighbour from the Cowards' sojourn in the Kentish marshes wanted to let quite a small Elizabethan farmhouse called Golden-hurst, in Aldington, a few miles inland from the stretch of coast between Dymchurch and Romney, which Noël knew well. It was set in acres of private land, had been wired for electricity, and showed great potential for extension and improvement. The rooms were cosy rather than grand, and their low-beamed ceilings were surely a problem for Noël, who was well over six foot. But the house seemed to him ideal, and the owner was asking just £50 for a year's rent. Soon Noël was dividing his time between Ebury Street and Goldenhurst, leaving his mother to oversee major renovations. He would gradually purchase more and more of the surrounding land, living at Goldenhurst for thirty years and transforming it into the country estate about which he had so long written, with the inevitable croquet lawn, the parties in which he would play on into the night, and the famously white-on-white interior design of Somerset Maugham's wife, Syrie. (Maugham was predomin-antly homosexual, and the couple would divorce in 1928.) Noël employed a gardener to plant ravishing borders, of which he took very little notice. Jeffery Amherst thought "he really regarded house and garden as a set, a framework".[44]

But despite the potential for recuperation at Goldenhurst, things suddenly unravelled. Only a few weeks into the run of *The Constant Nymph* Noël wept his way through a performance and then crum-pled onto the floor of his dressing room. The doctor injected him with strychnine, which was thought at the time to calm the nervous system. Noël left the production a week early, and Gielgud stepped in with his well-honed impression. Medical advice was to cancel everything and rest, but after a week in bed, during which Noël refused to see almost anyone, he insisted on going to New York to oversee rehearsals of *This Was a Man*. Work was, in many ways, an addiction and he sailed on 13 October 1926.

He and Jack settled in the Gladstone Hotel, ostensibly to get away from the noise of the Ritz. "I love being here", Noël told Violet, "and I'm taking everything very easily and being a good boy – Jack sends dearest love and is looking after me beautifully."[45] But any good intentions of rest and recuperation – "I've only been out late once since I arrived" – were soon ruined by the pull and pace of New York: "About twenty new buildings have shot up into the air since last year and five million more motor cars, consequently one can't move anywhere."[46] There were so many business plans that he and Basil Dean took an office with "Noël Coward Inc." written over the door. He had not been in New York a month when he found himself at an "enormous house party with all the Vanderbilts and Astors and Shufflebottoms", and a week later was at another "tremendous" gathering: "George Gershwin played and we all carried on like one o'clock".[47] Gershwin had just opened his musical *Oh, Kay!*, in which Gertrude Lawrence delivered "Someone to Watch Over Me" to a Raggedy Ann doll purchased by the composer at a local toy store, in conscious emulation of "Parisian Pierrot".[48] There was also the initiation of being introduced to Jack's parents, with whom Noël spent Thanksgiving at their home in New Jersey.

None of this can have helped the sudden rearrival of depressive episodes that speedily bleached the world of hope and colour, his head sluggish and woolly, his limbs aching, his nights plagued by insomnia. *This Was a Man* opened on 25 November at the Klaw, the very first theatre he had visited in New York, but he watched the auditorium slowly empty as the evening progressed. One of the actors, A. E. Matthews, was embroiled in unhappy affairs with two women and in Dean's opinion "knew less about the play at the final dress rehearsal than when he'd begun".[49] Noël wrote to Violet: "The play, dear, has all the earmarks of being a failure! Gladys and Jack and I sat grandly in a box on the First Night and watched it falling flatter and flatter." His initial reaction was characteristic: "I must admit we got bad giggles! They were all expecting something very dirty indeed after the English Censor banning it and they were bitterly disappointed."[50] Critics sharpened their knives; "meretricious" appeared in the very first sentence of the *New York Times* review.[51] The play would prove more successful in Europe: first in Berlin in 1927 (staged by Max Reinhardt), then in Paris a year later, when police had to be hired to hold back the crowds. But the taste of American failure was bitter and with the benefit of hindsight the harshest critic would prove to be Noël himself.

To Violet he was stoic. "I find on close reflection that I am as unmoved by failure as I am by success which is a great comfort. [. . .] I like writing the plays anyhow and if people don't like them that's their loss."[52] But this may have been a brave face. He and Jack spent a fortnight at a resort in the Allegheny Mountains in Virginia, "the most divine rest imaginable", but breaking off from work did not occur to him: "I lie flat on my back and write all the afternoon, I'm doing a lovely comedy for Marie Tempest which I shall finish in a week. [. . .] There is an awful married couple in the next room to us and they fight like cats – Jack and I spend hours with our ears glued to the wall."[53] But the eavesdropping did not turn his play into a prototype for *Private Lives*; instead he produced a historical comedy called *The Marquise*, in his own words "a tenuous, frivolous little piece", set in a French chateau during the eighteenth century: a count and a duke want their children to marry one another, but the children's affections lie elsewhere. The dialogue made no efforts to be anything other than contemporary Coward: "If I refuse I shall be sent to a convent or something dreadful." "Some convents are very accommodating, you know – an aunt of mine had heaps of lovers when *she* was in a convent." In its title character – the Marquise Eloise, who turns out to be the mother of both children, making their planned union incestuous – Noël had created a role for Marie Tempest that, they would both agree, was a jolly good one. But it was a play written as escape from an onslaught of depression that did not abate on his return to New York, on 8 December.

Matters came to a head and he began to feel so ill, physical and emotional symptoms once again eliding, that a doctor was called. "I am completely healthy", Noël reassured his mother,

but I am in a bad way as far as nerves are concerned – he said that I have been living on nervous energy for years and now it has given out and that I must go away at once! [. . .] I feel I must get away from all the people I know for a while, not only from the point of view of health but for my work as well. [. . .] Nerves are extraordinary things – I sleep for eleven hours and wake up dead tired with my legs aching as though I'd walked ten miles! It's not serious yet as I haven't had a break down but the Doctor says I'm on the verge of one. [. . .] I expect your vivid imagination is now at work conjuring up pictures of your beloved son gibbering like a maniac and telling everyone I'm not the Empress Eugenie, I'm Napoleon.[54]

Plans for a trip to Hollywood were abandoned in favour of a two-month recuperative voyage to the Far East. Noël was determined to go alone, as if the relationship with Jack did more to provoke than soothe. From New York the two of them crossed America, arriving in San Francisco on Christmas Eve and reuniting with Diana Cooper, who was touring America in Reinhardt's *The Miracle*. She wrote of having come across Noël in "a black bugger's dressing-gown" and "on the edge of a nervous breakdown".[55] The following day he left Jack, who admitted he was in a "highly emotional state", and sailed out east into the Pacific, where he was to spend New Year in the Territory of Hawaii before going on to Japan.[56] "Noël left", wrote Diana Cooper, "and on coming in after lunch we found his 'boy' crying in our sitting room, watching the boat sail out."[57]

The week on board the ship was one of the worst of his life. He descended into a state he afterwards called "despair" and his memories of the days at sea were hazy, bar a vague sense that he had tried, during one ghastly sleepless night wandering the deck, "to fling my miseries over the rail and into the past".[58] The cryptic phrase occludes whether this were a theatrical gesture of refreshment, or something closer to a suicide attempt. His state became so poor that he was eventually sedated by the ship's doctor, his depression clearly exacerbated by confinement within the unsteady walls of a ship, and by the strange claustrophobia of the open ocean. Afterwards he thought it an inevitable pay-off for the years of near-hysterical activity, but his condition may well have afflicted him had life taken a different turn; the periods of manic energy and shattering melancholia hint at bipolar disorder, although that may be too easy a posthumous diagnosis.

He became so run-down that when the ship docked at Honolulu on 31 December he had a high temperature. Scrapping any thoughts of going on to Japan, he threw himself into the care of his hosts,

Walter Dillingham (the "Baron of Hawaii Industry") and his wife, Louise. They instantly tried to set him on the rounds of lunches and whiskey that characterised their sunlit social life, but by this time, whether through fever or sheer mental distress, he was hearing noises in his head and losing his vision. He fled that same day to the Moana Hotel on Waikiki Beach, unable to take in the splendour of its columns and palm trees, and he awoke some time later to find himself attended by a doctor friend of the Dillinghams who restored him to health over the following week.

He recuperated at the Dillinghams' holiday ranch at Mokuleʻia, on the north shore of Honolulu. A long avenue of royal palms led up to the low white house with its sloping roof and columned porch, the hills beyond coated in eucalyptus trees.[59] He was tended by the caretaker and his wife, and by a soft-hearted bull terrier who toddled along to the beach with him every morning. "The island is exquisite", he wrote to Violet in January, "never too hot and never anything approaching cold – flowers in masses all the year round, particularly camellias and hibiscus and roses all wild!" His tone has a sense of childhood adventure – when writing from abroad he often signed himself "Robinson Crusoe" – but as the letter goes on it starts to judder and repeat itself: "deep blue ocean – bright green lagoon – dazzling yellow sand – enormous cocoa palms and scarlet hibiscus everywhere."[60]

Recuperating amid the scarlet hibiscus, he worked on a collection of essays that poured from him with such angry openness that it is unsurprising the volume – provisionally titled *Anglo-Saxon Attitudes** – never saw the light of day.[61] It defended a method of living that defied the expectations of society: heterosexuality, monogamy, parenthood. He supported birth control, decried "the propagation of children in large and satisfyingly unsanitary numbers", and attacked theatrical censorship, the hypocrisies of government, and the "deep rooted belief in most conventionally bred people that any sexual intercourse outside the bonds of matrimony is vile and wicked

---

* A phrase from Lewis Carroll's *Through the Looking-Glass*, later used for a 1956 novel by Angus Wilson.

and an offence against God and the state and society generally".
Marriage, he wrote, was no "sacrament", merely "an inadequate
social convenience". He occasionally pulled his punches – "I have
no wish at this point to launch into a discussion as to whether sex
abnormalities should be nationally recognised and accepted" – but
elsewhere was daring: "it is possible for the masses to read in any
newspaper an account of some police court trial weighed down
with sinister homo-sexual implications and written in execrable
journalese, and impossible to enjoy the privilege of reading Marcel
Proust's *Sodom and Gomorrah* in English owing to the translation of
this sincere and valuable contribution to literature having been
relentlessly vetoed".[62] The essays were carted back to England in his
luggage but Noël seems never to have attempted publication.

Through wealth, connections, and determination he had narrow-
ly avoided a spell either in a sanatorium or in a psychiatric hospital.
There were still patches of black depression, stimulated especially by any communication from home or from Jack. But he was
now determined to get well and he began to apply his customary
self-discipline to curing himself, deciding not to budge from his
luxurious solitary confinement until he was physically and mentally
restored. "People, I decided, were the danger. People were greedy
and predatory, and if you gave them the chance, they would steal
unscrupulously the heart and soul out of you."[63] This conclusion
was a turning point, the arrival of a deep-rooted scepticism that
would now lie at the heart of his worldview. It was a moment to
see vividly the unwanted side of the celebrity he had craved, and
he used his time alone to sort the wheat from the chaff among
his social circle, separating intimate friends from vulture fans. The
group of friends with which he surrounded himself would become
ever more important as a blanket of protection from the predatory
world.

Finally, in late January, he felt himself strong enough to cancel
his voyage to the Far East and return to New York, and then he and
Jack sailed for England, and Goldenhurst, and home.

CURTAIN

ACT THREE

SCENE ONE

"You can't cope adequately with your successes", declares Larita in *Easy Virtue*, "unless you realise your failures." Soon she would be proved cruelly prophetic.

For a while it had seemed as if nothing could dent public enthusiasm for Noël's work. Almost all of his back catalogue had stayed either in amateur production or on tour, and Kate Cutler had even deigned to join a tour of *The Vortex*, memories of her walk-out long forgotten. By the end of 1926 the newspapers reported that over three thousand performances of Noël Coward's plays had been given worldwide.[1] His literary reputation in Europe, where audiences were better acquainted with farces by Feydeau or the light comedy of Sacha Guitry, was even higher than in Britain. The distinguished German critic Alfred Kerr wrote that he had laughed for half an hour after the "breathtaking" *Hay Fever* and rated Noël among the top three European playwrights.[2] But in London approbation seemed to be on the turn, and Basil Dean thought it was Noël's own fault: "much of the ill-natured criticism that Noël suffered at this time was brought on by his youthful display of indifference to public opinion [. . .] his sang-froid on [opening nights] was mistaken for conceit and alerted the galleryites for counter-tactics. He sat in a stage-box in full view of the audience, reading telegrams handed to him by a deferential secretary."[3]

On his return to England he flung himself back into work with renewed fervour, beginning and then abandoning any number of projects; there are fragments in that year's notebooks for "high comedies" called *Day By Day* and *The Higher The Fewer*, both set in a theatre.[4] He also spent much of 1927 working on a novel called *Charade*, telling Arnold Bennett that he had "written 25,000 words but had destroyed it because it was done too hastily and carelessly".[5] The unfinished manuscript chronicles the life of a child performer called Sophie who acts in "fairy plays" and whose family runs a boarding house.[6] The impression is of a mind writing on autobiographical autopilot. His early and phenomenal fame meant that he lacked a real guide: a figure such as Somerset Maugham, twenty-five years his senior and a prime candidate for literary mentor, was now his competition or even his equal. Noël seems to have had no premonition, as he signed off on a trio of West End premieres for 1927, that he was about to put before the public a series of plays that would be found wanting in comparison to his previous successes. Partly he had given in to the persuasion of Basil Dean, who would direct two of the three and who seems to have thought the name of Noël Coward secure enough a money-spinner to merit the staging of any script that bore it. Noël also needed the money: on top of domestic expansion, he was funding not only friends and close family, but the livelihoods of an aunt or two.

The Marquise, written for Marie Tempest while on retreat in Virginia the previous year, opened on 16 February, the very day of his return to London, and had mixed reviews but a respectable run, Tempest's performance disguising what Noël later admitted were serious weaknesses in the glibness of the plot's untangling. He began a play called *Home Chat* on 28 June, finished it on 6 July, and it appeared on stage in October.[7] Named for the women's weekly magazine, it began with a train crash that sets off false rumours of an affair between two travellers, she married, he engaged, who do nothing to dispel the gossip in order to shock their respectable families, even enacting a passionate love scene which they know will be overheard. Eventually the woman, Janet Ebony, falls happily in love with someone else and goes off to live with him – not that the family believes *that*, either. The actors were sluggish, lines were forgotten, and there were boos from the audience that became louder when Noël appeared on the stage. "We expected better", somebody called from the audience, to which Noël replied, "So did I".[8] He intended the retort to refer to the manners of the audience, but many of the reviews hailed the honesty of his self-criticism: "he is", wrote *The Era*, "the one person to blame for a rather dull evening in the theatre."[9]

After thirty-eight performances *Home Chat* was closed (a 2016 revival was acclaimed as a "forgotten feminist piece" that showed

"Coward as the firebrand of his day").[10] The critics began to be more excited about the writer Frederick Lonsdale who, a leading librettist for the musical comedies of Noël's youth, had had a resonant success with his play *On Approval*: much was written about how Maugham and Coward were "yielding the central place in the limelight" to Lonsdale.[11] It was Noël's first London failure, and he and Jack escaped London to attend a production of *The Marquise* in Vienna on 4 November.[12] Flummoxed by the German translation, they were amazed to find the whole thing was being staged in modern dress. "It was somewhat shocking", Jack thought, "to see the heroine on a motorcycle, clad from head to foot in leather."[13]

But everyone had high hopes for *Sirocco*, a play written in 1921 on his very first visit to New York, and due to open in London on 24 November. "I have a feeling", Basil Dean told him, "that [it] may be the best success."[14] It was a catastrophe. For years the title was used as theatrical shorthand for failure: "How was it last night?" "Sirocco." Noël had revised the script and, fatally, the production was advertised as being of a new work. Set in Northern Italy and named for the strong Mediterranean wind from the Sahara said to make people irritable, *Sirocco* is about an affair between Sirio, an Italian painter, and Lucy, a married Englishwoman. They cause a mild scandal when dancing together at the central act's *fiesta*, which was staged with lavish spectacle. In the end, in a combination of freedom and despair, Lucy leaves both her husband and Sirio (revealed as a cad in the cold light of day) for an independent life in Paris, although the play, a prototype for *Easy Virtue*, is ambivalent as to where this newfound freedom will lead her.

That *Sirocco* was staged at Daly's Theatre, just off Leicester Square and previously devoted almost exclusively to musical comedies and operetta, was the first hint that all would not be well: the theatre's debt-ridden manager, James White, had poisoned himself five months before. Ivor Novello, despite disliking the script, had taken the lead role; Basil Dean had laughed openly in Noël's face at the suggestion that the author himself could be cast as an irresistibly attractive Italian. That year Novello had starred in two successful films directed by Alfred Hitchcock, *The Lodger* and *Downhill*, appearing bare chested in the latter. His presence guaranteed a crackle of almost hysterical excitement in the audience, many of whom had been queueing for first-night tickets since eight in the morning and, come curtain-up, were already exhausted. Nevertheless, he was expecting a great success, soothed by the ease of rehearsals and by early praise during previews, when his dressing room was thronged with friends who predicted a hit on the scale of *The Vortex*.

On the first night, the passionate love scenes of *Sirocco* were greeted with gales of laughter. There were boos at the end of the first and second acts. The third-act fight scene saw Novello throwing his co-stars around the stage, breaking crockery, and sweeping out with the line: "I go to my mother". The audience howled.[15] The final curtain calls were, said one reporter, "as exciting as a bull fight".[16] There was much appreciation for Frances Doble, the female lead, and the audience called repeatedly for "Bunny" (her nickname). Basil Dean stood in the wings positively beaming at the noise, which he had mistaken for rapturous cheering, and he told the perplexed stage management to raise the curtain again and again. Finally, Noël came on, shook hands with the lead actors, bowed to a storm of boos, and left. "He should not", continued the reporter, "have come on again and made a speech. The noisy members of the audience would have none of him."[17] He was shouted down by cries of "rubbish" and calls for "Bunny". A man in the stalls got to his feet and yelled at the booers in the gallery: "Be quiet you swine!"[18] Noël later described Doble bravely responding of her own accord to shouts for her name, but many thought it contemptible of him to have pushed forward, and hidden behind, someone at whom the audience was less likely to jeer. On the verge of tears, she began her prepared speech: "This is the happiest moment of my life. . ." Then Dean, finally cottoning on to what had happened, burst onto the stage in a temper and tried a speech of his own: "Ladies and gentlemen, if there *are* any gentlemen in the house. . .?"[19] The crowd was still shouting at him as the orchestra began to play the National Anthem.

One member of the cast thought the furore had threatened real danger: "the audience were really terrifying".[20] The actor Raymond Massey claimed to have witnessed "three different fist fights" after the show, and went backstage to find Noël sitting "with a rather sad

smile on his face. 'Isn't it charming?' he said. 'Such enthusiasm.'"[21]
Noël afterwards insisted that, as he left the theatre to drown his
sorrows at a stoic party held at Ivor Novello's flat, people spat at
him in fury. Also at the party was Edward Marsh, Winston Churchill's private secretary, who pronounced himself "seldom more
impressed than by the dispassionate courage, free from all trace of
self-pity, with which the two routed aspirants, neither of whom
would have been surprised to be told that he was irreparably done
for, discussed the failure and its causes".[22] The next morning Noël
was fully intending leave the country; by lunchtime he had cannily
decided the best thing to do was to be seen enjoying himself at The
Ivy for lunch, where he found Novello at a nearby table, genuinely
and infectiously cheery in the middle of an admiring crowd. Novello was loyal ever afterwards: "I must say Noël behaved superbly.
He was not going to let us face it alone. [. . .] I couldn't help
seeing the funny side of it all. I wanted to step forward and say to
the audience: 'Listen, dears, this is not the French Revolution.'"[23]
But he nevertheless thought *Sirocco* a death-blow to his career and
temporarily abandoned theatre for the movies.

The vociferous reaction to *Sirocco* is still hard to explain. "It looked
remarkably like the work of a 'claque'", argued one reporter. "I
do not see how it could have been otherwise. It was too well
organised. [. . .] I have long been aware that there is an 'anti-Ivor'
claque."[24] There may have been a hefty mismatch between Novello's
brooding silent presence on film and his flamboyant performance
on the stage, where he was barely experienced. His sexuality was
an open secret (film critics sneered at his "effeminacy") and the
uproar that greeted his portrayal of a red-blooded Italian could
have had a homophobic edge. The notion of theatrical etiquette had
also been a comparatively recent development. Not that long ago
Somerset Maugham, who publicly supported Noël over *Sirocco*, had
been jeered at the premiere of *The Circle*, and Henry James had been
booed off the stage at the opening night of his play *Guy Domville*,
thirty years before.

Some critics went back to see *Sirocco* again and many published
more temperate write-ups. Novello was "brilliant", the third act
"redeemed all that preceded", the evening left "a very definite

impression, despite its faults".[25] St. John Ervine in the *Observer*, unaware that the work was seven years old, argued that *Sirocco* was a sign of Noël's having matured, that the writing was a moral tract against the false allure of romance, and that the audience had, in effect, taken at face value what was clearly ironic. "The evening seemed to be a sad one, but it will probably prove to be the turning-point in Mr Coward's career. I regard *Sirocco* as the most significant and hopeful play he has yet produced."[26] J. M. Barrie told Noël that it was a "brilliant piece of work [. . .] the best of your things so far".[27] But the death rattle had sounded. At the second performance only two stalls seats were sold before noon and *Sirocco* closed after three weeks.[28] "I fear", wrote one columnist, "that those who have been prophesying that one day Noël Coward will write something really big are likely to turn out very minor prophets."[29]

In the end, Noël enjoyed telling the story of the first night of *Sirocco*, but he went through the following weeks in a blur of anger and distress. Matters were made worse by the fact that, in the last months of 1927, first *The Marquise* and then *Fallen Angels* opened unsuccessfully in America. He fought hard to cancel his next engagement, not least because Basil Dean was once again to be director and the partnership by now seemed cursed. This was to be an acting role in the American playwright Samuel Behrman's *The Second Man* – already a hit on Broadway with the Lunts. About a novelist with whom two women fall in love, it had appealed to Noël as a good vehicle for his talents, and a production had been on the cards for some time. The producers would not release him from the contract, and so he gritted his teeth, hoping to heal emotional bruises by losing himself in work. Expecting to be pelted with abuse on the first night, which fell on 23 January 1928, he was pleasantly surprised to gain an entrance round, and even more pleased when it was evident that the play was going down well. Noël's critical bête noir, Hannen Swaffer, barged his way into the dressing rooms after the show. "I've always said you could act better than you write", he pronounced, to which Noël shot back: "And I've always said the same about you."[30] More than one critic thought "S. N. Behrman" (who in reality sat in the stalls mightily pleased with the performance) was simply a pseudonym of Noël's, employed to save face.

Basil Dean, whom Noël half blamed for the pile-up of disasters, wrote to him: "what an impression your performance made upon me. It was one of supreme distinction, and in the true line of descent from the best sources of English comedy acting."[31] Their friendship had survived the year's buffetings but their professional relationship had not, and they would never work together again.

Scene Two

In other respects life in the late 1920s was happier and more profitable. Goldenhurst had expanded into a comfortable retreat. Violet pootled on, deaf enough to have mistaken the booing at *Sirocco* for enthusiastic cheering. Gladys Calthrop had returned from New York, her relationship with Eva Le Gallienne over. She had designed the sets for *The Second Man* and shuttled between London, where she kept a cold studio flat in Clerkenwell, and Kent, where she purchased a converted mill close to Goldenhurst – eventually she became the partner of Noël's gardener, Patience Erskine. She was a striking fixture at first nights, with her black bob and fashionable clothes, "her head held so high", Jeffery Amherst remembered, "one wondered if she might not be in danger of falling over backwards".[32] She took to driving her open-topped sports car haphazardly around London with her three Siamese cats on the back seat and in February 1928, her mind elsewhere, found herself stopped by a policeman on Buckingham Palace Road. For some time, and without realising, she had been driving happily along amid the funeral procession of Field Marshal Haig.

One excitement that had promised to soothe Noël's theatrical failures was the world of silent film, which had yet to be entirely ousted by the talkies. Three of Noël's plays – *The Queen Was in the Parlour*, *The Vortex*, and *Easy Virtue* – were filmed in 1927, although it was a fool's errand to reduce the dialogue to a series of brief intertitles (provided not by Noël but by writers such as Eliot Stannard or Roland Pertwee). *Easy Virtue* was filmed on location in Nice and directed by Alfred Hitchcock, Noël's exact contemporary, increasingly bankable after the success of *The Lodger*. Hitchcock later took credit for one of the more absurd intertitles, which appeared as Larita spotted a press photographer: "Shoot. There's nothing left to kill."[33] All three of the films suffered badly from censorship, which at times could make the Lord Chamberlain's views on the theatre seem positively louche. Ireland banned *Easy Virtue* altogether and in *The Vortex* an avowedly heterosexual Nicky Lancaster (played by Novello after Noël's screen test proved unpromising) was shown merely pretending to take drugs. Nicky's fiancée was played by Frances Doble, her double act with Novello now cursed by *Sirocco*. Adrian Brunel, directing, could do little either with the bowdlerised scenario or with his lead actress, Willette Kershaw, who lived on a diet of vegetable extract pellets and could not manage takes longer than twenty seconds.[34]

Noël, appalled at the changes to his scripts, left the world of film alone, and was instead determined to devote himself to another, long-planned, revue for Charles Cochran, who would hear no talk of cancellation despite recent debacles. As performances of *The Second Man* rolled happily on into 1928, the revue came to dominate the year. Back in 1926, Noël had begun to think seriously about writing a three-act musical comedy called *Star Dust*, a play-within-a-play conceived on a vast scale and featuring over forty named characters. Once again, he was satirising the theatre: the show was to feature a theatrical troupe rehearsing a romantic comedy called *Mary Make-Believe* about high-society holidaymakers gambling on the Riviera. Early drafts and sketches show a progenitor of Michael Frayn's *Noises Off*, with an irascible director rehearsing a group of highly strung actors: "You'll never get a laugh if you say it like that." "It's not funny anyway."[35] Abandoning *Star Dust*, Noël salvaged two of its songs, "Mary Make-Believe" and "A Room With a View", for the Cochran show, which became *This Year of Grace*. Elsie April, notating all the music, had her work cut out.

Of all Noël's revues so far staged, this was the one that most showed off its creator as a one-man band, writer of all the sketches, lyrics, and music, and even taking credit for some of the choreography, ostensibly by Max Rivers and by the Austrian dancer Tilly Losch. A Cochran–Coward revue now had a house style, with designs by Gladys Calthrop, a cast that included Maisie Gay and

Douglas Byng, a chorus of "Mr Cochran's Young Ladies", and what was said to be eight hundred gowns. The first night in London was on 22 March. That evening Noël began to rattle through *The Second Man* at such speed, in order to appear onstage at the revue's finale, that the audience was left reeling. Meanwhile, at the Pavilion, the curtain rose on *This Year of Grace*, to reveal a little boy standing outside a London tube station. He began to whistle, which set the whole company whirling into a dance.

Dance was the chief means by which Noël was able to explore the revue's unifying theme: the tug of war between old and new, sentiment and satire. Jazz ballets were contrasted with traditional Viennese waltzes and polkas that Tilly Losch danced not only on her feet but on her hands. Serious ballets were set against outrageous parodies of Diaghilev's choreography and of a touring group called La Chauve-Souris. Acrobats dangled over the stage and a song-and-dance routine was given by a child banjo player from St Louis, a "diminutive Negro comedian", as one paper had it, called "Snowball".[36] His real name was Edwin Harris: just ten years old, he was already a staple of revues in Paris and on Broadway. The stage name was frequently used as a pseudonym (alongside "black lamb" or "smoky kid") for Black performers of the day.

The sketches included depictions of the holidaying set on the Venice lido contrasted with a portrait of the lower-middle classes on a beach trip ("Is Mr Coward not a trifle superior here?" asked *The Era*).[37] Maisie Gay was a redoubtable cross-Channel swimmer; Maisie Gay was a policewoman chatting to a colleague: "My husband went to Australia." "On business?" "No, on purpose." One of the most successful scenes, and the most canny, was a series of brief parodies, updated as the run progressed, in which Noël skewered a raft of contemporary playwrights, showing how figures such as Barrie or Lonsdale would have treated a stock scenario. The pièce de résistance was when he turned the satire on himself in a parody of *Sirocco*: to a storm of booing, a leading lady fervently re-enacted Frances Doble's infamous first-night speech: "this is the happiest moment of my life!"

An ability to laugh at himself seemed to mend overnight what had threatened to be a permanent rupture between Noël and the critics, who heaped praise upon *This Year of Grace.* On and on it went: "the unmistakable trade mark of Noël Coward's genius"; "the most brilliant and generally satisfying revue I have ever seen". George Gershwin, on a visit to London that year, attended twice in a row with his brother, Ira, who wrote in his diary that it was a "great production for one man to do".[38] And in the *Observer* St. John Ervine, after finding a superlative for each letter of the alphabet bar "X", which stumped him, professed that "if any person comes to me and says that there has ever, anywhere in the world, been a better revue than this, I shall publicly tweak his nose".[39] Noël wrote to him: "I am broken hearted that you didn't like my revue – your notice in the *Observer* seemed so terse and cold. Bless you for it."[40]

On one point though, the critics were agreed: that while Noël's lyrics were brilliant, his melodies were unmemorable. Ironically, many of the revue's songs have remained among his most popular, their context forgotten: "Mary Make-Believe"; "World Weary" (added for the New York transfer); and most of all the dreamy idyll of "A Room With a View", sung through a large window by Jessie Matthews and Sonnie Hale who, scandalously, fell in love during the production. The last, its title borrowed from Forster's 1908 novel, Noël had written while recuperating in Hawaii and its swooping melody – "We'll bill and we'll coo, oo-oooh" – catches the smooth glide of the Hawaiian steel guitar, already popular in Broadway shows. The song was said to have particularly delighted the Prince of Wales, who asked for it to be played nine times during a charity ball at Surrey in June.[41]

Noël rushed to record six of the numbers before any other performers could get near the microphone, and while critics complained that he didn't "have the knack of singing to the wax" and lacked the vocal talents of Sonnie Hale, he had made the songs indivisible from, even unhelpfully shackled to, his own idiosyncratic delivery.[42] Jack Wilson was dismissive – "let's face it, he's not very good" – but the records are the first preservation of his aged and fluting sound, his rolled 'r's and elastic, elongated, vowels.[43] He sang with a head, rather than with a chest, voice, allowing him to tip into falsetto with almost no break, his vibrato a fluttering pulse that thins and cloaks the sound, his singing as crimped as his diction. As Penelope Fitzgerald has it, giving Noël a cameo in her novel *At Freddie's*, it was an "unmistakable toneless half-voice, a kind of satire on itself, blandly enticing".[44]

Most striking of all was the number "Dance, Little Lady". The little lady was danced by Lauri Devine as a contemporary flapper, unsmiling and vapid, while Sonnie Hale sang to her as a warning: "Though you're only seventeen | Far too much of life you've seen | Syncopated child . . ." Around her a crowd of dancers loomed from blackness, wearing papier-mâché masks designed by the 24-year-old Oliver Messel. It was a host of vacuous faces, eyebrows raised, smiling in a rictus grin. "Dance, dance, dance little lady | Youth is fleeting to the rhythm | Beating in your mind . . ." A sighting of a haunting Messel specimen from another show – grey-haired, heavy browed, as if from a Greek play – had given Noël the idea for "Dance, Little Lady".[45] But where Messel's masks usually allowed performers' eyes to appear, the collection he designed for *This Year of Grace* had painted eyes of wide clownish surprise, empty, even drugged, with dilated pupils swimming in a sea of white. Monochrome photographs do not show the bright colours of the dresses, made of a metallic celluloid that shone horribly in the stage lighting. Sonnie Hale's evening suit was made of oilcloth: stiff, shiny, imprisoning.

The decade's tension between the private and public self had given rise to a swathe of masking. Messel's had appeared in Diaghilev's ballets and were already a fixture of Cochran revues. Eugene O'Neill had recently thrilled Broadway with *The Great God Brown*, which made use of masks to demarcate its characters' different personas; Pirandello's eponymous six characters, searching for their author, were likewise masked at their 1924 premiere. "Dance, Little Lady" was reminiscent of a moment in E. Nesbit's *The Enchanted Castle*, favourite of Noël's childhood books, in which children put on a theatrical performance wearing "paper masks [. . .] their eyebrows were furious with lamp-black frowns – their eyes the size, and almost the shape, of five-shilling pieces".[46] And masks were familiar and resonant to contemporary audiences for other reasons: thousands of facially disfigured soldiers in London wore them, either fashioned in plaster by artists, or created through skin-grafts by pioneering plastic surgeons.

"Dance, Little Lady" is a tarantella, to be performed with a frenzy and hysteria designed to ward off horror. There is a sharp tension between music and lyrics. The former, its stolid 4/4 beat disrupted by tango-like cross-rhythms, caught the age; the latter mournfully admonished it, half sympathetic, half goading. But the initial blitheness of the tune (borrowed, Noël admitted, from Liza Lehmann's "In a Persian Garden") morphs into something sinister. The words hiss with sibilance — "So obsessed with second best" — and the folding and double-folding of internal rhyme create a distinct claustrophobia, as if the little lady were trapped in the lyrics' mirrored corridors. The syncopation can make the music limp rather than dance, as the song attempts to wrest the flippant mask from the girl's face lest she wound herself on the jagged edges of life's offbeat rhythm: "And when the lights are starting to gutter | Dawn — through the shutter — | Shows you're living in a world of lies."

One unexpected but passionate admirer of *This Year of Grace* was Virginia Woolf who, now forty-six, was renowned in literary circles for *Mrs Dalloway* and *To the Lighthouse*. She had met Noël, at the introduction of Sibyl Colefax, in early March 1928, just as she was writing the final chapter, even the final pages, of *Orlando*, her love letter to Noël's Ebury Street neighbour Vita Sackville-West.[47] "Did I tell you about Noël Coward?" Woolf wrote to Sackville-West.

He is in search of culture and thinks Bloomsbury a kind of place of pilgrimage. Will you come and meet him? He is a miracle, a prodigy. He can sing, dance, write plays, act, compose, and I daresay paint — he rescued his whole family who kept boarding houses in Surbiton and they are now affluent, but on the verge of bankruptcy, because he spends so much on cocktails.[48]

The *tendresse* between them lasted, to Woolf's surprise. It was as if his flamboyance were contagious. "I fell in love with Noël Coward", she told Sackville-West, and to her sister she spoke of "Noël Coward — with whom I am slightly in love — Why?"[49] Her reaction is good proof that, although some would never find a personality such as Noël's anything other than irritating, to others his company could be magnetic. The days of adolescent gaucherie had been taken over by a manner that, given his wealth and success, could hardly avoid a certain grandeur, and, given his age, was not free of self-aware precocity, but which also had charm, scintillating conversation and, as many testified, a surprising sincerity and seriousness. He had already perfected a social technique that would serve him well through life: by praising himself with such disarmingly blatant honesty, he gave the odd impression of humility. As the composer Ned Rorem would put it, many decades later, "his immodesty is generous".[50] Noël's was an odd mixture of wearing his heart on his sleeve and burying it deep within, so that necessary reticence about his private life combined with social gregariousness to create an intriguing combination of florid candour and unknowable reserve. For all his consciously moulded manner, he could also give the impression, in his emotional extravagance, of being entirely artless.

Unexpected as the friendship now seems, there are aspects of Woolf's personality that make the union a natural one. She had seen her fair share of 1920s party-going and had already drafted her play *Freshwater*, a satirical farce affectionately lampooning Victorian eccentrics. Both she and Noël had attended, and disliked, the premiere of Sitwell's *Façade*. *Orlando* combined satire, theatricality, even camp; there may be something revue-like about its series of scenes and set-pieces flashing across the centuries, its title character flinging off shackles of time and gender. Her meeting with Noël came just as she brought her time-travelling hero, now heroine, into 1928, and she sent Noël a copy not with an inscription, but with his name specifically added by hand – "if he will allow" – to the list of acknowledgements.[51] What she wished to acknowledge is uncertain: a sense, perhaps, that he was the personification of this year of grace, 1928. Noël read the novel later in the year, and wrote to her in gushing but genuine admiration: "I am still hot and glowing with it [. . .] If ever I could write one page to equal in beauty your "Frozen Thames" description [. . .] I should feel that I really was a writer."[52]

Noël could cherish his outsiderness even as he tried to woo the establishment, whom he wanted simultaneously to join and criticise. His was a surprising approach to the Bloomsbury Group, whose combination of intellectuality and modernism encapsulated much that he disliked. But the Group's social and sexual attitudes may have appealed to him, Woolf's fame was increasing, and he was clearly keen – at a time in his career when his revues and songs were more successful than his plays – to be accepted as a serious writer. "My real ambition" he told St. John Ervine, "is to write good stuff and not fritter away my talents on flippant nonsense."[53] Bloomsbury would offer acceptance as a creator of something other than frippery, with Woolf's encouragement clearly valuable. "I think you ought to bring off something", she told him, "that will put these cautious creeping novels that one has to read silently in an arm chair deep, deep in the shade."[54] Other forays into the Group were social successes: the artist Dora Carrington was "distinctly taken with Noël Coward" on their meeting that summer. She found him "gloomy and fascinating, with a face that shone like Bronze. I expect he uses a Pink-Brown powder."[55]

Carrington was not alone in being surprised by Noël's seriousness. He was dejected by British theatre, and to make matters worse, a Dutch production of *Fallen Angels* had been banned by the Burgomaster of The Hague. "[Noël] says the English theatre is so degraded", Woolf reported, "that he will not produce any serious work here in future. He says the middle classes make his life a burden. Old women in Gloucester write and abuse him for immorality. [. . .] So he is off to produce his plays in New York. There he makes £1000 a week, and he can say what he likes."[56] Three decades before the press officer of the Royal Court Theatre coined the phrase "angry young man", Noël was young and angry, disillusioned with the prurience of British society and determined actively to demolish establishment figures. "It becomes necessary", he fumed in an unpublished essay, "immediately to eliminate from one's mind the belief that Shaw and Ibsen are in the least important [. . .] The attitude of middle class England towards her few young embryonic artists is deplorable. [. . .] The fact that the war opened several windows wide, plunging the youth of every country involved in it into an appalling draught, must not be admitted for a moment – the grown-ups continue to insist blindly that everything is as it was, they wrap this threadbare shawl of consolation round their ageing shoulders, and slap the young ones a little harder."[57]

Noël was frequently described in the press as "that scintillating young modernist", but he thought nothing of trouncing what he called "the modern extremists".[58] His anti-intellectualism had taken firm route, and he was mistrustful of radical experiment in art or music. The following decade he would even bother to produce a book called *Spangled Unicorn*, in order to revive the figure of Hernia Whittlebot, now accompanied by a whole phalanx of mock-modernists (parodies of figures such as Radclyffe Hall or T. S. Eliot easily discernible). Partly he thrilled to any excuse to coin amusing dismissals of modern art without engaging with the art itself, much of which he thought "reminiscent of the average child's less successful efforts in a kindergarten drawing class".[59]

But his dismissal of modernism had a complex texture. Three times he had sat through Igor Stravinsky's ballet *Les Noces*, and his initial irritation with audience members, who he thought were pretending to like a ballet deemed fashionable by the intelligentsia, faded on prolonged exposure to the score: "those relentless rhythms – the angular discords of voice and pianos were undoubtedly stimulating – there was an almost fierce inevitability in the primitive semi religious monotony of the groupings [. . .] I was splendidly, tremendously moved." He would change his mind again, but conceded "that a few years hence I [may] be as genuinely appreciative of 'Les Noces' as I am of Gauguin at the present moment". In April 1931 Stravinsky would write to Noël suggesting a collaboration. Lorn Loraine sent a reply – "I have been unable to persuade Mr Noël Coward to enter into a collaboration with you" – and suggested that Stravinsky try H. G. Wells.[60] Quite what Stravinsky, who was then living in Paris, had in mind, is uncertain (his letter is lost). But Noël's revue ballets of the 1920s do not make the venture so unlikely. Stravinsky would compose for jazz band and for a Broadway revue, and Cole Porter had wanted to study with him.

In private writing Noël praised Wyndham Lewis and held up performances of Chekhov as his most entirely satisfying evenings in the theatre. Joyce's *Ulysses* he found a "work of tremendous force and virility" that had discovered "fresh psychological pastures"; it was the pale imitators of Joyce's style, as he perceived them, whom he deplored, not least the "painful gibberings" of Gertrude Stein.[61] And while Noël might have rejected the suggestion that his lyrics were indebted to T. S. Eliot (who also disliked Stein's writing and dismissed the term "modernism"), allusions accrue, especially in "Dance, Little Lady".* In their social history of interwar Britain, *The Long Week-End*, Robert Graves and Alan Hodge did not list Coward in opposition to the modernists of the day, but banded them together as among the 1920s' quintessential chroniclers: "Coward was the dramatist of disillusion, as Eliot was its tragic poet, Aldous Huxley its novelist, and James Joyce its prose epic-writer."[62]

Virginia Woolf wrote to Noël late in 1928: "Some of the things in *This Year of Grace* struck me on the forehead like a bullet. And what's more, I remember them and see them enveloped in atmosphere – works of art in short."[63]

Scene Three

Arthur Coward was now seventy-two, Violet sixty-five, and family life was not unquarrelsome. "How much better", Violet wrote to Noël in 1928, "to have [died] while you still loved me, and no crowds of grand friends and success had come between us! You think a lot of my making you unhappy but nothing at all of your making me unhappy." Nor was Jack's presence pacifying: "I remember twice before", she continued, "when Jack ran to you, to

---

* "And when the lights are starting to gutter | Dawn – through the shutter. . ." strikingly echoes Eliot's "Preludes" (1917): "And the light crept up between the shutters | And you heard the sparrows in the gutters. . .". Coward's song "Lorelei" is sung by a Rhinemaiden, her waters thronged with polluting liners whose sailors are no longer enchanted by her siren-call; the Rhinemaidens appear, in oil-clogged waters, in Eliot's *The Waste Land* (1922), with an identical metric scheme. "Lorelei" also recalls the "mermaids singing" in Eliot's "The Love Song of J. Alfred Prufrock", the vacillations of its narrator – "And time yet for a hundred indecisions, | And for a hundred visions and revisions" – finding another parallel in Coward's "Mary Make-Believe": "Her indecisions | Quite prevent her visions | Coming true."

make mischief between us, and I should have been warned. [. . .] I feel inside me that nothing will alter your opinion of me now, so there is nothing more to be said. I believe in your love, I must, for it is all I have left in the world, but it is not what it was, and I feel terribly alone."[64] Finally, Violet, whose temper could cool as rapidly as it could heat, was persuaded that Ebury Street could be sold, and although Noël continued to rent his suite of rooms in the building, Goldenhurst became the Cowards' chief residence. While Arthur was happy to potter about the garden, Violet was at a loose end, her life made fractious by the permanent installation in the house of her sister Vida.

Noël's brother, Eric, was trying at twenty-three to carve a niche in the world free not only from his brother's considerable shadow, but from the openness with which the family admitted to his lack of direction or talent. It has been suggested that he too may have been homosexual; his relationship with his first cousin, Leslie Makeham, was one of great intimacy. His relationship with his brother was distant, a mixture of emulative hero-worship and frustrated resentment. Often he made sure to avoid their paths crossing: "Leslie and I will come down on the 1.15, Noël will have plenty of time to have departed." As if in an attempt to grasp at a fleck of individuality, something for himself in a life consigned to the indexes of his brother's biographies, he added a small flourish to the spelling of his name, insisting upon "Erik". Eventually he found an unlikely job as a tea-planter in what was then Ceylon. The suspicion that the family was ridding itself of a cumbersome nuisance was never far from the surface. He wrote to his mother: "The obvious thing is for me to go out. You think so. [. . .] Noël is apparently prepared to provide £350 provided he hears nothing further on the subject. Well and good. [. . .] It's kind of Noël to be so liberal and I really do think he is anxious for me to go, but his hardness so gets the better of him that he trusts nobody and nothing that isn't a stone cold certainty. I know he has a pretty poor opinion of me."[65]

Erik sailed in the summer. Jack Wilson suggested that an outbuilding at Goldenhurst be renovated into a home for the family so that Noël and his entourage could take over the house proper. This was a cue for prolonged, aggrieved, and not entirely unfounded, accusations that Noël was ashamed of his family and wished to banish them from sight. In the event, a grand new wing was added, doubling the size of Goldenhurst, and Noël and Jack lived in it quite happily, leaving the family snug in the main house. Escape was welcome, and on 2 June Noël went to New York for a few weeks to prepare for the Broadway opening of *This Year of Grace*, in which he was to perform himself, taking over the roles played in England by Sonnie Hale. He added new sketches – one stuck its knife, rather disloyally, into Gladys Calthrop's work with the Civic Repertory Company – and spent time at a dancing school to get his choreography up to scratch. He returned to America in October for rehearsals, although the opening was delayed for three weeks while he recovered from a brief spate in hospital. "NOËL COWARD OPERATED ON", the *New York Times* reported. "Dramatist stricken in London. [. . .] The nature of the operation was not revealed."[66] The affliction in question was haemorrhoids.

After a preview run in Baltimore, the revue finally opened in Manhattan on 7 November. The dress rehearsal had been beset by every possible calamity, and the whole company, which now numbered seventy performers, became convinced the show was going to be a disaster. Jack Wilson "went home and drank some gin, took a bath, put on a dinner jacket, and went back to the Selwyn Theatre prepared for the worst".[67] The show was a smash hit. "Unless someone in America", wrote one reporter, "is able to do something that approximates Mr Coward's feat, we shall always feel that it was a mistake to break away from England back there in 1775."[68]

Noël never thought himself as good as Sonnie Hale in the show (a view with which both Charles Cochran and Jack Wilson agreed). An addition to the American cast, taking over Maisie Gay's comedy numbers, was Beatrice Lillie, known for her parodies of old-fashioned performance styles. Nerves in rehearsal made her, Noël thought, insufferable, but as she settled into the run a truer, calmer, and above all funny character emerged, and they struck up a devoted friendship, leading to press speculation of a romance. They made a wonderful double act, as when Lillie knocked on the door of Noël's room, feeling mischievous: "Hotel detective.

Have you got a gentleman in your room?" "Just a minute", Noël
replied. "I'll ask him." The two of them became the toast of New
York and her performance was acclaimed as comic genius. The
revue continued happily over Christmas until, in February 1929,
Noël was admitted to the Park East Hospital for another operation;
perhaps it was a recurrence of the previous year's unfortunate
malady, although his doctor gave interviews to the press about the
"severity" of his illness, and recommended he leave the production
and travel to recuperate. Noël sailed for a holiday in the Bahamas
in March 1929, and returned to England the following month, by
which time plans were well afoot for the final opening of this torrid
and transformative decade.[69]

The success of the revue was a prime opportunity for Noël to
open a new play that would silence for ever the boos of *Sirocco*.
Critics were despairing at the dearth of distinguished writers repre-
sented in the West End, which had all but ignored Ibsen's centenary
in favour of a plethora of musicals. There had been no recent
premieres by Barrie or Galsworthy; Shaw had written nothing since
Saint Joan; and Pinero's *A Private Room* had closed after three weeks.
But to be sole author of a musical had been an ambition of Noël's
for over a decade. He was perhaps looking, as the atmosphere
of post-war hedonism darkened into poverty and political crisis,
to reinvent his reputation as something other than a purveyor of
jagged modernity, perceiving a forthcoming need for the false
security of an imagined past. Anthony Hope's Ruritanian adventure
novels still sold well, and his mantle had been taken up by writers
such as Dornford Yates and Edgar Rice Burroughs. Georgette Heyer
was beginning her career and the 1930s would see the foundation
of Mills and Boon.

A scenario had been simmering at the back of Noël's mind for
some time, but had come to fruition in the summer of 1928 on
a visit to Gladys Calthrop's family solicitor. There he had heard a
new recording of Strauss's *Die Fledermaus* (1874) and on the journey
home had to pull the car to the side of the road in order to sketch
out a story, set in England and Austro-Hungary, that would enable
him to revive the genre of Viennese operetta. The action was told
in flashback: in 1929, a young woman called Dolly Chamberlain is

torn between her love for a poor musician and her engagement to a wealthy young man. Her predicament mirrors that of her friend, the elderly Sarah, Lady Shayne, who is shown half a century before, engaged to a dull nobleman, and eloping to Vienna with her music teacher, Carl Linden. Carl is eventually killed in a duel, leading Sarah to become "Sari Linden", a famous European singer performing her dead lover's music.[70] Soon Noël had the title: *Bitter Sweet*.

To resuscitate the form of operetta was a risky move. The genre had largely given way to revues and musicals. British composers of light opera such as Edward German and Sidney Jones had been relegated unhappily to the old guard, and it had been over twenty years since the success of Lehár's *The Merry Widow*. (*Bitter Sweet* is exactly contemporary with *The Poisoned Kiss*, a forgotten "romantic extravaganza" by Ralph Vaughan Williams that is thought to owe something to Noël's revues, its "fairy-play" scenario really a dig at the Bright Young People.) But Noël was undaunted and *Bitter Sweet*, much of which was written on ocean liners, was finished in time to go into rehearsal in London at the end of May 1929, with Noël himself directing. The three acts were interspersed with over twenty musical numbers for which Elsie April's help had been once again indispensable, to the extent that she became the operetta's dedicatee. Noël's knowledge of harmony was so untechnical that presumably his own accompaniments, worked out by ear as he went along, were neatened and notated by her, before being handed over to the uncredited orchestrator, Ignatius de Orellana, who composed the overture.

The musical score is something of a genuine fake, in that many of the songs were self-consciously pastiche (as opposed to parody). While ostensibly a departure from the American musical, Noël's score is filtered through the world of a composer such as Jerome Kern, with whom he had attempted to collaborate. While Kern, who was of Czech descent, had openly renounced Mittel-European scenarios, his *Show Boat* (1927) follows a similar trajectory to *Bitter Sweet*, combining elements of vaudeville and operetta. But *Bitter Sweet* is not musical mimicry for its own sake. Many of the songs belong to the internal world of the story, having ostensibly been composed by Sari's lover, Carl. The music mirrors the time-travel of the scenario, painting the waltzes of Vienna in the 1870s, the music-hall ballads of London in the 1890s, and finally the foxtrots of the present day, by which time the waltzes have lost their triple-time lilt and curdled into jazz. An 1890s party scene featured not only "Tarara boom-de-ay" but a daring quartet called "The Green Carnation", satirising the symbol of homosexuality and aestheticism worn by Oscar Wilde and his circle.* "Haughty boys, naughty boys [. . .] we are the reason for the 'Nineties' being gay." The *Oxford English Dictionary* gives the lyric as the second traceable attestation of "gay" used to mean homosexual; Noël was moulding language under the guise of satire, linking gayness with gaiety.[71] The number, shamelessly unnecessary to the plot and only grudgingly passed by the Lord Chamberlain, would cause no scandal at all, perhaps because it was clearly a parody, perhaps because audiences did not know what was being parodied.

Noël had conceived the role of Sari as a vehicle for Gertrude Lawrence, but she was the first to concede that she could not carry the vocal demands, which were finally handed to Peggy Wood (then thirty-seven, and later to play the Mother Abbess in *The Sound of Music*). So often in Noël's career had a frantic rehearsal period led to unexpected success, that the smoothness with which *Bitter Sweet* fell into place made him uneasy. Trips to Europe to cast a foreign tenor as Carl were useless, despite a mischievous desire to see a potential singer called Hans Unterfucker with his name in lights in the West End. Unterfucking – and, indeed, Oberfucking – are villages in Northern Austria.

The first night in Manchester, on 2 July 1929, was a tumultuous success; the first night in London, on 18 July, slightly less so, and Noël refused to make a speech, telling fans at the stage door that he "only came on when they booed".[72] Evelyn Laye took the lead role for the American run – "she certainly does knock spots off the

---

* The green-dyed flower had been immortalised by Robert Hichens's 1894 novel *The Green Carnation*, which had been withdrawn from circulation and was not republished until 1948, although – through figures such as Robbie Ross, Philip Streatfeild, or Charles Scott Moncrieff – Coward may have had opportunities to read it.

wretched Peggy!" – and was making her Broadway debut.[73] Noël, never one to let personal sympathy disrupt professional ambition, removed from the role of Carl not one but two well-meaning European tenors whose English (and acting talent) left something to be desired. Over every detail of his productions he was now not only in control but ruthlessly in charge. "I've had to fight every step of the way", he wrote to his mother. "They wanted me to alter everything and I wouldn't, now of course they're delighted and say they <u>knew</u> it was a success all along!"[74] His relationship with Florenz Ziegfeld, who produced the Broadway run, went from bad to worse, and the final straw came when smoking was forbidden in the theatre during rehearsals. Jack Wilson swore that he witnessed Ziegfeld running down Seventh Avenue imploring Noël not to abandon the production.[75] Noël smoked during rehearsals.

Noël seemed to expect success and greeted it calmly, writing to his mother from the Boston previews: "They stood up and cheered and screamed and that was that, here are some notices." The letter is blasé, but Evelyn Laye remembered that he had taken his curtain call in floods of tears. The first night on Broadway, on 5 November, was out of control, and police were called to hold back the traffic on Sixth Avenue. Noël reported "a complete riot. It was probably the most distinguished first night ever seen in New York, some seats were sold for as much as $150 each! [. . .] When I came on at the end they went raving mad."[76]

Despite a gush from the *New York Times*, the American production ran for four months, but in the West End – where James Agate, invoking Wagner as the only precedent for Noël's dual talent as composer and librettist, acclaimed the operetta as "stupendous" – *Bitter Sweet* ran for two years.[77] As early as 1926 *The Stage* had reported that Noël could command £1,000 a week when working, and the long run of *Bitter Sweet* meant that this earning power could be sustained year-round. There were breathless reports of his annual £50,000 – equivalent in terms of twenty-first-century income to over £15 million a year – and Jack Wilson thought the estimates were conservative.[78] Noël had become the highest paid writer in the world.

There were said to be twelve marriages among members of the

Bitter Sweet company during the run, and Evelyn Laye eventually travelled to London to take over the role of Sari. When he was in Britain Noël would occasionally make surprise appearances in the crowd scenes wearing a long beard, in an attempt to enthuse the exhausted, cabin-feverish, 150-strong cast.[79] The show was seen by well over a million people: 2 per cent of the entire country, given the population of the day. The death of Sari's lover, though perceived as mawkish by some, struck a chord with many audience members a decade on from the First World War. "The whole thing", wrote Ivor Novello, who was himself returning to composition, "is so full of regret — not only for that darling lover [Carl] who died but for a vanished kindly silly darling age."[80]

Predictions at the time were that it "will be played long after some of the Coward plays are dated"; in reality *Bitter Sweet* has remained a period piece, embedded in its era.[81] But the songs have flown free, not least "Zigeuner", nodding to Lehár's operetta *Zigeunerliebe*; "If You Could Only Come With Me", its sinuous melody painting the silver ribbon of the Danube; and "I'll See You Again", which came into Noël's head while stuck in a New York traffic jam, a waltz that illumines an innocuous phrase by placing the rhythmic emphasis on the word "you". The operetta's sentimentality is leavened by the tension with which Noël's restoration of a rose-tinted past is contrasted with his portrait of an increasingly desperate present. Noël may be as guilty as his characters of viewing the past with nostalgia, but in doing so he allowed his portrayals of the modern world to be concomitantly more caustic. The freedom to live as she chooses comes at a price, and Sari watches a new generation make the same mistakes, ending the show with a "cracked, contemptuous laugh".

One of the evening's greatest successes was the song "If Love Were All", delivered by Manon, a former lover of Carl's whom he has spurned for Sari.

I believe the more you love a man,
The more you give your trust,
The more you're bound to lose.
Although when shadows fall

I think if only –
Somebody splendid really needed me
Someone affectionate and dear,
Cares would be ended if I knew that he
Wanted to have me near.
But I believe that since my life began
The most I've had is just
A talent to amuse.[82]

The phrase "talent to amuse", chosen for the title of Sheridan Morley's biography and inscribed on Noël's memorial in Westminster Abbey, has become inextricably linked with its creator, who would not sing even excerpts from the number himself until 1951, and never performed it complete. But it is certain, as John Lahr has written, that "Noël Coward never believed he had just a talent to amuse".[83] If there is autobiography in the song, it is in its emotional wistfulness, its pining loneliness, its sense of being a warning to Jack Wilson that the trust Noël had placed in him was slowly being abused. They were to spend much of the following year apart, and Noël would shortly send him a telegram: "DARLING BAYBAY, DARLING JACK | JUST A KLEPTOMANIAC | PINCHING GIFTS FROM POPPA'S HOUSE | LIKE A PREDATORY LOUSE." It was as if Noël could only address fault lines in Jack's behaviour, and his own, in comic form, or in a number designed for a nostalgic musical. Even an expression of love came in a jokey couplet: "STILL, ALTHOUGH YOU SNATCH AND GRAB, | POPPA LOVES HIS DARLING DAB."[84]

SCENE FOUR

Noël had sailed for Manhattan for the American production of *Bitter Sweet* on 5 October 1929, just a fortnight after the London Stock Exchange had crashed. Gladys was with him, as were her Siamese cats, in whose company she now always insisted on travelling. "New York is as exciting as ever", he had written to his mother from his "very expensive suite at the Ritz".[85] The Chrysler Building, a few blocks south-east of the hotel, had just been erected and on 16 October officially became the world's tallest structure. The company had travelled to Boston on 20 October, and *Bitter Sweet* opened its trial week at the Tremont Theatre two days later. The stock market wobbled badly, losing 11 per cent of its value, and bankers called emergency meetings. The final Boston performance was on 26 October, and Noël returned to Manhattan the following morning.

The next day became known as Black Monday, and the day after, during which 16 million shares were traded on the New York Stock Exchange, was Black Tuesday. Billions of dollars were lost. It was the largest and most devastating market crash in American history. Crowds gathered in Wall Street, and well-dressed gentlemen who had been up all night were seen fast asleep in restaurants. Hotels and gymnasia were full of temporarily erected beds allowing stock-brokers to camp out, and speculators drove their grand automobiles through Manhattan in an attempt to sell them for ready cash. The New York streets were in chaos, and newspapers were hard to come by, so paper boys yelled the headlines across town. It was rumoured (falsely) that bankers were flinging themselves off skyscrapers. Noël wrote to his mother: "There's been a complete disaster on the New York Stock Market, everybody is losing millions." His own financial security did not make him especially sympathetic to others' misfortune: "poor old Syrie [Maugham] has lost practically all she had, but it really serves them right for gambling. Thank God Jack has invested my money in gilt-edged securities and never speculated, so I'm perfectly safe, but it really is horrible, people hurling themselves off buildings like confetti."[86]

The 1920s were over, not only as a decade but as an era. The Great Depression had begun. Noël might have felt vindicated, much of his work having attempted to imply that the post-war lifestyle of decadence and excess – of which he had enjoyed more than his fair share – was unsustainable. Nor had he been entirely unaware of the economic realities of life beyond the West End. One sketch from *This Year of Grace* was "The Miners' Day-Leave", featuring a backdrop specially painted by the artist Rex Whistler that showed a Lowry-scape of dark satanic mills looming in the distance. Noël was often more politically engaged than he let on, but political engagement was no more part of the Coward package than was deep intellectuality, and he made efforts to remove both from his public image: the scene was firmly cut in the move from Manchester to London. In his grim song "City", written for Cochran's 1931 revue, he would nevertheless convey the soul-destroying effects of urban poverty on individuality amid the shiny new metropolises of the world:

Only one among millions
Life's a sad routine [. . .]
Lonely, living in shadow, part of a machine
Rising from despair, the buildings are leaning,
Nearer, nearer each day, pressing life away. [. . .]

Noise and speed are conspiring to crucify me
Ever making me crawl for my daily bread
Never letting me rest till my dreams are dead.[87]

Noël's most popular plays and songs were thought to sum up the flippant meaningless of the decade. But his work had an in-built awareness of the age's ephemerality. A song seemingly intended for *This Year of Grace* but eventually cut, was "The Dream is Over", ostensibly about the impermanence of love, but speaking of a wider shift from giddiness to depression. The 1920s had been a decade of instantaneous success leading to sudden fall. A generation of young writers and actors had become famous almost literally overnight, yet most of them were destined for obscurity, not least Sutton Vane and Frederick Lonsdale, Noël's chief rivals as leading playwrights. Neither Margaret Kennedy nor Michael Arlen would replicate the success of *The Constant Nymph* or *The Green Hat*. In 1955, *Harper's Magazine* would publish an article titled: "Whatever happened to Michael Arlen?" He was finally found, dying of cancer after ten years of writer's block.

Arlen's novel, so reflective of the decade's atmosphere, ended with its heroine driving her car into a tree. Kennedy's finished with the death of its teenage protagonist. "This period", wrote Gladys Calthrop's lover Mercedes de Acosta, "seemed to produce people with an inner violence and an overcharged excess of emotion that marked them for a tragic end."[88] And so it had proved. Some of the major players in Noël's and the century's twenties were, by the decade's close, swiftly and painfully removed from the *dramatis personae* of his life. Leading actresses such as Jeanne Eagels and Meggie Albanesi died young, Eagels at thirty-nine of a drug overdose, Albanesi at twenty-four of a botched abortion.[89] The writer Hartley Manners, whose family had proved such an inspiration for *Hay Fever* on Noël's first, poverty-stricken, visit to New York, had died in 1928, of oesophageal cancer. Back in England, Noël's old friend Mrs Astley Cooper, now a widow in her seventies, lived on at Hambleton Hall, mourning the death of her eldest child, while the composer Irène Dean Paul watched her daughter Brenda, one of the brightest of the bright young things, sink yet further into drug addiction and bulimia, drifting from prisons to nursing homes.

Nineteen-thirty would prove a particularly cruel year. Charles Scott Moncrieff died of cancer at forty years old, and the South African journalist William Bolitho died suddenly of peritonitis not long before his fortieth birthday. Noël had befriended Bolitho in America and spent time at his chateau in France. The author of a hugely successful group biography called *Twelve Against the Gods*, Bolitho had a mind that Noël found among the most brilliant he knew and the friendship was clearly a formative one, cut off not long after it had begun. Ned Lathom had opened a small furniture shop in London, where he had met and eventually married one of the sales assistants, Marie Xenis de Tunzelmann, the orphaned, impoverished, famously beautiful, and recently divorced, daughter of a Russian nobleman.[90] They lived together in poverty in a flat in St John's Wood. Lathom's possessions were sold, his fortune spent. His tuberculosis worsened and he died in June, thirty-five years old. Noël's arch enemy, the critic Hannen Swaffer, wrote with grudging respect: "When Lathom was dying, neglected, you were closest, the only one who showed gratitude."[91]

Noël's work had provided both distraction from, and subtle reflection of, these tragedies lurking beneath high spirits, his remarkably explicit call for permissiveness and free love tempered by pragmatic concession of the difficulties and darknesses of such a route. The world, newly torn with motorcars and aeroplanes, was running at a speed by which he was simultaneously intoxicated and disturbed. His plays had offered different forms of escape from life's reality, through sex, drugs, humour, theatricality, nostalgia, all means by which an engagement with life could be deflected, or an alternative way of living sought. If there is a unifying theme to his work of the 1920s it is a sense of conflict: between youth and age, gaiety and cynicism, past and present, stasis and permanence. He was a mire of contradiction. Here was a puritan hedonist, an exemplar of the age who simultaneously decried it, a man of serious frivolity, a louche disciplinarian who combined gaiety and mournfulness, sentimentality and cynicism. The apotheosis of sophistication, he exemplified adolescence and immaturity. Frequenter of country-house weekends, having carefully worked his way into high society, he also led a public campaign against blood sports: "Englishmen stand round and enjoy seeing a small, helpless animal tortured to death. Can nothing be done about it?"[92] The author of several unsuccessful historical romances, he had sought to strip his era of its romance, to cast heady affairs in a clearer, more realistic, light: "Vows that have been spoken | When the tide is high | Lie around us broken | When the sands are dry."[93]

His was a modernity that expressed itself in mistrust of the modern, mourning the disappearance of a former age while guiding the inevitable domination of the new. Entrenched participant and foreign onlooker, simultaneously he had incarnated and disman-tled what Stella Gibbons called "the *myth* of the 'twenties: gaiety, courage, pain concealed, amusing malice".[94] In his fifties, from the other side of a world war, he dismissed such a mindset as a "phase we all went through [. . .] compared with Existentialism it becomes *Rebecca of Sunnybrook Farm.* We all got over this period in our mental growth, or most of us did, and I can't feel we were any the worse for it."[95] But, from within his first decade of adulthood, his view of the future was a vortex of frenzied, near-apocalyptic, prophesy. It was a frantically blasé vision of a new world: thrilling, inevitable, terrifying, and pointless.

NOËL COWARD [*in his late twenties, reading from his essay "Hurry, Hurry, Hurry".* . .]: The younger generation will live to see still greater scientific discoveries and still more labour-saving devices for the home and far briefer wars because the poisonous gases and acids and magnificent engines of destruction which are bound to be perfected within the next few years must certainly preclude the possibility of any battle lasting more than a few hours. It is an age of speed and wonderment and ceaseless surprises and one of the principle faults to be found with it is that in the inevitable process of elimination engendered by so much invention so many pleasant things are hopelessly lost and so many unpleasant things allowed to remain. The world is your oyster, remember – someone will achieve fulfilment and despair and triumph and death before you, so hurry – hurry, hurry, hurry – for there is no more time now to be lazy or energetic, or happy or miserable, or victorious or defeated. It has lately been proven that even the air, which we had hitherto regarded as a more or less incomprehensible but necessary convenience for breathing, is filled with voices and music and wailings and screechings; and through the medium of the radio the need of listening to them has crept insinuatingly into the hearts of ordinary people – gentle, peaceful people – this automatically created need of things is definitely one of the most sinister and frightening aspects of civilisation. The romance of machinery is too rapidly superseding the romance of personal contacts, and in the noise and rattle, people swirl along narrow country roads in gigantic charabancs and cover the fields and woods with dust and newspapers but it doesn't matter really because in a few years or so there won't be any fields or woods left, only villas and shops and cinemas and factories – an advanced and enlightened age of aeroplanes and speed and publicity and stucco and aluminium. It is an age of young old age and strangely old youth and very soon there will in all probability be no more old age any more and we shall in the very near future find ourselves injected with peculiar animal glands and be reconstructed and redecorated and rejuvenated and live on and on violently and hopefully, forcing from our minds day by day and year by year the steadily growing realisation of complete and utter futility . . .[96]

He is still talking as
THE CURTAIN FALLS

THE TIPSY CROW

———

A PLAY WITH MUSIC
IN TWO ACTS

CAST

NOËL COWARD, *a famous playwright and actor*

In London:
GERTRUDE LAWRENCE, *an actress*
SIR CHARLES COCHRAN, *a theatrical manager*
LAURENCE OLIVIER, *a young actor*
KEITH WINTER, *a young playwright*
LOUIS HAYWARD, *a young actor from South Africa*
COLE LESLEY, *Noël Coward's valet and assistant*
YVONNE PRINTEMPS, *a French actress and singer*

In America:
ALFRED LUNT, *an actor*
LYNN FONTANNE, *an actress, married to Alfred Lunt*
JACK WILSON, *a theatrical producer*

At Goldenhurst, Kent:
ERIK COWARD, *Noël Coward's brother*
VIOLET COWARD, *Noël Coward's mother*
ARTHUR COWARD, *Noël Coward's father*

Around the world:
JEFFERY AMHERST, *a journalist, and Noël Coward's old friend*
JOHN MILLS, *a young actor*
MARLENE DIETRICH, *a movie star*
GRETA GARBO, *a movie star*

The action takes place in London, Manhattan, South America, and the Far East.

TIME: 1930–1938 (opening, briefly, in 1943)

ACT ONE

PRELUDE

The scene is Oflag VII-B, a German prisoner-of-war camp in Eichstätt, about sixty miles north of Munich, in south-east Germany. It is 8 o'clock in the evening, some time in January, 1943. The Second World War has been raging for over three years, Singapore has fallen to the Japanese, and the Axis forces at Stalingrad are soon to surrender. An audience of some two hundred prisoners has gathered for the world premiere of a play by NOËL COWARD *called* Post-Mortem, *set partly in the trenches of the First World War, partly in the year 1930. The actor* DAN CUNNINGHAM *is in character as* PERRY LOMAS.

PERRY (CUNNINGHAM): There's still poverty, unemployment, pain, greed, cruelty, passion and crime. There's still meanness, jealousy, money and disease . . . The only real difference in Post War conditions is that there are so many men maimed for life and still existing, and so many women whose heartache will never heal. The rest is the same only faster, and more meretricious. The War is fashionable now, like a pleasantly harrowing film. Even men who fought in it, some of them see in it a sort of vague glamour, they've slipped back as I knew they would.[1]

The German guards encouraged the dramatic company that had formed in the camp: The Repertory Players. Among the prisoners were numerous professional actors, marshalled by the Canadian director Wallace Douglas. A theatre was erected, capable of seating two hundred, its stage oddly placed across one corner of the building. The guards made sure to sit in the front rows, taking the view that the more serious stagings – the prisoners even managed *Hamlet* – were benefitting from the help of the "master race". Costumes were sent in from the Munich opera, programmes were formally printed, and professional stage make-up was ordered from Berlin. There was even a theatre orchestra.

The actor Desmond Llewelyn (later famous as "Q" in the James Bond films) was twenty-nine, a graduate of the Royal Academy of Dramatic Art; he had been a prisoner of the Germans for three years. He was given a role in *Post-Mortem*, which had been written in April 1930 while the playwright, Noël Coward, was on a tour of the Far East. The script had been published but never staged. The younger actors, as had become routine, took on the female parts. Such enterprises were common in the camps: at Stalag IV-B in Mühlberg, on the banks of the river Elbe, one of the largest camps in Germany, Noël's 1941 play *Blithe Spirit* was being staged; at Stalag VIII-A in Görlitz, prisoners were having a riotous time with *Hay Fever*. And in the freezing German winter at Eichstätt, *Post-Mortem* was being given its very first performance, thirteen years after it had been written in the swaying cabin of an old P&O liner as its author, pausing to write between waves of sickness, sailed through the Red Sea from Ceylon to Marseilles.[2]

The trip had produced not only *Post-Mortem* but *Private Lives* and, while the former would never see a professional staging in Noël's lifetime, the latter became his most famous work. At first glance it seems remarkable, even bizarre, that the two plays were written within weeks of one another by the same author. *Post-Mortem* is unlike anything else he produced, either in topic or in treatment. "I know all about my facility for writing adroit swift dialogue and hitting unimportant but popular nails on the head", he told a friend, "and I thought the time had come to break new ground a little."[3] The play was inspired by R. C. Sherriff's *Journey's End* and, in its portrayal of the upper classes' indifference to the horrors of war, perhaps by Shaw's *Heartbreak House.* It was the product of political despondency and black depression. Twelve years on from the First World War, Noël was finally wrestling head-on with the fallout from the slaughter he had just avoided. Many friends, from Charles Scott Moncrieff to Geoffrey Holdsworth, had been wounded; Jeffery Amherst had been injured in the Battle of Loos, and Jeffery's closest friend, hit by a shell, was "left hanging in shreds of raw meat all over my face, hair and uniform".[4]

Post-Mortem opens in a dug-out in 1917, with a group of soldiers aghast at the sugar-coated portraits of British pluck perpetrated by the press. "They'll smarm it all over with memorials and Rolls of Honour [. . .] and it'll look so noble and glorious in retrospect that they'll all start itching for another war." The lead character, John Cavan, is soon fatally wounded and the play, pausing Cavan's life in its final seconds, spools forward to 1930, in a device that prefig- ures the dreamscapes and time slips of J. B. Priestley's Time Plays.* Cavan, half-ghost, meets his mother; his former sweetheart; and his father, an immoral press magnate and a thinly disguised portrait of the excessively powerful Lord Beaverbrook.[5] In the final scene, back in 1917, Cavan dies, becoming a statistic in a generation's futile sacrifice.

Post-Mortem belongs to the genre of interwar writing known in Ger- many as *Heimkehrromane*, "return-novels", depicting soldiers returning to a betrayed society. The play shows a United Kingdom that has become fascist in all but name, with Church, press, and state in col- lusion. All three are fiercely attacked, and Christianity condemned as a "threadbare legend", the meaningless worship of a "tin-pot God". Bishops, journalists, and politicians are shown working together to ensure the public burning of dissenting books. In 1930 the Nazis had yet to take power or stoke bonfires of "un-German" publica- tions, and Berlin had yet to be proclaimed the host of the 1936 Olympic Games, which would promote racial supremacy and anti- Semitism. But *Post-Mortem* prophetically describes the "competitive sporting spirit" as "being admirably fostered, particularly as regards the Olympic Games. A superb preparation for the next War, fully realised by everyone but the public that will be involved." The real object of the play's anger is not the First World War but the society to which it gave rise. "The war was glorious, do you hear me? Supremely glorious, because it set men free. Not the ones who lived, poor devils, but the ones who died. [. . .] War is no evil compared

---

* Priestley thought *Post-Mortem* "very fine and moving" and on 24 June 1932 he wrote to Coward suggesting they collaborate on a play about war. "The thing to do with war is to ridicule it [. . .] it is a job that wants doing and I believe you and I are the people to do it." Coward Archive, NPC-8884.

with this sort of living." One ex-soldier claims he would shoot his children if they refused to fight in any further conflict. "Try with all your might", Cavan responds, "to be brave enough to shoot them when they come back."

Post-Mortem would be published in 1931, receiving good sales and mixed but serious attention from the critics. But Noël made no attempts to have it staged (it would be televised, in 1968). It contained, he thought in hindsight, "some of the best writing I have ever done", but he found its arguments tangled and its tone hysterical and unsubtle.[6] His attitude towards sincerity, even his own, was mistrust. West End schedules had been studded with war plays during the 1920s, ever since Harry Wall's *Havoc* (1923), a story of love rivals in the trenches, sold so many tickets that it was made into a film and a novel. J. R. Ackerley's *Prisoners of War*, which explored homosexual desire among interned officers, had been produced to acclaim in 1925. *Post-Mortem* could simply have been Noël's pragmatic attempt to align himself with a major genre of contemporary theatre. But he may have noticed how the most successful war plays struck a tone of human grief rather than political anger. Somerset Maugham's condemnation of war, *For Services Rendered* (1932), would prove unpopular on its premiere; Seán O'Casey's anti-war and partly Expressionist evocation of the front, *The Silver Tassie* (1928), struggled to find audiences. O'Casey, whose actress wife had been in *Bitter Sweet*, had taken a vicious dislike to Noël and suggested that *Post-Mortem* remained unstaged simply because it would not be a money-maker. In this there may have been some truth, and Noël's ambitions − commercial success, critical praise, dramatic integrity − were conflicted.[7]

Noël may most of all have been hiding what was essentially a semi-autobiographical grappling with survivor's guilt. John Cavan is in love with nobody so much as his mother and has a childhood friend who, like Esmé Wynne, has converted to Christian Science. He searches for meaning in his temporary reprieve from the afterlife: "I'm trying to find a reason for survival." "Life is reason enough, isn't it?" "No, I don't believe it is." And later, "I never wanted to be born." Not long before *Post-Mortem* Noël had begun work on a novel titled *Julian Kane*. The book's eponymous anti-hero was to have become so bored with life that he put an end to it – suicide the result not of grand passion or tragic depression but simply of ennui, as if killing oneself were the apotheosis of fashionable lassitude. The novel was abandoned, its manuscript seemingly destroyed. But a shadow of it survives in *Post-Mortem*, in the role of the "thin and nervy" writer Perry Lomas, a survivor from the trenches. Lomas suffers from "a sort of hopelessness which isn't quite despair, not localized enough for that. A formless, deserted boredom." Visited by John Cavan's ghost, he is on the verge of suicide, and it is Cavan who hands him the gun. "Thanks", comes Lomas's reply, just before the shot rings out in the dark. "What's a little death among friends?"

"CITY"
from *Cochran's 1931 Revue*

Day in, day out,
Life will soon be over and done.
Where has it led and why?
Day in, day out,
Where is the moon?
Where is the sun?
Where is the open sky?
Ever seeking, and believing
There is hope for us all.

Sirens shrieking, progress weaving
Poor humanity's pall.
Iron, rot, steel, rust,
Speed, noise, death, dust,
Why should we work?
Why should we live?
Why should we even die?[8]

SCENE ONE

The Victoria Theatre in the Centre of Singapore, Wednesday, 2 April 1930.

The large white pillared building is resolutely Western, dominated by a tall clock tower at the centre. The performance is of Journey's End *by* R. C. SHERRIFF. *Onstage, the set is of a First World War trench.* JOHN MILLS *(playing the young soldier,* RALEIGH*) is standing at a desk, at which sits* NOËL COWARD *(playing his superior,* STANHOPE*). Offstage, crew are recreating the sound of gunfire.*

STANHOPE (COWARD): The one man I could trust — my best friend — the one man I could talk to as man to man — who understood everything — you think I don't care?

RALEIGH (MILLS): But how can you when . . .?

STANHOPE (COWARD): To forget, you little fool — to forget! D'you understand? To forget! You think there's no limit to what a man can bear?

The trip on which Noël had written both *Post-Mortem* and *Private Lives* had taken up the first five months of 1930. Jeffery Amherst, who was tired of his hectic life as a New York journalist, had agreed to meet him in Japan and accompany him on a tour of the Far East.

Noël's decision to go abroad was eased by the knowledge that his critical and monetary fortunes were restored by *Bitter Sweet*; he seemed to be fleeing the celebrity he had always wanted to achieve. His choice of travelling companion, and his decision to spend so long away from home, speak of rupture with Jack Wilson. In a few years he would write *Design for Living*: "You'd soon be all right if you got away from all this muck", one of its characters is told. "Get on a ship [. . .], never mind where it's going! Just get on a ship." It was a time for reflection, to which he had not been much given. He had lived in the moment, rattling from one production to the next, crossing oceans as frequently and carelessly as others might cross the Thames. He now had the money to retire, to live as he wished — but how he wished to live, beyond occupying a central spot in the public eye, was a question he could not answer. He had itchy feet, a need constantly to be on the move lest, in stopping to reflect, he did not like what he found. When he did permit himself introspection he showed ominous signs of buckling to the depression that had threatened to derail him a few years before. The old questions reared their heads: what now? What was there left to achieve? Although he professed indifference to critical disdain, he harboured not only a need for approval but a paranoia about disapproval, especially from the critics of the Beaverbrook press, who he was convinced disliked him on principle. Hannen Swaffer could be seen at first nights melodramatically re-enacting the duel scene from *Bitter Sweet*.

Travel was also a means of projecting the glamour on which his public image rested. He became the "face" of the Royal Portable Typewriter; adverts in newspapers were adorned with a picture of Noël carting it around the globe. He was tailoring a brand, of the globetrotting yet disciplined writer, as if to emulate Somerset Maugham, who had spent considerable time in the Pacific or Far East researching novels that depicted the twilight of European colonialism. When abroad Noël simply recreated his plush London life, staying in grand Westernised hotels or lavish first-class cabins, socialising with British consuls and governor-generals, and partying at embassies and clubs. He did not return from Japan with an interest in Noh plays or a passion for sushi; he frankly admitted that he disliked visiting historic sites and being assailed by information; he had a poor memory for landscape and tended to dislike foreigners: "Japan was enjoyable but the Japanese are rather irritating".[9] When travelling he considered countries as theatrical sets in which to give a performance. Even the noise of the sea became a sound effect, likened in his recollections to "the perpetual off-stage effect of rice in a sieve".[10] The boats in which he spent so much time during the first months of the new decade were floating auditoria: safely enclosed worlds, divided – like the strata of stalls, circle, and amphitheatre – into ranks of class, from the paying public to the lavishly costumed crew.

He had left San Francisco on 29 November 1929, sailing out west into the Pacific en route to Japan. Jeffery arrived on 16 December, Noël's thirtieth birthday. The two of them were united in their dislike of Tokyo and most of its inhabitants, whose inability to speak English annoyed them and whose own language sent them into uncontrollable giggles. "Silly little bastards" was Jeffery's dismissal; Noël settled for "little buggers".[11] They escaped the capital for the more beautiful landscape of Osaka and Nagasaki, and by late December they were in south-eastern Korea (then a single country in the Empire of Japan), and travelling up to north-eastern China. The cold was bitter, the landscape turned to ice, and it hurt to breathe. The British Consul in Mukden (now Shenyang) turned out to be the brother of *Bitter Sweet*'s musical director, and took them under his wing: they spent New Year's Eve at a Harlequinade Ball at the English Club, safe from the icy wastes outside.

China had just been unified and the Kuomintang was beginning a period of political "tutelage", but the warlords ruled supreme, and Japan was to invade the following year, using Mukden as the site of a staged attack blamed on Chinese dissidents. Noël and Jeffery were close enough to the Chinese–Siberian frontier to be aware of the Russian refugees who were braving the frozen Chinese winter in order to escape Stalin's agricultural policies. The pair went west to Peking on an unheated train with boarded-up windows, warming themselves with vodka and playing songs on the gramophone to ward off fierce-looking men in uniforms who barged into the shabby wooden carriages. Once, they heard gunshots, but stayed put.

Peking was a round of parties topped off with a visit to the Chinese Theatre, though Noël and Jeffery left before the opera started. In mid-January they went south to Shanghai, where, worn out by the day-long train journeys, Noël promptly caught influenza and retired to bed at his hotel. It was in Shanghai – "a cross between Brussels and Huddersfield" – that he made the acquaintance of three naval officers, "with whom we visited many of the lower and gayer haunts of the city".[12] (The sexual tourism of Far Eastern cities was renowned and there was little stigma attached to homosexual activity.) Noël eventually asked whether they might all travel on to Hong Kong in one of the ships of the Royal Navy, HMS *Suffolk*, then serving at the China Station and promoting British commercial interests in the Far East. When he was fourteen years old, he had lived and even marched with the Sherwood Foresters; now, and not for the last time, he installed himself with the navy.

So began Noël's strange love affair with the British navy. He claimed to have spent "some of the happiest hours of my life" travelling to Hong Kong on the naval ship.[13] Every detail thrilled him: the hum of the engines, the smell of the cabins, the rituals and discipline, the way in which the ship's band worked unsteadily through the hits of *Bitter Sweet*, the atmosphere's strange combination of theatre and boarding school (cocoa was taken before bed with the officer of the watch). He was being given a vicarious taste of the military life he had once escaped, now repackaged as spectator sport and theatrical ritual, free from arduous training or the horrors of warfare. Many of his male ancestors had been in the navy, and their seafaring had been upheld by his mother as the high point of his family's social position; even the uniform seemed to emulate the sailor suits of an Edwardian childhood. The ship's world was also a homosocial community and, for some, homosexual refuge. Noël was attracted by the disciplined masculinity and comradeship of the officers, but the naval uniform would become emblematic of camp, chorus lines of sailors appearing in everything from *Anything Goes* to Derek Jarman's film of *The Tempest*. Even *HMS Pinafore* had played on the inherent theatre of the navy, linking the nautical with the naughty amid those insular and secret floating worlds.

Such was the glory of their time at sea that when Noël and Jeffery arrived in the British colony of Hong Kong, on 3 February 1930, they became seriously depressed at bidding farewell to the ship. They left after only a week, departing for Vietnam and Cambodia, a region united as "Indo-China" and under French colonial rule. They arrived at Hanoi on 9 February, during the Yên Bái mutiny, which had begun north-west of the city. Vietnamese soldiers in the French army had rebelled in an attempt to overthrow the colonial regime, and the French had imposed a twelve-day curfew. Noël and Jeffery found themselves in Government Palace, dining lavishly to intermittent bursts of gunfire, which seemed to make little impression: "there was, it seems, some sort of revolution going on".[14] They left Hanoi as soon as possible, hiring a car and two drivers, and travelling down the narrow length of Vietnam to Saigon.

By the time of their arrival Jeffery was burning with fever. They were now over 3000 kilometres south of Peking and its frozen winter. The heat was intense. Somehow Noël found a doctor; somehow Jeffery was bundled into a clinic run by nuns where he lay beneath a mosquito net barely conscious. He had, they later found out, amoebic dysentery that could have proved fatal but, thanks to the diligence of the nuns, he recovered. Noël was left to discover Saigon, which he did from the comfort of the Grand Hotel's terrace, listening to the hotel orchestra work through a rag-bag of Puccini. When Jeffery was well enough they went north together, driving up through what is now Cambodia. Noël got over his antipathy towards historic tourist sites in a visit to Angkor Wat, a many-towered temple wreathed at sunset with a black smoke that turned out to be swarms of bats.

From Angkor they went in mid-March to Bangkok; naturally, the King of Siam had been at Eton with Jeffery, which secured them an introduction (the country's monarchy would be ended permanently by a military coup the following year). "Very sweet" was Noël's estimation of the King, "and [he] had read all my plays if you please!"[15] They took a ship down through what is now the Gulf of Thailand and on board Jeffery again collapsed. By the time of their arrival in Singapore, on 21 March, he was once again dangerously ill with dysentery and transferred to hospital.[16] Singapore was under British control and known as the guardian of the Empire's commercial interests; troops were garrisoned nearby and amid the rickshaws the streets were thronged with men in uniform. Noël, forced by Jeffery's illness to stay far longer in Singapore than the few days they had intended, was left to his own devices. Neither his increasing depression nor the permanent humidity was alleviated by the frequent thunderstorms.

Theatre came to the rescue, in the form of a touring troupe called The Quaints, who were putting on irreverent versions of Shakespeare at the Victoria Theatre in the city centre. During one of their performances the actor playing Hamlet had fallen ill, and the manager hastily substituted the final act of a contemporary comedy called *When Knights Were Bold*. The audience was said not to have noticed.[17] Among the company was twenty-two-year-old

John Mills. Noël attached himself to the troupe, surely pleased to be a celebrity figure at the centre of adoring acolytes: it was here that he first cultivated the use of his nickname "the Master", which Mills always took credit for inventing. That said, so did Jack Wilson, who not long before had watched Noël descend the Ebury Street staircase looking more than usually immaculate. "I unfortunately sardonically quipped 'Here comes the Master!'" Jack remembered. "In spite of my sarcasm, the label was picked up by the group, and they have called him the 'Master' ever since. He loves it [. . .]. Ironically enough, I became the only one close to him who refused to repeat the title."[18]

The Quaints were shortly to perform R. C. Sherriff's *Journey's End* which, set in the British Army trenches towards the end of the First World War, had opened in London the previous year. A film version was that month being shown in British cinemas, and the play had already become internationally popular. Bruce Carfax, acting the lead role of Captain Stanhope, had lost his voice. Would Noël take over? It was not a part to accept on a whim merely to alleviate boredom. Stanhope had been created by Laurence Olivier and was a character tormented with self-loathing, drowning the realities of war in alcohol. Noël, his memory apparently photographic, learned the lines in two days.

The production opened at the Victoria Theatre on 2 April 1930 and ran for a further two performances. Noël was under-rehearsed, and the military costume became almost unbearable in the heat, but he got through until, at the last moment, he dropped his heavy tin hat onto the groin of the dead young soldier Raleigh, played by John Mills. The curtain fell on a corpse sitting bolt upright and squealing with pain. Local reviewers described Noël's acting as if he were still in *The Vortex*: "we had an excessively neurotic young man, intensely emotional [. . . though] punctuated by effeminate gestures that were wholly inappropriate". One critic thought that "Stanhope is not a Noël Coward part", but others acclaimed his "flawless interpretation" and its "tangible, real tragedy".[19] Noël was invited to celebrate his success over lunch with the new Governor of the Straits Settlements, Sir Cecil Clementi, and his wife, Marie. She crossly told him that *Journey's End* was immoral, in that it had

showed the troops drinking. Surely British soldiers were tee-total
to a man. Jeffery Amherst, recovered and in attendance, gently put
her right. Noël took his revenge with a comic song about Lady
Clementi: "You're anti-sex in any form, or so I've heard it said |
You're just the sort who would prefer a cup of tea instead | You
must have been a riot in the matrimonial bed . . ." This he enjoyed
performing to Lady Clementi's social circle. "Oh disgraceful, disgraceful", they muttered. "Please, sing it AGAIN."[20]

On 5 April, the Quaints finished their season in Singapore with
When Knights Were Bold: "the performance was notable", read one
review, "for the appearance of Mr Noël Coward as one of the
ladies-in-waiting".[21] The next morning Noël and Jeffery left for the
British colony of Ceylon and its capital, Colombo. Noël's brother
Erik had been working there for eighteen months as a tea-planter
and met them off the boat, although the fraternal reunion takes up
less time in Noël's account of the trip than the sudden appearance
of Cole Porter, completing an Eastern tour with his wife, and only
too eager to share movie footage of their travels. By May, Noël
was back at sea and bound for Marseilles, sailing from Colombo
through the Red Sea and up through the Gulf of Suez into the
Mediterranean. Jeffery was preparing for a new life in the airlines
industry, and Noël, who had not been in England for nearly eight
months, was intent on organising the staging of a play he had
written in Shanghai, about a divorced couple who happen upon
one another in a French hotel.

The trip had also inspired his songwriting. On board the ship to
Marseilles almost all the passengers who approached him seemed to
want advice about the theatrical ambitions of their children; he took
his revenge in his famous number pleading with Mrs Worthington
not to put her daughter on the stage. Another song prompted by
his voyage, sketched out in his head during the long car journey
to Hanoi, proved equally immortal. The lyrics are of a tripping
dexterity designed to showcase impeccable diction, and the tune
and words of the refrain (riffing on a phrase about the English
thought to have originated with Kipling) have a claim to be among
the most memorable things he produced.

Mad dogs and Englishmen
Go out in the midday sun.
The Japanese don't care to.
The Chinese wouldn't dare to,
Hindoos and Argentines sleep firmly from twelve to one . . .[22]

The song, with its intricate lacework of rhyme, has gone down as
a light-hearted dig at colonial society which, on one level, it is.
But the object of its satire is evasive. Often Noël would incorporate
into performance a sprinkling of "native" gibberish − "Papalaka
boo", "Digariga doo" − and it is hard to know whether the fabricated patois is lampooning foreign vernacular or showing up the
Englishman's lazy idea of it. The lyrics manage at once to tease
and to venerate British colonialism and eccentricity. Poking fun,
from Noël, was a means of paying his respects, and he was quite
capable of mocking a way of life in which he inherently believed:
his conception of patriotism embraced the flippancy he believed
innate to the English character. In Indo-China he had always been
"deeply impressed by the admirable French colonization" (mainly
because it "enabled us to procure excellent coffee and rolls in the
remotest villages").[23] When Jeffery fell ill, Noël's chief source of
exasperation was the impossibility of finding a local doctor during
siesta hour. The rhyme was irresistible: "Englishmen detest a
siesta . . ."

The elusive, perhaps chimerical, quality of Englishness, which
Noël fought to exemplify and even to create, was becoming a
driving force in his work, and he would become supportive of, and
nostalgic for, the British Empire of his Edwardian childhood. "The
British Empire was a great and wonderful social, economic and
even spiritual experiment", he would write in 1957.[24] Imperialism
and camp are not mutually exclusive, and Noël had a liking for the
theatricality and ceremonial pomp of colonial life. Englishmen may
be mad enough to venture into the most intense heat. But that, the
song seems to be saying, is the kind of admirably potty discipline
on which the Empire was built. And over the Empire even the blazing noonday sun should never, Noël thought, be allowed to set.

"MAD DOGS AND ENGLISHMEN"

Mad Dogs and Englishmen
Go out in the midday sun.
The smallest Malay rabbit
Deplores this stupid habit.
In Hongkong
They strike a gong
And fire off a noonday gun
To reprimand each inmate
Who's in late.
In the mangrove swamps
Where the python romps
There is peace from twelve till two.
Even caribous
Lie around and snooze
For there's nothing else to do.
In Bengal
To move at all
Is seldom, if ever done.
But mad dogs and Englishmen
Go out in the midday sun.[25]

SCENE TWO

Two couples on the divided terrace of a beachside hotel; four actors restricted to a slice of stage as small as in anything by Beckett; the audience watching them placed by the play's surreal geography high above the sea, hovering vertiginously in space.

The novelty of the stage picture has been dulled by the familiarity of *Private Lives*. "It's astonishing as a piece of machinery", wrote the critic Susannah Clapp in 2010. "Within three-quarters of an hour a divorced couple, meeting each other while honeymooning with new partners, have rediscovered love and run off together".[26] By the end of the second act, hiding in a Paris apartment, the pair – Amanda and Elyot – are deep in a violent and screaming row. By the end of the third, tracked down by their abandoned spouses – Victor and Sibyl – they once again flee away together at curtain-fall. *Private Lives*, the high watermark of the 1920s mode of living and loving, captures a single revolution of an endlessly rotating wheel: love, marriage, honeymoon, quarrel, divorce, repeat.

Noël was adding to a popular genre of "divorce plays" that were harnessing the comedic potential of the evolving divorce laws.* In 1930, English law did not allow for divorce by mutual consent, and proof of violence or adultery was required. To marry a divorcee still had a whiff of scandal. *Private Lives* expands on a song Noël had written not long before, "Marriage is a fatal curse", and is a variation on a painful line tucked into the lyrics of *Bitter Sweet*: "Love crucifies the lover." Elyot and Amanda may be the first of his couples to be genuinely sexually infatuated with one another, but their sexual drive begets a dangerous passion: "We were so ridiculously over in love [. . .] Selfishness, cruelty, hatred, possessiveness, petty jealousy. All these qualities came out in us just because we loved each other [. . .] To hell with love." Amanda and Elyot can live neither with nor without one another and in this lies the comedy's tragedy.

Noël had long wanted to write a vehicle for Gertrude Lawrence, and she had been nagging him to get going. Often his plays were sparked by a particular image and, when he was in Japan, Lawrence had appeared in his mind, standing in a white dress on a hotel terrace. Around this vision a whole script had begun to construct itself, but he had learned to let ideas coalesce of their own accord, and did not rush, as once he would have done, for a pen and paper. Writing plays, for Noël, was a very different process from writing them *down*. *Private Lives* had been written down, by hand, in

---

* Early audiences would have recognised the play's ancestors: Victorien Sardou's popular *Divorçons* (filmed as *Let's Get a Divorce*) showed a passionate clandestine affair curdling on the lovers' marriage; Alfred Capus's *Les Deux Écoles* was a classic chamber comedy about a bored wife who prefers her ex's faithless passion to the decorous loyalty of her new husband. Shaw's *Overruled*, a one-act piece from 1912 that was frequently revived through the 1920s, even shows two cross-stitched couples colliding at a seaside hotel.

pencil, across four cold days in January 1930, as he recovered from flu and low spirits in the Cathay Hotel on the Bund in Shanghai, overlooking the Huangpu River. Noël set great store by promoting the legend of his fluency, and in some cases this was no more than legend. "Nobody knows better than I what agony [writing] is", he told Gladys Calthrop.[27] But the manuscript of *Private Lives* has a remarkably small number of corrections, the only major revision being the removal of a waiter from the first act.

Noël had little premonition that here was a comedy to outrank in popularity everything he had written or would write. He was concerned only with the evident vehicle it would be for the talents of its intended lead actors. "It's completely trivial", he told Gladys, "except for one or two slaps but it will be fun to play." Nor did he perceive the depths that would later be found in it, as if meaning had worked its way in without the author's noticing: "the whole thing is very flippant and gay". In many ways *Private Lives* seemed to him a warm-up to bigger and better things: "there is a sporting chance of something really dandy hatching out before I'm through". As his letter to Gladys continues, recounting his travels, it seems strange that *Private Lives* could have hatched from the same writer, whose default mode seemed to be silliness. "We pee ourselves a good deal. [. . .] It really was splitarsingly loverly."[28]

He had sent Gertrude Lawrence the script on 7 February, while still in Hong Kong. "I've worked very hard on it", he told her.

I think it is good, but God knows it's going to be very tricky to play. [. . .] we shall have to watch one another like lynxes to see that we don't overdo it [. . . and] use every subtlety and change of mood we are capable of, and the only place where we can really let go and enjoy ourselves will be the big quarrel scene at the end of the Act. I do think that will be fun, although probably slightly painful! I'm all for being really abandoned in the love scenes, and doing a few things that will give the old ladies a treat at matinees! Copulation has been the basis of the dear old British Drama for so long, we might just as well salute it. [. . .] however lightly we may happen to be playing, we can always switch to complete seriousness without too much of a jerk. [. . .] Perhaps you'll simply hate it, if so, send me a tactful subtle cable saying "Think Play Bloody Terrible" or something like that, and I shall understand.[29]

Charles Cochran was the first to respond: "GERTIE LIKES PLAY BUT NOT LAST ACT HOWEVER SHE WANTS TO DO IT". Three weeks later a telegram from Lawrence had arrived in Singapore: "HELLO DUCKIE READ PLAY TWICE AND ADORE STOP NOTHING WRONG THAT CANT BE FIXED."[30] Noël told her that only her performance would need fixing, and they bickered good-naturedly by cable throughout the rest of his Far Eastern tour, while she tried to extricate herself from another production. She was now thirty-two and a major star, known for her performances in revue. Her finances and her personal life were in disarray; she was engaged to a Wall Street banker whom she would never marry, certain that her career should take precedence. A lot rode for her on *Private Lives*, not least the importance of making money (which she would, after securing a cut of the profits).

Lawrence's double act with Noël became the defining one of both their careers, although they appeared together in just three productions. The friendship was born of mutual admiration and throve on effusive affection and hot-blooded quarrel. Like their characters they expressed liking through insult, and they were often discovered backstage in rows so intense that they had come to blows. Even this may have been stage-managed; much of their success arose from careful public presentation of their merry war. They were often photographed as mirror images of one another, cigarette holders brandished like weapons. Even her stylisation as "Gertie" was confected; those to whom she was close called her Gertrude or Gee. Lawrence never joined Noël's inner circle, and may not have wished to. But he found her witty, generous, loving, lacking in critical judgement, and passionately talented. Most of all he recognised in her a contradiction that was one of his own defining qualities, namely a combination of high spirits and world-weariness that seemed to have emanated from the difficulties of her early life. She had endured her father's alcoholism; her parents' divorce; a meagre income; poor health; and long years as a single mother while pursuing various short-lived relationships. "It's a very great pleasure to me to be of the faintest service to you over anything ever", Noël wrote to her, "for the simple reason that I love you very much."[31]

The two of them worked hard at *Private Lives* even before the fortnight of official rehearsals began, staying at Edward Molyneux's villa in France during the summer of 1930. (Onstage Lawrence would wear a trend-setting Molyneux gown of white satin that was featured on the cover of *Vogue*.) Lawrence's daughter, Pamela, now twelve, was turned out of the villa to make room for Noël and Jack Wilson. Gladys Calthrop began to work on the designs, and the cast was completed in the shape of Adrianne Allen and Laurence Olivier. Twenty-three years old, Olivier seemed to keep missing his chance at stardom. Having created the role of Stanhope in *Journey's End* at its one-off, Sunday-night, premiere, he had refused to continue in the part in favour of an unsuccessful comedy. The role of Victor was so clearly an also-ran that Olivier would never really enjoy himself during *Private Lives*, but the relationship between him and Noël was soon one of mutual adoration, and on Noël's side sexual attraction. But Olivier wanted a mentor rather than a lover: "I think Noël probably was the first man who took hold of me and made me think, he made me use my silly little brain. He taxed me with his sharpness and shrewdness and brilliance and he pointed out when I was talking nonsense, which nobody else had ever done before. He gave me a sense of right and wrong."[32]

Charles Cochran threw a great deal at *Private Lives*, and when in August 1930 the cast embarked on a five-week provincial tour prior to a West End run they did so in first-class luxury. Noël and Laurence Olivier were seen leading a full-scale food fight in one of the grand hotel dining rooms. During the tour, Noël was introduced to yet another Lawrence, no longer "of Arabia": T. E. Lawrence was now serving in the Royal Air Force under an assumed name, having withdrawn from public life. "Meeting you was such a surprise and pleasure to me", he told Noël. "I had often (and quite inadequately) wondered what you were like." He was enchanted by *Private Lives*, and seemingly by its creator. "The play reads astonishingly well. It gets thicker, in print, and has bones and muscles. [. . .] For fun I took some pages and tried to strike redundant words out of your phrases. Only there were none [. . .] Your work is like sword-play; as quick as light. Mine a slow painful mosaic of hard words stiffly cemented together. However, it is usually opposites that fall in love." Lawrence's notepaper was headed with his RAF number. "Dear 338171", Noël wrote to him from his Liverpool hotel room. "May I call you 338?"[33]

For the London opening, on 24 September 1930, the glittering new Phoenix Theatre was secured, and the building was unveiled by Cochran to a fanfare of uniformed trumpeters. Stalls tickets were sold for a record £2 (£130 today); there was even a very early form of air conditioning. The audience glittered. H. G. Wells was spotted taking his seat. "Was there ever", asked *The Tatler*, "a premiere so crashingly soigné?"[34] Where Noël was an actor of technique and precision, Lawrence was a performer of instinct and volatility, and would change from night to night, veering from inspired brilliance to over-played hysteria. The collision between the two modes of acting made their duets hell to perform but electric to watch. Noël thought Lawrence barely pretty, but she could enact beauty such that, on some evenings, he was stopped in his tracks. "These two", one reviewer would write, "play with words as sunshine with rippling water. Passionate clowns conjuring with heart-ache; incorrigible jesters slapping till it hurts."[35]

Mrs Patrick Campbell rushed round afterwards to Noël's dressing room. "Don't you just love it", she asked the gushing crowd, "when he does his little hummings at the piano?"[36] Amanda and Elyot reunite after hearing a "sentimental, romantic little tune"; at the premiere, and in most subsequent productions, Noël's song "Someday I'll find you" was used, a waltz that could have belonged to *Bitter Sweet*. Amanda's description became immortal: "Extraordinary how potent cheap music is."* But Noël Coward never thought of himself as a composer of "cheap music", any more than he thought his talent was solely to amuse. The line is an arch joke

---

* Lawrence often pruned "extraordinary" to "strange"; the line in the manuscript (Coward Archive, p. 38) runs: "It's awfully annoying to think how potent cheap music is."

at Noël's expense: audiences would have known that actor and composer were one and the same. But it encapsulates the play's dual-headed ability to be romantic while revealing the trappings of romance, conceding the dangerous effectiveness of sentimentality, and the fulcrum between the tender and mawkish on which much of his work had wobbled.

In the age of ever improving radio technology, Noël knew he could soon preserve forever not only the song but his clipped performance of the play's terse rhythms; he and Lawrence recorded chunks of the script for HMV just weeks after opening night. The record proves that he had written into the dialogue the sound of his own delivery. The surface of *Private Lives* is shiny and mirrored, as full of reflections as the English Channel on which Amanda and Elyot see rippling images of yachts by moonlight. "Are you happy?" he asks her on their reunion, to which she replies, "Ecstatically". Soon she leaves, to be replaced by Sibyl.

SIBYL: Elli, what's the matter?

ELYOT: I feel very odd.

SIBYL: Odd, what do you mean, ill?

ELYOT: Yes, ill.

SIBYL: What sort of —

ELYOT: We must leave at once.

SIBYL: Leave!

ELYOT: Yes, dear. Leave immediately.

SIBYL: Elli! [. . .] What's happened, what has happened?

ELYOT: Nothing has happened.

SIBYL: You've gone out of your mind.

ELYOT: I haven't gone out of my mind [. . .]

SIBYL: You're not drunk, are you?

ELYOT: Of course I'm not drunk. [. . .]

SIBYL: Hysterical nonsense.

ELYOT: It isn't hysterical nonsense. [. . .]

SIBYL: Do you mean that there's going to be an earthquake or something?

ELYOT: Very possibly, very possibly indeed, or perhaps a violent explosion [. . .] Don't quibble, Sibyl.[37]

Almost every major word or phrase is repeated, in an obsessive and nightmarish echoing that enacts the characters' cyclical dance to the music of passion. Amanda's "ecstatically" has been exploded, its shards studding the text in repeated exclamations of "Elli" and "ill". These are then echoed in "Sibyl", a name that nestles within the repeated "possibly" before appearing conjoined to "quibble".

The script, punctuated for rhythm rather than grammar, is not so much written as notated. *Private Lives* has an acoustic, a sound-world. Sonically, it could be by no other author. A constant use of adverbs – "terribly, terribly sweet" – pinches the dialogue into tiny emphatic phrases. A simile such as "lint white" (quite different to "as white as lint") crams in more consonants than seem possible. The frequent addition of "little" – "nasty little matrimonial bottle", "nasty little feet", "frowsy little hotel" – adds a permanent sneer, as if everything must be made trivial on principle, but is also a rhythmic technique, a musical grace-note. Even the idiosyncratic spelling of "Elyot" (the manuscript uses the more conventional "Elliot") rids the name of a superfluous syllable. Noël, as the critic Kenneth Tynan would put it, "took the fat off English comic dialogue; he was the Turkish Bath in which it slimmed".[38] He was also the metronome to which it beat time. Noël's ear was attuned to his era, and the contours of the writing capture the sound and diction of the Jazz Age, the bang and rattle of the motorcar as it drove over the remnants of a bygone world.

But the critics, almost to a man, thought that while the souf-flé had risen it would not keep. *Private Lives* was "dazzling and delectable" but would not "survive a decade".[39] The *Observer* pronounced it "a bad play in the sense that it would collapse before consideration in cold blood [. . .] an airy nothing". James Agate acclaimed "Mr Coward's genius" but took up the general view: "To talk even of Wilde", he wrote in *The Sunday Times*, "would be uncritical, for the wit of [Wilde] wears down the ages, and Mr Coward's hardly reaches the theatre door."[40] After the success of *Bitter Sweet*, *Private Lives* was perceived as a step backwards to the acid flippancy of Noël's apparently less mature work. "Mr Coward's most successful medium is always flippancy, and here he has chosen a theme in which he can be flippant all through." "This essay in flippancy . . ."; "a master of flippancy . . ."; "flippancy dances in the mask of wit."[41] The *Daily Mirror* nicknamed Noël "Prince Flip".[42] Not that anyone could doubt the popular success. The Prince of Wales came twice; the Queen of Spain and the Queen of Norway bumped into each other in the stalls.[43] The Lord Chamberlain wrote personally to Noël, their early sparring forgotten: "It is quite excellent and will give many people food for thought!"[44] The run could have continued a great deal longer than the three months to which Noël, wary of becoming stale, eventually agreed. He was earning £1200 a week from the run (just short of a weekly £400,000 today), but the play was exhausting to perform. During the central-act row tables were overturned, lamps and records smashed, and the couple rolled over and over one another in passionate fury as the Phoenix Theatre's new safety curtain slowly fell. With wonderful irony, it was decorated with Titian's *The Triumph of Love.*

That critics had missed a seam of sadness and violence since revealed by subsequent interpretations may be because the first production had missed it too. The premiere had its shivers of shock, not least in its frequent use of the phrase "make love", which for a year or two, especially in America, had begun to mean sex rather than courtship. Some of the love scenes were so explicitly played that a critic damned the kissing as "revolting"; and during Amanda and Elyot's discussion of atheism, "a faint cold wave" was said to pass perceptibly through the audience.[45] But Noël mistrusted those who would mine his texts for profundity, gravitas, or even "classic" status. Only in revival would performances tease out the play's violent imagery of acids and gases, earthquakes and explosions, of necks being wrung or broken: "You can consider yourself damned lucky I didn't shoot you"; "I'll knock your head off"; "I'll murder you"; "I should like to cut off your head with a meat axe". Noël's skill as a director was technical and in the spirit of an actor-manager; he devoted more time to blocking and verbal precision than to psychological delving of the script. This was partly a means of fending off the intellectual analysis he so mistrusted, and he made it a rule to dislike any figures (Restoration playwrights, Gilbert and Sullivan, Oscar Wilde, even Mozart) with whom he might be compared.

In the near-century since its premiere, *Private Lives* has been read as a stark exposé of heterosexual romance; an essay in high camp; an absurdist dream; a depiction of two halves of the same androgynous soul; a dark and violent exploration of human relationships in all their psychological instability; a bitter display of the love lives of the upper classes, well wadded from domestic or financial realities. Essays have been written about its encoding of homosexuality, contrasting Elyot's sexless love for the "completely feminine" Sibyl with his physical passion for the "gay"-faced A-man-da. The scepticism about romantic love that bubbles away beneath the glittering dialogue may also hint at an account of Noël's own relationships more honest and explicit than his memoirs could ever be: "I think very few people are completely normal really, deep down in their private lives." That the play can encompass such a wide range of interpretations, despite the precise, even imprisoning, nature of its specificities, speaks of the freedom within its restrictions, and of the ambiguities and profundities that can be glimpsed through the script's tight weave. *Private Lives* is not a flippant play; it depicts flippancy, which is employed as a *modus vivendi*, a means of dodging unhappiness and avoiding society. "You mustn't be serious, my dear one, it's just what they want." "Who's they?" "All the futile moralists who try to make life unbearable. Laugh at them. Be flippant. Laugh at everything, all their sacred shibboleths. Flippancy brings out the acid in their damned sweetness and light."[46]

The play exists in a world of surreal oddity, emotional topsy-turvydom, and moral emptiness, sealed off from an outside world, in which the stock market is crumbling and the world preparing for further conflict. Gladys Calthrop's sets for the second act had made liberal use of flat painted backdrops, as if the realism of the opening had given way to the dream-world of the couple's escape (curtains over doors in the scenery were painted on, as if for a puppet show or cartoon). A carnival of animals parades through the dialogue, which descends to Wonderland absurdity. Rats dance like Tiller Girls, shrimps are blown through ear trumpets, and there

is talk of the Royal London School of Bisons and a painted wooden
snake called Charles.* Some of the lines are now so famous as to
occlude their essential oddity, from the geographically unsound
description of Norfolk as "very flat", to Elyot's disturbing avowal
that "certain women should be struck regularly, like gongs", and
the code word Solomon Isaacs, shortened to "sollocks", that calls
time-out from a row.† "I'm so apt to see things the wrong way
round", Amanda says. "Morals. What one should do and what one
shouldn't." Life is oxymoronic – "perfectly horrible", "horribly
funny" – or just plain moronic: "Dear God, what does it all mean?"
But little effort is made to escape the cloud of apathy and point-
lessness: "Nothing's any use. There's no escape, ever." And later:
"Who cares?"

Amanda and Elyot are seldom played at the age the script suggests – "about thirty" – but they are of Noël's generation and their
youth is vital. They are Bright Young People moving into their
second decade of adulthood, and recognisable as such to its first
audiences as clearly as the characters of *The Vortex* had been just
seven years before. Lawrence even sported a pair of the infamous
"Lido pyjamas" worn on the beaches of Venice by the fashionable
set. Amanda is the poor little rich girl, the dancing little lady, and
is "marked for tragedy". She is of a generation permitted contraception and, as of 1929, the vote. But there is sadness embedded in
her political and sexual emancipation. "I suffered a great deal", she
admits, "and had my heart broken. But it wasn't an innocent girlish
heart. It was jagged with sophistication." She and Elyot epitomise a
generation caught between a past of slaughter and a future of overwhelming modernity: "aeroplanes then, and Cosmic Atoms, and
Television". Their conversation flicks constantly back to death; even

---

* Snakes aside, there are references to sharks, stags, bison, shrimps, cows, bulls,
   rats, flamingos, a leopard, a blind cat, a vixen, panthers, and a white elephant.
   In *Design for Living* (1932) Coward would be more self-conscious about his dramatic menagerie: "You've called me a jaguar and an ox within the last two
   minutes. I wish you wouldn't be quite so zoological."

† *Solomon Isaacs* is the title of a Victorian novel by Benjamin Farjeon, whose son,
   the drama critic and revue writer Herbert Farjeon, was a friend of Coward's.

in youth they feel that life is being lived against the clock: "what about after we're dead?" "What happens if one of us dies?" "Come and kiss me, darling, before your body rots, and worms pop in and out of your eye sockets." In one haunting moment, Amanda bursts out with a cry from the Psalms, as if she has wandered in from Shaw's *Saint Joan* (which concludes with the same line): "How long, Oh lord, how long?"

Private Lives is, in its way, as much of a post-war work as *Post-Mortem.* The hotels and casinos of Deauville, in which the play is partially set, had not long before been hospitals for wounded soldiers. Amanda and Elyot believe neither in God, nor in war, nor in man; they are of a generation permitted an angry despondency at a horror of which those who had experienced it first-hand could not speak. Sincerity is so deeply pointless that flippancy is the only option. Their *carpe-diem* spirit, which allows them to abandon their new partners on the spur of the moment and without a qualm, is matched by a sense that the *diem* is barely worth being *carpe*-d. Noël's first biographer, Patrick Braybrooke, would describe the play as an "intimate tragedy".[47] And the critic St. John Ervine, who had lost a leg in the war and who lived in almost constant pain, found it to be a "stern morality play", a continuation of Noël's virtuosic vivisection, his comedic post-mortem, of contemporary life:

Mr Coward might have been born to be the symbol of the youth that grew up in the War: bewildered, honourably angry, uninformed, willing to prevail, but in despair of any use in prevailing. Everywhere there was wreckage, and the young are more easily depressed than the middle-aged. They threw up their hands. Their catch-word was "What's the good?" They lost the expression of life from their faces and became creatures with masks.[48]

None of which is to ignore the fact that *Private Lives* can be terribly, terribly funny.

"SOMEDAY I'll FIND YOU"

Some day I'll find you,
Moonlight behind you
True to the dream I am dreaming
As I draw near you
You'll smile a little smile
For a little while
We shall stand
Hand in hand.
I'll leave you never;
Love you for ever;
All our past sorrow redeeming
Try to make it true.
Say you love me too.
Someday I'll find you again.

SCENE THREE

On 4 January 1931 the cast of *Private Lives* departed for the Broadway run, which opened three weeks later to more positive reviews than in London, although the admiration was still of "an admirable piece of fluff".[49] The part of Sybil had been taken over by Laurence Olivier's wife, Jill Esmond, but life imitated art and the relationship soon fractured. An unprecedented fortnight's break in the run, during which Gertrude Lawrence was given time to get over the final break-up of her marriage engagement, did nothing to dent sales. Lawrence's devotion to the theatre above all else, despite her yearning for the security of marriage, was a tug of war between domesticity and creativity with which Noël was familiar and which had been the subject of his earliest work. That he refused to perform with an understudy, allowing Lawrence a decent recovery period despite considerable financial loss, she thought a "wonderful thing".[50]

Jack Wilson, with his eye on a career in theatrical production, went along as company manager; he and Noël lived together on the top floor of a skyscraper south of Central Park. They escaped at the weekends to Connecticut, where the two of them purchased an American country retreat, going halves on the considerable price (Jack would eventually buy Noël out). Sasco Manor was a lavish pastiche of an English manor house, set into three acres of grounds close to the coastline town of Fairfield. But despite the prospect of an American domestic life with Jack, Noël once again refused to continue as Elyot longer than the allotted three months. Otto Kruger and Madge Kennedy took over *Private Lives* in April and column inches were expended listing how they failed to measure up to their predecessors. Noël was then offered the title role in *Hamlet* for a forthcoming Broadway production, which – surely wisely – he turned down, passing it over to Raymond Massey (now married to the original Sibyl, Adrianne Allen). Massey received poor reviews and the unorthodox production was a disaster, but he esteemed Noël for his generosity, noting that he made it a mission while on Broadway to care for the actress Constance Collier, then suffering from debilitating depression: "It was like Noël to arrive in New York for the production of his most successful play so far and to make an errand of kindness his first duty."[51] S. N. Behrman also noticed Noël's determination to cheer up the miserable, praising the way in which he elicited much-needed laughter by his habitual response to litanies of gloom: "And you're not getting any younger you know, either, dear!"[52]

In May 1931 Noël could finally return to London, where his families real and adopted had kept his various lives afloat. Goldenhurst and its land had grown almost beyond recognition, and was now a country estate. Violet, returning home from visiting Erik in Ceylon and increasingly concerned by her younger son's poor health, decided that she could no longer bear her relationship with Arthur and wrote him long and vitriolic letters telling him that it was all over. Arthur was moved to the other side of the house. Late the previous year Noël, finally deciding to give up his rooms at Ebury Street, had purchased the lease of a house on Gerald Road in London, which had been sitting empty.[53] The white-stucco building, a former coach house halfway between Sloane Square and Victoria, was barely five minutes' walk from Ebury Street. A staircase in the front hallway led straight to the vast double-height reception room on the first floor, where Noël soon installed a raised platform that ran the length of one wall beneath the quasi-proscenium of an exposed wooden beam; it was lit from behind by a huge curtained window. An upper mezzanine floor with interior windows overlooking the "stage" even served as a dress circle: he now had a domestic theatre built into the centre of his living space.

Syrie Maugham, in need of money after the Wall Street Crash, sorted the scenic design and set dressing; guests came in their droves to give him an audience; and eventually Noël was able to buy an adjoining mews house that Lorn Loraine could use as a backstage office, attending to the stage management of life.[54] A large scrapbook was obtained and bound in red velvet, and in it Noël's "family" would write down "Masterisms", so that even his private and domestic life seemed to be on show, his every word chronicled. Noël was by now insisting on "Master" as his preferred form of address, seemingly without irony, as if he had an unhealthy belief in the reality of his own myth – the border between self-belief and self-worship was unstable. "Two busts of Noël Coward stand under the lofty window", wrote a reporter, surveying the new home, "and there is a painting of Noël Coward in the entrance."[55] Nor was cruelty all that far from the surface, even if meant affectionately, as to the long-suffering Loraine: "Your eyes are safety-pinned to the bridge of your nose"; "you are just like a haddock"; "you are very old and very stupid".[56]

But it was to the rural solitude of Goldenhurst that Noël went when, in the spring of 1931, he immersed himself in his next, and largest, project. "I have fixed to open *Cavalcade* at Drury Lane", he told his mother in May, "and as it is not written yet, it looks like being a busy summer."[57] *Cavalcade* was to mark a decisive shift, both theatrical and political, in Noël's work. But threading a neat structure through his output is in many ways a pointless task, so haphazardly did his all-embracing creativity dart from project to project. *Cavalcade* was born from an ambition not for word-play but for spectacle, and its topic was of secondary importance. He had promised Charles Cochran a vast show on some theme or other – the Roman Empire, the Russian or French revolutions – that would be designed to test his skills as a director and choreographer on a scale to rival the epic vision of his friend Max Reinhardt. *Cavalcade* was to be a twist on the historical pageant craze that had begun at the turn of the century, usually depicting a romanticised Merrie England and sweeping panoramically through history from the Romans onwards, with casts of hundreds. One of Noël's very earliest works had been a pastiche of Louis Parker's pageant *Drake of England*. At a time when movies were regarded as a serious threat to the theatre, and auditoria were being converted into cinemas, the conception was a canny attempt to show that the West End could offer spectacle on a similar or even superior scale.

Not until a chance sighting of a photograph showing soldiers departing by ship for the Second Boer War did a structure begin to coalesce, namely a portrait of the last thirty years of English history (the span of Noël's own life), woven around a series of popular songs that, he was certain, would potently transport the audience to their recent pasts. A useful session with his friend Gladys Stern helped him decide the historical hooks on which the story would be hung: the Relief of Mafeking, the death of Queen Victoria, the sinking of the *Titanic*, the departure of troops to Flanders. Through this pageant of recent history he then threaded the lives of two families: the upper-middle-class Marryots, and their servants, the Bridges. The elder Marryot son goes down on the *Titanic*; the younger is killed in the war. The cross-stitching of the two social classes was an innovation when compared to popular family sagas such as Galsworthy's Forsytes or G. B. Stern's Rakonitz Chronicles, none of which paid attention to the staff that kept these well-to-do families afloat.[58] Even more daring was the introduction of a love affair between the children of each family, stretching across the class barrier.

At Goldenhurst, Noël and Gladys Calthrop kept a rigid schedule constructing the script and scene design simultaneously, such that one is really inseparable from the other, and Noël (though only afterwards) acknowledged her as co-creator. Over a thousand out-of-work actors auditioned; four hundred were chosen. John Mills, back from the Far East after his tour with the Quaints, was given the part of the Marryots' younger son, Joe. Rehearsals began in

September, and were mostly devoted to crowd control. Extras were divided into coloured groups, each member wearing a numbered plaque, so that Noël could direct from the stalls, shouting directions through a megaphone. The dress rehearsal took a week and Noël spent most of his time conquering his nerves. Elsie April was redoubtable at the piano and Cochran was a benign overseer, although he had to quell a strike in the chorus by announcing that demands for higher wages would result in the cancellation of the entire production. The overall budget, in today's money, was nearly seven million pounds.

So overwhelmed had everyone been by the sheer vastness of the project that the outside world had remained sealed off beyond the walls first of Goldenhurst and then of the Drury Lane Theatre. Back in August the Labour government, deadlocked over a budget crisis, had been replaced by a National Government drawn from all parties and led by Ramsay MacDonald. Rehearsals were already underway when, on 6 September, reductions were made to unemployment benefit. The value of the pound sterling, linked directly to the value of gold, came under threat over fears the budget was unbalanced and, after a run on gold, the pound sterling came off the gold standard on 20 September. Three weeks later, on 13 October, came the premiere of *Cavalcade*. Queues stretched around the theatre twenty-four hours before curtain-up. Noël managed to enter his first-night box as the band struck up God Save the King, so that it seemed everyone was standing for him. "One had a feeling", wrote the *Manchester Guardian*, "that Mr. Ramsay MacDonald ought to be in the box too and give us a few words."[59] Everything went well until one of the hydraulic lifts controlling the stage got stuck and threatened to derail the whole evening.

In all other respects, though, the spectacle was unparalleled. The passing years flashed up in lights over the proscenium arch. A contingent of volunteers left for South Africa by boat (there were Boer veterans in the audience). Queen Victoria's funeral cortège trundled past, indicated only by sounds offstage and a gathering of backs. The Marryots danced at a grand ball, and the stage flocked with gowns; they travelled to the beach, and an entire seaside resort was recreated. The soldiers departed for the Great War in a long trudge of uniformed extras, while war songs were delivered with increasing frenzy. The hubbub of Armistice Day in London filled the stage, omnibuses and all, as if Noël's personal memories had meshed indivisibly with theatrical display. News of the death of the Marryot children was brought in and their mother, Jane, was left alone on the stage, toasting the New Year: "Let's drink to the hope that one day this country of ours, which we love so much, will find dignity and greatness and peace again." *Cavalcade* ended with the entire company singing the national anthem beneath the Union Jack. Noël took his bow and – apparently with no idea what he was going to say – told the audience: "I hope that this play has made you feel that, in spite of the troublous times we are living in, it is still pretty exciting to be English."[60]

The audience was in raptures. The *Daily Mail* was in ecstasy. The evening, thought the paper, was a "magnificent play in which the note of national pride pervading every scene and every sentence must make each one of us face the future with courage and high hopes".[61] At the final curtain, wrote a reviewer in the *Illustrated London News*, "the auditorium looked like a devastated arena crowded with weeping women and shaken men. I was ready to fight anyone who wouldn't agree that Noël Coward is one of the greatest of living producers – not even Germany barred."[62] On and on it went: "No more lavish show has been seen in London." "One of the greatest stage successes of this generation."[63] George Bernard Shaw, who would soon embark on his most obviously Coward-esque play, *The Millionairess*, apparently thought it would be Noël's claim to historical permanence.[64] To others, though, *Cavalcade* seemed not only dramatically thin in its pathos and spectacle, but politically a betrayal. During the run Oswald Mosley would form the British Union of Fascists, his rallies at Olympia increasingly well attended. Writers such as Beverley Nichols and Ethel Mannin, with whom Noël had once seemed so aligned, angrily condemned the show for perpetuating the spirit of war, and characterised the rapturous response as the stirring of a mob into dangerous nationalist fervour.

On 27 October, two weeks after the first night, the National Government won a landslide victory in the general election, with the bulk of its support coming from the Conservative Party.

The success of *Cavalcade* was said to have contributed to the result. On 28 October, George V and Queen Mary, accompanied by their entire family, paid the show a well-publicised visit, and sealed its fate as an unexpected but welcome expression of patriotism, as if Noël had given up his Bright-Young-Thing ways and come over to the way of national pride. The aisles of the theatre were stuffed with extra chairs, and Jack Wilson was "in floods of tears the entire evening", rejoicing at the applause, which "bordered on hysteria".[65] The Duchess of York – later the Queen Mother – adored it: "marvellous, I think, as a Pageant and very moving".[66] Noël would remain irresistibly attracted to the company of royalty, the apotheosis of his social ascent.

In many ways the play's patriotism had been both planned and genuine. "I spent the whole evening", Gertrude Lawrence wrote to him, "with my hand tightly clasped in yours – <u>anything</u> just to feel that I might perhaps be of some subconscious support to you. As you say it's 'pretty exciting to be English'. But also it's pretty exciting to love you as I do!" He replied: "You know me well enough to know that when I stammered about it being pretty exciting to be English, I meant every naïve word. We're a strange race and we persist in getting a lot of things wrong but we do have our hearts in the right place."[67] This was a strange volte-face from one who had damned the hypocrisies of British society, which he had found wanting in comparison to the speed, glitter, and seeming liberality, of America. Noël was now expressing pride of a country that vilified his and many of his friends' sexuality and lifestyle. It may be that he was happy to bend his political views to the wind in which the majority seemed to be blowing: 1920s cynicism was becoming unfashionable. Or perhaps he was happy to put theatrical effectiveness above political consistency. He claimed to have regretted the inclusion of the Union Jack as soon as he read the reviews, but made no attempt to remove it from the production, and in part, the play had a patriotic climax because that made the best ending.

But *Cavalcade* is a more complicated, more inconsistent, show than a mere pageant of national pride. As one reviewer put it, "Mr Coward's patriotic sentiments are certainly not accompanied by a jingo rattle of drums".[68] Noël claimed to have been unaware of the general election, and soon resented the fact that *Cavalcade*, which had gone into rehearsal before the election was announced, would forever be painted as a play of patriotic sentiment. Its famous toast to the future of England is spoken by a woman who has been left childless and for whom the future is lonely and bleak. Underneath her speech, the sound of "sirens" is heard, ostensibly celebrating the New Year but carrying prophetic overtones of an air raid. The Victorian age is cast not as a sunlit upland of history but as an age of mistakes miserably replicated by ensuing generations, in a portrayal of the futility of repeated conflict and slaughter. Armistice Day was staged not in triumph but in regret, the bereaved mother lost amid "screaming humanity". Jane Marryot shouts hysterically to the departing troops: "Soldiers of the Queen – wounded and dying and suffering for the Queen!" Noël had originally intended to end the show simply with the Union Jack waving silently over an empty stage, more in mourning than in triumph.[69]

Even the finale's rendition of "God Save the King" is ambivalent, a twist on the theatrical rule by which each and every performance was bookended with the national anthem. And the sentiment of the anthem must be filtered through the scene that directly precedes it, which was described by more than one critic as "Expressionist". It had caused so many technical difficulties that Noël tried to cut it altogether during rehearsals, and it was Charles Cochran who insisted that it was essential.[70] A night club in 1930 filled with the vacuous dancing made familiar from Noël's revues (among the performers in the onstage band was the sprinter Jack London, Britain's first Black Olympic medallist, working as a pianist after an injury). Under blazing flashes of light, the Marryots were seen sitting alone, their hair silver, their faces aged. "Incurables" from the war were perched downstage, basket-weaving. Radios blared incessantly; news headlines were projected; jazz bands were heard playing over one another; Communists ranted; aeroplanes and steam-power machinery threatened to overwhelm the stage. The scene held a mirror up to society and reflected the hopes of a new century withering first into slaughter and then into frenzy.

The scene was scored to Noël's song "Twentieth-Century Blues". More strictly a march than conventional blues, the music was nevertheless widely credited for increasing the popularity of the blues in Britain. Covered by a singer such as Marianne Faithfull, its savage slither can seem more allied to the glittering violence of Kurt Weill than the wit of Cole Porter; the first four words of the chorus roam over more than an octave. *Cavalcade* was attended by Benjamin Britten and by Michael Tippett, eventually to become the leading classical composers of their generation and each in their different ways influenced by the blues.* "Magnificently produced", wrote the nineteen-year-old Britten in his diary, "and with some fine and moving ideas. Not a great play though."[71] Tippett, who had been thrilled by *The Vortex*, would be even more affected by the music of *Cavalcade*: "When you sing the blues, you do so not just because you are 'blue', but to relieve the blue emotions. When I heard Noël Coward sing 'Those twentieth-century blues are getting me down', he sang because the blues were doing exactly that and the singing of them is his means of discharging their effect."[72]

Cavalcade was an attempt to discharge society's war-weary blues, and to redefine patriotism as something separate from either militarism or nationalism. With hindsight it can be seen as a clear influence on Joan Littlewood's anti-war musical *Oh, What a Lovely War!* (1963), which Noël much admired; in 1939, Christopher Isherwood would group Noël with Owen and Sassoon as a trio who had taught him "to loathe the old men who had made the war".[73] The Oxford Union was soon to hold its famous debate, which, in passing the motion "This House will under no circumstances fight for its King and country", drove the controversial dispute between patriotism and pacifism. *Cavalcade* showed that the two were not

---

* Coward accused Britten of avoiding melody, but hugely admired his opera *Peter Grimes*. Britten's music festival at Aldeburgh in Suffolk held a celebration of Coward's seventieth birthday, and at one of Britten's final public appearances, his partner the tenor Peter Pears sang "I'll See You Again" from *Bitter Sweet*. Tippett acknowledged the influence of Coward on his opera *The Knot Garden* (1970) and titled his autobiography *Those Twentieth Century Blues*.

mutually exclusive. Rather as T. S. Eliot's 1934 pageant-play *The Rock* would offer religion as a unifying force to a divided society, Noël presented a belief in King and country as potential filler for the vacuum at modernity's war-wounded heart. Nineteen-thirty had seen the publication of Eliot's *Ash Wednesday*: "Consequently I rejoice, having to construct something | Upon which to rejoice." Noël had constructed an idea of nationhood in which to rejoice, as if to compensate for the failure of political machination and of romantic love. The national anthem was one potential answer to the questions he asked in the show's bleak final song.

"TWENTIETH-CENTURY BLUES"

Why is it that civilised humanity
Must make the world so wrong?
In this hurly-burly of insanity
Your dreams cannot last long. [. . .]

Blues, Twentieth-Century Blues, are getting me down.
Who's escaped those weary Twentieth-Century Blues.
Why, if there's a God in the sky, why shouldn't he grin?
High above this dreary Twentieth-Century din [. . .]
What is there to strive for,
Love or keep alive for? Say –
Hey, hey, call it a day.[74]

Scene Four

Noël's reaction to the uproar, the arguments, the acclaim, the success, was to flee. He left England to travel in South America on 29 October 1931, a day after the royal visit to *Cavalcade*, leaving the *Manchester Guardian* devoting columns to "Mr Coward's genius – a master at 32".[75] Apparently happier living from a suitcase, aware that absence was integral to the mystery of his public image, and longing for the strange no-man's-land of sea life, abroad, away,

Noël left the country to which *Cavalcade* had paid ambivalent tribute – and not with Jack Wilson but with Jeffery Amherst. Apolitical as he professed to be, he had little confidence in the temporary security of the election victory. "I compared [England] in my mind to a gallant, unimaginative old lady convalescing after an abdominal operation, unaware of the nature and danger of her disease."[76]

One of the attractions of the tour was that he and Jeffery were following in the footsteps of the Prince of Wales and his brother Prince George, the Duke of Kent, who had returned from their well-publicised trip to South America not long before their visit to *Cavalcade*. The Prince of Wales's love for Noël's work was well known, but Noël had not taken kindly to being ignored when their paths had crossed. His real affection was reserved for the Duke of Kent, whom he had first met in 1922. The Duke was bisexual and promiscuous and rumours of his love affair with Noël have become increasingly elaborate (the two of them paraded the streets in drag . . . the two of them were arrested on the suspicion of being rent boys . . . their love letters were stolen from Gerald Road . . .). An affair with a Duke would surely have been an attraction for Noël, and even more so with a Duke devoted to the navy. But Noël's eventual partner, Graham Payn, denied the rumour when he had no particular reason to do so, and fifteen letters to Noël from the Duke do survive, the earliest from 1930; they are both bland and formal, each one signed "Yours ever, George".[77] (To his friends, the Duke always signed himself "Georgie".) The Duke would marry Princess Marina of Greece and Denmark in 1934, and Noël became an intimate friend to both.

Jack Wilson meanwhile had begun an affair with the writer and socialite David Herbert that was an open secret in their circle: when in New York, they shared an apartment on East End Avenue. Hence, perhaps, Noël's travels with Jeffery, which would be undertaken by rail, boat, and mule over the next four and a half months, as they traversed a huge loop of South America. The Great Depression and the rise of fascism had reached South America too, and they arrived in Brazil – greeted by the open arms of Christ the Redeemer, completed just weeks before their arrival – to find a country led by a military junta after a revolution the previous year; the president's policies were broadly modelled on those of Mussolini. In Rio de Janeiro they befriended Daan Hubrecht, the son of the Dutch Ambassador. Twenty-one years old and in the throes of a tempestuous love affair with a married Englishwoman, Daan was more than ready to be taken under their wing, and it was soon decided that the three of them would travel on together.

In December they took a tugboat along the Paraná River, accompanied by a small and un-venomous pet snake that Noël had been given in São Paolo, and which lived calmly in his pocket until Jeffery accidentally killed it by giving it a sip of martini. Noël spent his thirty-second birthday on the boat, surrounded by the crates of green tea that were the merchants' stock-in-trade and gazing at starlit night skies or looking for piranhas and crocodiles in the water. Still he was unable, as he later admitted, to avoid a certain self-satisfaction at having achieved a life of such luxury and exoticism. Memories of dowdy boarding houses and dreary train journeys through foggy London were still fresh in his mind. The boat took them some 600 kilometres until, as the Brazilian summer began, they reached the Iguazú Falls on the border of Argentina and Brazil, which together form the largest series of waterfalls in the world. The mist of mosquitoes was such that on their arrival, filthy from the trip and longing for a bath, they saw very little. Arriving at Buenos Aires they became local celebrities after it transpired that the captain of their passenger ship, taking umbrage at their refusal or inability to keep to the strictures of the dress code, had imprisoned them behind bars in the lower-deck cabins, leading the crew to pass them food and cigarettes through the grille. Hubrecht returned to Rio (increasingly famous as an idle playboy, he nevertheless went on to work in Government Intelligence in the East Indies). Noël and Jeffery carried on alone, navigating fields of pampas and dust-storms in the warm but rainy summer months of January and February 1932, riding by mule through the Andes while endlessly trying to catch their breath in the high altitude.

At a station in Chile they found a passenger who had been crushed between two wagons of a train; he was, Jeffery recalled, in a bad state and perhaps dying. Noël speedily translated this to their happening upon "the bleeding torso and head of a young man who had been completely cut in half", but Jeffery's account focused mainly on Noël who, newly furnished with a well-stuffed first aid box, rushed dramatically to the scene in the hopes of injecting somebody with something. Chilean officials believed this well-supplied Englishman to be a doctor and were only too encouraging. Noël had to be dissuaded from causing the man (or, at least, the remaining half of him) further damage. It was in Chile that they could resume their love affair with the navy, and Noël spent most of his time with officers in hotel bars, admitting to "a couple of fairly libidinous 'guest nights'" with some of the sailors.[78] In February they went on to Peru by plane, seemingly Noël's first flight, but it made little discernible impression on him, luxurious novelty now being so easily available that it had become the norm. As was their habit, they coincided with political uprising and populist politics (a strike by a bakery workers' union in Lima was being violently suppressed). As was also their habit, they paid little heed: "some sort of revolution was in progress".[79] They sat in a hotel until it was over, before making their way to Cuzco: "where the Incas had such a delightful time", wrote Noël, "and it really isn't very central".[80]

He travelled from Panama to Los Angeles on 12 March 1932, leaving Jeffery to return to London.[81] Noël was now at his most content amid the solitude and inactivity of sea life, and it was during the apparently blissful voyage on board the small cargo boat, as it sailed from Colón to the West Coast of America, that he wrote *Design for Living*, having been casting around in his mind during the latter stages of his travels for the spark that would set a new play alight. About a love triangle, this was to be a vehicle to perform himself with Alfred Lunt and Lynn Fontanne, something he had promised the renowned couple when, ambitious and unknown, they had all first met in America eleven years before. The Lunts had been released from contractual obligations and were eager to get going, but the play would have to wait. Jack Wilson met Noël at Los Angeles and together they spent ten days in Hollywood.

Noël disliked the false and moneyed bonhomie of the place, with its hectic and ingratiating social life. But after the silent truncations of his early scripts, the movies were a world of exciting innovation that he was keen finally to conquer; the "talkies", once dismissed as a fad, were speedily becoming both standard and popular. A successful film of *Private Lives* had been made while he was abroad, starring Robert Montgomery and Norma Shearer, who took their fight scene so seriously that the former was knocked unconscious. The actors had privately filmed the stage performances in order to mimic the original delivery, and this may have been the reason for Noël's approval. But it was a movie of *Cavalcade* that took up most of his time. Almost nobody had shown interest in the project until an enthusiastic director of Fox Studios had fought for it. Noël spent hours vetoing various scriptwriters' ideas (eventually Reginald Berkeley would provide a faithful adaptation), and then departed for New York in April, leaving the movie to look after itself. Lack of enthusiasm from on high meant it was free from studio interference and permitted mainly to replicate the stage production. Noël adored the result and so, after a breathless publicity campaign – "Picture of a Generation!" – did the public and the Academy Award voters. *Cavalcade* would be declared Best Picture for 1933, but the rash of Coward adaptations it inspired were all unfaithful, or unsuccessful, or both.

In New York a read-through of *Design for Living* with the Lunts had an electric chemistry and American producers fell over themselves to secure the premiere, but Noël had first to return to England to work on a long-promised revue for Charles Cochran: *Words and Music*. Revue was still going strong in the new decade and although composers such as Cole Porter and Vivian Ellis were now enjoying increasing success with the form, Noël was still notorious for his ability to produce sketches, lyrics, and music single-handedly – hence the title, a reminder of his many talents. At the Manchester previews he would even briefly take on the role of conductor. The success of *Cavalcade* had been such that he now needed to brook no compromise with Charles Cochran, or even seek his advice, despite the impresario's misgivings at the revue's lack both of variety and of a major star.

Noël quickly employed Buddy Bradley as choreographer, making the show the first with an exclusively white cast ever to be choreographed by a Black dancer. John Mills joined the line-up, and so did a precocious fourteen-year-old called Graham Payn, whose audition had involved a rendition of "Nearer My God to Thee" accompanied by a tap dance. Payn saw an elegant man who was holding his cigarette very oddly. Noël looked at the ambitious little boy in an Eton suit with greased hair, flanked by a pushy mother swathed in fur, and may essentially have seen his childhood self looking back at him.[82] Payn's treble was powerful: footage of his teenage performances is quite startling, in that both sound (tremulous) and delivery (saucy) wouldn't have disgraced the leading soubrettes of the day.[83] He was employed, but neither of them could know that when he was cast in another of Noël's revues, over a decade later, the two men would begin a lifelong relationship.

Words and Music was a critical success, but it was less popular with audiences and played at the Adelphi Theatre from 16 August 1932 until February of the following year: not quite the long run for which all had hoped. With its simple black-and-white design scheme, there was little in the way of spectacle and it may be that *Cavalcade* had led people to expect something different. But *Words and Music* proved conclusively that, for Noël, satire and sentiment were two halves of the same coin. Among the sketches was one of the most daring he ever wrote: a parody of *Journey's End* featuring a Spanish-accented Captain Stanhope, which would have spoken, to contemporary audiences, of the recently proclaimed Second Spanish Republic and the growing shadow of the Spanish Civil War. There were chorus girls dressed in glittery army uniforms, and the scene ended with puffs of glitter shooting out of diamanté rifles, to the strains of "Deutschland Über Alles". Its only equal in fabulous poor taste, allying militarism with high camp, may be "Springtime for Hitler" from Mel Brooks's *The Producers.*

The revue found a home for "Mad Dogs and Englishmen" (sung by the actor Romney Brent), and among the other numbers was the immortal "Mad About the Boy", delivered by a series of star-struck women obsessing over a movie star whose glamour turns out to be confected: "He has a gay appeal | That makes me feel | There's maybe something sad about the boy."[84] The real sexual daring in the song was revealed when, in September 1932, Noël himself recorded it, without altering the lyrics. The weakness of his voice led to the record's never being released — perhaps an excuse, although by 1955, either through false memory or a more conscious effort to rid the song of sexual politics, Noël was writing in his diary that "I *never* sing [it] because (a) it is a woman's song, and (b) because it is too high for me".[85] The recording, now released, contradicts both propositions. And when mounting the eventual Broadway transfer, in 1939, Noël would attempt to add a verse sung by a young married man, equally obsessed: "Mad about the boy | I know it's silly | But I'm mad about the boy | And even Dr Freud cannot explain | Those vexing dreams | I've had about the boy." Psychoanalysis was receiving more public recognition in America and the new lines – a match for Cole Porter's gay innuendo – were a topical riposte to the increasingly prevalent notion of conversion therapy: "My doctor can't advise me | He'd help me if he could | Three times he's tried to psychoanalyse me | But it's just no good." The theatre's management deemed the additional lyrics too risqué to be permitted.

But *Words and Music* ended on a wistful note, and had been an attempt to show that the days of money-no-object spectacle and roaring excess were well and truly over. Back in November 1931 the "Red and White Party" in Regent's Park, in which food, costumes and décor had been a lavish display solely of red and white, had brought conclusively to an end the era of the Bright Young Things, whose lifestyle now seemed painfully divorced from the Depression's realities. In numbers such as "Children of the Ritz", Noël showed the party-going set coming to terms with the hardships of the new decade, and the revue ended with a group of young people leaving a party. "It's over." "What's over?" "The Party, silly, all that was part of the Party, now we're tired." Two months after *Words and Music* closed Hitler became Chancellor of the Third Reich, and in England Churchill was beginning to warn of the dangers of German rearmament. "I'm certainly all for disarmament", Noël told Beverley Nichols later that year, "providing that every other country is all for disarmament too. As now everything seems so chaotic in this delicious civilisation I should think that the really best thing to do is for all of us to slay each other as swiftly and efficiently as possible."[86]

News from home did little to alleviate this philosophy. A month

before *Words and Music* had opened, his brother Erik had been granted
three months' sick leave from his job at Ceylon: "Nothing serious
so don't worry masses of love".[87] But Noël was astonished by the
emaciated person who arrived in England. He installed Erik in a
nursing home, where a diagnosis was quickly made. Cancer, left
untreated, had spread and was now incurable. The prognosis was
kept from Erik, and he was transferred to Goldenhurst, though not
before Noël had to break the news to his parents, a discussion so
traumatic that he afterwards found the memory "intolerable".[88]
Erik's adoration of his mother had also reached near-romantic fervour, and Violet was helpless with distress. Distance had made the
siblings closer, and Erik's letters from Ceylon – his correspondence
equals his brother's wit and improves on his brother's grammar
– express his delight at the success of *Cavalcade* and report the frequent and generous gifts that arrived from Noël's chequebook. But
resentment had never entirely dissipated: "Noël I still haven't heard
from since I left home. But I suppose he is so busy grabbing money
with both hands and feet that he hasn't time to hold a pen as well.
[. . .] He is getting a Cadillac is he? For all his supposed patriotism
he seems to prefer most American things."[89]

Noël's frankly admitted guilt may have been assuaged by the fact
that he could at least fund Erik's care. But nor did he put life on
hold, and he left the patient to be tended by Violet and the nurses
in order to holiday in Europe through September and October, using
his tried-and-tested method of hitching a ride on a naval ship to
travel as far as Egypt. His sympathy was more with Violet than Erik,
who is not mentioned by name in any of his letters from the boat.
"I'm trying to take your advice about not thinking of you", he
wrote to her from Versailles. "Everything is so tragic and cruel for
you and my heart aches dreadfully for you but that's no good either
except that it proves even to me (who didn't need much proof) how
very very much I love you. [. . .] I'm saying several acid prayers to
a fat contented God the Father in a dirty night gown who hates you
and me and every living creature in the world."[90]

There was no thought of cutting back on work. That autumn,
under his supervision, a newly formed "Noël Coward Company"
toured a selection of his plays across the country, led by Kate Cutler

and with a young James Mason in the cast. Noël wrote them a one-act comedy, *Weatherwise*, adapting a short story he had published (in *Motor Owner* magazine) back in 1923. It prefigures *Blithe Spirit* in its take-off of spiritualism and, in its dark and savage humour, is a clear pastiche of Saki: sceptical Lady Warple attends a séance and becomes possessed by a demonic dog, eventually leaping at a doctor and mauling him to death. "Serves him right", someone comments, "for wearing such low collars." Nor was there any question of Noël's postponing his voyage to New York to open *Design for Living*. He left in November and rehearsed over Christmas. "Lynn and Alfred are simply superb and I think we're going to give the best acting in the world to the great American Public. It is bliss working with them." Taking a small role in the cast was a figure from his childhood, Philip Tonge, once the lead in *Where the Rainbow Ends* and now a jobbing actor on Broadway. Noël could not temper his glee at the way the tables had turned. "It does seem funny when I look back and remember how much in awe of him I was. Life certainly plays very strange tricks on people."[91]

He apologised to Erik: "I haven't written as much and as often as I should have but that's me all over – careless! [. . .] All my love to you and hand some out to everybody and get well soon." And, to his mother, on 10 January: "How wonderful if he could die quietly in his sleep [. . .] perhaps in the long run he will turn out to be lucky after all!"[92] Whether he was hoping for Erik's sudden recovery or hinting that death was a lucky escape is uncertain. Erik, twenty-seven years old, did die in his sleep, a week later, just two days before the Broadway opening of *Design for Living*. He was buried next to his brother Russell, in the churchyard at Teddington, and there was something oddly inevitable about his early departure from an overlooked life.

"THE PARTY'S OVER NOW"

The Party's over now,
The dawn is drawing very nigh,
The candles gutter;
The starlight leaves the sky.

It's time for little boys and girls
To hurry home to bed
For there's a new day
Waiting just ahead.
Life is sweet
But time is fleet,
Beneath the magic of the moon,
Dancing time
May seem sublime
But it is ended all too soon,
The thrill has gone
To linger on
Would spoil it anyhow,
Let's creep away from the day
For the Party's over now.[93]

CURTAIN

ACT TWO

SCENE ONE

The Ethel Barrymore Theatre, New York, on the evening of 2 January 1933.
The premiere of NOËL COWARD*'s new play,* Design For Living, *in which*
he is starring with ALFRED LUNT *and* LYNN FONTANNE.

GILDA (FONTANNE): Can't we laugh a little? Isn't it a joke? Can't we
make it a joke?

LEO (COWARD): Yes, it's a joke. It's a joke, all right. We can laugh
until our sides ache. Let's start, shall we?

GILDA: What's the truth of it? The absolute, deep-down truth? Until
we really know that, we can't grapple with it. We can't do a thing.
We can only sit here flicking words about.

LEO: It should be easy, you know. The actual facts are so simple. I
love you. You love me. You love Otto. I love Otto. Otto loves you.
Otto loves me. There now! Start to unravel from there.[1]

In a nutshell Leo gives the plot of *Design for Living*, in which Noël
grappled with the various permutations of a love triangle among
three artists: Gilda, an interior designer; Leo, a writer; and Otto, a
painter. Their Bohemian search for free love and their rejection of
the monogamy and morals of society scrape against a world that
would seek to censure their "disgusting three-sided erotic hotch-
potch" – as exemplified by the pointedly named Ernest, to whom
Gilda makes a misguided and short-lived marriage. Eventually she
rejects the importance of being earnest, returning to live and laugh
with Leo and Otto.

The ménage à trois was a natural subject for Noël. Alfred Lunt and Lynn Fontanne had been only one of the couples to which he, a born third, had become intimately attached. In France the previous decade he had spent time with Somerset Maugham, then shuttling between his lover Gerald Haxton and his wife Syrie (like Gilda, an interior designer). The daring of *Design for Living* came not in the conventional plot of the love triangle, but in his open depiction of Leo's and Otto's bisexuality. Noël's use of the word "gay" in the script was still a code that few could read, but it is clear from the start that the two men love one another. Their physical attraction is marked in the stage directions, and by the third act (temporarily abandoned by Gilda) they have travelled the world as a couple, fighting off their unhappiness, an increasingly camp double act.

Such sexual daring, at the outset of Noël's career, might have seemed all part of the general atmosphere, but in Britain and America the public mood was beginning to turn, and in cities such as Chicago and New York, where an openly gay culture had thrived over the previous decade, a crackdown was beginning. Prohibition would end half a year after the run of *Design for Living*, but far from creating a new mood of permissiveness, the grip of the Depression led to the evaporation of the tourist trades, and the nightclubs and bars in which gay life had been permissible did poor business and began to close. Police raids became more frequent and within a few years the nightlife of the 1920s would be all but eliminated. Homosexuals became indicative of a perceived social decay that was thought to have caused the economic downturn with its profligacy and extravagance, and they were considered a threat to traditional family hierarchies already imperilled by unemployment. Sexual crimes were whipped up by the press into homophobic hysteria. The situation was no better in London, where theatrical censorship was becoming stricter, and while the riotous sexual display of events such as the Chelsea Arts Club ball managed to continue, with Noël often in attendance, police surveillance and raids increased in frequency and severity.

A London premiere of *Design for Living* would have been impossible without major cuts, and the show was instead to open first in Ohio and then in New York. But even in America there had been efforts to tighten theatrical censorship. Within a year a production code would be introduced in Hollywood that prohibited elements of "perversion" in a screen story, and Mae West's *The Drag*, subtitled "a homosexual comedy", had been closed after ten performances, before it reached Broadway. Laws were soon to be passed in New York that would prohibit homosexuals from gathering in any state-licensed public place. *Design for Living*, staged during a turning point in public attitudes, was pushing against an increasingly conservative society and against criminal law.

That Noël got away with it, and with great success, was down to the star power of its three leads. Emotional ambiguity was tucked beneath comedic turns, and homoeroticism hidden within bisexuality: both men have genuine sexual feelings towards Gilda, and at one point Otto vaults over a sofa to make love to her. In theatrical circles rumours of the Lunts' extramarital affairs were rife, which gave the play a whiff of behind-the-scenes gossip. Lunt had even wondered whether it could be staged on an enormous bed, apparently one of his less risqué suggestions during rehearsals. The Lunts were brilliantly adept at fashioning their own legend. As with Noël, life was theatre and theatre life – their homes were compared to sets, their parties to cabarets, their friends to an audience. They were said to rehearse and to perform everywhere from the dinner table to the marital bed, and the latter, rumour had it, was for sleeping only. Theirs is thought to have been a sexless, almost fraternal, union, made closer by intense friendships with gay men and (possibly) by Alfred's homosexual infidelity.

Their critics and fans described their near-histrionic perform-ances in comedy, toying with the rhythms and stresses of every line. When Noël's equally virtuosic but rather more throwaway style was added into the mixture it became a potent one, the three actors meshing so neatly that during one performance, when Lunt skipped a line, he and Noël simply swapped roles without missing a beat. As if confirming where the sexual frisson in the intimate trio really lay, Noël gave Alfred a much easier time than Lynn, with whom he could fight as if performing *Private Lives*; his nicknames for the couple ("Grandpa" and "Grandma") seemed designed to expose the sexless nature of their relationship. Rehearsals were not devoid of tension or even of walk-outs ("I can't do it!" was Alfred's cry, "Get someone else!"), and Noël did not share the Lunts' habit of ripping the evening's performance to shreds in a late-night post-mortem. "I was *terrible* tonight!" one of them would moan, to which he would invariably respond: "Well, *I* was wonderful!"[2] But as the production toured to Cleveland, Pittsburgh, and Washington through January 1933 it seemed clear a success was brewing.

The opening night on Broadway, on 22 January, confirmed the suspicion. Noël was badly affected by the death of Erik and made it through only with the Lunts' support. He raged at the audience's perpetual mirth, finding them deaf to the play's more serious side, and critics, although almost unanimously approving, thought he had written nothing more than a vehicle for the leading trio. "Without the three luminaries who scamper through the leading parts, [*Design for Living*] would have a great deal less of the holiday glitter" wrote the *New York Times*.[3] The sexual daring was barely remarked, bar in *Vanity Fair*, which tore apart a "pansy paraphrase of [Shaw's] *Candida*". The reviewer, George Jean Nathan, then published a parody script, "Design for Loving", which not only featured characters of "tribade" (i.e. lesbian) tendencies, but had among its cast a "flagellant", a "hermaphrodite", and an "onanist". *Vogue* set the cat among the backstage pigeons by suggesting that Noël's performance was in a different league to the Lunts, at which point almost all of their friends sent tongue-in-cheek telegrams professing profound agreement. One common criticism was of the third act's superfluity. Cue Mrs Patrick Campbell's arrival in Noël's dressing room during the second interval: "Such a good play." And, over her shoulder as she left, "such a good ending".[4]

The tone of *Design for Living* is far less highly wrought than *Private Lives*, and lacks the latter's percussive, staccato, soundscape. Its feel is distinctly European, not only in the naming of the central trio – the writer, Leo Mercuré, is French – but in the nods to the sexual roundelays of Arthur Schnitzler or to the work of August Strindberg in rare comic vein: Strindberg's one-act *Playing with Fire*, which hints at the homoerotic undertones inherent to a love triangle, had been published in English in 1930. A riposte to those who, after *Cavalcade*, would tar Noël with a jingoistic brush, *Design for Living* presented a clash between artistic Bohemianism and conventional society – and, seemingly, the triumph of the former. Friends of the Lunts wrote to Alfred fearing he had been sexually corrupted by the play and its author. The designer Lee Simonson told him it was the "nastiest play" he had ever seen: "a demi-homo is the most disgusting of God's creatures [. . . and Noël] was the personification of the most loathing and revolting human being I have ever seen on any stage".[5]

But *Design for Living*'s primary concern is neither advocacy of bisexuality nor the life of the artist. It is clear-eyed about the romance of the Ivory Tower: "I'm far too much of an artist to be taken in by the old cliché of shutting out the world and living for my art alone." Its trio is too self-centred, too amoral, too dependent on money and success as the bedrock of their purportedly free lives, to be the object of their author's unalloyed approval. Come together in a love triangle, they are warned that it "won't last". The ménage à trois may be one answer to the modern search for alternative ways of living, but in its formation there is, by default, the inherent sadness of the spare part. "I'm not needed any more", Gilda concedes, aware of the overarching attraction between the two men. Otto attempts to reassure her: "We shall always need each other, all three of us." But she is certain: "The survival of the fittest – that's what counts." The reality of their polyamory is an "endless game of three-handed, spiritual ping-pong".

The search for freedom and honesty comes at a cost. Leo and Otto declare themselves free only when drunk, on bad sherry. The play's sleight of hand is that the characters' attempts to be true to themselves, and to one another, unfold alongside their increasing reliance on the artifice of camp. Leo is a writer of the thinnest of plays; Gilda a designer – or gild-er – interested in "the decoration of life"; Otto a painter trying to see beneath the surface portrait. Self-consciously they play at happiness as if acting a part – "we can pretend that we're happy" – taking refuge in façade, for fear of what they might find beneath: "We have a veneer though; it's taken us years to acquire." Their design for living is in its way as superficial and hopeless as the world of moral convention – Church, children, monogamy – that they wilfully reject. "It's all a question of masks, really", Leo concludes, "brittle, painted masks. We all wear them as a form of protection; modern life forces us to." The line is an echo of Wilde's *An Ideal Husband*: "What a mask you have been wearing all these years! A horrible, painted mask!"

Design for Living is also a psychological study of Gilda, and of her permanent dissatisfaction, as she tries on and then discards different lives, different loves, either within or outside of society. Like Nina Leeds, the heroine of Eugene O'Neill's *Strange Interlude* (a role created by Fontanne in 1928), she is caught between two men. Like Constance in Maugham's *The Constant Wife* (1926), she earns her own money working as a designer. Part of the play's daring is its concession that sexual freedom for women is the privilege of the financially independent. Rejecting her own "damned femininity", and dismissing humanity as a "let-down", when living as a designer in a shabby Paris studio she longs to be a "nice-minded British matron, with a husband, a cook, and a baby", wishing she believed "in God and the *Daily Mail* and 'Mother India!'". Yet when she is married to the dully respectable Ernest in an oppressively stylish high-rise apartment, her only option is to leave once again, to rejoin Otto and Leo. Her door is constantly slamming, her life a sequence of disappearing acts, as she flutters out "into the night like a silly great owl". Like Larita in *Easy Virtue*, or Amanda in *Private Lives*, she seems doomed to shuttle between different modes of living, different attempts at loving, in a perennial search for the ostensible freedom of the modern woman and the freethinking artist, perpetually desiring what she has not got.

Noël's strain continued through the run as he battled vocal infections. Ticket sales paid no attention to attacks in the press, but the worst of these had been virulent and even dangerous. Alfred Lunt would never again play a role of such sexual ambivalence. Noël made arrangements for Violet and Aunt Vida to join him in Manhattan, but soon removed himself from the city's melee, taking a woodland cottage in the Palisades. His celebrity was now such that he was forced to hire security, not least because America was in the grip of a wave of kidnapping scares, following the abduction and murder of the baby son of the aviator Charles Lindbergh. Noël employed an armed detective called Tommy Webber who accompanied him everywhere and sat in the wings of the Ethel Barrymore Theatre. Nor was this entirely paranoia; in

March, a young British actor living in New York called Frederick Manthorp sent Noël a threatening letter demanding £450, one of a number of blackmailing documents he despatched to wealthy celebrities.[6] Noël did not press charges. On 16 May, he went with Elsa Maxwell to the eighteen-month-old Empire State Building, only to be told by a trembling driver that they had been followed by a carload of gangsters and had to leave by another entrance under police supervision. The gangsters turned out to be autograph hunters.

He was persuaded to play for four months rather than his usual three, but he was struggling with laryngitis and counting the days. "Capacity and standees at every performance", he wrote to Gladys Calthrop, whose extravagantly chic sets had contributed to the success, "and very common people, dear – not our class at all – given to spitting and coughing and belching during the quieter passages."[7] Violet and Aunt Vida returned to England, *Design for Living* closed on 26 May, and Noël sailed out into the North Atlantic the following morning on a ship bound for Bermuda, where he joined a British naval cruiser. He was intending to make another tour of South America but after a few days in Panama, suffering once again from the gloom that overcame him when having to leave the camaraderie of the navy, he went on instead to Trinidad, his first visit to the Caribbean. From there he returned to England for the first time in over six months, his mind already buzzing with other projects. But he was never sure that audiences had fully understood, or sufficiently liked, the frolicsome and forlorn trio at the heart of *Design for Living*. Few grasped that the part he had written for himself was essentially a self-portrait: Leo, a chain-smoking writer accused of producing flimsy and sentimental plays, was openly bisexual, "thin and nervy", and given a name that was almost the mirror image of his own.

Noël was returning to a family still grieving the death of Erik, and to his own complex trios, his relationship with Jack Wilson fraying yet further even as they planned new business ventures. One of *Design for Living*'s cures for melancholy is to exist in the moment, to grope towards "a flicker of ecstasy sandwiched between yesterday and tomorrow". Another is laughter. Laughter is the recurrent refrain of the play, but it appears always as something dangerous, uncontrolled, hysterical, frightening – "If I once started, I should never stop" – and as the only real way to deal with unhappiness, which may be the funniest joke of all. At the end of their play Otto and Leo and Gilda "break down utterly and roar with laughter; they groan and weep with laughter; their laughter is still echoing from the walls as the curtain falls . . ."

Scene Two

In January 1934 Virginia Woolf wrote to her nephew. "I have to dine with [Sibyl] Colefax tonight to meet Noël Coward whose works I despise but they say he's very good to his old mother."[8] Her initially rapturous admiration of Noël's talents had cooled over the six years since they had first met.

> He called me Darling and gave me his glass to drink out of. These are dramatic manners. I find them rather congenial. [. . .] Then he played his new opera on Sibyl's grand piano and sang like a tipsy crow – quite without self-consciousness. It is about Brighton in the time of the Regency – you can imagine. He makes about twenty thousand a year, but has several decayed uncles and aunts to keep; and they will dine with him, he says, coming out of Surbiton, and harking back to his poverty stricken days.[9]

The "new opera", begun on his voyage back to England from Trinidad, was *Conversation Piece*, and was Noël in romantic mode, attempting to replicate the success of *Bitter Sweet* and to provide a vehicle for the star French soprano Yvonne Printemps. It was hardly calculated to appeal to Woolf or to the Bloomsbury Group, whose opinion of his work was going from bad to worse. Once, he had been a name of promising glitter on Sibyl Colefax's guest lists, but he was now a topic for critical discussion at her parties. Woolf continued to meet Noël occasionally until the war and their personal relationship remained warm. He especially loved *Flush*, her fictional biography of Elizabeth Barrett Browning's spaniel, and she responded to his praise with evidently genuine pleasure: "My heart leapt, that <u>you</u> should have liked that innocent story and I feel – not like a dog – like a cat that is purring all over, with pleasure at your praise and generosity."[10] She recounted a conversation with Colefax in her diary: "The truth was Noël adores me and I could save him from being as clever as a bag of ferrets and as trivial as a perch of canaries."[11]

Woolf's complex attitude towards Noël exemplified what came to be known as the "Battle of the Brows": an opposition between so-called highbrow and middlebrow art, cementing divisions that had been sown as early as Noël's quarrel with Edith Sitwell. He was by now passionately suspicious of the "intelligentsia" and of work he believed paid no heed to audience enjoyment, of art created for artists by the highly educated and the privately wealthy. In return, figures such as Woolf mistrusted Noël's facility, his craving for success and celebrity, the importance he placed on mere entertainment, the perceived vapidity of his work, and the apparently nationalist politics of *Cavalcade* at a time of political crisis. There was also the problem not only of his popular appeal, but of the way in which praise often tipped over (not without his nurturing and encouragement) into adulation: in 1934 a book appeared entitled *The Amazing Mr Noël Coward*. Aldous Huxley, for example, enjoyed Noël's company, finding him "much nicer and more intelligent when he's by himself than when he's being the brilliant young actor-dramatist in front of a crowd of people", but was sure that his gifts were "all out of the 6d box at Woolworth's [. . .] an omelette without eggs".[12] Evelyn Waugh had liked Noël well enough but was convinced he had "no brains", and back in 1926 W. H. Auden had sat through *The Queen Was in the Parlour* (not, perhaps, the best introduction) in abject disbelief. "Is it like this", he wrote to a friend, quoting Eliot, "in Death's other Kingdom?"[13]

Worst of all would be a review by the critic Cyril Connolly of Noël's first memoir, *Present Indicative*, on which Noël had worked through the run of *Design for Living*. The book, which would sell in the tens of thousands on its eventual publication in 1937, resisted neither name-dropping nor anecdote, but was surprising for its concession of debt, its self-criticism, and its honest account – the first in the public domain – of his patchy and undistinguished war service. In revealing the discipline and self-control that lay behind the popular image of the louche hedonist, the memoir contained as much to puncture as to inflate the bubble of his own legend: more than one critic commented with surprise on the unhappiness it revealed. But Esmé Wynne, now working as a novelist and living apart from her husband, berated him by letter for the book's inaccuracy, and in the *New Statesman* Connolly sharpened his knife, amazed by Noël's unabashed flight from intellectuality in pursuit of success. "It is almost always shallow, and often dull, and leaves us with the picture, carefully incomplete, of one of the most talented and prodigiously successful people the world has ever known [. . .] an essentially unhappy man who gives the impression of having seldom really thought or really lived."[14] Connolly had gone from Eton to Balliol, and his views cemented Noël's distrust, even loathing, of the literary establishment. Noël would take his literary revenge in his post-war play *Peace in Our Time*, which in its portrait of a fascist Britain included a character called Chorley Bannister, editor of a highbrow magazine called *Progress* (a thinly disguised version of Connolly's *Horizon*) and on very good terms with the local Gestapo.

By the early 1930s a new wave of experimental British dramatists was determined to disrupt, both theatrically and politically, what it perceived as a conservative realism of which Noël was now an apparent figurehead. In 1932 the Group Theatre had been founded, and would perform plays written by figures such as Auden or Christopher Isherwood. Yet Auden's *The Dance of Death* (1933), or the Auden–Isherwood collaboration *The Dog Beneath the Skin* (1935), were to make use of music hall and revue to create a form of entertainment that revealed what the *Manchester Guardian* called "the closeness of kinship between the modern poets Coward and Auden".[15] The *Observer* claimed that "Mr Noël Coward has never professed to be a poet, but there is better verse, in addition to finer satire, in *This Year of Grace* than in Mr Auden's [*Dance of Death*]."[16] The popularity of blues music in the wake of *Cavalcade* led to lyrics of Auden's such as "Funeral Blues". Woolf's last novel, *Between the Acts*, would feature a pageant staged at a country house that, to the strains of a jazz record, reflects the state of England. A novel such as Waugh's *Vile Bodies*, an exact contemporary of *Private Lives*, is positively Coward-esque in the way it reveals the mournfulness of the party-going generation while wrestling with the prospect of renewed global warfare.* Charles Cochran suggested to T. S. Eliot and Benjamin Britten that they collaborate on a revue, and Eliot's jazz-torn verse drama, *Sweeney Agonistes*, would be staged at the Group Theatre in 1934 with all but the lead actor in masks.

The false divisions were exacerbated by the fact that, in the mid-1930s, Noël was chiefly known as the creator of *Bitter Sweet* and *Cavalcade*. Of his earliest plays only *Hay Fever* had been revived in the West End; *Private Lives* was a four-year-old memory and *Design for Living* had not been seen in Britain. That Noël was now work-ing on *Conversation Piece*, a "romantic comedy with music" set in Brighton during the Regency, was not going to help his cause.[17] He had worked on the music in the second half of 1933, struggling especially over the central waltz, "I'll Follow my Secret Heart". The plot brazenly ignored the criticisms of those who dismissed his eagerness to entertain capacity audiences and earn a lot of money for doing so. Romney Brent, not long out of *Words and Music*, was to play Paul, an émigré from the French Revolution, who passes off a music-hall singer as his aristocratic ward so she can make a beneficial marriage – though their real love turns out to be for one another. Brent struggled during rehearsals and happily relinquished the part to Noël, who performed with the aid of a wig and a French accent that wouldn't have disgraced *Allo' Allo!* It was the first time Noël had written, composed, and acted the lead in, a musical, and the feat was thought to have had few, if any, parallels.

Conversation Piece opened in the West End on 16 February 1934. Yvonne Printemps's English was so poor that she learned much of

---

* Compare *Cavalcade*'s depiction of "screaming humanity" with Waugh's *Vile Bod-ies*, Chapter Eight: "All that succession and repetition of massed humanity . . ." The critic Ivor Brown linked *Private Lives* to the novel: "[The play's] characters might have wandered in from a story by Mr. Evelyn Waugh, [with] their vile bodies . . ." (*Manchester Guardian*, 25 September 1930, p. 17). Like *Post-Mortem*, *Vile Bodies* (which Coward admired) features a caricature of Lord Beaverbrook.

the script phonetically, but her star power won the day. Noël had no qualms about admitting that he had written a crowd-pleaser: "I am now giving an exquisite performance as a syphilitic French duke [. . .] the play itself I think is dull and garbled and I am faintly ashamed of it".[18] But depression-beleaguered audiences still craved escapist entertainment. Georgette Heyer's *Regency Buck* was published the following year and soon inspired a whole genre of Regency romance; in 1935 Ivor Novello would make a successful return to music with his *Glamorous Night*, set in a Ruritanian kingdom. *Conversation Piece* received more unanimously praiseful write-ups than had *Private Lives*. "If you cannot afford a ticket for this show", wrote the *Daily Telegraph*, "sell your wife's jewellery or your children's school books. You will never regret the sacrifice."[19]

But the run would be plagued by bad luck. In April Gladys Calthrop's appendix ruptured, and then, during a performance soon afterwards, so did Noël's. His role was taken over by Printemps's husband, Pierre Fresnay. Back at Goldenhurst, Arthur Coward nearly died of a lung complaint and was being kept alive by nurses and oxygen. Violet was now so deaf that she clutched an ear trumpet to her head. She and her sister Vida quarrelled so badly that Violet had to go to Monte Carlo and Vida to Madeira. Soon Printemps had filming obligations and *Conversation Piece* had to close. Its Broadway transfer, which would open in October starring Fresnay, lasted only six weeks. The *New York Times* unknowingly reached for Aldous Huxley's culinary metaphor: "Mr Coward has baked us another fluffy omelette".[20]

Noël's illness may have resulted from the strain of severing ties with Charles Cochran, his loyal producer and supporter for nearly a decade. They had had a number of disagreements over *Conversation Piece*, and their personal relationship was cooling. Cochran suspected, not without foundation, that Noël resented passing over a chunk of the profits, and Noël was now planning to set up his own production company. The end was cordial, and Cochran's public account of it was wrapped in a jolly story about Noël's explanatory letter having been eaten by his pet dog. The letter itself (once uncrumpled) had genuine warmth: "without your encouragement and faith in me and my work it is unlikely that I should have ever reached the position I now hold in the theatre, and that whatever may happen in the future, I feel that there is a personal bond between us which has nothing to do with business or finance or production. Please understand about all this, and continue to give me the benefit of your invaluable friendship."[21] But Cochran's reply was curt, and even thirty years later Noël was resentful of the impresarios who had launched his career. "Cochran, Charlot [. . .] I have been taken advantage of by all of them, and downright cheated by some of them."[22]

Noël's new company was a partnership with Jack Wilson and the Lunts. The project was chiefly Jack's; the money chiefly Noël's. The first production was to be of S. N. Behrman's comedy *Biography*, directed by Noël and starring Laurence Olivier, which opened in London in April 1934 and ran for only five weeks. Then came George Kaufman's and Edna Ferber's *The Royal Family*, their thinly disguised comic portrait of the Barrymore acting dynasty, which arrived in the West End in November as *Theatre Royal*, the Lord Chamberlain having panicked that Buckingham Palace would be offended by the original title. Olivier was once again cast, initially only for the pre-London tour, but the unnerving gusto with which he performed, nightly making an eight-foot jump from a balcony of the set, led Noël to ring round behind the scenes and ensure that the intended star replacement, Brian Aherne, was detained elsewhere.

Two more Jack Wilson productions were then announced. Neither would be a success, and each became entangled with the messes and sadnesses of Noël's personal life in the mid-1930s. The Lunts were to star in a new play by Noël, written during his recuperation from appendicitis and titled *Point Valaine*. And Noël was to act in *Ringmaster*, by a young Welsh writer called Keith Winter. Winter had started off as an eager fan: "You are a thrilling artist. I'm so grateful, dear Noël, for all the help and encouragement you have given me."[23] But soon the friendship became an affair. Winter was in his late twenties, already known for scandalous novels and for two hits on Broadway, *The Rats of Norway* and *The Shining Hour*. Intriguingly, given the opinion in which Noël was held by the so-called highbrows, Winter was intellectual and Oxford-educated. His plays and novels – hinting at erotic relationships between schoolboys or undergraduates – had ended his career as a teacher. The affair with Noël was brief, undocumented, and may have ended badly, for the intended professional collaboration was abandoned, and *Ringmaster* eventually opened under a different production company, starring Olivier as a wheelchair-bound hotel manager. It was a box office disaster, closing after just a week.

"I'm naturally depressed about *Ringmaster*", Winter wrote to Noël, "but I do understand."[24] He would soon publish his tragic novel *Impassioned Pygmies*,* a thinly disguised portrait of D. H. Lawrence that also featured "Andrew Jordan", a brilliant and wealthy playwright who has a lashing wit and is clearly homosexual. It was a cruel portrait of Noël – Jordan is described as a "galvanised corpse" – but one of the earliest to perceive the depths of grief that lay beneath the assurance. The novel reads as a rebuke at the end of an unhappy affair, an attempt to tell Noël about himself from the safe vantage point of ostensible fiction:

> The real Andrew Jordan was not the witty playboy known to the world, nor the odd mixture of sympathy and brutality, spectacular generosity and incredible meanness known to his friends, but a pathetic being who wandered desolately through the empty hills of his life, crying, begging, pleading for one thing and one thing only – to be loved. Finally you would have to know Andrew far better than he knew himself to realise that the love that he desired so passionately was the one thing he would never find, for the simple reason that he would have been quite incapable of recognising it, even if he had met it, so drastically had he poisoned himself with suspicion and disbelief.[25]

In the novel's final pages Andrew, pursued by a woman he cannot love and suffering from depression, drowns himself.

Winter denied the resemblance. "I can truthfully say that not once during the creation of the character did I think of Andrew as

---

* Cf. Siegfried Sassoon's "Everyman": "And then once more the impassioned pigmy fist | Clenched cloudward and defiant."

yourself", he told Noël. "Next time I am preparing to libel you, I'll send you a word of warning long in advance and I hope you'll do the same for me [. . .] What's a little libel between friends? Much love, Keithie." Noël was not sanguine. "I think your book is brilliant", he wrote, "[but] I must admit I'm embarrassed about Andrew Jordan because on every superficial point he seems to resemble me closely!"[26] He made no attempts to block publication, and critics easily recognised the disguise: "as a satirical portrait of Noël Coward, *Impassioned Pygmies* is first rate". There was open talk about the character's sexuality: "was he or was he not a homosexual?" asked *The Tatler*.[27] The book had potential to draw unwanted and even dangerous attention to Noël's private life.

Winter soon moved to Hollywood to work as a scriptwriter, most famously for Powell and Pressburger's *The Red Shoes* (he died in New Jersey, in 1983). It is unclear whether the affair predated or even overlapped Noël's attachment to the actor Louis Hayward, who after playing Simon Bliss in the revival of *Hay Fever* had been cast in *Conversation Piece*. Like Noël's eventual partner Graham Payn, Hayward was South African; he was in his mid-twenties and was already breaking into movies, gaining greater success with Noël's introductions. He was not homosexual, or not exclusively so, and would marry the actress Ida Lupino in 1938, the first of his three marriages. Later he would claim that a homosexual relationship with Noël was nothing but the latter's "unrealized fantasy".[28] But resisting Noël's often pressurising advances, given the older man's power and influence as regards the making, or breaking, of a young actor's career, was a difficult thing.

Noël could also offer a lifestyle of considerable luxury, and in August 1934 he and Hayward had gone on a holiday that seemed doomed from the off. They had chartered a yacht with the intention of sailing around the Mediterranean, and quickly ran into what Noël called "the worst hurricane in my experience – I was never so afraid in my life as then". The skipper succeeded in docking at Calvi, on the north-west coast of Corsica. On 6 September Noël and Hayward were in a café at L'Île-Rousse, a little further along the coast, when a second hurricane struck. The boat, moored off the Gulf of Girolata, was completely wrecked. Jack Wilson began to receive urgent telegrams reporting shipwreck, at which point Violet, getting wind of the news, sent more than a few frantic telegrams back to Corsica. The papers went to town: "NOËL COWARD REPORTED STRANDED." "SOS FOR MONEY." "MR COWARD'S CRUSOE PART." Noël had been in little danger. "Mr Hayward and I went out to the wreck and waded up to our necks in bilge water to try and save as much as we could", he told reporters. "The crew of four men were all saved, but apart from the loss of fourteen suits and about £3,000 in money and jewels nothing really dramatic happened."[29] Given the economic depression, this was a riskily blasé dismissal of the loss, in today's terms, of nearly a quarter of a million pounds.

The accident had been a strange metaphor for the fraught relationship between the two men, and matters can't have improved when Noël's *Point Valaine*, in which Hayward had a lead role, went into rehearsals in America later in the year, opening in Boston prior to a Broadway run in January 1935. Inspired by his trip to the Caribbean two years before, during which he had stayed in a whaling port – a "point baleine" – off the north-western coast of Trinidad, the play was set on a fictional island in the British West Indies. It was the first of a number of works Noël would set in the region, dealing with the fate of the British colonials as, rum punches served daily at six, they faced the slow twilight of Empire alone on their rainy island. *Point Valaine* attempted to be to the Caribbean what Somerset Maugham, the play's dedicatee, had been to the islands of the South Pacific; Bernard Shaw's most recent plays, *Too True to Be Good* (1932) and *The Simpleton of the Unexpected Isles* (1934), also took place on an obscure island at an outpost of the Empire.

Lynn Fontanne was to be Linda Valaine, an embittered missionary's daughter who has lost her faith: "I swear at God too! God damn him!" Widowed in the war, she runs a hotel on the island and, less out of love than from a desire to feel something in an unhappy existence, she begins an affair with Stefan, a Russian waiter (played by Alfred Lunt). Louis Hayward had been cast as a handsome young pilot, fifteen years her junior, who is soon besotted with her. That she gives in to the pilot's advances enrages Stefan, a part that comes into its own during a vicious third-act fight: he spits in Linda's face before killing himself. Linda's heart ices over once again on hearing the news: "I must see about engaging a new head waiter." Suicide – then illegal – is studded through the text. A guest at the hotel is writing a play about it; the pilot has witnessed a mechanic hang himself with a belt; Linda wonders "if it isn't braver to kill yourself really, in some circumstances, than to go on living".

The Lunts professed excitement and admiration at the script but were privately disappointed. Rehearsals were strained and, unusually, Gladys Calthrop's sets proved both cumbersome and ineffective. In Boston the rain machine packed up; in New York audiences flocked to the Ethel Barrymore Theatre, where *Design for Living* had been so successful, expecting the Lunts to give their familiar duet of studied wit. "The first night was awful", Noël told Violet. "I think they all expected a gay champagne comedy and that, most emphatically, they didn't get! The press was very abusive, three good notices and the rest awful. They do hate me breaking away and trying to do something different."[30] Among the vocal supporters were the *New York Times* and *The Times* in London, but in general there was considerable discomfort at Noël's explicit portrayal of a middle-aged – and middle-class – woman's sexual urge. The Lunts afterwards claimed they had predicted the failure, the only real catastrophe of their joint career, and it rankled with them always. Given that Noël was now invested financially in his productions, the implications of the flop were severe. "I have risen above it," he told Gladys Stern, who thought *Point Valaine* his best work yet. "I am flouncing off to China on Friday. [. . .] After all, Ibsen and Shaw got bad notices, didn't they, once? And what I always say is that we writers must be brave and true and stand by (not lie on) our convictions."[31]

Noël later decided that *Point Valaine*, which closed in March, had severe weaknesses. Its melodrama seems most to foreshadow the steamy gothic of Tennessee Williams, though without Williams's lyricism. Shorn of wit or quip, the tone is blunt, even violent, and purposefully so, a clear and conscious change in direction: "Poor little bastard" . . . "Go back to the mines, to the prisons, to the scum you came from . . . Go away and die." Horror mounts amid the chat of the hotel guests, among them a gay couple and a waspish middle-aged writer, Mortimer Quinn, who is apparently modelled on Maugham. But Noël more than once used Maugham as the ostensible base for what would seem more clearly to be self-portrait. Quinn, onlooker to the tragedy, affects "to despise human nature. My role in life is so clearly marked. Cynical, detached, unscrupulous, an ironic observer and recorder of other people's passions. It is a nice façade to sit behind, but a trifle bleak. [. . .] Perhaps I have suffered a great deal and am really a very lonely, loving spirit."[32]

But if there is self-portrait in the play, it may lie most clearly in Linda, an outsider caught between an abusive affair and a transient infatuation with gilded youth. She is taunted with the prospect of losing her heroic lover: "Then after a little he would write once more and say good-bye because he was going to be married, and that he would never forget you." To lose the love of a young man as he departed to be married was a familiar situation for Noël. Louis Hayward's relationship with a young American actress had been permanently damaged by his time with Noël on *Point Valaine*.[33] But he also pursued an affair with Natasha Paley, an exiled Russian aristocrat, which had the desired effect of enflaming Noël with jealousy.

Hayward soon left the stage permanently for Hollywood. "It really is lovely for him," Noël wrote, "and we are all very glad."[34] But when, in 1939, Hayward played the lead roles of King Louis and his twin brother in *The Man in the Iron Mask*, his performance as the foppish monarch was clearly a scathing burlesque of Coward-esque mannerisms: "I used to channel Noël and imitate him when I played gay parts".[35] After seeing the highly successful film Noël never spoke to Hayward again, and his account of the affair was pinched into a single, curt, diary entry about the "less agreeable memories of long ago when I chartered that bestial little yacht and set off with Louis Hayward, emphatically not one of the happier episodes of my life".[36] *Point Valaine* would have to wait until 1991 to be acclaimed by the *Guardian* as a "theatrical bolt from the blue", "fired with a raw, erotic passion almost unknown in English plays of the 1930s. [. . .] Never before or after did [Coward] write about sexual politics, and of an erotic relationship which vaults the frontiers of class and rank, with such power and such conviction."[37]

"I'll FOLLOW MY SECRET HEART"

I'll follow my secret heart
My whole life through.
I'll keep all my dreams apart
Till one comes true.
No matter what price is paid,
What stars may fade,
Above.
I'll follow my secret heart
Till I find love.[38]

SCENE THREE

"Once", wrote the playwright Frances Gray, "he showed us how the mask was made."

Gray describes the opening sequence of *The Scoundrel*, a movie by Ben Hecht and Charles MacArthur, in which Noël, low on funds after *Point Valaine*, was to take his first leading role. He was playing Anthony Mallare, a ruthless bastard of a publisher who is killed in a plane crash and permitted a ghostly month to find one person who mourns his loss. An early scene in which Noël emerges from the shower is a daring deconstruction of the Coward image: a bow tie is expertly knotted in time with the dialogue; long wet hair flops messily over his face and is meticulously slicked to his head, the comb wielded like a flick-knife. A receding hairline appears above a face prematurely aged for a man of thirty-five, etched with the grooves of cigarettes and strain. "Mallare", writes Gray, "was a simplified version of the Coward charm – a charm which gained intensity by the easy impudence with which it revealed its own artifice."[39]

Noël was frustrated by the long hours spent beneath rain machines or bobbing in tanks of water standing in for the ocean:

"It's so terribly, terribly monotonous, acting all day in front of a tired electrician and a lamp."[40] The film, only a moderate success, won an Academy Award for its screenplay, and intense adulation from female fans made it clear that Noël had become an unlikely heart-throb. But *The Scoundrel* did not launch his career as a movie star, although the soundtrack's liberal use of Rachmaninov's second piano concerto may have sparked an idea for *Brief Encounter*. He had anyway decided to reject more film roles; beneath his ambition and need for money lay a secure conviction that he was, first and foremost, a writer. He devoted the rest of 1935 to travel in the Far East and, on his return, to one of the most ambitious writing projects he would take on: not one play, but a series of one-act dramas to be presented under the title *Tonight at 8.30*, the timing altered as circumstances demanded.

The idea was born from a desire to showcase his versatility as a writer and performer, and to prove his ability to keep up with new playwrights on the block such as J. B. Priestley and the twenty-five-year-old Terence Rattigan, soon to launch his career with *French Without Tears*. The project was also intended to revive his partnership with, and rejuvenate the finances of, Gertrude Lawrence. Since *Private Lives* she had had considerable success in Cole Porter's *Nymph Errant* but she owed years in back taxes and was declared officially bankrupt. Noël and Jack were often called in by her managers to try to explain to her the necessities of economy, with little success. Her fee from the run would begin slowly to pay off her debt. Most of all Noël wanted to haul the one-act play back into fashion, and to find a means of competing with the newly introduced "double feature" in cinemas, where two motion pictures were shown for the price of one, in a variety programme that included newsreels, cartoons, and short films. *Tonight at 8.30*, like the variety programmes of his youth, would feature its leading duo performing in light comedy and in music hall, in serious drama and in "musical fantasy". Its scope and scale were risky and vast, but Noël's confidence in his talent and ambition seemed barely to quiver.

A first trio opened at the Opera House in Manchester, on 15 October 1935. The evening was book-ended by *We Were Dancing* (two married colonials briefly mistake the trappings of romance for love at first sight) and *Red Peppers* (a wistful paean to the dying art of music hall, featuring a not especially talented husband-and-wife vaudeville act). The centrepiece was *The Astonished Heart*,* a play, relayed in a series of flashbacks, that showed Noël had not abandoned the emotional intensity of *Point Valaine* in portraying passion's destruction, while telescoping into six scenes a scenario conventionally suited to a traditional three-acter. His role was that of a psychiatrist whose own mind is in turmoil and who, after realising that he cannot extricate himself from an affair with his wife's school friend (Lawrence), flings himself out of the window. He dies asking not for his wife but for his lover. His wife (played by Alison Leggatt) manages the situation with altruism and self-command, greeting the news of the death with a devastating "oh, dear"; the play, in many ways, is her tragedy. Where once Noël's wives had been in constant flight, now they were more likely to hold things together, resolutely maintaining stoicism and self-restraint. *The Astonished Heart* wrings from its scenario every drip of anguish and hurt, and with a thoughtful calm that is worlds away from farcical violence or acid repartee.

Noël hated acting in *The Astonished Heart*, but was otherwise in his energetic element. He and Lawrence again fought viciously behind the scenes but that was, still, the fuel for friendship: "EVERYTHING LOVELY STOP CRACKING ROW WITH GERTIE", he telegrammed Jack Wilson. "HER PERFORMANCE EXQUISITE EVER SINCE."[41] On 18 October, a second trio joined the line-up, opening with *Hands Across the Sea*, acclaimed by Terence Rattigan as "the best short comedy ever written": a naval captain and his wife host a dinner party, slowly realising that they have no clue who the guests are.[42] They try to work out what is going on by hiding their frantic communications to one another in song. The play was partly proof that the author of *Cavalcade* could still send up the English character. It was also clear to many that the hosts were closely based on Louis Mountbatten and his wife Edwina. Mountbatten was in his late thirties and had

---

* "The Lord shall smite thee with madness, and blindness, and astonishment of heart" – one of the "Curses of Disobedience" in Deuteronomy.

recently been appointed commander of a destroyer; back in 1932 he had invited Noël to join his boat in Greece before sailing on to Egypt. A member not only of the Royal Navy but of the royal family, and rumoured to be bisexual, he held irresistible attraction. Their teasing and jovial friendship – "please be careful with your zippers, Dickie dear [. . .] Love and kisses, Signal Bosun Coward" – would become closer during the Second World War.[43]

Fumed Oak took the evening from society salons to suburban sitting-rooms furnished with a dining table of the eponymous wood. Henry Gow, all but silent in the first act during a family quarrel, abruptly walks out in the second, exploding in a rant of vicious – and violent – fury directed against his wife and daughter. The comedy wrought from the argument, lacking the high style of *Private Lives*, is discomforting. Henry's views of women, and the pleasure he takes in raising his hand to them, leave a bitter taste. Noël professed to enjoy playing Henry's tirades more than anything in his career, but whether the sympathies of author and character are aligned is uncertain. Ending with the slamming of a door, *Fumed Oak* is almost a parody of Ibsen's *A Doll's House*; as Henry tries to escape the daily grind of family life, shouting about freedom and independence, his hysteria is simply ridiculous.

The evening ended with *Shadow Play*, a "musical fantasy" that seems to have been in Noël's mind for many years (a sketch of "Shadow Show" is in one of his earliest notebooks). What starts as a conventional "Noël Coward" script – a couple wanting to divorce after each has had an affair – disintegrates into something sui generis. The woman is deeply unhappy: "You mustn't be deceived by my gay frivolity, it's really only masking agony and defeat and despair." Returning from an evening at the theatre, she tries to sleep with the aid of three tablets. Her feverish dream passes in a sequence of flashbacks spliced with fragments of the musical she has just seen at the theatre; the dialogue loops and judders, is repeated, danced, sung, or performed in extended patches of complete darkness. Life, theatre, and memory mesh; love scenes are interjected with "stick to the script" or "you're skipping again". What is disjointed in the text was given coherence and innovation by the quasi-cinematic dreamscape of Noël's staging, with nightmarish silhouettes cast against a backcloth, as the actors scrambled in a makeshift changing room to the side of the stage, banging into one another in the dark so as to re-enter quickly and find their glaring pools of harsh white light.

The six plays, as they were then, set off on a wildly successful tour late in 1935, during which Noël replaced the innocuous opener, *We Were Dancing*, with *Family Album*, about a prosperous Victorian family working out how to secure its inheritance from a deceased father's many mistresses. The London opening, on 9 January 1936, cannily returned Noël and Gertrude Lawrence to the Phoenix Theatre, once home of *Private Lives*. Six days later King George V retired to his bedroom at Sandringham House. A play about a dying patriarch was suddenly impossible and *Family Album* was promptly removed from the bill. "There was a hush over England", Lawrence remembered. "People spoke softly; nobody made plans. Everyone waited for the bulletins which gave us news of the King's illness. We felt the imminent passing of an era. I had a small radio in my dressing-room at the theatre and would turn it on between acts to pick up the news from the B.B.C." On 20 January it was announced that the King was certainly dying; Lawrence and Douglas Fairbanks Junior (with whom she was having an unhappy affair) took a taxi to Buckingham Palace to stand with the crowds, "packed shoulder to shoulder in a silent, motionless mass".[44]

The next morning St Paul's tolled its largest bell for two hours, blinds were drawn across shop windows, and most men in the streets wore a black tie. The theatres closed. Noël found it "very dramatic and moving, and the Lying in State was quite indescribably beautiful".[45] But neither national mourning nor a collection of mixed reviews got in the way of *Tonight at 8.30*, which did excellent business until the summer, the world of the theatre well insulated from Hitler's annexation of the Rhineland, in March. By May, *Family Album* had been quietly reinstated, and a new pair added to create a third and final triple bill. Noël and Lawrence were now performing a total of nine plays in repertory, while she was filming during the day.* *Ways and Means* was a farce set on the Côte d'Azur, and *Still Life* (resurrecting the original title for *Hay Fever*) took place in a station refreshment room, where a married woman falls in love with a doctor from whom she must eventually part. Gertrude Lawrence removed her false eyelashes, messed her hair, wore no make-up and only the cheapest dresses, but it was no good. "Whatever she wore", Noël remembered, "she looked superb. We finally solved the problem by buying everything one and a half sizes too large."[46] It was a script to which he would return.

Tonight at 8.30 closed in June 1936 with a Broadway transfer scheduled for November. That the Spanish Civil War broke out the follow month seemed to register for Noël as little as would, later in the year, the Battle of Cable Street. Passionately opposed to Communism of any persuasion, he would no more think of going to Spain than he would have considered Orwell-esque travel in the North of England to report on the poverty of the Depression. The Civil War impinged on his life only when, later, a pleasure cruise had to be turned back at Gibraltar. In the summer of 1936 he set off for a holiday to Europe, where Mussolini's dictatorship had done little to damage the luxurious visits of wealthy tourists. In Germany the Berlin Olympics, as Noël had half-predicted in *Post-Mortem,* were promoting Nazi ideology, but the growing threat of fascism, at this stage, worried him less than the British constitutional crisis thrown up by the new King and his love for the American divorcee Wallis Simpson. Edward VIII, as he now was, continued to adore Noël's songs, but Noël's opinion of him, already poor, was lowered even further by what Noël saw as a selfish abandonment of duty. Decades later, interviewed by Truman Capote, Noël did not hold back on the man who had by then given up his crown to become the Duke of Windsor, and he diagnosed repressed homosexuality: "However well he pretends not to hate me, he does, though. Because I'm queer and he's queer but, unlike him, I don't pretend not to be.

---

* At a matinee performance, on 21 March 1936, Coward ran a quiet try-out of a new one-act comedy called *Star Chamber* (about theatrical types at an actors' committee), but by the evening performance it had been dropped, never to be staged again in his lifetime.

Anyway, the fag-hag [Simpson] must be enjoying it."[47]

He continued to profess that he cared little for politics, even if friends noted wryly that he was more than happy to pontificate about matters on which he was not well informed. Little could drag him from the theatre, and he found time to direct a West End production of *Mademoiselle*, a comedy by Jacques Duval, which opened successfully in September. The triumphant Broadway run of *Tonight at 8.30* then kept him in America from November until February of the following year. He had finally purchased a permanent home in New York, buying an apartment in the Campanile building on 52nd Street, overlooking the East River. But soon, during the flood-lit frenzy of *Shadow Play*, he started inexplicably to weep. A week's holiday did not prevent the lines running from his head when he went back to work, and he was still unable to perform. The papers were told he had laryngitis. "I barely got through the show and we realized it wasn't any good", he told Violet, "so all the advance booking was returned the next day and we closed for good."[48]

"THEN"
from *Shadow Play*

Then, love was complete for us
Then, the days were sweet for us,
Life rose to its feet for us
And stepped aside
Before our pride.
Then, we knew the best of it,
Then, our hearts stood the test of it.
Now, the magic has flown,
We face the unknown,
Apart and alone.[49]

SCENE FOUR

If the variety acts of *Tonight at 8.30* had a unifying theme, it was the tension between freedom and imprisonment, between romantic flight and familial duty. From the poignantly past-it vaudeville of *Red Peppers* to the decaying relationships of *The Astonished Heart*, the plays were marbled with impermanence: "Nobody can live without loving somebody, nobody can love without leaving somebody."

The breakdown Noël had suffered, from which, with rest and travel, he slowly recovered, coincided with a period of recalibration. Family life at Goldenhurst was strained by his father's strange behaviour: Arthur was lurching between periods of deep confusion and lustful ardour for a neighbour. And at Gerald Road in London, back in March 1936, a vital member of Noël's entourage had arrived in the shape of Leonard Cole, a stage-struck young man in his late twenties who had heard that a job was going spare at Noël Coward's residence and boldly put himself forward. The job turned out to be cooking and cleaning, but free entry to the theatre was a given, as was the steady stream of celebrities visiting the house. Cole was in his element and became utterly enamoured of his new employer, which suited Noël very well, as did the fact that Cole was homosexual, which assured safety and discretion. Cole plucked up courage to ask whether the situation was to be permanent. "Good God, yes", came the reply, "until the grave closes over us."[50]

Which was exactly what happened. From dogsbody Cole became valet, from valet he became a personal assistant, and from assistant he became Noël's Boswell, storing up anecdotes and observations that led, in 1977, to his writing a successful biography. Leonard Cole gave his life to Noël Coward, and even gave up his name. Noël decided he could not abide "Leonard", or even "Lesley", and insisted on a reversal despite an unwillingness, even unhappiness, on Cole's part. But "Cole Lesley" eventually stuck. Noël's control over those to whom he was close could be total, even as he inspired both loyalty and, often, love. Lesley played the role of permanently appreciative spectator that Noël craved, the relationship caught, sometimes awkwardly, between deep intimacy and necessary subservience, and complicated by the vast disparity in wealth between the two, which Noël seemed barely to comprehend. Lesley was both rock and, occasionally, whipping boy. In both wit and intellect he threatened to outrank Noël, but evidently he subdued his own talents to the extent that they could serve, rather than threaten, his employer's.

Also welcomed into the inner circle was the actress Joyce Carey, a good-luck charm in that, now in her late thirties but already specialising in aunts and spinsters, she was the daughter of Lilian Braithwaite, original star of *The Vortex*. She had inherited her mother's skill in delivering Noël's dialogue, having taken a small role in *Easy Virtue* in 1926, and she and Noël cemented their friendship when she stepped in at short notice to perform in *Tonight at 8.30*. Carey's was another example of a life given over to Noël Coward. She remained unmarried, and made no real efforts to capitalise on her success as a writer; her 1935 play *Sweet Aloes*, for which she used the pseudonym J. Malory, had run for over a year. Her impeccable diction contrasted brilliantly with her pleasingly filthy jokes; less fiery than Gladys Calthrop (with whom she didn't get on), less troubled than Gertrude Lawrence, she offered, and received from, Noël a warm love of the reassuringly sexless nature that he needed from his many and close female friendships.

His performance in *The Scoundrel* had also led to his close relationship with Marlene Dietrich, famous for her film *The Blue Angel*, who had contacted him to express admiration. She was being marketed as the German equivalent of the Swedish star Greta Garbo, whom Noël had recently met in Stockholm. Their ascent to stardom from working-class childhoods, Dietrich the daughter of a policeman, Garbo of a labourer, would surely have chimed with him, as would, in Dietrich's case at least, a careful honing of public image and a reliance on self-reinvention to combat box office failure. Both were bisexual, and each had had a romance with Mercedes de Acosta (once the lover of Gladys Calthrop). Dietrich loved the company of gay men and found Noël a fount of open-eared affection during a series of unhappy and overlapping affairs of which her husband, Rudolf Sieber, was entirely aware. Her flirtation with Noël, often conducted by letter, was self-consciously camp ("I see you every night and talk of you all day").[51]

But Greta Garbo was something different again. Noël wept at her famous performance in *Camille*, but within five years of their meeting she would retire from the screen altogether, humiliated by a cinematic flop and longing for anonymity. The notion of unwanted fame and success was so anathema to Noël as to make Garbo intriguing, although beneath her almost paranoid craving for privacy lay a pleasing gregariousness. She was soon added by the press to the lengthening list of women with whom he was thought to be romantically linked, and she spent the last decades of her life as his Manhattan neighbour in the Campanile building. She wrote to him in 1936 with apparent sincerity, wistfully wishing he could be not her groom but, intriguingly, her "bride": "Dear person it almost makes me wish the newspapers in this country was right. I am so dreadfully fond of you that I wish I could forget you. Can't think of anything more terrific than to fall in love with you. [. . .] I take the opportunity to ask if you will be my little bride."[52] Garbo suffered from depression; like Noël she seems to have been attracted by romance even as she conceded its falsity. Hers was the sadness inherent to a loving friendship that can find no sexual expression – and perhaps not for the want of trying. Even Cole Lesley was uncertain as to whether they had had an affair.

Noël was impatient with Garbo's craving for solitude. In *Design for Living* he had written "loneliness doesn't necessarily mean being by yourself". The more he added to the padded coat of his entourage, the more solitary he seemed; in 1934 he had written the song "I Travel Alone".* Jack Wilson had now met Natasha Paley, with whom Louis Hayward had had a brief affair. A first cousin of Tsar Nicholas II, she had emigrated to France and then America after the Revolution, briefly working as a film actress before becoming a socialite and model. Many of her lovers were primarily homosexual: Jean Cocteau had wanted to marry her. The couturier Lucien Lelong did marry her, but on their divorce she and Jack Wilson quickly announced their engagement. Wilson's work with Noël had made him rich, and the marriage offered Natasha American citizenship. Theirs was to be a sexless union, a marriage of convenience but also of friendship.

---

* Often taken to be autobiographical, the song (according to a note in a Chicago playbill from 1940) was written to be sung by Larita in a planned revival of *Easy Virtue.*

It may be that the announcement was simply a disguise to allow the affair with Noël to continue in private, public suspicions allayed. But it seems that Natasha's presence allowed Jack's relationship with Noël to settle onto a happier plain, a liberating shift from sexual passion to friendly affection, free from infidelities and recrimination. He had lost two lovers to Natasha, but he liked and supported her, slipping happily into his role of third party to another couple. Jack insisted that Noël attend the wedding: "I would be happier, of course, if – however simple the ceremony will be – and it <u>will</u> be simple – <u>you</u> could be there. Reasons for that I don't think I need explain." Noël's reply is lost, but Jack thought it "very sweet and very thoughtful and very complete, and [it] brings us both up to scratch again [. . .] we have been through some beauties in our day and I suppose we will manage to survive as in the past".[53]

Noël had begun a new relationship of his own, with the thirty-year-old actor Alan Webb, who had taken supporting roles in *Tonight at 8.30*. Webb was a perfect combination for Noël of theatrical ambition and naval training: after a period at the Royal Naval Colleges in Osborne and Dartmouth he had had a long acting apprenticeship at provincial repertory companies. He and Joyce Carey went on holiday with Noël to Nassau in the spring of 1937; they returned to a Britain bedecked with coronation festivity. Noël had always preferred George VI, as he now was, to his brother, who had formally abdicated the previous December. Noël was invited to the coronation, which took place on 12 May, a lavish public spectacle designed to display the might of Empire.

At Goldenhurst that summer Alan Webb became a frequent, even a belligerent, presence. Cole Lesley noted how he "enjoyed throwing spanners in works, in fact became famous, infamous rather, for it".[54] John Gielgud rather admired him for refusing to grovel: "Webb was a very caustic and brilliant actor, much under-rated. He was one of the few who dared to oppose Noël."[55] Webb was to take the lead role, and Noël was to direct him, in the Broadway transfer of *George and Margaret*, a new comedy written by the actor Gerald Savory and already running successfully in London. Noël and Alan sailed for New York on 1 September, arriving just in time to attend Jack Wilson's wedding, which took place in Connecticut on 8 September and was reported in all the gossip columns, Noël apparently a happy and eager best man.

Four days later there was news from Kent. Arthur Coward had died, eighty years old. The sole surviving of Arthur's three children, Noël had been able to provide a comfortable retirement for his father after decades of financial instability, but Arthur's last years had been ones of illness and quarrel. "I am so relieved", Noël wrote, "that he died peacefully and without any struggle. I am also really relieved that he died when he did. It would have been awful both for him and for us if he had dragged on indefinitely."[56] Arthur is preserved on Noël's home movies, a shadow, long-faced and unknowable, trundling the lawnmower across the gardens of Goldenhurst.

The first night of *George and Margaret* was the day after Arthur's death. Noël had by his own admission become bullying and irate during rehearsals, not least with Alan Webb, still a lone voice of challenge where others felt it their duty to indulge. This was partly a result of his having taken it upon himself to rewrite much of the script (the transfer did less good business than had Savory's unadulterated original). Cole Lesley was honest about Noël's increasingly short temper and capacity for tantrum or panic over the smallest of mishaps; he expected, even wanted, bad temper, as evidence of Noël's star power. Most of the rages were theatrical enough to be enjoyed by Noël and his audience; they led to the soothing praise that insecurity demanded. "When he was really and truly angry", Lesley wrote, "that was quite another matter. Then there would be an ominous quiet about him [. . .] As for his selfishness it was total; but if he only thought of himself and getting what he wanted when he wanted it, this was because he very genuinely believed that other people did, or should do, the same and were fools if they didn't."[57] There was little, in the end, even the feelings of closest friends, permitted to supersede in importance Noël's fierce devotion to his own talents.

Spells of gloom were only exacerbated by the failure of his next project, *Operette*, which instead of making capital from the new ground broken with *Point Valaine* or *Tonight at 8.30*, seemed intended

to win back his position as the unparalleled creator of musical
entertainment in the Mittel-European vein of *Bitter Sweet*. Given
the popularity of new American musicals by Cole Porter, Irving
Berlin, and Richard Rodgers, this was a daring reliance on audience nostalgia. "It's dangerous to be romantic", says Linda Valaine,
and so Noël seemed to think, while simultaneously deciding to
interleave his plays with musicals that many dismissed as trite. In
the summer he had holidayed briefly in Austria, meeting the singer
Fritzi Massary, whose performances in operetta had charmed him
on his first visit to Berlin, in 1923. Massary was of Jewish ancestry
and had left Germany to escape Nazi persecution shortly before
the declaration of the Third Reich. Noël, in a deliberate attempt to
provide her with work in London (he sent her a teacher to improve
her English), wrote specifically for her the lead role of *Operette*: an
ageing Viennese star, who is cast in an Edwardian musical comedy.
The show opened in London on 16 March 1938, the curtain rising
on a frothy haze of Viennese noblemen and ball-gowned ingénues,
just a day after cheering crowds had gathered in the Austrian capital
to witness Hitler announce the country's annexation.

Nostalgic paintings of faded worlds were popular, but they threw
into painful relief the fearsome reality. "This is just to let you
know", Noël wrote to the critic Alexander Woollcott, "that [*Operette*]
is a smash success."[58] But it was not. "Floperette" was an irresistible
pun for the critics and Noël later professed it the worst musical he
had produced. His song "The Stately Homes of England" was the
sole survivor of a show that closed four months later, never to be
revived. The first couplet – "The stately homes of England, how
beautiful they stand" – had been pinched from a nineteenth-century
poem by Felicia Hermans; the lyric then spins into a virtuosic
rhyming account, at once paean and parody, of the backbone of the
British upper class, and its ability to withstand flood, fire, and decay.
The song was prophetic of an era when the country's grand estates
were to be threatened by bombs or requisitioned as hospitals, and
then left gently to crumble in the new world that would emerge
after the war. Noël's satire poked fun at the aristocracy to which he
had worked hard to belong and which he hoped would endure; the
song may be the most satirical expression of genuine national pride

ever written. But the threat of war was a threat to the class system in which, now he had climbed to the top of its ladder, he had implicit, amused, faith.

"THE STATELY HOMES OF ENGLAND"

The stately Homes of England
Although a trifle bleak,
Historically speaking,
Are more or less unique.
We've a cousin who won the Golden Fleece
And a very peculiar frowling-piece
Which was sent to Cromwell's niece,
Who detested it,
And rapidly sent it back
With a dirty crack.
A note we have from Chaucer
Contains a bawdy joke.
We also have a saucer
That Bloody Mary broke.
We've two pairs of tights
King Arthur's Knights
Had completely worn away
Sing Hey!
For the Stately Homes of England.[59]

POSTLUDE

An account of Noël's life in the 1930s, so densely packed, threatens to dwindle to a schedule. To state nonchalantly that he wrote nine plays in the summer months of 1935 is to take his prolificness for granted, and to ignore the hours he spent at his desk, from eight in the morning until one in the afternoon, partying forgotten, Cole Lesley bringing in the coffee. Long hours were spent at the piano with Elsie April, still a loyal amanuensis. To talk of his going to New York or back again is to forget the hours on board smoky trains, the weeks at sea in swaying cabins where, smoking almost constantly, he littered the floor with cigarette boxes and butts. To say that a play "opened in January" does not take into account the real fabric of Noël's life: the weeks of rehearsal prior to each and every opening night; the sessions of line-learning; the long technical rehearsals in which actors stood, bored, beneath misbehaving spotlights; the paraphernalia of theatrical courtesy – flowers of congratulation or condolence, loving first-night telegrams despatched to enemies as well as friends – by which Noël set great store. An account of a long run rushes past the daily journey to the theatre, the repeated rituals of the backstage world, the smell of dust and make-up, the nervous nightly wait in the offstage darkness. In the dressing rooms of theatres in London and New York, next to the cards and bottles of cologne and champagne, the wireless had announced the death of one king, the abdication of another and the crowning of a third; it had spoken in its cut-glass tones of unemployment, of Mrs Simpson and Spain, of Franco and Hitler and Mussolini and, increasingly, the threat of another war – a war which, for Noël Coward, would really begin in 1938.

*Songs begin to play over one another.**

"I TRAVEL ALONE" (chorus)
The world is wide, and when my day is done
I shall at least have travelled free,
Led by this wanderlust that turns my eyes to far horizons.
Though time and tide won't wait for anyone,
There's one illusion left for me
And that's the happiness I've known alone.

"BRIGHT YOUNG PEOPLE"
You may deplore

---

* "I Travel Alone" was written in 1934; "Bright Young People" was a contribution to *Cochran's 1931 Revue*; "Never Again" was written for *Words and Music*'s American version, *Set to Music* (1939); "The Dream is Over" is a miscellaneous song written in the late 1920s.

The effects of war
Which are causing the world to decay a bit.
We've found our place and will play a bit in the sun.
Though Waterloo was won upon the playing fields of Eton
The next war will be photographed, and lost, by Cecil Beaton.

"TWENTIETH-CENTURY BLUES" (reprise)
Why is that civilised humanity
Must make the world so wrong?
In this hurly-burly of insanity
Your dreams cannot last long.

"THE PARTY'S OVER NOW" (reprise)
The party's over now . . .

"NEVER AGAIN"
Over now, the dream is over now. . .

"THE DREAM IS OVER"
I love you so, but the dream is over;
Days come and go, but the dream is over. . .

"I TRAVEL ALONE" (chorus)
When the dream is ended and passion has flown
I travel alone.
Free from love's illusion, my heart is my own:
I travel alone.[60]

THE CURTAIN FALLS

TINSEL AND SAWDUST

———

A WAR FILM

CAST

NOËL COWARD, *a famous playwright and actor*

In London:
GLADYS CALTHROP, *his close friend and a scenic designer*
LORN LORAINE, *his secretary*
JOYCE CAREY, *his friend, an actress*
VIOLET COWARD, *his mother*
COLE LESLEY, *his valet*
WINIFRED ASHTON ("CLEMENCE DANE"), *his friend, a writer*

HUGH "BINKIE" BEAUMONT, *a theatrical producer*
MICHAEL REDGRAVE, *an actor*
DAVID LEAN, *a film director*

WINSTON CHURCHILL, *eventually Prime Minister*
LORD LOUIS MOUNTBATTEN, *a naval commander*
ANTHONY EDEN, *a Conservative politician*
DUFF COOPER, *a Conservative politician, eventually Minister of Information*
ROBERT VANSITTART, *a senior British diplomat*
GEORGE LLOYD, *a politician, chair of the British Council*

In Paris:
CAMPBELL STUART, *British Director of Propaganda in Enemy Countries*

In America:
FRANKLIN DELANO ROOSEVELT, *the US President*
WILLIAM STEPHENSON, *a Canadian spymaster*
INGRAM FRASER, *a secret agent*
JACK WILSON, *a Broadway producer*

The action takes place across the world.

TIME: 1938–1945

1. INT. THE HOUSE OF COMMONS, LONDON — 13 JULY 1938

LIEUTENANT-COMMANDER FLETCHER
Can I ask the First Lord of the Admiralty what is the object of Mr Noël Coward's visits to the Fleet in connection with ship cinemas?

FIRST LORD OF THE ADMIRALTY, DUFF COOPER
Mr. Noël Coward has consented to serve as a member of the Committee of the Royal Naval Film Corporation, and the object of his recent visits to the Home Fleet, Mediterranean Fleet and the three depots has been to ascertain the type of film most appreciated by the personnel. No charges have fallen upon public funds or on those of the Royal Naval Film Corporation as Mr. Coward has generously met all expenses himself.[1]

2. LONDON; THE MEDITERRANEAN — SUMMER 1938

"Everybody is very well", Noël had written on 21 March 1938, "though slightly depressed by the activities of Mr Hitler." *Operette* was staggering to its end. "I am now going off to join the Navy for two months."[2] The "slightly" was characteristic understatement. The threat of a European war was growing almost by the week, but the new prime minister, Neville Chamberlain, sought to conciliate Germany and cement relations with Italy. To this policy of appeasement Noël, openly expressing his dislike of Chamberlain, quickly became passionately opposed. "I've never hated anybody in my life", he said much later, "except him. Even now I can't bear to look at his photograph."[3] Noël's friendship with his supposed rival playwright, Frederick Lonsdale, hitherto one of "respectful jealousy", withered into "unwavering and unforgiving hatred" after Lonsdale openly expressed his support of Chamberlain.[4]

Noël had professed himself in the First World War a pacifist, and it was a term he was reluctant to give up even as he came to feel that a conflict with the Nazis was both inevitable and necessary. "A pacifist has such terrible connotations, hasn't it?" he said, many years later. "It meant all those terrible pale ladies at the Albert Hall making speeches. But of course I'm a pacifist. Anyone with any sense is a pacifist. I think war is horrible [. . .] I can't bear war. I think war is idiotic. I've seen such an enormous amount of it."[5] What Noël repudiated was absolutist pacifism, and its universal rejection of violence and war regardless of the consequences. In this he was part of a small minority in 1930s politics. British public opinion had remained strongly against the prospect of war throughout the decade, and George Bernard Shaw, who early on expressed admiration for both Hitler and Mussolini, would continue to push for a peace negotiation.

But Noël believed that appeasement simply ignored or postponed the danger of the Nazi regime reaching England. "Nazism", he wrote, "rejects all belief in the brotherhood of man; its idea of humanity consists of one ruling race and a number of other races naturally and eternally inferior."[6] His travels had given him first-hand experience of the realities of dictatorships, and he cannot have been unaware of Nazi purges of homosexuals. His late friend William Bolitho was the author of *Italy under Mussolini*, which, published in 1925, was one of the first accounts to bring to public notice the horrors of the Fascist regime. *Operette* had been mounted to provide work for a Jewish refugee, and his friend Max Reinhardt, whose films were banned in Germany because of his Jewish ancestry, had emigrated to Britain after the Anschluss.[7] In Germany a full legal ban on the broadcast of "Negermusik" had been in place since 1935, demonising the jazz and blues that had been integral to Noël's work. A number of Black composers and musicians had been among his collaborators – Alberta Hunter had recorded "I Travel Alone" – and he had been one of the first white actors to perform for a charity ball in aid of the "Negro Actors' Guild". In New York he had "stopped traffic" by escorting his friend Essie

Robeson (wife of the singer Paul Robeson) to the NAACP* annual ball; she noted how Noël made sure to dance with her often, "to the confoundment of all those present".[8]

Noël had for years thought himself well positioned to exert an influence on national affairs, as documented by his letter to Louis Mountbatten during the Abdication crisis: "I should hate you to think that I am attempting to interfere with what doesn't concern me but as a matter of fact this does concern me. It most vitally concerns all of us. Is there any way in which the King could be persuaded to make, or have made, an official statement to the American Press?"[9] That same year, going on to Cairo after summer travels in Europe, he had thought himself (perhaps only half-ironically) "almost personally responsible for the Anglo-Egyptian treaty!"[10] Britain had withdrawn its troops from Egypt and when the treaty was signed in London the Foreign Secretary, Anthony Eden, asked Noël to host the party for the Egyptian delegation.

Noël's friendship with the Edens influenced his growing wish to engage politically. Eden – who as a young man had often been compared to a character in a Coward play – resigned from government in February 1938, protesting Chamberlain's policy of coming to friendly terms with Italy. Noël became a fixture of a coterie that clustered around Eden and Churchill, almost all prominently anti-appeasement. They were not without internecine disagreement and did not unilaterally dismiss diplomatic solutions to Hitler's aggression, but they were banded together by the British press as being in opposition to the government. The Conservative MP Robert Boothby lived close to Goldenhurst, and thought that Noël "cared about the political policies we pursued in the Thirties more passionately than anything else. Not unnaturally this bored the theatrical world. But he used to come over [. . .] and talk with me, alone, into the deep watches of the night. He knew, as I did, that it was the finish."[11] Other political figures in Noël's circle included the Conservative politician George, Lord Lloyd (once High Commissioner to Egypt and now president of the British Council), and Alfred Duff Cooper,

---

* "National Association for the Advancement of Colored People"

the First Lord of the Admiralty and one of Chamberlain's most prominent critics. Most important would be Sir Robert Vansittart, soon to be removed as Permanent Under-Secretary at the Foreign Office for advocating a strong stance against Germany, having long argued that Hitler would start another war.

In such groups Noël at first seems an odd fit. But crucially, many such figures were also men of the theatre. Noël had credited George Lloyd's views on Empire as an inspiration for *Cavalcade* and Lloyd (married but homosexual) had "attended all rehearsals". Randolph Churchill wrote that it was Lloyd whom "we have to thank that the author of that silly and degenerate play *Private Lives* should have blossomed into a genuine imperialist".[12] Duff Cooper was one of the few survivors of a set of aristocratic intellectuals that had suffered grievous losses in the First World War; an unrepentant philanderer, he had married the actress and socialite Diana Manners (whom Noël had befriended when touring *The Vortex* in America) and he counted among his acquaintances figures from Cole Porter to Fred Astaire. "Noël Coward is so nice and so wonderfully enthusiastic", Cooper had told his wife in 1927. "He described your [acting] as the most moving thing ever seen on the stage, after which I forgave him everything – being a bugger easiest of all."[13] And Robert Vansittart was a published playwright and novelist who had written dialogue and lyrics for movies. He entertained lavishly at his Mayfair home, and had first met Noël in 1922, finding him "a 'brilliant' boy, unknown and resolute to soar", and with "more sense of politics than is usual in the profession".[14]

Noël spent much of the spring and summer of 1938 travelling with the navy in the Mediterranean Fleet. He left England for Egypt on 27 March, and by 13 April he was in Jerusalem: "a fair fucker except for the Arabs and Jews fighting and me having to *faire* the *gentil* promenade surrounded by armed guards".[15] By the end of the month he was in Malta on a naval ship, and on official business. "An unusual mission is taking Mr Noël Coward to the Mediterranean. He has undertaken, on behalf of the Admiralty Film Committee, to investigate the film tastes of the Mediterranean Fleet, and write a report on the type of films the sailors would most like to see."[16] The committee, formed in January by Louis Mountbatten and Duff Cooper, was attempting to fit every ship in the navy with its own cinema and to work with studios to get the best films at a good price. Noël returned to England at the end of April, but by early July was back at Malta on HMS *Warsprite*, resuming his work for the committee.[17] Given naval rearmament was now well under way, it is extraordinary that time and space was made for a famous playwright to come and quiz the sailors about their tastes in film. It seemed almost to be a cover story, and so the newspapers started to suspect: it was rumoured that he was researching a pageant depicting the history of the navy.[18] Noël sent long reports to the Admiralty via Mountbatten of such banality as to make it surprising that the whole scheme was raised in Parliament: "I have not put down any Disney Cartoons because all and every Disney is sure fire".[19]

As early as 1937, Mountbatten had been quietly laying plans. Work for the film committee, he wrote to Noël, "was the solution we both agreed upon for getting you a footing in the Admiralty from which a much more important post could probably be made to develop if a War came".[20] Noël's urge to serve his country had begun to reach passionate, even grandiose, heights, as did his disdain for those who would not (on the outbreak of war, he scorned any and all conscientious objectors, among them Esmé Wynne's son, Jon, one of his growing number of godchildren). He wished to contribute to a second war what he had been unable to contribute to the first, and in such a way that he would, once and for all, be taken seriously as a public figure. This was a final renunciation of the Bright Young Things' refusal to engage politically, but it was also a chance to have a crack at the heroism instilled in him during his childhood, when once he had acted the part of a little boy who saved the world from war, and gone on adventures in the name of St George.

The prospect of war offered him meaning, in a way that artistic creation, so often churned out in the pursuit of success, never had. Wartime patriotism would replace interwar futility, and provide something to strive for, to love and keep alive for. The arrival of a conflict so long predicted and dreaded was almost comforting. Working for the government or for the navy, as he had every intention of doing, would be another step in his social ascent, and a powerful form of acceptance and belonging for a homosexual from the wrong side of the tracks. In time he would write to Jack Wilson from his first official war job: "What I am doing now is, to me, even more important than a successful play however well written [. . .] At the moment I can't feel that [art and theatre] matter quite so much as they did."[21] The Second World War was perhaps the first event in Noël's life which would spur him into seriousness, and lead him to drop his mask of flippancy, even if his sincerity nudged towards self-importance. Deep into the conflict, he would write in his diary of a conversation with Gladys Calthrop: "We decided that oddly enough now with disaster and probably destruction hanging over us we felt free and happy for the first time in years."[22]

3. FORO MUSSOLINI, ROME – SUMMER 1938

Noël left the navy at Venice before going on to Rab in what was then Yugoslavia, and at the end of June he stopped off at Rome, just weeks after Hitler and Mussolini had met in Italy as a show of German–Italian solidarity. Noël decided to attend a Fascist rally at the newly completed "Foro Mussolini", a massive stadium on the outskirts of the city capable of accommodating twenty thousand. Mussolini arrived to chants of "Duce", and Noël thought he was spilling out of his uniform "like an enormous, purple-red victoria plum [. . .] I burst into uncontrollable laughter."[23] His reaction, of ungovernable mirth in the face of fascist display, was both characteristic and revealing. His giggles did not trivialise the situation so much as reveal its frightening absurdity, using merriment not as a means of making mischief but as an uncloaking weapon. Even Hitler's physical appearance provoked "a belly laugh [. . .] I was unable to look at him on a cinema screen without giggling".[24] In *The Code of the Woosters*, published later that year, P. G. Wodehouse would employ similar tactics in his description of Roderick Spode, a would-be fascist dictator of Britain, who looks "as if nature had intended to make a gorilla, and had changed its mind at the last moment".

Noël's default mode of amusement nevertheless sat startlingly alongside his ambitions for serious political involvement. He had written to Gladys from Venice: "there are millions of queens here all in Lanvin shorts and when Lady Pound (my late hostess in the *Aberdeen*) [became] concerned at my inviting some of my 'fine friends' on board, I said – 'Take care of the Pansies and the Pounds will take care of themselves!' Wasn't it a lovely joke and nobody understood it but the Captain and he only dimly! *Oh la la la, comme la vie est* fucking *drole* and no error."[25] He would later argue that it was precisely this flippant demeanour that qualified him for undercover war work. Certainly he appears to have won the genuine, perhaps star-struck, respect of senior figures in the political establishment.

For Noël's travels to Europe that year and the next were undertaken at least partly to send back secret reports to Robert Vansittart. As early as 5 July 1938, responding to some lost communication, Vansittart wrote to him: "Your letter told me much in a small compass, particularly in regard to the attitude of some people. In fact it told me all I wanted to know. [. . .] I shall look forward to hearing more of your experiences directly you get back."[26] Vansittart was now serving as "Chief Diplomatic Adviser to His Majesty's Government", a politically meaningless title, but he was building a private detective agency collecting German intelligence, not least on German rearmament, to make the case against appeasement. The Secret Service was run-down and short of funds, its political antennae trained towards the Soviet Union, and Vansittart had to devise other ways of obtaining information, forming a secret nexus of bankers and industrialists, who were rich enough to pay their own expenses.

Vansittart's detective agency either worked with, or may actually have been, the "Z Organisation", founded in 1936 by Colonel Claude Dansey, who had been active in British intelligence for nearly forty years.[27] The organisation had become a shadow network kept entirely separate from the Secret Service, which it was intended to replace completely in the case of invasion. Its secrecy was therefore such that even in the intelligence service few were aware of its existence. Dansey – married but covertly homosexual – had a number of links to Noël: he had not only been the lover of Robbie Ross and Lord Alfred Douglas, but had worked at the War Office with Charles Scott Moncrieff.[28] Ruthless and unpopular, charming only when he wanted to be, he had set up secret offices on the Aldwych and, with the support and encouragement of Vansittart, was extending the scope of the Organisation across Europe. Its management was haphazard and its training was rudimentary; a motley group of unofficial agents, many recruited from gentlemen's clubs, was sent on rather random tours around Europe on one pretext or another, reporting back – not, it was later admitted, all that usefully – on what they had found.

To make the Z Organisation yet more appealing to Noël, it was developing a naval reporting system using British ships sailing to German and Italian ports. Figures from journalists to movie moguls were working for Dansey and Vansittart; their closest collaborator was the film director Alexander Korda, who used his company, London Films, as an excuse to visit sensitive areas while scouting for locations. Noël's contact with Dansey is hard to prove and his link with the Organisation, which he never publicly mentioned in his lifetime, was mainly through Vansittart.* But, in the year that the Organisation was formed, Alexander Korda announced that he was to direct *The Life of Charles II*, a film both scripted by, and starring, Noël. And of this nothing was ever mentioned again.[29] In the middle of the war Coward would write in his diary: "[Alexander] Korda came to talk to me. He is going to America next week. I gave him messages for X."[30]

As so often Noël had a model in Somerset Maugham, famous for his undercover work in the First World War. Espionage, ostensibly the act of an outsider looking in, was also, and by definition, a culmination of belonging, to one country over another. Any homosexual pre-Wolfenden was well used to a clandestine life of subterfuge and secrecy, and spying offered Noël Coward, adept at

---

* That Coward was among the few mourners at Dansey's funeral, at Bath in June 1947, is apocryphal. Coward's diaries for summer 1947 (Coward Archive, NPC-0445) reveal a crammed schedule recorded in almost hourly detail (he was performing eight times a week in a revival of his play *Present Laughter*) and there was no possibility of a trip to Somerset.

self-reinvention in changing times, a new role to play, and another
mask to wear.

4. LONDON; SWITZERLAND; NEW YORK — AUTUMN 1938

By late September war appeared to be upon Britain. Hitler had
demanded the Sudetenland entire, and Chamberlain refused. Noël
cabled Jack Wilson, who was in New York preparing the Broadway
run of Noël's 1932 revue, *Words and Music*: "GRAVE POSSIBILITY OF WAR
WITHIN NEXT FEW WEEKS OR DAYS STOP IF THIS HAPPENS POSTPONEMENT
REVUE INEVITABLE AND ANNIHILATION ALL OF US PROBABLE".[31] Evacuation programmes began and air-raid shelters were dug, and the
government, fearing gas attack, issued millions of gas masks. "As
I walked into the Eaton Place Depot in the City of Westminster",
wrote one journalist, "whom should I see but Noël Coward in the
clutches of an efficient female A.R.P. worker. He was holding his
mask gingerly in his hands, and was looking inside it as though it
contained some unpleasant liquor which it was his unpleasant duty
to consume."[32] On 29 September Chamberlain went to Munich
and by the next day it had been agreed that Britain and France
would permit Hitler's annexation of the Sudetenland. The Munich
Agreement was signed and Chamberlain brought back the peace
treaty between Britain and Germany to cheering crowds. Noël went
to the Tivoli Cinema on the Strand in order to watch Chamberlain's
speech. Ivor Novello was with him, and burst into tears of relief.
"Stop it!" Noël yelled, in a serious temper, "stop it immediately", and hit him hard on the arm.[33] "For me", Noël later wrote,
"the pre-war past died on the day when Mr Neville Chamberlain
returned with such gay insouciance from Munich."[34]

Churchill told the Commons that the Agreement was "a total
and unmitigated defeat". Duff Cooper resigned from the cabinet in
protest, and Noël sent him "deepest congratulations on the strength
and courage of your resignation [. . .] It is an odd sensation when
one has been faced with very probable destruction to discover how
much one really minds about such increasingly abstract problems

such as the honour of one's country. It is still odder and a great
deal more unpleasant to see thousands and thousands of English
people wildly cheering their own defeat. [. . .] How honoured I
feel at being able to write to you in these terms."[35] Noël had gone
in person to Westminster for Churchill's speech, and was spotted
"in the House of Lords lobby, giving contemplative eye to the
cavalcade of Peers, Bishops and commoners. They do say that Noël
is giving serious study to politics these days, and it is whispered
that he may yet take active part in the fray."[36] By early October the
rumour was gaining traction, and it was reported that he had been
"approached by certain political circles to enter Parliament. His
sympathies are with the Eden–Duff Cooper–Churchill element. So
far he has refused, but is still being subjected to blandishments, and
may yet yield."[37] By then Noël (who spoke French fluently) had
gone, on the secret orders of Robert Vansittart, to Switzerland. It was
a trip that went entirely unnoticed by the press, but Lorn Loraine
noted briefly in her diary, on 15 October, "N went Bern" and, on
22 October, "N returned from Switzerland".[38] Claude Dansey had
until recently lived in Switzerland and maintained a number of
agents there; he planned to move the entire Z Organisation to the
country if war broke out.

Noël's accounts of what he saw in Switzerland were innocuous,
and at this stage gathered and written up so informally that they
may barely count as the work of a spy – and Vansittart was still in
political limbo, his warnings barely listened to. Switzerland had just
withdrawn from the League of Nations, returning, after a period
of rearmament, to a state of neutrality; evidently Noël's assignment
was to report on whether Swiss attempts to preserve the country's
national identity from fascism were proving effective, despite the
influx of German and Italian propaganda. He wrote to Vansittart in
November 1938:

I snooped around a good deal and flapped my ears and I don't
think discovered much more than you know already which is A.
That the Swiss, although pretty scared, behaved and are behaving pretty well and very calmly. B. That the Nazi propaganda,
particularly in Zurich and Basel, is very strong but falling on the

stoniest of stony ground. C. In various conversations I had and listened to it was apparent that English prestige had dropped considerably but there was no violence about this, just a rather depressed acceptance of the inevitable. There was, of course, relief that war had been averted but also a certain surprised resignation that it should have been averted at such a price [. . .] I shall be in Washington for two weeks in January so just drop me a line when you have time and give me a few conversational leads or, if possible, defences.[39]

Amidst all the political crises the theatre may have been a distraction. *Words and Music*, now revised as *Set to Music* and starring Beatrice Lillie, was to open on Broadway early in the New Year. On 4 November Noël threw a farewell party attended by Anthony Eden before sailing to New York the following day (the Edens arrived in America to visit him a week later). On 24 November Vansittart contacted Noël again: "I think that the impressions you gleaned [in Switzerland] would be applicable to many other countries in Europe. I should expect you to have the same impression in the U.S., only more so. I shall be most interested to get your general impressions about this, for your range will be pretty wide, and it should furnish a good cross section. Try to get them on to the topic as much as possible, and let them rip."[40]

Noël had to dedicate himself almost entirely to the revue, and no reports of his trips to Washington survive. Despite a rapturous reception from early audiences and critics, and the addition not only of Lillie's star power but of new songs such as "I Went to a Marvellous Party", the sales for *Set to Music* quickly dwindled; it ran for fewer performances than *Operette*. It was as if European fear were being felt across the Atlantic and diminishing the appetite for such entertainment. Noël himself was living on edge, upbraiding the cast on their first preview, which led to a screaming row with Lillie. As the world held its breath in its year's reprieve from warfare, he finally faced the uncertainty in the only way he knew: first, to go to a Hawaiian beach, and then to return to Goldenhurst, and to work.

5. GOLDENHURST, KENT — SPRING 1939

There was a new Lord Chamberlain. Noël's old bête noire, Rowland Baring, was replaced, in 1938, by George Villiers, who finally passed *Design for Living*, not yet seen in London, for a West End performance. Noël relinquished the part of Leo to 31-year-old Rex Harrison, and the play would run for most of the year, the first sign that audiences could find Noël's humour a tonic in difficult times. In March 1939 Hitler annexed the whole of Czechoslovakia and ordered preparations for the invasion of Poland, whose independence Britain and France had promised to guarantee. War seemed all but inevitable, and Noël found the public mood of optimism both false and reprehensible. On 25 April he went again to Switzerland, perhaps to continue his work for Vansittart, but otherwise he spent the spring at Goldenhurst writing two plays, one after the other, with a view to staging them simultaneously in the autumn.[41] As he told Gladys Calthrop, "I have to write. I expect it's the creative urge in me just surging and surging and itching and farting, don't you?"[42] It was a gruelling schedule, involving dawn wake-up calls and many hours at the desk. Life was often solitary, the house still mourning Arthur. Noël's lover, Alan Webb, was mainly in London, performing the role of Ernest in *Design for Living*.

The titles of Noël's new double bill were from Shakespeare: *Sweet Sorrow* (eventually to be renamed *Present Laughter*) and *This Happy Breed*. The former was to be a comedy about the theatre, with Noël as Garry Essendine, a successful and solipsistic actor of light comedy. In this the play was both autobiographical and self-critical: political crisis put dramatic tantrums into perspective, and Garry suggests that actors are "just puppets", "creatures of tinsel and sawdust". *This Happy Breed*, by contrast, depicted a sweep of history through the eyes of one household: the Gibbons family lives through the great events between the First World War and the Munich crisis, from the General Strike to the Abdication. The producer was to be Hugh "Binkie" Beaumont, the young co-director of H. M. Tennent Limited, who was already well on the way to becoming one of the most successful managers of the West End. He was a match for

Noël in camp, charm, and extravagance, but craved no spotlight
for himself, preferring to be influential behind the scenes. Noël had
worked with him once before – on the ill-fated Broadway transfer
of Savory's *George and Margaret* – and their professional relationship
would be both successful and long-lived, even if their personal
one, underneath the necessary bonhomie, was much more wary.
Beaumont could be a tenacious enemy if he had decided not to be a
loyal friend. In the event war would delay the staging of both plays.
And while the comedy of *Present Laughter* enables it to transcend the
circumstances of its composition (it remains among Noël's hardy
perennials), *This Happy Breed* makes most sense when returned to the
political situation in which it was imagined.

The Gibbons family is lower middle class, and Noël was to play
the patriarch, Frank, a role that would show off his versatility and
his connection during a time of national crisis to the so-called
common man. Solidly middle-class critics would praise his successful depiction of the family, in whose living room all three acts take
place. But nearly a century later the Gibbons' dialogue – all dropped
'h's and plucky aphorisms, pronouncements invariably concluded
with "and that's a fact" – can seem shaky at best. Such diction had
served him best as terrain for satire, relegated to comic servants
and to a charity sketch in which he had rewritten *Private Lives* for a
warring couple "from the poorer and less cultured sections of society". To accusations that he had patronised his characters he replied
that his own background had been similar and he knew of what he
wrote. On domestic detail and family interaction the play could not
help but be convincing, and was not without tragedy (the Gibbons'
son is killed in a car crash). But Noël's own family had placed great
emphasis on gentility: his mother had been to finishing school,
and diction in the Coward household had never been anything but
precise. Clapham was a distant memory and it was a risky business
to attempt a portrayal of lives now so impossibly distant from his
own.

The Gibbons' daughter Queenie, fed up with the drudgery of her
life and its lack of opportunity, elopes in the dead of night, to her
parents' bitter grief. She cannot love the neighbour she is expected
to marry, and has fallen for a military man who is not of her

own class. The way in which Queenie's ambitions and intellect are stifled by the world into which she was born promises a forerunner of plays by Arnold Wesker, whose *Roots* (a "kitchen-sink drama" of 1959) would show its heroine struggling to escape a life of drudgery. Queenie upbraids her parents: "You don't believe in people trying to better themselves, do you?" Her parents respond with baffled anger, deriding her social aspirations, and in Queenie's ambitions to escape may lie the play's autobiography. But it is her fate to return to the house in Clapham, penniless, abandoned by her lover, and married to the neighbour for whom she cares little. *This Happy Breed* may be an indictment of a class system too rigid to be transcended by all but the most ambitiously talented (its author a case in point); but in showing that attempts to leap across class barriers are doomed to failure, its tone comes perilously close to implying that its characters should know their place.

When politics are to the fore, the Gibbons are mouthpieces. Communists are revealed as vacuous; a Labour victory decried. Frank, fearing German invasion, finds the Munich Agreement nothing but a sham: "I do not think it doesn't matter if millions and millions of innocent people are bombed! [. . . But] I've seen thousands of people, English people, mark you! carrying on like maniacs, shouting and cheering with relief, for no other reason but that they'd been thoroughly frightened, and it made me sick and that's a fact!" The speech was lucky to have evaded the censorship of the Lord Chamberlain's Office, which until the war sought to ban criticisms of the government's foreign policy, even censoring anti-Nazi sentiment. Frank delivers a long speech to his baby grandson about protecting the sceptered isle from foreign invasion:

> The people themselves, the ordinary people like you and me, know something better than all the fussy old politicians put together – we know what we belong to, where we come from, and where we're going. We may not know it with our brains, but we know it with our roots. And we know another thing too, and it's this. We 'aven't lived and died and struggled all these hundreds of years to get decency and justice and freedom for ourselves without being prepared to fight fifty wars if need be – to keep 'em.[43]

By the time of the war-delayed premiere, in 1943, the speech had
become a stirring boost to morale, a theatrically effective reminder
of the "British values" – hazily defined, perhaps rose-tinted – that
the war was being fought to preserve. But, written in 1939, and
rehearsed during the uncertain months in the run-up to war, the
text can be seen as against-the-tide propaganda, an explicit advo-
cation of a just and necessary war in the face of Nazi evil, and an
attempt to sway public opinion away from appeasement. This was
a war that Noël believed would be fought on the ground not by
aristocrats or artists but by what the play calls "ordinary people",
with their salt-of-the-earth stoicism and pluck. Where *Cavalcade* had
caught a working-class anger that bubbled beneath the service, *This
Happy Breed* was designed to reinforce social hierarchies. Noël had
escaped the class system only to insist on its necessity.

6. LONDON; POLAND; U.S.S.R.; FINLAND; SCANDINAVIA; FRANCE – SUMMER 1939

It was unprecedented. Noël Coward was to call a press conference
in his home at Gerald Road, something he had always vowed never
to do. "After a twelve years' abstinence from giving interviews to
the Press", wrote the *Daily Mirror*, "Mr Noël Coward had the boys
up again the other day. Whether he has reformed, or they have,
is beside the point."[44] The "boys" gathered in Noël's domestic
theatre in the first week of July, just as the southern part of England
– including Goldenhurst but excepting London – went dark to prac-
tise for an air raid. The conference was ostensibly to announce his
forthcoming double bill, but Noël also made a point of mentioning
not only his theatrical plans but his geographical ones, stating that
he was shortly to go on a tour of Poland, Russia, and Scandinavia.
True, one of his plays was being produced at the Theatre of Modern
Art in Warsaw.[45] But that Noël was taking himself to these dangerous countries at such a febrile time merely for his own pleasure,
or – as he later claimed in his autobiography – "to see for myself
a little of what was going on in Europe", was almost impossible to
believe.[46] Was the trip, asked a journalist, "because of your interest

in politics?" Noël replied, "I've never been there. One might as well take the opportunity now."[47] The papers were still suspicious: "[Warsaw] seems an odd choice for a holiday, but rumours of his interest in politics have been persistent."[48]

That Noël had broken his own rule about never giving official interviews indicates a resolution to draw attention to his movements, which were undertaken, at least in part, in order to send further reports to Robert Vansittart, although the Foreign Office was certainly aware of his travels, opening a file – "Coward, Noël, Visit to Warsaw" – that no longer survives.[49] Noël was calling the bluff of those who might accuse him of spying by pushing to its absolute limits the notion of hiding in plain sight. He even wrote a sketch about spies, called "Secret Service", to be performed in a revue at the end of the year. On 7 July 1939, he flew to Berlin and from there to Warsaw, where his main point of contact was the chargé d'affaires, Sir Clifford Norton, who had worked as Vansittart's private secretary. In Poland he gave every appearance of settling into his usual routine of ambassadorial junketing punctuated by good-humoured letters to his mother. But foreign diplomats had more than partying on their mind. While Noël was in Warsaw, Chamberlain announced that Britain would be determined to help Poland in the case of an attack, which seemed more than likely. Noël introduced himself to anyone who would talk to him, trying to gauge public opinion as to the inevitability of war. Most to whom he spoke conveyed a stoic fatalism.

It was a trip to the Free City of Danzig, a semi-autonomous city state on the coast of the Baltic Sea, that threatened the most danger. Danzig had been created by the Treaty of Versailles and, with a majority German population and a senate under Nazi control, was agitating to rejoin the Third Reich. A media campaign in Germany was pushing for the return of the city; the Nazis feared Poland's complying with the request, which would have denied them a pretext to attack. While Noël was in Warsaw, trying to work out how to travel north to the Baltic coast and cross the border, Britain extended its defence of Poland to include protecting the autonomy of Danzig. Noël had been tasked with delivering a letter to Carl Burckhard, the Swiss diplomat who was the League of Nations

High Commissioner for the city and was attempting to maintain its international status. Noël never disclosed the details of the mission, but Burckhard was in secret contact with the British about a forthcoming meeting with Hitler, and the letter could have been from Vansittart or his associates.[50] That said, Burckhard was also having an affair with Duff Cooper's wife, Diana, and Noël could just as easily have been playing go-between at the tail-end of their romance, to which the war would put an end. In mid-July, Noël managed to fly to the Polish city of Gdynia on the Baltic Sea, and Burckhard arranged for his safe passage into Danzig.

Burckhard got his letter, and talked with Noël for an hour as they walked through the crowded streets of Danzig, which were thronged with Nazi soldiers milling about in front of buildings draped in swastika banners. Keith Scott-Watson, the *Daily Herald*'s Danzig correspondent, later told Noël that "the whole Nazi entourage had been in a fine frenzy" about the visit.[51] Noël lunched with Burckhard's family before taking a terrifying flight back to Warsaw in an almighty storm, writing to Burckhard the following day with greetings more courteous than clandestine: "Vous etiez vraiment tres gentil avec moi [. . .] N'oubliez pas de venir a Londres s'il n'y a pas une guerre."[52]* On his return to Warsaw he was hosted by the famously social and elegant American ambassador to Poland, Anthony Biddle, and then, late in July, he took a long train journey 1200 kilometres east and, after huge delays at the border, arrived in Moscow, its streets filthy in the summer heat.

The Soviet Union was buckling under the Great Terror of Stalin's repression. Noël was visiting at a time when it was uncertain whether Stalin would side with Hitler in the event of war and Robert Vansittart's intelligence contacts were especially focused on the state of German–Soviet negotiations. It did not take Noël long to be overcome with rage at the effects of Stalinism, in polar opposition to Shaw's sense that Russia was a land of hope led by a giant. He spent time in Moscow and in Leningrad, staying

---

* "You were really very kind to me. Don't forget to come to London if there is not a war."

either with diplomats or in the bugged rooms of gone-to-seed hotels; in both cities he was promptly taken in hand by frightened line-toeing officials from VOKS, the society promoting cultural relations with foreign countries, and led on grim sightseeing tours to a constant spout of Soviet propaganda. "I was spied upon and followed everywhere because it was known that I had something to do with the British Embassy", he wrote to his mother. "I gave out discreet information about my new plays and the magnificent strength of the English Air Force! [. . .] The Russians, I need hardly say, opened everything and turned out all my clothes onto the platform. What they hoped to find out I don't know. I had any papers of importance in my hip pocket!"[53] He questioned almost everyone he met as to their real views of the Soviet way of life, but nobody dared express anything but support for the regime.

The prospect of Finland and Scandinavia was more enticing. These were countries intent either on political neutrality or on pacts of non-aggression, which the Axis powers would eventually break. Relations between Finland and the Soviet Union were particularly tense and at the border Noël experienced genuine fear that he would never be able to leave Russia. In Helsinki he found an atmosphere of peaceful stoicism, having slipped happily into the role of visiting celebrity; it was suggested he visit Jean Sibelius, grand old man of Finnish music, who was living deep in the countryside north of the capital and composing almost nothing. The meeting was awkward, made worse by the fact that Sibelius's English was as non-existent as his knowledge of Noël's work. Noël himself was in a panic, not (as is often said) because he thought he was in the company of Frederick Delius, but because his memory had confused the music of the two composers, to his regret. The two composers were often linked in the public mind throughout the 1930s (both were championed by the conductor Thomas Beecham), but perhaps Noël was capitalising on a half-rhyme that Cole Porter also found irresistible: "I can't take Sibelius | Or Delius | But I'd throw my best pal away | For Calloway."

In Sweden, Noël was apparently on theatrical rather than government business, and announced that he had "signed a contract with Mrs Pauline Brunius, director of the Swedish Dramatiska Teatern, to appear in Stockholm".[54] But he presented himself to Edmund Monson, the British Minister to Sweden, who asked him to carry the diplomatic bag (the legally protected container used to transport correspondence) into Oslo. Noël happily agreed, locking himself into his sleeper train and feeling official, though all he had to do was hand the documents to an anonymous Norwegian waiting on the platform. The romance of spydom had worn away to reveal the realities of long and uncomfortable train journeys. Nor was he altogether subtle when attempting to persuade neutral countries to side with the Allied Powers. Ferdinand Lunde, a leading Norwegian actor, wrote to Noël in anger about his "meen utterances about 'Hiss' and 'boo' and laughter to Hitler and Moussoline. [. . .] It is tactless to use our hospitality to try to make Britisk propaganda here, we will be neutral."[55] Stopping off briefly at Copenhagen, Noël flew to France in August, as if longing for a final desperate fling with a world soon to vanish forever, high society clinging on by its fingernails to the capes of the Riviera.

Time seemed to stand still and for a brief moment Noël made himself believe that peace was a possibility, seeing the interwar years as he had known them held briefly in amber: the hotels of Paris, Marseilles, and Cannes, with their balconies on which former lovers might yet reunite; his friend Joyce Carey holidaying in Antibes; Gladys Calthrop out sailing on a yacht; Somerset Maugham in his villa; Marlene Dietrich at a local hotel. "Then", he remembered, "I knew that there were no perhapses; that the destiny of the human race was shaped by neither politicians nor dictators, but by its own inadequacy, superstition, avarice, envy, cruelty and silliness, and that it had no right whatever to demand and expect peace on earth until it had proved itself to be deserving of it."[56]

7. ENGLAND — AUGUST–SEPTEMBER 1939

The meeting was to be at midnight.

Noël had returned to England on 19 August, and he went into rehearsals for *This Happy Breed* and *Sweet Sorrow* two days later.[57] On 23 August the Molotov–Ribbentrop Pact was signed, and nobody in the cast – which included Joyce Carey – thought the productions would ever reach the stage. On 26 August, Noël's first weekend off, he went to Goldenhurst, where Jack Wilson and his wife Natasha were staying. The following day, sitting amid the false security of lazy Sunday sunshine, Noël was summoned to the telephone by a very sceptical Cole Lesley, who thought the strangely accented voice on the other end of the line must be a prank caller. Noël was inclined to agree: the voice announced itself as belonging to Sir Campbell Stuart and insisted that Noël go at once to Gerald Road to meet him at midnight.

It was Noël's neighbour Bob Boothby who explained everything. Sir Campbell Stuart was a Canadian newspaper magnate, once managing editor of *The Times* and involved in propaganda work during the First World War; he was thought eccentric and was not popular. Noël was sceptical about working in propaganda, which he suspected would be Stuart's proposal, and longed for a more important wartime role, preferably with the navy. Boothby suggested they travel to London that evening together, and made arrangements to break the journey at Chartwell, the country house of Winston Churchill, whom Noël could ask for advice. "We found a small party", Boothby remembered, "and Churchill not in a very good mood. After dinner Noël cheered everyone up by sitting down at the piano and singing some of his songs to us."[58] Churchill's seventeen-year-old daughter, Mary, was star-struck by the whole evening, writing in her diary that "Noël Coward was charming and saucy".[59] Boothby thought that her father, by contrast, "never really liked or appreciated Coward".[60]

Churchill, now sixty-four, fond of Gilbert and Sullivan and of music hall, had long been a fan of Noël's work; oddly, he admired *Operette* most of all, telling his wife: "I have not yet lost the impression of that lovely play."[61] Two years into the war, touring the Atlantic in a destroyer, he would request a record of "Mad Dogs and Englishmen" so as to lead the crew in a rousing rendition, proving "that he knew the words and the tune" (he was said to have had a splendid row with Roosevelt over a misremembered Coward lyric). On the flipside of the record was the toast from *Cavalcade*: "When the last words were spoken [. . .] there was no sound in the ward-room but a deep, emotional 'Hear, hear!' from

Mr Churchill."[62] But in August 1939, shortly to join the war cabinet
and be reappointed First Lord of the Admiralty, he could be forgiv-
en for not making Noël Coward's wartime career a priority. He was
well aware of Robert Vansittart's intelligence work, and perhaps of
Noël's involvement in it, but his rather irritated advice was for Noël
to "get into a warship and see some action! Go and sing to them
when the guns are firing – that's your job!"[63]

Noël left Chartwell in a deep depression and arrived back at
Gerald Road in time for Sir Campbell Stuart's prompt arrival at
midnight. Stuart, he suspected, rather enjoyed promoting an air of
romantic secrecy for the sake of it. Since September 1938 Stuart had
been working under cover as chairman of a shadowy organisation
called the Department of Enemy Propaganda, known as "Department EH" – its unofficial London base was in Electra House on the
Victoria Embankment, where he was undertaking his official job
as chairman of the Imperial Communications Advisory Committee.
Stuart had been tasked by the Foreign Office to investigate different
propaganda systems and recommend what schemes might be used
in the event of war. He had staffed Department EH with broadcasters
and journalists, and his main talent scout for further recruits was
the popular crime novelist Valentine Williams; that Noël Coward
was chief on the department's wish list is not as surprising as it
first appears. The Foreign Office was already uneasy at the way in
which Stuart, a famously convivial host, was often seen conducting
business meetings at expensive restaurants.[64]

When war was declared Anglo-French relations would be of
paramount importance for Department EH, and Stuart wanted
Noël to represent him in Paris, creating a French branch of the
department, working in co-operation with the French Ministry of
Information, and shunting Allied propaganda of various kinds into
Germany. Noël, Stuart argued, had a high standing with the French,
and this was perfectly true: Coward and Shaw had recently been
announced as the most frequently performed British playwrights
in Europe. Everything was set up and ready to go, and Sir Hugh
Sinclair, founder-director of MI6, was fully in agreement. Noël was
to prepare almost immediately and would be given anything he
needed – bar a salary. That Noël was in a position to fund any war

service he undertook may have been one of his primary attractions.

Flattered as he was, Noël was unconvinced, still holding out for a naval role. After not that many hours' sleep, he wrote to Winston Churchill the next morning in a last-ditch attempt to lay out his wares.

> During the last "war to end wars" I'm conscious that I made little or no contribution – and that is something that has stayed at the back of my mind ever since. I was young and callow – but that was a reason not an excuse. This time I am determined to play as much of a part as the powers-that-be allow me. [. . .] What I miserably failed to convey to you was that this time I want to do something that will utilize whatever <u>creative</u> intelligence I've been blessed with. You, I know, took me to mean I wanted some glamour job in Naval Intelligence. My ambitions are not so high, and I simply want to clear the air on that score. You may count on my doing whatever I am called upon to do and to do it to the best of my ability.[65]

His was a strange tangle of hubris, guilt, and genuinely felt national duty. But nothing more from Churchill was forthcoming. That very day, 28 August, Noël visited the Foreign Office to see Robert Vansittart, who encouraged him to take the job in Paris.[66] (The Z Organisation was to be merged with the Secret Service, of which Claude Dansey became assistant chief.) By the time a letter from the Ministry of Information arrived telling Noël that he should engage in no other national service and await instructions, he had formally accepted Stuart's offer, but there was nothing to be done but continue with the two plays until war was officially declared.

Two days later, on 30 August, came the dress rehearsal of *This Happy Breed* (Noël in spectacles and grey-powdered hair as Frank Gibbons). On 31 August British civilians began to be evacuated from cities and towns, and *Sweet Sorrow* went into dress rehearsal (Noël in spotted dressing-gown as Garry Essendine). Early the next morning Hitler invaded Poland, and ambassadors from Britain and France informed Germany that unless troops were withdrawn, they would declare war. The atmosphere was so tense that Noël announced a cheering title change. *Sweet Sorrow* became *Play for Comedy*.[67] But the blackout was introduced in London, and theatres and cinemas across the country began to close. The cast gathered on the stage of the Phoenix Theatre and both productions were cancelled. On 2 September Noël was twice seen visiting the Foreign Office.[68] The following morning, he was joined at Gerald Road by David Drummond, who was to be his chief-of-staff in Paris. Together, at a quarter past eleven, they listened to Neville Chamberlain address the nation on the wireless.

8. BEDFORDSHIRE — SEPTEMBER 1939

"The mystery of Mr Noël Coward deepens", wrote the *Daily News*. "Ever since he called at the Foreign Office in the comings – and goings – of the week before the war, rumours have been (as we say) rife. He is popularly supposed to (a) be organising naval films, (b) be supervising the whole of British entertainment, (c) be writing another *Cavalcade*. He is credibly reported to be in Paris, Tunbridge Wells, Edinburgh, Brighton, Cincinnati and Nizhny-Novgorod."[69] Mr Noël Coward was actually deep in the British countryside, driving with David Drummond into Bedfordshire. They had set off almost as soon as Chamberlain's speech had finished. Drummond was thirty-two, a Scottish aristocrat who had been working in the City. The two got on well, thrown together during the journey when they had to take shelter in the basement of a nearby apartment block, not knowing that the countrywide wail of air-raid sirens was merely a drill.

Department EH had immediately mobilised at the declaration of war, setting up Country Head Quarters in the vast grounds of Woburn Abbey, a grand country house ten miles to the east of Bletchley Park and veiled in much greater secrecy.[70] The Abbey was home to the Duke of Bedford, from whom Campbell Stuart had leased a number of outbuildings earlier that year. En route to Woburn, Noël found that the ostensibly secret location was known to most of the locals, although the activity was disguised as "the Riding School Organisation". The gates were coiled with barbed wire, and official passes had to be shown to multiple layers of security guards. At the centre of the site the Duke continued to live his life of pomp and ceremony in the Abbey itself, while around him his land teemed with secret agents. Campbell Stuart had been in Paris, and he returned to Woburn that very day with the greatest difficulty in order to take up residence in its mock-Tudor folly, "Paris House", where he and Noël spent most of the first day of the war.*

Noël was impressed by Stuart's calm and affable management of proceedings, but the appointment was continuing to disconcert the Foreign Office. Stuart spent the first weeks of the war prioritising a luxurious lifestyle at Woburn Abbey, establishing a cinema, finding the nearest squash court and golf club, and driving up to London in flashy cars.[71] Noël and David Drummond returned to London, their heads whizzing with information as to Stuart's strategy for their work in Paris. Drummond was to go to France by boat with the luggage and Noël, after only a few days' preparation, flew to Paris by plane on the morning of 7 September, clutching a gas mask, a life belt, and a briefcase of official documents.

9. PARIS — SEPTEMBER 1939–JANUARY 1940

Noël's essentially comedic account of his wartime life in Paris was written with over fifteen years' hindsight and in the knowledge that the Allied Powers were going to win. Crossing the channel

---

* Previous accounts claim that Coward spent the day at Bletchley Park, meeting with Hugh Sinclair, Director of MI6, before being enrolled into "Section D". But Campbell Stuart's department was never based at Bletchley, and Section D was run not by Stuart but by Major L. D. Grand. Section D was researching non-military strategies by which the enemy could be weakened (sabotage, financial inflation, social unrest) and would have been an unlikely fit for Coward. Campbell Stuart was initially unaware of Section D's existence and when it was realised that the departments were duplicating work there was friction between them; in 1940 they would be amalgamated. It is also unlikely that Coward met Hugh Sinclair, who by September 1939, suffering from terminal cancer, was in the final weeks of his life.

in a four-seater aircraft in the first week of September, he had no such certainty, nor any sense of how long his services would be required. Cole Lesley had been permitted secretly to join him as valet (quietly becoming fluent in French), but otherwise the close-knit group with which Noël had surrounded himself for the best part of two decades was being split apart. Jack Wilson was to return to America and theatre production, leaving Violet and Aunt Vida at Goldenhurst, complaining about the blackout. Jeffery Amherst was to join the Coldstream Guards, Alan Webb would also be called up into the army, and Gladys Calthrop would serve in the Mechanical Transport Corps. It was back to a life of emotional solitude, amid days thronged with people.

The centre of Paris was dirty and empty, made eerily silent by the evacuation of the city's children. Squares and parks were given over to bomb shelters; streetlamps did not shine at night; stained-glass had been removed from churches and cathedrals, and windows were taped against bombs. The Louvre sat empty of artwork, and the great landmarks of the city were piled with sandbags. In the week of Noël's arrival, France invaded the Saarland in west Germany, but the attack fizzled out within days and the country withdrew, opting to fight a defensive war. The occasional air-raid warning sounded in Paris, and Noël never forgot the sight of Coco Chanel entering a shelter followed by a maid, who carried a gas mask on a velvet cushion. But no bombs fell. In France as in Britain, it was *la drôle de guerre*: the Phoney War. The French Army waited in the fortifications of the Maginot Line.

Noël pretty soon thought the job he had been sent to do was phoney as well. He was staying at the Paris Ritz, overlooking the Place Vendôme, and for now its pre-war life of luxury carried on as normal. His primary duty was to establish a link between Department EH and its counterpart organisations within the French Ministry of Information. One of the leading interwar dramatists in France, Jean Giraudoux, had become head of Paris's wartime propaganda office, and it was thought they would have much in common. Giraudoux had made the French adaptation of *The Constant Nymph* and his comedy *Amphitryon 38* had been a success for the Lunts in S. N. Behrman's translation. Working alongside him was the author André Maurois, and Noël could hold his own in literary discussions, or thought he could, betraying a knowledge of writers that in other circles he would dismiss: "we discussed Gide, Proust, Wilde and Verlaine before going on to propaganda".[72]

But the French propaganda office was in chaos. Giraudoux had no aptitude for administration and Noël soon thought that he "betrayed strong Fascist leanings" (he had retained affection for Germany and had been slow to recognise the Nazi threat, advocating a peace deal with Hitler). And while the job promised intrigue – Giraudoux "took me aside and told me secret, super secret plot" – the Service de l'Information, established in the Hotel Continental on the rue de Rivoli, was mired in pointless bureaucracy and received almost no governmental funding.[73] Giraudoux often walked out of staff meetings, bored, and he would be released from his duties within months. Maurois was in despair at the terrifying disorder.[74]

Noël had little chance of establishing worthwhile links with the French in such conditions, and to make matters worse he found communications from the English side almost impossible. Nobody seemed to know the code words he had so carefully learned to avoid detection on the tapped phone lines. In despair he flew briefly back to England on 10 October, in order to collar Campbell Stuart in person at Woburn Abbey and persuade him to come to Paris, which he did. Stuart still prioritised grand lunches and charming conversation, but he did set some wheels in motion. Noël moved out of the Ritz and into an apartment above a dress shop on the other side of the Place Vendôme. He and David Drummond set up a proper office in the Place de la Madeleine, working with a secretary, and more staff soon arrived from England. "What a very funny war!" he wrote in letters home.

It seems to have started with an armistice but what it will finish with God knows! [. . .] I'm working like a dog and have apparently done well as praise has come from on high. I am very very bossy indeed and am learning all sorts of new ways of getting what I want. My secretary frightens me dreadfully. [. . .] I have a lovely flat, 22 Place Vendome. No hot water and a Steinway. It's all most interesting. Paris is very dangerous. One may meet the horridest people at any moment, particularly the rich Americans who can't get home. I am getting an armed guard and have also ordered a boy scout for the office, so decorative don't you think, and desperately loyal.[75]

The chief priority of Department EH was the dropping of propaganda leaflets in Germany, and in London Stuart told the war cabinet that his "liaison in Paris" – namely Noël – "pressed me personally to attend a meeting [. . .] in order to discuss the preparations for the French leaflet campaign".[76] Planes were soon replaced by inflated cotton balloons that exploded mid-air to drop thousands of documents on the towns and cities below. Noël's office was responsible for the setting up of supplementary printing facilities that could produce up to a million leaflets at a time. "Noël Coward and I", remembered André Maurois, "plied our trade as writers and composed brochures to the best of our ability [. . . which] either did not open or fell into the water. After having laughed at this a bit, I felt myself close to tears."[77] Maurois promptly took a job elsewhere.

Otherwise Noël's duties focused on entertaining visiting VIPs and politicos, including the Duke of Windsor, as Edward VIII had become. The Windsors were known by the British government to have Nazi sympathies, of which Noël would afterwards claim he had always been disgustedly aware. It is possible that even in these ostensibly sociable meetings he was reporting back on what he saw and heard. "The work itself is frightfully interesting", he told his mother, "and I'm beginning to understand what it's all about." And to Gladys: "It really is quite enthralling when you begin to get below the surface a bit [. . .] It's a strange life and oh dear, what material for a writer!! [. . .] I have a lot of very secret information, because I am very mysterious and doing a very important job for my country but you couldn't expect me to tell you anything because you are so garrulous."[78]

Among the staff of Noël's office, acting as a liaison between Department EH and German refugees, was Group Captain Paul Willert, who often complained in his diary: "Noël still pretending hard to be important [. . .] he will never realise that people will not take him seriously over politics"; "Noël quite at his worst and [full] of riviera gossip." But eventually he became more admiring: "Noël enjoyed the pleasures of Paris but with his sensitive perception was not taken in. He gave small dinners at his flat [. . .] for guests of every kind. Artists, journalists, painters, writers [. . .] this was real propaganda of skill, and a source of information."[79] Among those invited to dine was Willi Münzenberg, a leading figure in the German émigré community in Paris, who had defected from the Communist Party and was passionately anti-Fascist. From this dinner grew the "Münzenberg seminars", informal meetings of Western agents held in a Paris restaurant in order to discuss the Nazi–Soviet pact.[80] Münzenberg would be imprisoned while trying to flee Paris in June 1940; he was found dead later that year.

What nobody then knew was that Paul Willert had Communist sympathies. He would eventually become a Soviet agent in America. One of the characters in Paris with whom he made contact was Otto Katz, working in French propaganda but actually one of Stalin's most infamous and influential spies. Katz's chief cover for espionage work was his justified reputation as a Bohemian playboy with a passion for theatre; Marlene Dietrich was among his lovers. Noël attempted to recruit him to work in the British office, in the knowledge that Katz was supervising Soviet agents while working for the French, and presumably hoping, given their mutual friends, that he would become a trusted informer. But by the end of 1939 Katz had been arrested by the French police and deported to America. In 1952 he would be tried as part of an anti-Semitic show trial in Prague, during which he admitted his wartime association with "the writer Coward", forcing Noël, who was tied by the Official Secrets Act, to broadcast an official denial. Katz was found guilty and hanged.[81]

10. INT. PRAGUE COURT ROOM — [FLASH FORWARD] 22 NOVEMBER 1952, SLÁNSKÝ TRIAL

PROSECUTOR
(in Czech)
When did you meet Paul Willert?

OTTO KATZ
(in Czech)
I was invited to a dinner in a restaurant near the Comédie-Française. During our first meeting Willert told me that he was working for the British Intelligence Service. He asked me to meet his chief, Noël Coward, who at the time held an important position in the British Intelligence Service. I lunched with Noël Coward in Willert's presence in a private room in a Paris restaurant.

PROSECUTOR
Who is this Coward?

KATZ
Coward is a British novelist and playwright whose works are very popular in the Anglo-Saxon world. In France in 1939 and during the War, Coward never hid the fact that he was working for the Intelligence Service. His appearance was full of confidence and vanity.

PROSECUTOR
What did you discuss at your meeting with Coward?

KATZ

Coward told me at the very beginning that
he knew about my collaboration with important French circles and named certain members
of these circles. He pointed out that this
method of collaboration did not meet the
present-day needs. He then appealed to me to
join him. I told him that I would think it
over and we agreed on a further meeting, at
which I pledged myself to work for the British Intelligence Service.

PROSECUTOR

When did you sign your pledge to collaborate with the British Intelligence Service?

KATZ

At our next meeting. We proceeded to Noël
Coward's office. Noël Coward welcomed me as
the new member of the British Intelligence
Service.[1]

11. PARIS; LONDON — JANUARY–APRIL 1940

By January 1940, having moved without much ceremony from his
fourth decade to his fifth, Noël was sure he had "never worked
so God damned hard in my life. I am delighted to have a job that
is most of the time passionately interesting."[2] He performed in
concerts for troops — he and Maurice Chevalier sang together at
the Maginot Line — and found himself moved when visiting the
French soldiers in their barracks: "The boys all practically babies,
magazines, portable gramophone, coloured pictures, naked women
etc, all rather touching." But when socialising with French actors or
singers he was "strangely ill at ease and remote talking to them, as
though they belonged to another world".[3] He also became involved
in the co-ordination of British and French broadcasting, and was

especially exercised by the workings of a radio station at Fécamp in Normandy that was controlled by the International Broadcasting Company; it had continued to work independently despite a national decree to centralise all broadcasts, and its location meant it could easily have provided enemy aircraft with bearings and information.

Noël wrote immediately to Anthony Eden, then Secretary of State for Dominion Affairs: "I do really feel very strongly about this as you know. It has been proved by expert opinion and beyond any shadow of doubt that this station is a danger to our coastal defences. Do, please, privately or publicly or any way you like, do something about this."[4] Noël began an extensive campaign to have it closed, becoming enraged by the fact that delays in the shut-down were caused by British and French grandees' being financially invested in the station. The matter reached the War Cabinet, who were told that the station was "a menace to national security [. . .] the danger of allowing a station so near the Channel to work on its own without any synchronising precautions was felt by the Air Ministry to be grave".[5] Eventually Chamberlain himself wrote directly to Daladier, and on 4 January 1940 Noël scrawled two excited words in the diary that he had begun to keep that year: "FECAMP CLOSED !!"[6]

The first disaster came when Peter Milward, a member of staff in Noël's office, was accused of homosexual activity and asked by his colleagues to leave. Noël went into a fury. "I explained it was no affair of ours if Peter liked Chinese mice provided he didn't bring them into the office", he wrote in his diary. "Determined Peter shall not be sent away on flimsy evidence of something that is nobody's affair but his." David Drummond had been the chief accuser and Noël "flew at him, really dreadfully. Told him a few of the facts of life in no uncertain terms, also told him his God-damned Christ-bitten innocence had wrecked the office." Drummond apologised and Noël regretted the whole affair. "I take back some of my spleen against the pure in heart when they are as genuinely good as David, which is rare. It's okay. I wish there wasn't so much innocence in the world."[7]

Then, on 19 February 1940, the *Daily Telegraph* published what seemed an innocuous article, reporting on Noël's efforts to organise a charity evening at the Paris opera in aid of Anglo-French canteens.

Its final line was to cause an uproar: "Mr. Noël Coward, who became a lieutenant, R.N.V.R.,* [. . .] is occasionally to be seen in the purlieus of the Rue Royale in the uniform of the 'wavy navy'."[8] Noël had turned down Mountbatten's offer of a naval rank back in 1938 and vigorously denied that he had ever worn naval uniform while in Paris. Perhaps untruthfully, for he had told his mother that "I shall have to have a uniform of some sort [. . .] made by my tailors. It will, I think, be naval!"[9] André Maurois clearly remembered having been summoned by the British ambassador to meet a "British naval officer who was to be in charge, together with myself, of a secret mission [. . .] I burst into laughter, for the messenger of the gods, most imposing in his naval uniform, was my friend Noël Coward."[10]

Either way, the damage had been done. That a playwright of his or any reputation should don the uniform at a time when some in the navy were seeing active service was all but unforgivable. Hannen Swaffer sharpened his pen for the *Daily Herald*. "Coward is an actor-dramatist, not a propagandist, not an expert on foreign affairs."[11] The *Daily Mirror* struck a similar line: "This Nelson of the footlights is [nothing but] an expert in the smart-Aleck frippery of the Mayfair drawing-room."[12] Reporters were sent to Paris in search of a scoop only to find the articles they sent home had been censored by the British Embassy, and the newly appointed Minister of Information, John Reith, gave orders that the French correspondents at the BBC were not to focus on Noël Coward.[13]

The scandal reached the prime minister. "Winston has written", Noël told his diary, "asking if there were any truth in the press story that I had been seen in the Rue Royale in the uniform. Was furious and made private vow to tackle Winston personally." He flew to London in early March, "rang up Winston's secretary and demanded appointment during next three days". On 12 March, "Winston received me. He was a trifle surly at first and a bit fried, however, I took the offensive and attacked him for imagining for a moment that I was capable of wearing a uniform to which I was not entitled.

---

* Royal Naval Volunteer Reserve

I also explained that I had refused rank in the R.N.V.R. last year. The conversation finished in a bag of amiability, he explaining the high respect in which I was held by HM Navy, and me congratulating him warmly on the great work he was doing."[14]

It was perhaps at Churchill's instigation, however, that the following day the Ministry of Information formally offered Noël a job as Director of Film Propaganda in London. But Noël "refused it, explaining that having got so far with the Paris job I couldn't leave it".[15] However, by the spring of 1940, having spent over half a year in Paris, Noël was restless, a situation worsened by the critical reports in the press. The job was dwindling in interest even as it increased in bureaucracy, and the dissemination of pamphlets was thought to be having little effect, especially when the Nazis began to characterise British aircraft as engaged in the dropping of leaflets rather than bombs. Noël's suggestion was to drop miniature Tricolores and Union Jacks that would stick to German buildings and the Air Ministry was said to be "delighted with confetti idea", but nothing came of it.[16] Soon he was telling the British intelligence officer Vera Atkins, who travelled regularly to Paris on code-breaking work, that he was "stuck among upper-class twits above Schiaparelli's shop, larking about with daft ideas about bombarding Berlin with postage stamps. They carry Himmler's profile to suggest he's getting ready to replace Hitler, and they have sticky bottoms to stick to the pavements, provided it rains!"[17] Another scheme of French propaganda was to drop carrier pigeons with messages tied to their legs. The five birds who bothered to fly home were found to be carrying rude replies from the Germans.

12. AMERICA — APRIL–JUNE 1940

On 6 June 1940 Campbell Stuart, perhaps happy to rid himself of a thorn in his side, wrote to Paul Willert: "Noël has put himself at the Minister's disposal, and will not be returning to Paris."[18] The previous month Duff Cooper had become an unwilling, and eventually unpopular, Minister of Information, and he proposed that Noël should take six weeks' leave and visit America in order to send back reports on the public mood towards developments in the war. Gauging the viewpoint of America was thought crucial and a number of writers were undertaking similar missions; Somerset Maugham, now living in Los Angeles, had been asked by the government to make patriotic speeches calling for America to aid Britain. Noël left Paris on 18 April 1940 so as to sail to New York from Genoa two days later. Passing through Italy even with a diplomatic visa necessitated getting himself into the ship as soon as possible and locking himself in his cabin until it sailed. He arrived in New York on 29 April, working his way not only through customs but through crowds of journalists whose questions he had to evade. Manhattan was a blessed relief after wartime Paris: the Lunts and the Wilsons were in New York, and he could briefly persuade himself that pre-war reality had returned.

Roosevelt had promised that America would remain a neutral nation and public support for isolationism was high; over 90 per cent of the populace were said to be against the States declaring war on Germany. Noël was as opposed to American isolationist policies as he had been to British ones. Realising that a report for Campbell Stuart could hardly be made up of theatrical gossip, he flew to Washington, quickly organising a place on influential guest lists where he could talk with senators, journalists, and even a justice on the Supreme Court. Robert Vansittart had sent Noël a long telegram hoping for information about the United States: "DEAR NOËL THIS CRITICAL MOMENT CALLS FOR DRAMATIC HANDLING OF WHICH BILL* AND I BELIEVE YOU ARE THE MAN TO CONVINCE GOVERNMENT STOP DOES WASHINGTON GIVE MORAL SUPPORT TO BERLIN STOP OPINION IN THIS COUNTRY COMPLETELY ON FENCE AND ALL DEPENDS ON TIMELY DIPLOMACY. [. . .] IF RESULT IS WASHINGTON BACKS LONDON—PARIS BENEFITS OBVIOUS STOP."[19] Gathering even unofficial reports counted technically as espionage, given America's neutrality. Most to whom Noël spoke seemed to think that American participation in the war

---

* Probably William "Wild Bill" Donovan, an American soldier and diplomat working in secret with Vansittart on the development of Anglo–American intelligence; he became head of the United States intelligence service in 1941.

would eventually become inevitable, a view he greeted with relief.

His colleague Paul Willert was the son of *The Times*'s American correspondent and was friendly with Eleanor Roosevelt, to whom he wrote a letter of introduction in the hopes that Noël would gain an audience with the president. Noël was duly invited to the White House for dinner on 7 May.[20] Roosevelt, increasingly worried about the Nazi threat and with a very weak hold on Congress, was trying to make a bipartisan foreign policy that would keep all sides happy. Noël was granted a private audience with Roosevelt and the two got on well.

> Had about a quarter of an hour with him alone; presently Mrs R came in, both of them treated me like an old friend with great charm and warmth. No alcohol consumed officially at White House, so president mixes a few snappy martinis himself before dinner. He has great personality, likes telling stories, loves ships of all sorts, his study is full of models and pictures of them, reasonably good dinner, me on president's right, he talked freely and well about the war, no glorifying, with obvious sincerity about the King and Queen. After dinner I sang a few songs and then talked to the president alone for nearly an hour. [. . .] Sure he is a first rate man.[21]

Noël flew back to New York the following morning, settling into a life of first nights and parties until, on 10 May, Germany invaded Holland, Belgium, and Luxembourg, as a prelude to its assault on France. That same day, back in England, Neville Chamberlain resigned and Winston Churchill became prime minister of a coalition government. Noël spent the next days with the Wilsons, glued to the American headlines, "Natasha in tears, me too a bit".[22] He cabled Campbell Stuart saying that he wished to return to Paris if at all possible, in order to resume his work for a war that was phoney no longer. The response came that everything in the Paris office was under control and that Noël should continue his work in America.

Noël dutifully organised another tour, and flew to New Mexico on 16 May before going on to California. But he spent the weeks in "feverish discontent"; he was, in effect, taking an impulsive dislike to any Americans he met, fed up with what he saw as a national mindset that promoted anti-British sentiment under the banner of a fake and ignoble pacifism.[23] Among his unpublished papers is a speech for an American broadcast, clearly designed to sway public opinion: "It is still, in certain sections of the United States, considered far-fetched even to visualise the possibility of Nazi domination here. I have heard many intelligent Americans argue clearly and concisely that such a situation could never possibly exist. [. . . but] as far as I can see the United States is at war now and has been for several months."[24] Along the way he gathered a list of lawyers and journalists whose views were in accord with his own and who might be utilised by the British government at a later date. But politically the tour was disappointing, and he let the trip settle into a pleasure jaunt. Discomfort at the contrast between American luxury and the news from Europe did nothing to prevent him making full use of the former; in Los Angeles he stayed with Cary Grant, who gave him a private chauffeur and valet. He nevertheless became convinced that the prospect of English actors and artists living out the war in America as artistic ambassadors – which they were often encouraged to do by the Embassy in Washington – was bad for American public opinion and for British morale, and accordingly cabled his reports to Duff Cooper: "ENGLISH ACTORS HERE [. . .] PRACTICALLY UNTAMEABLE STOP BELIEVE ME MORAL EFFECT OF PROMINENT ENGLISHMEN RETURNING HOME MAGNIFICENT PROPAGANDA FOR ENGLAND STOP AM CONVINCED POLICY OF KEEPING ENGLISHMEN HERE UTTERLY WRONG FROM POINT OF VIEW AMERICAN PUBLIC OPINION STOP."[25]

In this he accurately predicted the hostile criticism that would greet prominent British figures who had stayed in America and his reports were taken seriously. Lord Lothian (the British Ambassador) wrote to Anthony Eden (by then Secretary of State for War) that "Noël Coward, who has just been to Hollywood, is strongly of the opinion that the continued presence of young British actors in this country [. . .] is producing a bad impression. [. . .] I agree with Coward in thinking that it is a mistake." Eden's office responded that "we entirely agree with your views", and that while the

National Service Act did not apply to foreign residents, Lothian was to "take such unofficial steps as you can".[26] Noël, as if aware of the hypocrisy of sending his reports from Hollywood's beaches, meanwhile made plans to return to the East Coast, hoping eventually to return to Europe. Outside of Hollywood's golden bubble, the news from the war was disturbing. By the end of May, Allied soldiers had been cut off and surrounded by German troops, and were being evacuated from the beaches of Dunkirk.

He got to Manhattan on 24 May and "listened to appalling news. Had visions of Goldenhurst and Mother blown to bits. Jack arrived. [I had] a bad crying jag. The only bad one I had since the war. Jack very good and sympathetic."[27] Messages from Campbell Stuart awaited him. At Churchill's instruction Department EH was to be merged with other secret departments to form a single sabotage organisation under the leadership of the civil servant Frank Nelson. Given the winding-up of Stuart's activities (he retired into a life of charity work) and the frightening speed of Nazi progress into France, it is unlikely that anybody in the government thought Noël Coward's next move a priority. Duff Cooper was non-committal: "THINK YOU MIGHT BE MORE USE NEW YORK THAN PARIS STOP LEAVE YOU TO JUDGE WHETHER WORTH WHILE YOUR RETURNING".[28] This was tantamount to formal permission to live out the forthcoming Battle of Britain in American luxury, but Noël's dislike of those in the arts who had done precisely this was intense. Knowing full well he was returning to likely danger, he arranged to travel to Paris.

Suddenly there arrived an invitation from the Roosevelts to come again to the White House for dinner, and Noël flew to Washington on 4 June. "Spent an hour and a half alone with president. Dreadfully hot weather and he seemed pretty exhausted but his vitality was amazing. He talked freely about entire war situation and asked me to ask Winston Churchill personally from him not on any account to surrender the British Fleet! Thought this was rather far fetched and said so. [. . .] He went on at length about the idiocy of Chamberlain in the past, I agreed warmly."[29] Roosevelt told Noël he had been impressed by the Dunkirk evacuations, and that only the British could have fashioned such a crushing military defeat into a victory for the British character. Pondering whether a Nazi invasion of the United Kingdom were possible, he received in reply such an encomium to the glories of the British people that he wryly accused Noël – not without cause – of harbouring a patriotism that took refuge in blind faith rather than strategic knowledge. Noël also attended a conference with Harry Hopkins (an adviser on foreign policy who was living with the Roosevelts) and with Claude Pepper, a senator from Florida and a vocal advocate of American aid to France and Britain. Pepper wrote in his diary the next day: "Told Coward, who [is] in British service, to get Allies to appeal directly to us for aid."[30]

Incongruously, Noël took his leave of the White House early the following morning in the Roosevelts' bedroom: "Sat on President's bed and talked, mostly about Italian situation, he looked a bit tired."[31] Back in New York he wrote in gratitude: "Please allow me to say how much I admire your wonderful humour and sanity at a moment when the world is battering at you." Uncharacteristically he had written the letter in draft, from which he cut a great swathe of the patriotism that had seemed to irk the president:

I have encountered [in America] a number of people who appear sceptical both of Britain's resolve and her ability to face and overcome the extreme challenges we presently face. In my humble actor's way I have tried to convince them that, though we may inhabit a small island, we never have been or ever shall be a small people. Many years ago in a very different world in a curtain speech after one of my plays I heard myself saying that it was still pretty exciting to be English. I feel that today more than ever.[32]

Three days later, on 9 June, he was finally able to board a clipper bound for Europe, surrounded by an entourage of friends and colleagues whom, he could not help thinking, he might never see again: "Saying goodbye to Jack and Natasha agony. Unable to speak for a moment."[33] And he wondered what would await him on his return to a world of blackout and bombs.

13. PARIS — 9–14 JUNE 1940

That very day Cole Lesley, who had stayed behind in Paris, came out of a restaurant onto a French street and realised it was silent and deserted, bar a single car that sped past, stuffed with luggage and people, a mattress tied to the roof. Distant firing had been heard in the capital, and Parisians had jammed themselves into departing trains with no notion of where they were headed. Later in the evening, Lesley was rung by David Drummond, Noël's chief-of-staff, who ordered him to leave the country. Lesley packed what he could from the apartment and gathered the secret papers that Noël kept under the carpet. On the morning of 10 June, the French government fled Paris, and the roads were filled with vehicles that could barely move as tens of thousands left the city carrying what they could. Lesley had no exit permit and missed his train. Drummond arranged for him to be collected and the car took thirty-six hours to reach Tours, where the government had set up temporary headquarters. It took Lesley four more days to return to England, and he arrived at Gerald Road on 14 June, the day on which the German advance guard entered Paris. By that evening, a swastika hung from the Arc de Triomphe.[34]

14. LISBON; BORDEAUX; LONDON — SUMMER 1940

Noël's clipper was to take him from New York to Lisbon, where he hoped to catch a train bound for Paris. With him on the flight was the writer (later politician) Clare Boothe Luce, who was working as a war journalist. Arriving in Lisbon late in the evening, they headed up a small group going off in search of food. Luce had nurtured an infatuation with Noël since seeing him perform as a teenager, when she had rushed backstage for an autograph, but discovery of his sexuality — "what a pity he is a fairy" — had dismayed her. As they sat in the Lisbon café at midnight, drinking red wine, she watched him vent his desperation at American complacency and his passionate certainty that the British, unlike the French, would never surrender. Luce found his sincerity pompous, and her scepticism led him to back down: "I'm afraid that everything I say sounds rather like lines from *Cavalcade*, doesn't it?" He often delivered the speech from the pageant during the war – to friends, in broadcasts – as if the theatre of patriotic performance were truer to him than the realities of battle. But his fervour was contagious, and, sitting with Noël in the small Portuguese café, Luce herself ended up declaiming from *Henry V.* "How can we fail?" she asked him, as they parted in the early morning. "Darling", he replied. "I can't possibly imagine."[35]

Noël was still fully intending to catch a train to Paris, feeling that at the very least he would be able to help with the evacuation of his staff. He would have arrived in the French capital on the morning of 13 June, twenty-four hours before the Nazis, and found the government gone and his office abandoned. He would certainly have been arrested and perhaps have been shot. Only by the intervention of the British Ambassador to Poland, Walford Selby, was he finally persuaded of the danger that awaited him, and on 14 June Selby accompanied him on a flight to Bordeaux, apparently the last civilian aircraft to land in France for five years. News of Paris's fall reached them on the runway and Noël, uncertain as to whether any of his friends or colleagues had escaped, felt sick with worry. He got to England late that same evening, and by uncanny coincidence reached Gerald Road just a few hours after Cole Lesley. They forgot to draw the blackout curtains, for which Noël would be summoned to Westminster Police Court and fined £5.[36]

The following day, 15 June, all men born in 1911 – which included Lesley – received their call-up. Lesley went into the RAF, where he spent four years. But there was still the question as to what Noël might now do. His age would have allowed him to avoid national service of any kind.* The West End theatres had reopened and now would have been the time to organise, either

---

* The National Services act of 1939 imposed conscription on all males aged between eighteen and forty-one, but 41-year-olds did not receive a call-up until 21 June 1941, when men born between July and December 1900 were asked to register. Coward missed receiving his registration papers by dint of being born six months and a fortnight too early.

in London or on Broadway, the premieres of his unstaged plays. But he continued to burn with a desire to undertake serious war work at the highest level, dismissing any suggestion of jobs, either in the navy or in the Ministry of Information, that he thought too menial. Other figures in the theatre were finding important roles for themselves: J. B. Priestley had begun a series of propaganda talks on the wireless that were credited with strengthening civilian morale. As the weeks went by Noël bombarded friends and contacts, not least Duff Cooper at the Ministry of Information, with suggestions and requests, pointing out "the importance of finding some source of Governmental title for me, otherwise my value would be lessened".[37]

On 16 June he dined in a private room at the Savoy with Churchill and Cooper, eagerly enacting his strange role as go-between for the American president and the British prime minister.

> Delivered my message from Roosevelt to W.C. about the Fleet, which irritated him as I thought it would, but he looked tired, poor man, but he revived during dinner and became unreasonably pickled. Well, I congratulated him on his hills, valleys and beaches speech, he said "if only this war could be won by words, we should now be masters of the world". Pretty good. Was slightly depressed by a certain resentiveness in his attitude to America though with all we tried to do here I can't altogether blame him.[38]

Noël's friend George Lloyd was now suffering from terminal leukaemia, but he had been appointed Secretary of State for the Colonies and began to make efforts to find Noël gainful employment. He suggested that Noël could be sent to South America, ostensibly to lecture on behalf of the British Council, of which Lloyd was still director. The real plan was for Noël to report back in secret to the War Office. The Director of Military Intelligence, Frederick Beaumont-Nesbitt, wrote that "Mr Noël Coward will have opportunities of carrying out certain incidental work for this Directorate. This he has undertaken to do on the clearest understanding that such work will neither interfere with his programme nor be regarded as forming in any sense the purpose of his tour."[39] On 25 June Noël met Beaumont-Nesbitt to discuss "South American possibilities" and "had lesson in managing Colt automatic, highly perilous"; soon afterwards, he was introduced to various War Office officials "and we discussed shady side of my South American tour". Eventually he was taken "to meet Venezuelan Minister who was very winning but spoke no French and very little English. Conversation was entirely in Spanish and I must say I was surprised at how much I remembered."[40]

But by the middle of July the Council got cold feet. Noël lost his temper: "I was very cross and said that if the British Council didn't consider it a privilege to send me out for any purpose they could stuff it up. Went straight to Director of Military Intelligence who sympathised and said it wasn't the money question but that I must have the cover of the British Council." The South American plan was off. Noël rather suspected that he had enemies in government who had blocked the scheme. "Sick to death over this rot in high places", he wrote in his diary. "Bitterly disappointed in Winston Churchill and the whole lot. [. . .] God damn them, stinking, self seeking political rats."[41]

He channelled his frustrations into charitable work. Since 1934 he had been president of the Actors' Orphanage, a home set up the previous century for actors' children whose parents were struggling financially or were otherwise incapacitated. Few of the children were orphans; some were illegitimate; others were simply seen as a hindrance to their parents' careers. Noël had inherited the Presidency from Gerald du Maurier, and found the orphanage, at that point in Buckinghamshire, a harsh and grim institution that only accepted boys and was cloaked in an atmosphere of shame and deprivation. He had instantly donated £500 for a new dormitory (about £36,000 today), and agreed to take the job on the condition that he would be more than a figurehead, insisting on the intake of girls and introducing a school uniform and a new headmaster. In 1938 he had overseen the orphanage's move to a large house in Chertsey, south-west of London, and enlisted the help of wealthy friends and a star-spangled committee to fix (in the words of a recent account) "serious, multifarious problems" so as to end "a reign of terror".[42] He had continued to organise annual fundraisers and perform for the children, who recalled his visits with affectionate glee. The priority now, with the growing threat of air bombardment, was whether the orphanage should be evacuated.

Committees in England and America met in the summer of 1940 to discuss what should be done. Noël knew a thing or two about the inefficiencies of such meetings (hence *Star Chamber*, his short play about the management committee of a theatrical charity, which had made a one-off appearance in *Tonight at 8.30*). Eventually it was decided that the children under fifteen should be sent to New York, and it seemed yet another good reason why Noël's best plan was to return to America, where he could look for potential homes. A trip to the States had also been the advice of Duff Cooper at the Ministry of Information, who furnished him with a letter of introduction to the Ambassador in Washington, Lord Lothian. Noël booked himself a passage on the SS *Britannic*, which departed on 21 July, convoyed by five British warships as it sailed out from an as yet unbombed Liverpool, into the open sea.[43]

15. INT. THE HOUSE OF COMMONS, LONDON — 6 AUGUST 1940

COMMANDER SIR ARCHIBALD SOUTHBY

Can I ask the Prime Minister on what mission Mr Noël Coward is engaged by His Majesty's Government; from what Minister does he receive his instructions; and whether those instructions directed him to seek an interview with the President of the United States of America?

PARLIAMENTARY SECRETARY TO THE MINISTRY OF INFORMATION MR HAROLD NICOLSON

I have been asked to reply. Mr Noël Coward has gone to the United States on a short visit with the knowledge and approval of my right hon. friend. So far as I am aware, he did not seek an interview, but was asked to call on the President with whom he is on terms of personal friendship.

MR SHINWELL

What special qualification does Mr Coward possess to act as a kind of ambassador to the United States?

MR NICOLSON

Mr Coward is not acting in the function of an ambassador. His qualifications are that he possesses a contact with certain sections of opinion which are very difficult to reach through ordinary sources.

MR GRANVILLE
Does the Parliamentary Secretary recognise that this gentleman does not appeal to
democracy in America and does not represent
democracy in this country, and that he is
doing more harm than good, and will he bring
him back to this country?

CAPTAIN BELLENGER
Is the Parliamentary Secretary aware that a
feeling is arising in this country that if a
man has a certain publicity value and money,
he can get out of this country quite easily,
often on short visits, and probably not
returning, during a time when this country
is going through great stress and anxiety?

MR NICOLSON
I think that is grossly unfair.

MR DENVILLE
Is not Mr Coward only doing what any other
Britisher would do in another country, and
that is, speaking well of his own?[1]

16. AMERICA — JULY–OCTOBER 1940

While the passengers and evacuees were still boarding the SS *Britannic* waiting for departure, Noël had recognised somebody he had
briefly met while in Scandinavia the previous year. "Had drink with
a man called Fraser whom I met in Copenhagen", he wrote in his
diary on 20 July. "He says he is travelling with Lord Stonehaven
– obviously a cover for more nefarious activities." And then, two
days later, while they were at sea: "My suspicions were correct. He
is using Lord S as cover. He talked reasonably frankly, so did I. I
like his viewpoint but am not entirely sanguine about the setup he

works for, however, it is obviously efficient and energetic which
God knows is needed." And, two days later still: "Mask finally off.
I now know whom he works for and what he's up to, and very
fancy it is too." And finally, three days before the ship docked in
Manhattan: "Long talk with Fraser. Every card on the table, mutual
pact. Found this comforting. The future seems interesting if a trifle
perilous."[2]

Ingram Fraser was a former advertising executive who had
worked for MI6 in Scandinavia. On 22 July, while Noël and
Fraser were at sea, came the formal creation of Special Operations
Executive, a large secret organisation amalgamating smaller units
(including Campbell Stuart's Department EH). Its purpose was to
conduct espionage and sabotage against the Axis Powers; to, in
Churchill's words, "set Europe ablaze". Ingram Fraser was to be its
representative for a new enterprise in New York, working under
William Stephenson, a man who, Noël later wrote, "was to have a
considerable influence on the next few years of my life".[3]

Stephenson was a Canadian who became known by the code
name "Intrepid" (which he never actually used). Three years older
than Noël, and with a distinguished military record in the First
World War, he had accrued vast wealth by marrying an heiress
and through various business pursuits. Leaving Canada for England
he diversified his interests into industries from radio manufacture
to aircraft and the film world. As early as 1936 he had begun to
pass confidential information about Nazi rearmament to Winston
Churchill, and he had worked for Claude Dansey's Z Organisation.
On becoming prime minister, Churchill sent Stephenson to America
to work in British intelligence. Stephenson had sailed for New York
on the *Britannic*'s previous crossing from Liverpool, leaving England
on 11 June.

To the outside eye Stephenson had been appointed as director
of the British Passport Control Office, which he relocated at his
own expense to two floors of the Rockefeller Center. From here,
he was actually working as an unpaid liaison between MI6 and the
Americans, soon developing the vast organisation that was British
Security Co-ordination, its activities stretching across the world.
At the time of Noël's arrival in New York, Stephenson had had

only five weeks to develop the organisation.* He had little to work with but a secretary, an assistant, an office, and a brief to establish closer relations between MI6 and the FBI. Ultimately the aim was to increase American material aid to Britain with a view to bringing the United States into the war.[4] Noël and Ingram Fraser – who went by the code name "Oragio" – arrived in Manhattan on 30 July, and Noël, rather than going to his own apartment, booked into the St Regis hotel, where William Stephenson was to conduct a lot of his work.[5] The next day he made contact with the British Ambassador, Lord Lothian, with whom he was never likely to see eye to eye. Later that year Lothian would die from an infection for which, guided by the teachings of Christian Science, he refused treatment. He was a committed interventionist and a close friend of Robert Vansittart; crucially, he supported William Stephenson's activities.[6]

On 1 August, Noël flew to Washington for an early morning meeting with Roosevelt at the White House, partly to discuss the evacuation of children from England to America. "Talked to the President while he had his breakfast", Noël noted. "Was conscious that he was very preoccupied with election possibilities. Long talk [with Senator] Harry Hopkins, most friendly, he said I was in unique position and should tour the whole country."[7] Noël gave an impromptu press conference to the waiting journalists on his departure, claiming to be working as a "goodwill ambassador". He appealed to Americans not to send relief supplies of food to Europe, thus spoiling the British blockade. "If you would preserve liberty and freedom throughout the world, harden your hearts and close your eyes", he said. "If you feed Hitler's victims you feed Germany herself." Food supplies to Europe, he claimed, "would make it more difficult for us to win. The prospect is grim for the unfortunates, but this is a grim war."[8]

Back in New York the next day, Noël was taken by Ingram Fraser to meet William Stephenson, whom most knew as "Little Bill".

---

* Coward is often said to have visited "Camp X", a training school for under-cover agents created by Stephenson in Ontario, Canada. But the camp was not established until December 1941, by which time Coward was in England and he did not visit Canada during the war.

Stephenson was living in an incongruously chintzy apartment at Hampshire House, an exclusive "apartment hotel" on the southern edge of Central Park. "Momentous interview with B.S.", reads Noël's diary entry for 2 August. "Thought [him] first rate. Would trust him hundred percent."* He found that Stephenson's amazing energy and charisma (he had been a boxing champion, on top of everything else) made up for his noticeable lack of height and inspired both liking and loyalty. He would later say that Stephenson was the only man he had ever met for whom he would "go through fire and water".[9]

The liking was mutual. Stephenson was "greatly impressed by [Noël's] abilities, [and] wished to employ him on propaganda and other secret work in the Western Hemisphere".[10] He and Noël met four times in the first week of August alone, "apparently B.S. as well impressed with me as I was with him. [. . .] Long talk about future plans including organization in New York."[11] But these were almost hijacked by the furore over his public comments about American aid to Europe. Questions were raised in the House of Commons, and columnists in the *Sunday Express* and *Daily Mirror* were indicative of the general view in the press: "The despatch of Mr Noël Coward as special emissary to the States can do nothing but harm." "As a representative for democracy he's like a plate of caviar in a carman's pull-up."[12] American journalists were equally irate, and matters were made worse when he was seen attending a roller-skating party at the Rockefeller Center, thirty-six floors beneath William Stephenson's secret headquarters.[13]

On 8 August, Noël went again to Stephenson, in a panic. "I was worried at first because I thought S had been put off me by Parliamentary attack, actually he wasn't, but I spoke pretty strongly and I believe impressed him with the fact that even if disowned by the entire British Government I should still proceed to do all that I could in this country on my own!"[14] But in England he had

---

* In Coward's 1940 diary, "B.S." is used to refer to William "Bill" Stephenson, and "Oragio" to Ingram Fraser. I have emended the latter to "Fraser" for clarity.

become a liability, and Lord Lothian, who had received complaints from the Foreign Office about Noël's "inaccurate and misleading" comments, was forced to tell him so:

> We see no particular point in starting discussions on [relief supplies to Europe . . . The State Department] have been assured that you are over here on private business and that you are not working for the embassy or the Government. If you are questioned again on this point by the newspapers, perhaps you would make it clear that you are not a Government agent. As such, you would of course have to be notified to the State Department or risk imprisonment up to five years.[15]

Noël replied to apologise and promised silence – "I am most awfully sorry if it caused you any embarrassment" – but he also aired grievances:

> I cannot help feeling a trifle embittered by the fact that although I have given up all my own affairs in order to do anything in my power to help my country I mostly seem to be getting only kicks for it. Would it be possible to tell the State Department the truth, which is that I was sent over by the Ministry of Information to work, with your approval, at gauging various cross sections of American opinion and reporting on it? I think I should be only too delighted to register as a Government agent and I think it would do away with a lot of false rumour and wild surmise.[16]

By this time Noël's plans with Stephenson were even further afoot. "Was delighted to hear that he had cabled London to lay off me once and for all as I was doing a valuable job here. We discussed my tour and also plans for the future. He is definitely one of the few men I have met lately who inspires one with confidence. It was certainly miraculous luck meeting Fraser on the boat."[17]

It had been decided that Noël would travel once again through America, gaining access to anyone of influence and reporting back to Stephenson and British Security Co-ordination. Stephenson had already begun to recruit a phalanx of eminent figures from the arts or journalism to undertake such work, using their celebrity both as access and cover. Among them was Roald Dahl, who thought that Noël was too proud of working for Stephenson to keep the necessary secrecy: "Noël Coward would go all over the place saying 'I'm working for Bill Stephenson.' They all did that. I mean Coward made a huge thing of it. And he'd turn up in the salons in London and say 'Now, shhh, you've heard of this chap Bill Stephenson.' You know it's true. Any celebrity that passed through, Bill would try to see."[18]

On 13 August, Noël set off for California, where he again stayed with Cary Grant.[19] Along the journey he stopped where he could – Utah, Nebraska, Milwaukee, Chicago – happy to cut ribbons and make speeches and sing at the piano, while meeting and talking with senators and journalists to propagate the argument that America should help the British. "Some of the senators", he remembered, "did accuse me of being a spy. I said I would hardly be spying on my own people."[20] Even the visit with Cary Grant (an American citizen fiercely loyal to Britain, country of his birth) may have had the intent of subterfuge. Grant was also in Stephenson's employ and was attempting to find out if any Hollywood actors might be spying for the Nazis. "Long heart to heart with Cary", Noël wrote, "who is in a frenzy of conscience-stricken self justification about the war and, although very sweet, is very very silly."[21] Noël remained furious at the apathy of the acting world in America, and wrote bitterly that he "left California with the conviction that an air raid of 20,000 planes over Hollywood would be a happy and beautiful thing".[22]

He arrived in San Francisco in the third week of August, reuniting with Gertrude Lawrence, who had recently married a theatre producer and was staying nearby. (He had cabled his congratulations: "DEAR MRS A, HOORAY HOORAY, AT LAST YOU ARE DEFLOWERED. ON THIS AS EVERY OTHER DAY, I LOVE YOU, NOËL COWARD.")[23] On 21 August former president Herbert Hoover gave a speech at Palo Alto about the delivery of food to the starving populations of the Low Countries, and Noël, who had argued against doing precisely this, obtained an audience with him.[24] Hoover, who vociferously opposed American intervention in the war, flew into a temper on meeting Noël, attacking the British and their government. That same day William Stephenson sent a "most secret" proposal to the Foreign Office in London, listing Noël as part of a plan for an "authoritative means of repudiating Nazi propaganda in the United States".[25]

In the last weeks of August the Luftwaffe had begun to bomb British cities, and Noël arranged for his mother and aunt to travel to America, setting them up in his Manhattan apartment. On 5 September he joined them in New York, reporting to Stephenson what he had learned on his travels. "All my reports were written for him alone − nobody else. And whether anybody ever *will* see them or be anything but bored stiff, if they do, I doubt strongly."[26] Just three survive. Errett Cord, a business executive who owned several radio and television stations, he found to be "obviously a man of talent − business talent. [. . .] I would trust his judgment on international affairs only when the issues were very clear." Paul Smith, editor of the *San Francisco Chronicle* and still in his twenties, was "politically shrewd, realistic and knowledgable. His views on the war, which are reflected in his paper, are practically a hundred per cent pro-British [. . .] I am certain that if appealed to in the right way he would do anything in his power to help us either specifically or generally." The longest was on Hoover:

> his eyes are hard and small and I distrust his heart. His ego is obviously bruised and frustrated which makes him, not unnaturally, rather grumpy. I sensed in him a nostalgia for limelight [. . .] He stated unequivocally that Britain would have half of America against her if she relentlessly pursued the Blockade [. . .] My careful summing up of the whole interview brings me to the inescapable conviction that he must have been the hell of a dull president.[27]

Such work had not gone undetected. Isolationists had been angered by his presence and message, and the American Communist Party, which opposed any involvement in the conflict, dropped pamphlets across Illinois: "Noël Coward is only one of a whole gang of British agents disguised as actors, novelists, writers, lecturers, etc., who are working to drag the United States into the war."[28] In September he and Duff Cooper were attacked in the Senate by Rush Dew Holt Sr., a staunchly isolationist senator from West Virginia who argued that talk of Noël's apparently high contacts simply meant "he has a silk hat and can enter certain Park Avenue apartments".[29]

Noël was unable to contain his rage at the press reports, and at the inability of the British government to prevent them: "Personally would like a bomb to fall on the House of Commons during a full sitting [. . .] They are a lot of slimy little journalists [. . .] there is nothing of interest to write in this diary, only tears and depression and anger." Two days after his return to Manhattan, on the other side of the ocean, the London sky had clouded over with planes and the capital suffered the first of fifty-seven near-continuous nights of bombing. Noël fought hard not to sink into depression: "Listened to radio before dinner describing bombing of London and went swiftly upstairs for a brief crying jag. There are certain moments when the horror and anxiety rise too near the surface and a bright face is no longer possible. Don't think I betrayed too much about how I was feeling. Desperately worried."[30] He wrote to Gladys Calthrop, chief among those he loved and missed:

these last two weeks have obviously been hell and every minute fraught with anxiety and unimaginable imaginings, and it's sick my heart is with the longing to be with you. [. . .] I am now back in my apartment here working very hard, which is all part of the plan. [. . .] this filth that has been heaped upon me is really beginning to get under my skin. [. . .] if any mealy mouthed, cowering God can think out a viler year than this one, good luck to the bugger.[31]

America was engulfed in election fever: Roosevelt, running an essentially isolationist campaign, would defeat the Republican businessman Wendell Willkie. Noël's personal allegiance to Roosevelt prevented him from supporting Willkie, who favoured greater American involvement in the war. Reporting on the election had been among Noël's duties: "without being anti-Roosevelt", he wrote in his report on Paul Smith, "he favours Willkie strongly".[32]

In October sixty-eight evacuees from the Actors' Orphanage

arrived in New York, each one financially sponsored by wealthy celebrities in Noël's address book, and Noël settled them into the Edwin Gould Institute in the Bronx, where he had arranged they would stay for the duration. "Children well and happy", Noël wrote. "I felt really moved to see them. They were the last children to leave England and apparently had had a dreadful time and behaved beautifully. I talked to the elder girls and tried to mitigate their disappointment at not going to Hollywood."[33]

William Stephenson then suggested he should tour America under the guise of working for British War Relief, a humanitarian organisation that dealt with the supply of non-military aid to Britain. But the trip, as Noël wrote to Lorn Loraine, "would resemble, in many ways, the travelling I did to Poland and Russia just before the war, if you know what I mean, dear".[34] It was "all excellent cover", and Stephenson "suggested I could be very useful in Washington".[35] But eventually Noël jumped at the chance to escape America altogether, which came in the unlikely shape of Richard Casey, newly appointed as Australia's Ambassador to the United States, who suggested a tour of concerts across Australia and New Zealand. The prospect of undercover American travels was forgotten. Lord Lothian was supportive of the plan, but the suggestion caused ructions in the British government. Lord Hood, senior in the Ministry of Information, was bombarded by letters of objection: "I cannot think that Coward [. . .] will prove a good emissary", "Do you not think it would be better if he refrained from any further public appearance?" The Ministry opened a thick file on Noël and were tracking and discussing his every move, fearing him a liability; every critical article was carefully clipped and distributed. The biggest objection came from Churchill himself, and the British High Commissioner in New Zealand cabled that "THE PRIME MINISTER IS NOT ALTOGETHER ENAMOURED OF THE IDEA".[36] But Noël was determined to go, and the final person to sanction the trip was William Stephenson. "He is glad I am going but irritated that nothing better could have been found for me. He hinted at doings in the future when I have returned. I parted from him with regret."[37]

17. AUSTRALIA; NEW ZEALAND — OCTOBER 1940–MARCH 1941

"Oh Lornie", he wrote to his ever-faithful secretary, "it feels very strange and not entirely nice going further and further away but, because I've got a really good job to do, I must say I feel happier than I have felt for ages."[38] He had sailed from California on 16 October and, waiting out the three-week voyage, he admitted to his diary that he was "depressed, still uncertain in my mind about so much, myself in particular [. . .] Wonder if I am being spared something. Feel no particular presentiment beyond the one that is always in the wind. Gladys or Lorn or who? Sunset very beautiful this evening. There is obviously no real escape, ever."[39] The trip itself was peaceful bar a sudden diversion to Japan, where none of the English passengers was given permission to go ashore. Noël snuck out into Yokohama disguised as an American sailor ("visited several bordellos — everything drab and unhappy").[40] He wrote to Gladys from the middle of the ocean:

This is all quite different from what we thought it was going to be like isn't it? I wish you were here so very very much [. . .] My principal agitation is about you being safe; underneath I know that even that isn't so important measured against what we have, which is so far beyond safety and so comfortingly indestructible. However hard these strains and distances tug at us they've left it too late to pull us apart. There now I've gone and upset myself, that's me all over, up one minute and down the next, if you know what I mean, and oh, darling, you're the only one in the world who ever really does. I do hope the censor enjoys this.[41]

He arrived in Sydney on 16 November, to be greeted by a crowd of fans and reporters who would barely leave him alone for the duration of his stay. "I find myself here", he announced, "shorn of a supporting company, in a part in which I have been insufficiently rehearsed."[42] Britain's declaration of war had applied to Australia by default, and, although there was little public enthusiasm for the conflict, millions of Australian men had enlisted and were completing their training in the Middle East.

Noël was finally doing what Churchill had always said he should do: entertaining the troops. In the great heat of the Australian summer he embarked on a seven-week tour carefully planned for him by the government, who provided a small staff: accompanist, secretary, assistant, and press agent. The last must have been especially efficient, for Noël's appearances were both popular and well received. A military concert in Brisbane was attended by over fifteen hundred soldiers in training, who stood on the seats and on one another's shoulders, some even sitting atop the exposed rafters of the concert hall, in order to see him perform. During the course of a single day in Adelaide he was thought to have met or spoken to fifteen hundred people; as he left Sydney nine hundred women were reported to have clamoured for his autograph. Nurses asked him to sign their uniforms, and he was introduced to a family of koalas.[43]

He gave a series of weekly broadcasts on the ABC that became hugely popular, in which (when he was not disdaining French politicians) he described the overwhelming strength of the British character in the face of Nazi attack, such that Australians should think themselves proud to rush to the defence of the old country. "I am fareing very well", he reported to Duff Cooper, "and doing all I can to help keep alive the feeling for England. [. . .] I am feeling happier than I have felt for several months, because at last I feel I am doing something constructive [. . .] I am doing the level best I can, and intend to go on doing so until the damned war is won."[44] In January 1941, voiceless and exhausted, he sailed to Auckland to do the whole thing over again. His schedule was less intensive, although at Dunedin, in front of an audience of several thousand, he sang without pause for nearly two hours, soaking a towel with sweat between songs. Many of the concerts were fundraisers for the Red Cross, for which, by the end of the trip, he had raised – in today's value – over three quarters of a million pounds, even as he began to panic about his own finances, badly dented by his self-funded activities since the outbreak of war. A brief holiday in February found him trapped by a cyclone on various islands of the South Pacific. "This can be very down-getting at moments", he wrote to Gladys, "and I've had a lot of black-nesses."[45] By early March he was in a clipper en route to California, where his chief desire was to be reunited not with friends but with cigarettes, which had been on short supply. "Cigarette situation graver and graver", he had written, "hoarding them, and saving butts."[46]

The first months of 1941 had also been devoted to another kind of work. On 3 January he had been "racking my brains to think of a play to write for Jack. I must make some money this year. Got an idea just as I was going to sleep – an attack on the rich international set migrating to America during this last summer." Apparently it did not occur to him that his own luxurious trips in America would expose him to accusations of hypocrisy. The manuscript accompanied him through New Zealand and the Pacific islands, and he was sure he had "never worked so hard on a play in my life".[47] *Salute to the Brave* featured a young British woman who relocates her family to the United States for safety but ultimately returns to be at her husband's side in Europe. It contained such a scathing depiction of wealthy Americans and British ex-pats, partying on while London burned, that it is hard to believe it could ever have been a success in America. Set specifically in September 1940 and containing up-to-the-minute broadcasts from Churchill and detailed talk of the Willkie-versus-Roosevelt election, within weeks it had dated badly, and within a year it had dated impossibly, becoming irrelevant once the Japanese attacked Pearl Harbour.* Its final speech seemed

---

* Coward made efforts to have the play staged with Katharine Cornell and Tyrone Guthrie: "Really think [Katharine] might do *Salute to the Brave*, both she and Guthrie are mad about [it]." As late as April 1943, long after Pearl Harbour, he revised the play under the title *Time Remembered*, as if to remind audiences of a period when American involvement was not a given, and made plans for a production: "too good to be wasted". But Gladys Calthrop persuaded him to shelve it, and the play has never been produced. 1941 Diary (28 March); 1943 Diary (8 April), Coward Archive.

to be lecturing the audience as much as the characters: "We've all got to behave well and pretend it doesn't matter a bit. You see with a war on everybody's got to be brave in one way or another."

18. NEW YORK; BERMUDA — MARCH–APRIL 1941

Noël's Australian tour had raised his stock with the British government. Both the governor-general of New Zealand and the British high commissioner enthused to the Ministry of Information: "His versatility and charm won all hearts wherever he went [. . .] You know Noël Coward and you know, therefore the charm of his many-sided and vital personality." Duff Cooper wrote to Noël on 20 March 1941: "I hear on all sides that your visit to Australia was a great success [. . .] I hope this will hearten you in the work that you are doing, and that you will not worry about the criticisms which exude from the foul mouth of Hannen Swaffer and even lower creatures that crawl about the world. I look forward to hearing from you shortly as to how things are going and what your suggestions are as to your future activities." Cooper even began to gather a dossier of evidence to put before the prime minister, lest "the powers that be" tried to prevent Noël from undertaking any further work.[48]

But Noël had plans of his own. On 18 March 1941 he arrived in New York, and that very day he went straight to see William Stephenson: "Two hours discussion with Mr X. Terrific plans in progress – said I could decide on nothing until I'd seen [William] Casey in Washington".[49] Casey was head of the Secret Intelligence Branch of the Office of Strategic Services, and Noël duly travelled to Washington and Virginia. The suggestion was for him to become Director of Propaganda in Latin America for Special Operations Executive, which was now a year old and using Stephenson's offices in New York as its administrative headquarters in America.[50] South America was an important source of trade for the Axis Powers, and Stephenson was attempting to intercept a smuggling route between Rome and Brazil. "I agreed to the whole job", Noël wrote, "on condition that I be sent to London for a week or two. Everything okay. Very very excited. Feel at last I can be really utilised properly.

I am to pick my own staff in London if possible. [. . .] Gladys would be invaluable. Absolutely delighted."[51]

The British Minister of Economic Warfare, Hugh Dalton, took political responsibility for Special Operations Executive. His private secretary, Hugh Gaitskell (later Labour leader), consulted MI5 about Stephenson's proposal: "It has been suggested that Noël Coward might be a suitable person for us to employ [. . .] I should be grateful for the views of MI5 on this." There was no objection: "We know of no reason why you should not employ Noël Coward. I expect you know that he has already done work for some departments."[52] But Hugh Dalton himself was having none of it. "A stupidity proposed regarding Noël Coward", he wrote in his diary. "I react violently against it. Someone over there has gone much beyond his authority. The man is utterly unsuitable and attracts publicity everywhere. I am told that it will upset X if I say no. I say I will risk that. C.E.O.* rather weak on this. Thinks the man is very intelligent and amusing. This is a relic of pre-war Mayfair judgments. No use now! [. . .] C.E.O. remarked this morning that of course he is a 'roaring pansy'."[53]

Dalton gathered together a sheaf of unsympathetic articles about Noël and scrawled on them in red pencil: "an indiscreet stinker, off his proper beat". Hugh Gaitskell then enclosed them with a letter to William Stephenson:

Dear 48000.† I hope and believe that you will not have been distressed by the Minister's unwillingness to agree to the appointment of Noël to take over Special Operations propaganda in the Americas. [. . .] The real point is that, rightly or wrongly, Noël Coward is greatly suspected in the House of Commons by members of all three parties. Further, Noël is known to be fairly intimate with a number of politicians here who may or may not be well disposed towards the S.O. Organization. [. . .] We

---

* The Chief Executive Officer of Special Operations Executive, the diplomat Gladwyn Jebb. "X" is William Stephenson.

† Stephenson's code name (48 for America, 0 marking him as head of the organisation, and 00 for "highly classified").

cannot disregard accusations of indiscretion, which have come
to us from various sources. One of these sources, I may tell you
in confidence, is no less a person than Campbell Stuart. [. . .]
If [Coward] does come, we can only say that we have nothing
whatever to do with him."[54]

On 30 March, Noël was told that "London had called to postpone
my visit for a week. Feel there is something sinister behind this.
Everybody completely reassuring. [. . .] Discussed plans. I think
I was reasonably creative. Feel very happy. These people good to
work with."[55] What he did not know was that he was now being
watched in America, his movements of interest to the FBI, who
noted on 31 March that on the previous day "NOËL COWARD,
British playwright, visited [redacted] at Hotel".[56] But by that time,
Noël had left for England, after a "final interview with Grand Mogul
in which I expressed doubts about the London end which were
waved away".[57]

The clippers of British Imperial Airways made their 21-hour
Atlantic crossing by way of Bermuda and Lisbon. The route had
led Stephenson to establish a Bermuda station, which took over the
direction of Secret Service officers in the region and apprehended
suspicious travellers moving between the United States and Latin
America. The island also contained a large censorship office and
Bermuda was essentially the first posting of Noël's new job. His
host was Hamish Mitchell, a Secret Service agent in Stephenson's
employ stationed on the island.[58]

But it was in Bermuda that a telegram from Special Operations
Executive was waiting for him. It had been sent first to William
Stephenson, who had forwarded it to Mitchell.

APRIL 2ND. FOLLOWING FOR NOEL COWARD.

A. REGRETTABLE PUBLICITY GIVEN TO YOUR VISIT LONDON BY ENTIRE
BRITISH PRESS WHICH WOULD INCREASE ON YOUR ARRIVAL UNFORTUNATE-
LY MAKES ENTIRE SCHEME IMPRACTICABLE.

B. COMPLETE SECRECY IS FOUNDATION [OF] OUR WORK AND IT WOULD
NOW BE IMPOSSIBLE FOR ANY OF OUR PEOPLE TO CONTACT YOU IN
ENGLAND WITHOUT INCURRING PUBLICITY.

C. WE ARE ALL VERY DISAPPOINTED AS WE HAD LOOKED FORWARD TO
WORKING WITH YOU BUT THERE ARE NO FURTHER STEPS TO BE TAKEN.[59]

Noël was "utterly stunned", and wrote in his diary that evening.

> Still hard to believe I have been let down so thoroughly. Long
> talk with Hamish who was very sympathetic. Absolutely bitched.
> Must obviously return to New York to find out what it's all
> about. Determined to go on to London. God what enemies I must
> have. Suspect whole thing has been done in by Beaverbrook plus
> Churchill. Angrier than I've been for years. [. . .] Heartbroken at
> being let down by the boys but suspect it is not their fault. [. . .]
> God knows what will happen but blood will flow.[60]

Noël never found out the truth of what happened and blamed
Churchill ever afterwards. But the prime minister had never been
informed of the aborted plan. "I decide", Hugh Dalton wrote, "that
I will <u>not</u> say anything to the PM on this personal case. It would
show weakness. [. . .] NC is coming back to England all the same,
but the whole deal is off, to my great relief [. . .] Meanwhile those
who know NC this side must neither run after him nor tell him
anything."[61]

19. LONDON — SPRING AND SUMMER 1941

Noël had not been in England for nearly nine months. He returned,
on 9 April 1941, to a country transformed. A uniformed Gladys
Calthrop met him at Bristol, which had been described by its mayor
as "the city of ruins"; the two of them drove together to London.
During his absence, the house in Gerald Road had been occupied by
Dallas Brooks, a tall and athletic Australian who had been second-
in-command at the now-defunct Department EH and involved with
Noël's propaganda work in Paris; he was now directing the Political
Warfare Executive, yet another secret propaganda organisation.[62]
    Lorn Loraine had booked Noël a luxurious suite at Claridge's
Hotel, where exiled monarchs were living out the war in style. But

after just one plush night amid the art-deco rooms, conscience got the better of him, and he moved into Gerald Road's spare bedroom. The house had remained standing, but around it the streets were gap-toothed with bomb damage, and reeked of fire and smoke. The pavements of Belgravia were traversed by sleep-deprived pedestrians and piled high with sandbags and bricks and heaps of timber and broken glass. Barrage balloons lumbered through the skies, which were scribbled with the vapour trails of bombers, and the trains that steamed in and out of Victoria Station had to avoid the crumbling walls and fallen pillars and the stretches of track that had buckled or melted away.

Life seemed both lonely and purposeless. The British press, from the depths of the Blitz, had not agreed with the Australian reporters as to the success and importance of Noël's tour and laughed bitterly at reports of his exhaustion. Goldenhurst had been requisitioned by the army; a Sunderland regiment had set up offices in its cocktail bar, their desks incongruously erected in a room hung floor-to-ceiling with autographed photos in gilt frames. "Felt a bit heartbroken", he wrote on visiting, "and oppressed by ghosts."[63] His mother was still in America; most to whom he was close had been called up. He immediately organised press conferences in the spirit of damage control, correcting misinformation about his travels in a tone that didn't quite escape petulance.

With both Ingram Fraser and William Stephenson (eventually knighted for his vital role in the decryption of the Enigma ciphers) he would remain in close contact long after the war. But Anthony Eden had all but ignored him after the poor publicity of his American tour; George Lloyd had died earlier in the year; Duff Cooper had with relief given up work at the Ministry of Information. Robert Vansittart was now working as chief adviser to Special Operations Executive, where Noël was no longer welcome. The pair discussed plans to collaborate on a film, a parallel to *Cavalcade* but set in Germany and presumably intended to show the history of a barbarous people.[64] Vansittart was notoriously anti-German, arguing that the Nazis were merely the latest manifestation of the country's continuous aggression. Noël's brief period of military training had instilled a similar dislike: "there is something about the Teutonic mentality that grates on my nerves [. . .] possibly their fundamental lack of humour".[65] But these plans came to nothing, and Noël was both angry and desolate, now that the prospect of the important work he had craved seemed to have dried up. How the little boy had cried when, at school award ceremonies, he had won no prizes.

The Blitz would last for another month, but Noël and Dallas Brooks were able to share Gerald Road for only five days. On the evening of 16 April, Noël was dining with the Mountbattens at the Hungarian Restaurant, which, housed in an underground room on Lower Regent Street, advertised itself as "the SAFE restaurant, bomb-proof, splinter-proof, blast-proof, gas-proof, and boredom proof". Travel had cossetted Noël from the terrors of a major air raid, and he sat in the restaurant quite calmly, listening to the wail of the siren, and the distant thump of falling bombs. Advised to stay where he was, he instead found a taxi in Trafalgar Square, which drove him at pace the two miles to Gerald Road. Noël noticed his lack of fear as they shot through darkened streets lit only by the intermittent explosions, along the Mall and past Buckingham Palace, the machine guns firing into a sky striped with searchlights as if in some grotesque parody of theatrical lighting. When he reached Gerald Road, he found that much of South Eaton Place – onto which backed both his house and its adjoining offices in Burton Mews – was on fire. Glass and rubble lay between him and his front door. The blackout had made the carrying of a pocket torch a necessity; with its aid he managed to enter the pitch-dark house, where he found Dallas Brooks bruised and cut by a swinging chandelier.

Noël's next move – by his own account – was to see if they could administer aid to wounded neighbours. But then a bomb fell very close to the house, blowing out most of the windows and doors. The large skylight in the roof rained down upon them, and the ceiling of the adjoining building in Burton Mews fell in. They were able to get outside, where fire-fighters were already dousing blazing houses on South Eaton Place and on Ebury Street, site of his former home. And even here, standing in the eerie silence that came between explosions, his home in ruins, fire and water all around him, he overheard the conversation of two young women picking their high heels through the rubble – "You know, dear, the trouble with all this is you could rick your ankle" – and, flippant to the last, found himself laughing.[66]

He and Brooks were finally able to get to Gladys Calthrop's house on Spenser Street. It had been the heaviest raid on London since the start of the Blitz, lasting eight hours, carried out by 685 planes, and killing over eleven hundred people. The following day he returned to the wreck of his home. "People still standing about with white papery faces – no one complaining, just looking. Lots of people still buried. Probably no hope for them. Felt aware of deep rage. Drove off in a taxi to try and find somewhere to live."[67]

There was little that most owners of damaged property could do other than submit a claim for compensation and throw themselves on the mercy of friends or relatives. Noël on the other hand could afford to move instantly into the Savoy Hotel, where once, as a child actor, he had been taken for tea parties and where, over twenty years ago, he had celebrated the cessation of a war to end war. The Savoy had remained defiantly open, maintaining its luxurious world in the face of staff shortages, bombs, and rationing. It had its own air-raid shelter, into which protestors would occasionally smuggle themselves, disgusted by the way in which the wealthy were insulated from the damage and privations of war. The protection of affluent lifestyles at the best hotels gained a nickname in the press: Ritzkrieg. Noël will also have been attracted by the Savoy Grill's being the dining room of choice for Churchill and the War Cabinet, although wartime restrictions had led to a five-shilling limit on the price of a meal.

The weeks after the bomb fell on Gerald Road were a whirl of social engagements during the day and raids during the night, a period of which Noël afterwards could remember little, as if numb. When a bomb blew in the doors of the Savoy Grill, he rushed to the piano, defiant, and perhaps not entirely unconscious of the fact that the hotel – realising the important role he could play in maintaining residents' moods – would soon upgrade him to its best suite at no extra charge. The Savoy also became the scene of a new love affair, with the thirty-three-year-old actor Michael Redgrave, who, married with two children, had admitted his bisexuality to his wife, the actress Rachel Kempson. Cambridge-educated, acclaimed for his work in Shakespeare, he was an odd fit for Noël. Earlier that year he had been banned from broadcasting on the BBC owing to his advocacy of a peace deal with the Germans and close co-operation with the Soviets, views which angered Noël in the extreme.

But attraction superseded political disagreement. Each addressed the other as "china", the euphemism for sex in Wycherley's Restoration comedy *The Country Wife.* Redgrave, who was building a successful movie career, had spent much of that year filming the lead role in Carol Reed's *Kipps.* "Michael is staying here at the Savoy as he is finishing his film", Noël noted in his diary. "Very dashing."[68] It would be a fractious relationship, and Noël, nearly ten years older, often lapsed into lecture-giving. "I have amongst other things been bearing in mind your strictures", Redgrave wrote to him. "You needn't have been quite so abusive about it because my colossal vanity is readily pierced [. . .] invective may sharpen your darts, but it does make you aim wildly [. . .] when we are in love with someone it is not so much that we idealise their good qualities but rationalise their defects."[69]

Noël was not content merely to enjoy life with Redgrave at the Savoy. He had a reputation to win back, and the chief option available was to return to the theatre. On New Year's Eve, he had made a promise to his diary: "I intend to write in 1941, really write. I can't afford to waste these years. [. . .] I am not going to devote all of myself to this bloody war any longer."[70] The theatres were able to reopen once the bombing had decreased in severity, and such was the speed at which he wrote that he would have a comedy up and running just weeks after the end of the Blitz, some while before Terence Rattigan would score successes either in sombre wartime mode (*Flare Path*) or with light comedy (*While the Sun Shines*). The popularity of musicals during the conflict was clear, but Ivor Novello had already opened *The Dancing Years*, one of the bestselling shows of the war, and Noël may have scented stiff competition. He settled on a comedy – about death.

On 21 April he had an "idea for comedy and would try to get away and write it [. . .] Title: *Blythe Spirit.*"[71] He and Joyce Carey went off to Wales, arriving on 2 May and settling into so strict a routine that the thing was done and dusted eight days later. (He took little heed of the fact that the holiday was meant to be a writing retreat for them both, instead using Carey as a sounding board and leaving her no time to work on her own project.) The new play broke all his strict rules about letting an idea percolate in the mind. *Blithe Spirit* went from brain to page in under a fortnight, and would be on a stage in Manchester a month later. "It is a special occasion", Noël told the first-night audience. "Because it proves that in spite of blitzes, discomforts, inconveniences, and alarms, the English Theatre can still function. [. . .] Our audiences can still laugh and applaud and enjoy themselves and I want to say in conclusion how proud I am to have been able to make even the small contribution of this play towards our universal valiant determination to get on with the job."[72]

He had used the familiar Coward plot, a reworking of *Private Lives*. Charles Condomine is a writer torn between his first wife, Elvira, and his second, Ruth. Elvira makes an unwelcome return into his life, and he must choose between his tormenting passion for Elvira and his comfortable domestic set-up with Ruth. The twist of *Blithe Spirit* is that Elvira just happens to be dead. Her ghost has appeared with the aid of a local psychic called Madame Arcati, whom Charles has asked to hold a séance as research for a book. Elvira sabotages Charles's car, hoping he will die and join her forever in the afterlife, as if the Orpheus myth has been turned inside out: the dead must return to fetch a lover from the world of the living. But the car is driven first by Ruth, who – like the heroine of Michael Arlen's *The Green Hat* – is involved in a fatal crash, and promptly returns as the play's second ghost.

That a wartime production should dare to treat death with such flippant nonchalance was the risk on which *Blithe Spirit* would live or die. At the first night in London, on 2 July, audiences had to pick their way across an enormous crater that had been blown into the pavement outside the Piccadilly Theatre. The "lull" in bombing had begun, but army leave had been banned in the early summer of that year and box offices were suffering. Costumes and even make-up were rationed; timings were sent haywire by disrupted train schedules and by the need to perform as much as possible during daylight. Auditoria were hung with warning signs that lit up during air raids, and those who wanted to leave were asked to make quietly for the nearest shelter. Newspapers noted that the first night had a carefully tailored pre-war atmosphere, although nobody wore evening dress. At Noël's curtain speech a lone heckler yelled "rubbish!" from the dress circle, to which he replied, "thank you", although she continued to shout about his recent absence: "Why did you run away?!"[73]

The play lived. Its London run lasted longer than the war and by the end of the year Jack Wilson had opened an equally success-ful production in New York. Most critics thought it touched by comic genius. Graham Greene, reviewing for the *Spectator*, found the whole thing a "weary exhibition of bad taste", but the novelist Rosamond Lehmann, who would spend her old age immersed in spiritualism, wrote a prompt rebuttal: "Never having to feel, we never have to shudder. [. . .] if *Blithe Spirit* is in bad taste, then I am led to conclude, not for the first time, that I like bad taste."[74] Noël's reputation had been rebuilt almost overnight. "Winston was raving about *Blithe Spirit*", he wrote happily, "and told Beaverbrook in front of Anthony [Eden] that I had been disgracefully treated by the Press."[75] Much of the success was due to the performances: the husky voiced Cecil Parker as Charles, Fay Compton as Ruth, and Kay Hammond, lit by a green-tinged follow spot, as Elvira. Most successful of all was Margaret Rutherford as Madame Arcati, a role she had originally turned down, unhappy with its flippant treatment of spiritualism, in which she was seriously interested. Rutherford was a stalwart supporting actress whose performance in *Blithe Spirit* – which Noël disliked – made her famous.

Noël had models aplenty for Arcati.[76] She wears "barbaric" jew-ellery, a word he often used to describe the necklaces of Gladys Calthrop and Hernia Whittlebot. On board a ship in the Pacific, earlier in the year, he had befriended "Marcella Hicks, an elderly, tubby, over-made-up old girl who is a spiritual medium [. . .] her sole companions seem to be those who have passed on".[77] But most of all there was Winifred Ashton, an acclaimed writer who produced work – novels, plays, screenplays – under the pseudonym

Clemence Dane, and who now had a firm place among his closest friends. Her fame had outstripped his own when they first met: she had had early success with plays such as *A Bill of Divorcement* or her 1917 novel *Regiment of Women*, which explored life in a girls' school with daring implications of lesbianism. Her most popular book, *Broome Stages*, followed a theatrical dynasty over two hundred years.

Noël became a permanent fixture of the salon she kept at her home in Covent Garden with her partner, Olwen Bowen-Davies. Larger than life in almost every sense, she had worked briefly as an actress, and had been potential casting for Arcati. Her eccentricity was legend; friends adored the way in which she innocently larded her conversation with outrageous *double entendres*. On top of writing she had trained as both sculptor and painter at the Slade, and when the building opposite her flat was set ablaze by a bomb she asked the firemen not to extinguish the flames until she had got everything down on canvas. Dane was almost too eccentric to be entirely a shoo-in for Arcati, who combines her psychic pretensions with a jolly-hockey-sticks briskness, splicing faux-Oriental frippery with a tweedy good sense.

To forge comedy from the world of spiritualism was novel. On its first outing George Orwell, reviewing for *Time and Tide*, found *Blithe Spirit* "the best thing [Coward] has done for a long time past" and a "devastating [. . .] satire on spiritualism". Arcati's world of Ouija boards and crystal balls was not, to wartime audiences, simply crackpot entertainment, but remnants of a religious movement that had had serious traction in living memory. The slaughter of the First World War had given rise to an interest in spiritualism that was at one point thought to have more followers than the Anglican Church, among them Hannen Swaffer. Bereaved parents wrote best-sellers about communicating with dead sons; Arthur Conan Doyle became a devout believer; Noël's mother had sought the advice of a spirit medium when worried about her son's career. Noël had little truck with such beliefs, and *Blithe Spirit* sought to nip their resurgence in the bud even as another wave of mourning and loss surged across the world. The play called the spiritualists' bluff. As Orwell wrote, "suppose one simply accepts the whole thing as truthful! It is then that the fundamental uninterestingness of what

the spiritualists have to say [. . .] comes out."[78] Noël had mined
for comic potential the basic conception of scenes in *Hamlet* (which
Arcati is fond of quoting) and *Macbeth*: one character can see another
who is invisible to the rest of the cast, while being visible to the
audience. The supernatural is then treated with worldly logic. Elvira
drives into Folkestone to catch up with old friends. She even admits
to being afraid of ghosts.

Blithe Spirit, like *Private Lives*, welcomes a number of readings, chief
among them homosexual allegory. Charles Condomine, mired in a
sexless marriage with the starchy but clear-eyed Ruth, is suddenly
confronted by his attraction to the "gay charm" of Elvira, as if having
to face up to his sexual nature. Elvira's name means "truth". But
eventually, escaping both his wives, he leaves for a life of freedom,
rejecting the trappings of both sex and marriage, and questioning
monogamous union of any kind. He employs the licence of the
artist to live as he wishes, free from the destroying pull of passion
and the hampering necessities of domesticity: "I'm going a long
way away [. . .] I'm free, Ruth dear, not only of Mother and Elvira
[. . .] but free of you too and I should like to take this farewell
opportunity of saying I'm enjoying it immensely." *Blithe Spirit* was
written at a time in Noël's life when, with Michael Redgrave married to another, Noël apparently had no single emotional or sexual
partner. He was travelling the world during a time of war, and
travelling alone.

But Condomine, author of cheap thrillers with titles such as
The Unseen, is also a very bad novelist, his feeble powers on the
decline. The play is not a paean to the artist's rejection of society's conventions. Noël had seen too many alternative lifestyles,
at their peak in the interwar years, descend into unhappiness and
unsustainability, not least his own. Elvira's death occurred in the
early 1930s, ending her life of monied leisure and sexual freedom.
Blithe Spirit can be thought of as "Bright Young Things: The Sequel,
or 'What Amanda Did Next'". Elvira is a dancing little lady now
speaking from beyond the grave, but still wearing a lifeless mask,
of – in Noël's description of the first production – "dead white
make up with a little green in it".[79] The focus of her life was "going
to parties [. . .] why shouldn't I have fun? I died young didn't I?"

She laughed herself to death, sudden hysteria at a wireless broadcast leading to a heart attack; but she is a surprisingly wounded poltergeist: "They're only ghost tears – they don't mean anything really – but they're very painful." Charles meanwhile is the archetypal anti-hero of Noël's earlier work – "I really must ask you not to be flippant, Mr Condomine" – attractive, facetious, hot-tempered, easefully mingling violence and sexuality. He once hit Elvira with a billiards cue and is revealed to have been promiscuous, a serial adulterer to both his wives. If the part is self-portrait (Charles is addressed as "Cowardy custard") then Noël had been unsparing. Once, his male roles had encapsulated the times, but Charles is facing his comeuppance, as if it were about time he, and perhaps his author, grew up: "In your younger days this display of roguish flippancy might have been alluring – in a middle-aged novelist it's nauseating."

By the end, the ghosts of both wives have been exorcised, and yet Charles is still aware of their invisible presence, as if they have become drawing-room Eumenides, bringing about his disintegration.* From the start he has thought himself "going mad", has behaved like a "lunatic", is told he will be in a "strait-jacket" in a situation that is "madness, sheer madness". He must, quite literally, grapple with his demons; the word "demonic" nestles in his surname. The final curtain descends on the two invisible shades wreaking havoc in his home: around him, in a series of *coups de théâtre*, ornaments smash, the clock strikes sixteen, and curtain poles fall, wrenched by invisible hands. The scene, written in the last weeks of the Blitz while Noël's own home lay beneath a blanket of dust and glass, was a daring portrayal of domestic ruin. Charles prepares to leave, unrepentant, professing his freedom – and in many productions he actually *does* leave. David Lean's film version

---

* T. S. Eliot's *The Family Reunion* featured a young man, Harry, racked with guilt after the death of his wife and pursued in the drawing room of a country house by the avenging Furies, who, as with *Blithe Spirit*'s ghosts, can also be seen by his servant. Where Condomine's reaction is to depart in nihilist and solitary triumph, Harry's is to discover religious vocation. *The Family Reunion* was premiered, unsuccessfully, in 1939; Michael Redgrave played Harry.

has him crash the car and join his wives as a ghost to live in some
spectral threesome, as if the afterlife were an ultimate Bohemia
from which convention could be rejected.

But the original script keeps him onstage, the rake's progress
having finally arrived in bedlam. Able to make "an inventory of my
sex life", Condomine seems most of all a reckless Don Giovanni,
forever pursued by his spurned Elvira. He ends the savage farce that
is *Blithe Spirit* about to be dragged down into hell by a ghost from
his past. Outside of the theatre, which rocked with laughter over
nearly two thousand performances, the city lay in ruins.

20. LONDON; ORKNEY ISLANDS; ICELAND — SUMMER–AUTUMN 1941

Legend had it that on bombsites across the country, amid the
craters, and the piles of buckled timber, dense carpets of green
spoon-shaped leaves were taking root and blooming, that June,
into pink-dotted white flowers: *Saxifraga x urbium*, known as London
Pride. The plant gave Noël the idea for a song, which came to him
as he sat on a damaged platform at Paddington, watching people
carry on with life despite the crunch of broken glass underfoot.
He had been strangely elated by his return to England. As he told
his mother, who was still in America, "I wouldn't have missed
what's going on here for anything in the world. The ordinary
people are so wonderful and there is a new vitality all over the
country, particularly in the badly blitzed areas, which are dreadful
but somehow quite magnificent at the same time. It makes one very
proud to belong."[80] The belonging of war was one of the conflict's
attractions, as he exchanged the bitter solitude of the satirist for the
stoic comradeship of national endurance. But his attitude towards
the "ordinary people" could be more lofty than neighbourly. Back
he went, through the Blitzed streets, to his suite at the Savoy.

He worked hard on "London Pride" for nearly a month (far
longer than he ever officially claimed), wrestling for weeks with
both music and lyrics until Elsie April took dictation of the finished version on 24 June. The song has the harmonic basis of

the Westminster chimes and is woven from a street-sellers' cry – "Won't You Buy My Sweet Blooming Lavender" – and from the opening phrase of Deutschland über Alles, as if to seize and reclaim an enemy anthem. War songs were becoming powerful weapons of propaganda and morale. "London Pride" would exemplify the defiant mood of a city in which, ironically, Noël had spent only a few months of the war. In his thirties he had written lyrics about the modern city with a kind of exhilarated doom, depicting alienated souls trapped in a burgeoning metropolis that blocked out the sun: "iron, rot, steel, rust | speed, noise, death, dust". Now he portrayed the British capital in roseate dawn light, ignoring the piles of bricks and corpses to conjure an entirely romanticised picture of a city untouched not only by war but by modernity: "See the coster barrows, the vegetables and the fruit piled high"; "Early rain, and the pavement's glistening | All Park Lane in a shimmering gown. | Nothing ever could break or harm | The charm of London town."

Noël's war songs were unusual in that they often lacked either nostalgia or optimism. This would serve him well when, after the Fall of Singapore the following year, the apparent sentimentality of Vera Lynn's performances led to the cancellation of her radio programme, lest she soften the virility of listening soldiers. Noël instead welded wit to the war song in "Could You Please Provide Us With a Bren Gun?", a comedy lampooning wartime muddle. Loss of material after Dunkirk had led the army and marines to be prioritised when it came to weaponry, and the Home Guard found themselves using outdated weapons. (Twenty years later *Dad's Army* would give the song a new lease of life.) Noël left unfinished a number mocking the government itself: "Never did so many know so little about so much!"[81]

In July Michael Redgrave enlisted in the navy as an ordinary seaman, and the night before his departure he spent with Noël. His wife, Rachel Kempson, was calm in her upset:

Noël said to me: "I have loved Michael, but he is very difficult, and you must have had your difficulties." I told him that in fact he, Noël, had upset me greatly [. . .] the night before Michael went to Plymouth. I had wanted to spend the evening with Michael, but he had spent it instead with Noël. Noël said that he hadn't wished to hurt me, and that it was no use having regrets about what you have done, but he had found Michael so irresistibly charming. I couldn't but agree with him.[82]

Noël had become a third figure in Redgrave's marriage. Kempson openly admitted her (Platonic) feelings – "I loved Noël" – and she longed to work for him, "because it would have meant being directed by him and spending time in his company".[83] She spent much of the war touring in *Blithe Spirit*, and made sure to inform her husband's lover of their movements. "Rachel called up to say that Mike had gone", Noël wrote. "A little chilled by the news – shall miss him."[84]

Redgrave tried to see Noël when he could, but their meetings were not altogether happy. "Please forgive my behaviour while on leave and if possible forget it", Redgrave wrote to him. "I was pretty unhappy and worried about a number of things [. . .] I had looked forward to it so much that I was almost ill with excitement." Their relationship was not to last, and Noël, all too used to the evanescence of his affairs, seems to have imparted to Redgrave his belief in love's impermanence. "You have so often said", Redgrave wrote, "that you looked forward to us being friends always. I would like that."[85] Noël, for all his neuroses, was not one to bring love affairs to an end with arguments and silence; he was still in contact not only with Jack Wilson but with Alan Webb, and he may even have greeted the transition from lover to friend with relief. In 1971, knighted and eminent, Redgrave would tell him: "You are always in my thoughts – or more exactly hardly a day goes by, believe it or not, when I do not chance to think of you."[86]

Redgrave's presence at Plymouth was an enticement for Noël to work hard on another project, a war propaganda film suggested to him by a trio of movie producers. Initially wary, Noël had given in when offered complete artistic control, realising that this could well be an opportunity to serve the navy to the best of his ability: as writer, actor, director, and composer of the score. He was quick to see the increasing power of the screen. "In our brave new world of the future", he had argued during one of his Australian broadcasts, "I think the radio and the movies might exercise a much greater influence on man's education than they have done hitherto."[87] With the Battle of Britain over, the Battle of the Atlantic remained one of the country's most critical struggles, and the navy, which had provided cover during the Dunkirk evacuation, was an important focus of propaganda attention.

In May, during the evacuation of Crete, Louis Mountbatten's destroyer, HMS *Kelly*, had been bombed and sank, killing half the crew. Noël heard the story straight from the mouth of Mountbatten, and he realised that the potential for screen adaptation was irresistible. Mountbatten, initially wary that the film would be too closely modelled both on him and the recent disaster, eventually offered help and encouragement, and Noël travelled to the bombed wrecks of dockyards from Newcastle to Portsmouth. In August he spent a fortnight's research trip at sea, visiting the Home Fleet in the Orkney Islands and going as far as Iceland. This was his first travel with the navy since before the war, and the conviviality of naval life had given way to real danger. The Home Fleet was responsible for keeping German ships from breaking out of the North Sea, and Noël sailed blithely through a minefield on a vessel whose anti-submarine detection had broken down: "it was all fraught with delicious peril and laced with gin".[88]

The house at Gerald Road had been repaired to the extent that, on his return, he could move back in, and it was while he was working on the movie script in the studio that, on 16 October, two police officers arrived at his front door.

**21. INT. BOW STREET POLICE COURT, LONDON
— 30 OCTOBER 1941**

MR GEOFFREY ROBERTS
Is your full name Noël Peirce Coward?

NOËL COWARD
Yes.

MR ROBERTS
What is your private address now?

NOËL COWARD
17, Gerald Road, SW1.

MR ROBERTS
Until this matter was brought to your
attention in the Summer of 1941, had you any
knowledge of the existence of these Regulations at all?

NOËL COWARD
No.

MR ROBERTS
Had you the slightest idea that you ought
to have surrendered your dollars or registered your American securities?

NOËL COWARD
No.

MR ROBERTS
Do you in fact ever interest yourself in
finance or business at all?

NOËL COWARD
Never, if I can possibly avoid it.[1]

22. LONDON — OCTOBER–NOVEMBER 1941

Just before the outbreak of war, while Noël had been rehearsing his unstaged double bill, new financial regulations had been brought in to mobilise all foreign currency, in cash or investments, owned by British citizens. Dollars, for example, had to be offered straight to the Treasury against payment in sterling; stocks and bonds could not be sold abroad unless the proceeds were offered to the Bank of England. Even sending pounds abroad was controlled; hence the difficulties experienced by British parents trying to fund evacuees in America. Noël, apparently unaware of the rules, owned over £20,000 worth of American dollars, in cash and investments, that he had not registered or offered to the government. To fund his travels in the States he had also sold, without government consent, £11,000 of securities. The upshot was two trials, first at the Bow Street Police Court on 24 October and then at Mansion House the following month, of which the worst potential outcome would be fines totalling over £80,000. This was a sum to which he did not have immediate access, and imprisonment was not impossible.* "Feel sick with anxiety", he wrote, outraged that nobody conceded how much of his American money had gone towards work for the British government. "Terrified of what's being done in America behind my back."[2]

The authorities were keen to make an example of a celebrity not being offered special treatment: the Savoy Hotel had been taken to court for flouting wartime restrictions; there had been an improbable scandal over the omission of luxury cheese from wartime rationing; and Ivor Novello would eventually be imprisoned for

---

* The figures in today's values (2023): Coward had not registered dollars to the tune of some £700,000; he had sold over £300,000 in securities; and faced a maximum fine of over £3 million.

misusing petrol coupons. Noël suspected that someone in government was deliberately targeting him in revenge for his bad publicity the previous year. But the reality was more mundane, as proved by a police report written for the Treasury. "One of the officials at the Bank of England was reading, during a bout of influenza, Noël Coward's autobiography *Present Indicative.* He noticed that Chapter 17 begins with the words: 'Jack, having already wisely invested a lot of my money in American securities . . . ' and he accordingly sent the book to the Foreign Exchange Control of the Bank of England with a view to their investigating the matter."[3] Had the official in question not caught flu the matter might never have come to court. As it was, the prosecution quietly gathered evidence for nearly a year before bringing the case, and the Ministry of Information refused to be drawn on whether or not Noël had been travelling on official business.

Noël employed a good defence lawyer, Geoffrey Roberts, and kept his cool during the trials, well advised by George Bernard Shaw, who had written in sympathetic support. The prosecution could only gape at his financial naivety, and credulity was further stretched when he swore on oath that even his close involvement with the evacuation of children to America had given him no sense of restrictions imposed on foreign currency. In cross examination he could make no mention of any projects undertaken for William Stephenson, whose activities remained secret to all but the very highest levels of government: "All the truth of my war activities came out except the secret stuff."[4] In his diary he had noted, for one trip, "expenses to be paid by Stephenson", which may explain his wariness in drawing attention to foreign finances. But it became clear that not only Jack Wilson but accountants in America and in England had been guilty of gross negligence, and that Noël looked on money with his customary mistrust of sincerity. "I know it does seem most awfully stupid", he said in court, "but I am afraid I must admit to that extreme stupidity. I did not give the matter any thought at all [. . .] Looking back now it seems to me very remiss on my part − but that is the actual truth."[5]

The first magistrate was sympathetic, the second much less so,

and excerpts from Noël's autobiography and private correspondence were read aloud, to reporters' glee. It emerged that his foreign
expenditure since the outbreak of war had amounted to well over
a million dollars in today's money: "every dollar of that", said
the judge, "should have come to this country and been used by
this country". The examination also threatened to divulge details
of his private life, as he had to admit to sharing (and paying for)
the house in Connecticut with Jack Wilson. "It is only fair to say",
conceded the first magistrate, "that, though lost to the Government,
[the money] has not gone into Mr Coward's pocket. [. . .] I am
very much impressed – and I think it is the dominant feature in
this case – by the fact that he went abroad with the knowledge,
asset and approval [. . .] of the Government."[6] Noël was roundly
criticised for his financial negligence, found guilty on all charges,
and fined, in today's values, around £90,000, the bulk of it for not
registering his foreign investments (the least serious offence, but
the one to which the second trial had been devoted).

Noël came home and wrote in his diary: "It's over now and as
far as I am concerned, the Lord Mayor can take a flying fuck at
a galloping mule."[7] Geoffrey Roberts thought the conduct of the
trials had been the "most frightful BALLS", telling Noël: "I have
always had such an admiration for your work and I now have
an equal admiration for your courage and good humour when
you're in a 'jam'."[8] The case was heavily reported in the press,
revealing Noël's vast income and luxurious lifestyle at a time when
the average wage in England was around £320 and income tax at
50 per cent. But reports were surprisingly sympathetic, and even
the *Daily Mirror* grudgingly admitted that somehow the case had
"touched the public heart-strings, [despite its] touching the public
purse-strings".[9]

The negligence was good evidence of the way in which Noël's
love for Jack Wilson had translated into a handover of total financial
control for nigh-on two decades, his trust cemented by Jack's pru-
dency during the Wall Street Crash. For Noël, it had been "one of
the most horrible and humiliating ordeals of my life", and he felt
"sickeningly ashamed", as he told Jack: "I am now going to tick
you off as you have never been ticked off before. [. . .] Fortunately

my own personal integrity is unimpeachable, although my own
personal idiocy [. . .] was only too apparent."[10] Jack's explanation
and apology was spread over five pages: "I was heartsick and miserable [. . .] I must ask you to continue the faith that you have always
shown in my judgement and to believe that anything that was
done, rightly or wrongly, was done with integrity, with justice,
with the sincere desire to promote the best interests of your life."
He pointed out that Noël had always been determined to pay full
tax on his British earnings, a situation that many British actors
working in the States had avoided by taking American citizenship.

Noël determined to take more financial control, but he could not
stay cross with Jack for long and he soon returned to his customary
state of helpless affection. "Your letter really was a fair treat", he
wrote to him. "Extremely comforting to me because it showed that
you really and truly understood."[11]

23. LONDON; BUCKINGHAMSHIRE — AUTUMN 1941– SPRING 1942

His name clear, his pride and his finances wounded, Noël could
resume work on the film that became *In Which We Serve*, which he
thought "the most important job, from every point of view, that
I have ever done".[12] He became so immersed that when, after the
attack on Pearl Harbour in December 1941, America joined the
war, he barely had time to rejoice.

He was a happy member of a close quartet, who all called him
"father": Anthony Havelock-Allan was to produce; cinematog-
raphy was by Ronald Neame; and co-directing with Noël was the
thirty-three-year-old editor David Lean, making the first film of his
legendary career. Noël was to direct the actors, Lean to be in charge
of the camera. The decision was made to use black-and-white,
avoiding garish Technicolor and giving the film a documentary feel,
emulating the newsreels that would bookend its cinema screenings.
The script began life as an epic encompassing almost the entire
history of the navy, and Noël told Jack Wilson that it "would have
made *Gone With the Wind* look like *Three Little Pigs* and have played

at least three and a half hours".[13] He was despatched for cuts and revisions, eventually settling on the structure of the finished film. Mountbatten and HMS *Kelly* were thinly disguised as Captain Kinross and HMS *Torrin*. As the Captain and his crew cling to the life raft in the sea, awaiting rescue, the film was to travel, via flashback, into the memories of the various sailors, the screen rippling and dissolving as if the camera had disappeared beneath the water.

For this the navy had to give its permission, and Mountbatten was a vital support. The press, who had not forgotten the naval-uniform farrago of the previous year, took against the project and trashed it before it had begun, especially when it became clear that Noël Coward, of all people, was to play Mountbatten. That the film was specifically dramatising the sinking of the *Kelly* had to be officially denied, at Mountbatten's request. Nobody need have worried about too close a resemblance, for despite his best efforts Noël was to play the captain more or less as Noël Coward, delivering all the lines at speed in his smoky hoot, not really convincing either as a husband and father, or, slender and slick in his pristine uniform, as an officer. There were concerns that a sinking ship had no place in a propaganda film. The Admiralty complained to the Ministry of Information; the Ministry of Information complained to the Admiralty. In the end Mountbatten took the script directly to the King to make sure proceedings were smooth but when, after the war, Noël gleefully included this fact in his memoir, he was formally asked to remove it. "One never", Mountbatten told him, "quotes any action which the King may have taken behind the scenes."[14]

Finances were nevertheless slow. Noël, taking on only his second speaking role in the cinema, was not a bankable movie star; to some in government he was an entirely unsuitable character to be involved with such a project. A cast was slowly gathered, and for even the smallest roles six potential actors were seen for half an hour each. Domestic life on the Home Front was led by Joyce Carey and, as Kinross's wife, by Celia Johnson (her first full-length film). Noël angrily vetoed James Mason, on account of his conscientious objection. Among the sailors were to be John Mills and, making his film debut and mistakenly omitted from the credits, nineteen-year-old Richard Attenborough. As a young unknown, he found

Noël self-deprecating and supportive; as a legend of British cinema, many years later, he proclaimed him "the kindest, most generous person I have ever encountered".[15]

Three weeks before filming began, Noël took the highly unusual step of sending a copy of the script with a personal note to each and every member of the crew. Shooting began in February 1942, at the Denham Film Studios in Buckinghamshire. Noël and Gladys Calthrop (who designed the domestic interiors) lived side by side in a grim pair of local cottages, living on "sardines, baked beans, Worcester Sauce, etc".[16] Everyone was nervous and when the actor William Hartnell (eventually the first Doctor Who) arrived late, only half-dressed, the cast quaked as Noël calmly called for silence and had him fired from the production. Over the long filming days tempers continued to fray and Noël was taut with tension. Ronald Neame found him startlingly serious beneath the frivolous veneer, noting his refusal to suffer fools at all, leave alone gladly. He remembered a conversation in which Noël "quietly related how he feared one day waking up to find his talent had disappeared. He was concerned that time was running out, and he hadn't yet fulfilled his potential."[17]

It became clear to most that David Lean had always to answer to his co-director and lead actor, who tended to side with the cast in any disagreement and who, they noticed, asked to be lit in a certain way to disguise his receding hairline, visible even beneath the naval cap he wore, Mountbatten's own. A third of a destroyer had been built of wood in the studios, 200-feet long and weighing one hundred tonnes; the sea scenes were done in tanks of tepid dirty water that reeked, and the actors were smeared in a filthy gloop, meant to represent fuel, which thickened under the heat of the lights. "I went in first in order to set a good example", Noël wrote. "Tank water now putrid, so much that I was a little bit sick, but persevered, submerged myself, swallowed quarts of it, and generally set the best example I could."[18] The actors overheard him mutter: "There's dysentery in every ripple".[19] Everyone complained of the cold to such an extent that Lean refused to get too near the tank lest he be pulled in, and eventually the water was mistakenly heated to boiling point. Noël asked if the crew had confused the actors with lobsters. Mountbatten, visiting the set, thought the conditions rather worse than in the Mediterranean.

The effects of the film were epic and novel; the means by which they were achieved haphazard and dangerous. The navy provided hundreds of extras, many of them wounded veterans; the footage of German aircraft, rather than employing models, used real captured planes supplied by the RAF and protected, during filming, by British pilots to prevent them being fired upon. (The bombs dropped on the ship, however, were recognisably British. Letters were written.) Underwater machine-gun fire was managed by shooting dozens of condoms from a long pipe, to great effect. A wall of water crashing over the ship emerged with such force that part of the set collapsed beneath its weight. Then, on 23 May, an electrician, Jock Dymore, not realising that a tin of fake gunpowder was still burning hot from a previous take, lifted the lid and it exploded. "Five men badly burnt", Noël wrote. "All taken to hospital. Everyone too shattered to work in the afternoon." The next day: "Jock Dymore died this morning. The other two, Sid and Ronnie, are in a very grave condition. Went with David to see them but they were having blood transfusions. [. . .] They are pretty bad but I think they will be all right. Of course they looked terrible, painted with gentian violet and dreadfully swollen." Lean noted that Noël, shocked and upset as he was, would countenance no delay in the filming schedule.[20]

When the money ran out nobody dared tell Noël; eventually Sam Smith, a producer at British Lion, footed the bill after viewing some promising rushes: the budget (in today's values) approached twelve million pounds. Omens seemed good when, in April 1942, Mountbatten arranged for an appreciative royal family to visit the studios. "The King spoke to the Prime Minister at dinner last night", Mountbatten told Noël, "and said how thrilled he had been by what he had seen and the Prime Minister spoke in glowing and affectionate terms of you. He told the King that he had been immensely impressed by the number of senior officers who wished you had a commission in the Navy and that he had come of late to think very highly of you."[21]

Finally it was done, and the premiere came on 27 September 1942. The film had been made at such speed that veterans from the sinking of the *Kelly* could attend, their memories of the tragedy only a year old. Noël's name appeared in the opening credits seven times in different capacities. Critics spoke in terms of the "best war film ever made" and the same team moved quickly on to films of *This Happy Breed* and *Blithe Spirit*. Approval came from the Mountbattens, the King and Queen, Roosevelt, even Anthony Eden, who thought Noël had "never done anything so big as this [. . .] no other living man could have done it".[22] Churchill complained about the scrambled chronology and said he found it hard to follow, although this may be explained by the fact that during his private screening the Battle of Libya started and he kept leaving to make calls.[23] As unlikely a fan as T. S. Eliot wrote of "the excellent Noël Coward film".[24] Suspicions from the Admiralty melted away, and new naval recruits would be shown the movie as an induction. The army asked for a film of its own. Noël would be given an honorary Academy Award for the production and when the movie opened in America, the New York office of William Stephenson's British Security Co-ordination was all but deserted. Everyone had gone off together to see it.[25]

The small number of movies already made about the war – *The Lion Has Wings*, *Target for Tonight* – had been, essentially, propaganda documentaries. *In Which We Serve* set a new standard for, even created, the genre of the semi-fictional "war movie", and became the model on which so many of its successors, especially during the post-war craze for such films, would be based. Eighty years on, its propaganda – the blessings heaped upon the navy, the rousing speeches, the celebration as German ships are sunk and German sailors drowned – must be returned to its context to be accepted. As a portrait of Noël's beloved "ordinary people" the film often resorts to central-casting chipper sailors, who know their place in the ship's hierarchy; as a portrait of Mountbatten, it is hero-worship. Noël had always been willing to accept Mountbatten's carefully honed self-portrait as peerless national hero, and Mountbatten's involvement in the failure of the Dieppe Raid, just weeks after the premiere, did not dent his adulation.

But what has survived of the film, aside from its technical impressiveness, is its attention to domestic life in the Second World

War, the way it creates a mosaic (781 scenes) of epic spectacle and domestic miniature. Celia Johnson, as Mrs Kinross, is given a long speech about the plight of the naval wife. A woman says a brisk final goodbye to her husband on a heartbreaking note of domestic detail: "I won't forget to get the mower mended." A wife and mother natter through the air raid that will kill them. Kinross carefully learns the addresses of dying men, that their families can be informed; news of survival comes in a two-word telegram – "OK. LOVE" – and news of death is greeted with "Oh – oh, I see." The camera lingers over faces in a crowd, on workers building a ship, on the filthy faces of sailors each of whom, in a final scene of daring length, Kinross greets by name. The result is a film of individuals, rather than cannon fodder; an attempt, as in *Cavalcade*, to bring within the bounds of its patriotism an honest concession of the horrors, rather than the glories, of warfare.

24. ENGLAND — SPRING 1942–SPRING 1943

Violet Coward was still in New York, nearing eighty and unhappy. Noël, stressed by *In Which We Serve*, had been in low spirits, and they had quarrelled badly by letter over the many months of preparation and filming. Finally he had erupted at her suggestion that the British government was mishandling the war and that he would be better off in the United States. "You must NEVER", he wrote, "while you are in America, speak against this country or even against the government which is apparently doing its not very inspired best; because if you do you are letting me down very badly." At this, Violet lost her temper: "You neglected me for months, because you had no time to write, and then found time to type pages of a pompous lecture at me. How dared you! [. . .] This letter will doubtless be torn to shreds like all my letters have always been by your immediate circle, but I must keep my reputation for being the 'wicked old woman' you have always called me. Please don't bother about my coming home."[26] Like all their arguments, this one eventually cooled, and Noël made arrangements for her safe return to England, installing her in a rented cottage not too far from Goldenhurst.

As filming had continued, so had the tragedies of war. The actress Beatrice Lillie's only son was killed in action on a naval ship, and on 30 March 1942 Gladys Calthrop's son, Hugo, a captain in the Royal Engineers, was killed in Burma aged just twenty-six. His mother had not been a fixture of his life since his early childhood, but the tragedy was a great shock to Gladys, who spent much of the rest of her life battling onslaughts of severe depression, for which she eventually underwent electric shock therapy. "I brought her home to dinner", Noël wrote, "and feel low and wretched. There is nothing to be done but play up to her own supreme integrity. Hugo was young, good-looking, intelligent, and nice. [. . .] I know [Gladys] is more deeply unhappy than ever before in her life. [. . .] Perhaps such integrity can be regarded as compensation for a lot, but this constant killing of the young enchanted is a hell of a price to pay."[27]

Five months later, on 20 August, in the run-up to the premiere of *In Which We Serve*, Noël had taken over the part of Charles Condomine in *Blithe Spirit* for a fortnight, his first acting role in five years. Just days into the run, on 25 August, came the death in a plane crash of his beloved Duke of Kent, whom he had seen or spoken to almost weekly during filming, driving the two miles from Denham Studios to the Kents' home. He stood by the graveside in tears. "It is never difficult to believe", he wrote, "that someone young and charming and kind is dead. They are always dying. The Duke of Windsor and Hannen Swaffer, etc., remain alive but Prince George has to die by accident."[28] Visiting the Duke's widow, Princess Marina, he wept in her arms, his bereavement of an intensity that gives credence to rumours of a past affair: "She cried and so did I and we confessed how we had dreaded seeing each other and how glad we were that the shock was over. My heart aches for her. [. . .] I slipped into his room when she had gone to change, just to look round. But it was dreadfully empty. [. . .] The thought of him sits on top of everything all the time. This of course, will fade, but at the moment it is sickeningly sad."[29] Journalists soon began to turn up at Gerald Road, "to ask me if there was any truth in the rumours that are now strong in Fleet Street that I am engaged to the Duchess of Kent".[30]

Noël had retreated into a numb apathy about the war, cushioning

himself once again in the world of the theatre, safe from the failures and humiliations of his attempts – perhaps misguided, he had
begun to concede – to work in any other capacity. A secret meeting
at Claridge's with William Stephenson, who was visiting London
that summer, was more of a social call. "He suggested I make a
tour of South America. I refused, a little sadly. I shall do better by
doing my own job. Perhaps I started the war with rather too high
hopes."[31] On 18 June he had a secret meeting with Bill Donovan,
who five days earlier had been appointed head of American intelligence, and with John Winant, the American ambassador.[32] Such
meetings were perhaps the reason why the FBI began to keep a close
eye on his British movements. The manager of the Cleveland Office,
Leiland Boardman, wrote to the director, J. Edgar Hoover, that one
of his agents had attended a party "at [redacted]'s place on the Isle
of Wight", and that "the usual crowd was there including NOËL
COWARD and his American friend". But the agent could not have
been more wrong, reporting back his bizarre sense that "Coward
[. . .] favour[s] appeasement and friendship with Germany".[33]

The most exciting prospect on the horizon was a heavy hint
from Louis Mountbatten that the King had personally nominated
Noël for a long-rumoured knighthood. "You know how little I
want anything like that", Noël told him, truthfully or otherwise.
"My rewards are so tremendous anyway. [. . .] The fact that the
'honour' question was the King's own idea obviously touches me
deeply and I am immensely pleased. [. . .] I only wish secretly that
it could be a little different from the usual award on account of that
particular accolade having fallen rather into disrepute lately through
being so very indiscriminately bestowed. The fact of it being the
King's wish of course makes the whole difference and so that's
that."[34] But a few weeks later Winston Churchill told the King,
"with considerable personal reluctance", that Noël's court case the
previous year had been "one of substance" and that a knighthood
"so soon afterwards would give rise to unfavourable comment".[35]
Homophobia has been mooted as a reason for Churchill's blocking the knighthood, but although Churchill argued against the
legalisation of homosexuality, even advocating medical treatment,
he maintained close friendships with figures in the arts and in

government of whose sexuality he cannot have been unaware. Some were given official honours, including his private secretary, Edward Marsh. Knighthoods were not expected for playwrights, and none had received one since Pinero in 1909; nor would they until Noël was finally offered the honour, over twenty-five years later. But he was said to have wept when Mountbatten regretfully informed him that the honours list of 1943 would not contain his name.

His focus was now the organisation of a theatrical tour. Binkie Beaumont was in control of H. M. Tennent Ltd, after the death of Tennent himself, and had become one of the most powerful men in British theatre. He suggested a massive tour that would finally bring to the stage the dormant scripts that Noël had written just before the war: *This Happy Breed* and, as it was now permanently titled, *Present Laughter*. To these *Blithe Spirit* was added to make a triptych called *Play Parade*, with Noël performing a trio of contrasting lead roles across a weekly eight performances: Frank Collins, Garry Essendine, and Charles Condomine. He began to make plans for a fourth play – a one-acter about spying called *With My Little Eye* – but these were eventually dropped.[36]

The tour opened in Blackpool in September 1942 and would run for twenty-eight weeks before, in April 1943, *Play Parade* came into the West End. "It is extraordinary", Noël wrote, "how completely concentration on the job wipes all extraneous things from the mind. I know that men are fighting and dying all over the world and I am concerned with whether I get the laugh on a certain line [. . .] Perhaps what I am about to do will make people laugh and enjoy themselves enough to compensate any further feeling of frustration which I have had since the war started, except for those first months in Paris when I really felt I was working."[37] The cast, which included Joyce Carey, was a happy and convivial one, the only difficulty being Beryl Measor (playing Madame Arcati), who was not always sober during her performances and had a habit of travelling to Blackpool when she was meant to be in Manchester. Playing wives in all three productions was Judy Campbell, famous for her performance of "A Nightingale Sang in Berkeley Square" in a 1940 revue. She became an especially beloved friend (soon after the run ended she married a lieutenant-colonel; one of their children is the actress Jane Birkin). The anecdote she told with the greatest affection in later life was of Noël slipping his hands into her bra backstage. Describing herself as "absolutely in love with him", she was not affronted but delighted; after so long in one another's company, there may have been a sexual frisson to their theatrical chemistry, although Noël professed it nothing but a hand-warming technique.[38]

Warmth was indeed in short supply. Bombing raids were infrequent, but touring life was arduous. Petrol was available only for absolutely essential work and never for private use. *Play Parade* visited twenty-one locations across Britain, and the actors crossed the country on unheated trains with blacked-out windows and lightbulbs daubed in blue paint; they handed in their ration books to the various frozen hotels after navigating unknown pitch-dark bomb-mangled streets; stage management dealt inventively with the challenges of clothing coupons. In seaside towns a ten o'clock curfew was in force and walks on the promenade could not be made without permission from a local officer. Coal could only be obtained for bedroom fires on receipt of a valid doctor's certificate, and Noël marvelled at how many of the company suddenly developed symptoms of one kind or another, and crowded into local clinics claiming they had colds, or pneumonia, or both. Even the theatres were unheated and, at one venue in Scotland, Noël complained to Joyce Carey and Judy Campbell that "I had been unable to hear myself speaking owing to the chattering of their teeth. In the second act, to our immense relief, the theatre caught on fire."[39]

Not that Noël had entirely jettisoned extravagance. A valet called Herbert Lister had temporarily replaced Cole Lesley, and Harold Nicolson, visiting Leicester, found Noël in the bath, with Herbert "opening countless scent bottles" (Noël, no method actor, wore perfume even when acting in *This Happy Breed*). "There was a large apparatus in the corner, in front of which Noël, clad only in a triangulo, seated himself with an expression of intense desire and submitted himself to five minutes of infra-red, talking gaily all the while. So patriotic he was, so light-hearted, and so comfortable and well-served. He is a nice, nice man."[40] Noël, for his part, noted that Nicolson looked "less like a summer pudding than the last time I saw him".[41] But the tour contained its sadnesses, too; in Bath, in October, he travelled to see Maisie Gay, star of his early revues and the creator of Hernia Whittlebot, now confined to bed with fibromyalgia and experiencing what Noël saw was a "slow lingering painful death".[42] That month brought news of the death of Marie Tempest. Figures from his youth were falling away.

At the end of each performance, at the request of the Director of Naval Intelligence, Noël made a "security speech", of the careless-talk-costs-lives variety, perhaps more theatrical than effective, but much enjoyed by the audience. Adding to the already exhausting timetable, he agreed to give matinee concerts with Judy Campbell in munitions factories and hospitals; the two of them were now performing something or other, without break, nearly fourteen times a week. In hospitals they toured the wards and she noted the care Noël took at bedsides, talking at length with wounded soldiers.[43] But factory audiences – often as large as four thousand – were often unresponsive or confused and Noël, exhausted, became bitter, his admiration of the working man forgotten: "I have no real rapport with the 'workers', in fact I actively detest them *en masse* [. . .] they are obtuse and slow-witted and most outrageously spoilt."[44] By the spring he was suffering with jaundice and ceded his triumvirate of roles to his understudy, spending a month in Cornwall so as to be ready for the West End season, and slowly turning from yellow to pink.

The travails were sweetened by the fact that, on the tour, they had enjoyed mainly full houses, and when, on 29 April 1943, *Play Parade* came into the Haymarket Theatre in London, the season was a triumph with critics and audiences. In June Churchill attended in secret, flanked by two plain-clothes detectives.[45] *Blithe Spirit* was a known entity; *This Happy Breed* had settled into a morale-boosting portrait of a British family; and *Present Laughter* introduced to a London audience for the first time the character of Garry Essendine, who, on the verge of turning forty, is essentially facing a mid-life crisis. A comedy actor of dazzling vanity, he is preparing to tour Africa, and suffers a nightmarishly farcical few days in which women want to seduce him and a crazed young playwright with dubious opinions comes to worship at the altar. *Present Laughter* laid out, via its dazzling comedy, the corroding effects of fame and the dangers of charisma. "Is he happy do you think? I mean really happy?" someone asks of Essendine. It is he who says: "there's something awfully sad about happiness, isn't there?"

Present Laughter is a pastiche of a farce, consciously employing the tricks of its trade (lost latchkeys, slammed doors). It also offered yet another new design for living: a tangle of sexual and Platonic cross-currents, a "family" united by Bohemianism rather than blood. Essendine is the solipsistic sun around which his entourage is slavishly in orbit. Enough was known about Noël's life that devoted admirers would have been able to join the dots: here was Noël Coward himself in a disguise as thin as the silk of his dressing-gown, attended by his camp valet and his devoted secretary. A manager and a producer make intermittent appearances, as does Essendine's ex-wife Liz (performed and inspired by Joyce Carey). Together they form a Bohemian quintet unaware that the world has left them behind. Written in the months leading up to the war, *Present Laughter* may have been an attempt to preserve the Coward "family" before the fighting separated everyone, perhaps forever.

In the 1920s the play could have been a cruel portrait of upper-class egoism; twenty years later, it showed a faded world. The group is threatened from the outside by the appearance of Joanna Lyppiatt. A "hundred per cent female" and intent on seducing Garry, she threatens to split everything apart (as Natasha Wilson had once done by marrying Jack), and to derail Essendine's self-control. There are hints of Garry's bisexuality, as he enthuses over an actor's "strapping shoulders and tiny, tiny hips like a wasp"; Lyppiatt was changed to a man for a London production in 2019. But *Present Laughter* abides by the rules of comedy, and ends in the "if-only" world in which farces, neatly unravelled, usually conclude, awoken from the nightmare. Parting is such sweet sorrow that Garry and Liz decide finally to reunite, tiptoeing off together as the curtain falls, in flight once again. The neatness of Noël's architecture infuses *Present Laughter* with a consciousness that life does not conform to the rules of light comedy.

Essendine is vain, petulant, childish, and pontificating, reliant on the hero-worship of his followers (his surname is an anagram of "neediness"). He fears the onset of age, is touchy about his thinning hair, and knows that "youth's a stuff will not endure".* He brandishes the weapons of charm and wit to keep the world at bay, and to save him from having to engage with almost anything or anyone. He is on the run from the truth, while simultaneously in quest of it, and friends tell him things about his character he does not wish to know. As a self-portrait, this was a brazen, even lacerating, admission of faults − or a means of rejoicing in them. In some ways *Present Laughter* is a more open autobiography than the printed memoirs.

But *Present Laughter* second-guesses the trap of too biographical a reading (and actors as different from Noël as Donald Sinden, Albert Finney, and Andrew Scott have shown that the character can transcend its original). Little is revealed about Garry Essendine, and the play's concern is just how much there *is* to reveal. Its comedy is based on its essential contradictions, between truth and artifice, revelation and obfuscation. Above all, *Present Laughter* is about the life of an actor, and whether emotional autonomy is possible for "a puppet of tinsel and sawdust". The more Garry surrounds himself with acolytes (just once is he left alone on the stage) the more solitary he becomes: "I'm so lonely sometimes, so desperately lonely." In a later musical, *The Girl Who Came to Supper*, Noël would descant on the same theme: "I'm a lonely man − a victim of my destiny | A sawdust puppet on a string. | [. . .] Nobody to care or even dream | That the heart behind this royal mask I wear | Is beating out a melancholy theme."

In 1937 Somerset Maugham had published his novel *Theatre* (filmed as *Being Julia*), in which a successful actress is told: "You don't know the difference between truth and make-believe. You never stop acting." So it is for Garry, who is besieged by the accusation that, even offstage, he is giving a performance − "You're acting again!" − in a life of fakery and solitude. It was a quality

---

* "What is love? 'tis not hereafter | Present mirth hath present laughter | What's to come is still unsure [. . .] | Youth's a stuff will not endure." *Twelfth Night*, Act II, Scene 3

Cecil Beaton perceived in Noël: "He never lets up acting for a moment."[46] Garry is open: "I'm always acting", he admits. "Watching myself go by – that's what's so horrible – I see myself all the time eating, drinking, loving, suffering – sometimes I think I'm going mad." In *Easy Virtue*, Larita had bemoaned the same condition: "I wonder if it's a handicap having our sort of minds [. . .] watching ourselves go by." Unless such melancholy is nothing but a good performance. Garry tells a young woman with whom he has had a fling: "You're not in love with me – the real me." But his quest for the "real me" is oddly fruitless, in that the worlds of life and theatre have blurred so dangerously, selfhood swallowed by the silk dressing-gown. "You were acting when you pretended to be cross," he is told. "But when you said good-bye to me so sweetly, that other morning, then you weren't acting. The mask was off then, wasn't it? Wasn't it?"

25. LONDON; NORTH AFRICA; MIDDLE EAST; SOUTH AFRICA; RHODESIA; FAR EAST – JULY 1943–AUGUST 1944

When, during the First World War, Noël had been called up into the army, the part he had been rehearsing had been taken over by a young actor called Leslie Howard. Roles in *Gone With the Wind* and others had turned Howard into a movie star; he and Noël had filmed advertisements for the National Savings Movement at Denham Studios. On 1 June 1943 Howard, in Portugal on propaganda work, had caught a plane from Lisbon to Bristol that was shot down by the Luftwaffe over the Atlantic, killing everyone on board. Noël thought about Howard's death as if picking a wound. "Imagined all too vividly poor Leslie's last moments. Such a horrible way to die, cooped up with a dozen people in a plane and being brought down into a rough sea. It can't have been so very quick. There must have been lots of time to think and be frightened."[47]

In the weeks following Howard's death Noël wrote, as if in response, his song "Don't Let's Be Beastly to the Germans":

Don't let's be beastly to the Germans
When our victory is ultimately won
It was just those nasty Nazis who persuaded them to fight
And their Beethoven and Bach are really far worse than their bite
Let's be meek to them
And turn the other cheek to them
And try to bring out their latent sense of fun.
Let's give them full air parity
And treat the rats with charity
But don't let's be beastly to the Hun![48]

Play Parade closed on 3 July (*Blithe Spirit* continued without him). The following day Noël went to Chequers to visit Churchill, who insisted on hearing the new song again and again. It was a genial evening – even Churchill performed – and Noël sang on into the night. The prime minister had understood that the object of the song's satire was the appeasement movement. Noël had no intention of arguing that, post-war, there should be an effort not to repeat the severity of Versailles reparations. "If I were still Minister of Information", wrote Duff Cooper, who was now unemployed after an unsuccessful transfer to Singapore, "I should insist upon [the song's] being broadcast nightly because its message is one that is much needed by all the silly, sloppy, sentimental shits who form such a formidable section of our fellow countrymen."[49]

But the political point that lay beneath the song's Billy-Bunter diction eluded most of its critics. A member of the Women's Auxiliary Air Force wrote to the *Daily Mirror* that she was "bitterly disgusted and ashamed" at Noël's leniency towards the Germans, to which the *Mirror*, who had gradually adopted an anti-appeasement stance, responded defending his "excellent" satire: "You dumb-wits, don't you know what satire is? Are you so ignorant?"[50] Complaints flooded in, from pacifists and warmongers alike, the song dismissed alternately as unforgivably lenient or absurdly bellicose.[51] In the end the recording was put on hold by HMV, and the BBC, who weathered a lot of the critical storm, temporarily banned it from the airwaves. The ban was lifted for a single performance in which the line "build their bloody fleet" then caused its own mini-scandal.

The fuss over the song may be one reason why Noël chose once again to leave England, this time for the best part of a year. He was also fleeing heartsickness. It was easier, perhaps, to love Jack Wilson from afar. "I have missed you most grievously", Noël wrote to him that summer, "and I think that you have missed me more grievously still. [. . .] I would give so very, very, very much for just a few hours with you."[52] British Security Co-ordination had had one final go at employing him: "Bill Stephenson telephoned", Noël wrote on 20 July, "and asked me when it would be possible for me to go to Canada."[53] But his priorities lay elsewhere. "I would like to go to the Middle East and do a bit of entertaining. This travelling is not to satisfy my wanderlust but because I know I can do good by hopping about and entertaining people."[54] The obvious route would have been to make himself available to the Entertainments National Service Association, established in 1939 to provide entertainment to the armed forces. But Noël held a grudge against ENSA, which had a reputation for substandard shows ("Every Night Something Awful"). The Association had been co-founded by Basil Dean, with whom he had not worked since the disaster of *Sirocco*, and given that its personnel were required to wear uniform, he risked a repeat of the ridicule that had dogged him earlier in the war.

With the support of Brendan Bracken, who had replaced Duff Cooper as the Minister of Information, he organised a tour of areas that were not covered by ENSA, leaving England for Gibraltar in late July 1943, well supplied with traveller's cheques to ensure his financial activities were above board. The Ministry of Information had demanded approval of any and all songs he was to perform, which Noël grudgingly gave, vowing to make his own decisions once he was out of England. The trip returned him to the navy and his attempt at a synthetic military life. Travelling on HMS *Charybdis*, he was on deck when the ship was suddenly shot at by enemy aircraft: "the noise was terrific and gunfire scorched my face". But even here he seemed unable to tell the difference between war and a war movie: "I felt singularly detached and almost expected to hear David's voice saying 'cut'."[55] En route to Malta, he witnessed a ship being sunk in the Mediterranean, thinking it like a "film without the sound track".[56] (The *Charybdis* would be torpedoed a few months later, killing over four hundred.) The military man was another role to play, and he would be photographed on his tours, sheltering from the sun beneath his pith helmet, high-waisted shorts voluminous above white socks pulled to his knees, the spotlessness of the outfit betraying the fact of its being a costume.

He would be abroad until October, sailing from Gibraltar to Algeria and then moving east in the vicious summer heat across North Africa and into Egypt. In Algeria he was introduced to Dwight Eisenhower, commander of the Allied Forces across the Mediterranean and overseeing the invasion of Sicily. Mountbatten had arranged the introduction: "I know how busy you are but [. . . Coward] is one of the outstanding people of our country."[57] Eisenhower found Noël "most interesting and a very attractive personality. In fact we started talking at such a great rate, I am afraid he will think I am a bit on the garrulous side."[58] Reaching Cairo, Noël was persuaded to fly on to Iraq, where the Persia and Iraq Command had little to no entertainment.

The Allies had achieved victory in the North African campaign just a few months before, and hospitals were crammed with the wounded. Noël fell into an arduous routine, giving as many as three concerts a day, often to thousands of troops, and visiting hospital after hospital, watching clouds of flies gather in the heat, and admiring spotless uniforms and British courtesy amid the primitive sanitation. Malaria was rife. The comedian Leslie Henson, co-founder of ENSA, saw one such visit and wrote in his diary: "He went from bed to bed, listening to the woes of each patient and, strangely enough, telling them that he had suffered from most of the troubles they were enduring. As he left one ward to visit the next one, one of the soldiers called out, 'Wait till he gets to the VD cases.'"[59] The clearest memory Noël retained from the tour was of sitting by the bedside of a wounded soldier, and holding his hand until he died.

Noël returned to England on 10 October, but would stay for fewer than two months, his time mainly devoted to planning another tour, this time to South Africa. On 2 December he sailed first of all to Manhattan, on a ship crammed with GIs and, in

consequence, no alcohol (he took secret supplies). He found the
atmosphere of American life unchanged, war or no, and enjoyed
playing "Don't let's be beastly . . ." to an appreciative Roosevelt at
the White House. He spent most of his time either in the company
of Roald Dahl, who was supplying intelligence from Washington
to Churchill, or visiting the evacuated orphans in the Bronx. There
was also a chance to reunite with William Stephenson, and it is
possible that, given his forthcoming travels, Noël hoped once again
to be of use to British Security Co-ordination. But Stephenson was
concerned only with Noël's health. "I dined with dear Mr Mysterious on Christmas Night", Noël wrote to Lorn Loraine, "and he
said it was idiotic of me to attempt a strenuous tour of South Africa
without having a rest first, and that one of his staff had a house
in Jamaica and that he would make all arrangements which he did
with paralysing efficiency."[60]

Noël accordingly spent the first fortnight of 1944 in a house in
the mountains of Kingston, enjoying various pleasure jaunts with
the agents of British Security Co-ordination, before embarking on
the journey to South Africa. This took nearly a fortnight, travelling
into South America in order to fly from Brazil to Ghana, and then
down through Africa, giving concerts all the while. "Moths as big
as your titties", he wrote to Lorn. "Nothing but rather attractive
mud houses and very, very black people indeed with very long
things hanging down in front, if you know what I mean."[61] Finally
he arrived at Pretoria, on 2 February. En route he had reunited
with Bert Lister, the valet who had replaced Cole Lesley and who
proved an efficient and invaluable assistant during the tour; Noël
thought him "one of the sweetest characters I have ever met in my
life, unfailingly good about everything" – not least the fact that his
daughter was born while they were away.[62] The pianist Norman
Hackforth, with whom he had briefly worked a few years earlier,
was to be his accompanist, and they became a close duo. "Dear
Mister Coward was sweetness and light", Hackforth wrote later,
"gentle as a lamb, and the easiest person in the world to get on
with, *always provided* that he was surrounded by unflagging devotion,
unswerving loyalty, and absolute total perfection [. . .] If any one
of these simple prerequisites was lacking, a wounded tiger at bay

would, by comparison with the discountenanced Master, seem like a dear cuddly little kitten."[63]

Noël was to travel all over South Africa and Rhodesia for more than three months. The British Press sent journalists to attend in secret, apparently hoping to see him booed off the stage, but the performances were a success. He admitted to feeling both nervous and inadequate, and, most of all, tired (in Cape Town he appeared in some forty concerts in just nineteen days). The Union of South Africa was supplying troops to the Italian Campaign, and the prime minister, Jan Smuts, had been appointed a field marshal of the British Army (there was even a plan to make him prime minister, should Churchill become incapacitated). He was a white supremacist who supported racial segregation, and Noël found the country taut with unrest and fear: "aware also that my strong contempt for any sort of racial discrimination might, if expressed, however casually, imperil the success of my tour, I decided to sidetrack the subject wherever possible".[64] But he admired and liked Smuts enormously, and even more so when Smuts defended him against a query in Parliament as to why he was travelling in such luxury.

For the concerts he interleaved hits from his back catalogue with recitations of Clemence Dane's poetry and his own verse about an air raid: "Lie in the Dark and Listen | It's clear tonight so they're flying high | Hundreds of them, thousands perhaps, | Riding the icy, moonlit sky . . ." He could also try out new work: "Uncle Harry" (a comic song written in Jamaica, about a missionary rather too susceptible to sins of the flesh) and, best of all, "a new song called 'Nina', designed to kill South American rhythmic numbers for all time".[65] This was a pastiche rumba about an Argentinian senorita who won't dance, and by implication, won't do a lot of other things. The song was written on one of the long journeys across South Africa, with Hackforth notating the melody − the insistent beat of the rhymes landing with the thrusts of the dance it parodies − and creating an accompaniment. On Nina's first outing Noël was barely able to remember the lines:

She said "I hate to be pedantic but I'm driven nearly frantic
When I see that unromantic, sycophantic lot of sluts

Forever wriggling their guts.
It drives me absolutely nuts."

By the end of the tour Noël had not been in England for five months, and he had already begun the journey home when, stopping in Kenya in May 1944, he received a request from Mountbatten, now Supreme Allied Commander in South East Asia, to travel to India and Burma and entertain the Fourteenth Army. Formed late the previous year, the so-called "Forgotten Army" was responsible for operations against the Japanese. The nickname was partly owing to ENSA, who would not assume full responsibility for troop entertainment in the region until the end of the year. The climate was difficult, and there were significant health risks. But Noël could deny Mountbatten nothing, and on 16 May he sailed to Ceylon in order to travel up to Calcutta. Mountbatten was beleaguered, and relations with his American colleagues were not good. The arrival of a patriotic British entertainer seemed only to confirm his poor judgement, and Noël did not help matters by having a public scrap with James Somerville, commander-in-chief of the navy and Mountbatten's main foe.

Nor did Noël decide to temper the audacity of his performances. While in Calcutta he wrote, and sang, "I Wonder What Happened to Him", a satire of the British Raj that led to a certain amount of grumbling from elderly generals. Not that he remotely believed in Indian independence, but the song was good proof that in his view nothing was off limits to be mined for comic potential: "Whatever became of old Bagot? | I haven't seen him for a year.| Is it true that young Forbes had to marry that Faggot | He met in the Vale of Kashmir?" The last verse is closer to the bone today than it would have been to the soldiers of the Fourteenth Army in 1944:

Do you, do you remember young Phipps
Who had very large hips
And whose waist was excessively slim?
Well, it seems that some doctor in Grosvenor Square
Gave him hormone injections for growing his hair
And he grew something here, and he grew something there

I wonder what happened to her – him?

Noël may have read about the earliest examples of sex reassignment surgery during the 1930s, but the song precedes by some years the first high-profile cases in Britain or America.

Bert Lister meanwhile had fallen ill (dangerously so, with typhoid) and was left behind, but Norman Hackforth had joined him, and together they set off, travelling north through India and what is now Bangladesh into Burma. Things got off to a bad start when the American general Joseph Stilwell refused to provide any transport for Noël, which Mountbatten took as a personal insult. When Noël arrived to perform at the Lido Road, an overland connection between India and China being built mainly by African-American troops, he was booed off the stage by an audience that made little of his humour or patriotism. Noël blamed the sound of the traffic and the troops' lack of sophistication; he wrote with wry bitterness in his diary of microphones that "made me sound like Donald Duck", or of overhearing one soldier say "he's a clever bugger but he can't sing".[66] Unbeknownst to Noël, Stilwell eventually ordered his men to show approval. "If any more piano players start this way", he wrote to a friend, "you know what to do with the piano."[67] Noël's style did not promise to be as effective or suitable as that of Vera Lynn, who was finishing a long tour of Burma (their paths did not cross).

But as the concerts went by he hit his stride. Mountbatten had warned him about the conditions. It was monsoon season, and the world was reduced to rain and mud and humidity. Villages were under siege from the Japanese, and Noël had to be flown over enemy lines in small planes that delivered supplies. Otherwise he and Norman drove through the steaming jungles in a jeep jammed with mosquito nets and camp beds and a miniature piano that fell badly out of tune. They slept in bamboo huts, on the lookout for snakes, shaving in tin basins on a tripod. Falling on his face in the mud, Noël was overheard: "I'm most frightfully sorry but it's the fucking awful weather!"[68] Concerts were given in isolated camps or hospitals erected in wooden huts with no nurses and sometimes no flooring but the mud. Wounded soldiers lay under mosquito nets reading magazines or staring at the roof. Noël watched operations carried out with primitive equipment, and he watched men die. He performed under tarpaulins; he performed in the rain; he performed, on one occasion, very close to the Japanese lines, battling with the sound of nearby gunfire in front of rows of soldiers who sat cross-legged in the mud. Mosquitoes and midges settled on the microphone "like caraway seeds on a bun", and the wind, when it changed direction, brought with it the smell of Japanese corpses, stacked nearby in a clearing. Noël vomited into a bucket between shows.[69] In the end he came down with a fever but continued to sing. Norman was indefatigable. The bucket overflowed in the wings.

In the summer Noël returned to India, spending a further month touring and living in grander conditions, although, in Bombay, a lorry turned in front of his limousine, which slammed into a tree and knocked him out cold. Departing the town of Digboi in Assam he watched the plane in front of his explode into flames, killing its twelve passengers. Meanwhile an anonymous letter was sent to an ENSA officer: "I do feel extremely violent over the whole of Noël Coward's tour." The objection was that many of the concerts had raised funds for troop amenities. "Noël Coward, or any other star coming out to India to entertain the troops, comes out to entertain and not to collect funds. [. . . Everyone has] joked quite openly that Noël Coward wishes to go back to England not only with statistics showing the number of troops that he has entertained, but also the number of rupees that he has raised, in order that the Mr may be substituted for a Sir."[70] ENSA continued to complain that Noël had refused to perform under its banner, and one of its officers wrote that Noël had been an "infernal nuisance [. . .] he is giving some shows in big centres to pay expenses of his tour and in Delhi complained that the price of his seats was too low". But he admitted that "all the first-hand accounts of his performances I have had were that he had a very good reputation".[71] To Bill Erskine, a major assigned to assist Noël in Madras, the experience of travelling with Noël was as memorable as a love affair, which, given the tone of the letter Erskine wrote to him in July 1944, it may have briefly been: "When you had roared out of my life this morning, I waited until no one was looking and then tiptoed out of a dream. On assignment to you I came with the idea of carrying out the desires of my General, whom I adore. Later I revelled in the privilege of serving a great artist, later still – a friend. This morning I wept a little and was not ashamed. Wherever you go my thoughts are with you, and I pray that your memory may be as great as your heart."[72]

Reaching Ceylon, Noël, who had lost two stone over the tour, suddenly collapsed during a long drive. His final shows were cancelled, for which he always felt guilty, but Mountbatten wrote in gratitude: "I realise that it was at great personal inconvenience that you came on to South East Asia from South Africa, and that the tour you undertook was terribly strenuous. [. . .] the greatest value your visit will have is to make the men feel that they are not forgotten by the people back home."[73] Noël had indeed raised funds, to the tune of tens of thousands of pounds. But the tour – even if the notion of an official reward were at the back of his mind – was undertaken with an energy born of a genuine need to help, and of a belief in the importance of entertainment at a time of hardship. He refused to fob off audiences with a performance as makeshift as his surrounds, demanding from himself a level of stamina and professionalism that stalled only once, when, seeing soldiers passing around smutty photographs during an impromptu concert, he lost his temper.

Finally, in August, he was able to start the journey home, on plane after plane, to India, to Egypt, to Morocco, to England, where the bombs had once again started to fall.

26. LONDON – AUGUST 1944–MAY 1945

During the Blitz you had not heard the bomb that would kill you. But in June 1944, while Noël was abroad, the terrifying buzz of the V-1s (or "doodlebugs") had begun. By the time he was back in England, the V-2s (long-range ballistic missiles) promised further destruction. Noël arrived at Paddington on 17 August, full of praise for the troops in Burma. "The guts and fortitude of these men is terrific", he told the waiting press. "Their cheerfulness is beyond words. I have seen much heroism in the war, but nothing like this."[74]

A few days before his return, Noël's *Middle East Diary* had been published, covering his four months in North Africa and Iraq the previous year. The result was a book in which his love of the social round, of sunlit bathing and luxurious receptions in far-off cities, was all too evident. He appears to have had no awareness that to publish an account of such a life, even as the bombs fell once again onto an exhausted Britain, risked at best ridicule and at worst accusations of hypocrisy. He had not been shy of expressing his contempt for those who had spent the war abroad. Had the book included the more serious privations of his later travels, in India and Bombay, its atmosphere would have been very different. The English reviews were ambivalent, noting that Noël's globetrotting made little dent on his worldview. "He sees so much – and so little", wrote Ivor Brown in the *Observer*, "he has travelled far more than most men of his age, and yet, when he writes, it always has to be of the same little world." But the book had its defenders. "When the reader penetrates through the social atmosphere of the trip, he can see these pages for what they really are", argued *The Sunday Times*, "a record of a man determined to give service in the way for which he is best fitted [. . .] it is no light undertaking for an entertainer to travel thousands of miles under exceedingly difficult conditions."[75]

But when the book was released in America, in November, all hell broke loose. The diary contained glowing accounts of American troops, all of whom "were behaving as cheerfully and courteously as our own men", and attacked the British press for its misleading account of GIs, "who deserve nothing but the best from us". But on page 140 there was an account of visiting a hospital in Tripoli, and the damage was done: "I talked to some tough men from Texas and Arizona; they were magnificent specimens and in great heart but I was less impressed by some of the mournful little Brooklyn boys lying there in tears amidst the alien corn with nothing worse than a bullet wound in the leg or a fractured arm."[76] Oddly, the line is not present in the handwritten manuscript. Beverley Nichols flew to his defence in print, healing a frostiness resulting from his attack, earlier in the war, of Noël's departure for America. Noël stayed calm: "I was 3,000 miles away [when the diary was published] and considered the whole thing bollocks anyway."[77] But "cancel culture" predates the advent of social media.

On 15 November a resolution of the Brooklyn City Council called on New York producers and publishers to halt the performance or issue of any play by Noël Coward. Most of the New York press ran fierce attacks on his work and character, and the *Brooklyn Eagle* said that "dozens of indignant mothers, wives and sweethearts kept this newspaper's phones busy with lashing rebukes of the actor-playwright".[78] Samuel Dickstein, a Congressional Representative from New York, stood up in the House and announced that he would use his influence as chair of the House Committee on Immigration "to keep Mr Coward from again visiting this country [. . .] we American people don't like the trashy books he is circulating throughout this country, threatening our fine men. If he tries to come back here, I'll see that he spends all of his time on Ellis Island until a boat comes to take him back."[79] (Dickstein himself was later revealed to be a Soviet spy.) An account of the uproar landed on the desk of William Stephenson in New York, and his secretary, Grace Garner, mildly pointed out that the incendiary lines had been quoting Keats. "The Americans didn't know the reference. I said to Sir William, 'that's the Ode to a Nightingale'.* They took it out of context."[80]

When the row erupted Noël was in France, having finally agreed to perform for ENSA in Paris and Brussels at a concert for Allied Troops. Paris had been liberated in August, but he found the city painful, full of memories. He was introduced to Jean Cocteau, who was enraptured by the meeting. "Je veux t'entendre chante et récite un poème dans notre langue", he wrote to Noël, "Ne m'oublie pas. Je t'aime et je t'embrasse."[81]† But Paris was embroiled in guilt and recrimination; colleagues and friends – Sacha Guitry,

---

* "Perhaps the self-same song that found a path | Through the sad heart of Ruth, when, sick for home, | She stood in tears amid the alien corn."

† "I want to hear you sing and recite a poem in our language. Do not forget me. I love you, I embrace you."

Maurice Chevalier – were caught up in accusations of collaboration. Noël returned to his old flat, which had been requisitioned by the Gestapo and ransacked; now it was filthy and deserted. His maid, Yvonne Garnier, had salvaged a lot of his clothes and books, but his French teacher, Blanche Prenez, an inspiring figure from his time in the city, had disappeared. Noël later heard that she had joined the Resistance only to be arrested and tortured; she had died of TB on her release from prison.

On his return, he thought it best to lie low, especially when questions were once again raised in Parliament as to the funding of his performances abroad. That autumn he took the lease on a secluded Victorian villa called Sydney Lodge in Alfold, a village on the border between Surrey and West Sussex, which served him as a country retreat until the end of the war.[82] A revival of *Private Lives* had opened successfully in the West End and, running happily alongside *Blithe Spirit*, seemed to show that, though there was no appetite for his ruminations on American troops, his comedies were still popular. And he worked meanwhile on his final project of the war, which would turn out to be the most successful of all. He was searching for another project for the big screen. The films of *Blithe Spirit* and *This Happy Breed* met with critical success but were thought disappointing in comparison with the experimental techniques of *In Which We Serve*; after seeing *Blithe Spirit* Noël apparently turned to Lean and said calmly "you've just fucked up the best thing I've ever written".[83] With Lean and Ronald Neame he formed the company Cineguild, partly to ensure he would have complete control over future projects.

On 5 September 1944 he had noted: "my idea is for [Lean] to do *Still Life*" – one of the plays in *Tonight at 8.30*, hailed on its premiere as a "small masterpiece".[84] He had begun a screenplay two days later, and after a fortnight's uninterrupted work, finished on 23 September, having produced a script that is now familiar from hundreds of broadcasts; from parodies by Victoria Wood and homages by Alan Bennett; from remastered screenings and stage adaptations and lists of the movies you should see before you die.[85] Where the one-act play had been set entirely in the café of a railway station, the screenplay unfolded the story into a full-length movie, told as an illustrated monologue: a longed-for but imaginary confession, to a loving but dull husband, of his wife's passionate, unconsummated, affair. Laura Jesson's conventional middle-class family life has been suddenly interrupted by a chance meeting with a married stranger, Alec, with whom she falls in love. Her lover is a doctor shortly to move to South Africa, and they part knowing they will never see one another again.

Filming began during the first, freezing, months of 1945. The Coward leading lady had shifted from the inspired eccentricity of Gertrude Lawrence in a Molyneux gown to the subterranean emotions of Celia Johnson in a sensible coat. Johnson's restraint was a perfect match for Noël's technique, at its most pronounced in *Brief Encounter*, of allowing the emotional action to take place in unspoken harmony to the perilously bland melody of the words. (In *Present Laughter* Garry Essendine had been seduced with a discussion of Beethoven symphonies; the lovers of *Brief Encounter* fall for one another as Alec tells Laura about his medical research specialism of pneumoconiosis, which by some alchemy is imbued with the erotic charge of the most highly wrought love scene.) Alec was to be played by Trevor Howard, almost unknown as an actor, and although everyone came to admire his performance, his inability to understand the character's sexual reticence led to tense filming days. Johnson, eight years his senior, wrote privately that he was "rather pleasant but pretty stupid (shhh)".[86]

Joyce Carey was the haughty manageress of the tea room, permitted – as the middle-class characters are not – openly to flirt with Stanley Holloway's stationmaster. Cockney stereotypes, certainly, but a vital counterpoint to the passion quietly playing out in the corner of the café. Station scenes were filmed on the frozen platforms at Carnforth station in Lancashire, chosen for its distance from the South Coast, so that warning of an air raid would be sufficient to extinguish the filming lights. The cast and crew were officially listed as evacuees. Otherwise the actors went to Denham studios, and Noël, although he was less involved in the actual filming, supervised almost every aspect of the production, down to the soft furnishings of Laura's living room and the dismissal of the actress Joyce Barbour, miscast as chattering Dolly Messitter, who unwittingly forbids the parting lovers a final moment alone. Everley Gregg, who had played the role on stage, was a successful replacement.

Another aspect of the film over which Noël exerted absolute control was the soundtrack. Rachmaninov's second piano concerto was forty-five years old, already celebrated as a classic; its composer – dismissed by Madame Arcati as "too florid" – had only recently died. Noël was insistent that there would be no specially composed score, an unusual choice for the time and one that outraged the musical supervisor, Muir Matheson. It was to pacify Matheson that the soundtrack exists *within* the narrative, surging from the wireless as Laura sits unhappily with her husband, who understands the warm-blooded passion of the music not at all; he asks for it to be turned down. *Brief Encounter* is infused with the Rachmaninov, which becomes a third character in the room, flooding the film with a Russian outpouring of the romantic soul even as the affair is thwarted by English reticence and repression. The soliloquy of the conflicted housewife is injected with a transfusion of something closer to a Russian tragedy of doomed adultery. As Laura sits in the café, alone, wishing herself dead, the camera tilts vertiginously and she runs onto the platform to throw herself under a passing train, as if to become a British Anna Karenina, a role recently played on film by Greta Garbo, with a script by Clemence Dane.

But Laura can no more kill herself than she can leave her husband and children to elope with her lover. The 1920s world of elopements and suicides has been replaced by British restraint. Cole Porter had written "Let's Do It" in 1928, which could be a motto for *Private Lives*; but the philosophy of *Brief Encounter* is closer to "Let's Not Do It". Noël, who had once dismissed marriage as an "inadequate social convenience", had not suddenly come to respect the world of family and stability and the thick patterned curtains of suburbia. (Nor had David Lean, who was to marry six times.) The film is not a sudden disavowal of his early portrayals of unorthodox sexual and domestic set-ups, but part of his continual questioning of the dictates of society, of the self-sacrifice of marriage, and of the shapes into which love is so often required to fit. Alec longs to live in sunnier climes, as if conceding that in a country other than

England they would feel less tied by convention and duty. Where
the heroines of Noël's early plays had had the financial capability
to search for sexual freedom and domestic independence, Laura
has little possibility of abandoning her family, and – crucially – no
wish to; she is one of the first of Noël's protagonists to be tied
by the binds of parenthood as well as marriage. Her love for the
unknowable, even ominously blank, Alec (who rarely appears on
screen without her) is romanticised, a fairy tale built on sand. She is
in love with the idea of love, and of what Alec represents: another
life she might have had. Hers is a love that is ultimately forbidden
– by circumstance, by society – and *Brief Encounter* is the writing of
a man whose affairs were still prohibited by law.

By the time the film was released, the world would be at peace.
Brief Encounter is set in 1938 but is suffused with the mood of war, of
the brief encounters that had occurred behind the smokescreen of
the blackout curtains. An early preview (with an audience formed
of local soldiers who laughed hysterically throughout) promised
disaster, but the film eventually received such good reviews that it
was advertised in northern industrial towns as being worth seeing
"in spite of" the critical praise. Award nominations were to follow,
as were long runs in cinemas American and English. Ireland banned
it. Its release came at a hinge in the country's history, catching
audiences at the moment when the strangely permissive atmosphere of the war, its dangerous excitements and liberations, were
sliding into a time which would see women returned to a life of
domesticity, and homosexuals persecuted. Few in the audiences of
Private Lives had reunited with a former lover in the grand hotels
of the Riviera; but many viewers of *Brief Encounter* had experienced
affairs behind the blackout, and now faced a return to the drudge
of loving, domestic, passionless routine. "You've been a long way
away," says Laura's husband in the famous closing lines. "Thank
you for coming back to me." But as the Rachmaninov soars and she
weeps on his shoulder, we wonder if she has done any such thing.

The last weeks of March (which saw Noël once again appearing
in Paris for ENSA) had brought the Allied invasion of Germany,
and the final bomb attack on British soil. Roosevelt died in April,
and Noël mourned his loss. On 4 May the BBC announced news of

German surrender in Northern France, and filming on *Brief Encounter* up in Lancashire was temporarily paused. Celia Johnson wrote to her husband that "excitement became intense at lunch-time by the report that all Technicolor cameras had gone to the Palace and bets were laid and work haphazard on account of having to rush out to listen to the radio between every shot".[87] The previous evening, Noël had dined with Winston Churchill at a small dinner party. Churchill arrived late and turned sharply on Noël: "*You've* blotted your copy book" (referring to the *Middle East Diary*). "Oh sir", Noël replied. "Please don't be beastly to Noël Coward."[88] Churchill burst out laughing, and all was well.

That Noël made Churchill laugh was his saving grace. The two had had an uneasy relationship, and Churchill's admiration for Rattigan's *Flare Path* can only have fanned the flames. But Noël had warmed towards the prime minister and now, with peace imminent, he suddenly became weak with admiration and gratitude. The party toasted Churchill, who "was immensely touched and simple about it. It was a strange but, I suppose, very natural moment. There he was, gossiping away with us, the man who had carried England through the black years, and he looked so well and cheerful and unstrained, and in addition was so ineffably charming, that I forgave him all his trespasses and melted into hero-worship."[89]

Five days later Churchill announced that the war in Europe was over. For the second time in his life Noël wandered around the London streets on the declaration of peace, amid the crowds, and the flags, and the ringing of bells. He had a drink with the cast of *Blithe Spirit*; he listened to the wireless at Clemence Dane's flat. People came and went. He went out into the streets again at twilight; the façade of Buckingham Palace was illumined and people sang and cheered. The King and Queen came out onto the balcony. But for Noël, the peace he had so long desired and fought for was an anti-climax. He was tired, bruised and buffeted by triumph and attack, by the thousands of performances he had given across the world, by the attacks on his domestic life, the deaths, the bombs. Much of his life he had spent in a search, not always successful, for meaning and purpose. The attainment of victory threatened a return to pre-war nihilism. "Nothing matters really", says Laura in

Brief Encounter, "neither happiness nor despair." When the atomic bombs were dropped on Japan, he would write of the weapons that could "blow us all to buggery. Not a bad idea."[90] Amid cheering crowds celebrating victory in Japan, he could not rejoice: "felt desolate remembering all the people who have gone".[91] For the second time in his life, he was emerging from a war without having seen active service and he would be unable to expound in any detail the nature of his work in Paris and America.

He wrote to Joyce Carey: "So now it's over, and I suppose I should share the general jubilation but somehow I don't. I never for a moment doubted that we should win, somehow or other, no matter how black things seemed. We British are at our best in adversity. We won the war but my concern is – how shall we win the peace?"[92]

27. BERLIN, LONDON — SEPTEMBER 1945

On one of his periodic flights over the Channel from Paris to England, he had looked through the small window at the white cliffs not of Dover but of Eastbourne. "'This,' I said to myself, 'is what the Nazis will see when they come. It will be upon all this that those fine-looking de-humanised young robots will drop their bombs.' And a rage boiled up in me, a primitive violent hatred of which I had no idea I was capable."[93]

In the event the Nazis had not come. But in September 1945 it was reported that a small booklet had been discovered in the Berlin headquarters of the main office of Reich security. The *Sonderfahndungsliste G.B.* – "Special Search List Great Britain" – was a secret list of those British residents who, in the event of Nazi invasion, were to be arrested. Its 2,820 names had been compiled in 1940, and among them was almost everyone with whom Noël had been involved during the war: Churchill, naturally, but also Robert Boothby and Robert Vansittart, Claude Dansey and George Lloyd. His own name was on page thirty-four, ninety-sixth of the "C" entries, a few rows beneath Duff Cooper. Noël had been in Paris at the time, but the Germans believed him to be in London at an "unknown" location, and he was wanted specifically by Amtsgruppe VIG1, a department evaluating intelligence material. When questioned by reporters he laughed the matter off. Even during the war, after he had escaped returning to Paris during the Nazi invasion, he tended to state in print that he had been due to arrive in the French capital on the same day as Hitler, which would have been "highly embarrassing for them both". Humour, he maintained, was an important weapon.

Also on the list was his friend Rebecca West. She had written to him in loyal support when he was attacked in the press: "I can't quite see what more you could do for your country, except strip yourself of all your clothes and sell them for War Weapons Week, after which your country would step in and prosecute you for indecent exposure."[94] On the release of the Gestapo's list, she sent Noël a telegram: "MY DEAR THE PEOPLE WE SHOULD HAVE BEEN SEEN DEAD WITH."[95]

THE DESERT

——

SHORT STORIES

CONTENTS

THE PEACE

The cheering was near hysterical, with cries of "author" and shouts of "bravo", and on his appearance he silenced the audience of the Lyric Theatre in London with his hand, that evening of 22 July 1947:

> Ladies and gentlemen, on behalf of us all, thank you so very much for your thrilling and heartwarming reception of our play. [. . .] Sixteen years ago, on the first night of *Cavalcade*, I said that I hoped that the play would make the audience feel that it was still a pretty exciting thing to be English. I still stubbornly believe that, and I hope passionately with all my heart that my countrymen, and whatever government may be in power – [*laughter*] – will allow me to go on believing it until the end of my days. Thank you.[1]

Noël Coward's new play, *Peace in Our Time*, was all set to be a big hit, not least in the eyes of its author, who was heartened by the sheer volume of its first-night reception. The two acts bulged with over thirty characters, though the set was a single one: a pub in Chelsea that becomes the secret headquarters of the British Resistance, it having become gradually clear that the Battle of Britain has been lost, not won, and the Nazis have invaded. The play was one of the earliest entries in the long list of titles imagining an Axis victory. Information is drip-fed through wireless broadcasts in chilling news reports from the BBC Home Service, describing Hitler processing in state along the Mall. A concentration camp (Stalag 23) has been built on the Isle of Wight and the royal family is held prisoner. The publican's daughter, Doris, an active member of the Resistance, is arrested and tortured by the Gestapo; her body, broken and beaten and barely alive, is dumped in the pub and she dies in the arms of her howling mother. The final curtain falls to the violent but triumphant chaos of the British liberation, a German guard tied to a chair and accidentally machine-gunned by fleeing Nazis as the National Anthem blares from the wireless.

In 1939 his friend Clemence Dane had published a novel, *The Arrogant History of White Ben*, predicting an England buckling to fascism. But Noël admitted his real model had been *When William Came*, a 1913 novel by his literary hero, Saki, chronicling life in London under German occupation. Where Saki had written before the Great War and knowledge of its outcome, Noël wrote with hindsight. His original title was *Might Have Been*, but he settled on (mis)quoting Chamberlain's speech after Munich. The play is partly a work of self-justification in its argument that the anti-appeasers were right all along: "we were dancing in the streets because a silly old man promised us peace". It will have sent a chill through its first audiences in its depiction of a horror so closely and recently avoided. Churchill's assassination is announced and, not eighteen months after the liberation of the concentration camps, a German officer lays out plans for the liquidation of British Jews. But in showing the British dividing into factions of resistance and collaboration, the script was an attack not only on the Nazis but on left-wing intellectuals, who are pitched against Noël's now-familiar portrait of an idealised working class, willing to fall into patriotic speeches at a moment's notice. Noël's ear for his assumed class had been accurate; his depiction of the world in which he had grown up now seemed awry.

Binkie Beaumont had overseen a lavish production, directed by Noël's former lover Alan Webb; among the cast were actors, later famous, such as Alan Badel, Kenneth More, and Dora Bryan. Noël's hopes for a big success were not even dented by the presence at the first night of a writer called Townley Searle, who showered the audience with leaflets protesting Noël's politics and drawing attention to the fact that he, too, had published a play with the same title on the same topics. But the *Daily Telegraph* provided the sole rave review: "This play cannot possibly fail. It is too moving, too exciting, too deft – and too timely."[2] The remainder of the critics united in their sense that a good idea had been submerged beneath melodrama and polemic, and *Peace in Our Time* closed after five months. So soon after the war, with rationing still in place, audiences may have wanted only merriment from Noël Coward. However, *Sigh No More*, his first revue in over a decade, had appeared

in August 1945; and an escapist operetta called *Pacific 1860* opened
at Christmas the following year, marking the reopening of the
bomb-damaged Theatre Royal, Drury Lane. Neither had been a
success.

Revues had been among the most popular wartime entertainments and they would continue to be successful into the fifties
(even Harold Pinter would provide sketches). But *Sigh No More* had
had a strained rehearsal period and Noël did not mourn its early
demise. His sketches had included a pastiche pageant of the Merrie
England variety, written in cod-Elizabethan verse, and "Nina" found
her theatrical home. He had taken the unusual step of working
with co-authors, in the form of composer Richard Addinsell and
actress Joyce Grenfell. In her mid-thirties and already admired for
her comic monologues, Grenfell had known Noël since she was a
child, and toured with ENSA during the war at his suggestion. She
had refused to appear in the film of *This Happy Breed* owing to its
caricature of Christian Science, which she practised devotedly. In
Sigh No More she had particular success with Noël's song "That is the
End of the News", listing a family's medical afflictions dressed as a
schoolgirl with plaits. But she found his dictatorial tendencies as a
director difficult to bear, especially when he ruthlessly cut much of
her and Addinsell's material before the first night. She found herself
desirous of his approval – "He said I was the most professional
thing he'd ever seen. Oh, I did like that" – but felt that he couldn't
resist "hurting where he knows it will make the most sting. It's a
form of bullying and power. [. . .] I wonder if he has a heart?"
She had another reason for her dislike. "It is definitely a pity", she
wrote to her mother, "that the man who represents this country
[during war] should be famous as a 'queer'".[3]

Operettas were also holding their own despite the success of
American musicals such as *Annie Get Your Gun*, which were settling
into long West End runs. Noël never thought himself in competition with figures such as Richard Rodgers or Irving Berlin,
and *Oklahoma!* he considered "quite one of the loveliest evenings I
have ever spent in the theatre [. . .] a deep and abiding theatrical
pleasure".[4] *Pacific 1860* had been consciously old-fashioned, set on
a British Colonial island in the nineteenth century. Mary Martin,

soon to create lead roles in *South Pacific* and *The Sound of Music*, had been miscast as Elena Salvador, a visiting opera singer who falls in love with the son of a plantation owner. Noël found a place in the score for his song "Uncle Harry", which sat oddly amid the mixture of romantic duets, waltzes, and gypsy melodies. Musicals in similar vein — Vivian Ellis's *Bless the Bride* or Ivor Novello's *King's Rhapsody* — were still pulling in audiences, but *Pacific 1860* ran for only four months, beset by problems. Noël fell out with Mary Martin, and the island setting threw into stark relief the cold of the theatre: fuel shortages led to the box office's being lit with candles. Three years later, in 1949, Noël would try again with a musical called *Ace of Clubs*, providing a more American mood with a scenario of nightclubs, sailors, gangsters, and chorus girls (among them a young June Whitfield). Some of the songs — "Sail Away", "I Like America" — have found a life of their own, and the lyrics showed Noël had not lost his touch: "On first meeting Bonaparte | She murmured 'Hell's bells! | You let down the tone, apart | From anything else!'" But he would be booed at the curtain call, to his mystified distress.

A sadly familiar pattern had set in: rows in rehearsal, numerous rewrites, indifferent or even hostile reviews, and a short and unprofitable run leading to straitened finances. Of the near-twenty stage works that Noël Coward wrote after the war, only a handful could be called a success, and only two were ever to gain a foothold on the list of his plays that, today, are even infrequently revived. Many were never to be staged again. It was a vicious cycle, in that Noël's talents had arguably been fuelled by an acclaim which, when absent, left him adrift on a sea of productivity, driven by the need to keep earning money and by a dogged refusal to drift into theatrical memory. He stuck to his guns, sure that criticism (from friends as well as from newspapers) was misguided, and certain there had been no decline in the quality of his output. But the work was not flowing as easily as once it had. "I know nothing so dreary", he had written, struggling with *Sigh No More*, "as the feeling that you can't make the sounds or write the words that your whole creative being is yearning for."[5] It was one of the few admissions he left on record of the difficulties of creative endeavour.

Some of his earlier hits were holding their own. *Present Laughter* was revived in spring 1947, with Noël as Garry Essendine (performing in French, he took the show to Paris the following year, with much less success). In 1948 Tallulah Bankhead would take *Private Lives* on a tour of America, claiming to have done the play everywhere but underwater. Noël admired her performance more than the work of the Hermiones Baddeley and Gingold when, in 1949, they competed outrageously for laughs in a London revival of *Fallen Angels*. "A terrific success", he wrote in his diary. "Livid."[6] But an attempt to get *Point Valaine* up and running in London lasted for just thirty-seven performances, and *Blithe Spirit* had finally come to an end. Critics argued that even successful revivals were kept afloat by star actors rather than innate buoyancy. The plays seemed flimsily amusing chronicles of a world not yet distant enough to make them period pieces. Art deco was out of fashion. The daringly androgynous outfits of the 1920s had been superseded by Dior's resolutely feminine New Look.

From the depths of war Noël had spoken of rebuilding society with near Utopian fervour. "How more than strange if, from the midst of this carnage, this welter of violence and death and shattered hopes and lost illusions, a real progressive, constructive ideal should emerge! An ideal beyond the destructive fingers of little, cruel men; an ideal detached from the fantasies of national conquest; an ideal capable of inspiring a little more kindness and comradeship in mankind and a little less business sense."[7] Sentiments such as these could easily be mistaken for one of J. B. Priestley's "Postscripts" (his Sunday-night wartime broadcasts to which almost half the population tuned in). But Priestley's Utopia was a socialist one, and he welcomed Attlee's welfare state. Noël's "progressive, constructive" post-war vision, by contrast, was to put things back how they had been, rather than build anew. Peace had brought with it a world in which Noël Coward did not belong, and he did not want to. As a dramatist he had required excess – financial, political, sexual – to both chronicle and criticise. The post-war world offered asceticism, restriction, and domesticity, and he could not work out how to function successfully within it. "How I should hate to be young again", he had written in 1941, but the man who had reached stratospheric success in his early twenties did not know how *not* to be young.

He had felt himself a spokesperson first for the Age of Youth, and then for the British as a whole, clinging to the success of *Cavalcade*, now fifteen years old and never revived. His article on the British victory had appeared in the *Daily Mail* alongside speeches by Winston Churchill and by the King, as if Noël Coward, at least in his own mind, were banded with them in some unlikely trio, leading the country. But such currency and popularity seemed no longer possible. He had lost the knack or the taste for self-reinvention. To have caught so accurately the voices of one generation may have meant that, by default, he would be at cross-purposes with the voices of a next. His impatience with the younger generation was exacerbated by nostalgia for his own youth, and he measured everything against the days when he had conquered the theatrical world. Bitter nostalgia can be traced even in the song titles of his lightest musicals: "This is a changing world" (from *Pacific 1860*), and "Nothing lasts for ever" (from *Ace of Clubs*). Only in his mid-forties, he had lived several lives, and his face was prematurely aged even as, in his diary each year, he meticulously listed his birthday presents like any child. He had not changed with the times, but the times had changed him.

Most of all his politics were at odds with the prevailing wind. The Communist Party of Great Britain was at the height of its influence, but he continued to condemn Stalin's regime in the Soviet Union, long before the Hungarian Uprising in 1956 would lead many in the arts to follow suit. Mourning Churchill's temporary absence from government, he resented Clement Attlee's Labour Party and its values, turning down Attlee's strange invitation that they might collaborate on a film about the atomic bombs.[8] Noël would resign from the board of the Festival of Britain, a cultural event intended as a tonic for a nation undergoing social and economic reform in which he did not remotely believe. The lyrics and plays he would write over the next fifteen years were often hampered by his desire to criticise the new political world. In *Sigh No More* the "Burchells of Battersea Rise" proclaim: "We may find if we swallow the Socialist bait | That a simple head cold is controlled by the state." And to a 1952 revue he would contribute a parody of a war song, "There Are Bad Times Just Around the Corner", which encapsulates his feelings about contemporary life and politics:

There are black birds over the greyish cliffs of Dover,
And the rats are preparing to leave the BBC [. . .]
If the Reds and the Pinks
Believe that England stinks
And that world revolution is bound to spread,
We'd better all learn the lyrics of the old "Red Flag"
And wait until we drop down dead.
A likely story
Land of Hope and Glory
Wait until we drop down dead.

Evelyn Waugh's *Brideshead Revisited*, published in 1945 and acclaimed by Noël as "exquisite",[9] showed that there was still literary mileage in nostalgia for aristocracy and disdain of the welfare state.* But Noël was attempting to resuscitate, rather than obituarise, a lost world of which he felt himself a custodian. Theatrically and politically, the radical seemed to have become the reactionary. His ardent support for his own generation's fight for a wider kind of life had made him unsympathetic to the next generation's social causes – social equality, decolonisation – which he openly despised. As a young writer he had scorned established values of decency, cheerily lambasting the notion, say, that women should not get drunk.

---

* Coward was on increasingly friendly terms with Waugh. "I wish we met more often", Waugh wrote to him in 1950, in response to exhilarated letters about the *Sword of Honour* trilogy and *Helena*, a historical novel of Imperial Rome. "Appreciation from fellow writers is the only kind worth having and we are usually too shy to express it." (Coward Archive, NPC-9873-4.) In 1955 Coward told Clemence Dane: "Evelyn Waugh came to dinner, what a strange little man he is; I like him but as you know I have always been puzzled how anyone as intelligent can accept the dogmas of the RC faith and he didn't, perhaps he couldn't, enlighten me. On the contrary he told me that he was a bored and unhappy man so now I am more mystified than ever." (Dane Letters, OSB MSS 245 Box F.)

Chief among the qualities he now valued was the ideal of "good behaviour", of "behaving beautifully", phrases that toll admiringly through his diaries. Proud of the ambition and self-reliance that had led him to success without the connections of public school or a university education, he was now claiming that "the much maligned 'old school tie' is as essential a part of our heritage as anything else".[10]

And so his character, always volatile, gives some impression of hardening into bitterness, resentment, even self-importance. Capable as he was of bearing grudges, he had usually been happy to shrug off feuds and quarrels with those who mattered to him, as when Rebecca West had apparently spoken ill of him behind his back and then written in mortified apology. "I didn't worry a bit", he had replied, "your quoted remarks were so unlike you that I never believed them for a moment! All love dear."[11] But insecurity as to his reputation could sharpen quips from teasing to malice, his manner made more difficult by the fact that, when calmer, his praise was fulsome, and so nobody knew what to believe. He grew angry with the press and the public – and, by extension, with the country as a whole. "England", he wrote, on the reception to *Peace in Our Time*, "does not deserve my work. [. . .] I have a sick at heart feeling about England anyhow."[12] Even America, which had once seemed to him a country of dazzle and freedom, had sharply fallen in his affections, and its citizens joined the various groups (left-wing intellectuals, socialists, younger writers) which his plays now made it their business to attack. Waking up on one of the first mornings of 1947 he realised he was "in a still, dark rage".[13]

Friendships began to suffer. Beloved friends from the past – Gertrude Lawrence, Ivor Novello, Elsa Maxwell – began to irritate more than please. Relations with his musical assistant, Elsie April, went from bad to worse. She was now in her early sixties, grieving the death of one of her children, her hands and feet twisted with arthritis. "I'm glad our association is at an end", she wrote during the first of many quarrels, "I was such an outsider. You listened to so many behind my back and I hurt."[14] Her health and spirits declined. "I think I would be better in a place for old 'has beens'. I can't walk alone, and I must be a trouble." Noël was riled by her accusations: "I have treated you not only with fairness but with generosity and I am deeply disappointed and surprised that you should think otherwise for a moment. My financial liability to you finished with the cheque I sent you last Autumn but as I have been fond of you for many years and as you say you are in need of money will you please accept the enclosed cheque for £50, as a gift from me, with my love." And she was grateful: "I can cheerfully have a breakdown or a holiday and know that things are safe. I feel still too excited to realize. My love to you and always remember I am your friend always, always."[15] Noël began to work on his songs with an amanuensis called Robb Stewart, one of his accompanists during the war, but it was an unhappy and short-lived collaboration. April's health deteriorated rapidly, and she died in 1950.

Others, though, continued to find Noël as energetic and warm as ever. His post-war life and opinions are mainly chronicled by diaries that were a specific outlet for a bitterness not omnipresent day to day. He still worked hard for the Actors' Orphanage, and it was often he who made attempts to patch quarrels with protestations of continued personal affection. A long letter to Mary Martin, in the fallout from their rows over *Pacific 1860*, ends its pages of advice, accusation, apology, and justification, with nothing but personal warmth: "I deeply hope that we shall meet again and again and again and I do send you my best wishes always."[16] He was still full of energy and fun, lavish with gifts, generous with praise, combining in his letters vitality, silliness, and extravagant, contagious, affection. Graham Greene had continued to attack him in the *Spectator*, castigating not only his work but his apparent flight from England during the Blitz. It was a sign of how Noël could mingle temper with good humour that his response, sent directly to Greene, was in comic verse. The two men found that, when they actually met, they liked each other. Old friends were loyal and loving; new friends were delighted by him. In France in 1950 he would meet the writer Molly Keane, on whose work he was an influence (though her novel *Conversation Piece* predates his play of the same name). She found he had a unique way of "giving one the feeling that he enjoyed one", and delighted, as did so many, in a life-enhancing wit that remained genuinely spontaneous. "I am devoted to you", he told her on a holiday when they were both in the sea, "but nothing can make me swim beside you to the raft while you are doing that Margate breast stroke."[17]

The crucial pleasure of Noël's post-war work was the rearrival in his life of Graham Payn, whom he had cast in *Sigh No More*. The little boy who had performed in *Words and Music*, back in 1932, was now twenty-seven. His life had uncannily mirrored Noël's own.[18] A boy soprano, he had been a Lost Boy in *Peter Pan* and an alumnus of Italia Conti's stage school; after his parents' divorce, he had lived with his mother, who was a match for Violet when it came to fierce ambitions for a son's stage career – although determination, Payn thought, had outstripped maternal affection. Payn had returned to his native South Africa briefly as a teenager, but had come to England just before the war; the slight trace of a South African accent clipped his voice as sharply as Noël's own. A ruptured hernia led him to be discharged from the army and he had become a jobbing actor-singer in revues and musicals. "Graham Payne [*sic*] came for a drink," Noël had noted in his diary for 1941. "Pleasant but obviously <u>very</u> ambitious."[19] By the time *Sigh No More* went into rehearsal, Noël was in love, and their quickly formed relationship would be lifelong. Friends noticed that he had fallen for Graham with a force nobody had seen since his first days with Jack Wilson, although they worried that Graham would depart soon enough, leaving Noël bereft. But Graham, crucially, was even-tempered and uninterested in jealousy or possessiveness.

Payn, despite Noël's early misgivings, did lack ambition. By his own admission, it was Noël's support, rather than any exceptional talent, that lifted him from stalwart company member to leading man. Noël was at a loss to understand the unambitious, and the fact that Payn was content to sit on his professional laurels, although it helpfully stripped the relationship of competition, would become a point of contention between them. Noël thought nothing of listing Payn's faults in meticulous detail. One explanation for Noël's poor critical reception in the 1950s could be his newfound muse, who provided an emotional contentment that rid him of creatively fruitful anguish, and a reason to embark upon a series of star vehicles for which the young actor was not always best suited. Payn took

romantic leads in *Pacific 1860* and in *Ace of Clubs*, neither of which
secured his career; even worse was a Broadway revival of *Tonight
at 8.30* in February 1948, in which Payn was cast opposite Gertrude Lawrence in six of the plays. Noël directed, blind to Payn's
struggles with the virtuosity and energy required from the highly
varied selection of roles. He made sure to introduce the first-night
audience to a major new talent, which threw further into relief
the stark reality. Payn "lacks the master's sting and stage rapacity",
wrote the *New York Times* in one of the politer reviews, "with Gertrude Lawrence outdazzling the material".[20] The production closed
after three weeks.

For Payn's performance in *Sigh No More* Noël had created the
wistful song "Matelot", and although Payn was not a sailor, the
song made him one in Noël's imagination: "Matelot, Matelot,
where you go, my heart will follow." Payn's affairs had previously
been with women ("Jean Louis Dominic right or wrong", run
the lyrics, "ever pursued a new love, till in his brain, there beat a
strain, he knew to be his true love.") But, as he said later, "I loved
the man totally. At first I only saw the public Noël, fascinating
but distant. But I grew to love him as I got to know him, saw
the compassion behind the wit, sensed the vulnerability. I realised
I wanted nothing more than to share my life with this remarkable man, to help protect him as best I could."[21] If the protection
would eventually extend to helping Noël through other, unhappier,
affairs, then so be it. ("Never mind if you find other charms, here
within my arms you'll sleep, sailor from the deep . . .") Once the
first flush of infatuation was over, his love for Coward became
more domestic, even filial; his nickname was "little lad". Graham
was also content to exist as a couple within a larger group, which
provided him with a companionable coterie that made up for his
childhood's lack of family life. "We *were* family. Not your conventional Victorian family, granted, but in many respects something
better, more alive, because we *chose* each other. We got together and stayed together because we wanted to be together. [. . .]
Each of us was vulnerable in our own way, I suppose. We'd had
to pick ourselves up early in life and make what we could of
the hand we'd been dealt. We sensed that quality in each other.

It brought us together and kept us together in a cocoon that kept the world out."[22]

But the family had its problems. Lorn Loraine's husband, Rupert, after years of suffering from Parkinson's, had had a seizure in a public swimming pool, and drowned. "All those years during which she has never grumbled but has gone home to that dreary atmosphere", Noël wrote. "And now she is free."[23] Free, he may have meant, to devote the rest of her life to him, with her two children now in their twenties. Gladys Calthrop, still suffering from depression, had a nervous breakdown, from which she recovered in a London nursing home. Noël had been inclined to blame her design work for his theatrical failures, and they fought bitterly, but he was distraught at her condition: "it is terrible to see someone you love in any sort of mental state".[24] And Clemence Dane continued to live in Covent Garden, at the pinnacle of her professional success; she won an Academy Award for screenwriting in 1945. But her relationship with Noël was growing competitive, and she was outraged at his cavalier treatment of Richard Addinsell, her close friend, during *Sigh No More*. Finally she told him what she thought of him, accusing him of a solipsism worthy of Garry Essendine. He apologised, examined his conscience . . . and thought her accusations unjust. But it was he who made efforts to rebuild the relationship. "Now all is well. I am glad. I would have hated to lose a friend I valued."[25]

Cole Lesley had been discharged from the RAF and had moved into the rebuilt mews house at the back of Gerald Road, his role in Noël's life shifting from valet to, for want of a better word, assistant. There was never any question of a friendship on equal footing, yet there were few who knew Noël more intimately. Crucially, Lesley found Graham Payn immediately likeable, full of fun and good humour, although noticed that "his I.Q. as such was not spectacularly high; Noël more than once calling him an illiterate little sod to his face". Payn's innocent irreverence had, as if unwittingly, sliced through the protective veneer of Noël's public character. He and Lesley got on so well that the latter soon spoke in terms of a "threefold relationship", although the singer Dorothy Fellowes-Gordon thought that, once sexual passion had faded, Noël was followed about by "two slaves, Graham and Coley. Wherever Noël went, they went too, as kind of attendants."[26] Nevertheless, Noël and Payn were functioning as a couple, and – for the first time in Noël's life – romantic love had coincided with at least an attempt at domestic contentment.

Goldenhurst was standing empty, its garden overgrown (eventually Patience Erskine, Gladys Calthrop's partner, moved in and saw to its maintenance). In October 1945, after months of house-hunting, Noël had finally moved in to a rented property in St Margaret's, a seaside village near Dover, which he used as a weekend and holiday home. The house, known as "White Cliffs", stood right on the shingle beach of St Margaret's Bay, so close to the sea, Cole Lesley remarked, "that it was almost in it".[27] Plain white with a red-tiled roof, it was the least interesting in a row of white art-deco buildings that had been damaged by army occupation; there were mines in the bay, and barbed wire and invasion defences now disfigured a once-fashionable seaside retreat.

Post-war restrictions did not permit Noël to take over the entire row of houses as he would have liked, but he was able to ensure *simpatico* neighbours by giving friends and family the money to move in. Lorn Loraine had half of one house, Cole Lesley the next, and Violet Coward lived alone in the bay after the death of her sister Vida. Gladys bought a home nearby. Even the initially primitive nature of camping out in White Cliffs before it was wired for electricity or fully decorated gave Noël pleasure. He employed a couple who kept house and lived in a garden cottage, although the optimistic mood of refreshment that suffused the new set-up dissolved into tragedy when an oil stove set fire to the cradle of their baby, who was killed. First the press and then even Parliament questioned the building works, which were heavily restricted after the war, but, given he leased rather than owned the property, Noël's permits were in order, even if his pride were dented. He and Graham got a cat and two poodles, "Matelot" and "Joe", mourning deeply the premature death of Matelot. The walls were hung with newly purchased artworks and little expense was spared. But post-war taxes were high. "Obviously I am not going to see much of the money that I make", he wrote bitterly. He raised Lorn's salary, which he could charge against tax. "I would rather Lorn had some of [my money] than anyone in the world."[28]

Jack Wilson was continuing his career on Broadway, as both producer and director, overseeing American stagings of Noël's work while leading big Broadway premieres such as *Gentlemen Prefer Blondes* and *Kiss Me Kate*. But he was growing increasingly reliant on alcohol, and was furious with jealousy at the arrival of Graham Payn in Noël's life. Nearing fifty, white-haired, he looked, Noël thought, "like an old man".[29] Their correspondence became less frequent and when they did write it was to air grievances. "We are dismally unaware of what is in your heart", Noël told him, "there must be something wrong somewhere [. . .] please answer with absolute candour and leave nothing out."[30] Wilson professed "deep, deep, deep unending love", but concern made Noël anxious and short-tempered. Privately Gertrude Lawrence complained to Jack: "I wish [Noël] didn't get so angry."[31] In September 1947 Noël wrote *Long Island Sound*, a play adapting an earlier short story, but Jack's fierce dislike of the script drove another wedge between them even when others, including Binkie Beaumont, agreed with his appraisal.

It was a weekend-in-the-country comedy, featuring an English author on a tour of the States and invited to stay on New York's Long Island. Expecting peace, he experiences chaos (as had once happened to Noël when invited to a Hamptons mansion by a wealthy hostess). More and more guests arrive, each a too-thinly disguised portrait of real actors or society figures, the comedy often at Americans' expense. At moments Noël was in his element – "you remind me of someone I loved very much; he had sinus trouble" – but he came to agree that it was a one-joke play, overextended, and it was never staged in his lifetime. Persuading theatregoers that wealthy American socialites were vapid and self-obsessed was pushing at an open door, and during a time of food and alcohol shortages, an on-stage cocktail party was the stuff of fantasy. The surprisingly explicit rendering of clearly homosexual actors would have struggled to survive in the increasingly unpermissive theatre of the decade.

But Jack's appraisal was painful, and things got worse when he began publically to criticise Payn's struggles in *Tonight at 8.30* and place various obstacles in their way. "A quiet dinner with Graham", Noël wrote, "interrupted by the arrival of Jack, who [. . .] succeeded in upsetting Graham and our hitherto peaceful evening. I made a joke of it at the time, but when I got home I was sick." It transpired that Wilson had made yet more mess with Noël's American finances, overpaying taxes, and Noël – habitually blind to faults in those he loved – was badly shocked, even if few others were. "I feel this is the end of the friendship between Jack and me. So many things add up over the years [. . .] It is a bitter revelation that I can no longer trust him. [. . .] I am sick at heart."[32] Noël threatened to put an end to their association once and for all, Jack apologised and promised to do better, Noël relented, and so they went on. It was a proof of the lyric he had written for *Bitter Sweet*, twenty years before: "I believe the more you love a man, the more you put your trust, the more you're bound to lose . . ."

THE ISLAND

Noël Coward had been dazzled by the Caribbean ever since his first visit, to Trinidad, back in 1933. One of the few hit numbers in his musical *Ace of Clubs* was a lyric espousing his personal philosophy that, in the face of emotional or professional trauma, the best option was escape.

> When the storm clouds are riding through a winter sky
> Sail away, sail away
> When the love light is fading in your sweetheart's eye
> Sail away, sail away
> When you feel your song
> Is orchestrated wrong
> Why should you prolong your stay?
> When the wind and the weather blow your dreams sky high
> Sail away, sail away, sail away

The song, its melody deceptively blithe, the echo of its haunting refrain disappearing into the distance like a ship on the horizon, was a geographical metaphor for his use of flippancy as a defence against emotional introspection. By the time it was written, late in 1949, his plans to leave the seemingly hostile worlds of either England or America were well advanced. Winter cold had brought on painful rheumatism, and he was agitated by demands on his time and energy.

In the harsh post-war winters of rationing and fogs the prospect of a more congenial climate was especially attractive to one who loved intense heat. Bermuda, north of the Caribbean, had been the first location of the potential espionage work he had craved and, on his first visit to Jamaica in 1944, recuperating at William Stephenson's instruction, he had been given the loan of a house owned by Ivar Bryce, a secret agent in Stephenson's employ. Jamaica had provided not only the paradisiacal landscape of winter sun and unspoiled white-sand beaches during the bleakness of war, but also the glamorous secrecy of the spying community. To make the island yet more appealing, Stephenson himself now lived in Hillowton, a grand house in Montego Bay on the fashionable north coast of Jamaica, where the completion of an airport in 1947 had led to its becoming a popular winter escape for the wealthy (and a comfortable exile for pro-Nazi British). Ivor Novello had managed to buy one of the few properties in the area with no view, and the writer Ian Fleming had finished building Goldeneye, his villa on the edge of a cliff in Oracabessa where, in 1952, he would begin work on *Casino Royale*, the first of the James Bond novels.

Noël had occasionally come across Fleming (a friend of William Stephenson, and Celia Johnson's brother-in-law) in England. In search of a retreat in March 1948 after the disastrous revival of *Tonight at 8.30*, he had arranged to rent Goldeneye for three months. When he and Graham Payn arrived at the house they found its interiors so bland and uncomfortable that Noël, who thought it reminiscent of a hospital ward, promptly christened it Goldeneye, Nose and Throat. But he adored their stay and by April, he had purchased a plot of land on a hilltop close to Port Maria, a few miles east along the coast from Fleming's estate. It was the view of the sea from on high that he found irresistible, with the Blue Mountains in the distance and the town of Port Maria glimpsed through the plantations of banana and coconut: "we look for eighty miles over sea and mountains and it's always doing quick changes like me in *The Constant Nymph*".[1] Noël set to work with Ian Fleming's architects almost immediately, designing a property that was to be called "Blue Harbour". A fortnight later, he had also purchased (for, in today's money, no more than £5,000) an even more entrancing plot a thousand feet higher up the cliff, with the ruins of an old stone observation post once owned by Henry Morgan, a nefarious seventeenth-century governor of Jamaica. Here Noël planned to build the smaller retreat for himself that became "Firefly", intending either to sell or rent "Blue Harbour" or give it over to friends.

It would take nearly a year for Blue Harbour to be completed and when Noël returned to Jamaica early in 1949, he found that it had not been built into the hillside in layers, as he had stipulated, but was merely a white cube above the sea, generous with windows

but furnished by the designer in a taste Noël found insupport-
ably suburban. (Both the architecture and interiors of his Jamaican
properties would remain surprisingly basic, suffering the double
attack of sun and humidity.) But the salt-water swimming pool,
the prospect of further improvements, and the beauty of the island
itself soon submerged any disappointments and Noël nearly wept
with the enchantment of it all.

The spate of recent professional failures meant that his finances
were not what they had been, and Firefly would have to wait.
His Rolls-Royce was sold to fund the Jamaican works, but there
was the promise of further income from a movie of *The Astonished
Heart* (expanding the play from *Tonight at 8.30*), which went into
production while he was abroad. Noël had released David Lean
from their production company with a generosity for which Lean
was always grateful, and the film was instead directed by Terence
Fisher and Antony Darnborough, with Michael Redgrave as the
dying and adulterous psychiatrist. On seeing the rushes when back
in London, Noël did not let personal affection for Redgrave soften
his conviction that he was disastrous casting, and he took over the
part himself, playing opposite Margaret Leighton and Celia Johnson. But the film, although it provided much-needed cash, was a
commercial failure, ironically hampered by Noël's performance –
and it failed to help Graham Payn, given a small role, into a movie
career. Redgrave admitted to mild schadenfreude, while admitting
that, thanks to Noël, he didn't "lose a penny" of his fee.[2]

For the rest of his life Jamaica was to be Noël's escape from such
disappointments, especially during the British winter, and Blue
Harbour, to which two guesthouses were soon added, became a
popular destination for his ever-increasing circle of friends. Theatre
legends, film stars, writers, even royalty (all prized members of
Noël's social life) would join him for trips of sunlit leisure and
expansive hospitality, although most admitted that Noël did not
notice the difference between good and bad food and was as happy
with custard as caviar. "One marvellous thing about Jamaica", he
told Alec Guinness, "is that there are absolutely no insects and
nothing poisonous on the land." Guinness pointed to something
dark by the side of the pool, and asked what it was. "I haven't the

foggiest", said Noël, after scrutinising it closely. It was a scorpion. Noël's eyes, thought Guinness, "were shut to many things he didn't wish to face".[3]

As at White Cliffs, beautiful scenery inspired Noël's passion for painting, which he was taking with increasing seriousness, despite his famous dismissal of his "touch-and-Gauguin" efforts.[4] Winston Churchill, a similarly enthusiastic amateur artist, would visit Jamaica and erect an easel alongside Noël's, persuading him to jettison watercolour in favour of oils, to which Noël's fearsome allergy necessitated working with gloves or paper bags over his hands. Gladys Calthrop purchased a house there that she would never actually use; Max Beaverbrook also bought on the island, and he and Noël had a tentative rapprochement. But Cole Lesley refused to drop everything and accompany Noël to help with the move into Blue Harbour. He feared a breakdown after the strain of the war years, and was pursuing a new relationship in London. This small but vital act of independence was a quietly important moment in his life with Noël, who tended to get into a temper whenever Lesley voiced any grievance.

Jamaica's attraction was not solely the life of sunshine, nude swimming, rum punches, and local marijuana (of which Noël disapproved). Ian Fleming used Goldeneye as the location for an affair with the married socialite Ann Charteris, who became his wife when she left her husband, Lord Rothermere; Noël would be a witness at the wedding, on Jamaica in 1952. But the Flemings' was not a faithful marriage. She pursued an affair with the eventual Labour leader Hugh Gaitskell; he eventually fell in love with Blanche Blackwell, the local Jamaican heiress from whose family Noël had purchased the land intended for Firefly. The bed-hopping interwar lifestyle that had thrived in ocean liners or the bars of the Ritz, in the grand hotels of Deauville or the flats of Mayfair, had found a sealed-off part of the world in which to continue. But it was a self-conscious, even synthetic, recreation of a pre-war lifestyle and in using the island and its claustrophobic intrigues as dramatic fodder, Noël risked cutting himself off yet further from British and American audiences, for whom such stories were increasingly irrelevant.

Jamaica also offered protection for his life with Graham.

In London distracted wartime attitudes towards homosexuality had given way to intolerance. David Maxwell Fyfe would become home secretary in 1951 and begin a crackdown on homosexuals in the public eye. Life on an island separated from London by five thousand miles of open ocean was a sunlit escape for those who could afford it, and a homosexual community thrived in the Caribbean. The designer Edward Molyneux would buy a home on Jamaica (he and Noël promptly quarrelled), and Oliver Messel eventually nursed painful arthritis amid the lush beauty of Barbados. Ian Fleming's wife Ann became distinctly uncomfortable at what she perceived to be a homosexual enclave, thinking that Noël's attraction to Ian Fleming had a sexual element. Her feelings towards Noël were never sanguine, and she made matters worse by telling the press that he had come to Jamaica to lick his wounds after theatrical failure, an indiscretion that threatened a permanent breach. But he offered the Flemings use of a house in St Margaret's Bay and, in December 1951, when he decided to move back into Goldenhurst, they purchased White Cliffs for themselves.

With the success of the Bond novels Fleming's career flourished just as Noël's seemed on the decline, a tension their friendship, intensified by their time in the Caribbean, survived. Noël enjoyed teasing Fleming about his crowded, energetic, and entirely heterosexual love life, managing to puncture glooms and passions with a near-flirtatious mockery that did not seem to offend. Fleming shared with James Bond a distaste for gay men, who are dismissed in *Goldfinger* by the fictional spy as the result of men having mopped up the femininity discarded by female emancipation: "pansies of both sexes were everywhere [. . .] a herd of unhappy sexual misfits – barren and full of frustrations". But this did not step him befriending figures such as Noël or the writer William Plomer, perhaps to minimise competition in a small sexual playing field. Noël found himself comforting women (among them the novelist Rosamond Lehmann) who travelled to Jamaica expecting love and romance, only to realise that Fleming was interested solely in sex. He managed to double-book wife and mistress into the same trip, and his attempts to cheer Lehmann by throwing a live squid into the bedroom led her to flee to Blue Harbour.

Most of all, Noël shared with Ian Fleming a political disenchantment. Both were nostalgic for empire and pre-war values. James Bond's politics are Coward-esque in their criticism of "the welfare state politics [that] have made us expect too much for free", and the Bond novels were fiercely patriotic and generally anti-American. The two of them made of Jamaica a time capsule in which the imperialist world they longed for could be preserved. Noël remained fervent in his support for the "great social experiment" of the British Empire, his views perhaps born of unwavering loyalty to Churchill and Mountbatten. He bemoaned the Labour government's efforts to address Indian independence. "Anyone who fondly imagines that [India] is within a hundred years of successful government must be dotty", he had written in his diary during his Far East tour in 1944. "I do wish our high idealed humanitarians from Bloomsbury and the Labour Party could take a few drives through these suburbs."[5] Gandhi's assassination, in January 1948, had been "a bloody good thing but far too late".[6]

The Colony of Jamaica would not gain independence until 1962, and while some middle-class Jamaicans were resolutely Anglophile and committed to British rule, this was by no means the general view. The influx of rich tourists and the increase in grand hotels and private beaches barring locals only served to heighten segregation. Noël's view of Jamaicans was often stereotypical and condescending: "Coloured people are naive and easily led and, if propaganded cleverly, could change their smiles into snarls overnight."[7] He employed a large and loyal staff to whom he was warmly attached, but this did nothing to alleviate the feudalism of the island under British rule. Nevertheless, his streams of visitors bolstered the local economy and he gave over some of his land for use by the community. Using funds from an American philanthropist, he would set up a scheme called "Design for Living", providing local employment through the formation of a weaving business. At one dinner party he got into a screaming row with a neighbour called Louise Blackton who argued that segregation was a conspiracy theory. "She became loopy and started squealing frenziedly about propaganda and White Trash and [arguing] it was quite untrue that the Southern whites were unkind to the negroes.

I mentioned the horrible photograph in *Time* magazine recently, of a white man in Alabama kicking the face of a negro on the ground."[8] In 1951 Hurricane Charlie would become Jamaica's deadliest natural disaster of the twentieth century, and Noël threw himself into fundraising to rebuild local villages, handing over thousands of dollars from ticket sales. He also decried the "foolish edict" that Princess Margaret would dance with no "coloured person" during her visit: "Jamaica is a coloured island and if members of our Royal Family visit it they should be told to overcome prejudice".[9]

He wanted to use the periods in Jamaica to work as well as sunbathe: "I am going through one of my periodical worry phases about time and how little there is of it; there is so much that I want to write."[10] He had published a volume of short stories, *To Step Aside*, at the beginning of the war and in May 1951 would bring out a second, collecting six tales, mostly of theatrical life, under the title *Star Quality*. Reviewing in the *Telegraph* was John Betjeman, who thought it a "modest and excellent book", the dialogue without equal but the prose clotted: "there are, for instance, so many gins and whiskies in these stories that the reader finishes feeling drunk".[11] Beneath the studies of showbiz bitchiness, for which the stories have more than sneaking admiration, were streaks of mournfulness, not least in the account of a woman terrified of flying to whom, not long before take-off, people say the most unhelpful things. The volume evinced Noël's now characteristic conflict between loyalty to British values and scorn for the middle classes who upheld them, his condemnation perhaps stemming from fear of a life he had escaped.

"Mr and Mrs Edgehill" stood apart from the rest, its title couple at once the object of ridicule and sympathy (when the stories were filmed in 1985, the roles were taken by Judi Dench and Ian Holm). Colonial life on a Pacific island offers them meaning and beauty in a way their drab marriage back in England – they have lost a baby – never could. They look sadly upon the British flag, wondering how long it will fly above the island, and are thrilled to receive a photograph of the royal family. After a Japanese invasion they are rescued by a British naval ship. Written during Noël's travels during the war, the story is unequivocally pro-colonial, a portrait of a stoic and dutiful lower-middle-class couple upholding British rule. But it is also a distant ancestor of Paul Scott's novel *Staying On* (1977), about a British couple living in India after the country's independence. The Edgehills cannot stay on, but there is pathos in their patriotism, as without their commitment to the Empire their lives are stripped of meaning and purpose: "'Never mind, old girl," he said softly. 'It was lovely while it lasted.' She returned the pressure of his hand, and tried to smile, but it was not a great success, so she turned her face toward the open sea and did not look at the island any more."

The Edgehills' first posting is to the fictional island of "Samolo", the setting of a play in *Tonight at 8.30* and of *Pacific 1860*. Spurred on by his time in Jamaica, Noël was now acting on a longstanding ambition to develop this fictional creation. He worked out in detail the island's topography and geography, and even the rudiments of a language; the island's volcano was Fum-Fum-Bolo. This was an odd, almost wilfully contrary, project to embark upon, in its focus on the infidelities of the colonial set. And where his earlier scripts had been written quickly and fluently, moving from brain to script and onto the stage in a matter of months, the birth of his Samolan plays was protracted. What became *South Sea Bubble* began life in the spring of 1949 as *Home and Colonial*, and was retitled *Island Fling* for a tiny run (just eight performances) in Connecticut two years later; it would not reach the West End until 1956. Hindsight makes it astonishing to find the *New York Telegraph* praising *South Sea Bubble*, in its brief American run, as "a funnier and better play" than *Present Laughter*.[12] It is unrevivable in the twenty-first century, from its made-up Samolan language ("Somba Kola um Doka! Somba Gulana koob!") to its depictions of the islanders, one of whom speaks pidgin English and is wound into sexual frenzy by performing on ancient war drums.

The meat of the plot revolves around the progressive governor of Samolo, Sir George Shotter, and his wife, Sandra, whom he despatches to charm an imperialist local, Hali Alani, so as to persuade him that the island should move to self-government. But Sandra's approaches to Alani soon descend into his alcohol-fuelled attempt at seduction, which she escapes first with a performance of a hockey song from schooldays at Roedean, then by smashing a bottle over his head. The scene had potential to shock, but was designed to show that Sir George's notions of Samolan independence are a great deal too progressive for their own good. Even his attempts to fit out the island with public conveniences are derided by an Anglophile local. "Most Samolans are still Empire minded", says one of Shotter's colleagues. "They've been happy and contented under British rule for so many years."

The American production was directed by Jack Wilson, and Noël blamed him for its failures. "BESEECH YOU", Jack cabled, "IN ALL SINCERITY NOT TO COME OVER TO SEE THE PLAY [. . .] YOU WILL DETEST MY DIRECTION [. . .] IT WILL ONLY LEAD TO UNPLEASANTNESS BETWEEN US." It led Noël finally to withdraw from their professional partnership, after nearly thirty years of collaboration. "I am bitterly hurt and angry", he wrote to Jack. "Have you ever had a good honest look at your feelings for me? [. . .] There is so much about you I wish I knew."[13]

THE BUTLER

On 26 October 1951 the Conservatives won the election with a comfortable majority. Winston Churchill, seventy-seven years old, was once again prime minister, and Anthony Eden returned as foreign secretary. As with *Cavalcade*, a shift in the country's politics had coincided with a successful Noël Coward opening. *Relative Values*, his first new comedy in the West End since *Blithe Spirit*, opened on 29 November. "Well, well, what a surprise!" he wrote in his diary. "Rave notices. [. . .] This should mean a smash hit – very nice too."[1]

In truth the reviews had been guarded. *Relative Values*, its three acts taking place entirely in a country house in Kent, seemed a return to solid home territory for its author. Few critics could argue that the script was anything other than old-fashioned and most thought its cast – led by Gladys Cooper and under Noël's direction – was propping up something flimsy. The rehearsals had been sorely tested by Cooper's difficulty with line-learning, and she had to surmount a mistrust of Noël in place since, thirty years before, she had seen him, bumptious and noisy, tearing around the hotel in Davos as he planned his very first revue. But the run of *Relative Values* would last for over a year, the play sitting more comfortably in a world where Attlee's government had stuttered to its end.

Blithe Spirit or *Present Laughter* had depicted members of a leisured class cut off from the realities of a changing and conflicted world, caught in life's melancholy farce, and unaware of their own impermanence. It is, in the end, the servant Edith (revealed to have psychic powers) who brings about the Condomines' downfall. But *Relative Values* was no Chekhovian portrait of the fading inhabitants of a grand house, grappling with their own decline; the story was calculated to celebrate the decline of socialist values. The Earl of Marshwood is to be married to the Hollywood actress Miranda Frayle, who turns out to be the sister of his mother's maid, Moxie. To avoid having to work as a maid for her own sister, Moxie is reluctantly persuaded to disguise herself as a grand friend of the family. But the Earl's engagement is soon called off. Moxie can return to being a servant, and the household's butler explains what her brief attempt at transcending her own class has been about: "a social experiment based on the ancient and inaccurate assumption that, as we are equal in the eyes of God, we should therefore be equally equal in the eyes of our fellow creatures. The fact that it doesn't work out like that and never will in no way deters the idealists from pressing on valiantly towards Utopia." The play ends with the butler's *Cavalcade*-esque toast: "I drink solemnly to the final, glorious disintegration of the most unlikely dream that ever troubled the foolish heart of man – Social Equality."

The wily butler was an obvious descendant of the title character in J. M. Barrie's *The Admirable Crichton*, in which a resourceful butler, shipwrecked with his employers, assumes the position of leader. But Crichton believes in the class system, and on his rescue reverts to being a butler. If Noël's servants are the heroes of *Relative Values* – "There's nothing inferior about Moxie, social or otherwise", says the Countess – they are so because they have no desire to be anything other than servants. Harold Hobson, acclaiming the "the best [play Coward] has written for several years", thought that *Relative Values* proved its author no less of a rebel than *The Vortex*, even if the object of his satire had changed: "he looks round for the modern conventions that have replaced the shibboleths of a generation ago, and having found them, pulls the trigger of his satire with the old insolent gaiety".[2] The entertainment value, over subsequent revivals, has seldom been denied. "If you can hear the sound of Bow Bells from Sidcup", Moxie tells her sister, who has fabricated sob stories about their childhood, "you must have the ears of an elk-hound!" But satire against social equality has aged less well than satire against social convention, and a 2014 production led to accusations of "rancid snobbery [. . .] a musty, tribal relic in praise of the class system".[3]

Had *Relative Values* appeared just five years later, it would have struggled to find a place amid the politics and success of "kitchen-sink" realism. But Noël's values were not entirely at odds with theatregoers of the 1940s, who kept *Relative Values* afloat for well over a year. British theatre was in an interim period. Somerset Maugham had written nothing for the stage since 1933, but

Frederick Lonsdale could still draw crowds with murder mysteries or light comedies. In 1947 William Douglas Home would have a hit with *The Chiltern Hundreds*, which also dropped a vulgar American into the British aristocracy, and featured a butler with aspirations for a political career; he must "give up being an MP and learn to keep your place". Verse drama was having its brief moment in the sun: between 1946 and 1955 Christopher Fry wrote seven plays and three translations, most staged successfully in the West End or Broadway, and the American premiere of Fry's *The Lady's Not for Burning* was produced by Jack Wilson.

Fry's work, about which Noël had mixed but not entirely critical feelings, was heavy with symbolism and ostensibly far from the world of *Relative Values*. But Fry, also a musician, had written songs for André Charlot's revues and for films starring Ivor Novello, and it was even suggested that Noël take the lead role in his play *Venus Observed*. In September 1950 Noël had tried his hand at a verse drama of his own called *Flights of Fancy*, in which, after a plane crash, the passengers find themselves as ghosts on a mountain, not knowing which of them is dead. "One of us is dreaming all this | The rest are dead as mutton!" The man whose dream the play turns out to be "gradually draws from everyone present his or her reasons for lying and cheating and showing-off". The first scene survives:

> I'm getting sadly young, my brain's confused
> I can't look back as once I could and see
> Those other days before the Christians came
> And made the world untidy with lament
> And self abasement. All their craven prayers
> And moral attitudes and shrill complaints
> Have cluttered up the globe and made it small
> And querulous, lacking in charm and grace.[4]

But (perhaps wisely) Noël left such plays to Christopher Fry and to T. S. Eliot, who had returned to writing drama in verse after the war.* Drawing on Greek tragedy and Christian philosophy, Eliot's plays were often wrapped in the traditional dress of the stately-home comedy. His apparent dismissal of Noël – "I do not suppose for a moment that Mr Coward has ever spent one hour in the study of ethics" – gained fame through Noël's reply: "I do not think that would have helped me, but I think it would have done Mr. Eliot a lot of good to spend some time in the theatre".[5] But Eliot's line, which he also applied to Shaw and Pinero, came from his "Dialogue on Dramatic Poetry", in which two fictional interlocutors tentatively debate. One gives Noël's own retort: "But why should a dramatist be expected to spend even five minutes in the study of ethics?"[6] Noël had actually found Eliot's *The Cocktail Party* "absolutely lovely until the last act", and Eliot wrote to the author of a book on his stageworks: "I particularly enjoyed the comparison with Noël Coward which nobody else has thought of and which seems to me to the point."[7]

It was Terence Rattigan, though, who seemed to be enjoying almost uninterrupted success, and who, now in his forties, was a candidate for Noël's chief rival. Where Noël had seen no active service, Rattigan had served in the RAF, an experience that inspired *Flare Path* and its popular film adaptation, *The Way to the Stars*. Alternating between comedy and drama he had established himself as a heavy-weight, with *The Winslow Boy*, *The Browning Version*, *The Deep Blue Sea*, and *Separate Tables* following hard on one another's heels between 1946 and 1954. The two men got off to a bad start. Binkie Beaumont had persuaded Noël to invest financially in Rattigan's wartime comedy *Love in Idleness*, which Noël savaged when invited to an early performance; the same thing happened with Rattigan's 1949 play on Alexander the Great, *Adventure Story*. Rattigan had wanted to carve

---

* The number of Coward's abandoned writing projects from the 1950s indicates a new restlessness and uncertainty. *Flights of Fancy* is one of nearly thirty incomplete scripts held in the Coward Archive, including plans for a vast "Samolan Operette"; scenes written in blank verse; a comedy set in the world of movies; hints of a new double act with Gertrude Lawrence; and a proto-Ayckbourn play called *Semi-Detached*, in which dramas set in two neighbouring households – one Bohemian, one very much not – play out simultaneously.

his own niche as a serious writer of a younger generation, and dismissed Noël as the purveyor of pompous patriotism and trivial songs. It did not help that Jack Wilson had produced the successful Broadway run of *The Winslow Boy* not long before *Tonight at 8.30* was so disastrously revived in New York. But Noël had nothing but admiration for Rattigan's major plays, which shared with his own a focus on sexual frustration in a repressed world, born from their author's homosexuality. Rivalry shifted into a friendship that would be strengthened when Rattigan's own work fell out of fashion, and in 1956 he described Noël as "a phenomenon, and one that is unlikely to occur ever again in theatre history".[8]

Rattigan's *Love in Idleness* had starred Alfred Lunt and Lynn Fontanne, and Noël's criticism may have arisen from an urge to restore them as the leading interpreters of his own work. They remained among his closest friends and were as popular as ever, particularly in England, where they had spent much of the war. With both *Relative Values* and a revival of *The Vortex* a respectable success, Noël was spurred quickly on to produce a comic vehicle for the Lunts, *Quadrille*, which he completed in January 1952; it opened in London in September. Beneath the Victorian setting, the plot was similar to *Private Lives*, this time focusing on the abandoned couple, rather than the eloping one. The Lunts were to play a pair of left-behind spouses, who fall in love with one another. Not until the end did *Quadrille* really broach what could have been its most interesting and perhaps most autobiographical theme, of newfound passion in later life (Lynn Fontanne was now sixty-five, not that anybody knew): "If only you and I were younger! If only there were more time." The Lunts enjoyed rehearsing in Jamaica, although they could not help faltering at the writing. This was Noël in a mode that *The Times* would dismiss as "romantic fustian".[9] And indeed: "I will love you for ever, until the end of time". . . . "Did you hear, behind my words, the pounding of my stricken heart?"

The play managed to charm American critics when the Lunts, after indecision, requests for rewrites, and consequent epistolary quarrel ("We love you and believe in your honesty" . . . "I love *Quadrille* very, very, much" . . . "We all loved *Quadrille* very much" . . . "I won't re-write one line" . . . "It naturally makes me unhappy that my motives should be misunderstood by you two who I have loved so much for so many years" . . . "Fuck, Fuck, Fuck") eventually took the production to Broadway with some success.[10] But the British reviews, dismissing overwritten and outdated material rescued only by a talented cast, were among the worst Noël had received since the war. *Quadrille* nevertheless ran in London into the following year, surviving not only poor reviews but the great smog that, in December 1952, descended upon London and, Lunt wrote, "filled the theatre like grey chiffon [. . .] we acted as though under the sea".[11]

Quadrille's popularity was helped by its designs. *Relative Values* had been the first of Noël's productions on which Gladys Calthrop, frail after her breakdown and finding it hard to take account of post-war shortages, had not worked. *Quadrille* required the ornate costumes of British and American aristocracy in the 1870s (Lunt's character was an American railway engineer given to muttering "Hell and damnation!"), and sets ranging from French villas and railway stations to the drawing rooms of Belgravia. "Wrote rather a difficult letter to Gladys", Noël noted in his diary, "explaining why I did not want her to do the dresses."[12] She took it well, he thought, and was happy to work on the smaller project of illustrating *The Noël Coward Songbook*. It was the end, not of their friendship, but of a collaboration that had spanned thirty years and nearly as many productions. Her work on a dramatisation of Vita Sackville-West's *The Edwardians* did not stop the production failing in the West End. She had, essentially, retired.

Quadrille was to be designed by Cecil Beaton, his first collaboration with Noël. Forty-eight, he had established himself as one of the country's leading photographers, especially of the Bright Young People and the royal family; he had moved into stage design after the war. He had never entirely liked Noël, admitting that his mistrust arose from jealousy: "I admire everything about his work [. . .] Why, then, have I hated him? [. . .] I was envious of his success, of a triumphant career that seemed so much like the career I might have wished for myself." Meeting Noël on a ship late in 1929, he had been suspicious of such calculated, and literal, self-regard. "You should appraise yourself", Noël had told him.

"I take ruthless stock of myself in the mirror before going out."[13] Beaton was nervous of being subsumed into a clique, which he called "the Ivor, Noël naughty set. They're rather cheap and horrid and yet sometimes very nice." He had rejoiced in Noël's critical failures, and once claimed to have left England in order to escape the irritating songs of *Bitter Sweet*. Meeting Noël in Calcutta during the war, he recoiled from his politics: "Noël shouted and said he had become more and more imperialistic and would like to beat the black and yellow buggers down the street."[14]

But they had also spent an evening together so open and intimate that Beaton never understood why it didn't firmly cement their friendship. He too found that, criticise Noël as he might, he wanted to be liked and praised by him, and his company inspired affection, even if the liking did not outlast time spent in his presence. "Noël was extremely generous and, at once, said some kind things about my recent work. I was pleased. Life suddenly had a glow [. . .] Noël was being completely frank and opening himself up to me on a platter."[15] He told Noël that *Quadrille* was his "best play to date" and "a masterpiece of its sort" (a view with which its author agreed). "Nothing on earth that I know of would prevent me from doing the job."[16] Binkie Beaumont's offer of 12 per cent royalties didn't hurt, either. But despite Noël's pleasure in Beaton's elaborate designs, theirs would never be an entirely easy relationship, although Beaton admired Noël's sangfroid during rehearsals made crotchety by the Lunts' habitual nerves: "How is it you're not harassed and pulling out your hair?" To which the reply came: "It doesn't do you any good and it's bad for the hair."[17]

The box office success of *Relative Values* and *Quadrille* had been overshadowed by tragedies to which these plays made little concession. Pre-war glories were further distanced by the deaths of major figures from Noël's early life. In January 1951 Charles Cochran had died after being trapped in a scalding bath. The following month Ivor Novello had made a success, as composer and actor, with *Gay's The Word*, a musical comedy that managed what Noël had found impossible: to incorporate successfully the style of the American musical, and bravely to parody its composer's earlier, more sincerely romantic, operettas. But on 6 March 1951, a month after the opening, a few weeks after Noël had praised him in the press, and an hour after the curtain came down on a performance, Novello had suffered a fatal heart attack. He was fifty-eight. "I don't know when I have been so astonished and dismayed", Noël wrote to the Lunts. Clemence Dane made a bust of Novello's head in bronze, capturing the profile that Noël had famously declared was equalled in beauty only by his own mind. "Shattering news", he wrote to her. "There is really nothing much to say, is there. You know how deeply fond of him I've been for over thirty-five years; beneath all the irritations and the embarrassment and tiresomenesses he was gay and generous and a darling and I shall miss him always. I do wish that just for a moment people would stop dying off."[18]

Then, while *Quadrille* was opening its preview run in Manchester, Gertrude Lawrence fainted backstage after a Saturday matinee on Broadway of *The King and I*, in which she had made the greatest success of her musical career. Her triumph was sharpened for Noël by the fact that he had declined the offer either to direct the show or to play opposite her as the King. She was found to be suffering from advanced liver cancer and by the day of a planned operation she was in a coma. She died on 6 September 1952, fifty-four years old. They had shared an American lawyer, Fanny Holtzmann, who telephoned him with the news, "incoherent and in floods. All she could say was that Gertie knew she was dying and had spoken of me. I dined with Gladys, and then came home and wrote an obituary for *The Times*. This was agony and I broke down several times."[19]

He had last seen her in April, in New York. He had been wounded by her poor opinion of *South Sea Bubble*, which he had written for her; she longed for another comic double act. They had often quarrelled: "if I have hurt you", she wrote to him over an unknown disagreement, "you <u>must</u> know it was not intentional".[20] But theirs was a friendship sustained over four decades, and it had weathered the voltage of their combined tempers, egos, talents, as well as (Noël thought) the dullness of her husband. His published praise of her unique contribution to his work annoyed the Lunts, but he didn't care. "We have grown up in the theatre together, and now she is suddenly dead and I am left with a thousand memories of her, not one of which will ever fade. I have loved her always,

31. *Bathers on the Rocks*, by Philip Streatfeild. Oil on canvas, 99 x 152 cm, 1914.

32. *The View* from *Firefly*, by Noël Coward. Oil on board.

33. Papier-mâché masks by Oliver Messel (held at the Victoria & Albert Museum, London), similar to those used in Coward's 1928 sketch "Dance, Little Lady" (see plate section 1, photo 17).

34. Claude Dansey, founder of the secret "Z Organisation", for whom Coward worked in 1938.

35. British diplomat Robert Vansittart, to whom Coward reported when beginning his espionage career.

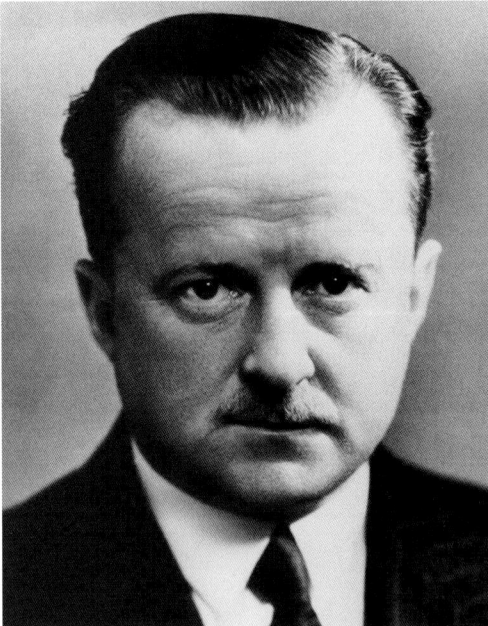

36. The politician Duff Cooper.

37. Spymaster William Stephenson (his 1942 passport photo).

PLAY PARADE

From September 1942 to April 1943, Coward performed leading roles in three of his plays during a gruelling nationwide tour.

38. As Charles Condomine in *Blithe Spirit*, with Judy Campbell as the ghostly Elvira.

39. As the vain Garry Essendine in *Present Laughter*.

40. As Frank Gibbons in *This Happy Breed*.

41. "The most important job . . . I have ever done." In 1942 Coward was screenwriter, director, and lead actor for the war film *In Which We Serve*. After the survivors of HMS *Torrin* have been rescued, Captain Kinross (Coward) takes the dying testimony of his men, among them a young Richard Attenborough.

42. Entertaining the men of the Eastern Fleet on the aircraft lift aboard HMS *Victorious*, Trincomalee, Ceylon, 1 August 1944, with Norman Hackforth accompanying.

43. Cole Lesley (born Leonard Cole): Coward's devoted valet, assistant, friend, and (eventually) biographer.

44. Graham Payn, performing "Matelot" in Coward's short-lived revue Sigh No More (1945). During the run they fell in love and would stay together for the rest of Coward's life.

45. "You've been a long way away . . . Thank you for coming back to me." A lobbycard for Brief Encounter, 1945.

A STORY OF THE MOST PRECIOUS MOMENTS IN A WOMAN'S LIFE!

J. ARTHUR RANK presents

NOEL COWARD'S

Brief Encounter

A NOEL COWARD-CINEGUILD PRODUCTION

starring

CELIA JOHNSON   TREVOR HOWARD

WHOSE PERFORMANCE WAS VOTED THE BEST OF THE YEAR 1946 BY THE NEW YORK CRITICS

STANLEY   JOYCE
HOLLOWAY * CAREY

Thrill to RACHMANINOFF'S CONCERTO No. 2 as played by EILEEN JOYCE

Directed by DAVID LEAN   In charge of Production Anthony Havelock-Allan and Ronald Neame

A PRESTIGE PICTURE released through UNIVERSAL INTERNATIONAL

46. "Mad Dogs and Englishmen go out in the noonday sun."
Coward photographed in the Nevada desert during his wildly
successful cabaret performances in Las Vegas, June 1955.

47. The spartan but sunlit surrounds of Firefly, Coward's solitary
Jamaican retreat, higher up the hill from Blue Harbour, his larger
property on the island.

48. "Mad about the boy. . ." The actor William Traylor, with whom Coward had a tormented affair in 1958.

49. At the first-night party for *A Song at Twilight*, London, 14 April 1966, Coward's last major play and his final acting role.

50. Collecting the longed-for knighthood at Buckingham Palace, with Gladys Calthrop (left) and Joyce Carey, 13 April 1970.

51. **Ghost of Noël Coward, winking**
Maggi Hambling
oil on canvas, 2019 to 2020
21 x 17 inches

as herself and as an artist."[21] Lawrence's widower wrote to him: "Gertrude loved you so very dearly, and always had such respect for you too. Seeing you always made her happy."[22]

The final death which would recalibrate life, severing links to the past, was longer expected. After Noël had given up White Cliffs and the properties at St Margaret's Bay, Violet Coward had moved into a flat in London not far from Gerald Road. She was in the last years of her eighties, alone after the death of her sister, increasingly bent and frail, stone deaf and almost blind. She found partings from Noël, sole surviving of her three children, hard to bear. Work on *Relative Values* and *Quadrille* was overshadowed by his worry about her physical state, but she would hold on for another eighteen months, until cancer was finally diagnosed. On 1 July 1954 he would write in his diary:

Mother died yesterday at a quarter to two. I went round at eleven o'clock and she recognized me for a fleeting moment and said "dear old darling". Then she went into a coma. I sat by the bed and held her hand until she gave a pathetic little final gasp and died. I have no complaints and no regrets. It was as I always hoped it would be. She was ninety-one years old and I was with her close, close, close until her last breath. Over and above this sensible, wise philosophy I know it to be the saddest moment of my life.[23]

THE DESERT

He stood in the desert, spotlit by the noonday sun, which cast a long slender shadow across the cracked sand. He was immaculate in a double-breasted black suit and bow tie, carnation in his button-hole, handkerchief in his chest pocket, cigarette in a long holder, thin hair greased back from a face of lined leather, two inches of gold-linked cuffs poking from the impeccably tailored sleeve on which he refused to wear his heart. Even in the dusty heat of Nevada, he was the exemplification and originator of a national character unrumpled by physical discomfort or the foreign culture of a far-away country. It was a kind of psychological imperialism, covering the world maps not with the red-marked territory of a rupturing geographical empire, but with a more enduring, perhaps illusional, export: Englishness.

It was the summer of 1955, and Noël Coward was being photo-graphed for *Life* magazine by the legendary Loomis Dean. They were about fifteen miles from the city of Las Vegas where, performing a cabaret into the small hours of the night before, he had embarked upon the fashioning of his next legend. The image of the black-suited figure, alone in the great stretch of desert, captured the way in which, since the end of the war, Noël Coward had ploughed his own unfashionable furrow, clinging hard to a way of life regardless of its absurd difference to the inimical landscape around him.

He was more solitary than he had ever been. Finally orphaned, in his mid-fifties, he was cut loose from family ties. Las Vegas was a long way from Teddington, where he had buried his mother in the churchyard, not five minutes' walk from his babyhood's home. Noël had had all his teeth out; "Firefly" had finally begun to be constructed in Jamaica, high above Blue Harbour; George VI had died. Noël had watched the coronation on television. The six-feet-three Queen Salote Tupou III of Tonga was driven through the pouring rain in an open-top carriage, sitting next to the diminutive Sultan Ibrahim IV of Kelantan. Famous as the comment became, Noël denied ever having described the sultan as "her lunch".

For the coronation season, in spring 1953, he had taken the lead role in George Bernard Shaw's 1928 satirical comedy, *The Apple Cart*, the first time in a quarter-century he had appeared on stage in a work he had not written himself. Shaw had died three years earlier, and the play, full of lengthy monologues, had been an unlikely choice for Noël, cast as King Magnus, who outwits a cabinet aiming to strip the monarchy of political influence. A massive opening speech he had learned at Blue Harbour: "Every Jamaican seagull now knows it. They call it out as they go past."[1] He had got through the first night, in May 1953, on painkillers after an attack of lumbago, and there were complaints about his lack of projection. But the combined star power of Shaw and Coward was still of a voltage to ensure good sales, and Harold Hobson, his most support-ive critic, wrote that he had given to Shaw's wit "a sly flippancy that made it human as well as dazzling".[2] In the audience was Lila Field, the first person to have put him on the stage. Now she was old, and ill. "You are always the Goldfish to me", she wrote to him in September, a few months before she died.[3]

Nineteen fifty-four had been devoted to another musical, *After the Ball*, an adaptation of Wilde's *Lady Windermere's Fan* that after disastrous rehearsals and mainly indifferent reviews had managed a five-month run in the West End, from June to November, while Noël was mourning the death of his mother. His attitude to Oscar Wilde had become ever more hostile: "what a tiresome, affected sod".[4] Wilde's play, in which Lady Windermere suspects her hus-band of having an affair with a woman who is actually her mother, had influenced *Easy Virtue*. But as the basis for a Noël Coward music-al many had thought it an odd fit. (Ironically, and long before *My Fair Lady*, Noël had turned down the suggestion that Shaw's *Pygmalion* would make a good musical.) Australian dancer Robert Helpmann, directing *After the Ball*, soon realised that the combination of two very different forms of wit was like "having two funny people at a dinner party. Everything that Noël sent up, Wilde was sentimental about, and [vice versa . . .] It didn't work."[5] Noël had passed over script-writing duties to Cole Lesley, while focusing himself on the lyrics and music, which he wrote in Jamaica with Norman Hack-forth as his musical assistant. Spending so much time abroad meant that he was unable to supervise rehearsals, and when he saw the show for the first time it had already toured for six weeks. Graham Payn had stayed in England to take a small role, and Mary Ellis, praised for her performance in Rattigan's *The Browning Version*, was cast as Lady Windermere's disgraced mother. Nearing sixty, she no longer had a secure singing voice, which, Noël told the Lunts, sounded "like someone fucking the cat. I know that your sense of the urbane, sophisticated Coward wit will appreciate this simile".[6] He had become ever more ruthless in his attempts to improve the show and he fired Norman Hackforth as musical director. "It was a cruel thing to do", Hackforth admitted, "and in the final issue, I shall never believe that it made any difference."[7]

Hackforth, who was made seriously ill by the stress and the shock of his dismissal, was all the more dismayed because of the close link he had forged with Noël, not only during wartime tours but during the series of cabaret performances that had led to the bookings in Las Vegas. Since 1951 he had been Noël's accompanist for an annual show at the Café de Paris in London. The fashionable nightclub had reopened after repairing its bomb damage, and the star performers it attracted were a far cry from the days when Master Noël Coward had joined Miss Eileen Dennis in stately dances there, during the First World War. The Café had been redecorated in honour of Marlene Dietrich's debut, but the managers had not jumped at the suggestion that Noël perform. "For Marlene", Noël said, "it's cloth of gold on the walls and purple marmosets swinging from the chandeliers. But for me – sweet fuck all."[8] Still: "nothing ever quite equalled the magic of that first night", Hackforth remembered of the Café concerts. "He was undoubtedly the greatest man of the theatre in this century, and a faultless immaculate performer." Noël was paid not in money but in paintings, calling his December seasons "my Christmas Boudin".[9] The popularity of the shows had been such that, not long before the death of the King, he was asked to recreate the full-length cabaret in the royal family's drawing room. Princess Margaret performed, too.

But Boudin canvases, although helpful tax-wise, did not help his bank balance which, given the series of failures and not-quite-successes, were struggling to maintain his life on Jamaica and the renovations on Goldenhurst, now an estate of more than a hundred acres. Income from the publication of his second autobiography did not prevent his soon being in debt to the tune of £19,000; half a million today. (The memoir, designed to rebut criticism of his wartime travels, had ended up salting the wound. "He trips over platitude, stumbles into pomposity, and even falls under suspicion of snobbery", wrote *The Times*. "It is not by Mr Coward that we want to be told [about] the Union of South Africa.")[10] So when, in November 1954, the legendary American agent Joe Glaser had appeared in his dressing room with the suggestion of work in Las Vegas, and offering a fee that, in terms of 21st-century income, would amount to a weekly half-million dollars, Noël had to accept.

On 1 June 1955 Noël arrived in Las Vegas for the performances, accompanied by Cole Lesley and wary of the dry desert air and the surprisingly high altitude that threatened to wreck the voice of visiting singers. Millions of tourists were now pouring in and out of the city to use the gambling halls, and to see the grand hotels and illumined billboards of the Las Vegas Strip, which by the summer was shimmering in the intense heat. Between the lights and the pylons there were still "for sale" signs on increasingly valuable plots of unbuilt land. North of the city there was a nuclear weapons testing site, which became its own tourist attraction: guests would book viewing platforms from which to watch the explosions from a supposedly safe distance. Mushroom clouds hovered above the neon.

Noël was to perform at the Desert Inn, built late the previous decade by the casino owner Wilbur Clark, who had run out of money and been bailed out by the gangster Moe Dalitz. While Clark was the public face of the resort, only the fifth to open on the Strip, Dalitz kept a quiet hand on proceedings. Most of the Las Vegas venues were in the employ of local gangsters, who took a cut from the vast amounts of money that surged through the casinos, very little of which was ever officially declared. Big-name acts – from Mae West to Ronald Reagan – were hired to attract rich customers and keep them in the hotels spending money. Noël was being paid not from ticket sales but from illicit gambling profits. "The gangsters", Noël wrote, "are all urbane and charming. I had a feeling that if I opened a rival casino I would be battered to death with the utmost efficiency and despatch, but if I remained on my own ground as a most highly paid entertainer that I could trust them all the way."[11]

His calculatedly British act was a risk to set in front of wealthy American audiences. But he had made careful preparations in advance, working with a vocal coach. In New York and Hollywood he and his booking agents ensured that he was sent on the celebrity party circuit in order to sign up star support. Frank Sinatra advertised Noël's appearances on the radio and then chartered a plane in order to send glitzy guests to Nevada, among them Lauren Bacall and Judy Garland, who soon added "If Love Were All" to her repertoire. Zsa Zsa Gabor arrived and for some reason Noël never fathomed sent a giant bright-pink teddy bear to his hotel room.

In the Inn's "Painted Desert Room" guests sat between the muralled walls eating Filet Mignon, which was included in the six-dollar ticket price. The stage was made up to look, not all that convincingly, like the Café de Paris. NOEL COWARD was spelled out in flashing lights, and chorus girls set the scene. Dry ice recreated a London smog rather too authentically, and the front tables began to cough. The chorus sang a medley of songs about London, the platform was raised a few feet behind the mist, and Noël – who performed for half an hour at suppertime and then again at midnight – entered to a snatch of "I'll See You Again". Had the programme continued in solely nostalgic vein it could have been a disaster, but after forty seconds he launched into "Dance, Little Lady", switched to "Poor Little Rich Girl", and then sang wistfully to the audience, in a manner that implied neither he nor they agreed, that the most he had was just a talent to amuse. The medley ended with a rambunctious account of "Play, Orchestra, Play" from *Tonight at 8.30*, and once he had begun the comic songs, polite applause had turned to wild laughter. Cole Porter, sitting in the audience and still in perpetual pain two decades after his riding accident, happily accepted being the butt of Noël's jokes in "Nina": "She declined to Begin The Beguine when they besought her to | And with language profane and obscene she cursed the man who taught her to | She cursed Cole Porter too."

His singing voice had strengthened and deepened with age, taking on the quality that Kenneth Tynan described as being like "a baritone dove", the songs emerging "with the staccato, blind impulsiveness of a machine-gun".[12] His bright (false) teeth gnashed through the jokes beneath eyebrows constantly raised, and even his first bow would be accompanied by the removal of an imaginary speck from his eye. Hands emerged from his cuffs to whirl around his head like birds, or rushed to his ear to underline the rudest jokes by rubbing a lobe slowly between thumb and forefinger. "Mad Dogs and Englishmen" shot by at a gabble of astonishing clarity; his hips waggled to Nina's rumba; newer songs fizzed and thrummed. "A Bar on the Piccola Marina" depicted a middle-aged widow's rediscovery of sex, lapsing into strains of Neapolitan song, the 'r's rolled with elan:

> Where love came to Mrs. Wentworth-Brewster
> Hot flushes of delight suffused her
> Right round the bend she went, picture her astonishment
> Day in, day out, she would gad about
> Because she felt she was no longer on the shelf
> Night out, night in, knocking back the gin
> She cried "Hurrah, Funiculi, funicula, funnic-yourself".

Norman Hackforth had not been able to acquire a permit to work in America (Noël quietly paid him the fee he would have received), and on Marlene Dietrich's recommendation the musician Peter Matz had taken over, producing brilliant accompaniments that injected new life into the songs. The set finished with "The Party's Over Now", Noël's arms spread wide to acknowledge the applause.

He wrote in his diary on the morning of 12 June: "I have made one of the most sensational successes of my career and to pretend that I am not absolutely delighted would be idiotic. I have had screaming rave notices and the news has flashed round the world."[13] Given the jibes he had received at the Café de Paris, the acclaim of the American press served to increase a nagging suspicion that Britain had turned its back on him. The reviews had indeed been sensational and Noël performed for a month to packed houses.

Inevitably he fell ill, and using an assumed name he checked into a hospital for three days and read *War and Peace*. His finances were restored on a spectacular scale, a recording was a bestseller, and he went off to Hollywood as famous in America as he had ever been, besieged by party invitations and job offers. He turned down roles in a number of movies, including *The Bridge on the River Kwai*, but would accept a small cameo in *Around the World in 80 Days*.

He had also been commissioned for a series of television specials, for (in today's money) a fee close on five million dollars: such exorbitant sums were necessary to lure stars onto the small screen. He was contracted for three episodes of *Ford Star Jubilee*, a series shown once a month on CBS. The first was *Together with Music*, a song-and-dance concert to be performed, live, with Mary Martin. Their arguments over *Pacific 1860* were not quite forgotten and reignited when she arrived for rehearsals in Jamaica with her husband in tow, whom Noël absolutely hated. The special was filmed in front of an invited audience in New York in October 1955 and Noël, beneath a shiny helmet of hair, delivered his songs straight to camera with an energy so voracious as to give his charm an almost menacing edge. He finished with a medley of show tunes in duet with Martin, whirling himself fearlessly into the finale's Charleston. They reached an audience of millions, although the ratings were not as high as producers had hoped. The second episode was to be *Blithe Spirit*, in which Noël, his leg numbed after treatment for an abscess, played Charles Condomine while struggling with the demands of his leading ladies Lauren Bacall and Claudette Colbert. (The latter may have been smarting from the week-long American production of *South Sea Bubble*, in which she had been the lead.) He insisted that Graham Payn take a small part, but this was one of the only requests with which producers – who had accepted demands for unprecedented rehearsal time – did not acquiesce, and the role went to Noël's childhood rival, Philip Tonge. The following year the third episode would be filmed, with Noël playing Frank Gibbons in a shortened version of *This Happy Breed*, but only after he had flown to New York in a snowstorm and a panic to win over producers who, dismayed by the ratings, had got cold feet and threatened cancellation. With Edna Best and a young Roger Moore in the cast, it would prove the biggest critical triumph of the three.

Newfound success in America had arrived partly because Noël had embraced and heightened the incongruity of his wry British manner amid the glitz of Las Vegas and Hollywood. But his world of camp and innuendo, although a tonic to worldly audiences at expensive casinos, had been a risk in McCarthyite America. He had fought with television producers who asked for certain double entendres to be cut. His rewriting of Porter's "Let's Do It", mentioning the Kinsey Report, was especially risqué: "In Texas some of the men do it | Others drill a hole and then do it." But he never included the line "I believe the more you love a man . . ." when singing "If Love Were All". Homosexuality was perceived by many American psychiatrists as a mental illness, and at a time of communist witch-hunts gay men were thought a likely target for Marxist blackmail and were being fired in their droves from government. Eisenhower had made it illegal for the State Department to employ homosexuals and Gore Vidal's novel *The City and the Pillar*, about a homosexual coming of age, had led to scandal and blacklisting.

"To regard homosexuality either as a disease or a vice", Noël thought, was "archaic and ignorant"; he was certain that objections to its legalisation by groups of "bigoted old gentlemen" were nothing but "uninformed prejudice" that "will cause irremediable suffering". But he was steadfast in his belief that discretion was paramount and that flagrantly expressed sexuality did nothing but harm. Even his increasing dislike of Oscar Wilde may have resulted not only from political disagreement – his own philosophy was poles apart from Wilde's socialist worldview – but from a sense that Wilde had set back the homosexual cause. He wrote in his diary:

The police are empowered to frame private individuals, to extort terrified and probably inaccurate confessions and betrayals from scared young men. [. . .] What is to prevent a stranger to whom I have given a lift in my car from going to the police? [. . .] Any sexual activities when over-advertised are tasteless, and for as long as these barbarous laws exist it should be remembered that homosexuality is a penal offence and should be considered as such

socially, although not morally. This places on the natural homo a
burden of responsibility to himself, his friends and society which
he is too prone to forget. [. . .] The human urge to persecute is
always at the ready. When there isn't a major war in progress to
satisfy man's inherent sadism, the Jews must be hounded, or the
Negroes, or any nonconforming minority anywhere.[14]

His fear, if uncharitable, was genuine and not without reason. The
Evening Standard's theatre critic had attacked "bachelors" such as Noël
and Terence Rattigan who had never known the fulfilment of a
wife and children.[15] An American magazine called *Rave* published
an article titled "Las Vegas' Queerist Hit", in which it claimed
that Noël was the highest-paid British "tulip" and had been seen
wooing young RAF officers. In Las Vegas he had met the bisexual
singer (and heart-throb) Johnnie Ray, who visited him in Jamaica.
Top Secret, another gossip magazine, dropped heavy hints: "Johnnie
Ray's Caribbean Caper".[16]

To be outed in public now threatened fearful consequences. It
may be no coincidence that the atmosphere of persecution had led
to a decline in the reception and the daring of his work. James Agate
had been blackmailed by a young guardsman, and Cecil Beaton had
been interviewed by Scotland Yard. In 1953 Noël's friend the writer
Rupert Croft-Cooke had been imprisoned for indecency, and John
Gielgud was arrested for cottaging. Noël had written to Gielgud in
support and sympathy, but privately he was frustrated.

A day of horror. [. . .] This imbecile behaviour of John's has let
us all down with a crash. He was only knighted a few months
ago. [. . .] I am torn between bitter rage at his self-indulgent
idiocy and desperate pity for what he must be suffering. [. . .] If
only John had been caught decently in bed with someone, then
there would have been a sympathetic reaction and people might
have been forced to think seriously about the injustice of the anti-
homosexual laws, but this descent into dirt and slime can only
do harm from every point of view. The lack of dignity, the utter
squalor and the contemptible lack of self control are really too
horrible to contemplate. How <u>could</u> he, how <u>could</u> he, have been

so <u>silly</u>. [. . .] This tirade of mine seems terribly self-righteous but I have worked myself into a fury. Poor wretched John, so kind and humble and sensitive and what a bloody, bloody fool.[17]

And a frightening rumour was gaining traction in Jamaica:

Apparently the Tourist Board, headed by Cy Elkins,* have started a big drive to eliminate all homosexuals, or those <u>suspected</u> of being homosexuals from the island. [. . .] Elkins has taken it upon himself to clean Jamaica from this vile stain and is determined that anyone with the slightest suspicion of unconventional sex habits must not only be refused admission to all hotels but also, if possible, refused admission to the island! [. . .] Needless to say, all the queer young men in Jamaica are in a state of understandable jitters. Incidentally they have all been behaving idiotically for years. They have been in the habit of driving over to Kingston in carloads and having fairly promiscuous rendez-vous with coloured boys at a certain hotel. [. . .] I have lived here with the utmost discretion since 1947 and whatever unpleasant gossip there may be concerning me must, like *Rave*, be entirely fabricated. However, I think the situation needs watching carefully and I intend to keep my ear firmly to the ground.[18]

By the end of 1954 over a thousand men had been imprisoned in Britain for homosexual acts, and although the Wolfenden Committee had recommended legalisation, it would be over a decade before any change in the law. The same year had brought the "Montagu case", which saw the gay writer Peter Wildeblood sentenced to prison, along with the landowner Michael Pitt-Rivers and the Conservative peer Edward Montagu. But when Terence Rattigan got up a petition for their release, Noël refused to sign.

Within the walls of the Desert Inn, his cabaret act had offered a hidden layer of double meanings, a good dose of the implicit that

---

* A Canadian entrepreneur who owned hotels in Ocho Rios such as the famous Jamaica Inn.

also hinted at the way in which mob rule lay beneath the razzy public face of the city. Kenneth Tynan described Noël's cabaret performances as "public and private personalities conjoined", but the figure of Noël Coward, Englishman and cabaret star, who stood cool and collected in the desert sunshine in front of Loomis Dean's camera, was still a construct.[19] Finishing his sets at one in the morning, he was rarely awake to see the noonday sun, which was so hot that touching the handle of a car door without gloves singed the fingers. Driving back to Las Vegas from the shoot, sweating in the scorching car surrounded by buckets of ice, he threw away his cigarette, took off his suit, and, free of his sweltering costume, sat in his underwear.[20]

THE ENTERTAINER

On 25 April 1956, at the Lyric Theatre in London, the curtain rose on the first British production of Noël Coward's *South Sea Bubble*, revealing the verandah of Government House in the fictional British colony of Samolo. A fortnight later, on 8 May, the curtain rose at the Royal Court Theatre in Chelsea on *Look Back in Anger*, a new play by twenty-six-year-old John Osborne: a cramped attic flat in the Midlands, two men reading the Sunday papers, a woman ironing.

The difference could not have been more marked and exemplified what was seen as the theatrical revolution led by the so-called Angry Young Men, the title under which writers such as Osborne, Arnold Wesker, and Kingsley Amis were soon grouped. Kenneth Tynan, for two years an influential reviewer at the *Observer* who had criticised Noël's recent work, wrote that he could not love anyone who did not wish to see *Look Back in Anger*, which depicted the unhappy marriage and life of Jimmy Porter, a disaffected – and working-class – young man. Tynan was among the few voices of enthusiasm in a barrage of criticism, but the play announced a new wave of social realism, intended to wash away the old-fashioned world of Noël Coward and his contemporaries. It was also noticeable that for decades the most powerful men in British theatre – Rattigan and Novello and Coward, Somerset Maugham and Binkie Beaumont – had been homosexual. The leaders of the new generation (Osborne and Pinter, Wesker and Amis) were not. "How queer *are* you?" Noël would ask Osborne in 1966. "Oh", Osborne good-naturedly replied. "About twenty per cent."[1] The Royal Court pointedly abandoned curtain calls for playwrights. The Bright Young People had been ousted by the Angry Young Men.

In truth there was no overnight revolution. *The Reluctant Debutante* played to packed houses in the West End all through 1956. A musical version of Rattigan's *French Without Tears* was a four-performance disaster but *Ross*, his 1960 drama about T. E. Lawrence, would run for two years. And while reviews were decidedly mixed for Noël's *South Sea Bubble*, which had finally reached a British production seven

years after it was written, it ran steadily until Christmas and the
Daily Express thought it Noël's best in years. The success was aided
by performances from seasoned members of his personal and professional troupe such as Alan Webb and Joyce Carey, but the main
attraction was its lead actress, Vivien Leigh, star of *Gone With the
Wind* and *A Streetcar Named Desire*. She had recently played Lavinia in
Titus Andronicus, who, tongue cut out and hands cut off, uses a staff
to write the names of her attackers in the sand. On the night Noël
attended, Leigh dropped the staff. He went round to her dressing
room: "Hello, butterstumps!"

Leigh had taken the part of the Governor's wife in *South Sea Bubble*
only after requesting extensive rewrites to the original script, which
she thought weak. Married to Laurence Olivier who, thirty years on
from *Private Lives*, Noël now considered the greatest living actor bar
none, she was having an affair with the actor Peter Finch and had
not long recovered from a serious nervous breakdown. In August
she had to withdraw from *South Sea Bubble* when, forty-two years
old, she became pregnant. "I am SO SO happy for them", Noël
wrote, "although a teeny bit apprehensive on the tot's account. To
be born into such a turbulent *menage* might possibly be far from
cosy, what with Daddy shrieking 'Fuck' and bellowing *Macbeth*, and
Mummy going briskly round and round different bends."[2] Leigh
had a miscarriage just a day after leaving the production, resulting
in a period of debilitating depression.

Noël had hoped that Leigh would play the role in America,
and soon discovered that both Olivier and the producer, Binkie
Beaumont, had known about the pregnancy long before he had.
The three of them quarrelled badly, and insult may have been
added to injury by the fact that Olivier was able to ally himself
to the new generation in a way Noël never could. The actor who
had thrilled wartime audiences with his patriotic performance as
Henry V would soon score astonishing success as Archie Rice, the
title character in Osborne's *The Entertainer*. But Noël's ability to row
was matched only by his capacity for reconciliation: "the only
thing that's left is three people who love each other very much and
always did and always will". Like almost all his quarrels, this one
ended with his peculiar brand of lavishly insulting affection.[3] To

Olivier he wrote "give my dearest love to Puss [Leigh] and tell her
that she's a wicked, dull, common, repulsive pig and I never want
to see her again except constantly".[4] Noël and Olivier communicated in a bizarre theatrical lingo of foul-mouthed baby-talk, with
"cunt" clearly a term of endearment. Letters addressed to "Darling
Noelie-Poelie" or "Dearest darling Larryboy" are signed "Your
adoring fuck-pigs".[5] In Noël's more private writing Leigh's travails
inspired a cruel impatience: "Fond as I am of her and sorry as I feel
for her, I would like to give her a good belting."[6] But Blue Harbour
had been always on offer as a place for rest and recuperation, and
almost all her illnesses and incarcerations were accompanied by a
rain of gifts from him. One of his "get well" cards was "all I had
to hang on to at that dreadful time", and she kept it in her purse
for the rest of her life.[7]

Despite the success of *South Sea Bubble*, Noël was not sanguine about
the arrival of the Angry Young Men: "I am very old indeed and
cannot understand why the younger generation, instead of knocking
at the door, should bash the fuck out of it."[8] He was not entirely
dismissive of new playwrights and, although he disliked Osborne's
later work, professed himself "genuinely thrilled" by *Look Back in
Anger*, which he found "full of vitality and rich language".[9] Arnold
Wesker's *Chips with Everything* was "bitter, exciting, and moving".[10]
But even Shelagh Delaney's brave portrayal of homosexuality in *A
Taste of Honey*, her seminal account of a teenage girl's family life in
working-class Manchester, could not persuade him that the play
was anything other than a "squalid little piece about squalid and
unattractive people".[11]

American imports he seemed determined to dislike on principle,
and while he praised *A Streetcar Named Desire* (having befriended Tennessee Williams), Arthur Miller's *Death of a Salesman* he found "boring
and embarrassing".[12] Absurdist theatre provoked even greater ire. In
1955 Samuel Beckett's *Waiting for Godot* had had its British premiere,
and the Royal Court would soon champion the work of Eugène
Ionesco. Noël was not attracted even by the music-hall origins of
Beckett's tramps – "pretentious gibberish [. . .] it made me ashamed
to think that such balls could be taken seriously" – and Ionesco he
simply thought was "not a playwright".[13] Harold Pinter's earliest

plays – *The Dumb Waiter* or *The Birthday Party* – contained elements of the absurd and Noël found them "completely incomprehensible and insultingly boring".[14]

Disgruntlement with the avant-garde was part of his newest role: the witty curmudgeon. His was a short memory, as if he had forgotten the days when his own radical eruption into the theatre had been brushed off by conservative reviewers as a passing fad. It had been many years since anyone had considered Noël Coward an angry young man, but his own plays had depicted disaffected youth across the class spectrum, fighting against the morals of a previous generation. Only in hindsight have hidden similarities, rather than obvious differences, become clear. Mutual friends thought that Osborne had specifically used Noël as a model, and Kenneth Tynan noticed how often they both employed the disparaging use of the word "little".[15] Noël's dismay at post-war society matched Osborne's, and looking back in anger (or, at least, in regret) was the essence of his own post-war attitude. The sad comic patter of Archie Rice in Osborne's *The Entertainer*, his music-hall routines a metaphor for the country's decline, owed something to the past-it performers in Noël's *Red Peppers*. Noël and Osborne had grown up in similar households not far from one another in Surrey, and Osborne, like Kingsley Amis, was privately educated and had a clear nostalgia for Edwardian values.

Nor was Noël able immediately to discern the impact of his own writing on Pinter, who wrote dialogue of similar economy, rhythmic precision, and subterranean implications. In *The Dumb Waiter* two hitmen wait in a basement for their instructions and find orders for Greek dishes in the eponymous elevator: "Macaroni Pastitsio. Ormitha Macarounada." "What was that?" "Macaroni Pastitsio. Ormitha Macarounada." Pinter had followed the advice of Otto in *Design for Living*: "Any word's ludicrous if you stare at it long enough. Look at 'macaroni'." Even Beckett's *Endgame*, in which the elderly Hamm is attended by his loyal servant, can be seen as a post-apocalyptic flipside of *Present Laughter* and its ham actor. ("Nothing is funnier than unhappiness", says Nell in *Endgame*; "there's something awfully sad about happiness", says Garry in *Present Laughter*.) Beckett's *Happy Days* ends to the nostalgic strain of a bitter-sweet Viennese waltz.

And: "I suggested a little jaunt to celebrate, to the Riviera or our darling Grand Canary" is a line not from Noël Coward but from Beckett's *Play*. Noël was unable or unwilling to concede that rebellion was the final proof of influence. Younger playwrights, even if they hoped to explode his style of theatre, had nevertheless built on the rubble.

Noël's life had settled into a comfortable pattern: winters in Jamaica, summers at Goldenhurst, punctuated by trips to Europe and America. He lunched with Rebecca West or the Mountbattens or the Duchess of Kent; he met the Queen Mother and her daughter and son-in-law at parties, his admiration for royalty past and present now extending to an increasingly forgiving attitude towards the Duke and Duchess of Windsor. In America Marlene Dietrich would drive him to and from the airport, and Noël would try not to notice how a decrepit Jack Wilson peered out at the world through a mist of alcohol. Firefly was now complete, and the spartan single-bedroomed building, a small box of white stone and concrete looking more like a gun emplacement at Dover than a luxurious Caribbean retreat, provided isolation in which to work before he descended to socialise with whichever guest was bobbing in the pool at Blue Harbour. Ian Fleming privately thought Firefly a "near disaster, and anyway the rain pours into it from every angle and even through the stone walls so that the rooms are running with damp. He is by way of living alone up there and Coley has to spend half his time running up and down in the car with ice and hot dishes of quiche Lorraine! A crazy set-up."[16] Clemence Dane visited and, dramatically enacting the way in which Marlowe had been stabbed, managed to jab a fork into her own neck.

In Britain standard income tax was at a flat rate of roughly 40 per cent, on top of which the highest earners paid a hefty surtax. Noël's annual tax bill could reach, in terms of today's income, millions of pounds, a situation he found monstrously unfair and which, with his capital mainly in property (he had invested in other building schemes on Jamaica) led him to move from overdraft to overdraft. He had a poor grasp of his own finances, which made him testy with agents and managers, and paranoid about his future security. The instability of the actor's life, and the memory of his childhood's money struggles, were never far away. By late December 1955 he had decided to give up his English domicile and, on the advice of his accountants, move to the British dependency of Bermuda, a short flight north of Jamaica and an offshore financial centre with no personal or corporate income tax. Accountants and agents slowly began to put the plan into action and early in 1956 he had travelled to Bermuda house-hunting. Spithead Lodge was an eighteenth-century pirates' warehouse in Warwick Parish that had belonged to Eugene O'Neill. Built in sugary pink stone and with a white roof and shutters, it sat on a jetty above the water of Hamilton Harbour, and Noël spent a happy spring moving in. As *South Sea Bubble* went into rehearsals in March he had sold Gerald Road and then, the following month, Goldenhurst, auctioning off the houses' contents and telling himself that it was all a grand new beginning. His two Steinways were shipped to Bermuda; he gave up membership of his London clubs; and the presidency of the Actors' Orphanage was handed, in a more honorary capacity, to Laurence Olivier. Lorn Loraine was to work from her own home.

In order to lose his residential status in England he had to live outside of the country for an entire tax year (meaning he never saw *South Sea Bubble*). After this he would be able to return only for an annual three months. By June, he was back in Bermuda, "up to my arse in shavings and old china", and trying to learn to fend for himself: "A disaster with the chocolate shape. In my fluffy way I added the cornflour paste to the boiling milk instead of *viva voce*" – sic – "and the whole thing became stodgier than *Murder in the Cathedral*."[17] He was happy and excited, especially by his newfound financial security – although Spithead had been bought with a mortgage and Goldenhurst sold for less than the asking price. It would be years before prominent rock stars and actors would move to Monte Carlo or the Caribbean to avoid high taxes, and Noël was among the first high-profile instances of a wealthy celebrity giving up his British domicile. The phrases "tax exile" or "tax haven" had yet to be coined. Both Gladys Calthrop and Laurence Olivier criticised him for what seemed a hypocritical abandonment of a country he had professed to love. Gladys thought the plan "smells of exile to some degree and I wonder if you have thought of how this will feel

[. . .] this very important step is being taken a bit blithely. [. . .] These are things that – caring deeply for your happiness, knowing you pretty well after all this time, and loving you – I must say."[18]

Noël admitted to Olivier that he had suffered "a beastly time over it" and hated "the idea of having no actual home in England". But he was also defensive: "I have not gone away from being English and bloody proud of it. [. . .] I have not evaded paying English tax by this move. My Company will pay English tax on all my English earnings [. . .] what I have done is to avoid paying any more surtax which, if I had continued to be domiciled in England, would have completely crippled me and left no cushion at all for my old age which is due to begin next Tuesday. [. . . Now] I can really get on with my primary job which is to become a better and better writer and a more tolerant and compassionate human being. I do not, I hasten to add, intend to give up being witty as all fuck and pretty as a picture."[19]

The press condemned him, and the accusations led to fierce debate as to whether British tax rates were too high or deterred ambition and enterprise. It was reported that Noël was escaping years of unpaid back taxes, a rumour that the Inland Revenue had to deny officially. Noël wrote to *The Times* to clarify and complain: "all this Press hullaballoo regarding my private affairs has distressed me considerably [. . .] I consider this action as entirely justifiable and requiring neither defence nor vindication."[20] His taste for melo-dramatics didn't always help. "I just dare not set foot on British soil for fear the Income Tax people will get at me", he told the *Daily Mirror* from an outward-bound boat. "Out there is the country I love. But if I leave the ship I am faced with poverty."[21] Ronald Searle drew a cartoon of him, cigarette holder aloft, bags packed, with the caption: "I'll never see you again".

Noël spent his enforced year-long absence from England shut-tling between America and the Caribbean; in New York he gave up his riverside apartment in the Campanile and would thereafter rent in The Sutton Collection, two blocks north. But he was strained and irritable, and the physical exertions of the moves had left him, he knew, gaunt and tired. Foreign domicile made it all but impossible for him to work on the staging of his plays, which would now often begin with previews at Dublin in order for him to attend. Such was the case with his next project, a comedy he had dreamed up six years before and had finally written over a fortnight in the spring of 1955. *Nude with Violin* opened in London on 7 November 1956 and ran for over a year. Osborne or no Osborne, by the end of 1956 Noël Coward had two productions running simultaneously in the West End.

But to those who found Noël's post-war work feeble and reactionary, *Nude with Violin* only confirmed their apprehensions. "Described as a comedy, it emerged as a farce, and ended as a corpse", wrote the *Evening Standard*.[22] Set in the Paris studio of a famous French artist who has recently died, the play is a comic attack on modern art. Forty years later Yasmina Reza's *Art* (1994), about a large all-white canvas worth an astonishing sum, would treat the same theme with more ambivalence as to the state of contemporary painting. Noël's artist is explicitly a fraud, his lauded and valuable paintings – whether from his Farouche, Circular, Jamaican, or Neo-Infantalist periods – having been created in truth by a Russian princess, a Jamaican evangelical, and a schoolboy.* Noël had fun with Graham and Cole working on the canvases for the production, but Graham's rendering of the title painting was destroyed. The producers thought it obscene.

The action is controlled by the lead character of the artist's Jeeves-esque valet who, like the butler in *Relative Values*, delivers a final, moralising, speech on those who earn their living by "writing without grammar, composing without harmony and painting without form". Wit tips into alarming anger: "the rot will spread like wildfire. Modern sculpture, music, drama and poetry will all shrivel in the holocaust." *Nude with Violin* promises more introspective, even autobiographical, themes than eventually appear, hinting at an exploration of the relationship between an ageing artist and his devoted servant-cum-companion, and a consideration of

---

* In *South Sea Bubble*'s West End run, the Samolan characters were performed in heavy make-up by Alan Webb and the Welsh actor Ronald Lewis, but for *Nude with Violin* the Jamaican painter was played by Thomas Baptiste, a Guyanese-born British actor and singer.

posthumous reputation and artistic integrity. But it has little consistency, attacking not only cultural pretension but the philistinism of the painter's estranged and suburban family, who sell off the fakes for huge sums. Nor is the art skewered with any precision, the object of the play's ire being its broad-brush conception of pseudo modernity.

At best *Nude for Violin* was a vehicle for a star actor to have fun with the role of the valet, and John Gielgud was eventually cast after both Rex Harrison and Yvonne Arnaud (who would have necessitated rewrites) turned it down. Gielgud, also the director, had not yet managed to ally himself with contemporary playwrights and was known primarily as a classical actor; his appearance in a new comedy and in modern dress was worthy of remark. He had never quite lost his wariness of Noël, instilled by his days understudying in *The Vortex*, and he had recently recovered from a breakdown after his arrest. Perpetually loyal to Binkie Beaumont, he convinced himself at the time that *Nude with Violin* was "the best thing Noël has written in years", but spent the too-brief rehearsal period mistrusting the script and his own performance.[23] When Noël saw the production in Dublin he found it fussy and promptly took over. Gielgud generously marvelled at the speed and effectiveness of Noël's improvements, but soon professed himself foolish to have taken on a second-rate work.

By the end of the year Britain's global reputation had been badly dented by the Suez Crisis, a sign to Noël that he had been right to leave a country on the decline. Anthony Eden's reputation was damaged, and he was suffering from cancer, recuperating from an operation at Ian Fleming's home on Jamaica. He resigned as prime minister early in 1957, and Noël thought his successor, Harold Macmillan, a promising appointment. And so Noël Coward, exiled from England, wrote and painted and learned how to sculpt in clay, on one island or another, in the Neverland's endless sun.

THE ACTOR

"My secret news", Noël Coward wrote in his diary on 26 October 1957, "is that I fear that Old Black Magic has reared itself up again. This is stimulating, disturbing, enjoyable, depressing, gay, tormenting, delightful, silly and sensible."[1] He had fallen in love.

He had decided to take *Nude with Violin* to America and to perform the role of the valet himself, marking his first acting role on Broadway in over two decades. He felt sure that American audiences would welcome his return, and he had lost no confidence in the play despite the largely negative critical reaction in Britain. The production would also be a means of finding work outside of England, where he now spent his annual three months in a hotel, cross with the press and feeling deracinated. Rehearsals began in New York in October, prior to a Broadway opening the following month. A brief tour in Delaware and Philadelphia promised big success, but it did not come. "There is no avoiding the conclusion that the wit is limp and tarnished", wrote the *New York Times*. "The raillery is almost completely lacking in the crackle, spring and audacity that put Mr Coward at the lead of the British comedy writers."[2] Business dwindled and even over Christmas the company was playing to half-empty houses. A sudden convulsion in his emotional life had coincided with huge professional disappointment.

The young actor William Traylor had auditioned for the small role of an American journalist. Only Noël, already mad about the boy, had wanted to cast him, and the part, quickly expanded, was Traylor's Broadway debut. Twenty-six years old and originally from a small farming town in Missouri, he had been trained at the prestigious Actors Studio. Noël had no time for the method acting espoused by its director, Lee Strasberg, but it made no difference to his feelings for William Traylor. The company watched him pursue the younger man with ardour and frustration, noticing that he flew into a rage when Traylor attempted a romance with a young actress in the cast.[3] Traylor was not exclusively homosexual and seems to have been a lost soul, suffering from depression, drinking heavily, and struggling to break away from an intensely religious upbringing. But he did reciprocate Noël's affections to some degree, and they began a tormented, and necessarily secret, affair.

Noël's relationship with Graham Payn, while steadfast, had lost its sexual passion. Graham's career was still stagnating and Noël had been slow to realise "how deeply unhappy he is [. . .] This really tore me in two."[4] The move to Bermuda led them to spend more time apart and Graham, nearing forty, was now sharing a London flat with Cole Lesley. He, Graham, and Noël were living as an intimate trio, with Noël the triangle's tip, but it was a Platonic unit. Noël, thought Graham, "was vulnerable to the temptations of a brief infatuation but his pleasure was always outweighed by the irritation he felt at losing control of his emotions. It didn't happen often, and it made no difference to our relationship, that's really all there is to say."[5] Cole had accompanied Noël to America and tried to help as best he could, pained by the perceptible agony after the "sleepless night when the loved one hadn't kept a promised tryst, or the telephone hadn't rung as had been pledged. Why, Noël wanted to know, should these idiotically small things cause an actual physical pain, an ache which he literally could feel and from which he had suffered throughout his insomniac night?"[6]

Noël was open in his belief that he did not know how to love. Or that, like his childhood self, he loved too much and too hard. "To me, passionate love has always been like a tight shoe rubbing blisters on my Achilles heel. [. . .] I wish to God I could handle it, but I never have and I know I never will."[7] In *Easy Virtue*, over thirty years before, he had given Larita the painful admission that she was "so tiresome in love. We hammer at it, tooth and nail until it's all bent and misshapen." In 1967 he would use the same metaphor in a poem: "I am no good at love | I batter it out of shape [. . .] I lie alone in the endless dark | Knowing there's no escape." Certainty as to love's impermanence, instilled in his boyhood, led him to cling with tighter grip. "I am no good at love | I betray it with little sins | For I feel the misery of the end | In the moment that it begins."

Amid post-war insecurity he was now insatiable for proofs of love: "to love and be loved is the most important thing in the world".[8] His habitual conclusion to letters – "love, love, love, love, love" – seemed more a command than a sign-off.[9] To be loved was a form of control; to be in love was to lose control. Sexual success was a means of counteracting professional failure, and a reassurance of attraction in the face of increasing age. Weight loss in preparation for *Nude with Violin* had left him more gaunt than svelte, and after cutting what hair he had remaining he looked, he thought, "like Yul Brynner's aunt".[10] (Kenneth Tynan was more charitable: "If his face suggested an old boot, it was unquestionably hand-made.")[11] Sex had begun to play a role in Noël's life entirely separate from his emotional affairs, a functional transaction that interrupted briefly the tidiness and control of the industrious and disciplined life he otherwise espoused. Young actors would find themselves the object of a discreet enquiry or even a reassurance that they had nothing to fear. Among his one-night lovers were Gore Vidal and the American composer Ned Rorem, who thought him in search of tenderness rather than wild passion. Noël even seemed to conduct a sexual life through Graham, who became a third, physically more involved, party in the fling with Vidal.[12]

Despite the geographical and financial upheavals of the previous year, Noël had managed to write another "Samolan" play, called *Volcano*. This was a portrait, in the thinnest of disguises, of Ian Fleming's unfaithful marriage and his supposed affair with his neighbour in Jamaica, Blanche Blackwell. To the rumble of the volcano, a charming philanderer shuttles between a vengeful wife; a lover from the past; and an unhappily married younger woman. Noël hoped to persuade Katharine Hepburn to star, but Binkie Beaumont, perhaps fearing libellous retribution from the Flemings or the wrath of the Lord Chamberlain at the tangled sexual web, thought the script subpar and the characters unsympathetic, and said so.* The bitter taste of *Volcano*, which was permanently shelved, stems from its depiction of love as a burning lava-flow. The promiscuity of the central lothario wreaks havoc and wrecks

---

* Few critics thought the play a lost masterpiece when it finally reached the West End, in 2016, a year before Blackwell (who denied the affair) died, aged 104.

lives, and turns on its head the daring renunciation of conventional monogamy in Noël's early work. In *Private Lives* Elyot is certain: "Let's blow trumpets and squeakers and enjoy the party as much as we can." In *Volcano* the central character is pilloried for his "shrill, boastful trumpeting".[13] The irony was that, soon after the ageing writer had completed this repudiation of sexual freedom, he found himself once again in the agonies of a frustrated desire that reached a corrosive and destructive pitch.

The affair with William Traylor disappears from view behind his diaries' accounts of continual professional frustrations. Binkie Beaumont thought he was entitled to a cut of the American sales for *Nude with Violin*, and Noël thought he wasn't. Exhausted, Noël slipped in the shower and took a wedge out of his nose, nearly choking on the blood, which soon covered the bathroom floor. The New York winter was freezing and by Christmas Eve Noël's voice had given out completely. Refusing to let an understudy perform, he cancelled five shows, leading to financial loss. He staggered on into the new year, battling laryngitis, at which point he tried to cure himself not with rest but with further industry, the only medicine he knew. *Nude with Violin* was to transfer to California and be performed in repertory with *Present Laughter*, with Noël as Garry Essendine. William Traylor was cast as Roland Maule, the pompous young playwright whom Garry decides to teach a lesson. Dismiss method acting as Noël might, the frustrations of character and actor seemed to integrate, even as Essendine dismissed sex as "vastly over-rated". Rehearsing the two massive roles left him on the verge of a breakdown and at the end of January, "at the lowest ebb that I have been for many years", he collapsed.[14]

Then, on the morning of 3 February 1958, he was woken early by Cole Lesley. "He told me that Bill Traylor had got blind drunk on Sunday night, gone home, and swallowed a whole bottle of sleeping pills and was now in the Roosevelt hospital on the danger list. [. . .] Bill had come home at about 2 a.m. high as a kite, gone into the bathroom, then returned and had a crying jag and then collapsed in a dead coma." Traylor had been with a friend, who phoned not an ambulance but the police. "They tied Bill to a chair with sheets in order to get him down the stairs, and took him to the hospital where he was stomach pumped and put in a strait-jacket." Noël went straight to the hospital that afternoon.

> He was thrashing about stark naked in a caged bed, and looked
> ghastly. [. . .] I gripped Bill firmly by the shoulders and shook
> him like a rat and said over and over again with tremendous
> intensity, "You have got to get yourself onto that stage tomorrow
> night", "You have got to get yourself onto that stage tomorrow
> night." This apparently penetrated, for it is all he remembers of
> that day. [. . .] Meanwhile all the papers ran the story.[15]

The patient was soon discharged, and Noël brought him home, spending much of the week in mournful discussion with Traylor's mother. "Bill himself is mortally ashamed", he wrote. "I am still not sure <u>why</u> he did it or if he really meant to kill himself or was merely doing it as a sort of drunken 'some day you'll be sorry' gesture. If so, why? He gave me a garbled explanation about feeling insecure and ashamed of this but none of it quite rang true."[16] Traylor recovered in time for the performances in Los Angeles and San Francisco which, conversely, were more successful than in New York. But Noël thought he was living in a "recurring nightmare". Self-recrimination was surely inevitable, which, in his diary's account, expressed itself in unsympathetic anger.

> Bill is still suffering from a sort of moral hangover and is what
> might be described as "moody". I must say with every reason. He
> hasn't yet, as far as I know, dared enter the confessional to explain
> that in a fit of drunken idiocy he tried to fuck up his immortal
> soul. I presume he will ultimately and will be told to say a few
> "Hail Marys" and do some light penance. What a lot of blithering
> nonsense it all is. His moods of introspective despair are definitely
> mitigated by the fact that he has had some good notices.[17]

He may have needed anger, not only to quench guilt and distress, but to keep his love and desire at bay. When the run came to an end, in March, "Bill rang me up from Hollywood and said his 'Goodbye, thank you' piece very sweetly, and he already sounded long ago and far away".[18] There was something neatly metaphorical about the way in which the flight that finally carried Noël away to Jamaica was nearly knocked out of the sky by a massive storm. His feelings for Traylor abated only slowly, and in his correspondence he found an introspection and tenderness that his diaries had not permitted. "I have only myself to blame for being 'lonely as a cloud' and missing you like hell", Noël wrote to him from Firefly, in the tenderest and most open of his letters to survive.[19]

> Now all is peace and sunshine and I am trying, not as yet very successfully, to adjust myself to a slower tempo. I have slept and slept and dreamed too much. I can remember – I can remember – the months of November and December [. . .] and the ecstasy and the nightmare. I know I couldn't bear to live it all over again but I wouldn't be without it. Of course I regret much of my own foolishness because I should have been old enough to know better, but if I had been old enough to know better none of it would have happened and if none of it had happened I should not be happier and more contented and a good deal duller and dryer. My only valid excuse is that, at moments, the pain was unendurable and when the heart is in pain it is liable to strike out.
>
> There are so many many things I want to say to you now that we are so far away from each other, but only one of them really counts and you know what that is.
>
> Take care of yourself and never never run away again whatever happens. Too much fear is running away, and too much gin is running away, forswear them both my very dear. Think tenderly of me and wrap yourself in your <u>very</u> expensive raincoat and press sturdily on. Les Beaux Jours, Les Beaux Jours, j'étais si malheureux.*

---

* Happy Days, Happy Days, I was so unhappy. Cf. Coward's story "Mr and Mrs Edgehill": "She remembered a phrase that she had read years ago in a book of historical memoirs, a phrase spoken by a dying French actress of the eighteenth century who had achieved triumph and fame and been reduced to penury. 'Ah les beaux jours, les beaux jours, j'étais si malheureuse!'"

Traylor's reply evinces neither anger nor regret. A year later he would marry the actress Peggy Feury, and Noël attended the wedding, gifting the couple one of his paintings (they soon moved to Los Angeles and founded an influential acting school).[20] He also sent a photograph, inscribed by hand not with his own verse but with a quotation from Swinburne. It was rare for him to reach for the words of another. "Time remembered is grief forgotten, | And frosts are slain and flakes begotten, | And in green underwood and cover | Blossom by blossom the spring begins." Traylor's letter appears to consider his suicide attempt as stemming from depression, rather than from an affair that, however often it had tipped into frustration or unhappiness, was evidently born of genuine affection.

How are you my darling? [. . .] I've had what one would say [was] the worst year professionally that could be conjured up and yet I still have that blind faith thing. As to my state of mind I've coped and I'm glad to say rather well. At least I'm sane and damnit it will happen. I just reread those lines and they are about as lucid as this ink – what I'm trying to say is that it hasn't been good at all but I've tried to be a little more objective about it and have for the most part stayed on top of the depression. God this does sound like an introduction to Psychology 1 for Freshman students. I'm not going to talk about it anymore since I'm doing such an abominable job of it. [. . .] As I write there is a lot of time remembered and it is a rare pleasure to remember – for my life would not be worth it, were I not able, now and then, to turn back the clock all the way.

Bill.[21]

THE MOUNTAIN

Noël Coward, nearing sixty, looked at the world and disliked what he saw. "We are still worshipping at different shrines, imprisoning homosexuals [. . .] People are still genuflecting before crucifixes and Virgin Marys, still persecuting other people for being coloured or Jewish or in some way different from what they apparently should be. [. . .] The Pope still makes announcements against birth control. The Ku-Klux-Klan is still, if permitted, ready to dash out and do some light lynching."[1] Cole Porter had finally had his leg amputated and Noël visited him in hospital. Grace Forster, mother of his old friend Stewart and inspiration for *The Vortex*, was "dying slowly in a tatty nursing home", and he went to her bedside.[2] Laurence Olivier was on the verge of leaving Vivien Leigh, who continued to struggle with drinking and depression, and Noël found himself listening to the woes of each, managing to maintain the friendship of both, and hoping above all – in the event fruitlessly – to keep the marriage together. "Marlene is alternating between flashing about in white ermine and scrubbing floors and changing diapers for her grandchildren", he wrote during an American trip. "The weather is humid and I am humid. My lower plate has been fixed satisfactorily and no longer gives me cancer of the jaw every time I eat a meringue."[3]

Already he was homesick for Europe, quickly losing patience with the climate and solitude of Bermuda, where he could hear passing pleasure cruises pointing out Spithead Lodge to tourists. He holidayed in France, idly house-hunting. The love affair with William Traylor, once out of his system, seemed to provoke a period of calm and industry. "After those gruelling six months in America it has taken a while to uncoil the springs", he told Clemence Dane. "But this has been accomplished at last, and now I am raring to go once again."[4] Few flecks of passion or grief can be discerned in the numerous projects that, all through 1958, crossed the pianos and desks that he had scattered across the world. A novel was beginning to take shape, as were poetry and short stories. He wrote a play about actresses in a retirement home; he agreed to do an English adaptation of Feydeau; he began to work on a musical set on a cruise liner; and as if to prove that there were simply no genre he could not master, composed the score of a half-hour piece for London Festival Ballet. The year ended with a trip to cold London, where he promptly caught pneumonia, recovering in time to attend *Peter Pan* and *Where the Rainbow Ends*, both shows still running nearly half a century after he had capered entrancingly among the Lost Boys as the Zeppelins dropped their bombs.

His translation of Feydeau, *Look after Lulu!* – the first English version of *Occupe-toi d'Amélie!* (1908) – fared badly when it opened on Broadway in March 1959. Some of Noël's earliest work had been written in an attempt to enthuse London audiences about French farce, but Feydeau had fallen from fashion until after the war, when the French actor-director Jean-Louis Barrault had led revivals at the Comédie-Française. It was at Barrault's suggestion that Noël set to work, thinking the play could be a vehicle for Vivien Leigh, although owing to Leigh's precarious health the role, to Leigh's dismay, was first given to Tammy Grimes. The title character was a cocotte, tricked into a mock (actually real) wedding by a friend in whose care she is left when her lover goes to war. Cole Lesley, whose French was better than Noël's own, was an invaluable assistant, almost co-writer, but Noël's heart was not in it, and he believed the original play so untidy as to consider the adaptation little more than a rescue project. The Broadway production ran for only a month.

By April he was in sunnier climes, acting in *Our Man in Havana*, Carol Reed's film of Graham Greene's novel. Location filming in Cuba, just months after Castro's revolution had ousted Batista, was its own pleasure and excitement, as was working with Alec Guinness and Ralph Richardson. Castro's officers milled about the grand hotel with machine guns on their laps, and lorries drove through the streets transporting prisoners in chicken-wire cages. Eventually a summons came from Castro himself, but after a ninety-minute wait, the actors realised they had been stood up.[5] Noël surely enjoyed the secret irony in playing the role of Hawthorne, a senior agent in the British Intelligence Service (tightly furled umbrella, trilby, tiepin, pocket square) who recruits Guinness's mild-mannered vacuum salesman in a gentleman's lavatory. Given the sexuality of the two actors and the atmosphere of the decade, it was a charged location. Greene introduced Noël to Ernest Hemingway, who was living partly in Cuba and in his last years of alcoholism and illness. But Hemingway found Noël's gossipy conversation unbearable, and fled his company.

The film had been worth it for the fee (£1,000 a week) but the experience did not lead Noël to accept the role of Humbert Humbert in Stanley Kubrick's forthcoming adaptation of Nabokov's *Lolita*. Inspired as the casting could have been, Noël didn't countenance having anything to do with a novel he had found "exceedingly pornographic and quite disgusting".[6] He pondered bringing out a "Noël Coward" cologne instead. *Lolita* was also a far cry from his ballet, *London Morning*, which had been dictated to Peter Matz and orchestrated by the composer Gordon Jacob. The premiere came in mid-July 1959, at the Festival Hall in London. "Is there nothing you can't do?" he was asked by a journalist at the first night. "I could not dance in my ballet", he replied.[7] The lead dancers − Anton Dolin and Jeanette Minty − were prestigious, and the music (dramatising the to-and-fro of children, locals, guards, and tourists in front of Buckingham Palace) was a medley of horn-pipes and marches culminating in a rousing rendition of "London Pride", with brass at full whack amid peals of bells. He took eight curtain calls, but reviewers thought the evening old-fashioned both in music and style: "a teeny-weeny indulgence in elderly jokes and flag-wagging".[8]

A fortnight later, on 29 July, *Look after Lulu!* opened in London. Vivien Leigh had been able to take over the title role, and illumined by her performance the play was more successful. Before transferring to the West End it opened at the Royal Court Theatre, which hoped to stabilise its finances with a sure-fire crowd-pleaser from a known name. The production should have been an announcement that bridges were being built between Noël Coward and contemporary theatre. Like the original production of *Look Back in Anger* it was directed by Tony Richardson, part of the "New Wave" of British directors and associated with kitchen-sink realism. Among the cast was George Devine, co-founder of the English Stage Company and a champion of challenging new writing from Samuel Beckett to Edward Bond. But the combination of Noël's verbal wit with Feydeau's physical farce (characters hiding under beds and in bathrooms) had still not entirely melded, and Cecil Beaton's sets were thought handsome but overbearing. Within seven years John Mortimer would have much greater success with a translation of Feydeau's *A Flea in Her Ear*.

Between the American and British productions of *Look after Lulu!* Noël had finally decided to abandon Bermuda for good. His accountants suggested that Geneva would be the most financially prudent location, free of currency restrictions and with low taxes. Early in 1959 he had registered as a "subsidiary resident" of Geneva, while remaining domiciled in Bermuda, which he promptly fell in love with all over again now he was facing imminent departure. But in June he and Cole Lesley, after seeing a promising advert in the *Telegraph*, had gone in search of a new home at Les Avants, a village in the Vaud canton to the West of Switzerland, high above Montreux and reached by car or tiny railway. The chalet, set into four and a half acres of garden, was run-down and, Noël thought, ugly. But the views of Lac Léman in the distance surrounded by snow-tipped Alps were astounding. Noël bought it for £12,000 and was excited by the prospect of Switzerland's clean mountain air on his beleaguered lungs. The Bermudan life was left behind, his Chevrolet was shipped from Jamaica, and he decided not to care that a girls' finishing school just beneath them threatened noise and distraction.

Within not too long he would ensure a splendid set of neighbours in the form of soprano Joan Sutherland and her husband, conductor Richard Bonynge, whom he met on an Atlantic crossing the following decade and for whom he played estate agent, helping to broker their purchase of Chalet Monet, a little further up the mountain. Sutherland paid her debt by making a record of his more romantic songs that, although she insisted they were surprisingly operatic, did not sell as well as expected. Charlie Chaplin's estate was a twenty-minute drive south, and Vladimir Nabokov would soon be an unlikely local resident, setting up home in the Montreux

Palace hotel. He and Noël never met, but Nabokov was tickled by the local community of Humbert Humberts potential or actual, for James Mason, who took the role in Kubrick's *Lolita*, lived only a few miles away.

Joan Sutherland's home was positively rococo in its opulence, but Chalet Coward, as it became known (Noël had considered "Chilly Chalet"), was less extravagant. It contained Noël's eccentric stabs at interior decoration, hardly the last word in grandeur, and more Victorian than art deco: red ceiling over the stairs, cream walls, sofas and chintz and coloured carpets, books (and bathrooms) everywhere, and the piano loaded with framed photographs.[9] Walls were papered with posters and sheet music, and he created a studio to paint in. Light-blocking fir trees were removed – and conservation laws ignored. Noël was said to have silenced journalists clamouring to know why he had moved to Switzerland with two words: "Adore chocolates!"

Come the autumn audiences for *Look after Lulu!* had dwindled. By the time his furniture arrived at Les Avants from Bermuda in a heavy November blizzard the show had closed. Cole Lesley, mostly in charge of proceedings, panicked at Noël's more expensive choices and tried to take control of the budget without anyone noticing. Vivien Leigh spent Christmas with them in the chalet, mostly in tears. Gladys Calthrop joined them for New Year, and Noël – sending out hundreds of Christmas cards, each with a picture of himself – was happy with the new home, which he would keep for the rest of his life. His exile remained a metaphor for the way in which he seemed unable to find a place in British theatre, powerless to wrestle his talent into true reinvention. The Conservatives won the 1959 election and Noël thought it served Labour right.

Nineteen-sixty would bring the publication of his novel *Pomp and Circumstance*, one of two on which he had worked intermittently; the other, about the French Resistance, he abandoned, resolutely avoiding the serious. The book was a final gasp of his "Samolo" period, opening in the "gargantuan mauve blanc-mange" of Government House and showing the ex-pat community thrown into frenzy by an impending visit from the Queen and Prince Philip (who never appear). The narrator is Grizel Craigie, wife of an official and as convinced as her creator that the "dear Samolans" – to whom "sexual indulgence is as natural, enjoyable, and unimportant as eating mangoes" – have no wish or need for self-government and are loyal to the British crown. A duchess has an affair with a man called Bunny; chickenpox spreads; a clearly lesbian couple seemed to some reviewers, unaware of Noël's back catalogue, to be a flailing attempt at modernity. "Altogether", wrote *The Times*, "this would be an excellent novel for a deckchair at Ilfracombe."[10] It found a place on bestseller lists but was hardly a book to announce to a newly permissive decade that Noël Coward was back to stay.

But where once this seemingly endless period in the critical desert had enraged him, now he was mellower, happier – or so he claimed – to take refuge in work, sure that audiences would stay loyal even if he assumed he would never again be the subject of critical praise. It was Kenneth Tynan, savaging *Look after Lulu!* in the *New Yorker*, who had sounded the play's death knell on Broadway. He had first met Noël back in October 1951 and they could not help but like and admire one another, although Noël raged in his diary when Tynan invariably demolished his premieres. Watching one of his many and beloved cats on Jamaica crunch up a lizard, he wished "the lizard had been Kenneth Tynan".[11] But the day after filing his hatchet-job, Tynan was dining at Sardi's, looked up, and saw Noël come in, alone. There was nowhere to hide, and Noël came across to Tynan's table.

"Mr T," he said. "You are a cunt. Come and have dinner with me."[12]

THE WINGS

Noël Coward had high hopes, and high regard, for *Waiting in the Wings*, his play set in a retirement home for elderly actresses. He thought it a "Chekhovian lark", containing scenes among the best he had written, and it marks a veer away from camouflaged polemic (what his friends and even he referred to as a "finger-wag") and into a "late" phase of his writing. The script is shadowed by a consciousness of mortality, of houses being set in order before the final exit.[1] Premature, perhaps, given it was written in his late fifties. But not long after his sixtieth birthday he had suffered from phlebitis in one of his legs, and soon afterwards became severely congested in one of his lungs. He would do little to improve his health, despite doctors' orders, and after half-hearted attempts to give up cigarettes reverted to smoking his way through the days, refusing to take exercise but continuing to exhaust himself with travel and work.

In April 1960 Lorn Loraine was diagnosed with breast cancer and had a mastectomy. "Do <u>not</u>", he told her, "repeat <u>not</u>, allow the faintest thought of economy to enter your fluffy little head. Remember this is your master speaking and your master is accustomed to getting his own way. [. . .] There is to be <u>no</u> nonsense about the money side. Dear N.C. Limited pays <u>everything</u>. [. . .] The only thing that profoundly saddens me is that in future it will have to be Lorniebub, instead of Lorniebubs, but we must face these sorrows bravely."[2] But he was frightened: "I am well aware that we are all nearing the end of our lives but I don't want Lornie to go away yet."[3] *Waiting in the Wings* felt valedictory.

Noël longed for it to be a success, not least because it would be one in the eye to Binkie Beaumont, who, thinking the script old-fashioned, had refused to produce it. Old faithfuls such as Gladys Cooper or Edith Evans would have been natural casting, but Beaumont reported they had turned the play down, having never shown them the script. Financially secured by *West Side Story* and *My Fair Lady*, he agreed with Noël's estimation of younger playwrights, but conversely, wary of seeming safe and conventional, began to alienate himself both from Noël and from Terence Rattigan. His demands over the American production of *Nude with Violin* had been, Noël thought, "morally indefensible". Their friendship was "far more important than any contractual obligations in the world", but Beaumont's duplicity drove a wedge between them.[4] Michael Redgrave, in partnership with his lover and assistant Fred Sadoff, had founded a production company and eagerly accepted the new play. Noël's one-time affair with Redgrave did not smooth their disagreements during rehearsals, but by the time the preview run had opened in Dublin, on 8 August 1960, he was full of excitement. On his arrival in Ireland the crowds of photographers made him feel like a movie star. Local reviews were so enthusiastic that American newspapers flew their critics over to London for the premiere.

The action is set in "The Wings", a charity-run retirement home, and its creaking plot is of secondary importance to its conjuring of a world, and its tribute to a generation of actresses who in youth enchanted the Edwardian stage and in late middle-age toured with ENSA during the Second World War. Now, they do not belong, and are as "happy as you could expect a bunch of old women to be when the tide of life has turned away from them and left them high and dry watching the dark shadows growing longer and longer and waiting for the grave". Noël knew about the sniping of the elderly, the neuroses of ageing actresses, and the internecine battles of charity committees. The play has fun with all three. This was territory later claimed by writers such as Alan Bennett or Ronald Harwood; the latter's *Quartet* (1999) – about retired opera singers – owes *Waiting in the Wings* a great deal. From the sitcom *Waiting for God* to Bernice Rubens's novel *The Waiting Game*, the old people's home has become a familiar setting for bittersweet comedy, but Noël was among the first to mine its potential. John Arden's *The Happy Haven*, set in its eponymous home and featuring young actors in aged masks, would appear at the Royal Court the following year.

The play was an opportunity to bring together distinguished stars of Noël's youth, marshalled by the pioneering director Margaret Webster, who praised him professionally without qualification. They had difficulty gathering the performers – most of her suggestions turned out to be dead – but eventually they found the leads in the form of Marie Lohr and Sybil Thorndike, who thought it the best new work she had ever done.[5] Both the dialogue and the rehearsals were steeped in faulty memories, theatrical quarrel, and professional rivalry. Noël had provided a supporting role for Graham Payn, who seemed to take in good humour the fact that his own career had been all too obvious a model for the part, a former actor now secretary to the "The Wings", who has "little hope of becoming a star". Thorndike was Lotta Bainbridge and Lohr her fellow resident May Davenport. Their frostiness is explained by the past, as if Amanda and Sibyl have reunited in old age long after the final curtain of *Private Lives*: Lotta ran off with May's husband. Slowly their old-age, age-old feuds are resolved.

Waiting in the Wings can seem an exercise in nostalgia, or even an exercise in self-pity on the part of its ageing and out-of-fashion author, gullibly in thrall to the fakery of theatrical glamour. It is balanced on a knife-edge between a sentimental portrayal of fading faculties and a sugar-coated reassurance that old age isn't so bad after all. The eldest resident even enjoys the loving attentions of a gentleman caller. The cast list is made up of game old things poignant with fading stardom, mostly in control of their faculties and all in control of their bladders. But *Waiting in the Wings* is startlingly clear-eyed about the melancholy and cruelty of old age: "We haven't many years left and very, very little to look forward to." Noël would not have risked any explicit portrayal of physical indignities, but was honest about psychological ones. One of the actresses has dementia, and is living in her mind and in Shakespeare, lapsing into tears, confusing life with theatre. "It's a very nice house isn't it?" she is asked, referring to The Wings. "Capacity", she replies. Eventually she sets her room on fire, and is taken away. Those left behind discuss her plight. "I expect she's to be envied really. At least she doesn't realise what a bore it is, all this sitting about and waiting."

The sentimentality is almost always self-conscious. "Milton!" declaims a resident, quoting Wordsworth. "Thou should'st be living at this hour: England hath need of thee." Another sardonically mutters: "Curtain." The scene that risks nostalgia most acutely is a champagne-fuelled sing-song around the piano, for which Noël had written a new lyric: "We shall still be together when our life's journey ends." But the song is dismissed by one resident as "sentimental poppycock". After its final chord an elderly Irish actress crumples to the floor with a heart attack: "Mother of God, it's happening – it's happening to me." The curtain falls on her corpse with a line of cynically black humour straight out of Noël's earliest plays, which had often pondered whether it were better to be dead than alive: "The luck of the Irish!"

At moments *Waiting in the Wings* shows Noël clawing his way back to the style of *Private Lives*: "She was born in Winnipeg and then her whole family moved to Montreal." "Is it large?" "Winnipeg?" "No – her family." But sugariness and inconsequentiality were the accusations of near unanimously hostile reviews when, on 7 September 1960, *Waiting in the Wings* opened in the West End. "I have never read such abuse in my life", Noël wrote. "To read them was like being repeatedly slashed in the face."[6] The *Financial Times* thought the whole thing "nauseating", and even the most positive write-up, in the *Manchester Guardian*, found little to praise but bitchy wit.[7] Nevertheless, business remained healthy through a six-month run. "I cried buckets", John Betjeman wrote to Noël, "and smiled through the tears and cried again. It is an infinitely subtle and warm-hearted play."[8] But it was not a smash hit, and did not seem to anyone a sudden return to form for Noël Coward. A production in New York, in 1999, would be a star vehicle for Lauren Bacall and Rosemary Harris, but both the onstage death and the fire were cut, as if the revival had produced what Noël might have been expected to write.

It is with the character of Lotta Bainbridge that *Waiting in the Wings* takes its place as an entry in Noël's career-long dismissal of convention. Its twin themes are the impossible tussle between career and family, and the belief, daring even today, that water can be thicker than blood. Lotta is one of his younger characters – Judith Bliss, Amanda Prynne, Larita Whittaker – grown old. She exemplifies the professional and personal struggles of Gertrude Lawrence, as if the play conferred on Lawrence the old age she had been denied. "Nothing worth having is ever handed to you gratis", Lawrence had written, unable to give up the stage for a life of marriage and motherhood, and usually at loggerheads with her daughter. "The price of my career [. . .] has always been my personal happiness."[9] Approaching old age too soon, Noël, who began the play shortly after his tormented affair with William Traylor, was equally familiar with the personal sacrifices of professional dedication.

Like many an actress, Lotta is without a pension and struggling for money and work, wondering who she is without the theatre. The breadwinner of her family, she had a talent that outstripped her husband's, an imbalance he could not forgive and which wrecked the marriage. She has long prioritised freedom and independence over motherhood, and has been estranged from her son for seventeen years. He arrives in the third act, and invites her to live with him in Canada.* "You keep on making almost defiant statements", she tells him. "'I am your son.' 'You are my mother.' Do you really believe that they mean much?" She rejects the offer, choosing instead, despite the indignities and the solitude, to stay among her chosen family of actors, in their crumbling retirement home. "I was in deep despair, lonely and hopeless and feeling as if I were going to prison, and now, after a year of prison, I feel suddenly free. Isn't that curious?" So she and her chosen family, humour and memory their tonic, wait in The Wings – neither for Godot nor for God.

Noël's own sense of impending death, even at sixty, was leading him to take stock. He had given up on critical approval – "I really do seem to be without honour in my own country" – but was in good spirits: "I must remember to count every happy day as a dividend. I've had a wonderful life."[10] His chief resolution, as 1960 slipped into 1961, was to complete and stage the musical on which he'd been working for the last few years and which, after various iterations, had become *Sail Away* (the title song recycled from *Ace of Clubs*). He had enjoyed returning to the piano, and may have felt less estranged from the world of musicals than he did from

---

* With uncanny prophecy, he is named Alan Bennet. But the script was complete before the success, in August 1960, of *Beyond the Fringe*, which would have first brought Alan Bennett to Coward's attention.

contemporary playwrights; he had adored both Lionel Bart's *Oliver!*
and Lionel Bart. (Bart loved Noël, "unreservedly and uninhibitedly
[. . .] up until now I was the only person I would run to the
ends of the earth for. There is now one other – you.")[11] He had
abandoned any ambitions for operetta in favour of a big escapist
Broadway show. That the designer, Oliver Smith, had worked on
everything from *Oklahoma!* to *My Fair Lady* was an announcement
that Noël was writing in a different, more modern, key. With the
help of Peter Matz's orchestrations, the score is more redolent of
Richard Rodgers and Frank Loesser than of Novello or Lehár. It is
surprising that Noël had waited until this late in his career to plumb
the dramatic and comedic possibilities of an ocean liner, on which
much of *Sail Away* takes place, but then Cole Porter's *Anything Goes*
had been stiff competition.

The promise of the musical sweetened the pill when *Waiting in
the Wings* closed early in 1961. That January, still in a rage about
the state of modern drama, Noël published an article in *The Sunday
Times*. Under photographs of Shelagh Delaney, Arnold Wesker, and
Samuel Beckett, the essay let rip, offering "a little gentle advice
to the young revolutionaries of today [. . .] Consider the Public".
Noël was safely in Jamaica, tending to Ian Fleming, who was suffering from flu, with more assiduity than Fleming's wife thought
strictly necessary. The paper's correspondence pages bristled. "How
refreshing to read Noël Coward's castigation of the revolting and
sordid rubbish inflicted on so much of today's theatre." "Can he
not accept the fact that his day is now over?" "My one thought after
seeing *Waiting in the Wings* was of geronticide."[12] But Noël wasn't
finished. The following week brought "The Scratch-and-Mumble
School", and a week after came "A Warning to the Critics". He
expended a number of column inches arguing that it was much
easier to play a working-class character than an upper-class one.
"For any experienced actor who has mastered the poetic nuances
of Shakespearean verse and the intricate subtleties of modern high
comedy, 'Dear Old Dad' in a kitchen-sink drama is the equivalent
of a couple of aspirins and a nice lie-down."[13]

Even Kenneth Tynan had recently admitted that British theatre was
in a rut, torn between left-wing writers and conservative audiences;

he pointed out that angry new plays offered few solutions to the problems about which they raged. But Noël's articles, fiercely attacked by dramatists and critics alike, were self-destructive, and confirmed to many that he should now be permanently put out to pasture. He had written them in the spirit of a final immolation, as if to bow out in a blaze of unrepentant glory: "It saddens me to think that my career is over and done for."[14] Conversely, this led him to spend much of the spring fine-tuning *Sail Away* with care and determination. The show was to open on Broadway in October, and he spent the summer in New York directing rehearsals, with the help of choreographer Joe Layton.

In the supporting role of Mimi Paragon, a brash American divorcee who is a hostess on the ship, he had cast Elaine Stritch, then thirty-six and already Tony-nominated. Stritch, raised a strict Catholic, was heavily reliant on alcohol to conquer her considerable stage fright. She had a habit of disappearing during rehearsals but Noël, as if recognising the nervous desperation from which her neuroses sprang, remained confident in her talent and was soon thrilled with her performance. Her dry wit gave fresh life to his lyrics, as when Mimi studies an Italian phrasebook and bemoans the failure of the Tower of Babel: "If it hadn't been for that | Bloody building falling flat | I would not have had to learn Italiano. | And keep muttering 'Si, si' | And 'Mi Chiamino Mimi' | Like an ageing Metropolitan soprano!" Noël also had fun with comic vignettes of the liner's passengers, especially an old married couple, given a song to themselves in the London transfer: "We're a dear old couple who DETEST one another | We've detested one another since our bridal night | Which was squalid, unattractive and convulsive | And proved beyond dispute | That we were mutually repulsive."

The pre-New York tour was so successful that advance sales were immense, more than paying off the huge investment in the show from the American heiress Helen Bonfils. But the romantic lead, played by the opera singer Jean Fenn, seemed out of place: "she is cursed with refinement", Noël told Gladys Calthrop, "and does everything 'beautifully'. Oh dear, I long for her to pick her nose or fart and before I'm through with her, she'll do both."[15] But in the end Noël took the riskily last-minute decision to merge two roles into one. Fenn's part was cut entirely and much of its material handed to Stritch. What could have been trite in the hands of a lyric soprano was transformed by Stritch's husky mezzo, which was marinated in cigarettes and alcohol and world-weary pizzazz. In England and America she would carry the show, brassy and camp in the comic numbers ("Why Do The Wrong People Travel-Travel-Travel?") and moving in the romantic ones. Noël's lifelong disillusion about love, exacerbated by old age, had found its way into the lyrics: "Need it be such unbearable sadness to face the truth? | Love, with its passionate madness, belongs to youth. | Later than spring, our values change, my dear | It would be strange, my dear | If they should stay." Stritch's own love life was unhappy, and her Catholicism had led her to turn down marriage proposals from divorced men. She was desperately in love with the homosexual actor Rock Hudson, and would not marry until she was fifty. She and Noël were kindred spirits, and she later said of him: "he was one of the saddest men I've ever known".[16]

The Broadway run did only middling business and was overshadowed by Noël's rows with his American business manager, Charles Russell, who, when starting out as an actor, had had a small part in *In Which We Serve*. Noël begrudged him his high percentage of ticket sales and they had begun to quarrel badly; there followed months of legal wrangling with Russell and his partner Lance Hamilton, in order to end the association. "Unless", Noël wrote, "[there is] a secret contract binding them to me for life, in which case I shall commit suicide."[17] When the show came into London in 1962, it circumvented disappointing reviews to run for over two hundred and fifty performances, and Noël would go to Australia to supervise a production there. But he thought that despite strong individual numbers a thin script meant *Sail Away* was never greater than the sum of its parts.

He would write just one more musical. Terence Rattigan's *The Sleeping Prince* was ten years old and familiar to audiences through its film version, *The Prince and the Showgirl*, starring Marilyn Monroe. Noël had turned down a role in the film, but accepted the invitation to contribute music and lyrics to a musical version, titled *The Girl Who Came to Supper*, which would premiere on Broadway in December

1963. Set in 1911, and about an American chorus girl's involvement with the Prince Regent of Carpathia, it was an opportunity to combine Ruritanian romance with an array of Cockney tunes, and was a gesture of loyalty to Rattigan and to nostalgia in general. But in the wake of *My Fair Lady* it seemed paltry fare, and when at the time of its previews President Kennedy, whom Noël had met and liked during the run of *Sail Away*, was assassinated, the glitz of the Broadway opening was diminished. Noël, shocked and upset, had hastily to replace an early number about regicide called "Long Live the King". The critics were mildly more enthusiastic than they had been for *Sail Away*, but audiences did not flock and the show has never been produced in England. The following year Noël would sanction *High Spirits*, a musical version of *Blithe Spirit* by Hugh Martin and Timothy Gray, and was so keen on the duo's work that, assisted by Graham Payn, he directed both the American and the English productions, with Beatrice Lillie and Cicely Courtneidge as his Arcatis. On Broadway the show was nominated for a clutch of Tony Awards and enjoyed a decent run; in London the reviews were dreadful, and the show didn't last three months.

It seemed impossible for Noël to work on a project that delighted both the critics and the public. It is a moment at which to consider an alternative history, to imagine a sudden heart attack in the winter snow of Les Avants felling Noël Coward in his early sixties, and giving his biographers the task of charting a terminal professional decline. He had not been forgotten – productivity had seen to that – but it seemed uncertain whether, and for what, he would be remembered. The seemingly final rupture with the golden age of his career had come in October 1961, when Jack Wilson, after years of heavy drinking and little work, had a heart attack and died in his bedroom at home. He was sixty-two. Noël struggled to remember the young man with whom he had been so passionately in love. "I was shocked and startled", he told Lorn Loraine, "but little more than that. I haven't loved him for so many years, and the last few of them he has been only half-alive anyway."[18] On one of their final meetings, seeing Jack so weak from drink and heart trouble that he could not stand, Noël had wept in the car on the journey home.[19] Jack's wife, Natasha, had written to Noël in despair, "aghast and speechless with horror" at the state into which their lives had dwindled. "I will pass over all the outrages [. . .] he had hallucinations and delusions about seeing strange masked people bursting into his room and preventing him to sleep!" Noël offered her Blue Harbour for recuperation, and she was "infinitely grateful".[20]

Noël's heart was hardening, metaphorically and (according to his doctors) literally. "Of course I am sad", he wrote. "Of course I feel horrid inside. But not nearly so much as I might have. To me he died years ago. [. . .] This growing old! This losing of friends and breaking of links with the past. One by one they go – a bit chipped off here, a bit chipped off there. It is an inevitability that one must prepare the heart and mind for. I wonder how long it will be before I make my last exit."[21]

THE LIVING MASK

A Suite in Three Keys

A VERY CLEAR DAY
A RECKONING UNDER THE MOON
THE PERFORMANCE OF HIS LIFE

CAST

NOËL COWARD, *a playwright and actor, ageing and eminent*
COLE LESLEY, *his devoted assistant*
GRAHAM PAYN, *his intimate companion*

A Very Clear Day:
EDITH EVANS, *an eminent actress*
MAGGIE SMITH, *a young actress of increasing renown*
EDITH SITWELL, *an ageing poet*
JOHN OSBORNE, *a playwright*
HAROLD PINTER, *a playwright*
QUEEN ELIZABETH THE QUEEN MOTHER

A Reckoning under the Moon:
VIVIAN MATALON, *a young director*
IRENE WORTH, *an American actress*
LILLI PALMER, *a German actress*

The Performance of his Life:
LORN LORAINE, *Noël Coward's secretary*
JOAN HIRST, *her assistant*
GEOFFREY JOHNSON, *Noël Coward's American manager*
GLADYS CALTHROP, *Noël Coward's oldest friend, a retired designer*
PETER COLLINSON, *a film director*
MICHAEL CAINE, *an actor*
KENNETH TYNAN, *a theatre critic*
HUGH "BINKIE" BEAUMONT, *a theatre producer*
MARLENE DIETRICH, *a German-born actress and singer*

The action takes place chiefly in London, New York, and at Noël Coward's Swiss chalet.

TIME: 1963–1973

A VERY CLEAR DAY

25 April 1966; the Queen's Theatre, London. Onstage, the sitting room of a private suite of a luxurious hotel in Switzerland. The performance is the premiere of NOËL COWARD*'s short comedy,* Come Into the Garden, Maud, *one of a new trilogy called* Suite in Three Keys. COWARD, *wearing a loud checked suit, is acting the role of* VERNER CONKLIN, *a wealthy (and married) American. Opposite him is the German actress* LILLI PALMER, *playing* MAUD CARAGNANI, *a wealthy British-born socialite with whom* VERNER *intends to elope.* COWARD, *at sixty-six, looks ten years older, and, beneath a white hair-piece, ten years older still. The audience is star-studded; critics scribble in aisle seats.*

VERNER (COWARD): All I know is I've fallen in love with you, and all I *want* to know is whether you've fallen in love with me. It's as simple as that. Once that's clear all the other complications can be taken care of. Have you? – Or rather could you – do you think – be in love with me?

MAUD (PALMER): Yes Verner. I think I could, and I think I am. Falling in love sounds so comprehensive and all embracing and violent. It's the stuff of youth really, not of middle-age, and yet – and yet . . .[1]

Suite in Three Keys *was to be Noël's final stage appearance, and he could hardly be accused of bowing out with a lack of ambition. Each play of the trilogy was set in the same luxurious suite of a Swiss hotel and written to be performed by the same trio of actors, with Noël joined by Irene Worth and Lilli Palmer. Two minor characters were common to each: the handsome waiter Felix, and an offstage figure called Mariette. Two short dramas – *Come Into the Garden, Maud* and *Shadows of the Evening* – form a contrasting double bill, the first about an American couple visited by an Italian socialite with whom the man elopes, and the second focusing on a man dying of cancer whose wife and mistress call a truce so as to spend his remaining months with him. These were to play alternately with the full-length *A Song at Twilight*, about an ageing writer forced to confront his past. If the *Suite*'s sole comic piece was about how to live, then its two companions were about how to die.

The new decade had brought with it a reversal in Noël's fortunes that arguably transformed his writing. Back in May 1963 the enterprising young director James Roose-Evans had mounted a production of *Private Lives* at the Hampstead Theatre Club, of which he was founder-director. Three years old, the Club had staged the double bill of Harold Pinter – *The Room* and *The Dumb Waiter* – which Noël had so disliked, but the plays had given the small theatre a considerable reputation. In its new home of a Portakabin in Swiss Cottage, Roose-Evans had made the case for *Private Lives*, which had not been staged in London since the war, as something more than a dated comedy, casting the young actors Edward de Souza and Rosemary Martin. Daringly, he put the whole thing in modern dress, and references to the Duke of Westminster were changed to Aristotle Onassis. Martin was twenty-six and wore trousers; she danced the Twist, not the Charleston.

"It is a long time", wrote Harold Hobson in *The Sunday Times*, "since I passed in the theatre an evening of such exuberant and troubled pleasure."[2] His argument was that a theatre championing writers such as Pinter was exactly the right location for a Coward revival, and in praising the script's perfection he invoked not only Congreve but Samuel Beckett. It was at Hobson's urging that Noël, on his way from Switzerland to a holiday in Thailand, was persuaded to stop in London for a few days in order to see a matinee. Noël's mind was full of preparations for *The Girl Who Came to Supper*, and his flying visit to England (where, having transferred his domicile from Bermuda to Switzerland, he was now permitted to spend six months each year) was taken up with meeting the Queen Mother for dinner at the Savoy later that day. Pleased as he was with the revival of *Private Lives* he found it slightly inelegant and had no conception that the updating would be especially important.

Soon the producer Michael Codron brought the staging into the West End, and Roose-Evans insisted on retaining the lead actors, refusing any big-name replacements. Noël was in San Francisco by the time of the first night, but Cole Lesley rang him with a report of the reviews. "Has there ever been a better play of its kind written in English?" asked the *Telegraph*. *The Times* argued that the script transcended the 1930s; the warring couple now seemed "timeless figures of fun". Not everyone agreed with the case for *Private Lives*'s profundity, and with the indifferent reactions to *The Girl Who Came to Supper* and *High Spirits* still to come, it was not an overnight renaissance for Noël Coward. But it was the beginning of a rediscovery of his earlier work by a younger generation. The *Guardian* noticed how, while older members of the audience were grumbling about the updated costumes and the way in which "Someday I'll Find You" was sung with a noticeable lack of romance, the stalls were full of "the young knocking themselves out and laughing like crazy at how witty a thirty-three-year-old play can be".[3]

Private Lives settled into a long run, and fitted the West End of the early 1960s, where bitter social realism was already being challenged by the seriously playful. *A Severed Head*, J. B. Priestley's adaptation of Iris Murdoch's novel, was enjoying a run of over one thousand performances. Murdoch had fashioned a tangle of six privileged middle-class characters in almost all its possible sexual permutations, using the conventions of farce to question whether it is really possible to transcend conventional morality in the name of sexual freedom. The novel and play were harbingers of the sexual revolution, and the parallels with Noël's early work now seem unavoidable. Murdoch apparently loved Noël's approaching her at the Connaught Hotel and professing undying admiration, although Princess Margaret appeared and cut their meeting short. Forty years after the Bright Young Things had rejected the conventions of their parents, a new decade of liberation would see the emergence of the women's liberation movement, the legalisation of homosexuality, and various anti-establishment countercultures peopled by disaffected youth searching for escape through free love and drug use. *The Vortex* was successfully televised by the BBC, and had increasing relevance as a portrait of a generation groping unhappily at different forms of escape against a backdrop of potential destruction. The threat of nuclear war shadowed the swing of the sixties, and discussion of the atom bomb in *Private Lives* was horribly resonant to audiences who, the previous year, had lived through the Cuban Missile Crisis.

Noël's reaction to the stand-off had been one of mordant sarcasm. "This, my darlings, means war! Isn't that fun?" The atomic bomb he thought "far too vast a nightmare to be frightened of".[4] Among the many paradoxes of Noël Coward is the fact that this by now avowedly old-fashioned conservative found renewed relevance during a period defined by its radicalism and change, and – from October 1964 – by its Labour government. Returning regularly to his island or his mountain, he seemed ever more remote from reality and most of all from youth culture. But he became an icon to leaders of a younger generation whose work and style he professed to dislike. The sixties would see a satire boom, led by the popular revue *Beyond the Fringe*. Back in 1924 a reviewer had written that "it is almost entirely Mr Coward's doing that irony and revue have been introduced", and Noël's kinship with the deadpan monologues of Peter Cook or the satirical cabaret of Dudley Moore was obvious.[5] In Jamaica he would be introduced to Twiggy, whose short hair and tiny frame highlighted the parallels between twenties and sixties fashion; they became friends, and he hoped she might play Elvira.[6] (She did, in 1997.) The Beatles he thought overrated, and his opinion would be confirmed when he heard them live in July 1965 and was overwhelmed by the noise and hysteria of the audience. He went backstage but, aware of his opinions, they refused to see him. This he thought proof that they were not only talentless but graceless, although Paul McCartney (who eventually recorded "A Room With a View") came to find him and make peace.

But to Dave Davies, lead guitarist of the Kinks, Noël was a "master songwriter whose view of English culture resonated with us"; his brother Ray, the band's lead singer, met Noël in Singapore and thought him "a great writer and musician in his own right", taking to heart Noël's advice: "always keep a smile on your face when singing about anything that makes you angry".[7] Popular sixties groups such as the Bonzo Dog Doo-Dah Band seemed partly to be modelling themselves on him in their juxtaposition of avant-garde pop with traditional jazz and music hall; and comic songs by Spike

Milligan or Bernard Cribbins were bestselling records throughout the decade. Noël even chose Cribbins's "Hole in the Ground" as his favourite track on *Desert Island Discs* (above Rachmaninov's second piano concerto). By the 1970s, even during the punk era of rock music, a singer-songwriter such as Ian Dury would openly confess his debt with lyrics such as "Noël Coward was a charmer | As a writer he was brahma." Joe Cocker made an album called *Mad Dogs and Englishmen.*

Noël was a reminder to the new decade that sexual intercourse, *pace* Larkin, had not begun "between the end of the 'Chatterley' ban and the Beatles' first LP", and that the journey to the liberations of the sixties had not been a continual upward trajectory but a zig-zag of eras, alternately permissive and intolerant, with which Noël had been in daring dialogue. The Lord Chamberlain's office was finally relaxing its censorship of the British stage. Noël had seen and admired Joan Henry's 1960 play *Look on Tempests*, an account of an upper-middle-class man accused of gross indecency. Many of the successful dramatists whose careers took off in the 1960s – Edward Albee, Joe Orton, Peter Shaffer – were homosexual. Orton's *Entertaining Mr Sloane* was admired and funded by Terence Rattigan; it opened in the West End in 1964, and was closer to Noël's alliance of black comedy and camp than any hit production of the previous decade. Albee had had a huge success with *Who's Afraid of Virginia Woolf?*, and while Noël thought Albee "talked quite a lot of cock", he found the play itself quite brilliant. In 1964 Albee elected to introduce a collection of Noël's scripts in America. "Mr Coward writes dialogue as well as any man going; it is seemingly effortless, surprising in the most wonderfully surprising places, and 'true' – very, very true."[8]

Albee had been astonished to find that most of Noël's scripts were out of print in the United States and when, in 1964, ITV invited Noël personally to introduce a new series under the title *A Choice of Coward*, plays such as *Design for Living* or *Present Laughter* were, for many, new discoveries. On the whole the productions received rave reviews (Hattie Jacques, established *Carry On* star, was Madame Arcati). And just as *High Spirits* was beginning its successful run on Broadway, Laurence Olivier scheduled *Hay Fever* for the opening season of his newly founded National Theatre Company at the Old Vic, making Noël the first living dramatist to be so honoured. Exhausted by work on three troublesome musicals in as many years, Noël was initially reluctant to direct: "I would rather undertake to play *Peer Gynt on Ice* than show one actor, however talented, how to walk across the stage."[9] But he was persuaded, because the cast, as he told them on the first day of rehearsals, "could play the Albanian telephone directory".[10] His childhood neighbour Edith Evans was Judith Bliss, and among the younger actors were Lynn Redgrave, Derek Jacobi, Maggie Smith, and her soon to be husband, Robert Stephens.

Smith, who had begun her career in revue, was cast as the seductive Myra Arundel and her combination of high camp and intense melancholy made her the perfect "Coward" actor, capable of expressing truth through, rather than despite, the brilliant mannerism of her performances; she confessed her stylistic debt to her close friend Kenneth Williams, himself a Coward devotee. It was no coincidence that she excelled at the National in Restoration comedy, even though Noël continued to insist he hated the genre, refusing the offer to direct Congreve's *Love for Love* at the Old Vic. Smith and Robert Stephens were marketed as the Lunts' inheritors, and would eventually channel the breakdown of their marriage into violently comic renderings of *Private Lives* and *Design for Living.* Understanding that Noël found humour in the most unremarkable of words, Smith made even innocuous phrases immortal, famously bringing the house down with her mournful drawl: "this haddock's disgusting".

In rehearsals Edith Evans was flustered and nervous, thinking herself too old for the part and apparently threatened by Smith's talent, and devastating send-up of her imperious style. "The classic example", Noël told Joyce Carey, "was her insistence on saying 'On a <u>very</u> clear day you can see Marlow'. Finally, when I had corrected her for the umpteenth time, pointing out that the 'very' was very <u>very</u> superfluous to my intent, I heard myself saying 'No, dear, on a <u>clear</u> day you can see Marlow — on a <u>very</u> clear day you can see Marlowe and Beaumont and Fletcher.' Which I was rather pleased with."[11] Memories of his youthful performance in *The Knight of the Burning Pestle* ran deep; an attention to the minutest detail of his dialogue ran even deeper. During early previews Evans was coaxed out of hotel rooms only by blistering lectures from Noël, and by accounts of how good Maggie Smith had been when standing in as Judith Bliss.

Hay Fever opened in London in October 1964 and its massive success eclipsed the West End failure of *High Spirits*. Olivier to Noël: "OH MY LOVELY BOY ISNT IT GREAT GREAT GREAT AND LOVELY LOVELY LOVELY GLAMOROUS AND EARTH SHAKING. BRAVOS TO MY BELOVED ONE — AND — ONLY PRETTIEST AND BEST. OH I AM SO HAPPY HAPPY HAPPY." Noël to Olivier: "WHAT A FRIGID UNGENEROUS LITTLE TELEGRAM."[12] A West End revival of *Present Laughter* was scheduled, the first in nearly twenty years. In the *New Statesman* Ronald Bryden argued that Noël was "a national treasure" and "demonstrably the greatest living English playwright".[13] Noël bought himself a Mercedes Benz, placed his income in a Credit Suisse account at a rate of 7.4 per cent tax, and basked in his newfound success and solvency. On 30 November he presented a television tribute for Winston Churchill's ninetieth birthday, at Churchill's personal request. "When it was finished", Clementine Churchill told Noël, "Winston clamoured for more."[14]

Noël ended 1964 in metre-deep snow at Les Avants, his career having been transformed over the previous eighteen months. He was tired by intense activity and the incessant news of death, not only of figures from his early life – Cole Porter, Elsa Maxwell – but of Ian Fleming who, a heavy drinker and smoker, had suffered a fatal heart attack in August, aged just fifty-eight. Noël did not regret having turned down firmly the opportunity to play the title character in *Dr. No*, the first of the Bond films, but he grieved bitterly the absence of his neighbour on Jamaica. A trip to Capri to celebrate his sixty-fifth birthday had been dreary, but he enjoyed his Switzerland Christmas, which he spent quietly with Cole Lesley and Graham Payn, while beginning to make notes for a third memoir, *Past Conditional*, which he would never finish. He and Cole slid down the mountain on sledges each day, and sat together afterwards, back at the chalet, companionably sharing *The Times* crossword. The newspaper's front page, in January the following year, announced Churchill's death.

There had never been a reversal of fortunes quite like it in the history of British theatre. (Terence Rattigan, in ill health, had retired to Bermuda to work mainly in screenwriting.) Ironically Noël did not think that the new decade offered any particular sign of society's improvement, and he continued to rail against the abolition of the death penalty, against youth culture – "I despise the young" – and the scandal of the Profumo affair. Even the promise of sexual liberation led to nothing but suspicion. Taken to the resort of Fire Island, off the coast of Long Island in New York and known as a liberal refuge for homosexual travellers, he was appalled, thinking the place "macabre, sinister, irritating and somehow tragic".[15] Nor was everything he did unanimously acclaimed. His subservient broadcast to Churchill, in which he addressed the former prime minister as "Sir" throughout, led to critical attack, and a further short story collection, *Pretty Polly Barlow*, was as poorly reviewed as the film of the title story that would be made in 1967.

In an eternal fight with the onset of age, and now suffering with a stomach ulcer, a blocked artery in his leg, and endless teeth trouble, he visited the Swiss surgeon Paul Niehans, developer of a cellular therapy popular with celebrities who could afford it. Nearly forty years before, Noël had predicted just such a treatment in a newspaper article: "We shall in the very near future find ourselves injected with peculiar animal glands . . ." In *Private Lives* Elyot asks Amanda whether she would be "young always? If you could choose?" "Not", she replies, "if it meant having awful bull's glands popped into me." "Cows for you, dear", says Elyot. "Bulls for me." Niehans actually favoured sheep (Merino sheep from New Zealand, specifically), and cells from embryos were injected, expensively and painfully, into the buttocks of Noël Coward, who wasn't sure he noticed any discernible effect. The treatment is now categorically dismissed as quackery and in 1965 Noël eventually resorted to surgery and had a face-lift. During the operation he had a small heart attack, something he found out only later.

Secured by success he could make other, less painful, ventures into restoration. Almost all his projects were now streaked with argument, from the rupture with Binkie Beaumont and Charles Russell to rows with both Beatrice Lillie and Cicely Courtneidge during rehearsals for *High Spirits* (Lillie's husband had been summoned to give Noël a piece of his wife's mind). Rather than settling for all-purpose niceness, Noël could exist only at the extremes of his character, continuing to combine surges of temper with great flights of generosity and kindness. The actress Madge Titheradge had died after suffering severe arthritis for twenty years; he and the Lunts quietly pooled resources to pay for her cortisone injections.[16] Younger actors discovered he enjoyed taking the role of father-confessor. Anna Massey, daughter of Adrianne Allen and Raymond Massey, was in her late twenties and recently divorced from Jeremy Brett, who had left her for another man. She found Noël's care and advice indispensable, noting that his "caustic humour" completely disappeared when she was in need of comfort: "he showed me a side of himself that I suspect few people knew existed".[17] Billie Whitelaw, sharing a dressing room with Maggie Smith at the National, thought him "unexpectedly humble" and "liked him enormously, which astonished me, since when I first came down from the North, people like Noël Coward and Terence Rattigan were high on the list of those who, in our arrogance, ignorance and youthful hubris, we wanted to sweep into the Thames."[18]

He also made efforts to patch old quarrels. "I very much fear", he admitted to Graham Greene, "that you and I got off to a sticky start all those years ago. You clearly thought my attitude to life was a little *soufflé*-ish and I must confess I found yours occasionally *al dente* [. . . but] you are without doubt one of the finest writers in the language."[19] Back in 1962 he had finally approached Edith Sitwell, forty years after sending her up in *London Calling!*. "DELIGHTED", she wired in answer. "FRIENDSHIP NEVER TOO LATE." They had met later that year, he peering at Sitwell from behind dark glasses after conjunctivitis; she in turban, fur coat, and slippers. He apologised for having hurt her feelings, and afterwards sent her a painting and his *Collected Short Stories*. "There are no short stories I admire more", she replied, enclosing a book of her own by return.[20] "Three-quarters of it is gibberish", Noël privately thought. "I must crush down these thoughts otherwise the dove of peace will shit on me." He was pleased to have closed their long argument, having found her "completely charming, very amusing and rather touching".[21]

But they could not make up for lost time: Sitwell died in December 1964.

The most valuable bridges mended were with the Angry Young Men. Noël's constant attacks on plays he disliked led John Osborne finally to crack: "I have always had the profoundest respect for you, both for what you do and as a unique and moving figure on our landscape. You are a genius. However, I think it is impertinent to pass judgement on other writers in this lordly way to gaggles of sniggering journalists. It is undignified, unkind and unnecessary." Noël professed himself "grateful" for the letter, which gave him "a sharp and much deserved jolt [. . .] forgive me if I have inadvertently hurt you or even irritated you".[22] The letter came with an invitation both for lunch and for a closer friendship, and Osborne made efforts to mount a production of *Design for Living*: "I've been mad about it for years".[23] When, at the end of the decade, he suffered a bad bout of depression, Noël sent him a valued telegram: "MAY I REITERATE I LOVE YOU".[24] Political and theatrical disagreements with Arnold Wesker were also soothed by friendship and mutual admiration, and although Noël refused to fund Wesker's touring festival Centre 42, he would agree briefly to perform, his false teeth gritted, in scenes from Wesker's *The Kitchen* for a Royal Court fundraising gala. It was a symbolically healing appearance.

In Harold Pinter too, despite early misgivings, Noël found an unlikely kindred spirit. He had had a Damascene conversion on seeing Pinter's *The Caretaker* in 1960, and he began to come round to this exciting new voice: "a sort of Cockney Ivy Compton-Burnett". On the face of it the play, a power struggle between two brothers and a tramp, was "everything I hate most in the theatre [. . . but] the writing is at moments brilliant and quite unlike anyone else's [. . .] I think I'm on to Pinter's wavelength".[25] Soon he was acclaiming Pinter as the "only one of the *soi-disant* avant-garde who has genuine originality", and Pinter told him that "yours is an opinion for which I have an immeasurable respect".[26] Noël contributed £1000 to the film of *The Caretaker*. Similarities of style and technique between them were becoming more apparent and, after Noël's death, Pinter would stage *Blithe Spirit* at the National, arguing that it was a heftier work than its author ever admitted. "Noël

Coward calls this play an improbable farce," he told the actors. "I just wish to make one thing clear – I do not regard it as improbable and I do not regard it as a farce."[27]

Sixty-five years old, Noël permitted no let-up in his schedule, and castigated Graham Payn, who now had a London flat of his own when he was not in Jamaica or Switzerland, for remaining "pathologically idle".[28] Travelling to New York and London, Noël rehearsed the revival of *Present Laughter*, oversaw the replacement of Edith Evans by Celia Johnson in *Hay Fever*, and attended *The Crucible*, finally coming round to Arthur Miller and professing the play thrilling. He then went with Cole Lesley to Jamaica where, in February 1965, the "dear darling Queen Mother" was to pay a visit. The island buzzed with police and rumour. Noël's friendship with her, despite his misty-eyed adoration of royalty, had become genuinely close, although he sometimes found it aggravating to be on best behaviour. "It isn't that I have a basic urge to say 'fuck' every five minutes, but I'm conscious of a faint resentment that I couldn't if I wanted to."[29] She enjoyed the company of gay men, from Benjamin Britten to Cecil Beaton, her acceptance highlighting their dual-headed social status as establishment outsiders.

Noël oversaw every detail of the visit. Lunch (coconut curry, fish mousse, rum cream pie) was to be held not at Blue Harbour but at the rather more basic and intimate surrounds of Firefly Hill. The Lunts came, as did his neighbour Blanche Blackwell. "I am at her feet", Noël wrote deferentially of the Queen Mother, his tongue nowhere near his cheek. "She did me great honour."[30] He was duly thanked enthusiastically and she invited him to Sandringham to hear a "famous Russian cellist (I can't spell him)". Noël asked her whether he should brush up his Russian, which was "limited at the moment to 'How do you do?', 'Shut up you Pig', and 'She has a White Blouse'."[31] History does not record whether Mstislav Rostropovich was ever treated to Noël's array of Russian phrases or indeed whether he stayed on for the dinner during which Noël and the Queen Mother led a rousing rendition of "My Old Man Said Follow the Van".

After the Queen Mother's departure Noël worked quietly in Jamaica on *Suite in Three Keys*, finishing *A Song at Twilight* on 27 March

1965. That day Clemence Dane, now in severe ill health, put on some make-up, tied a purple scarf around her head, and threw a small party for her friends. She died the next morning. Her departure was hard to bear, and Noël's grief was exacerbated by guilt over their various rows and the fact that she had not lived to read his last letter to her. "One more old friend gone – the cupboard is getting barer."[32] He wrote to her partner, Olwen, offering financial support. "It's just like you", she replied, "and gave me such a warm feeling. But I'm quite all right – <u>really</u> – Winifred has left everything to me and the accountant is letting me have any money I need. [. . .] Winifred always spoke of her time in Jamaica as the happiest holiday she'd ever had."[33]

In May he flew to London in order to film a small part in *Bunny Lake is Missing*, Otto Preminger's film adaptation, more admired now than it was at the time, of Merriam Modell's novel about a mother searching for her missing daughter. Among the cast were Laurence Olivier as a detective, and the young actor Keir Dullea, soon to appear in *2001: A Space Odyssey*. ("Keir Dullea, Gone Tomorrow", was Noël's view.) Noël played a slimy landlord, "an elderly drunk, queer masochist! Hurray! That's me all over."[34] "He's a bloody pervert if you want my opinion sir!" says a policeman about the landlord. "Please," says Olivier's detective, "he works for the BBC." Noël used a cable-knit jumper, his own voice, and a misbehaving Chihuahua, telling it sharply that it would never make another Lassie.

The rest of the year he devoted to *Suite in Three Keys* and to solitary travel, spending September in Rome and Switzerland before, in October, flying to Bombay and then sailing south-west to the Seychelles. India he found uncomfortable, and he mourned the demise of colonialism while managing to enjoy the experience, now rare, of being entirely alone. He arrived in the Seychelles on 21 October, read *Martin Chuzzlewit* in the warm rain, and began to learn his lines. But in early November he was suddenly taken into hospital with suspected food poisoning. Within a fortnight he had become ill once again, with what turned out to be amoebic dysentery. Amidst the beauty of the island he stayed in his hotel vomiting and suffering severe diarrhoea, and the weight fell from him. He got himself onto a boat for India and from there flew to Geneva, arriving on 3 December. The man whom Cole Lesley found collapsed on a chair at the airport was gaunt and emaciated, and so frail he could not stand. Weeks of rest at Les Avants were no miracle cure, and although he felt better, the dysentery marked the beginning of his health's slow and final decline. *Suite in Three Keys* was now, he knew, to be a swansong and he became ever more determined to act in London for one final time.

Binkie Beaumont was not yet sixty, but he shared Noël's devotion to sunbeds and cigarettes and, frequently drunk, was now wizened, as feared as fawned upon. Noël Coward's return to the West End, where he had not appeared in a play of his own since 1947, was too big an opportunity for Beaumont to pass up, despite their recent rows. Glen Byam Shaw, director of what became the Royal Shakespeare Company, was approached to direct, but he found both short plays weak. His experience would have given the triptych classical polish. Vivian Matalon, for whom they eventually settled, was still in his thirties and had none of Byam Shaw's pedigree; he had spent his childhood in Jamaica before working as an actor. He had followed the general trend of dismissing Noël as trivial, but *Suite in Three Keys* was an irresistible offer and, early in 1966, he and the two lead actresses travelled to Switzerland to begin preliminary rehearsals. But, on 17 January, Noël collapsed, the dysentery having returned, and more severely than ever, complicated by a kidney infection.

He was taken to a clinic in Lausanne, and sometimes he felt it unlikely he would ever leave. Graham was working in London, but Cole visited almost every day, unfailing in loyalty and what was now, surely, love. Noël's depression, worsened by strong medication, became so severe as to make him consider suicide, although antibiotics and rest slowly did their work as he lay, reading and reading – Flaubert, Jane Austen, E. Nesbit – and wondering whether he would ever be able to fly to London. In February the papers brought the news that the Sexual Offences Act, legalising homosexual activity between men over the age of twenty-one, had passed its second reading in the Commons. "Nothing will convince the bigots", Noël wrote, "but the blackmailers will be discouraged and fewer haunted, terrified young men will commit suicide."[35] But that year's general election brought a dissolution of Parliament that delayed the passage of the bill, and it would be over a year before any change in the law.

Noël's main worry was that the *Suite* would never happen. "I'm so sorry, so sorry that I've put you all out of work", he said to Lilli Palmer and Irene Worth. Vivian Matalon visited him. "He really startled me", Matalon remembered, "by saying 'Oh God curse my aging body', and tears ran down his face."[36]

A Reckoning Under the Moon

14 April 1966; the Queen's Theatre, London. Onstage, the sitting room of a private suite of a luxurious hotel in Switzerland. The performance is the premiere of NOËL COWARD*'s two-act play,* A Song at Twilight, *one of a new trilogy called* Suite in Three Keys. COWARD, *wearing a dark suit, is acting the role of* SIR HUGO LATYMER, *an eminent writer. Opposite him is the actress* LILLI PALMER, *playing* CARLOTTA GRAY, *his former lover.* COWARD, *at sixty-six, looks ten years older, and, with a white wig and moustache, ten years older still; he bears a curious resemblance to William Somerset Maugham. The audience is star-studded; critics scribble in aisle seats.*

HUGO (COWARD): The implications behind all the high faluting rubbish you have been talking have not been lost on me. The veiled threat is perfectly clear.

CARLOTTA (PALMER): What veiled threat?

HUGO: The threat to expose to the world the fact that I have had, in the past, homosexual tendencies.

CARLOTTA: [*calmly*] Homosexual tendencies in the past! What nonsense! You've been queer as a coot all your life, and you know it![37]

A Song at Twilight began life as a braver play than it eventually became. Even in performance Noël had a lapse, either of memory or of nerve, and cut the section in which Carlotta accuses him of homosexuality. During the run, and in the published text, he omitted the phrase "queer as a coot".

The play's first stirrings had been in 1959, when Noël had written out a scenario with the title *The Sixth Veil*.* Planned seven years before the legalisation of homosexuality, and in the shadow of his affair with William Traylor, it promised to be the most daring of anything he had written, being about a love triangle between three men, one of whom is married and another of whom kills himself. Noël wrote:

> The audience becomes aware that John and Owen have been lovers; that Trevor Blair was in love with Owen and is deeply jealous of John; and that Owen more than probably took his life in a fit of jealous despair over John's marriage with Judith. Trevor explains that he has in his possession a number of letters taken from Owen's flat and written by John. The production of these letters could involve John in a criminal action. Trevor makes it clear that his object is 1) blackmail and 2) the hope of breaking up John's marriage.[38]

Lorn Loraine, whose advice he found invaluable and often acted upon, told him she had "thought a lot about this play outline" and felt it needed "restraint and no sign of melodrama". She wondered "whether it would be a good idea for Trevor to have had an affair with Owen Fletcher but to be <u>really</u>, all the time, deeply and jealously in love with John".[39] No further hint of *The Sixth Veil* survives, and Noël seems to have lost the courage of his convictions, perhaps swayed by the need to maintain his newly eminent reputation. It is certain that the Lord Chamberlain would have refused *The Sixth Veil* a licence.

But, when writing *A Song at Twilight*, he kept both the topic and the rough structure of *The Sixth Veil* and retained the element of blackmail in the appearance of old letters. Sir Hugo Latymer is an ageing and globally famous writer of novels and plays; knighted where his creator was not, he is tired by the "constant strain of

---

* Presumably an allusion to James Mason's 1945 film *The Seventh Veil*, in which a doctor suggests that, while Salome removed all seven of her veils willingly, human beings protect themselves with a final layer of deep secrecy.

having to live up to [his] self-created image". Ill, petulant, and vulnerable, he is married to Hilde (Irene Worth), a German who was once his secretary, and the two snipe enjoyably at one another. He awaits a visit from an old flame, a second-rate actress called Carlotta Gray whom he has not seen since "she appeared briefly as a Mother Superior in an excruciatingly bad film about a nun with a vast bust". Hilde absents herself on Carlotta's arrival, and the two former lovers reminisce. The plot was partly inspired by David Cecil's 1964 biography of Max Beerbohm, which related a visit by a "flesh and blood *revenant* from [Beerbohm's] past" in the form of actress Constance Collier, once his lover. Beerbohm and Collier looked at old photographs. "Is that *us?*" she cried. "Are they really *us?*"[40]

For the whole of its first act, *A Song at Twilight* seems to be a play about ageing artists reflecting mournfully and waspishly on the past. Carlotta has had a miscarriage, and both her husbands have died, the first in an air crash, the second in the war. Hugo, meanwhile, is making sure (perhaps too late) that his obituaries will say what he wants them to. "You are remodelling your public image", Carlotta points out. "The witty, cynical author of so many Best Sellers is making way for the Grand Old Man of Letters." So far, so autobiographical, and Hugo is a mouthpiece for Noël's own views: "I detest the young of today. They are grubby, undisciplined and ill-mannered." He has given in to old age, sinking into maudlin resignation; Carlotta fights, resorting to make-up and plastic surgery. She, in a way, is more like Noël than Hugo; her wit is the more Coward-esque, and she is often accused of flippancy, which "in a woman of more mature years [. . .] is liable to be embarrassing".

Carlotta is writing her autobiography and wants permission to publish Hugo's amorous correspondence (rather as Mrs Patrick Campbell had once pestered Shaw for permission to print their love letters). At the first act's melodramatic curtain she leaves mentioning nonchalantly that she also owns three of his love letters to a young man called Perry Sheldon, who she knows was the "only true love of your life". *A Song at Twilight* modulates to a portrait of Hugo wrestling with his lifelong closeted homosexuality, and is partly an indictment of the blackmail suffered by gay men such as the critic James Agate and many others. Carlotta threatens to hand the letters over to a prospective young biographer. Forcing Hugo into a moral awakening, she becomes a vengeful ghost, another of Noël's drawing-room Furies.* The play quotes Heine's poem "Lorelei", about a siren song that leads to the drowning of a boatman, and Carlotta threatens to submerge Hugo with her siren call of truth. Noël had once written his own "Lorelei", a song in which a Rhine-maiden forces a sailor into "a reckoning soon, under the moon".

Hugo is forced into his own reckoning under the moon (a recurring image in the script). Carlotta does not "consider [homosexuality] a crime", arguing that the "law has become archaic and nonsensical". But he predicts that "when the actual law ceases to exist there will be a stigma attached to 'the love that dare not speak its name' in the minds of millions of people for generations to come". Such open discussion, with its clear call for a change in the law, was hugely resonant. Younger writers had tackled the topic: John Osborne's *A Patriot for Me*, about a blackmailed homosexual in the Austro-Hungarian Empire, had been denied a licence by the Lord Chamberlain, and the Royal Court had to turn itself into a private members' club for the performance. But it was something different again for such dialogue to be heard in a starry West End play written by an apparently conservative doyen of British theatre. Much as he eschewed political causes, Noël openly called in the press for homosexuality's legalisation, telling the *Sunday Telegraph* that the current law was "stupid, quite barbarous".[41]

Noël recovered from his illness to the extent that, in March 1966, he was able to travel to London, where he moved into the Savoy, under strict instructions not to wear tight shoes; his heart was weak,

---

* The presence of Carlotta makes the play closer to Ibsen than to Chekhov, a link Coward may be hinting at with his use of the name "Hilde" (Hilde Wangel is a recurring Ibsen character). Ibsen's final play, *When We Dead Awaken*, takes place at a spa hotel overlooking a fjord, and features an ageing sculptor, unhappily married, and confronted by a ghost from his youth who forces him to discuss the cost of his fame. *Pillars of the Community* is an earlier Ibsen work, in which an ex-lover appears from the past, threatening to expose an eminent business-man's life of lies.

and his circulation poor. Vivian Matalon had always been irritated
by Noël's pronouncements on acting, especially when they were
of the don't-bump-into-the-furniture variety. But he was pleasantly
surprised during rehearsals, noting how often Noël castigated himself: "It doesn't feel true", or "does the reading of the letters seem
real?" Matalon loved working with Noël the writer – "the easiest,
least defensive writer I have ever worked with" – and marvelled
at how easily he agreed to cuts and changes to the script. Noël
the actor was a different story, and the routine response to any
suggestion was "I don't agree, dear". Matalon found him "witty,
yes, and kind and generous and warm". But: "it is his sadness that
I remember more vividly than anything else. What despair in his
characters' lives had made it impossible for them to speak to each
other without being devastatingly witty?"[42]

Lilli Palmer had heard that, where professional disagreements
were concerned, Noël could be ruthless and cruel even towards his
friends, and on some days they were barely on speaking terms. He
was still subject to relapses of illness, made worse by the fact that
Cole Lesley, on whom he was now completely dependent, came
down with bronchitis that nearly turned into pneumonia. Noël
moved into a rented apartment in Knightsbridge in time for the
premiere, on 14 April, of *A Song at Twilight*; the double bill of *Shadows
of the Evening* and *Come Into the Garden, Maud* followed ten days later. It
was a gruelling schedule, and on matinee days he would perform
all three. His efforts in rehearsals to discard his pile of mannerisms
in favour of emotional nakedness and simplicity, his refusal to rely
on his long-practised technique, paid off. "Coward's art as an actor
has never been so fine", wrote the reviewer in *The Stage*, "so surely
and subtly tempered, so pointed and shining in theatrical effect, so
intelligent, expressive and alive."[43]

Noël admitted that the strain made him feel "physically like
death", but that "the most incredible thing has happened. The
Press notices have on the whole been extremely good." The plays
were "the work of a master playwright"; "a strong plea for homosexual tolerance"; "no one contributes more to this display than
Mr Coward himself whose wrecked appearance and perfect physical co-ordination display his ability to convey intense personal

feeling".[44] There were doubts, and by general agreement *A Song at Twilight* cast its companions into the shade. "I was held throughout", wrote W. A. Darlington in the *Telegraph*, "once things began to happen, but I should have enjoyed it a lot better if I had been made to believe in any of the people."[45] But after the long period of critical suspicion, Noël was euphoric. "I feel a warmth and a genuine 'love' emanating from the front of the house at every performance. I have been away too long, but it is truly moving to come back to my age-old job again, more triumphant and more loved than ever. My heart is very cosy and warm and gratified."[46]

Once, during a performance of *The Goldfish* in 1911, a little girl called June Tripp had forgotten her lines, and a little boy called Noël Coward had smugly prompted her. Fifty-five years later, as he ate mashed prunes standing in as caviar, he forgot his lines during *A Song at Twilight* and had to rely on Lilli Palmer for a whispered prompt. When the curtain fell he muttered to her: "Thank you, darling Prussian cow."[47] Vivian Matalon came round once a week, finding Noël in a dressing-gown surrounded by crowds, and observed "the exhaustion and the relief, as he began to remove the make-up – figuratively, and actually".[48] While subsequent commentators have felt that emotional honesty was simply not comfortable terrain for Noël Coward, and that the dialogue of *Suite in Three Keys* can read like a parody of his earlier work, the reviews of the first production ensured that he could end his career in a blaze of glory.

When, in 1969, the critic Sheridan Morley wrote the first authorised biography of Noël, its subject blocked any mention of sexuality. But the autobiographical resonance of *A Song at Twilight* was clear to its earliest audiences. Noël, for whom control and self-control were so important, was taking control of his own image before he died. "You would prefer to be regarded as cynical, mean and unforgiving", Hugo is told, "rather than as a vulnerable human being capable of tenderness [. . .] think how surprising it would be for posterity to discover you had a heart after all." Hugo's lover Perry Sheldon has clear touches of Jack Wilson: an alcoholic, he died of leukaemia prematurely aged. Hugo grieves that his own "capacity for loving" has been expended on false relationships and that the object of his greatest love proved worthless. "You waved me like a flag", Carlotta tells him, "to prove a fallacy." Now he faces death, friendless and tormented, after a life of lies. The prominent theme of the play is the emotional and artistic cost of not being true to oneself.

But in this *A Song at Twilight* is hardly autobiographical at all. Within the legal limits of their age Noël's earliest works – *Semi-Monde*, *Design for Living* – had not dodged his sexuality. He had never considered marriage and he did not think his writing lacked either quality or truthfulness. The play, hinting at differences between creator and creation, is more self-exoneration than self-portrait. Latymer is closer (as many realised) to Somerset Maugham, although Noël had made sure not to imitate Maugham's stammer. The two had seen each other occasionally over the years, and they had both relied on Professor Niehans's ovine injections, although Maugham's face in his final unhappy decade became crumpled and sunken, and Noël referred to him as "the lizard of Oz".[49] The friendship had lost any traces of competition and become loving, partly because Noël continued to admire, and concede his debt to, Maugham's work. "Neither age nor custom has withered nor changed your infinite kindness, wit and gaiety", Noël wrote to him, "I love you very very much and that's that."[50]

Maugham's memoirs had made no mention of his male partners, Gerald Haxton and Alan Searle, and, after her death in 1955, he had bitterly attacked his ex-wife, Syrie, in print. Noël had always supported Syrie and was enraged by Maugham's decision to adopt Searle as his son, a means of transferring inheritance from his biological daughter. Noël had begun *A Song at Twilight* before his final visit to Maugham, who, at ninety, was suffering from dementia. "Willie has become a small, lachrymose, yellow bird", Noël told Rebecca West, who was working actively to clear Syrie's name. "I was apparently the first person he had recognised for four months. But recognize me he did and burst into tears. He made sense only now and then, and to watch him stammering, flicking his fingers, and trying so desperately to organise his failing mind was agonizing. It was impossible to forgive him his many trespasses. He's certainly paying for those now in his interminable nightmare."[51] Maugham died three months later, on 16 December 1965, Noël's sixty-fifth birthday. Noël felt his actions unforgivable, and *A Song at*

Twilight is partly an act of literary vengeance, written at the bitter end of what had been a long friendship. "Maugham hated people more easily than he loved them", Noël explained in an interview. "I love people more easily than I hate them."[52]

But the play has a scope wider than autobiography or revenge. Hugo Latymer can stand for a generation forced to live in the human bondage of secrecy, and there are parallels with many gay men in Noël's social circle who had married, and not always entirely for camouflage: Cole Porter, Michael Redgrave, even Jack Wilson himself. The play shifts key once again with the return of Hugo's wife, Hilde. She married him after losing the love of her life, a German Jew, in a concentration camp. "I was not in love with [Hugo]", she announces calmly.

> I knew that he could never be in love with me. I also knew why, and was not deceived as to his reasons for asking me. I recognised his need for a 'façade'. [. . .] I have often been unhappy and lonely. But then, so has he. The conflict within him between his natural instincts and the laws of society has been for most of his life a perpetual problem that he has to grapple with alone. [. . .] He has made his career and lived his life in his own way according to the rules he has laid down for himself.[53]

Hilde is a character of dignity and the play's one real truth-teller. Her loyalty to Hugo is the closest thing to redemption that *A Song at Twilight* offers. She may be Noël's tribute to a generation of wives: Rachel Kempson, Linda Porter, Natasha Wilson (now living alone and going blind), each sharing her life with a gay man. *The Sixth Veil* was to have finished with a scene between a repressed homosexual and his wife, in order to show the depth of her "love and understanding", and "how much her loyalty means to him in the present crisis".[54] As the abandoned wife in *Shadows of the Evening* has it: "There are so many different degrees of loving." Hugo ends *A Song at Twilight* in tears, reading his letters to Perry. But he is not quite alone – Hilde returns to sit with him. At a time in his life when Noël seemed most trapped by his own legend, he had written a portrait of the artist as an old man, finally confronting the dangers of masquerade.

The Performance of His Life

25 April 1966; the Queen's Theatre, London. Onstage, the sitting-room of a private suite of a luxurious hotel in Switzerland. The performance is the premiere of NOËL COWARD*'s short play,* Shadows of the Evening, *one of a new trilogy called* Suite in Three Keys. COWARD, *wearing a dark suit, is acting the role of* GEORGE HILGAR, *who is dying. With him are* IRENE WORTH *and* LILLI PALMER, *the former playing George's wife, the latter his mistress with whom he now lives. Together the two women, old friends, have resolved to bury their differences in order to be with him in his last months.* COWARD, *at sixty-six, looks ten years older, and, with thinning hair and "ill" make-up, ten years older still. The audience is star-studded; critics scribble in aisle seats.*

GEORGE (COWARD): I'm quite content to die believing only in life itself which seems to me to be quite enough to be going on with, and I have no complaints either except an immediate resentment that I am only to be allowed to go on with it for such a little while longer.

ANNE (WORTH): If that's how you feel, hang on to it. No words can help, from me or anybody else.

GEORGE: On the other hand if, in three months' time, I suddenly find myself in some tinsel heaven or some gaudy hell, I shall come back and haunt you. But don't let go of my hand – don't let go of my hand.[55]

Noël Coward spent the last years of his life in flight, waiting for death. The first to let go of his hand would, he knew, be Lorn Loraine, whose illness was incurable, although she would hold on for longer than anyone predicted. His London office was now, in Lorn's frequent absences, controlled by her long-time assistant,

Joan Hirst, who grew used to the strange rituals of working for Noël Coward, learning to refer to "the Master" and to endure her own nickname ("Stop and Fetch"). Efficient and trustworthy, Joan became as valuable to Noël as Lorn had been. In America he had a new manager, Geoffrey Johnson, who had trained as an actor and worked in a minor capacity on Noël's American musicals; he soon began to deal with all Noël's American affairs. In his thirties, handsome and unassuming, "gentle Geoffrey" would be the last addition to the Coward family, a frequent visitor to Switzerland and Jamaica, adored by and adoring of his new employer.

The years settled into their peripatetic routine, as Noël moved between hotels and apartments in New York and London, retreating at intervals either to Les Avants or to Firefly. Diary entries dwindled, his handwriting shrivelling. News from Vietnam did little to improve his belief in the human race. "They've lost the war", he told journalists. "They should get out and shut up."[56] An interviewer asked his age. "Fifty-six", he replied confidently, then corrected himself. "What am I saying? I mean sixty-six. I've been fifty-six years on the stage."[57] The border between life and theatre was as porous as ever, and made more so when casting began for a biopic of Gertrude Lawrence. Julie Andrews was to play the lead, and both Peter Cook and Ian McKellen were considered for Noël, but preference was given – at Noël's request – to his godson Daniel Massey. At Les Avants, Chalet Coward was a theatre unto itself. Two Italian men, partners who doted on a poodle whose fur they dyed apricot, acted as chef and butler. Cole Lesley's duties were relieved by the arrival of an out-of-work actor called Calvin Darnell, who was too reliant on alcohol; he was promptly replaced by Peter Arne, who was too reliant on rent boys and also dismissed.*

Graham Payn had finally been persuaded to give up on his acting career and to spend his time running the life of his former lover, in partnership with Cole. "He has a loving and loyal heart", Noël wrote, "and no future anywhere but with me."[58] It was a final

---

* In 1983, Arne was beaten to death by a homeless man to whom he had been providing food.

reeling-in of a loved one; loving and being loved by Noël Coward left little room for a life of one's own. A tall young man called Guy Hunting, promptly christened "Large Lord Fauntleroy", arrived to take on secretarial duties, and found himself wryly amused by life at Les Avants. Noël spent his mornings in bed and refused exercise on principle, smoking menthol cigarettes and eating from a tray and drinking more heavily than was good for him. Hunting noticed that "the only activity that seemed to be ignored by the inhabitants of the Chalet Coward was sex".[59] In *Pomp and Circumstance* Noël had written of his now entrenched philosophy that "physical passion is surely the slyest and wickedest joke played by nature on the human race"; he was relieved by the way old age and physical infirmity had allowed him finally to escape what he had always considered the destructive force of sexual love. A few years before, he had written to Cole Lesley from Morocco of local young men who "only wish for <u>one</u> thing, which alas I am unable to provide. However, affection is what counts."[60] His existence in Switzerland was oddly humdrum in its mindless luxury, but interrupted by flurries of temper or panic at any hint of problem or disruption. Cole or Graham would expertly balance subservience and efficiency.

The enclosed world had its own rituals and vocabulary, increasingly reliant on baby-talk. Cole was now invariably Coley, Toley, or even Tinkerbell. Noël and Graham, alumni of *Peter Pan*, had laced into their communications phrases from the nursery and the Neverland. "Much of it could be shortened and used as a code", Cole remembered. "'That's Nana's bark when she smells danger', for instance. A sotto voce 'Nana's bark', from Noël at, say, a business meeting, would be enough to warn Graham and me to beware."[61] In *Waiting in the Wings* Graham had played a character who is homosexual and obsessed with *Peter Pan*: "That's because you've got a mother-fixation. All sensitive lads with mother-fixations worship *Peter Pan*." And so the three of them grew older and younger, alone on their mountain, which in the spring was carpeted with narcissi appearing beneath the melting snow.

From the safety of bed Noël, worrying about the unlikely scenario in which he would outlive his companions, made vague attempts to return to England and enjoy a coda of national-treasure status in his home country. But his health continued to trouble him, and by November 1966 he was in hospital in excruciating pain, with a kidney stone that had to be cut out. "My scar is sensational and I can't wait to show it to you", he wrote to Gladys Calthrop, just after Christmas. "I've never had such pain in my life. But now all is well. [. . .] I can now relax and contemplate my navel which I am relieved to see is still there."[62] But circulatory troubles from a failing heart were damaging his short-term memory, and when a Broadway production of *Suite in Three Keys* was planned there was no question of his being able to perform.

He turned instead to writing, adapting his 1951 story "Star Quality" into a play that both he and Binkie Beaumont eventually agreed was not worth staging (it follows the rows between leading actress, temperamental director, and naive playwright, from rehearsal to first night). He finished a quartet of new stories and gathered his verse into a first official poetry collection called *Not Yet The Dodo*; both volumes would appear in the same week, in November 1967. Reviewers were unsurprised by the longing for pre-war values, the castigation of youth, and the dexterity of rhyme and rhythm (the way in which strict rhyme pinches together lines of loose metre and unequal length makes the verse redolent of Stevie Smith, a great favourite of his).[63] Both the longest story and the longest poem were a depiction of upper-class frolics on a cruise liner; among the verse were nostalgic reminiscences of his childhood. There were other autobiographical themes too: no story ended without a death, and the books are characterised by affairs, not always happy, between couples of mismatched ages. One poem rails against "humourless refugees from alien lands | Seeking protection in our English sanity". "And how much of the taxable year do *you* spend in sane England?", the *Observer*'s critic asked Noël rhetorically. "'Not yet the dodo'. Dangerously near I'd say."[64]

In the spring of 1967 Noël began a new script, called *Age Cannot Wither*. Its first scene implies a light comic piece – in the vein of *Fallen Angels* – about the annual reunion of three middle-aged women who bicker agreeably the more they drink. The second scene, still unpublished, hints at a shift into a darker, though still comic, key. Jasper, grandson of one of the women, has left his wife for an antiques dealer called Bobbie. Attitudes to this news differ wildly, from accusations of degeneracy to calm understanding.

NAOMI: Is there a woman involved?

MELISSA: No. That's what's so appalling. It's a man.

JUDY: He can't have gone off with a man! He's my godson.

STELLA: Perhaps he forgot.

JUDY: Do you mean to tell me that Jasper of all people goes in for that sort of thing. He's six foot two and an all-round athlete.

STELLA: You can't go by that. The Greeks were all-round athletes and look how they used to carry on. [. . .]

NAOMI: I can see clearly that you are much more shocked by it than I am, but that perhaps can be accounted for by the difference in our generations. I have a feeling that only the very old or the very young are capable of understanding the social and moral values of these strange times. [. . .] Much has been learned and disclosed in our day about the waywardness of the human heart. There is nothing left for us but to profit from this and learn from it as much tolerance as possible. [. . .] Jasper is not in the least degenerate.

MELISSA: Even if those emotions happen to be decadent and abnormal?

NAOMI: If they are genuine they can't be abnormal.[65]

The play is a companion piece to the long title poem in *Not Yet The Dodo*, about upper-middle-class parents coming to terms with their son's homosexuality. Acceptance is part of their national character: "We British are a peculiar breed | Undemonstrative on the whole | It takes a very big shock indeed | To dent our maddening self-control."

But Noël gave up *Age Cannot Wither* after two scenes, unable to focus. Laurence Olivier had prostate cancer; Vivien Leigh had tuberculosis; Lorn Loraine was getting weaker by the day. Leigh died on 8 July, and Noël refused to read at her memorial service, thinking he would not be able to get through it without breaking down. The Sexual Acts Bill was passed a few weeks later, and theatrical censorship would be abolished the following year. As if to confirm to his detractors that he had lost permanently the daring of his youth, Noël – who had once decried the blue pencil of the Lord Chamberlain – told David Frost in a television interview that he regretted the demise of censorship.

He escaped to New York the following month to film the small part of Caesar in a disastrous musical version of Shaw's *Androcles and the Lion*; a few months later came the equally disastrous *Boom!*, an adaptation by Tennessee Williams of his play *The Milk Train Doesn't Stop Here Anymore*. The film, directed by Joseph Losey, was intended as a vehicle for Elizabeth Taylor and Richard Burton, and Noël – who loved the friendliness and professionalism of its stars – enjoyed the few days in Sardinia. But Williams's mystical scenario, about a dying woman visited by a mysterious young man, translated oddly to cinema. Noël was the Witch of Capri (originally female, now altered to Noël Coward playing himself in an impeccable suit), who imparts ominous information about the man's being an "angel of death". The theme struck close to home when, on 21 November, Lorn Loraine, friend of half a century, died of cancer at seventy-three. Noël attended her memorial service, "well and simply done and quite intolerable. I staggered blindly away."[66]

Nineteen sixty-eight would be a happier year. He could not banish grief, but was determined to enjoy the time he had left. He wrote to Gladys Calthrop with his well-honed brand of stoic and jolly nihilism: "Don't go cunting about saying that nothing is worth while, because we all know bloody well that it isn't, but there's always an apple and a good book."[67] When in England he was finding more to enjoy in British theatre, from Tom Stoppard's *Rosencrantz and Guildenstern are Dead* to Alan Bennett's *Forty Years On*, both of which he loved, as he did the work of Alan Ayckbourn. In the spring he was well enough to take Cole and Graham on one last massive holiday – and to experience a final blast of tropical heat – across Southeast Asia, Australia, and the islands of the South Pacific. He had returned to London by the summer and went to Dublin in order to work on his final movie, *The Italian Job*. The director, Peter Collinson, had lived from the age of fourteen at the Actors' Orphanage, his behaviour often leading to threats of expulsion from which he had been saved by heart-to-hearts with Noël.

The two were fond of one another, and his casting of Noël in the part of criminal mastermind Mr Bridger, who runs an empire from within his prison cell, was inspired. Michael Caine was the Cockney crook Charlie Croker – "You were only supposed to blow the bloody doors off!" – who forms a gang to steal gold from an armoured truck that ends up teetering on the edge of a cliff.

Noël was an unlikely partner for Michael Caine, chief player in a generation of working-class actors challenging conventional wisdom about acting technique and received pronunciation. But Noël loved working with Caine, who thought his co-star was "God". The film quickly encapsulated its era. Despite the prevalence of anti-establishment protests, the Swinging Sixties had made patriotism cool, and like the James Bond films, *The Italian Job* was a case in point, with its red-white-and-blue Minis, its theme song envisaging England as "the self-preservation society", and its attack on "Europe [and] the Common Market". Unpredictable to the last, Noël actually believed in Britain's joining the common market, precursor to the European Union, and he had once been asked by Churchill to work for the United European Movement. But, cleverly sending up his own character, he was a perfect fit for *The Italian Job*, wandering the prison corridors in a purple silk dressing-gown and reading a crisp copy of the *Telegraph*, his every appearance accompanied by "Rule, Britannia" on a harpsichord, and his prison cell pasted with pictures of the royal family. There is even a hint of his sexuality. "Everybody in the world", he says crisply, "is bent."

The Italian Job seemed to cement Noël's status as national institution. He did very little during 1969, worried most of all by Graham Payn's suffering a small cerebral haemorrhage while driving down the hill from Firefly. Graham made a full recovery, but it was a frightening experience. "I'm already dreading my 70th birthday celebration week", Noël told Gladys. "Perhaps I could arrange a tiny heart attack."[68] *Private Lives* was to tour America; the BBC, who had never honoured a living writer so extensively, televised a selection of his plays. Richard Attenborough hosted a Coward Gala at the National Film Theatre and the Queen Mother threw Noël a birthday lunch at Clarence House that, falling ill, she was unable to attend. Noël made do with the Queen, who gave him a cigarette case. Her mother sent a cigarette box, and her sister varied things up a bit with some cufflinks. Critics of every kind were flown over to Switzerland for a round of advance interviews. "If," wrote one, "beneath the cavalcade of masks [. . .] there is a real person, 'the Master' is very careful not to let him stick his head out in public."[69]

Noël had recently written and performed in his most open, most emotionally naked, plays. Asked what he most wants in life, the dying man in *Shadows of the Evening* replies "truthfulness", just as, in *The Vortex*, Nicky Lancaster had wanted to "realise the truth". But Noël had now retreated within his own myth so deeply as to lose sight of himself, or to become (as Oscar Wilde describes a butler in *An Ideal Husband*) a "mask with a manner". *A Song at Twilight* had been partly inspired by Max Beerbohm, whose story "The Happy Hypocrite" provided a model for Noël's old age: it is about a man who wears a mask for so long that his face takes on its contours. Hunter Davies, writing a profile of Noël for *The Sunday Times*, wondered afterwards "if I actually interviewed Noël Coward or was it someone acting Noel Coward. Is there anything under the cool, charming mask?"[70] It seemed as if, rather like Peter Shaffer's conception of Mozart in *Amadeus*, talent had chosen the strangest, and occasionally silliest, of vehicles in which to take root. The performance was as precise as ever: the cigarette held between fingers always curled, never straight; the wrist accentuated with a gold chain; the light flashing from a signet ring; the corrugated voice issuing from cords of smoked silk. He gave audiences and journalists what they wanted, from Wilde-esque epigrams – "conceit is an outwards manifestation of inferiority" – to lofty dismissals of "the masses – they'd rather play Bingo". And, always, his graceful concession when interviewers apologised for raking over the same old territory: "Not at all. I'm fascinated by the subject."[71]

The playwright David Hare would suggest that Noël was afraid of thought.[72] But what Noël seemed to fear most of all was being seen to think. The mask was pulled tight over his considerable capacity for introspection, his well-stocked mind, his fluent command of French and Spanish. Cheerfully – and surely falsely – he told journalists that he thought Nabokov had written *Dr Zhivago* and that one of the Beatles was called John McCartney. "I've never even seen

Hamlet", he informed the *Observer*, which was nonsense. But a comparison of *The Vortex* with Shakespeare's play had strayed too close to the serious, and had to be shot down. Just once he admitted that, during periods of writers' block, "sometimes you wish you had a revolver to put yourself out of your misery".[73] As Mr Bridger in *The Italian Job* he had let a Cockney accent occasionally sabotage his otherwise impeccably manicured delivery, and with a slight underbite had hinted at the savagery that lay behind the dressing-gown. And during his performance as Noël Coward similar flashes of something sharper, an interest in the darker recesses of the human soul, could suddenly appear – just as when, in Saki's short stories, a burst of violence stabs through the varnish of comedy. "I've always been fascinated by surgery. In New York I used to go to the hospitals to see them at work. Perhaps some people couldn't bear that sort of thing. I love it. The violence on the operating table is terrifying." Hunter Davies pressed him on this surprising admission. "Have another brandy", came the answer, as Noël disappeared from view once again.[74]

The charm had worked its magic. "I've never met a mind as quick as his", wrote John Heilpern in the *Observer*.[75] And on one thing Noël was honest. "I am not", he said, "'with it'. Things are changing all the time: the *haut monde* is not so haut, or so smart or so exclusive. There is a general leavening of all the classes. London is a bit more honky-tonk, the provinces are more garish. But on the whole I would say that it's not at all a bad thing."[76] Kenneth Tynan's risqué revue *Oh! Calcutta!*, with its sex-related sketches and nudity, he left at the interval. David Hare's 1970 play *Slag* – written with Coward-esque fluency in three days – was "five good scenes and one terrible one". Noël's appearance backstage at premieres could take on the atmosphere of a royal visit, but Hare was proof that there was still considerable dissent among the new generation as to Noël Coward's near deified status. Hare later said that "when I think of Coward, I have to stick pins in my palms to remember not to despise him".[77]

But there was little room for dissent when Noël travelled to England for what he had come to think of as "holy week", in December 1969. He moved into the river suite at the Savoy, whose doorman was interviewed about him by the BBC. Kenneth Williams appeared on television, "scattering lines from Coward lyrics like handfuls of confetti". John Gielgud gave long interviews, "lapsing disconcertingly into the past tense as though we were recording an obituary". Kenny Everett, DJ on the newly created BBC Radio 1, paid tribute, and journalists who arrived with good intentions of giving Noël a hard time found that their hostility evaporated as a result of "the man's enormous personal warmth". The *Telegraph* thought he had now "obviously become part of history".[78] At midnight on 15 December 1969, the Phoenix Theatre, site of the original *Private Lives*, held a special performance, the stalls packed with friends and colleagues. At four in the morning, after hours of tributes and performances, Noël came from his box onto the stage, and the audience stood for him. Later that evening there was dinner at the Savoy for 300 guests. The BBC sent television cameras; Mountbatten gave the toast; Olivier tried to give a speech and was overcome. Evelyn Laye sent seventy sausages to Noël's suite.

It was Mountbatten who provided the best birthday present. He had been the driving force in finally ensuring Noël's knighthood and in January 1968 had written to him: "I feel I ought to start moving to put you in for one of our two highest possible decorations, the Order of Merit or the Companionship of Honour." He asked Noël to write his own citation. "Of course no-one will ever know that you helped me personally and I will say I have dug all this out from my own records and my personal knowledge of you." By November 1969, the recommendation was in the "machine", but the Chairman of the Honours Committee reported considerable objection, "because of your residence abroad for tax reasons". Mountbatten eventually went to the royal family, thanking Noël "for permission to show my summary of the iniquitous way you were treated in your [wartime] law cases to the Queen". Noël tried to remain calm: "Whatever honour I may or may not get, it will never measure up to the honour you have done me in your efforts to procure it for me."[79] The Committee asked for full transcripts of the two trials before the invitation was formally given. Noël Coward's knighthood was announced in the New Years' Honours for 1970.

On 25 January 1970, Noël, back in Switzerland, made his last entry in the diary he had kept for thirty years.

Nothing particularly momentous has occurred during the last few weeks beyond the fact of me becoming seventy, an idea to which I have at last, reluctantly, become accustomed. I don't look seventy, I don't feel seventy, but what I am is seventy, so fuck it. This is our last day here. Tomorrow we fly to London and sit about waiting for me to be dubbed, which ceremony takes place on February 4th. Then we go to New York for about ten days and, at long last, my beloved Jamaica where I shall put myself down and encourage the sun to demolish the pale green patina which at the moment disfigures me. [. . .] No "cloud has pissed across the sky", and everything looks very rosy. That really is the extent of my news for the beginning of 1970. One cannot expect such tranquillity to last but I'm all for making the most of it while it's here. [. . .] Well, roll on 1970 and try to be as well disposed as possible.[80]

The journals were put away. The knighthood had been achieved; the plays and songs written. He would produce almost nothing more for the final three years of his life. He slips further into his legend, increasingly invisible, evading his biographers.

Coward accepted his knighthood wearing a top hat, flanked by Gladys Calthrop and Joyce Carey in full fur. There was to be no question of appearing with Graham Payn openly acknowledged as his partner. After another bout of birthday celebrations in America, there was little to do but drift through the days and the lunches and the supper parties. At airports he was whisked through customs in a wheelchair. In Jamaica he was now cared for devotedly by a local couple – Miguel Fraser and his wife Imogene – who lived in a lodge close by. Later that year he was hospitalised with pleurisy, and he would spend his last months swollen with medication. In 1971 he was awarded his first and only Tony, a special award presented to him by Cary Grant. His timing was still impeccable and only after a long pause, finger aloft, did he begin his speech: "this is my first award, so please be kind". (Laughter, applause.) "I would like to say to you that I have been in the theatre for sixty years. And the most rewarding thing in the world is to be appreciated by one's own people. And often, when I have given a performance of incredible brilliance, the civilians have come round" (hand flapping in amused dismissal) "and I've said to a few of my 'pro' friends, who were skittering about, 'stay where you are'. Because what *I* like, is praise from my peers. [. . .] I'm so proud to be here, and receive this, and thank you all" (arms stretched wide) "so much."[81]

In May 1971 he was back in London, and Kenneth Tynan saw him at the Savoy Grill. Tynan, instrumental in the renewed appreciation of Coward's work, never reneged on his view of the post-war plays but had become a support which Coward had warmly to appreciate. Tynan recorded an anecdote in his diary, "to demonstrate that Noël's wit really was impromptu". The death of General de Gaulle had been announced on the radio, and Coward was informed of the news by a journalist who wondered "'what he and God are talking about in heaven'. 'That,' Noël replied, 'depends on how good God's French is.'" At the Savoy, Tynan watched from afar, seeing Coward accompanied by Graham Payn, Gladys Calthrop, and Joyce Carey. "How sad that Noël should cherish this drab circle – nice enough people, but so second rate. [. . .] He can hardly hobble [. . .] an old man on the last of his legs. Probably I shall not see him again."[82]

Nor would he. It was a time of new triumphs and last meetings. In July 1972 a revue opened in the West End called *Cowardy Custard*, telling the story of Noël Coward through his songs and memoirs. His life had finally become a play. With Una Stubbs and Patricia Routledge in the cast, the latter more than a match for Beatrice Lillie in her glorious rendition of "Marvellous Party", it ran for four hundred performances. In September John Gielgud directed Maggie Smith and Robert Stephens in *Private Lives*, and Coward thought that Smith had effaced memories of Gertrude Lawrence in the part, telling the press that, if he tried to put his feelings into words, he would burst into tears. Binkie Beaumont threw a first-night party at his London home, the last time he and Coward saw one another. Later that month Cecil Beaton paid a visit to Les Avants. "Without losing any of your pepper", he wrote to Coward, "you have become so <u>kind</u>."[83] He expressed similar sentiments to Gladys Calthrop, after Coward's death: "Unlike some people he became nicer and nicer. And he was so wonderful to his friends."[84]

And so, at nine o'clock in the evening, on 14 January 1973, Noël Coward stood with Marlene Dietrich at the bottom of a flight of stairs in the foyer of the New Theatre in midtown Manhattan. He was the guest of honour at a special performance of another revue taken from his work: *Oh Coward!* His back was bent, and his feet shuffled, and he faced the difficult task of climbing the stairs to take his seat in an auditorium high above street level. He had planned to bring Katharine Cornell, the first actress he had ever seen perform on Broadway when, half a century before, he had first visited New York. But she was in poor health, and he had visited her during this, his last trip to America. "I remember he was very ill", she said afterwards. "All actors fall by the wayside. But go on."[85] Marlene Dietrich, at seventy-two, was increasingly reliant on painkillers and alcohol, but she stepped into the breach. "We have to get up there", she said to Coward, pointing at the staircase, and they began the climb. "It's going to be all right", she said to him. "We have made it this far, dear love."[86] And so they had, she the daughter of a police lieutenant, he the son of a music salesman, who had once cut out pictures of actresses from magazines and stuck them to his bedroom walls. The long climb up the stairs was an irresistible metaphor but also a physical reality. Coward was accompanied by Geoffrey Johnson and by Geoffrey's partner, Jerry Hogan. "The two males frankly put our arms under his," Geoffrey remembered, "and actually were really lifting him up each step of the stairs. Marlene sighed with relief when we managed to get to the summit."[87]

They took their seats in the sixth row of the stalls, amid a strobe of flashing cameras, as the audience stood for the guest of honour. It was a mild January by New York standards, but nevertheless cold; the audience was a mass of fur. It was a Sunday evening, Broadway actors were enjoying their night off, and tickets were by invitation only. Friends and colleagues were arrayed around him in the tiny theatre: John Gielgud, Joan Sutherland, Douglas Fairbanks, Ethel Merman, Gloria Vanderbilt . . . It was like some Proustian party

(Coward had recently reread Proust, with considerable misgivings) in which everybody seemed to be masked. But they were the masks of old age. Coward appeared on the stage at the end, and then got into a limousine mobbed by fans and was driven away. He was soon to travel to Jamaica where, on 22 March, he would hear of Binkie Beaumont's death. Beaumont was just sixty-four; he had returned home drunk and hit his head on the fireplace. The news – marking the end of an intense and often argumentative collaboration – would be a shattering blow. Gladys Calthrop, closest of friends for sixty-two years, would write to Coward on 25 March: "Darling dearest dear. I know you'll mind dreadfully – it is indeed hard to believe as happening and hard to think of the theatre without Binkie."[88] But Coward would not live to read the letter.

Before he left New York, he had time to give the manuscript of a poem he had written the previous year to the Actors' Fund of America, where it would be sold in a charity auction. The handwriting was crabbed and runic, and the verse alluded to John Keats's sonnet "When I have fears . . .", a poem that, in *Brief Encounter*, Laura knows by heart, helping her husband when it appears in a crossword puzzle.

> When I have fears as Keats had fears
> Of the moment I cease to be
> I console myself with vanished years
> Remembered laughter, remembered tears
> The peace of the changing sea
> And remembered friends who are dead and gone
> How happy they are I cannot know
> But happy am I who loved them so.[89]

Keats's fear was not of death, but of dying before his work was done. Coward had no such fears. He had written all that he had to write, perhaps more, and now he was living in his memory. Using words and music, he had created a world. Its boundaries were narrow, but like all worlds it had its own rules and its own diction. (The *Oxford English Dictionary* credits him with over twenty coinages.)

It was a world that had managed to convince many of its realism. But nobody in life speaks to one another in dialogue as lacquered as in Coward's plays. His stage was populated by puppets of tinsel and sawdust, with consonant-rich names: Essendine, Condomine, Heseldyne. The presence of the puppet-master was so obvious as to stamp every line with an authorial presence – simultaneously disenchanted and genial, sour and sentimental – and the resulting consciousness of theatre. It was a generous dramatic universe, prising amusement from bleakness, and it was created as a home for a character called Noël Coward, whose own life had been another dramatic entry in his oeuvre of alternative designs for living, and whose manner, so often imitated, would remain curiously inimitable. Now, the plays and songs would have to learn how to survive without their creator. Their very ephemerality would lead them to endure. "Any artist", Beverley Nichols had written of Coward in 1925, "who catches the exact echo of any period will hear his work echoed and echoed down the centuries."[90] Kenneth Tynan had agreed, writing in 1953: "Even the youngest of us will know, in fifty years' time, exactly what we mean by 'a very Noël Coward sort of person.'"[91] But did Tynan mean the cynic or the romantic, the radical or the reactionary?

Coward's was a life that straddled centuries and was caught between worlds; he epitomised an age, foresaw its transience, charted its decline, regretted its loss. His was a radical and revolutionary conservatism, in its concession that preservation is fuelled by change. His plays are united by a moral search for freedom and for truth (two words that are studded through almost every play he wrote): the freedom to live and love as one chooses, true to oneself, within or outside of society and its conventions, in duos or trios or groups, with men or with women, the definitions of masculine and feminine widened, the nuclear family discarded. The gay quartet of green-carnationed aesthetes in *Bitter Sweet* are "exquisitely free from the dreary and quite absurd | moral views of the common herd". Carl Linden, in the same operetta, is told he should be "free always, because you're an artist"; Condomine in *Blithe Spirit* pronounces himself "free", as do the men in *Design for Living*. Sorel in *Hay Fever* wants to be "earning my own living somewhere – a free agent – able to do whatever I liked without being cluttered up and frustrated by the family".

But Coward was a writer tarnished by too much reality. He charts the pain and sacrifice inherent in freedom, and the solitude of the artist's restless and unending search. Freedom, by the end of his life, involved liberation from what he considered the pain of love; his eventual ideal was to be, as in *The Astonished Heart*, "free of love, free of longing, a new life before you and the dead behind you". Even Nicky Lancaster in *The Vortex* had wished his generation "weren't so free"; in *Brief Encounter* the lovers are not "free to love each other"; in *Sirocco* the heroine professes herself "free – God help me". Garry Essendine, Noël's clearest self-portrait, honestly admits: "I am not free like other men to take happiness when it comes to me."

Unlike Tynan, Coward could not see fifty years into the future, and he claimed not to care about posterity, which would soon winnow his bulging collected works. What would he have made of "Mad About the Boy" becoming the theme for a Levi's jeans advert, or of Neil Tennant's curating a 1998 album that reinterpreted his songs for a new century, with The Divine Comedy laying "Marvellous Party" above a thumping techno beat? What barbs might Coward's diary have recorded at the prospect of actors such as Chewitel Ejiofor or Rupert Everett performing Nicky Lancaster, the lights fading on Everett as he injected heroin into his arm? Or of Lindsay Duncan and Alan Rickman stretching *Private Lives* to its full extent of joy and pain, as I, eleven years old, sat entranced in the audience? Or of Andrew Scott reworking Garry Essendine for a new generation in a production that mined the text for melancholy, and swapped the gender of Essendine's seducer, Joanna Lyppiatt? Coward never agreed with the view that the plays were simply cloaked accounts of homosexual relationships. Graham Payn – who argued that Coward's male characters were often unconvincing compared to his female – would, when running the estate, close down all-male productions. To argue that Coward wrote entirely in code teeters dangerously close to a belief that gay writers' portraits of women can never entirely convince. In encompassing the plight and fight of homosexuals across his lifetime, he had been among the foremost chroniclers of a search for liberation in which women and gay men were united.

Most of all, the world of Noël Coward was one of contradiction: meaningful in the flippant shallows, trite in the sincere depths, authentic only in pretence, and impossible to catch in the act of profundity, which creeps in on the sly. At a time when Freud was recalibrating society's conception of depth by pursuing the idea of the unconscious mind, Coward made a case for the sparkling, sensuous, surface. Pretence had had to be at the heart of his way of life, as an actor and as a homosexual. But Noël Coward never hid in plain sight; he revealed himself through flagrant disguise. The world of masquerade and theatre is where the truth he spent his career demanding can often be found: the illusion of a reality more real than real life.

In Beverley Nichols's novel *Crazy Pavements*, published the year before Coward created his dancing little lady and her flippant mask, a character builds a "hall of masks", to show the true faces of his friends. What matters in Noël Coward is not what lies beneath the mask but the mask itself. In *Operette* a character sings: "Throughout my lonely youth, I knew too much reality | So now my only truth is artificiality." Dismiss Oscar Wilde as he would, Coward had inherited Wilde's belief that the gravest things in life were too important to be taken seriously; that triviality was the only thing about which one should be truly in earnest; and that performance is something inseparable from authenticity. As Wilde put it: "Man is least himself when he talks in his own person. Give a man a mask, and he will tell you the truth."[92]

AN AWFULLY BIG ADVENTURE

——

A Late Play

CAST

NOËL COWARD, *a world-renowned actor and writer*

VIOLET COWARD, *Noël Coward's mother*

ESMÉ WYNNE-TYSON, *a writer and philosopher in increasing ill health*

GRAHAM PAYN, *Coward's partner*

COLE LESLEY, *his assistant and intimate friend*

GEOFFREY JOHNSON, *his American manager*

MIGUEL FRASER, *his Jamaican valet*

DESMOND GORDON, *the groundsman of his Jamaican estate*

The Biographers:

SHERIDAN MORLEY (1941–2007)

CLIVE FISHER (1960–)

PHILIP HOARE (1958–)

OLIVER SODEN (1990–)

The fluid action can take place on a single set depicting Firefly Hill in Jamaica.

The scene is the stage of the Duke of York's Theatre in London, Christmas 1913.

What you see is the Neverland. You have often half seen it before, or even three-quarters, after the night-lights were lit. The figure who has emerged from his tree is MASTER NOËL COWARD, *dressed as* SLIGHTLY *in a fur coat and top hat, his boots striped in pink and black.* SLIGHTLY *is conceited. He thinks he remembers the days before he was lost, with their manners and customs. It is impossible to tell whether he is thirteen or thirty or seventy.*

SLIGHTLY: My mother was fonder of me than your mothers were of you. Peter had to make up names for you, but my mother had wrote my name on the pinafore I was lost in. "Slightly Soiled"; that's my name.

A lady falls out of the sky. It is SLIGHTLY*'s idea that they shoot her: the Wendy-bird. She falls to earth to lie unconscious at their feet. Her resemblance to* NOËL*'s mother,* VIOLET, *is pronounced.*

SLIGHTLY: This is no bird. I think it must be a lady.

TOOTLES: When ladies used to come to me in dreams I said, "Pretty mother", but when she really came, I shot her!

The lady stirs; the arrow has caught in a button. PETER PAN *thinks the button is a kiss.*

SLIGHTLY: I remember kisses; let me see it. *(He takes it in his hand.)* Ay, that is a kiss.

TOOTLES: But if she lies there she will die.

SLIGHTLY: Ay, she will die. It is a pity, but there is no way out.

She rises, comes centre-stage. A date somewhere on the set appears: 1913.

VIOLET COWARD: It seems almost incredible I think, that I should have been destined to be the mother of a genius! But as it happens I am! A friend of mine, whose husband was an electrical engineer, asked me if I would go to the Coliseum with her, to see a thought reader, called Anna Eva Fay. She had created a tremendous sensation in America and the Coliseum was packed every performance. My friend's husband had had a lot of copper wire stolen and said if she could find out who stole it he would give her a nice present – she had already been twice to the Coliseum to ask Anna Eva Fay but had had no answer to her question. Well off we went together, and sat in a crowded balcony, the whole place was packed. Presently a man came around among the people with slips of paper, for you to write your question on. I was not going to ask anything, but my friend persuaded me to, and as at that time I was being a good deal pestered by relations and friends about letting Noël be on the stage, instead of at school, and had doubts in my own mind as to what was the wisest thing to do, I wrote on my slip, "Shall I keep my son Noël Coward on the stage, or not?" The slip was torn off and given to me and I kept it for years. Then there was a hush, and Miss Fay came on to the stage with her male assistant. She spoke a few words and then sat on a chair and the man put a sheet over her. She held out her arms like a ghost and answered one or two questions and then called out: "Mrs Coward! Mrs Coward!" My friend prodded me in the ribs, and I had to stand up, and she shouted out: "You ask me about your son Noël Coward. Keep him where he is, keep him where he is. He has great talent, and will have a wonderful career!" I was entirely flabbergasted. My friend pulled me down and we immediately wrote what she had said on a piece of paper so as not to forget a word of it. But my feelings were beyond words – how could she know and why should she have answered me amongst so many people! My relations and friends were very sceptical about Noël and his cleverness. But I knew perfectly well that Anna Eva Fay was right. She only answered a few more questions and then collapsed and was taken out.

Pause.

And my friend was again disappointed about her copper wire.[1]

ESMÉ WYNNE-TYSON *appears, a young woman. Divorced, she is a writer and a devoted, not to say missionary, Christian Scientist. The date changes: 1932. The setting is, ostensibly, Firefly Hill on Jamaica, but the "Neverland" set will serve.*

ESMÉ [*to Noël*]: I found our rules of palship in an old desk the other day. Would you like a copy? It's terribly funny and shows what complete children we were in some ways, even at fifteen. I'm afraid, however, the "religion" clause has been violated. So, where do we stand legally?

NOËL [*reading from it*]: "We must not talk RELIGION unless it is inevitable. We must swear by 'HONOUR AS A PAL' and hold it THE most sacred of bonds in the world. We must tell each other what we think about the other's appearance or behaviour. NO ONE, not even our Parents, may keep us from one another."

As the two of them speak, time passes and they age, fractionally. They do not address one another face to face, but stand at either side of the stage, looking straight ahead. It should not always be entirely clear that they hear one another. The date begins to scroll, hits 1952.

ESMÉ [*to herself*]: Went to lunch with Poj. We talked for an hour and a half. Very sweet.

NOËL [*to himself*]: Stoj reappeared from the past and came to lunch. Fattish with white hair. She was very cheerful and somehow touching because she talked more absolute nonsense than I have ever heard in my life. Her development from a bouncing, sexy, determined girl into this arid, muddled, moralising, elderly crank is fascinating. It is her complete compensation for being a failure as an actress, as a writer and as a wife. It is also a supreme compensation to her for my career of nasty, enviable, materialistic success. Yet she is an amiable enough creature.[2]

ESMÉ [*to Noël*]: You know, it's impractically impossible to talk really seriously face to face with you. I believe it's a sort of psychological armour. And it certainly has its points – and disadvantages, the chief of them being that you always see other people with a layer of artificiality over them. You prefer them like that, depth being uncomfortable. I used to think your habit of evading a logical issue to an argument through abuse or humour was weakness. I'm now convinced it's a protective armour.

NOËL [*to Esmé*]: I fear we shall never see human life eye to eye and tooth to tooth and cheek to cheek and bottom to bottom. It is my considered opinion that the human race (*soi disant*) is cruel, idiotic, sentimental, predatory, ungrateful, ugly, conceited and egocentric to the last ditch and that the occasional discovery of an isolated exception is as deliciously surprising as finding a sudden brazil nut in what you *know* to be five pounds of vanilla creams. You may well imagine that with such a jaundiced view I am a very unhappy creature but this is not so – I have a very nice time all told and enjoy life keenly – perhaps I only *think* I'm happy – perhaps I shall suddenly find Jesus, but I still have the grace to hope, both for his sake and for mine, that I don't! I don't believe I am thinking very differently from the way I have always thought.

ESMÉ: Might that not indicate a slight lack of progress?

NOËL [*lighting a cigarette*]: My philosophy is as simple as ever. I love smoking, drinking, moderate sexual intercourse on a diminishing scale, reading and writing (not arithmetic).

ESMÉ: Your memory appears to fail you. You say "I love smoking, drinking . . ." but in the most clear-sighted period of our close companionship, you did neither, thinking it was more original and sensible not to.

NOËL: I have a selfless absorption in the well-being and achievements of Noël Coward. I do not care for any Church (even the dear old Mother Church) and I don't believe there is a Universal Truth and if you have found it you're a better man than I am, Gunga Din. I have built myself a little house in Jamaica on the edge of the sea where I eat bread-fruit, coconuts, yams, bananas and rather curious fish and where I also lie in the sun and relax.

ESMÉ: I like your Jamaican diet, except for the fish. Why take it out on the fish?

NOËL: I am pegging on with my nose to the grindstone and my shoulder to the wheel and also with a great deal of love for my childhood playmate, whom I should like to see again. If I should happen to "pop" tomorrow I have no complaints – I have had a very happy and full life with enough sadness here and there to highlight the happiness. You have found peace and content in research and solitude. A rare treasure. Whether or not the truths you have discovered are transferable is not the point. The point is that *you* have discovered them. Or It. But *don't*, dear perennial reformer, waste *too* much mental time trying to impart it because that, my darling, leads to disillusion, irritation, discouragement, a thorough upset of your spiritual acids and frequently spots on the back.

ESMÉ: Aren't you a bit unrealistic in your advice to me not to impart what I know? It really isn't just a cosy "piece of mind" I've found. It is the answer to what I believe are fundamental questions. Bits of us remain just the same as they were fifty years ago, and we're probably right to keep to them, instead of meeting and disagreeing on many issues.

NOËL: Oh dear, *I* wish we saw each other more often. Let's have a try when spring breaks through again! Don't be put off by this elegance. It's all a hideous mockery. [*an exquisitely timed pause*] I *still* pick my nose.

The date hits 1960. They are ageing now, perceptibly, as the lights begin to dim. ESMÉ *is suffering from Parkinson's disease.*

ESMÉ: I wonder if you remember us standing in a field during that awful *Charley's Aunt* tour, realising (as I see it was now) power.

NOËL: I think we both decided then and there (if not before) that we were going to get what we wanted and, both being determined characters to say the least of it, we succeeded.

ESMÉ: We admitted to each other that we felt within us the power to achieve anything, and your integrated wish was to have the world at your feet, theatrically speaking. There is a fairy-tale quality about our two wishes that would make a wonderful book.

NOËL: I remember, I remember so very very well that long ago day in that far away field. "And the — something — bells chime to the sentinel Angel of the Watch who smiles to heaven and answers back, 'All's well, sweet bells, all's well.'" *Charley's Aunt*, act three. Thank God for my classical education.[3]

1970, now.

ESMÉ: Look after your **infant self**, still much loved by his Stoj.

NOËL: I am of course delighted to have the knighthood. So from now on I shall expect a great deal more deference from you than I have received in the past. You must never sit in my presence — unless I happen to have thrown you out onto the sofa. [*more quietly*] All loving love, my darling old pal. Your devoted old Sir Poj.

It is 1972. The light on ESMÉ *goes out.*
It is 1973. The light on NOËL COWARD *begins slowly to fade.*[4]

Enter GRAHAM PAYN, COLE LESLEY, *and* GEOFFREY JOHNSON, *with two members of the staff at Firefly Hill,* MIGUEL FRASER *and* DESMOND GORDON.
They reminisce. Firefly/Neverland, still.

COLE: Every detail of the hours we spent with Noël during the last four days of his life is etched on the memory. Because of the news of Binkie's death one's sensitivities to everything were heightened; an extra awareness of the beauties of the visual world, for Firefly

Hill was looking its loveliest. From where we sat with Noël on his verandah, vividly perceptible against the sea and blue sky, the tulip trees we planted so long ago were in abundant scarlet blossom. Emotions too were more susceptible; there was an extra edge to our laughter and our sadness.

GRAHAM: Coley and I were unwilling to accept the fact of Noël's rapid deterioration, so at Firefly and Blue Harbour we soon slipped back into the old routine.

GEOFFREY: But he was getting so fragile. I wanted to go up to him and smack the cigarettes out of his mouth. That wasn't the only thing that was affecting him, but he wasn't taking care of himself *at all*. I think he'd lost the will.

MIGUEL: One day, Master sitting here and he ring the bell for me. I come and he say, "Help me up, Miguel." I say, "What's the matter, Master? You sick?" He say, "No Miguel, I'm drunk." I take him to his bed and undress him. He say, "Ah Miguel, you're better than a mother to his child."

COLE: When we arrived on that last evening, Graham again gently steered him away from Binkie's death. We could not know that this was the last evening we should ever spend together, but even had we known and had planned it, it could not have been more peaceful or more quietly happy, or more perfectly evocative of the countless evenings we had spent witnessing the Firefly pageant.

GRAHAM: There were drink and chat and lots of laughs. Noël had always enjoyed privacy but lately it had become a necessity which Coley and I respected. Messing around during the day, evening drinks up at Firefly, waiting for the white owl to signal the arrival of dusk. Then the fireflies . . .

COLE: They looked as though someone had carelessly scattered a necklace and left it lying, sparkling in the dark. We all agreed that we had had a lovely evening and the magic of Firefly Hill had been as potent as ever. Noël over the years had had great fun, from time to time, speculating on what his last words would be. Would they be Famous Last Words? Of course, he said, he would like to utter something frightfully witty. In the event, the last words Noël spoke to Graham and me were as simple and for us as touching as he could have wished. He called – we were halfway down the steps of his verandah – "Good night, my darlings, I'll see you tomorrow"—

GRAHAM: [*slightly overlapping*] – Noël called out, "Goodnight, my darlings. See you in the morning!" We left him sitting in his chair on the terrace, his wire-rimmed glasses perched on the end of his nose and a copy of E. Nesbit's *The Enchanted Castle* propped up in front of him, with *The Would-Be-Goods* close by.

COLE: The events of the next day remain perfectly clear in my mind, yet I find difficulty in giving a lucid account of it, how Geoffrey, Graham and I got through it.

MIGUEL: My wife passing by round 6 a.m. and she hear moaning from the bathroom. She come get me. First I don't want to go cause he get very mad if he disturbed but she say, "Something wrong there." I go to the door and say, "Master, Master, let me in . . ." but he don't answer so I get a ladder and break the shutter and see Master lying on the bathroom floor. I tell my wife, "Go quick to Blue Harbour and fetch Mr Payn and Mr Lesley." I pick Master up and take him to the bed. He was rubbing at his chest.

COLE: I was wakened by Firefly's "head man", Jaghai, knocking on my door. His face was sad and stricken. "Master very sick" was all he said. Graham and I scrambled into some clothes.

MIGUEL: Master open his eyes and say, "Miguel, where's Mr Payn and Mr Lesley." I say, "They coming, sir", then he reach up and pat me twice on the shoulder and say, "Never mind, Miguel, never mind." I know he's gone. His teeth come out so I put them back, then I come to the balcony. The car arrive with Mr Payn and Mr Lesley.

COLE: Miguel was standing motionless on the verandah outside Noël's rooms, his cheeks wet with tears.

MIGUEL: I call and say, "Master gone, sir." Mr Lesley say—

COLE: "Stop it Miguel. Don't say that."

MIGUEL: I say, "It true sir, Master gone sir." Mr Lesley put his hands on top of his head and he go spinning around on the lawn with tears streaming down.

Pause.

GRAHAM: In true Jamaican fashion, Miguel continued to embroider his narrative over time. Sometimes Noël's last words were changed to, "No, it's too early. They'll be asleep," but the truth will never be known, since Miguel is now dead, murdered in some local disagreement.

The lights fade on MIGUEL.

COLE: We went in to Noël's room and it was true. Noël lay with his head on the pillows looking for all the world as though he had gone comfortably to sleep. What had he been reading? We hurried to see and there, on his table, were two E. Nesbits; he had read halfway through *The Enchanted Castle* and left it lying open.

EDITH NESBIT [*either faintly appearing or in voiceover, reading aloud*]: "There were three of them – Jerry, Jimmy, and Kathleen. Of course Jerry's name was Gerald, and not Jeremiah, whatever you may think, and Jimmy's name was James . . ."

GEOFFREY: I was staying in another guest house on the property. Blue Harbour was deserted when I went up. I found one of the servants and they told me what had happened. So I asked if he could drive me up, because it's not within walking distance. So he did. Noël was still in bed. And of course Coley and Graham were in very bad shape, so I tried to do whatever I could.

DESMOND: I was coming up to work, I don't remember the date, early morning it was about. And I saw Mr Payn in there and Mr Cole in there, so they stopped right at my foot, and I saw that they was crying. So I said, "What wrong?" "Oh Desmond, oh Desmond, Master die, Master die." So we went in the room, that same room there, and I see him stretch out on the floor there. So the doctor came up and attend him. And the car come and take him away and carry him to Kingston.

GRAHAM: But after they'd taken the coffin away, they had to come back. There'd been some muddle, so they had to return and then set off all over again. So Noël did two exits. Absolutely typical.

GEOFFREY: There was no decision about where they were going to bury him. Should he be buried in Switzerland, should he buried in London? But then we decided to bury him right there. Especially as all of a sudden the press started to arrive. It seemed *incredibly* fast. The British press were there *so* fast. And they were milling around, trying to be polite. And then the American press started; they checked into this terrible little hotel down in Port Maria, doubling up in rooms.

COLE: Noël's burial, three days after his death, took place at four in the afternoon; perhaps the loveliest time of all, when the heat of the day is over and the sun is westering.

DESMOND: Two weeks after, they bury him. Right down there. The body come and they carry it in the church, the church by the right-hand little building down there. And all of us carry him down there and bury down by the grave there. I helped carry him to the grave down there, six of us. We digged out the grave. And the concrete — the mason man do that.[5] [*He leaves*]

Long pause.

NOËL: The only thing that really saddens me over my demise is that I shall not be here to read the nonsense that will be written about me and my works and my motives. There will be books proving conclusively that I was homosexual and books proving equally conclusively that I was not. There will be detailed and inaccurate analyses of my motives for writing this or that and of my character. There will be lists of jokes I never made and gleeful misquotations of words I never said. *What* a pity I shan't be here to enjoy them!⁶

Another group enters: NOËL COWARD*'s biographers.*⁷
SHERIDAN MORLEY, PHILIP HOARE *and* OLIVER SODEN *form a rough line.*
COLE LESLEY *joins them.*

SODEN: Coward had died of a heart attack on 26 March 1973, which oddly (given he was born on 16 December) gave him an identical birthday *and* death-day with Beethoven, whose music made him giggle.

LESLEY: On May 24th, 1973, a Service of Thanksgiving for the life of Noël Coward was held at St Martin-in-the-Fields. Lord Olivier read Noël's early verse and his Last Poem. Yehudi Menuhin, a lone figure in the chancel, played for his friend from Bach's Solo Sonata in E major. Sir John Gielgud – the incomparable voice – read Shakespeare's Sonnet 30.

GIELGUD [*in voiceover*]: But if the while I think on thee dear friend | All losses are restor'd, and sorrows end.

LESLEY: Sir John Betjeman, Poet Laureate, composed and spoke the address.

BETJEMAN [*in voiceover*]: "We are all here today to thank the Lord for the life of Noël Coward. | Noël with two dots over the 'e' | And the firm decided downward stroke of the 'l'. | We can all see him in our mind's eye | And in our mind's ear | We can hear the clipped decided voice."

MORLEY: And then, on March 28th 1984, came the ultimate national accolade: in the presence of more than a thousand people, Queen Elizabeth the Queen Mother unveiled a memorial stone at Westminster Abbey. It read simply "Noël Coward, Playwright, Actor, Composer, 16 December 1899 – 26 March 1973. Buried in Jamaica. A Talent to Amuse."

JOHN LAHR [*the eminent critic, passing through, holding his book* Coward The Playwright, *muttering*]: Noël Coward never believed he had just a talent to amuse. The day Sheridan and I see eye to eye on theatre, gallstones will be jewellery.[8] [*He leaves.*]

MORLEY [*oblivious*]: All that London lacks now is a Noël Coward Theatre, and I cannot believe it will be too long before we get one.

SODEN: Indeed. What Morley knew as the Albery Theatre became the Noël Coward Theatre in 2006. Originally the New Theatre, it was the site of Noël's [*corrects himself*] – Coward's – West End debut as a playwright.

HOARE: The disposal of Coward's estate was precisely indicated in his nine-page will. Despite wild speculation that he had left £10 million, the figure was nearer £275,000. The bulk of the estate went to Graham Payn and Cole Lesley. In 1980, Cole Lesley died of heart failure, leaving Graham Payn as sole heir to Coward's estate. Gladys Calthrop moved to Markham Square in Chelsea. Resolutely elegant to the last, she was often seen strolling across the fashionable King's Road, her head as high as ever. She died in 1980, aged eighty-six. Joyce Carey continued to act on stage and film until the age of ninety. She died in March 1993. Jeffery Amherst died, aged 93, in March 1993.

SODEN: Graham Payn lived into the new century, having stayed on at Les Avants, editing and writing books on Noël Coward, and running the Coward Estate with his partner, Dany Dasto. He had given Firefly to the Jamaican National Heritage Trust, but the building became seriously run-down until Blanche Blackwell's son Chris – a record producer – purchased and restored it into, as they say, a "writer's house museum". Blue Harbour is a hotel. Les Avants has recently been sold. Graham died in November 2005, eighty-seven years old.

Exit GRAHAM PAYN.

The final member of the Coward family was Geoffrey Johnson, whom I met and interviewed in New York, late in 2019. The man whom Cole Lesley called "Gentle Geoffrey" was still gentle, and still handsome, even in his late eighties. The walls of his small Manhattan apartment were hung with Coward's paintings, and he delighted in his involvement with the Coward Estate. He'd become a renowned casting director and after the death of his partner, Jerry, he lived alone. We emailed occasionally during his long isolation over the Covid pandemic. He died in 2021, ninety-one years old.

Exit GEOFFREY JOHNSON.

HOARE: The task of writing the authorised biography was given to James Pope-Hennessy, whom Coward had known since 1943. He was homosexual and pray to "rough trade". Unwisely boasting of the large advance he had received for the book, which he told the *Evening Standard* he had not yet banked, he was found dead in his Ladbroke Grove home with a silk stocking around his throat.

SODEN [*trying to keep a note of smug correction from his voice*]: Well . . . he died in hospital, in January 1974, choking on his own blood from a lip wound after being attacked by three men.

HOARE: When the *Standard* breezily printed the amount of my own advance, I made sure the chain was on the door.

SODEN *looks glum. Says nothing.*

Responsibility for the book fell to Cole Lesley. Published in Britain in 1976 as *The Life of Noël Coward* it was well received as an affectionate and revealing account of his former master, but not revealing enough, said some. The first obstacle to my own biography was a substantial one, in the shape of Sheridan Morley, author of the first serious biography of Coward, published in 1969, four years before Coward died. What would he make of an upstart like me? To my relief, he not only didn't mind, he was positively encouraging. I then heard that a writer called Clive Fisher was about to publish his own account of Coward's life. But an appalling sense of schadenfreude overcame me when I learned that Coward's estate had taken against Fisher and were refusing him access to or permission to quote from Coward's unpublished work.

CLIVE FISHER [*enters, reading from his 1992 book,* Noël Coward]: "Samuel Beckett is one of the most overrated playwrights of recent times . . ."

SODEN *raises an eyebrow. Collects himself.*

MORLEY: The explanation of Coward's long and close friendship with Gertrude Lawrence is that in many ways he was very like her . . .

FISHER [*interrupting*]: It is hard to imagine they had a great deal in common, or even a great deal to offer each other; beyond the stage door they were simply business associates.

SODEN [*as if to silence their argument*]: Philip Hoare's biography came out in 1995. On the dustjacket of my copy are several quotations saying it was so good we'd never need another. I took the dustjacket off and threw it away. Hoare hasn't written another cradle-to-grave biography since, which may be a salutary lesson. He writes about whales now. Among other things. [*Turns to* HOARE, *probably with a sycophantic note in his voice*] "Dear Philip, if I may? I hope you won't feel this to be a communication from a horrendous usurper when I say that I've now been contracted to write a new book on Coward, which I assume I shan't finish for a number of years? I'm convinced that the need to look again at Coward, twenty-four years on from your biography, is not at all about trying to trounce previous books . . ."

HOARE: "Dear Oliver. Twenty-four years? Of course it's time! Very best. Philip."[9]

Together, the biographers begin to read from their books.

MORLEY: "So from the very beginning the legend of Noël Coward is destroyed by the facts . . ."

LESLEY: "One winter Monday morning in 1947, Noël Coward and I set out . . ."

FISHER: "Most biographies are about what people become, but a few – Noël Coward's among them – are about what people choose to be . . ."

HOARE: "With impeccable timing, Noël Coward was born on 16 December 1899, just in time to catch the fleeting grandeur of the old century . . ."

SODEN: "Violet Coward doted on her son. He was blond-haired . . ."

The lights fade on the biographers.

NOËL COWARD *and* VIOLET COWARD *have been here all this while.*
NOËL, *naturally, should be centre-stage.*
Choice of background music from NOËL'*s songs at director's discretion.*

VIOLET: We must go.

NOËL: Yes.

VIOLET: Shall we swim or fly?

NOËL: Wendy, do you think you could swim or fly to the island without me?

VIOLET: You know I couldn't, Peter, I am just a beginner.

NOËL: The kite! Why shouldn't it carry you?

VIOLET: Both of us!

NOËL: It can't lift two.

VIOLET: I won't go without you. Let us draw lots which is to stay behind.

NOËL: And you a lady, never! Ready, Wendy!

The kite draws her out of sight across the lagoon.

To die will be an awfully big adventure.

Pause.

[*more himself*] I am neither impressed by, nor frightened of, death. I admit that I am scared about the manner of my dying. I hope not to have to endure agonizing pain or violent panic, but even if I do have to face these things, there is nothing I can do about it, and I can only hope that my life will be interesting and fully lived until the moment I have to say goodbye to it.[10]

The conversation between NOËL COWARD's *characters can be heard either in voice-over or using projection.*

ELYOT: What about after we're dead?

ELVIRA: Not dead — "passed over". It's considered vulgar to say "dead" where I came from.

AMANDA: I think a rather gloomy merging into everything, don't you?

ELYOT: I hope not, I'm a bad merger.

AMANDA: You won't know a thing about it.

ELYOT: I hope for a glorious oblivion, like being under gas.

GARRY ESSENDINE: I don't give a hoot about posterity. Why should I worry about what people think of me when I'm dead as a doornail, anyway?

SIBYL: I wish I were dead!

With increasing hysteria.

JUDITH BLISS: I wish I were dead!

FLORENCE LANCASTER: I wish I were dead!

LAURA [*quietly*]: I want to die – if only I could die.

Pause.

NOËL: Death seems to me as natural a process as birth; inevitable, absolute and final. If, when it happens to me, I find myself in a sort of Odeon ante-room, queueing up for an interview with Our Lord, I shall be very surprised indeed.[11]

He makes to leave, but stops to watch an eleven-year-old boy enter, dressed as PRINCE MUSSEL, *the court jester, in a play called* The Goldfish *by* MISS LILA FIELD. *The boy speaks.*

PRINCE MUSSEL: Do you call me merry? Bah – you cannot read below the surface – my heart is breaking, and still I must laugh, laugh, and keep the ball of merriment rolling![12]

THE CURTAIN FALLS

Noël Coward (*right*) as Prince Mussel, the court jester,
in *The Goldfish*, 1911.

Acknowledgements

"There are hundreds of ways of describing unkindness and meanness and little cruelties. A sly dig at the right moment can work
wonders. But just try to write of generosity. Try to frame in words
an unrelated, motiveless gesture of sheer kindness and you are lost."

Noël Coward, *Present Indicative*

A great deal of this book was written during the various lock-
downs of the Covid-19 pandemic. I do not think this would have
been possible without the generosity, knowledge, and care with
which librarians and archivists across the world provided digitised
manuscripts, answered queries, and – when eventually possible –
welcomed me in person. My profound thanks to the following:
Beinecke Rare Book and Manuscript Library, Yale University (Rebecca Maguire; Natalia Sciarini); Bodleian Libraries, Special Collections
(Oliver House); British Library; Cadbury Research Library, Uni-
versity of Birmingham (Mark Eccleston, Hamda Gharib); Churchill
Archives Centre, Churchill College, University of Cambridge
(Jessica Collins); Columbia University, Rare Book and Manuscript
Library (Jennifer B. Lee and Tara Craig); Franklin D. Roosevelt
Presidential Library (Virginia Lewick); Getty Research Institute;
Harry Ransom Center, University of Texas at Austin (Eric Colleary);
Hartley Library, Archives and Special Collections, University of
Southampton (Mary Cockerill, Lara Nelson); Historical Society of
Pennsylvania (Steve Smith); Houghton Library, Harvard Universi-
ty; Howard Gotlieb Archival Research Center, Boston University

(J. C. Johnson); King's College London, Archives (Hannah Gibsoni); The London Library; London School of Economics and Political Science, Library (Francesca Ward); McFarlin Library, Department of Special Collections and University Archives, University of Tulsa, Oklahoma (Abigail Dairaghi); Morris Library, Special Collections, University of Delaware (Valerie C. Stenner); National Archives, Kew, UK; National Archives, MD, USA (Brigitte Flynn); New York Public Library (Doug Reside); Paul Sacher Stiftung (Heidy Zimmermann); The Rosenbach Museum and Library, Philadelphia (Jobi O. Zink); Somerville College Archives, University of Oxford (Kate O'Donnell); Sutton Local Studies and Archive Centre; University of Regina Archives, Canada (Elizabeth Seitz); West Sussex Record Office; Wisconsin Historical Society (Lee Grady).

I would like especially to acknowledge the financial support of the London Library's astonishing undertaking to provide books by post during the pandemic, and the financial assistance of its Carlyle Membership Scheme.

For help, support, and information of various kinds, my grateful thanks to Dominic Alldis; Douglas Atfield; Michael Berkeley; John Bridcut; Philip Clark; Bill Chubb; Jeremy Day-O'Connell; Artemis Cooper; Stephanie Feury; Jean Findlay; Barbara Gardner; Georgia Glover; Sally Groves; Simon Guerrier; Maggi Hambling; Tim Hart; June Henry; Mark Hickman; Thomas Hischak; Richard Hughes; Bruce Hunter; John Hunter Knowles; Jack Macauley; Kika Markham; Edward Mendelson; Susan Ferrier MacKay; Jim McCue; Lucinda Mason Brown; Laura Milburn; Douglas Murray; Emma Nichols; Barney Norris; Victoria Orr Ewing; Therese Oulton and Peter Gidal; Alan Pally; Matthew Parker; the late Jill Paton Walsh; Howard Pollack; Arianne Quinn; Clare Reihill; Tom Roberts; Elisa Rolle; Julian Rota; Judith Sale; Alan Scherstuhl; John Simpson; Beverley Slopen; Jeoffry and Maud Soden; Allan Spence; Richard Streatfeild; Geoffrey Streatfeild; Ann Tonkin and Warren Langley; Susan Traylor; Elizabeth and Francis Tregear; Tilly Vacher; Stephen Walsh; Christopher Wilson; Stuart Wright; Pippa Vaughan.

My bibliography will make clear the extent to which I have depended on others' work. I hugely valued the generosity with which Philip Hoare, Coward's previous biographer, greeted the news of this book and I need hardly say how reliant I have been on his (pre-internet!) research. He sent me the handwritten manuscript of Violet Coward's memoir, given to him by Graham Payn – a gesture not only helpful but generous, and one I dared to interpret as a blessing. The Noël Coward Society, founded in 1999 to celebrate Coward's life and work, provided support in the form of reassurance that Coward still had fans and admirers globally; the Society's magazine, *Home Chat* (ed. John Hunter Knowles), is full of Coward trouvailles and threw up a number of fascinating articles and interesting leads. Brad Rosenstein's exhibition, *Noël Coward: Art and Style* (held at the Guildhall in London in 2021), not only entertained but enlightened. The *Noël Coward Music Index* (currently online at noëlcowardmusic.com) is a jaw-dropping feat of research by the late Alan Farley and by Dominic Vlasto, and was for me a crucial resource.

It was my privilege and pleasure to meet Coward's American manager, the late Geoffrey Johnson, both in London and in New York; a day in his company was enough to convey a sense not only of his enthusiasm and love for his former employer but of his gentle and joyous spirit.

The Noël Coward Archive Trust and the Noël Coward Estate (run by Alan Brodie Representation) provided unstinting help while generously giving me a free hand. I could not be more grateful to Alan Brodie, tireless facilitator and supporter of this book, as also to Sophie Alonso, Carrie Kruitwagen, and Alison Lee. The Trust's Cultural Development Officer, Robert Hazle, made research a pleasure with his endless and uncomplaining help, hosting me at the Coward Archive's various locations; ferrying documents from one venue to another; providing information, photographs, encouragement, and, most valuable of all, good company. Coward was so prolific a writer that the Trust's loan of his collected works was indispensable.

This book was commissioned by Alan Samson at Weidenfeld, assisted by Simon Wright, and I am more than grateful to them. On Alan's departure, Ed Lake inherited the project, and instantly suggested the title that had been hiding in plain sight – a great gift. He read the manuscript with wit and care and has proved the perfect editor, ably assisted by Georgia Goodall who oversaw every corner of this epic project with patience and brilliance. Natalie Dawkins provided invaluable help with photographs; Sue Lascelles was a meticulous copy-editor; Kirsty Haworth got me through the nitty-gritty of copyrights. I'm indebted to Anne O'Brien for proofreading so carefully; to Christopher Phipps for the marvellously navigable and detailed index; and to Input Data Services for typesetting this complex project.

Thanks as always to my agent Ian Drury and all at Sheil Land.

I have relied more heavily than is considerate on the company and encouragement of friends – in particular Eileen Atkins, Roger Savage, Ruth Smith, and Lucy Walker – who during times of solitude and frustration offered wise help and support, both practical and emotional, with the manuscript and with life (which often seemed the same thing). They made both things infinitely better.

I could not write without the support of my parents, Louise and Ian Soden. I could not do much at all without Yrja Thorsdottir. To them, as ever, love and gratitude always.

PERMISSIONS

All Noël Coward's words and writings, published and unpublished, are © N. C. Aventales AG, successor in title to the Noël Coward Estate, c/o Alan Brodie Representation Ltd (abr@alanbrodie.com). Use is by arrangement with Alan Brodie Representation and the Noël Coward Archive Trust, to whom I am extremely grateful. Extracts from *Collected Plays* (1999–2018), *The Complete Lyrics* (1998), *Collected Short Stories* (1985), *Collected Revue Sketches and Parodies* (1999), and *The Complete Verse* (2011) are included by arrangement with Methuen Drama, an imprint of Bloomsbury Publishing Plc. Excerpts from *The Sickle Side of the Moon: The Letters of Virginia Woolf, Volume 5, 1932–1935* by Virginia Woolf (published by Chatto & Windus, © Quentin Bell and Angelica Garnett, 1994) are reproduced by permission of The Random House Group Limited. Extracts from the writings of T. S. Eliot are included by kind permission of Clare Reihill and Faber and Faber Ltd. Unpublished letters by Duff Cooper and by

Diana Cooper are included by kind permission of the Trustees of the Duff and Diana Cooper Archive. I am grateful to Susan Traylor and Stephanie Feury for their permission to include the letter from William Traylor; to Tilly Vacher for permission to use the letters of Esmé Wynne-Tyson; and to Dame Joan Plowright, Lady Olivier, for permission to use Laurence Olivier's words on Noël Coward.

All photographs are included by kind permission of the Noël Coward Archive Trust, with the following exceptions. Photo 3: Richard Bebb Collection / Bridgeman Images; 4, 17: University of Bristol Theatre Collection / ArenaPAL; 5: The Dulwich College Archive (by kind permission of the Governors); 9, 10, 11: National Portrait Gallery; 12, 20, 25, 34, 44: Mander and Mitchenson / University of Bristol Theatre Collection / ArenaPAL; 13, 19, 27: Sasha / Hulton Archive / Getty Images; 15: Culture Club / Getty Images; 16: James Abbe Collection; 18, 42: Imperial War Museum; 21, 46, 50: Bettman / Getty Images; 23: Hulton Deutsch / Getty Images; 26: Performing Arts Images / ArenaPAL; 28, 30: Mary Evans Picture Library; 29: Popperfoto / Getty Images; 33: Charlie J Ercilla / Alamy / Thomas Messel; 35: Library of Congress / Getty Images; 36: ullstein bild Dtl / Getty Images; 39, 40: Gwen Watford Collection / Bridgeman Images; 41: Dairy Herald Archives / Getty Images; 45: LMPC / Getty Images; 48: Susan Traylor; 49: David Cairns / Express / Getty Images; 51: Maggi Hambling; at p. 548: Trinity Mirror / Mirrorpix / Alamy.

While every effort has been made to trace or contact all copyright holders, the publishers would be pleased to rectify at the earliest opportunity any errors or omissions brought to their attention.

NOTES

Noël Coward could never bring himself to glance at a footnote, "after John Barrymore expressed the opinion that having to look at a footnote was like having to go down to answer the front door just as you were coming". I offer endnotes in the hope that post-coital tristesse is preferable to *coitus interruptus*.

Manuscript sources are only cited where there is no published version. Dates in square brackets indicate undated documents for which a date has been determined or estimated. Unpublished quotations from Coward's diaries (of which the originals are at Yale) I have cited to copies held at the Noël Coward Archive in London. In cases where the Coward Collection at the Cadbury Research Library, University of Birmingham, duplicates documents at the Noël Coward Archive, I have cited the latter.

Unless stated, the author is Noël Coward; recipients of letters are given only if unmentioned in the main text.

PROLOGUE
[1] "On Poetry and Drama" (1954), in Eliot, *Complete Prose*, 8, p. 17.
[2] Beaton, *Self-Portrait with Friends*, p. 12.
[3] Rorem, *The Nantucket Diary*, p. 6.
[4] *Diaries* (31 Dec. 1969), p. 679.

THE RAINBOW
[1] Since renumbered to 131.
[2] Coward (Violet), *Reminiscences of Noël*, Coward Archive.

[3] Lesley, *The Life of Noël Coward*, p. 185.
[4] *Autobiography*, p. 290.
[5] Lesley, *The Life of Noël Coward*, p. 185.
[6] See 1901 Census, in which Arthur S. Coward is listed as "music publisher's clerk". Coward thought that a maid from his later childhood, Emma Adams, had cared for him since his birth, but the census listing implies that she did not appear until the Cowards moved to Sutton

a few years later.

7 See "The Vaccination Acts", *Middlesex and Surrey Express*, 13 Feb. 1901, p. 3.

8 Coward (Violet), *Reminiscences of Noël*, Coward Archive.

9 By 1911 "St Margaret's" in Worcester Road was no longer functioning as a school, nor had it been in 1901, nor is a Miss Willington traceable in either census. It is possible that the institution and its head teacher were disguised in Coward's account.

10 *Cherry Pan*, Notebook 19, Coward Archive, NPC-0293.

11 [1907], *Letters*, p. 18.

12 See Stella King, "Noël Coward", *The Times*, 26 July 1966, p. 15.

13 Coward (Violet), *Reminiscences of Noël*, Coward Archive.

14 Selfe was a leading light in various amateur operatic and musical societies. See *Norwood News*, 15 May 1909, p. 5; *The Referee*, 26 Apr. 1908, p. 5. Also "The Chapel Royal", *The Musical Times and Singing Class Circular*, 1 Feb. 1902, p. 91.

15 *The Magnet*, Vol. 1, No. 1 (1908), cover.

16 Coward remembered the whole family making a trip to watch Kaiser Wilhelm II take part in the races of the Cowes Week Regatta (*Autobiography*, p. 43) but the Kaiser did not visit Cowes after 1895, and relations between the two countries were already deteriorating.

17 She inherited around £380 (just short of £40,000 in today's money). See *Wills and Probate 1908*, p. 108.

18 [1909], *Letters*, p. 19.

19 *Morning Post*, 30 June 1909, p. 1.

20 *Daily Mirror*, 7 Sep. 1910, p. 5.

21 Coward (Violet), *Reminiscences of Noël*, Coward Archive.

22 June, *The Glass Ladder*, p. 9.

23 June, *The Glass Ladder*, p. 9.

24 Mac Liammóir, *All for Hecuba*, pp. 8–9.

25 June, *The Glass Ladder*, p. 12.

26 *Westminster Gazette*, 28 Jan. 1911, p. 13.

27 "Lord Chamberlain's Department", 1912. National Archives, T 1/11384/2320.

28 de Valois, *Come Dance With Me*, p. 30. Ninette de Valois did not appear in *The Goldfish* as is sometimes stated.

29 As related by the 1911 census, which gives Arthur's profession as "travelling salesman".

30 See June, *The Glass Ladder*, pp. 14–15.

31 *Autobiography*, p. 20.

32 *Autobiography*, p. 21.

33 Gingold, *How to Grow Old*, p. 32.

34 "Where The Rainbow Ends", *Sunday Times*, 15 Dec. 1912, p. 6. The review refers to the production's first revival.

35 Coward (Violet), *Reminiscences of Noël*, Coward Archive.

36 See Dyan Colclough, "British child performers 1920–40", in Arrighi (ed.), *Entertaining Children*, p. 76.

37 See Hawtrey, *The Truth at Last*, pp. 300–301.

38 Coward described the friendship as beginning in "Spring 1914" (*Autobiography*, p. 32), but Violet Coward remembered that by 1912 the pair were collaborating on plays and in

1914 Wynne was sent to a Belgian convent, by which time Coward was sending her weekly letters. See Wynne-Tyson, *Finding the Words*, p. 133.

39 Wynne is usually described as having been an established child star but *Where the Rainbow Ends* was only her second appearance, following Maeterlinck's *The Blue Bird* (at the Haymarket Theatre, in December 1910) in which she had played not the lead but an uncredited walk-on. See "The Blue Bird", *The Times*, 20 Dec. 1910, p. 12.

40 The script is lost; it is described in Coward (Violet), *Reminiscences of Noël*, Coward Archive.

41 Gingold, *How to Grow Old*, p. 33. See also Hawtrey, *The Truth at Last*, p. 303, and *The Stage*, 1 Feb. 1912, p. 18.

42 *Letters*, pp. 29-30.

43 [Summer 1912], *Letters*, p. 18.

44 *Autobiography*, p. 24.

45 Dean, *Seven Ages*, p. 100.

46 *Autobiography*, p. 27.

47 See Coward's "Introduction" [1967] to Saki, *Complete Works*, p. xii.

48 *The Era*, 25 June 1913, p. 7.

49 Quoted in Lesley, *The Life of Noël Coward*, p. 22.

50 Tynan, *Tynan on Theatre*, p. 286.

51 Field, *The Goldfish*, p. 4.

52 Mac Liammóir, *All for Hecuba*, p. 7.

53 Chase, *Peter Pan's Postbag*, p. vi.

54 "The Little Theatre", *The Times*, 28 Jan. 1911, p. 12.

55 Mac Liammóir, *All for Hecuba*, p. 7.

56 See Morley, *A Talent to Amuse*, p. 26.

57 Notebook 2, Coward Archive, NPC-0186.

58 *Autobiography*, pp. 33–4.

59 Watts, *Mrs Sappho*, p. 79; Geoffrey Holdsworth, "The Boy Dramatist", *Daily Dispatch*, 3 May 1920; Mannin, *Confessions and Impressions*, p. 116.

60 [June 1914], *Letters*, pp. 32–3.

61 14 Mar. 1960, *Letters*, p. 47.

62 Shepard, *Drawn from Life*, p. 134.

63 See *The Era*, 29 Jan. 1910, p. 14. At one of Streatfeild's studio gatherings Oscar Wilde's "Endymion" was performed.

64 Streatfeild's sketch of the actor Peter Upcher – made in a style similar to his surviving drawing of Coward – is reproduced in *The Tatler*, 15 Nov. 1911, p. 52. (Upcher, a member of the "Junior Follies", was nineteen but in Streatfeild's drawing looks considerably younger.) Coward was present when the child actress Phyllis Monkman (1892–1976) sat for Streatfeild for her portrait (see *Autobiography*, p. 31). For accounts of Streatfeild's performances see *The Stage*, 11 July 1912, p. 21 and 28 Mar. 1914, p. 8; and *The Scotsman*, 30 Mar. 1914, p. 8.

65 See Guerrier, *Family Memories* (written by Streatfeild's great nephew).

66 Philip Hoare, "Something mad about the boy", *Independent*, 11 Apr. 1998. "[Streatfeild] had studied with the American John Singer Sargent, the fashionable portrait painter of the time [. . .] Philip used to claim that some of Sargent's portraits were entirely his." Guerrier, *Family Memories*.

67 *Bathers on the Rocks*, 1914, discovered by Philip Hoare, to whose work on

Streatfeild I am particularly indebted (see Hoare, *Noël Coward*, pp. 32–6).

68 The gun was found in right-handed Buchanan's left hand. See reports of the case in *Sheffield Daily Telegraph*, 13 June 1912, p. 11; *Dundee Evening Telegraph*, 13 June 1912, p. 2.

69 Sydney Oswald [Lomer], *The Greek Anthology, Epigrams from Anthologia Palatina XII translated into English Verse*, privately printed, 1914. The volume has been reprinted by Hermitage Books (Norfolk, 1992).

70 See Cooper, *The Sexual Perspective*, Chapter 2; and Michael Hatt, "'A great sight': Henry Scott Tuke and his models", in Desmarais (ed.), *Model and Supermodel*, pp. 89–104.

71 Wilfred Gabriel de Glehn, *Mavis Yorke Dancing in Where the Rainbow Ends*, 1913.

72 Hawtrey, *The Truth at Last*, p. 302.

SERVICES RENDERED

1 [Aug. 1914], *Letters*, pp 25-6. Minor cuts silently implemented.

2 Walpole, *Extracts from a Diary*, p. 14.

3 [*c.* Sep.-Oct., 1914], *Letters*, p. 28.

4 [*c.* Sep.-Oct., 1914], *Letters*, p. 28, with "Somers" for "Lomer".

5 [*c.* Sep.-Nov., 1914], *Letters*, p. 28, with "Somer's" for "Lomer's".

6 Streatfeild eventually left an estate of £828 (around £82,000 today); see *Wills and Probate, 1915*, p. 351. Also "Supplement" to *The London Gazette*, 9 Nov. 1914, p. 9124, and Philip Hoare, "Something mad about the boy", *Independent*, 11 Apr. 1998.

7 See *Hansard*, 4 June 1951.

8 The chronology and location of Coward's stay at Pinewood Sanatorium are uncertain. Coward remembered it as being in Wokingham, Berkshire (*Autobiography*, p. 36), but matters are complicated by undated letters written when he was evidently staying with Dr Etlinger in Cranham, near Stroud in Gloucestershire (Lesley, *The Life of Noël Coward*, pp. 24–5). Dr Frederick Kincaid Etlinger was the superintendent of Cotswold Sanatorium in Cranham until 1913 (see J. K. Whitton, *A History of the Cotswold Sanatorium Company Ltd*, privately printed, 1998). That year he and his family moved to the Pinewood Sanatorium in Berkshire; he transferred to Matlock House Sanatorium in Derbyshire in 1918. It seems that Coward visited the Etlingers in Cranham in *c.* 1912 simply for a holiday (the couple were family friends, and the letters outline activities too strenuous for a tubercular boy undergoing a rest cure).

9 "My son contracted Trench Fever and in Mar. 1915 had to be removed to hospital; after months of great suffering, and a major operation, he died in a nursing house at Norbury on the 3rd June 1915 and was buried with military honours in Streatham Cemetery." Arthur Streatfeild to McCulloch Christison, 30 May 1921 (Dulwich College Archive). Many details of Streatfeild's last months are taken from this letter. See also Hoare, *Noël Coward*, p. 44; Guerrier, *Family Memories*; Imperial War Museum

Bond of Sacrifice, HU 118697.
Streatfeild's older brother, (Arthur
Herbert) Morton Streatfeild, died of
TB in 1893, aged sixteen.

[10] *Autobiography*, p. 37.

[11] Eva Astley Cooper's memoir, quoted
in Hoare, *Noël Coward*, p. 39.

[12] Hawtrey, *The Truth at Last*, p. 315.

[13] "Introduction" [1967] to Saki,
Complete Works, p. x.

[14] See Langguth, *Saki*, p. 182.

[15] "Where The Rainbow Ends", *Observer*, 2 Jan. 1916, p. 9.

[16] "Fairies at the Garrick", *The Times*,
28 Dec. 1915, p. 10.

[17] Braybrooke, *The Amazing Mr. Noël
Coward*, p. 23.

[18] *Autobiography*, p. 39.

[19] *Autobiography*, p. 39.

[20] To Violet Coward [w/b 10 Apr.
1916], Coward Archive.

[21] Related in Hoare, *Noël Coward*, p. 49
(quoting writer Robin Maugham's
unpublished diary).

[22] [w/b 24 Apr. 1916], Coward
Archive.

[23] [Jan.–June 1916], Coward Archive,
and *Letters*, pp. 34–6.

[24] [Jan. June 1916], Coward Archive,
and *Letters*, pp. 34–6.

[25] To Violet Coward [w/b 29 May
1916], Coward Archive.

[26] Castle, *Noël*, p. 32.

[27] 27 Oct. 1930, Coward Archive,
NPC-5334.

[28] See Castle, *Noël*, pp. 32–3. There
were no raids on London during
the two-week run, so Courtneidge's
memory of bombs disrupting
the first night cannot be entirely
accurate. Details of all zeppelin raids
during the First World War are
taken from www.iancastlezeppelin.
co.uk (accessed Apr. 2020).

[29] Castle, *Noël*, p. 33.

[30] Drake, *Blind Fortune*, p. 28.

[31] "The Happy Family", *The Times*, 19
Dec. 1916, p. 11.

[32] See Notebook 18, Coward Archive,
NPC-0198; also "Scripts" and "Song
Collaborations", in Wynne and
Coward Collection, THM/287/6, 8.

[33] Coward (Violet), *Reminiscences of Noël*,
Coward Archive.

[34] Record of Service Paper, John
Robert Warre Ekins. National
Archives, Airmen's Service Records,
1912–1939.

[35] Notebook 18, Coward Archive,
NPC-0198.

[36] To Violet Coward [spring 1923],
Coward Archive.

[37] See *The Stage*, 20 Sep. 1917, p. 17;
Cambridge Daily News, 18 Sep. 1917,
p. 4.

[38] *Lyrics*, p. 17.

[39] [Aug. 1917], *Letters*, p. 51.

[40] [Aug. 1917], *Letters*, p. 51.

[41] *Autobiography*, p. 233.

[42] Notebook 17, Coward Archive,
NPC-0197.

[43] "The Saving Grace", *The Times*, 11
Oct. 1917, p. 11.

[44] See *The Era*, 13 Feb. 1918, p. 22.

[45] *The Era*, 23 Jan. 1918, p. 6.

[46] In January 1917 Coward was giving
his address as Clapham Common;
he inscribed 111 Ebury Street in a
notebook on 13 December 1917
(Coward Archive).

[47] See *Surrey Mirror*, 29 Mar. 1918,
p. 1. Coward remembered the play

as being written by Hazel May and produced by H. K. Ayliff (see *Autobiography*, p. 53). Both were actors in the production; the playwright was A. G. Rhode and the producer E. Holman Clark.

48 As in Castle, *Noël*, p. 32.

49 See East Surrey Regiment, Recruitment Register, Mar. 1918, Surrey History Centre, 2496/28.

50 "Record of Service Paper". Soldiers' Documents, First World War, National Archives, WO 363/C 1415.

51 *Autobiography*, p. 56.

52 Medical categories listed in *Registration and Recruiting*, War Office, Aug. 1916; quoted in *Hansard*, 20 June 1918, Vol. 107, p. 608.

53 The camp is described in Hibberd, *Wilfred Owen*, Chapter 10.

54 *Autobiography*, p. 56.

55 Notebook 15, Coward Archive, NPC-0195.

56 See Notebook 48, Coward Archive, NPC-0299. The song has hitherto been dated 1915, but its notebook draft seems to have been written in 1918; no earlier version survives.

57 "The Boy Dramatist", *Daily Dispatch*, 3 May 1920. See also Carey (pseud. Holdsworth), *The Rest is Lies*. Holdsworth was not, as has been assumed, homosexual; his memoir bemoans the rise of homosexuality after the war, and his friend Alec Waugh recalled his search for "dusky damsels" while travelling in the South Sea Islands.

58 Notebook 19, Coward Archive, NPC-0293. Bar the shared concept of Pan's having a daughter, the novel bears no relation to Coward's earlier play *Pan's Daughter*.

59 For chronology see Coward's "Medical Report on an Invalid", Soldiers' Documents from Pension Claims, National Archives, WO 364/822: "Admitted to GMH Colchester on 26/6/18."

60 "Medical Report on an Invalid", Soldiers' Documents from Pension Claims, National Archives, WO 364/822.

61 "Opinion of the Medical Board"; "Casualty Form Active Service"; "Award Sheet – First Award"; "Proceedings on Discharge", Soldiers' Documents from Pension Claims, National Archives, WO 364/822.

62 14 Aug. 1918. John Lane Company Records, Box 60, Folder 1.

63 *The Regimental Roll of Honour and War Record of the Artists' Rifles* (London: Howlett and Son, 1922), pp. 38-42. Coward is entered (as "N.C. Coward") on p. 444.

64 *Autobiography*, p. 72.

65 "Office in charge of Infantry Records to Noël Coward, 9 Dec. 1919." Soldiers' Documents, First World War, National Archives, WO 363/C 1415.

66 *Autobiography*, p. 67.

67 *Autobiography*, p. 68.

68 "G.B. Stern on Noël Coward", unidentified clipping in West Papers, Gen. MSS 105, Box 42, f. 1504.

69 Watts, *Mrs Sappho*, p. 78.

70 See Watts, *Mrs Sappho*, p. 79.

71 Watts, *Mrs Sappho*, pp. 78–9.

72 Mannin, *Confessions and Impressions*, p. 117.

[73] Byng, *As You Were*, pp. 158–9.

[74] Sassoon, *Siegfried's Journey*, p. 83.

[75] See Findlay, *Chasing Lost Time*, pp. 173–4.

[76] Watts, *Mrs Sappho*, p. 78.

[77] See Hoare, *Noël Coward*, pp. 33–4.

[78] Ogilvy, *Once a Saint*, p. 95.

[79] *Cherry Pan*, Notebook 19, Coward Archive, NPC-0293.

[80] The day is described in Richard Nelsson, "The War is over!", *Guardian*, 2 Nov. 2018.

LES ANNÉES FOLLES!
Part One

[1] See "The Victory Ball", *The Times*, 28 Nov. 1918, p. 9; and "Miss Billie Carleton's Death", 4 Dec. 1918, p. 3. The dialogue is taken verbatim from transcripts of the case in *The Pall Mall Gazette*, 14 Feb. 1919, pp. 1–2.

[2] The handwritten script is undated; the typescript is dated 26 February 1919.

[3] *Early Plays*, Coward Archive, NPC-0122. Kit Saville was originally to have been called Katt Saville, leading to the play's working title of *Copy Katts*. This play has occasionally been confused with *The Unattainable* (as in *Plays*, 9, p. ix). An early, untitled, draft of *The Dope Cure* is in Notebook 48 (Coward Archive), which also contains *The Unattainable*.

[4] Notebook 24, dated 29 Aug. 1918, Coward Archive, NPC-0201.

[5] Notebook 20, Coward Archive, NPC-0294.

[6] *Early Plays*, Coward Archive, NPC-0122.

[7] Esmé Wynne to Noël Coward, 1966 (Wynne-Tyson, *Finding the Words*, p. 145).

[8] *Gloucester Citizen*, 22 Jan. 1919, p. 8.

[9] See Notebook 48, Coward Archive, NPC-0299.

[10] *Early Plays*, p. 23, Coward Archive, NPC-0122.

[11] Notebook 17, Coward Archive, NPC-0197.

[12] He was still in the cast on 28 May 1919, but the following week's theatre listings, published on 4 June, quietly omit his name. See *The Globe*, 25 Nov. 1918, p. 9; *The Era*, 28 May 1919, p. 10; and *The Era*, 4 June, 1919, p. 12.

[13] *The Last Trick*, in "Scripts", Wynne and Coward Collection, THM/287/6. As if to set the record straight on his mother's behalf, Esmé's son, Jon Wynne-Tyson, added a memorandum explicitly noting the co-authorship.

[14] Notebook 14, p. 13, p. 28, Coward Archive, NPC-0096.

[15] 29 Aug. 1919, *Letters*, p. 57.

[16] See Findlay, *Finding Lost Time*, pp. 186–8.

[17] *Autobiography*, p. 81.

[18] *Globe*, 22 July 1920, p. 5.

[19] Only the critic Neville Cardus worked out that beneath a veneer of brazen inconsequentiality, Coward was sending up the idle rich. The "broad grin", thought Cardus, was "no longer so fashionable in our theatre as it was", and he argued that Coward was already beginning to move comedy on from the broad brushstrokes of *Charley's Aunt*.

Manchester Guardian, 4 May 1920, p. 13.

20 *The Sphere,* 21 July 1920, p. 24.

21 *The Tatler,* 4 Aug. 1920, p. 28; St. John Ervine, "I'll Leave It to You", *Observer,* 25 July 1920, p. 9.

22 *The Sphere,* 21 July 1920, p. 24 (and *Oxford English Dictionary*).

23 As in *Sunday Mirror,* 25 July 1920, p. 7.

24 Printed in *Hull Daily Mail,* 23 July 1920, p. 7.

25 See *Exeter and Plymouth Gazette,* 24 July 1920, p. 6; *Globe,* 22 July 1920, p. 5; *The Era,* 5 May 1920, p. 6.

26 *Exeter and Plymouth Gazette,* 24 July 1920, p. 6.

27 *The Era,* 11 Aug. 1920, p. 8; 24 Nov. 1920, p. 8.

28 *Autobiography,* p. 84.

29 George Bolton, "Polly With a Past", *The Times,* 3 Mar. 1921, p. 8.

30 "Duchess of Oporto coming", *New York Times,* 4 June 1921, p. 3.

31 Amherst, *Wandering Abroad,* p. 57. See also Philip Hoare, "Obituary: Earl Amherst", *Independent,* 10 Mar. 1993.

32 See "Princess Braganza...", *New York Times,* 11 June 1921, p. 14.

33 *Autobiography,* p. 89.

34 "Flourishes Pistol...", *New York Times,* 11 June 1921, p. 1.

35 "New York Diary", *Letters,* p. 59.

36 Nicholson, *Singled Out,* p. 204.

37 George Bolton, "Polly With a Past", *The Times,* 3 Mar. 1921, p. 8.

38 "New York Diary", *Letters,* p. 60.

39 "New York Diary", *Letters,* p. 61.

40 *Autobiography,* p. 90.

41 De Acosta, *Here Lies The Heart,* p. 131. The address is inscribed in

Coward's 1921 notebooks (Coward Archive).

42 See *New York Times,* 19 Jan. 1921, p. 27.

43 [Sep 1921], *Letters,* p. 62.

44 Courtney, *Laurette,* p. 261.

45 [Sep. 1921], *Letters,* p. 63.

46 *Autobiography,* p. 96.

47 See "Croker sails...", *New York Times,* 29 Oct. 1921, p. 12. In Coward's telegram to his mother, dated 29 October, "sailing next week" must mean "spending next week at sea" rather than "departing next week" (*Letters,* p. 67).

48 *Autobiography,* p. 102.

49 Marie Stopes to Humphrey Verdon Roe, 4 and 5 Nov. 1921 (Briant, *Marie Stopes,* p. 152).

50 Sep. 1921, *Letters,* p. 63.

Part Two

1 The story was recounted to John Hunter Knowles, to whose work on Lathom I am indebted. See www.lathomangel.com (accessed July 2020); Knowles, "Ned Lathom", *Home Chat,* Feb. 2001, pp. 3–4; and David Sudworth, "Lathom Calling!", *Local Life,* Nov/Dec 2014, pp. 28–30.

2 *Independent,* 1 Oct. 2000.

3 Among the working titles for *The Queen Was in the Parlour* were *Nadya* and *Souvenir* (Coward Archive). For *The Happy Harlot* see Notebook 32, Coward Archive, NPC-0253.

4 *Pall Mall Gazette,* 1 June 1922, p. 4. The brief mention of the play in *Autobiography* (p. 115) wrongly implies that the production took

place in 1923.

5 *Illustrated Sporting and Dramatic News*, 24 June 1922, p. 22.

6 See Hand and Wilson, *London's Grand Guignol*, pp. 239–41.

7 Maxwell, *R.S.V.P.*, p. 151.

8 See Notebook 34 (Coward Archive, NPC-0255) for chronology. The play exists in many forms and once under the title *Do Let's Talk About It*. It is often described as being based on Coward's novel *Cats and Dogs* but bar the presence of the "Poj and Stoj" roles – friends rather than siblings in the novel – it does not closely follow the novel's plot.

9 Castle, *Noël*, p. 159.

10 George Bernard Shaw, "Shakespeare: A Standard Text", *Times Literary Supplement*, 17 Mar. 1921, p. 14.

11 Quoted in Lesley, *The Life of Noël Coward*, p. 57.

12 Wynne-Tyson, *Finding the Words*, p. 134.

13 *Mild Oats* was hitherto thought to have been unproduced, but see *Western Daily Press*, 21 Sep. 1922, p. 8. The cast is not listed, although presumably the roles were taken by Coward and by Ann Trevor. *The Last Resource* was licensed by the Lord Chamberlain on 5 January 1923. The script is in the Lord Chamberlain's Plays, LCP 1923/2.

14 *Pall Mall Gazette*, 27 Jan. 1923, p. 4.

15 3 Dec. 1922, *Letters*, p. 77. Coward told his mother "Charlot arrives on Dec. the 3rd to discuss business" (Coward Archive).

16 See Notebook 37, Coward Archive, NPC-0257, and Coward's letter to his mother, c. Nov. 1922: "It will be very thrilling to hear all my songs done by a good orchestra won't it? The title is L.S.D.!" (Coward Archive.)

17 "Bottles and Bones" had been performed by George Grossmith and then placed in a revue called *The Curate's Egg*. A show called *The Co-optimists* had featured two of Coward's lyrics, set to music by Melville Gideon and performed by a topical chorus of dancing revolutionary Marxists.

18 5 Dec. 1922, *Letters*, p. 79.

19 To Violet Coward [Dec. 1922], *Letters*, p. 76.

20 To Violet Coward [12–13 Dec. 1922], *Letters*, p. 81.

21 Notebooks from 1915 contain the poems "Columbine and Harlequin" and "Pierrot and Pierrette" (possibly in Esmé Wynne's handwriting). The working title for "Parisian Pierrot" was "Fantasy beneath the moon" (Coward Archive.).

22 Morley, *A Talent to Amuse*, p. 69.

23 See *Autobiography*, p. 103, which mentions "grinding out an adaptation of a French play for Denis Eadie". *The Love Habit*, a version of Louis Verneuil's *Pour avoir Adrienne*, was produced by the actor-manager Dennis Eadie in February 1923. The script was credited to the leading man, Seymour Hicks, although one critic mentioned "the low comedy of Mr Hicks and Partner" (*Pall Mall Gazette*, 8 Feb. 1923, p. 8).

24 [Spring 1923], Coward Archive.

25 [Apr. 1923], *Letters*, p. 81.

26 He first noted down the title in mid 1922, and told his mother he wanted "time for *The Vortex*" later that year (*Letters*, p. 76).

27 [Spring 1923], Coward Archive.

28 [Spring 1923], Coward Archive.

29 Sketches for *Catherine* are in Notebook 42; *Sweet Pepper* is in Notebook 9; a script of *Fallen Angels* dated 28 October 1923 is in Notebook 44, Coward Archive. Eventually Norman MacDermott would direct his own adaptation of *Sweet Pepper* at the Everyman Theatre in 1925, a year after staging *The Vortex*. See also Coward's letters to his mother (spring 1923, Coward Archive): "*Sweet Pepper* seems to be developing all right"; "You'll be pleased to hear I'm not doing *Sweet Pepper*."

30 *Collected Revue Sketches*, p. 1.

31 See Sarah Whitfield, "Elsie April, 1884–1950", at https://www.rncm.ac.uk/blog/elsie-April-1884-1950/ (accessed 23 Feb. 2021), and "She Helped Noël Coward to Success", *Leicester Evening Mail*, 18 Mar. 1950, p. 7.

32 3 Dec. 1922, *Letters*, p. 77.

33 The Astaire burlesque is described in *Illustrated Sporting and Dramatic News*, 29 Sep. 1923, p. 19.

34 "London Calling", *The Times*, 5 Sep. 1923, p. 8. Many accounts of *London Calling!* include the revue's use of a "shadowgraph", an early form of 3-D that required the audience to wear tinted glasses. But this was not mentioned in any review or in Coward's memories of the production. Confusion seems to have arisen with the *Ziegfeld Follies*.

35 See *The Tatler*, 30 Nov. 1923, p. 49.

36 *Collected Revue Sketches*, pp. 17–19. See also Faye Hammill, "Noël Coward and the Sitwells: Enmity, Celebrity, Popularity", in *Journal of Modern Literature*, Vol. 39, No. 1 (Fall 2015), pp. 129–48.

37 "Another old dame making a sad muddle of modern slang" (*The Stage*, 6 Sep. 1923, p. 6). *The Sketch* (26 Dec. 1923, p. 28) thought similar.

38 Findlay, *Chasing Lost Time*, p. 173.

39 Glendinning, *Edith Sitwell*, p. 80.

40 Pearson, *The Sitwells*, p. 187.

41 *The Sphere*, 30 Oct. 1926, p. 24.

42 Sitwell, *Selected Letters*, pp. 29–30.

43 Nevinson, *Paint and Prejudice*, p. 234.

44 I'm grateful to Stuart Wright for this identification, hitherto unknown. In Wright's private collection are a copy of *Chelsea Buns* inscribed in Calthrop's hand "with the undying admiration of Gaspard Pustontin" and another belonging to Calthrop with Coward's inscription: "I can't write much in this dear you were responsible for half of it. Noël."

45 *Daily Herald*, 29 Nov. 1924, p. 4.

46 *Collected Revue Sketches*, p. 4.

47 *Plays*, 8, p. 77.

48 "Olympic arrives…", *New York Times*, 28 Feb. 1924, p. 24. The ship departed on 22 February (see Passenger Lists Leaving UK, 1890-1960). Also *Daily Mirror*, 16 Feb. 1924, p. 7.

49 See Pollack, *George Gershwin*, p. 159.

50 "New Play by Mr Noël Coward", *The Times*, 24 Mar. 1924, p. 10.

51 *New York Times*, 30 Mar. 1924, p. 1 (giving "Tarantam"); *Daily Telegraph*, 6 Mar. 1924, p. 15.

52 *Lyrics*, p. 62. See also Stephen Banfield, "Scholarship and the Musical: Reclaiming Jerome Kern", *Proceedings of the British Academy*, Vol. 125 (2004), pp. 183–210. Sketches and lyrics for *Tamaran* are spread across three notebooks (9, 41, and 44, Coward Archive), often appearing alongside sketches for *The Vortex*, implying that work began some time in 1923. Sketches made in 1924 for *Dream a Little*, also set in Tamaran, are in Notebook 40, Coward Archive, NPC-0260.

53 [Mar. 1924], *Letters*, p. 62 and Coward Archive.

54 Coward also contributed material for Fred Astaire to perform in a revue called *Yoicks!* which opened in June, and Charlot's *Revue of 1924* came into the West End from Broadway in September.

55 *Autobiography*, p. 125.

56 See Notebook 45, Coward Archive, NPC-0265. The corrections and edits decrease in frequency as the play goes on.

57 See Notebooks 44 and 45, Coward Archive, NPC-0264-5.

58 See Notebook 46, Coward Archive, NPC-0266.

59 See MacDermott, *Everymania*, pp. 67-8, and correspondence between MacDermott and Coward, 12 Nov. 1924, Cadbury Research Library, COW/3/N/1/44/1.

60 Notebook 41, Coward Archive, NPC-0261.

61 *Autobiography*, p. 103.

62 See Virginia Berridge, "The Origins of the English Drug 'Scene', 1890–1930", in *Medical History* (1988), Vol. 32, pp. 51–64.

63 *The Stage*, 5 Feb. 1925, p. 18.

64 As related in "Noël Coward at 29", *New York Times*, 11 Nov. 1928, p. 1, p. 4.

65 MacDermott, *Everymania*, p. 68.

66 MacDermott, *Everymania*, p. 68.

67 MacDermott, *Everymania*, p. 68.

68 See Lord Chamberlain's Plays, LCP CORR 1924/5862, and Hoare, *Noël Coward*, p. 133.

69 MacDermott, *Everymania*, p. 68.

70 7 May [1925], Richmond Autographs sale listing (accessed 7 Feb. 2021).

71 MacDermott, *Everymania*, p. 69.

72 See correspondence between MacDermott and Coward, 14 Nov. 1928, Cadbury Research Library, COW/3/N/1/44/1.

73 The scene quotes, in order (with a few minor cuts silently implemented): *Westminster Gazette*, 26 Nov. 1924, p. 5; *The Times*, 26 Nov. 1924, p. 8; *Observer*, 30 Nov. 1924, p. 11; *The Times*, 26 Nov. 1924, p. 8; *Daily Telegraph*, 27 Nov. 1924; *Daily Graphic*, 29 Nov. 1924; *Daily Mirror*, 27 Nov. 1924, p. 5, 1 Dec. 1924, p. 9, and 3 Dec. 1924, p. 17; *Westminster Gazette*, 29 Nov. 1924, p. 9; *Gentlewoman*, 13 Dec. 1924, p. 13; *Daily Mirror*, 26 Nov. 1924, p. 18; *Northampton Chronicle*, 16 Dec. 1924, p. 2; *Western Mail*, 17 Dec. 1924, p. 6; *Daily Telegraph*, 17 Dec. 1924, p. 10; *The People*, 21 Dec. 1924, p. 8;

Shaw, quoted in Morley, *A Talent to Amuse*, p. 95; *Aberdeen Press*, 17 Dec. 1924, p. 2; *Lyrics*, p. 73; *Westminster Gazette*, 19 Dec. 1924, p. 5; *Sunday Post*, 21 Dec. 1924, p. 11; *Daily Mirror*, 19 Nov. 1924, p. 9; *Western Daily Press*, 29 Oct. 1924, p. 6; *Complete Verse*, p. 73; *Westminster Gazette*, 5 Dec. 1924, p. 4; *Daily Mirror*, 26 Nov. 1924, p. 18; Mannin, *Young in the Twenties*, 33; *Lyrics*, p. 73; *Sunday Mirror*, 30 Nov. 1924, p. 9; *Lyrics*, p. 73; *Complete Verse*, p. 73; Mannin, *Young in the Twenties*, p. 34; *Lyrics*, p. 73; *Autobiography*, p. 136.

THE MASK OF FLIPPANCY
Act One

[1] Braybrooke, *The Amazing Mr Noël Coward*, p. 63.

[2] *Yorkshire Post and Leeds Intelligencer*, 28 Nov. 1924, p. 7.

[3] 29 Oct. 1924 (quoted in Pollack, *George Gershwin*, p. 159).

[4] See Harding, *Gerald Du Maurier*, p. 138.

[5] James Agate, "The Vortex", *Sunday Times*, 30 Nov. 1924, p. 4.

[6] Castle, *Noël*, p. 65.

[7] As on the playbill for the American premiere of *The Vortex*, Sep. 1925.

[8] Castle, *Noël*, p. 65.

[9] Quoted in Morley, "Introduction" to *Plays*, 3, p. xxi.

[10] Bennett, *Journals*, p. 153.

[11] *Daily Mirror*, 1 Apr. 1925, p. 9.

[12] *A Marvellous Party*, Noël Coward Foundation Film, 2020.

[13] Nichols, *Are They The Same At Home?*, p. 100.

[14] Unpublished foreword (1927) to

Beverley Nichols's *Are They The Same At Home?*. Notebook 29, Coward Archive, NPC-0250.

[15] *Leeds Mercury*, 23 Feb. 1926, p. 4.

[16] 25 Jan. 1925, Coward Archive, NPC-0715.

[17] 18 Feb. 1928, Coward Archive, NPC-0666. See also Bennett, *Journals*, p. 253.

[18] *Westminster Gazette*, 11 Nov 1926, p. 6.

[19] *Autobiography*, p. 164.

[20] Ivor Novello, "Are You Afraid?", *Daily Mirror*, 15 May 1938, p. 12.

[21] A habit described in *Westminster Gazette*, 15 Sep. 1927, p. 4.

[22] *Chelsea News and General Advertiser*, 13 Mar. 1925, p. 5. See also "Noël Coward's Fascist Secret", *Antiques Trade Gazette*, 9 June 2014.

[23] See Byng, *As You Were*, p. 98.

[24] Gielgud, *Gielgud on Gielgud*, p. 78.

[25] Coward, *Autobiography*, p. 143.

[26] See Byng, *As You Were*, p. 96.

[27] Massine, *My Life in Ballet*, pp. 164-5.

[28] *On With The Dance*, first night programme, Mar. 1925.

[29] Quoted in García-Márquez, *Massine*, p. 191.

[30] See *The Times*, 1 May 1925, p. 12.

[31] Among other exceptions are Vaughan Williams's *A London Symphony* (1914), which its composer argued was not designed as a sonic portrait of the city, and Elgar's *Cockaigne (In London Town)* (1900–1901), but both predate the technical advance of postwar cities.

[32] *Morning Post*, 1 May 1925.

[33] *Sporting Times*, 25 Apr. 1925, p. 7.

[34] Quoted in Israel, *Miss Tallulah*

Bankhead, p. 104.

[35] Bankhead, *Tallulah*, p. 121.

[36] Bankhead, *Tallulah*, p. 130.

[37] See Israel, *Miss Tallulah Bankhead*, p. 193; and Brian, *Tallulah, Darling*, p. 14.

[38] *Westminster Gazette*, 23 Apr. 1925, p. 7.

[39] To Violet Coward, 11 Nov. 1926, *Letters*, p. 127.

[40] *Manchester Guardian*, 31 Aug. 1925, p. 7. See also *Westminster Gazette*, 31 Aug. 1925, p. 5.

[41] *Shields Daily News*, 31 Aug. 1925, p. 3.

[42] Coward was referring to *Still Life* in Feb. 1925 (see *Letters*, p. 111). For *Gardening* see the draft in Notebook 45, Coward Archive, NPC-0265.

[43] Notebook 44, 9 June 1923, Coward Archive, NPC-0264.

[44] *Plays*, 1, p. 68.

[45] See *Plays*, 1, pp. 50–51.

[46] *Manchester Guardian*, 9 June 1925, p. 14.

[47] As quoted in *Norwood News*, 5 Mar. 1926, p. 8.

[48] *Manchester Guardian*, 9 June 1925, p. 14.

Act Two

[1] De Acosta, *Here Lies the Heart*, p. 131.

[2] See Schanke, *That Furious Lesbian*, p. 77.

[3] See Van Vechten, *The Splendid Drunken Twenties*, p. 94.

[4] See Castle, *Noël*, p. 71.

[5] *New York World*, 18 Sep. 1925, quoted in Bankhead, *Tallulah*, p. 111.

[6] As told to St. John Ervine in *Nottingham Evening Post*, 26 Mar. 1930, p. 4.

[7] *New York Times*, 13 Sep. 1925, p. 1; 17 Sep. 1925, p. 20.

[8] Dean, *Seven Ages*, p. 269.

[9] See *New York Times*, 13 Sep. 1925, p. 1, and 23 Sep. 1925, p. 22.

[10] *Autobiography*, p. 156.

[11] *New York Times*, 5 Oct. 1925, p. 25.

[12] See Hoare, *Noël Coward*, p. 153.

[13] Michael Arlen to Coward, 1 Apr. [1930?], Coward Archive, NPC-0543.

[14] *New York Times*, 8 Dec. 1925, p. 28.

[15] "From Ibsen to Coward", *Manchester Guardian*, 14 Mar. 1928, p. 12.

[16] Quoted in Wilson, *Noël, Tallulah, Cole and Me*, p. 28.

[17] *New York Times*, 28 Feb. 1926, p. 1.

[18] See, for chronology, "Olympic Brings the First Contingent", *Dundee Courier*, 3 Apr. 1926, p. 5.

[19] Glendinning, *Rebecca West*, p. 103.

[20] Wilson, *Noël, Tallulah, Cole and Me*, pp. 20–3.

[21] Notebook 14, Coward Archive. The line seems to be a draft of an unsent letter, the recipient unreadable.

[22] *The Graphic*, 26 May 1928, p. 20.

[23] Lesley, *The Life of Noël Coward*, pp. 92–5.

[24] Nichols, *Twenty-Five*, p. 253.

[25] Diana Cooper to Duff Cooper, 4 Mar. 1927, Cooper Papers, GBR/0014/DUFC 1/13/18.

[26] See Connon, *Beverley Nichols*, pp. 268–9.

[27] *Plays*, 6, p. 65.

[28] *The Bystander*, 23 June 1926, p. 23.

[29] *Westminster Gazette*, 11 Nov. 1926, p. 6.

[30] See *The Tatler*, 11 Aug. 1926, p. 4:

"Noël Coward is at the Palazzo Rezzonico."

31 Wilson, *Noël, Tallulah, Cole and Me*, p. 48.

32 Quoted in *Dundee Courier*, 6 Apr. 1926, p. 4.

33 *Westminster Gazette*, 11 Nov. 1926, p. 6.

34 *Weekly Despatch*, 17 Oct. 1926, p. 17.

35 See Castle, *Noël*, p. 88.

36 Peters, *Mrs Pat*, p. 389.

37 *The Times*, 15 Sep. 1926, p. 10.

38 *Autobiography*, p. 169.

39 *Weekly Dispatch*, 19 Sep. 1926, p. 9.

40 Wilson, *Noël, Tallulah, Cole and Me*, p. 31.

41 Findlay, *Chasing Last Time*, p. 211.

42 Connon, *Beverley Nichols*, p. 272.

43 *Sunday Post*, 14 Oct. 1926, p. 13.

44 Amherst, *Wandering Abroad*, p. 202.

45 28 Oct. 1926, *Letters*, p. 126.

46 To Violet Coward, 3 Nov. 1926, *Letters*, pp. 127, 126.

47 To Violet Coward, 11 and 18 Nov. 1926, *Letters*, p. 128.

48 See Pollack, *George Gershwin*, p. 736.

49 Dean, *Seven Ages*, p. 324.

50 25 Nov. 1926, *Letters*, p. 129.

51 *New York Times*, 24 Nov. 1926, p. 27.

52 25 Nov. 1926, *Letters*, pp. 129–30.

53 To Violet Coward, 1 Dec. 1926, Coward Archive.

54 14 Dec. 1926, *Letters*, pp. 131-2.

55 Diana Cooper to Duff Cooper, 23 Dec. 1926, Cooper Papers, GBR/0014/DUFC 1/13/18.

56 Wilson, *Noël, Tallulah, Cole and Me*, p. 41.

57 Diana Cooper to Duff Cooper, 25 Dec. 1926, Cooper Papers, GBR/0014/DUFC 1/13/22.

58 *Autobiography*, p. 128.

59 See www.dillinghamranchplan.com (accessed Mar. 2021).

60 To Violet Coward, 4 Jan. 1927, *Letters*, pp. 135–6.

61 The collection is in Notebook 28 (Coward Archive, NPC-0249), with handwritten entries dated from late 1926 and early 1927, using titles such as "Hay-Tossing", "The Times We Live In", "Intellectual Snobbery". Only a single essay seems to have been published, under the title "Hurry, Hurry, Hurry", in *The Daily Graphic*, 11 June 1927, p. 4.

62 From "Hay-Tossing", Notebook 28, Coward Archive, NPC-0249. In this essay Coward laid out his theory that celibacy before marriage led to a state of sexual ignorance culminating in a young couple forcing themselves "embarrassed and terrified into the bridal bed", although he makes clear that he was not advocating "unbridled sexual licence […] it takes a mind far above the average to be able to indulge physical desires absolutely freely". He goes on: "No one can blame authors for making the most of suggestive silences and the effective compromise of dotted lines at crucial moments when the infinitely less harmful method of saying straight out what they mean is vigorously denied them."

63 *Autobiography*, p. 178.

Act Three

1 As reported in *Belfast Telegraph*, 1

Nov. 1927, p. 8.

[2] See Mander and Mitchenson, *Theatrical Companion*, p. 152.

[3] Dean, *Seven Ages*, p. 308.

[4] Notebook 5, 1927, Coward Archive, NPC-0188. There are also brief sketches for plays called *High Comedy* and *Noblesse Oblige*.

[5] Bennett, *Journals*, p. 219.

[6] *Charade* is in Notebook 5, Coward Archive, NPC-0188.

[7] See Notebook 5, Coward Archive, NPC-0188. The working title was *To Err is Human*.

[8] As reported in *The Era*, 2 Nov. 1927, p. 1.

[9] *The Era*, 2 Nov. 1927, p. 1.

[10] *Daily Telegraph*, 17 Sep. 2016, p. 19.

[11] *Westminster Gazette*, 9 Sep. 1927, p. 6.

[12] The play was translated as *The Sins of Youth*. See also *Western Mail*, 14 Nov. 1927, p. 6.

[13] Wilson, *Noël, Tallulah, Cole and Me*, p. 43.

[14] 6 Sep. 1927, *Letters*, p. 141.

[15] See Noble, *Ivor Novello*, pp. 124–5.

[16] *Dundee Evening Telegraph*, 25 Nov. 1927, p. 10.

[17] *Dundee Evening Telegraph*, 25 Nov. 1927, p. 10.

[18] *Westminster Gazette*, 25 Nov. 1927, p. 7.

[19] Dean, *Seven Ages*, p. 311.

[20] Noble, *Ivor Novello*, p. 125.

[21] Massey (Raymond), *A Hundred Different Lives*, p. 73.

[22] Marsh, *A Number of People*, p. 371.

[23] Noble, *Ivor Novello*, p. 125.

[24] *The People*, 27 Nov. 1927, p. 12.

[25] *The Sketch*, 7 Dec. 1927, p. 36.

[26] *Observer*, 27 Nov. 1927, p. 15.

[27] 18 Feb. 1928, Coward Archive, NPC-0666.

[28] *Weekly Despatch* 11 Dec. 1927, p. 13.

[29] *The People*, 27 Nov. 1927, p. 12.

[30] Massey (Raymond), *A Hundred Different Lives*, p. 77.

[31] [Jan. 1928], *Letters*, p. 144.

[32] Amherst, *Wandering Abroad*, p. 200.

[33] McGilligan, *Alfred Hitchcock*, p. 92.

[34] Brunel, *Nice Work*, p. 131.

[35] Notebook 43, 1926, Coward Archive, NPC-0263.

[36] See *The Era*, 28 Mar. 1928, p. 1 (from which many details of the evening are taken). "Snowball" was the character for which the vaudevillian performer Stepin Fetchit became famous, in the 1931 film *The Galloping Ghost*.

[37] *The Era*, 28 Mar. 1928, p. 1.

[38] See Pollack, *George Gershwin*, p. 736. George and Ira Gershwin wrote their own song "The Lorelei" a few years later, nodding to Coward's "Lorelei" in *This Year of Grace*.

[39] *Illustrated Sporting and Dramatic News*, 31 Mar. 1928, p. 30; *The Sphere*, 31 Mar. 1928, p. 22; *Observer*, 25 Mar. 1928, p. 4. *The Times* (23 Mar. 1928, p. 12) wanted "more sugar and less pepper in Mr Coward's dish", but the *Daily Telegraph* (23 Mar. 1928, p. 80) thought it was "impossible to overrate" his versatility.

[40] 27 Mar. 1928, Ervine Papers, Box 1, Folder 4.

[41] "Played nine times at ball", *Londonderry Sentinel*, 23 June 1928, p. 6.

[42] *Bedfordshire Times and Independent*, 22 June 1928, p. 12.

[43] Wilson, *Noël, Tallulah, Cole, and Me*, pp. 55–6.

[44] Penelope Fitzgerald, *At Freddie's* (1982), Chapter 8.

[45] A mask from 1927 is held by the Victoria & Albert Museum in London, with a note from Messel: "Mask that Noël Coward saw and gave the idea for Dance Little Lady."

[46] E. Nesbit, *The Enchanted Castle* (1907), Chapter 6.

[47] For chronology see Woolf, *Letters*, 3, p. 454, p. 471, and Woolf, *Diary*, 3, pp. 176–7.

[48] 25 Mar. 1928 (Woolf, *Letters*, 3, p. 478).

[49] 16? Oct. 1928 (Woolf, *Letters*, 3, p. 546); 12 Mar. 1928 (Woolf, *Letters*, 3, p. 471).

[50] Rorem, *The Later Diaries*, p. 7.

[51] The copy appeared at Christie's in 2019 (Auction 17706).

[52] Oct. 1928, *Letters*, p. 151.

[53] [Spring 1928], *Letters*, p. 150.

[54] 20 Nov. 1928, *Letters*, p. 152 (misdated 28 Nov).

[55] Carrington to Poppet John, Aug. 1928 (Carrington, *Letters*, p. 343).

[56] Woolf to Roger Fry, 16 Oct. 1928 (Woolf, *Letters*, 6, pp. 523–4).

[57] "Anglo-Saxon Attitudes", *c.* 1927, Notebook 28, Coward Archive, NPC-0249.

[58] *Leeds Mercury*, 11 June 1925, p. 4; Notebook 28, Coward Archive, NPC-0249.

[59] Notebook 28, Coward Archive, NPC-0249.

[60] Quoted in Joseph, *Stravinsky Inside Out*, p. 31. Stravinsky and Coward had mutual friends in the form of Léonide Massine and Lord Berners, the eccentric composer and novelist, either of whom could have suggested the collaboration.

[61] "Intellectual Snobbery", Notebook 28, Coward Archive, NPC-0249. See also: "Mr James Joyce has set up a daunting standard for the young in his *Ulysses*. The obvious streaks of genius in this analytical tome have been magnified out of all proportion." "Insanity in Art", 3 Aug. 1924, Notebook 31, Coward Archive, NPC-0252.

[62] Graves and Hodge, *The Long Week-End*, p. 147.

[63] 22 Nov. 1928, *Letters*, p. 152.

[64] [*c.* 1928], Coward Archive.

[65] [Spring 1928], quoted in Lesley, *The Life of Noël Coward*, pp. 119–20.

[66] *New York Times*, 28 Aug. 1928, p. 31.

[67] Wilson, *Noël, Tallulah, Cole and Me*, pp. 55–6.

[68] Laffey, *Beatrice Lillie*, p. 81.

[69] See *New York Times*, 12 Feb. 1929, p. 22; 25 Feb. 1929, p. 29.

[70] The story has its beginnings in a piece called *Concerto*, written as a potential scenario for film a few years before, but rejected by Michael Balcon. *Concerto* is set predominantly in France in 1857 and features a young noblewoman, Alix de Cabruché, officialy betrothed to Paul de Valazon but having an affair with an opera singer called Katyan Landor. Discovering the affair, Paul challenges Katyan to a duel. In *Bitter Sweet* the duel results in the lover's death but in *Concerto* Katyan survives and makes his living as a violinist

in a café orchestra. Alix grows old and unhappy, and reads of Katyan's death in the newspapers. The film was to have been in flashback after a contemporary prologue in which Alix's diaries and letters were discovered. "Noël Coward Miscellaneous", Coward Archive. *Bitter Sweet* – replacing Coward's working title of *Sari Linden* – was originally suggested by Basil Dean as a potential title for *The Queen Was in the Parlour* (Dean, *Seven Ages*, p. 302).

71 *Lyrics*, p. 114.

72 *Autobiography*, p. 207

73 To Violet Coward, 6 Nov. 1929, *Letters*, p. 162.

74 23 Oct. 1929, *Letters*, p. 160.

75 Wilson, *Noël, Tallulah, Cole and Me*, pp. 55–6.

76 To Violet Coward, 23 Oct. and 6 Nov. 1929, *Letters*, p. 159, p. 162.

77 James Agate, "Bitter Sweet", *Sunday Times*, 21 July 1929, p. 6.

78 *The Stage*, 15 Apr. 1926, p. 15; Wilson, *Noël, Tallulah, Cole, and Me*, p. 24.

79 See *The Era*, 12 Nov. 1930, p. 9.

80 Novello to Noël Coward, July 1929, *Letters*, p. 156.

81 Braybrooke, *The Amazing Mr Noël Coward*, p. 130.

82 *Lyrics*, p. 110.

83 John Lahr, "Watching Himself Go By", *London Review of Books*, 4 Dec. 1980.

84 *Letters*, p. 91.

85 13 Oct. 1929, *Letters*, p. 159.

86 To Violet Coward, 29 Oct. 1929, *Letters*, p. 94.

87 *Complete Lyrics*, p. 139.

88 De Acosta, *Here Lies The Heart*, p. 131.

89 Albanesi, *Meggie Albanesi*, pp. 197–8. Coward wrote to Albanesi's mother: "If anyone in the world deserves eternal happiness it is Meggie, and perhaps because she was such a darling to us here we may be given the chance of meeting her again."

90 See *New York Times*, 18 March 1928, p. 21.

91 Hannen Swaffer, "You are the Limit", *John Bull*, 30 July 1932, p. 10.

92 *Daily Mirror*, 21 Feb. 1924, p. 15.

93 *Lyrics*, p. 120.

94 Lesley, *The Life of Noël Coward*, p. 82.

95 To Beverley Nichols, 1957 (quoted in Lesley, *The Life of Noël Coward*, pp. 123–4).

96 From Notebook 28 (the mooted essay collection *Anglo-Saxon Attitudes*) and published as "Hurry, Hurry, Hurry", in *The Daily Graphic*, 11 June 1927, p. 4 (minor cuts silently implemented).

THE TIPSY CROW
Act One

1 *Plays*, 2, p. 158.

2 For an account of the performance see *The Sketch*, 22 Mar. 1944, p. 23; *The Scotsman*, 12 Nov. 1943, p. 6; and mgoodliffe.co.uk (accessed July 2021).

3 To T. E. Lawrence, 19 June 1931, *Letters*, p. 214.

4 Amherst, *Wandering Abroad*, p. 53.

5 The structure of *Post-Mortem* is thought to have influenced collaborations between W. H. Auden and Christopher Isherwood such

as *The Ascent of F6* and *On the Frontier* (1938). See Lawrence Normand, "Modernity and Orientalism in the Ascent of F6", *Modern Philology* (May 2011), p. 555.

6 *Autobiography*, p. 227.

7 Coward was in America during the runs of *The Prisoners of War* and *The Silver Tassie*.

8 *Complete Lyrics*, p. 138.

9 To Violet Coward, 12 Jan. 1930, *Letters*, p. 168.

10 *Autobiography*, p. 216.

11 Amherst, *Wandering Abroad*, p. 118. See also pp. 115–29.

12 To Violet Coward, 31 Jan. 1930, *Letters*, p. 170; *Autobiography*, p. 219.

13 *Autobiography*, p. 219.

14 Amherst, *Wandering Abroad*, p. 123.

15 To Violet Coward, 13 Mar. 1930, *Letters*, p. 173.

16 The chronology is from "A Famous Visitor", *Malaya Tribune*, 22 Mar. 1930, p. 8.

17 *The Straits Times*, 26 Nov. 1930, p. 10.

18 Wilson, *Noël, Tallulah, Cole, and Me*, p. 43. See also Mills, *Up in the Clouds*, p. 126.

19 *The Straits Times*, 3 Apr. 1930, p. 12; *Malaya Tribune*, 3 Apr. 1930, p. 8. See also "The Quaints", *Malaya Tribune*, 31 Mar. 1930, p. 8.

20 Amherst, *Wandering Abroad*, p. 128.

21 *The Straits Times*, 7 Apr. 1930, p. 12.

22 *Complete Lyrics*, pp. 131–2. The exact phrase isn't to be found in Rudyard Kipling, although in *Kim* (1901) there is the line "only the devils and the English walk to and fro without reason" and later "we walk as though we were mad – or

English". See also *Field*, 4 Oct. 1902, p. 49: "Residents in India [...] aver that only Englishmen and mad dogs go the hot side of the pavement." *Leeds Mercury*, 4 June 1914, p. 4: "There is a saying in tropical latitudes that 'only mad dogs and Englishmen walk in the sun'." *Gentlewoman*, 26 Aug. 1911, p. 20: "There is a great deal of truth in what foreigners say as to only Englishmen and mad dogs venturing out in the heat of the day."

23 *Autobiography*, p. 131.

24 *Diaries* (3 Feb. 1957), p. 348.

25 *Complete Lyrics*, pp. 131–2.

26 Susannah Clapp, "Private Lives; King Lear; Ghost Stories", *Observer*, 7 Mar. 2010, p. 34.

27 Undated, Calthrop Papers, MS201/1/9.

28 12 Feb. 1930, *Letters*, p. 171.

29 7 Feb. 1930, Cadbury Research Library, COW/3/N/1/35. The letter, a typescript copy with no surviving original, is dated 7 January – a clear mistake, as the postmark is Hong Kong, where Coward arrived on 3 February (see *Letters*, p. 169).

30 Correspondence with Charles Cochran (Feb. 1930) and Gertrude Lawrence (25 Mar. 1930), Cadbury Research Library, COW/3/N/1/35.

31 [1932], Lawrence Papers, Columbia University, Box 1, Folder 54.

32 Interview with Kenneth Tynan, 1967. See Ziegler, *Olivier*, p. 45.

33 *Letters*, pp. 210–14. Later Coward decided that he had found Lawrence a humourless show-off, with a

charm that could only be repaid by "a certain arid loyalty. We had, of course, nothing in common." *Diaries* (19 Mar 1955), p. 260. Lawrence was equally capable of discrediting Coward behind his back: "his music's no good; vitality is all that he's got really". Hoare, *Serious Pleasures*, p. 188.

34 *The Tatler*, 22 Oct. 1930, p. 22.
35 *The Tatler*, 22 Oct. 1930, p. 23.
36 Recounted in Lesley, *The Life of Noël Coward*, p. 139.
37 *Plays*, 2, p. 15.
38 Programme note to *Hay Fever* (National Theatre, 1964 revival), quoted in *Letters*, p. 719.
39 *The Tatler*, 22 Oct. 1930, p. 23.
40 Ivor Brown, *Observer*, 28 Sep. 1930, p. 15; James Agate, *Sunday Times*, 28 Sep. 1930, p. 4.
41 *Western Morning News*, 27 Sep. 1930, p. 8; *Bystander*, 8 Oct. 1930, p. 16; *Graphic*, 4 Oct. 1930, p. 30; *Observer*, 28 Sep. 1930, p. 15.
42 *Daily Mirror*, 28 Sep. 1930, p. 11.
43 *The Stage*, 30 Oct. 1930, p. 12.
44 27 Oct. 1930, Coward Archive, NPC-5334.
45 *Daily Mirror*, 28 Sep. 1930, p. 11; *Graphic*, 4 Oct. 1930, p. 30; *The Sphere*, 25 Oct. 1930, p. 32.
46 *Plays*, 2, p. 43.
47 *Sunday Times*, 28 Sep. 1930, p. 4; Braybrooke, *The Amazing Mr Noël Coward*, p. 135.
48 *Observer*, 16 Aug. 1931, p. 8.
49 Quoted in Mander and Mitchenson, *Theatrical Companion to Coward*, p. 217.
50 Lawrence, *A Star Danced*, pp. 185–6.
51 Massey (Raymond), *A Hundred Different Lives*, p. 120.
52 Behrman, *People in a Diary*, p. 55.
53 "Mr Noël Coward, the actor-playwright and Society man, is one of the latest to buy a Gerald Road House. I hear he will soon move into it from the house with the bright red door which he has occupied for years." *Sheffield Daily Telegraph*, 8 Jan. 1931, p. 4. As late as October 1930, Coward was still addressing his letters from Ebury Street (*Letters*, p. 213).
54 See historicengland.co.uk (accessed 27 July 2021), List Entry number 1385697.
55 *Bradford Observer*, 4 July 1939, p. 6.
56 "Masterisms", in "Noël Coward Miscellaneous, 1931", Coward Archive.
57 [May 1931], *Letters*, p. 222.
58 *Cavalcade* seems an obvious ancestor of the 1970s television show *Upstairs, Downstairs*, but the similarities are, according to its creators, Eileen Atkins and Jean Marsh, coincidental (Eileen Atkins, personal communication).
59 *Manchester Guardian*, 14 Oct. 1931, p. 8.
60 *Autobiography*, p. 239.
61 *Daily Mail*, 1 Nov. 1931, quoted in Mander and Mitchenson, *Theatrical Companion to Coward*, p. 235.
62 *Illustrated Sporting and Dramatic News*, 24 Oct 1931, p. 26.
63 *Daily Mirror*, 14 Oct. 1931, p. 12; *Aberdeen Press and Journal*, 14 Oct. 1931, p. 6.
64 For Coward's influence on *The Millionairess* see Christopher Wixson,

"Acts of Revision: Bernard Shaw, Noël Coward, and 'Born Bosses'", *Journal of Modern Literature* (Summer 2017), pp. 166–85.

65 Wilson, *Noël, Tallulah, Cole and Me*, p. 82.

66 Elizabeth, The Queen Mother, *Counting One's Blessings*, p. 192.

67 Oct. 1931, *Letters*, pp. 182–3.

68 *Manchester Guardian*, 14 Oct. 1931, p. 8.

69 Braybrooke, *The Amazing Mr Noël Coward*, p. 155.

70 See Harding, *Cochran*, p. 146.

71 Britten, *Journeying Boy*, p. 108.

72 Tippett, *Those Twentieth Century Blues*, p. 275.

73 Isherwood, *Diaries*, p. 5.

74 *Plays*, 3, p. 110, pp. 156–7. The script does not specify the inclusion of Communists in the staging, but many reviewers mentioned their presence; see for example *Manchester Guardian*, 21 Oct. 1931, p. 6.

75 *Manchester Guardian*, 1 Nov. 1931, p. 15.

76 *Autobiography*, pp. 240–41.

77 "Royal Letters", Cadbury Research Library, COW/4/I/2/642a. See also Thornton, *Royal Feud*, p. 403. I'm grateful to Christopher Wilson for further information.

78 *Autobiography*, p. 262.

79 Amherst, *Wandering Abroad*, p. 138.

80 To Violet Coward, 21 Feb. 1932, *Letters*, p. 273.

81 See *Liverpool Echo*, 12 Mar. 1932, p. 4.

82 See Payn, *My Life with Noël Coward*, pp. 1-3.

83 From British Pathe, FILM

ID:3421.12 (available on YouTube, accessed 18 May 2020).

84 *Lyrics*, p. 160. "Mad Dogs and Englishmen" had first been heard in a non-Coward revue on Broadway, *The Third Little Show* (1931), sung by Beatrice Lillie.

85 *Diaries* (10 Nov. 1955), p. 292.

86 Nov. 1932, *Letters*, p. 368.

87 Erik Coward to Violet Coward, July 1932, *Letters*, p. 280.

88 *Autobiography*, p. 284.

89 Erik Coward to Violet Coward, 18 Dec. 1928 and 29 June 1932, Coward Archive.

90 Sep. 1932, *Letters*, p. 281.

91 To Violet Coward, 10 Dec. 1932, *Letters*, p. 284.

92 Jan. 1933, *Letters*, pp. 286–7.

93 *Complete Lyrics*, p. 160.

Act Two

1 *Plays*, 3, p. 16.

2 Peters, *Design for Living*, p. 120.

3 *New York Times*, 29 Jan. 1933, p. 1.

4 Amherst, *Wandering Abroad*, p. 199.

5 Peters, *Design for Living*, p. 127.

6 *Daily Herald*, 3 Mar. 1933, p. 11; *New York Times*, 22 Feb. 1933, p. 27.

7 5 Apr. 1933, *Letters*, p. 288.

8 Woolf to Quentin Bell, 24 Jan. 1934 (Woolf, *Letters*, 5, p. 273).

9 Woolf to Quentin Bell, 15 Feb. 1934 (Woolf, *Letters*, 5, pp. 276-7).

10 22 Nov. 1933, Coward Archive, NPC-10145 (and *Letters*, p. 151, misdated 1928).

11 Woolf, *Diary*, 4, p. 279

12 Murray, *Aldous Huxley*, p. 209; Woolf, *Diary*, 4, p. 259.

13 Carpenter, *W.H. Auden*, p. 165.

[14] Quoted in *Autobiography*, p. xi.

[15] *Manchester Guardian*, 14 Apr. 1939, p. 7.

[16] *Observer*, 19 Jan. 1936, p. 15.

[17] The title alludes to a genre of group portraiture popular in the eighteenth century. *Conversation Piece* is often said to be inspired by *The Regent and his Daughter* (1932), by Dormer Creston, the pen name of Dorothy Julia Baynes. The book gave Coward a sense of period, but is a work of non-fiction, chronicling the life of the Prince Regent and his daughter Charlotte, and it bears no resemblance to the play's scenario.

[18] To Alexander Woollcott, 3 Apr. 1934, *Letters*, pp. 294–5.

[19] *Daily Telegraph*, 17 Feb. 1934, p. 8.

[20] *New York Times*, 24 Oct. 1934, p. 24.

[21] Cochran, *Cock-A-Doodle-Do*, p. 105. See also Harding, *Cochran*, p. 151.

[22] *Diaries* (17 Mar. 1961), p. 467.

[23] Feb. 1934, Coward Archive, NPC-10075, 10079.

[24] Undated, Coward Archive, NPC-10078.

[25] Winter, *Impassioned Pygmies*, pp. 116-7.

[26] [Autumn 1935], Coward Archive, NPC-10089-90.

[27] *The Tatler*, 13 May 1936, p. 40. See also Slide, *Lost Gay Novels*, p. 193.

[28] Barry Lane, Hayward's manager, in online blog, 26 May 2008, www.coffeecoffeeandmorecoffee.com/ archives (accessed 9 Sep. 2021).

[29] *Yorkshire Post and Leeds Intelligencer*, 7 Sep. 1934, p. 3.

[30] Jan. 1935, *Letters*, p. 306.

[31] 5 Mar. 1935, *Letters*, p. 306.

[32] *Plays*, 6, pp. 149–50.

[33] See Anderson, *Louis Hayward*, p. 15.

[34] To Violet Coward, c. Jan. 1935, *Letters*, p. 309.

[35] Anderson, *Louis Hayward*, p. 18.

[36] *Diaries* (18 May 1969), p. 677.

[37] Nicholas de Jongh, "Coward's Brush With Danger", *Guardian*, 7 June 1991, p. 36.

[38] *Complete Lyrics*, p. 163.

[39] Gray, *Noël Coward*, pp. 1–2.

[40] *Daily Mirror*, 1 Mar. 1938, p. 11.

[41] Feb. 1936, *Letters*, p. 185.

[42] Rattigan, "Noël Coward", p. 5.

[43] 21 June 1934, *Letters*, p. 283.

[44] Lawrence, *A Star Danced*, p. 22.

[45] To Alexander Woollcott, 6 Feb. 1936, *Letters*, p. 339.

[46] Stella King, "Noël Coward", *The Times*, 26 July 1966, p. 15.

[47] Truman Capote, "Indelible Exits and Entrances", *Esquire* (Mar. 1983), quoted in Lownie, *Traitor King*, p. 269.

[48] 11 Mar. 1937, *Letters*, p. 349.

[49] *Complete Lyrics*, p. 179.

[50] Lesley, *The Life of Noël Coward*, p. 187.

[51] Marlene Dietrich to Coward, 31 July 1935, *Letters*, p. 315.

[52] [Spring 1936?], *Letters*, p. 337 (the last sentence mistranscribed).

[53] Jack Wilson to Coward, 10 June, 29 June, 1937, Cadbury Research Library, COW/3/N/2/58/1.

[54] Lesley, *The Life of Noël Coward*, p. 198.

[55] Interview in Hoare, *Noël Coward*, p. 274.

[56] To Violet Coward, 14 Sep. 1937, *Letters*, p. 355.

[57] Lesley, *The Life of Noël Coward*, p. 193.

58 21 Mar. 1938, *Letters*, p. 355.

59 *Complete Lyrics*, p. 189.

60 *Complete Lyrics*, p. 132, p.139, p. 145, p. 160, p. 197, p. 120.

TINSEL AND SAWDUST
Scenes 1–9

1 *Hansard*, 13 July 1938, Vol. 338, cc. 1302-3.

2 To Alexander Woollcott, 21 Mar. 1938, *Letters*, p. 355.

3 John Heilpern, "Coward at 70", *Observer*, 7 Dec. 1969, p. 40.

4 Donaldson, *Freddy Lonsdale*, p. 210.

5 "Noël Coward Talks to Edgar Lustgarten, 1972", printed in *Home Chat* (Apr. 2002), p. 7.

6 "Intended American Broadcast", Coward Archive, NPC-10364.

7 See also Coward's condemnation of anti-Semitism in *Autobiography*, p. 299.

8 Duberman, *Paul Robeson*, p. 147. Eslanda "Essie" Robeson had known Coward since admiring his performance in *The Vortex*, and he guided her through her marital difficulties in the early 1930s: "Noël Coward had been marvellous to me, had come often to the flat to talk with me, dine with me, and I had been out with him." (p. 615). See also Hoare, *Noël Coward*, pp. 260–61.

9 19 Nov. 1936, *Letters*, p. 340.

10 To Violet Coward, [summer 1936], *Letters*, p. 341.

11 Rhodes, *Bob Boothby*, p. 154.

12 *Weekly Dispatch*, 27 Aug. 1933, p. 10.

13 9 June 1927, Cooper Papers, GBR/0014/DUFC 1/7/5.

14 Vansittart, *The Mist Procession*, p. 313, p. 346.

15 To Gladys Calthrop, 14 Apr. 1938, *Letters*, p. 356.

16 *Lancashire Evening Post*, 31 Mar. 1938, p. 4.

17 *Daily Mirror*, 6 July 1938, p. 4.

18 *Weekly Despatch*, 24 Apr. 1938, p. 3.

19 7 July 1938, Mountbatten Papers, MB1/C58.

20 15 Sep. 1937, Mountbatten Papers, MB1/C58.

21 Jan. 1940, *Letters*, pp. 389-92.

22 1940 Diary (15 June), Coward Archive, NPC-0641.

23 *Autobiography*, p. 279.

24 *Autobiography*, p. 278.

25 23 July 1938, *Letters*, p. 357.

26 5 July 1938, *Letters*, p. 373, misdated 1939. (See Coward Archive, NPC 9763.)

27 See Read and Fisher, *Colonel Z*, pp. 165–80; Jeffery, *MI6*, p. 316; Andrew, *Secret Service*, p. 343. There is some disagreement as to Z Organisation's level of independence from the Secret Service and the extent of Vansittart's involvement.

28 See Findlay, *Chasing Lost Time*, 139.

29 The film was to have R. C. Sherriff as co-writer. See *Weekly Dispatch*, 1 Nov. 1936, p. 14.

30 1942 Diary (20 Mar. 1942), Coward Archive, NPC-0454. See also John Simpson, "Noël Coward was a spy, too", *Spectator*, 17 Dec. 1994, p. 26.

31 12 Sep. 1938, *Letters*, p. 360.

32 *Central Somerset Gazette*, 7 Oct. 1938, p. 2.

33 Heilpern, "Coward at 70", p. 40.

34 *Autobiography*, p. 296.

35 3 Oct. 1938, Cooper Papers, GBR/0014/DUFC 2/14.

36 George Munro, "Noël with the Peers", *The Era*, 6 Oct. 1938, p. 1.

37 *Sunday Mirror*, 9 Oct. 1938, p. 2.

38 Cadbury Research Library, COW/3/L/1/5.

39 5 Nov. 1938, *Letters*, p. 370 and Coward Archive, NPC-9762.

40 24 Nov. 1938, *Letters*, p. 371.

41 The trip is mentioned in Lorn Loraine's 1939 diary, Cadbury Research Library, COW/3/L/1/6.

42 23 July 1938, Calthrop Papers, MS201/1/7.

43 *Plays*, 4, p. 291.

44 *Daily Mirror*, 5 July 1939, p. 13.

45 "Noël Coward has arrived in Warsaw, where one of his plays is being produced at the Theatre of Modern Art." *The Stage*, 13 July 1939, p. 11.

46 *Autobiography*, p. 297.

47 *Bradford Observer*, 4 July 1939, p. 6.

48 *The Bystander*, 12 July 1939, p. 5.

49 Foreign Office Index, National Archives, FO 409.

50 See Colvin, *Vansittart in Office*, p. 334.

51 *Middle East Diary*, p. 78. Scott-Watson's report is frequently misattributed to Lawrence Durrell (as at *Letters*, p. 373).

52 [July 1939], Burckhardt archive, G 1406-1.

53 21 July 1939, Cadbury Research Library, COW/4/K/1/2.

54 *Daily Mirror*, 1 Aug. 1939, p. 25.

55 Ferdinand Lunde to Coward [Aug. 1939], Coward Archive, uncatalogued.

56 *Autobiography*, pp. 320–21.

57 The chronology of *Autobiography*, in which Coward remembers a fortnight's rehearsals before the productions were cancelled (p. 239), is awry. See *Cambridge Daily News*, 22 Aug. 1939, p. 2: "Mr Noël Coward arrived on the scene in Town to-day to meet the members of the cast of his two new plays."

58 Boothby, *Recollections of a Rebel*, pp. 78–9.

59 Lady Soames, diary, 27 Aug. 1939, Churchill Archives Centre, GBR/0014/MCHL 1/1/1.

60 Boothby, *Recollections of a Rebel*, pp. 78–9.

61 Gilbert, *Winston S. Churchill, Companion Volume V,* p. 1095.

62 Morton, *Atlantic Meeting*, p. 62.

63 *Autobiography*, p. 325.

64 See Rankin, *Churchill's Wizards*, p. 314, p. 430; Graham, *British Subversive Propaganda*, Chapter Two.

65 28 Aug. 1939, *Letters*, pp. 374–5. It may be that Coward never sent the letter.

66 "While Ministers were arriving Mr Noël Coward emerged from the Foreign Office and drove away." *Bristol Evening Post*, 28 Aug. 1939, p. 20. Also *Letters*, pp. 376–7.

67 "'Play for Comedy' is the new title for what was to be called 'Sweet Sorrow'." *Aberdeen Evening Express*, 31 Aug. 1939, p. 11.

68 See *Daily News*, 2 Sep. 1939, p. 6.

69 *Daily News*, 15 Sep. 1939, p. 8.

70 See Robinson, *The Country House At War*, pp. 114–17.

71 See Graham, *British Subversive Propaganda*, p. 34.

72 1940 Diary (2 Mar.), Coward Archive, NPC-0641.

73 1940 Diary (8 Feb.), Coward Archive, NPC-0641. Coward also worked with Giraudoux's son, Jean-Pierre, who "bored me to tears, very self important and in my opinion needs a healthy kick in the bottom [… he was] ill mannered and overbearing, added to which he was growing a disgusting looking mustache and his breath smelt." (1940 diary, 17 Jan., 1 Feb.)

74 See Maurois, *Call No Man Happy*, pp. 252–4.

75 To Clemence Dane [Oct. 1939], Dane Letters, OSB MSS 245 Box F.

76 Stuart Papers, Box 2.

77 Maurois, *Memoirs*, p. 226.

78 Sep.–Oct. 1939, *Letters*, pp. 377–80.

79 Willert, 1940 Diary and "Autobiographical fragment", Willert Collection.

80 See Miles, *The Nine Lives of Otto Katz*, p. 229.

81 See Miles, *The Nine Lives of Otto Katz*, pp. 1-8, p. 229; *The Times*, 24 Nov. 1952, p. 5; *Diaries* (23 Nov. 1952), p. 202 ("I vaguely remember meeting him in Paris in 1940").

Scenes 10–14

1 *Proceedings of Slánský Trial, Prague, 1952*, Czechoslovak Home Service, pp. 104–6. Cuts silently implemented.

2 To Alexander Woollcott, 26 Jan. 1940, *Letters*, p. 389.

3 1940 Diary (6 Apr., 11 Jan.), Coward Archive, NPC-0641.

4 1 Feb. 1940, National Archives, AIR 2/4208.

5 Stuart Papers, Box 2.

6 1940 Diary (4 Jan.), Coward Archive, NPC-0641. ("Daladier had signed and Fecamp would be closed at midnight." 1940 Diary, 3 Jan.)

7 1940 Diary (16-18 Feb.), Coward Archive, NPC-0641.

8 "British Artists at Paris Opera?", *Daily Telegraph*, 19 Feb. 1940, p. 6.

9 29 Sep. 1939, Cadbury Research Library, COW 4/K/1/1.

10 Maurois, *Memoirs*, p. 226.

11 *Daily Herald*, 27 Mar. 1940, p. 5.

12 *Daily Mirror*, 20 Apr. 1940, p. 6.

13 Reported in *Daily Herald*, 27 Mar. 1940, p. 5.

14 1940 Diary (8 Mar., 9 Mar., 12 Mar.), Coward Archive, NPC-0641. See also Winston Churchill Engagement Diary, Mar. 1940, George Washington University Libaries, digital transcription, 194003 (accessed Nov. 2021).

15 1940 Diary (13 Mar.), Coward Archive, NPC-0641.

16 1940 Diary (11 Mar.), Coward Archive, NPC-0641.

17 Stevenson, *Spymistress,* p. 115.

18 6 June 1940, Willert Papers.

19 30 Sep. 1939, Cadbury Research Library, COW/4/I/1/1.

20 Information and chronology are from "Day by Day", a project of the Pare Lorentz Center at the FDR Presidential Library, listing FDR's daily activities 1933–1945 (fdrlibrary.marist.edu/daybyday). Also at the meal were Frank Porter Graham (one of Roosevelt's economic advisers) and the director of a federally supported arts programme, Edward Bruce.

21 1940 Diary (7 May), Coward Archive, NPC-0641.

22 1940 Diary (10 May), Coward Archive, NPC-0641.

23 *Autobiography*, p. 373.

24 "Intended American Broadcast", Coward Archive, NPC-10364.

25 [May 1940], Coward Archive, uncatalogued.

26 National Archives, FO 371/24230.

27 1940 Diary (24 May), Coward Archive, NPC-0641.

28 31 May 1940, Coward Archive, uncatalogued.

29 1940 Diary (4 June), Coward Archive, NPC-0641.

30 Pepper's diary for 1940 (5 June), Pepper Papers, Florida State University Libraries, FSU_MSS197901.

31 1940 Diary (5 June), Coward Archive, NPC-0641.

32 6 June 1940 (including draft), *Letters*, pp. 397–8.

33 1940 Diary (9 June), Coward Archive, NPC-0641.

34 See Lesley, *The Life of Noël Coward*, pp. 212–13.

35 Morris, *Rage for Fame*, pp. 386–7, p. 536. Coward and Luce had seen one another a great deal in Paris, but he remained unsure about her: "She is clever, pretty and quick as a knife, but I wouldn't trust her. I think she has a basic bitchness which she isn't even aware of." 1940 Diary (16 Mar.), Coward Archive, NPC-0641.

36 "Mr Noël Coward Forgot Curtains", *Westminster and Pimlico News*, 5 July 1940, p. 3.

37 1940 Diary (19 June), Coward Archive, NPC-0641.

38 1940 Diary (16 June), Coward Archive, NPC-0641. "[Coward] would like to see you tonight if you can spare the time", wrote Churchill's private secretary in a memo, "as he has been staying with the President." *Letters*, p. 400, but misdated 14 July. The original (14 June 1940) is in the Churchill Papers, Churchill Archives Centre, GBR/0014/CHAR 20/4B176. Coward's name is not entered in Winston Churchill's engagement diary for June 1940 (George Washington University Libraries) and the meal at the Savoy was evidently off the record.

39 Frederick Beaumont-Nesbitt to George Lloyd, 9 July 1940, *Letters*, p. 400.

40 1940 Diary (25 June, 2 July), Coward Archive, NPC-0641.

41 1940 Diary (12 July, 4 July), Coward Archive, NPC-0641.

42 James, *The Importance of Happiness*, back cover.

43 See report in *New York Times*, 30 July 1940, p. 3.

Scenes 15–20

1 *Hansard*, HC Debate, 6 Aug. 1940, Vol. 364, c. 55.

2 1940 Diary (20 July, 22 July, 24 July, 27 July), Coward Archive, NPC-0641.

3 *Autobiography*, p. 391. Coward revealed the extent of his work for William Stephenson in a 1973 interview, made when he was in severe ill health, which needs to be treated with some scepticism:

"I had to go to St Ermin's Hotel in Caxton Street [...] this was the Special Operations Executive. [...] And Little Bill [Stephenson] was there, very calm, with those sort of hooded eyes watching everything." Yet Special Operations Executive was not founded until 22 July 1940, by which time Coward was en route to America, not to return to England until 9 April 1941, when his association with any form of espionage was over, and his reputation within the Executive poor. Possibly Coward had visited the hotel prior to summer 1940 (when it was used by, among others, Section D) but his diary makes it clear that his first meeting with Stephenson was on 2 August 1940. In his 1973 interview he also claimed that "in Latin America, I reported directly to Bill Stephenson while I sang my songs and spoke nicely to my hosts". But Coward visited South America only for a few days during the war (en route to Africa on a concert tour in 1944), long after he had been prevented from working for Stephenson. See Stevenson, *A Man Called Intrepid*, pp. 97–8, p. 199.

4   See Nigel West, "Introduction", in Stephenson, *British Security Coordination*, pp. ix–xx; Hyde, *The Quiet Canadian*, p. xiii.

5   Most of Coward's letters from the trip are on the hotel's headed notepaper. Some reports have Stephenson actually living at the hotel, but most put him in a nearby apartment, which Coward's recollections support.

6   Stephenson, *British Security Coordination*, p. xxvii.

7   1940 Diary (1 Aug.), Coward Archive, NPC-0641.

8   Most British papers ran the reports of Coward's statements taken from the Press Association. I have quoted *Daily Mirror*, 31 July 1940, p. 2; *Bradford Observer*, 31 July 1940, p. 6; *Yorkshire Post and Leeds Intelligencer*, 3 Aug. 1940, p. 1.

9   As mentioned to Roald Dahl. See Sturrock, *Storyteller*, p. 206.

10   Hyde, *The Quiet Canadian*, p. 187. Hyde's book, the first biography of Stephenson, was written with its subject's support and approval; Stephenson sent Hyde copies of Coward's *Future Indefinite* during research (see Hyde Papers). William Stevenson's better-selling *A Man Called Intrepid*, for which Coward was interviewed, is considered a less reliable account.

11   1940 Diary (5 Aug.), Coward Archive, NPC-0641.

12   Quoted in Calder, *Beware the British Serpent*, p. 97 is more generally, pp. 89–105.

13   *Daily Mirror*, 5 and 8 Aug. 1940, p. 4. Roller-skating party: *Sunday Mirror*, 11 Aug. 1940, p. 3.

14   1940 Diary (8 Aug.), Coward Archive, NPC-0641.

15   [Aug. 1940], Coward Archive, NPC-10396.

16   21 Aug. 1940, Coward Archive, NPC-10397 (and *Letters*, p. 407, in which the recipient is misidentified

as Robert Vansittart).

[17] 1940 Diary (11 Aug.), Coward Archive, NPC-0641.

[18] Macdonald, *The True Intrepid*, p. 262.

[19] *Yorkshire Post and Leeds Intelligencer*, 13 Aug. 1940, p. 1.

[20] Stevenson, *A Man Called Intrepid*, p. 199.

[21] 1940 Diary (20 Aug.), Coward Archive, NPC-0641.

[22] To Clemence Dane, 12 Sep. 1940, Dane Letters, OSB MSS 245 Box F.

[23] *Letters*, p. 186. See, for chronology, *Liverpool Echo*, 6 Aug. 1940, p. 6; *Daily Mirror*, 27 Aug. 1940, p. 2.

[24] Hoover's presence in Palo Alto: *Lancashire Evening Post*, 21 Aug. 1940, p. 3.

[25] "A Proposal", 21 August 1940, National Archives, FO 1093/238. The proposal was forwarded from British Security Co-ordination to an anonymous source, presumably Hugh Dalton, head of Special Operations Executive, and thence to Henry Hopkinson, private secretary of Alexander Cadogan, Under-Secretary for Foreign Affairs. P. G. Wodehouse and Somerset Maugham are also named among fifteen suggested writers.

[26] Interview with William Stevenson, 1973, quoted in *Letters*, p. 403.

[27] "Errett Cord", "Paul Smith", "Herbert Hoover", Coward Archive, NPC-10364-6.

[28] Quoted in *Letters*, p. 405.

[29] *Evening Despatch*, 26 Sep. 1940, p. 5.

[30] 1940 Diary (15 Sep.), Coward Archive, NPC-0641.

[31] 12 Sep. 1940, *Letters*, pp. 412–13.

[32] "Paul Smith", Coward Archive, NPC-10365.

[33] 1940 Diary (7 Oct.), Coward Archive, NPC-0641.

[34] 1 Oct. 1940, *Letters*, p. 414.

[35] 1940 Diary (20 Sep., 30 Sep.), Coward Archive, NPC-0641.

[36] Correspondence with Lord Hood, September 1940, and further documents in "Lecturers for Empire Publicity", National Archives, INF 1/543.

[37] 1940 Diary (11 Oct.), Coward Archive, NPC-0641.

[38] 20 Oct. 1940, *Letters*, p. 420.

[39] 1940 Diary (25 Oct.), Coward Archive, NPC-0641.

[40] 1940 Diary (30 Oct.), Coward Archive, NPC-0641.

[41] 20 Oct. 1940, Calthrop Papers, MS201/1/22.

[42] *His Talks in Australia*, p. 1.

[43] Quotes and information are from *Brisbane Telegraph*, 25 Nov. 1940.

[44] 3 Dec. 1940, National Archives, INF 1/543.

[45] 28 Feb. 1941, Calthrop Papers, MS201/1/25.

[46] 1941 Diary (19 Jan., 11 Feb.), Coward Archive, NPC-0452.

[47] 1941 Diary (3 Jan., 3 Mar.), Coward Archive, NPC-0452.

[48] Duff Cooper to Coward, 20 Mar. 1941 (and correspondence with New Zealand government and Viscount Cranbourne), National Archives, INF 1/543.

[49] 1941 Diary (18 Mar.), Coward Archive, NPC-0452.

[50] In his 1973 interview, Coward claimed to have discussed the

appointment with Churchill. "I'd had a confusing talk with Winston Churchill before I left. [...] He'd got it into his head that Bill Stephenson was aiming for Mata Hari and he kept saying, 'No use, you'd be no good – too well known.' I said, 'That's the whole point. I'd be so well known nobody will think I'm doing anything special.' And Winston just kept shaking his head and insisting I'd never make a spy. Eventually I got it through to him – I was fluent in Spanish and could do the whole of Latin America, where the Germans were very active preparing their campaigns in the United States. And so that's where I started." (Stevenson, *A Man Called Intrepid*, p. 199.) Nevertheless, the whole Latin American scheme had been definitively called off before Coward was back in England and able to talk with Churchill.

51 1941 Diary (27 Mar.), Coward Archive, NPC-0452.

52 Correspondence between Hugh Gaitskell and Roger Hollis, Apr. 1941, Dalton papers, 2/7/3/55, 63.

53 Dalton, diary (28 and 30 Mar. 1941), Dalton papers, 1/24. See also Dalton, *The Second World War Diaries*, pp. 177–8 and Hyde, *Secret Intelligence Agent*, p. 164.

54 4 Apr. 1941, Dalton papers, 2/7/3/56.

55 1941 Diary (30 Mar.), Coward Archive, NPC-0452.

56 *Letters*, p. 406.

57 1941 Diary (30 Mar.), Coward Archive, NPC-0452.

58 See Stephenson, *British Security Coordination*, p. ix, p. xxviii. "Stay Bermuda with Hamish Mitchell", 1941 Diary (Apr.), Coward Archive, NPC-0453.

59 Coward Archive, 10401. The manuscript has been torn off in one corner to omit any details of (presumably) William Stephenson or the work of Special Operations Executive. Cole Lesley (*The Life of Noël Coward*, p. 217) claims the original telegram – of which, no trace – was written in cypher.

60 1941 Diary (2 and 3 Apr.), Coward Archive, NPC-0452.

61 Dalton, diary (30 Mar., 5 Apr. 1941), Dalton papers, 1/24.

62 Coward never discovered that Brooks had been one of the figures involved in blocking the South American plans. "The Brig [Brooks] thinks I should get the PM – also alleged to be a friend of NC – to agree that he is unsuitable. [...] I am inclined to suspect that Brig B is trying to create a situation in which the PM will say I ought to take the chap." Dalton, diary (30 Mar. 1941), Dalton papers, 1/24.

63 1941 Diary (12 Apr.), Coward Archive, NPC-0452. See also *Sunderland Daily Echo*, 28 Dec. 1940, p. 1, and, for chronology, "Noël Coward flies home", 10 Apr. 1941, p. 3.

64 See Vansittart and Coward correspondence, Vansittart Papers, GBR/0014/VNST II/1/13.

65 *Autobiography*, p. 278.

66 *Autobiography*, p. 415 (and see pp. 414–16).

[67] 1941 Diary (17 Apr.), Coward Archive, NPC-0452.

[68] 1941 Diary (27 and 23 June), Coward Archive, NPC-0452. The diary entry contradicts Redgrave's memory – in his autobiography – of first meeting Noël on 3 July 1941.

[69] 25 Jan. 1942, *Letters*, pp. 441–2.

[70] 1940 Diary (31 Dec.), Coward Archive, NPC-0641.

[71] 1941 Diary (21 and 22 Apr.), Coward Archive, NPC-0452.

[72] "Blithe Spirit First Night Speech", Coward Archive, NPC-2032.

[73] See the account in *Yorkshire Post and Intelligencer*, 4 July 1943, p. 2.

[74] "Blithe Spirit", *Spectator*, 11 July 1941, p. 34; "Rosamond Lehmann letter", *Spectator*, 18 July 1941.

[75] 1941 Diary (11 Oct.), Coward Archive, NPC-0453.

[76] Radclyffe Hall's interest in the occult, and consultation of a medium to ask forgiveness of a spurned lover recently deceased, has also been suggested as a model; see Castle, *Noël Coward and Radclyffe Hall*, pp. 73–106. In W. B. Yeats's *The Words Upon the Window Pane* a séance is held by a mercenary medium, Mrs Henderson; apparently an imposter, she conjures the spirit of Jonathan Swift after snoring her way through a trance. The play, published in 1930, was given its Broadway premiere while Coward was in New York late in 1932.

[77] 1941 Diary (21 Feb.), Coward Archive, NPC-0452.

[78] *Time and Tide*, 12 July 1941.

[79] To Jack Wilson, 18 July 1941, *Letters*, p. 430.

[80] 18 July 1941, *Letters*, p. 432.

[81] Mentioned in 1941 Diary (1 July), Coward Archive, NPC-0453.

[82] Kempson, *A Family & its Fortunes*, p. 210.

[83] Kempson, *A Family & its Fortunes*, p. 210.

[84] 1941 Diary (15 Oct.), Coward Archive, NPC-0453.

[85] 25 Jan. 1942, *Letters*, pp. 442–3.

[86] Aug. 1971, Coward Archive, NPC-9160.

[87] *His Talks in Australia,* p. 40.

[88] To Jack Wilson, 18 Sep. 1941, Cadbury Research Library, COW/3/N/2/58/2.

Scenes 22–27

[1] "REX v NOËL PEIRCE COWARD", transcript, Mountbatten Papers, MB1/K92.

[2] 1941 Diary (16 Oct.), Coward Archive, NPC-0453.

[3] Director of Public Prosecutions to R. W. A. Speed at the Treasury, 12 Nov. 1941, National Archives, TS 27/515.

[4] 1941 Diary (30 Oct.), Coward Archive, NPC-0453.

[5] Transcripts and summaries of both cases are kept in the Mountbatten Papers, MB1/K92.

[6] Mountbatten Papers, MB1/K92.

[7] 1941 Diary (7 Nov.), Coward Archive, NPC-0453.

[8] [Nov. 1941], Mountbatten Papers, MB1/K92.

[9] *Daily Mirror*, 8 Nov. 1941, p. 2.

[10] 31 Oct. 1941, 5 Feb. 1942, *Letters*, p. 451, p. 463, p. 464.

[11] 11 Dec. 1941, 1 Jan. 1942, Cadbury Research Library, COW/3/N/2/58/2.

[12] 1941 Diary (30 July), Coward Archive, NPC-0453. I have drawn on accounts in Neame, *Straight From the Horse's Mouth*, pp. 56–72; Brownlow, *David Lean*, pp. 151–68; Mills, *Up In The Clouds*, pp. 260–71.

[13] 18 Sep. 1941, Cadbury Research Library, COW/3/N/2/58/2.

[14] 11 Sep. 1953, Mountbatten Papers, MB1/H66.

[15] Attenborough, *Entirely Up To You*, p. 124.

[16] To Jack Wilson, 18 Sep. 1941, Cadbury Research Library, COW/3/N/2/58/2.

[17] Neame, *Straight From the Horse's Mouth*, p. 61.

[18] 1942 Diary (2 and 10 Mar.), Coward Archive, NPC-0454.

[19] Brownlow, *David Lean*, p. 161.

[20] 1942 Diary (23 and 24 May), Coward Archive, NPC-0454.

[21] 16 Apr. 1942, Mountbatten Papers, MB1/C58/17.

[22] 20 Oct. 1942, *Letters*, p. 478.

[23] As described by Mountbatten's letter to Coward, 29 Oct. 1942, Mountbatten Papers, MB1/C58/24.

[24] T. S. Eliot to John Hayward, 8 Nov. 1942, private collection.

[25] MacDonald, *Intrepid's Last Secrets*, p. 261.

[26] 1941–2 correspondence, *Letters*, p. 454, p. 457. The row in all its glory is in *Letters*, pp. 451–8.

[27] 1942 Diary (21 Apr., 24 May), Coward Archive, NPC-0454.

[28] *Diaries* (26 Aug. 1942), pp. 16–17.

[29] 1943 Diary (23 May); 1942 Diary (27 Aug.), Coward Archive, NPC-0441, 0453.

[30] 1943 Diary (17 Nov.), Coward Archive, NPC-0442.

[31] 1942 Diary (18 June), Coward Archive, NPC-0454.

[32] "On leaving X I saw Bill Donovan and Winant", 1942 Diary (18 June), Coward Archive, NPC-0454.

[33] L. V. Boardman to J. Edgar Hoover, 25 Aug. 1942, FBI Archives, 100-1198. A previous FBI report, from June 1941, noted "NOËL COWARD" on a list of potential "agents of a foreign country".

[34] 2 Nov. [1942], Mountbatten Papers, MB1/C58.

[35] 29 Dec. 1942, *Letters*, p. 471.

[36] "Started planning a spy comedy called *With my Little Eye* (this for Play Parade)". 1942 Diary (9 June), Coward Archive, NPC-0454.

[37] 1943 Diary (16 Sep.), Coward Archive, NPC-0442.

[38] Hoare, *Noël Coward*, p. 334.

[39] *Autobiography*, p. 436.

[40] Nicolson, *Diaries and Letters*, p. 283.

[41] 1943 Diary (20 Feb.), Coward Archive, NPC-0441.

[42] 1942 Diary (9 Oct.), Coward Archive, NPC-0455.

[43] See Hoare, *Noël Coward*, p. 333.

[44] *Diaries* (6 Nov. 1942), p. 19.

[45] See correspondence with Churchill's secretary F. D. W. Brown, Coward Archive, NPC-3951.

[46] Beaton, *The Unexpurgated Diaries*, p. 38.

[47] *Diaries* (2 June 1943), p. 21.

[48] *Complete Lyrics*, p. 207.

[49] Cooper to Coward, 8 July 1943,

Coward Archive, NPC-4490.

[50] *Daily Mirror*, 23 July 1943, p. 6.

[51] Gerald Savory, whose play *George and Margaret* Noël had directed, argued that the song's chief defect was that it "satirized and lampooned groups of citizens who do not believe that emulating the Nazis' brutality will prove any solution to the problems of what is to be done with Germany when victory is won". *New York Times*, 25 Oct. 1943, p. 3; 21 Nov. 1943, p. 220.

[52] 19 July 1943, Cadbury Research Library, COW/3/N/2/58/2.

[53] 1943 Diary (20 July), Coward Archive, NPC-0442.

[54] 1942 Diary (14 Apr.), Coward Archive, NPC-0454.

[55] 1943 Diary (22 July), Coward Archive, NPC-0442.

[56] *Autobiography*, p. 446.

[57] 3 July 1943, Mountbatten Papers, MB1/C28/252.

[58] Eisenhower to Louis Mountbatten, 5 Aug. 1943, *Letters*, pp. 489–90.

[59] Quoted in Merriman, *Greasepaint and Cordite*, p. 171.

[60] 9 Jan. 1944, *Letters*, p. 494.

[61] 29 Jan. 1944, *Letters*, p. 497

[62] 1944 Diary (27 Jan.), Coward Archive, NPC-0456.

[63] Hackforth, *"And the next object…"*, p. 83.

[64] *Autobiography*, pp. 465–6. Smuts had been in enthusiastic correspondence with Brendan Bracken at the Ministry of Information about the tour, expressing "the view that the visit by Coward would be useful and successful"; Bracken agreed that the visit would "do good", and told Coward on 21 September 1943 that he was "delighted" by the whole tour. National Archives, INF 1/543.

[65] 1944 Diary (28 Mar.), Coward Archive, NPC-0456.

[66] 1944 Diary (6 June, 24 May), Coward Archive, NPC-0456.

[67] Tuchman, *Sand Against the Wind*, p. 452.

[68] Merriman, *Greasepaint and Cordite*, p. 247.

[69] *Autobiography*, p. 485.

[70] Anonymous to E. Dunstan [1944], Coward Archive, NPC-10380.

[71] Merriman, *Greasepaint and Cordite*, p. 247.

[72] 21 July 1944, Coward Archive, uncatalogued.

[73] 29 July 1944, *Letters*, p. 501.

[74] Quoted in *Liverpool Evening Express*, 7 Aug. 1944, p. 3; *Manchester Evening News*, 17 Aug. 1944, p. 8.

[75] *Observer*, 13 Aug. 1944, p. 2; *Sunday Times*, 13 Aug. 1944, p. 3.

[76] *Middle East Diary*, p. 84, p. 145, p. 140.

[77] To Jack Wilson, 17 Jan. 1945, Cadbury Research Library, COW/3/N/2/58/3.

[78] "Brooklyn Indignant", *Telegraph*, 14 Nov. 1944, p. 5.

[79] *New York Times*, 15 Nov. 1944, p. 29.

[80] Macdonald, *The True Intrepid*, p. 284.

[81] 14 Nov. 1944, Coward Archive, NPC-4395.

[82] Coward's time at Alfold seems to have escaped notice: he moved in October. See 1944 Diary.

[83] Neame, *Straight From the Horse's Mouth*, p. 82.

84 *Sunday Times*, 24 May 1936, p. 323.
85 David Lean said that not a line
was written by anyone other than
Coward, but Ronald Neame took
credit for some of the dialogue,
and Anthony Havelock-Allan,
producing, always claimed that
the adaptation was written solely
by "David, myself and Ronnie".
The title was Gladys Calthrop's
suggestion. But it is hard to imagine
that Coward exerted anything other
than the utmost control over every
last detail of the dialogue, and his
diaries relate his working on the
script, carefully and alone, through
September 1944. See Brownlow,
David Lean, pp. 194–5. The 1944
Diary (Coward Archive, NPC-
0458) shows Coward reading *Great
Expectations*, which he passed on to
Lean as a potential project (it would
be made, successfully but without
Coward's involvement, in 1946).
"Our next plan", Coward wrote, "is
an original story, *Spring Song*, a day
in the life of London, entirely shot
in the London streets." Nothing
came of it.
86 Fleming, *Celia Johnson*, p. 174.
87 Fleming, *Celia Johnson*, p. 201
88 Juliet Duff, "Winston: The Family
Man", *Sunday Times*, 31 Jan. 1965,
p. 11.
89 *Diaries* (2 May 1945), p. 26.
90 *Diaries* (8 Aug. 1945), p. 37.
91 *Diaries* (15 Aug. 1945), p. 37.
92 To Joyce Carey, 15 Aug. 1945,
Letters, p. 510.
93 *His Talks in Australia*, p. 23.
95 31 Oct. 1941, *Letters*, p. 429.

95 14 Sep. 1945, Coward Archive,
uncatalogued.

THE DESERT
The Peace

1 First-night speech of *Peace in Our
Time*, 22 July 1947, British Library.
2 *Daily Telegraph*, 23 July 1947, p. 5.
3 Grenfell, *Darling Ma*, pp. 293–4, p.
158.
4 1943 Diary (9 Dec.), Coward
Archive, NPC-0456.
5 *Diaries* (19 May 1945), p. 31.
6 *Diaries* (19 Dec. 1949), p. 138.
7 *His Talks in Australia*, p. 41.
8 See 1945 Diary (1 Oct.), Coward
Archive, NPC-0444.
9 "A lovely book with really exquisite
writing. He handles his Catholic
propaganda so delicately that it is
almost painless. A fine achievement." 1945 Diary (18 June),
Coward Archive, NPC-0444.
10 *Middle East Diary*, p. 141.
11 Undated, West Papers, Gen MSS
105 Box 7, f. 213.
12 *Diaries* (23 Sep. 1947), p. 92.
13 *Diaries* (3 Jan. 1947), p. 77.
14 17 June [1930s?], Coward Archive,
NPC-0301.
15 1945–6 correspondence, Coward
Archive, NPC-10532, 0317.
16 To Mary Martin, 28 Jan. 1947,
Letters, p. 526.
17 Phipps, *Molly Keane*, pp. 181–2.
18 See Hoare, *Noël Coward*, pp. 357–9.
19 1941 Diary (9 Sep.), Coward
Archive, NPC-0453.
20 *New York Times*, 21 Feb. 1948, p. 8
21 Gyles Brandreth, "Noël Coward and
Friends: Interview with Graham

Payn", 1999 (gylesbrandreth.net/ blog/2018/4/26/Noël-coward-friends, accessed Feb. 2022).

22 Payn, *My Life with Noël Coward*, p. x.

23 1942 Diary (1 Sep.), Coward Archive, NPC-0455.

24 *Diaries* (10 Sep. 1948), p. 60.

25 *Diaries* (23 Dec. 1946), p. 73.

26 Lesley, *The Life of Noël Coward*, pp. 236–7; Hoare, *Noël Coward*, p. 359.

27 Lesley, *The Life of Noël Coward*, p. 234.

28 1943 Diary (3 April), Coward Archive, NPC-0441.

29 *Diaries* (5 Feb. 1952), p. 188.

30 25 Feb. 1946, Cadbury Research Library, COW/3/N/2/58/3.

31 Wilson to Coward, 25 Mar. 1946; Lawrence to Wilson, 7 Nov. 1950, Cadbury Research Library, COW/3/N/2/58/3.

32 *Diaries* (8 Oct., 12 Oct. 1948), p. 93, p. 95.

The Island

1 To the Lunts, 27 Feb. [1949], Lunt Papers, MS 662, Box 2, Folder 17.

2 Redgrave, *In My Mind's Eye*, p. 187.

3 Guinness, *Blessings in Disguise*, p. 201.

4 Interviewed on *Person to Person*, CBS, 27 April 1956.

5 1944 Diary (3 June 1944), Coward Archive, NPC-0457.

6 *Diaries* (30 Jan. 1948), p. 103.

7 1955 Diary (10 Nov.), Coward Archive, NPC-0473.

8 1963 Diary (5 Aug.), Coward Archive, NPC-0483.

9 *Diaries* (15 Jan. 1954), p. 254.

10 *Diaries*, 6 May 1947, p. 85.

11 *Daily Telegraph*, 4 May 1951, p. 6.

12 20 August 1951, quoted in Mander

and Mitchenson, *Theatrical Companion to Coward*, p. 415.

13 [June 1951], Cadbury Research Library, COW/3/N/2/58/4. The letter exists in three drafts, decreasing in bitterness, and it is not clear which was sent. On 28 June 1951 Wilson replied: "We are of course desolate with grief. Natasha has been in floods of tears all the morning, and I have remained dry-eyed, but very, very sick inside."

The Butler

1 *Diaries* (29 Nov. 1951), p. 181.

2 *Sunday Times*, 2 Dec. 1951, p. 2.

3 Michael Billington, "Relative Values", *Guardian*, 14 Apr. 2014.

4 *Flight of Fancy*, 28 Sep. 1950, Cadbury Research Library, COW/3/N/1/12.

5 Philip Howard, "A brief encounter with The Master", *The Times*, 13 Nov. 1969, p. 3.

6 "A Dialogue on Dramatic Poetry" (1928), in Eliot, *Complete Prose*, 3, p. 397.

7 *Diaries* (11 Feb. 1950), p. 142; T. S. Eliot to Charles Brooks, 25 Feb. 1944, private collection. Eliot's lover, Emily Hale (a drama teacher at Vermont) had performed Elvira in *Blithe Spirit* in 1946.

8 Rattigan, "Noël Coward", p. 6.

9 *The Times*, 13 September 1952, p. 2.

10 *Letters*, pp. 555–63.

11 Peters, *Design for Living*, p. 248.

12 *Diaries* (26 Feb. 1952), p. 190.

13 Beaton, *Self Portrait with Friends*, p. 11, p. 12.

14 Vickers, *Cecil Beaton*, p. 39, p. 289.

[15] Vickers, *Cecil Beaton*, p. 90.

[16] 16 Mar. 1952, *Letters*, p. 551.

[17] Vickers, *Cecil Beaton*, p. 357.

[18] 8 Mar. [1951], Dane Letters, OSB MSS 245 Box F.

[19] *Diaries* (6 Sep. 1952), p. 198.

[20] 7 Nov. 1950, Coward Archive, NPC-7738.

[21] *The Times*, 8 Sep. 1952, p. 6.

[22] 18 Oct. 1952, Coward Archive, NPC-0225.

[23] *Diaries* (1 July 1954), p. 239.

The Desert

[1] John Heilpern, "Coward at 70", *Observer*, 7 Dec. 1969, p. 40.

[2] Harold Hobson, *Sunday Times*, 10 May 1953, p. 11.

[3] 9 Sep. 1953, Coward Archive, NPC-5785.

[4] *Diaries*, 14 July 1946, p. 60.

[5] Castle, *Noël*, p. 213.

[6] 24 May 1954, *Letters*, p. 582.

[7] Hackforth, *"And the next object…"*, p. 168.

[8] Kenneth Tynan, "Exit a man…", *Observer*, 1 April 1973, p. 13.

[9] Hackforth, *"And the next object…"*, p. 148, p. 158.

[10] *The Times*, 31 Mar. 1954, p. 10.

[11] *Diaries* (3 Dec. 1954), p. 246.

[12] Tynan, *Tynan on Theatre*, p. 287.

[13] *Diaries* (12 Jun. 1955), p. 269.

[14] *Diaries* (10 Nov. 1955), p. 291.

[15] See Tynan, *Diaries*, p. 312.

[16] See *Rave*, Oct. 1955; *Top Secret*, Aug. 1957, p. 10.

[17] 1953 Diary (23 Oct.), Coward Archive, NPC-0470. The entry bears no resemblance to an apparent diary entry on Gielgud's arrest published by Sheridan Morley in 2001 (see Morley, *John G*, p. 252), which I was unable to locate.

[18] 1955 Diary (10 Nov.), Coward Archive, NPC-0473.

[19] Tynan, *Tynan on Theatre*, p. 287.

[20] See Jon Thurber, "Desert Dandy", in *Los Angeles Times*, 17 December 2005.

The Entertainer

[1] Heilpern, *John Osborne*, p. 135.

[2] To Lorn Loraine, 17 July 1956, *Letters*, p. 615.

[3] To Laurence Olivier, 14 Feb 1957, *Letters*, p. 619.

[4] 12 Jan. 1957, *Letters*, p. 617.

[5] See correspondence with Olivier, Coward Archive.

[6] *Diaries* (19 Aug. 1955), p. 280.

[7] Vickers, *Vivien Leigh*, p. 216.

[8] *Diaries* (17 Feb. 1957), p. 349.

[9] *Diaries* (13 Oct. 1957), p. 365.

[10] *Diaries* (13 May 1962), p. 505.

[11] *Diaries* (5 May 1959), p. 408.

[12] *Diaries* (1 June 1949), p. 128.

[13] *Diaries* (6 Aug. 1960; 2 May 1960), pp. 444–5, p. 436.

[14] *Diaries* (27 Mar. 1960), p. 431.

[15] See Heilpern, *John Osborne*, p. 20.

[16] To Ann Fleming. 11 Feb. 1956 (Fleming, *The Man With The Golden Typewriter*, p. 115).

[17] To Gladys Calthrop, July 1956, Calthrop Papers, MS201/1/39-40.

[18] 14 Jan. 1956, Coward Archive, NPC-1788.

[19] 12 Jan. 1957, *Letters*, p. 617.

[20] "Mr Noël Coward's Decision", *The Times*, 2 Oct. 1956, p. 9 (see also *The Times*, 26 Sep. 1956, p. 7).

[21] *Daily Mirror*, 18 May 1956, p. 3.

[22] Quoted in Croall, *John Gielgud*, p. 423. See also pp. 422–4.

[23] *Letters*, p. 620.

The Actor

[1] *Diaries* (26 Oct. 1957), p. 366.

[2] *New York Times*, 15 Nov. 1957, p. 36.

[3] See Hoare, *Noël Coward*, pp. 441–5.

[4] *Diaries* (21 July 1957), p. 361.

[5] Brandreth, "Noël Coward and Friends".

[6] Lesley, *The Life of Noël Coward*, p. 95.

[7] *Diaries* (1 Dec. 1957), pp. 368–9.

[8] *Diaries* (8 Dec. 1950), pp. 160–61.

[9] A suggestion first made by Peter Conrad in the *Guardian*, 2 Dec. 2007.

[10] To Clifton Webb, May 1947, *Letters*, p. 633.

[11] Kenneth Tynan, "Exit a man...", *Observer*, 1 April 1973, p. 13.

[12] See the (explicit) account in Tynan, *Diaries*, p. 359.

[13] Michael Billington first noticed this precise antithesis (*Guardian*, 17 Aug. 2012).

[14] *Diaries* (26 Jan. 1958), p. 374.

[15] 1958 Diary (8 Feb.), Coward Archive, NPC-0476.

[16] 1958 Diary (8 Feb.), Coward Archive, NPC-0476.

[17] 1958 Diary (16 Feb.), Coward Archive, NPC-0476.

[18] 1958 Diary (30 Mar.), Coward Archive, NPC-0476.

[19] [Mar. 1958], Coward Archive, NPC-10825.

[20] Susan Traylor, personal communication.

[21] 10 Jan. 1960, Coward Archive, NPC-9689.

The Mountain

[1] *Diaries* (1 May 1958), p. 378.

[2] 1959 Diary (28 June), Coward Archive, NPC-0477.

[3] To Lorn Loraine, 16 Sep. 1958, Cadbury Research Library, COW/4/1/3/1.

[4] 16 Apr. 1958, Dane Letters, OSB MSS 245 Box F.

[5] See Guinness, *Blessings in Disguise*, pp. 203–4.

[6] *Diaries* (26 Apr. 1959), p. 407.

[7] *New York Times*, 15 July 1959, p. 26.

[8] *Manchester Guardian*, 15 July 1959, p. 5.

[9] I'm grateful to John Hunter Knowles for his You Tube video ("Chalet Coward Les Avants", accessed May 2021), an invaluable help to one who could not get to Switzerland in person and which preserves footage of the interiors before a recent sale.

[10] *The Times*, 3 Nov. 1960, p. 15.

[11] *Letters*, p. 699.

[12] Kenneth Tynan, "Exit a man...", *Observer*, 1 April 1973, p. 13.

The Wings

[1] To Margaret Webster, [Jan. 1960], *Letters*, p. 664.

[2] [Apr. 1960], Cadbury Research Library, COW/4/1/3/1.

[3] *Diaries* (22 Apr. 1960), p. 434.

[4] [Oct. 1957], *Letters*, p. 638.

[5] Webster, *Don't Put Your Daughter on the Stage*, p. 314.

[6] *Diaries* (11 Sep. 1960), p. 447.

[7] Collated in Mander and Mitchenson, *Theatrical Companion to Coward*, p. 486.

[8] 3 Jan. 1961, Coward Archive, NPC-0763.

9 Lawrence, *A Star Danced*, p. 185.

10 *Diaries* (1 Jan. 1961), p. 461.

11 24 Oct. 1960, 7 July 1964, Coward Archive, NPC-1015, -1266.

12 *Sunday Times*, 22 Jan. 1961, p. 34.

13 See *Sunday Times*, 15 Jan. 1961, p. 23; 22 Jan. 1961, p. 23; 29 Jan. 1961, p. 24.

14 *Diaries* (5 Feb. 1961), p. 464.

15 21 Aug. 1962, *Letters*, p. 679.

16 As told to John Lahr, in Lahr, "Introduction", p. xi.

17 To Lorn Loraine, 26 Feb. [1962], Cadbury Research Library, COW/4/1/3/1.

18 [Nov. 1961], Cadbury Research Library, COW/4/1/3/1.

19 See *Diaries*, p. 315.

20 Feb., 9 Aug. 1957, Coward Archive, NPC-10047, -10049.

21 *Diaries* (2 Nov. 1961), pp. 485–6.

THE LIVING MASK

1 *Plays*, 5, p. 529.

2 *Sunday Times*, 5 May 1963, p. 41.

3 *Telegraph*, 4 July 1963, p. 14; *The Times*, 26 Apr. 1963; *Guardian*, 4 July 1963, p. 7.

4 *Diaries* (24 Oct. 1962; 12 Jan. 1963), p. 516, p. 525.

5 *Yorkshire Evening Post*, 27 Sep. 1924, p. 6.

6 See "Twiggy on her friendship with Noël Coward", *Independent*, 17 Nov. 2015.

7 Davies, *Living on a Thin Line*, p. 117; Ray Davies interviewed in *Hampstead and Highgate Express*, 28 June 2013.

8 Edward Albee, "Introduction" [1964] to Coward, *Three Plays* (New York: Dell Publishing, 1965), p. 5.

9 To Laurence Olivier, 15 Apr. 1964, *Letters*, p. 720.

10 Coveney, *Maggie Smith*, p. 88.

11 [Nov. 1964], *Letters*, p. 722.

12 *Letters*, p. 723, and Coward Archive, NPC-1476.

13 A review of *Hay Fever* [1964], quoted in *New York Times*, 8 May 1983, p. 1.

14 2 Dec. 1964, Coward Archive, NPC-4338.

15 *Diaries* (14 Sep, 2 Sep, 1963), p. 545, p. 543.

16 See correspondence with the Lunts, 1951, Lunt papers, MMS 662, Box 2, Folder 17.

17 Massey (Anna), *Telling Some Tales*, pp. 83–4.

18 Whitelaw, *Who He?*, pp. 91–2.

19 [Aug. 1959], *Letters*, p. 660.

20 Autumn 1962, *Letters*, pp. 84–7. See also Salter, *The Last Years of a Rebel*, pp. 156–8.

21 *Diaries* (21 Nov. 1962), p. 518.

22 24 May 1966, *Letters*, pp. 234–5.

23 Osborne to Coward, 3 Aug. 1968, Coward Archive, NPC-8635.

24 Heilpern, *John Osborne*, p. 190.

25 *Diaries* (3 Aug. 1965, 2 May 1960), p. 605, p. 436.

26 *Diaries* (29 July 1962), p. 510; Harold Pinter to Coward, 27 July [1961], Coward Archive, NPC-7004.

27 Hall, *Diaries*, p. 236.

28 *Diaries* (10 Apr. 1964), p. 562.

29 *Diaries* (27 Jul. 1969), p. 679.

30 *Diaries* (28 Feb. 1965), p. 593. Also *Letters*, p. 725.

31 Elizabeth, The Queen Mother, *Counting One's Blessings*, p. 530 and 530n.

32 *Diaries* (4 Apr. 1965), p. 596.

33 14 Apr. 1965, Coward Archive, NPC-1523.

34 To Gladys Calthrop [May 1965], *Letters*, p. 731.

35 *Diaries* (13 Feb. 1966), p. 624.

36 Vivian Matalon, "After the Joking", *New York Times*, 24 Feb. 1974, p. 1.

37 *Plays*, 5, p. 410.

38 "The Sixth Veil", scenario, Cadbury Research Library, COW/3/N/1/41.

39 10 Feb. 1960, Cadbury Research Library, COW/4/1/3/1.

40 Cecil, *Max*, pp. 492–3.

41 Hugh Curnow, "Coward by Coward", *Sunday Telegraph*, 22 May 1966, p. 6.

42 Vivian Matalon, "After the Joking", *New York Times*, 24 Feb. 1974, p. 1.

43 *The Stage*, 21 April 1966, p. 13.

44 *The Stage*, 21 April 1966, p. 13; *The Times*, 15 April 1966, p. 16.

45 *Daily Telegraph*, 15 Apr. 1966, p. 21.

46 *Diaries* (19 Apr. 1966), pp. 629–30.

47 Palmer, *Change Lobsters and Dance*, p. 360.

48 Vivian Matalon, "After the Joking", *New York Times*, 24 Feb. 1974, p. 1.

49 Connon, *Beverley Nichols*, p. 272.

50 [early 60s?], Maugham Papers, Box 1, Folder 35.

51 29 Aug. 1965, West Collection.

52 Hugh Curnow, "Coward by Coward", *Sunday Telegraph*, 22 May 1966, p. 6.

53 *Plays*, 5, p. 439.

54 "The Sixth Veil", scenario, Cadbury Research Library, COW/3/N/1/41.

55 *Plays*, 5, p. 471.

56 John Heilpern, "Coward at 70…", *Observer*, 7 Dec. 1969, p. 40.

57 Stella King, "Noël Coward", *The Times*, 26 July 1966, p. 15.

58 *Diaries* (24 Nov. 1966), p. 641.

59 Hunting, *Adventures of a Gentleman's Gentleman*, p. 127.

60 [Apr. 1960], *Letters*, p. 671.

61 Lesley, *The Life of Noël Coward*, p. 23.

62 27 Dec. 1966, Calthrop Papers, MS 201/1/65.

63 Coward's unpublished diaries record his enjoyment of her work; in 1937 he had written to her publisher to request copies of her *Novel on Yellow Paper*, saying it was "a brilliant and original book, although at moments a trifle self-conscious. As an exposé of Stevie Smith's mind it is extraordinary and she has a wise, witty and entrancing mind." 7 Jan. 1937, McFarlin Library, University of Tulsa.

64 John Coleman, "Coward at Sea", *Observer*, 3 Dec. 1967, p. 27.

65 *Age Cannot Wither*, Cadbury Research Library, COW/1/A/3.

66 *Diaries* (3 Dec. 1967), p. 657.

67 [late 1960s?], Calthrop Papers, MS201/1/31.

68 25 Feb. 1969, Calthrop Papers, MS201/1/66.

69 Philip Howard, "A Brief Encounter with The Master", *The Times*, 13 Nov. 1969, p. 3.

70 Hunter Davies, "Life and Opinions of Noël Coward", *Sunday Times*, 16 Nov. 1969, p. 49.

71 Howard, "A Brief Encounter…", p. 3; Davies, "Life and Opinions…", p. 49.

72 David Hare, "And against…", *Times Literary Supplement*, 1 Oct. 1982, p. 14.

[73] Mel Gussow, "Coward", *New York Times*, 11 Feb. 1970, p. 38.

[74] Davies, "Life and Opinions…", p. 49.

[75] John Heilpern, "Coward at 70", *Observer*, 7 Dec. 1969, p. 40.

[76] Stella King, "Noël Coward", *The Times*, 26 July 1966, p. 15.

[77] Hare, *Obedience, Struggle and Revolt*, p. 43.

[78] "Celebrating Noël", *Sunday Telegraph*, 14 Dec. 1969, p. 11.

[79] 1968–9 correspondence, Mountbatten Papers, MB1/K92.

[80] 1970 Diary (25 Jan.), Coward Archive, NPC-0482.

[81] Archive footage discovered on YouTube (accessed June 2022).

[82] Tynan, *Diaries*, p. 371, p. 48.

[83] 7 Sep. 1972, Coward Archive, NPC-0902.

[84] 9 Apr. 1973, Calthrop Papers, MS201/3/6.

[85] Dierdre Carmody, "Katharine Cornell stars in the role of raconteur", *New York Times*, 11 Jan. 1974, 18.

[86] *New York Times*, 15 Jan. 1973, p. 20 (an article from which many details of the evening are taken). See also Lesley, *The Life of Noël Coward*, pp. 471–2.

[87] Geoffrey Johnson, personal communication, 27 Jan. 2020.

[88] 25 Mar. 1973, Coward Archive, NPC-5177.

[89] *Complete Verse*, p. 351. The poem exists in a longer version but was auctioned in its original, shorter, form.

[90] Nichols, *Are They the Same at Home?*, p. 98.

[91] Tynan, *Tynan on Theatre*, p. 288.

[92] In "The Critic as Artist", 1891.

AN AWFULLY BIG ADVENTURE

All text in this section is formed of verbatim quotations, with cuts silently implented but nothing added.

[1] Coward (Violet), *Reminiscences of Noël*, Coward Archive. Anna Eva Fay did a brief run of performances at the Coliseum in London, in January 1913. "In the second part", a review described, she was, for no apparent reason, wrapped up in a white sheet, through the folds of which she waved a thin hand and in a high voice gave answers to questions which members of the audience had written and put in their pockets." (*Pall Mall Gazette*, 14 Jan. 1913, p. 7.) Miss Fay was soon to be publically outed as a fraud whose audiences were rife with stooges relaying what was written on the slips of paper.

[2] *Diaries* (6 June 1950), p. 194.

[3] *Diaries* (27 July 1969), p. 678.

[4] From correspondence between Noël Coward and Esmé Wynne-Tyson, spanning 1936 to 1970. *Letters*, p. 31, pp. 39–46 and Wynne-Tyson, *Finding the Words*, pp. 130–48.

[5] Cole Lesley's words are from Lesley, *The Life of Noël Coward*, pp. 473–81; Graham Payn's from Payn, *My Life with Noël Coward*, pp. 243–5 and from Gyles Brandreth, "Noël Coward and Friends: Interview with Graham Payn", 1999 (https://www.gylesbrandreth.net/

blog/2018/4/26/Noël-coward-friends, accessed February 2022). Desmond Gordon's interview is in Salewicz, *Firefly*, p. 117; Miguel Fraser's in Susan Ferrier MacKay, "Blithe Spirit's Bastion", *The Globe and Mail*, 2 Dec. 1983, p. 15 (I'm grateful to Susan Ferrier MacKay for sending me a copy of this article, and for her recollections). Geoffrey Johnson's memories are from an interview with the author, 29 Oct. 2019.

6 *Diaries* (19 March 1955), p. 260.

7 See Lesley, *The Life of Noël Coward*, pp. 480–1, p. xvii; Hoare, *Noël Coward*, pp. 518–23, p. 1; Morley, *A Talent to Amuse*, p. 320, p. 169, p. 1; Fisher, *Noël Coward*, p. 233, p. 25, p. 7. Additionally, Hoare's words are taken from his article "Unbuttoning the Master", *Independent*, 18 Nov. 1995, and from his correspondence with the author, May 2019.

8 John Lahr, "Watching himself go by" (and subsequent correspondence), *London Review of Books*, 4 Dec. 1980.

9 Philip Hoare, correspondence with the author, May 2019.

10 *Diaries* (19 Mar. 1955), p. 260.

11 *Diaries* (19 Mar. 1955), p. 260.

12 Field, *The Goldfish*, p. 1.

BIBLIOGRAPHY

Diaries, letters, and editions are listed by author rather than by editor. Place of publication is London unless otherwise stated.

PUBLISHED WORK BY NOËL COWARD

Autobiography: Present Indicative [1937, pp. 1–244]; *Past Conditional* [1986, pp. 245-91]; *Future Indefinite* [1954, pp. 291–496]. Methuen, 1986, reissued 1999.

Collected Plays, 9 vols. Bloomsbury, 1979, second revised edition, 1999–2018.

Collected Revue Sketches and Parodies, ed. Barry Day. Methuen, 1999.

Collected Short Stories. Methuen, 1985.

The Complete Lyrics, ed. Barry Day. Methuen, 1998.

The Complete Verse of Noël Coward, ed. Barry Day. Methuen, 2011.

His Talks in Australia. Melbourne: Specialty Press, 1940.

The Letters of Noël Coward, ed. Barry Day. Methuen, 2007.

Middle East Diary. New York: Doubleday, 1944.

The Noël Coward Diaries, ed. Graham Payn and Sheridan Morley. Weidenfeld and Nicolson, 1982.

The Noël Coward Songbook. Michael Joseph, 1953.

Play Parade: The Collected Plays, 6 vols. William Heinemann, 1961–2.

Pomp and Circumstance [1960]. Methuen, 1999.

Screenplays, ed. Barry Day. Bloomsbury, 2015.

Three Cod Pieces: A Withered Nosegay [1922]; *Chelsea Buns* [1924]; *Spangled Unicorn* [1932]. Methuen, 1984.

Tonight at 8.30: Ten one-act plays [1936]. Methuen, 2009, second edition, 2014.

OTHER PUBLICATIONS

Albanesi, Maria. *Meggie Albanesi by Her Mother.* Hodder and Stoughton, 1926.

Aldrich, Richard Stoddard. *Gertrude Lawrence as "Mrs. A".* Odhams Press, 1955.

Amherst, Jeffery. *Wandering Abroad: The Autobiography of Jeffery Amherst.* Secker and Warburg, 1976.

Anderson, Mary Ann. *Louis Hayward: Beyond the Iron Mask.* Albany: BearManor Media, 2016.

Andrew, Christopher. *Secret Service: The Making of the British Intelligence Community.* Heinemann, 1985.

Arrighi, Gillian, and Victor Emeljanow (eds). *Entertaining Children: The Participation of Youth in the Entertainment Industry.* New York: Palgrave Macmillan, 2014.

Attenborough, Richard. *Entirely Up To You, Darling.* Hutchinson, 2008.

Bankhead, Tallulah. *Tallulah: My Autobiography.* Victor Gollancz, 1952.

Beaton, Cecil. *Self Portrait with Friends: The Selected Diaries of Cecil Beaton, 1926–1974.* Weidenfeld and Nicolson, 1979.

———— *The Unexpurgated Beaton Diaries.* Phoenix, 2003.

Behrman, S. N. *People In a Diary: A Memoir.* Boston: Little, Brown, 1972.

Bennett, Arnold. *The Journals of Arnold Bennett, 1921–1928*, ed. Newman Flower. Cassell, 1933.

Braybrooke, Patrick. *The Amazing Mr Noël Coward.* Denis Archer, 1933.

Briant, Keith. *Marie Stopes: A Biography.* The Hogarth Press, 1962.

Britten, Benjamin. *Journeying Boy: The Diaries of the Young Benjamin Britten, 1928–1938*, ed. John Evans. Faber and Faber, 2009.

Brownlow, Kevin. *David Lean: A Biography.* New York: St Martin's Press, 1996.

Brunel, Adrian. *Nice Work: The Story of Thirty Years in British Film Production.* Forbes Robertson, 1949.

Byng, Douglas. *As You Were.* Gerald Duckworth, 1970.

Calder, Robert. *Beware the British Serpent: The Role of Writers in British Propaganda in the United States, 1939–1945.* Montreal: McGill-Queen's University Press, 2004.

Carey, Martin (pseud. Geoffrey Holdsworth). *The Rest is Lies.*

Cobden-Sanderson, 1932.

Carpenter, Humphrey. *W. H. Auden: A Biography*. George Allen and Unwin, 1981.

Carrington, Dora. *Carrington's Letters*, ed. Anne Chisholm. Chatto and Windus, 2017.

Castle, Charles. *Noël*. W. H. Allen, 1972.

Castle, Terry. *Noël Coward & Radclyffe Hall: Kindred Spirits*. New York: Columbia University Press, 1996.

Cecil, David. *Max: A Biography*. Constable: 1964.

Chase, Pauline. *Peter Pan's Postbag: Letters to Pauline Chase*. William Heinemann, 1909.

Citron, Stephen. *Noël & Cole: The Sophisticates*. Sinclair Stevenson, 1992.

Cochran, Charles. *Cock-a-Doodle-Do*. J. M. Dent, 1941.

Colcough, Dyan. *Child Labor in the British Victorian Entertainment Industry: 1875–1914*. New York: Palgrave Macmillan, 2016.

Colvin, Ian. *Vansittart in Office*. Victor Gollancz, 1965.

Connon, Bryan. *Beverley Nichols: A Life*. Constable, 1991.

Cooper, Emmanuel. *The Sexual Perspective*. 1986, second edition. Routledge, 1994.

Courtney, Margaret. *Laurette*. New York: Rinehart, 1955.

Coveney, Michael. *Maggie Smith: A Biography*. Weidenfeld and Nicolson, 2015.

Croall, Jonathan. *John Gielgud: Matinee Idol to Movie Star*. Methuen Drama, 2011.

Dalton, Hugh. *The Second World War Diaries*, 1940–45, ed. Ben Pimlott. Jonathan Cape, 1986.

Davies, Dave. *Living on a Thin Line*, with Philip Clark. Headline, 2022.

DeAcosta, Mercedes. *Here Lies The Heart*, 1960. Reprint edition, Salem, New Hampshire: Ayer Company, 1990.

Dean, Basil. *Seven Ages, An Autobiography 1888–1927*. Hutchinson, 1970.

Denis, Brian. *Tallulah, Darling: A Biography of Tallulah Bankhead*. Sedgwick and Jackson, 1980.

Desmarais, Jane; Martin Postle; William Vaughan; Martin Vaughan (eds). *Model and Supermodel: The Artists' Model in British Art and Culture*. Manchester: Manchester University Press, 2006.

DeValois, Ninette. *Come Dance With Me: A Memoir 1898–1956*. Hamish Hamilton, 1957.

Donaldson, Frances. *Freddy Lonsdale*. William Heinemann, 1957.

Drake, Fabia. *Blind Fortune*. William Kimber, 1978.

Duberman, Martin B. *Paul Robeson*. New York: Ballantine Books, 1989.

Dunn, Waldo Hilary. *R. D. Blackmore: The Author of "Lorna Doone"*. Robert Hale, 1956.

Eliot, T. S. *The Complete Prose of T. S. Eliot*, ed. Ronald Schuchard et al, 8 vols. Baltimore: The Johns Hopkins University Press, 2021.

Elizabeth, The Queen Mother. *Counting One's Blessings: Selected Letters*, ed. William Shawcross. Macmillan, 2012.

Field, Lila. *The Goldfish: A Fairy Play in Three Acts*. Mills and Boon, 1910.

Findlay, Jean. *Chasing Lost Time: The Life of C. K. Scott Moncrieff*. Chatto and Windus, 2014.

Fisher, Clive. *Noël Coward*. Weidenfeld and Nicolson, 1992.

Fleming, Ian. *The Man With The Golden Typewriter: Ian Fleming's James Bond Letters*, ed. Fergus Fleming. Bloomsbury, 2015.

Fleming, Kate. *Celia Johnson: A Biography*. Orion, 1991.

García-Márquez, Vicente. *Massine*. Nick Hern Books, 1996.

Gielgud, John. *Gielgud on Gielgud: Early Stages* [1939]; *Backward Glances* [1989]. Hodder and Stoughton, 2000.

———— *Gielgud's Letters*, ed. Richard Mangan. Weidenfeld and Nicolson, 2004.

Gilbert, Martin (ed.). *Winston S. Churchill, Companion Volume V, Part 3: The Coming of War, 1936–1939*. Heinemann, 1982.

Gingold, Hermione. *How to Grow Old Disgracefully*. Victor Gollancz, 1989.

Glendinning, Victoria. *Edith Sitwell: A Unicorn Among Lions*. Weidenfeld and Nicolson, 1981.

———— *Rebecca West*. Weidenfeld and Nicolson, 1987.

Graham, Kirk Robert. *British Subversive Propaganda during the Second World War*. Switzerland: Palgrave Macmillan, 2021.

Graves, Robert and Alan Hodge. *The Long Week-End: A Social History of Great Britain, 1918–1935*. Hutchinson, 1985.

Gray, Frances. *Noël Coward*. Macmillan, 1987.

Greacen, Robert. *The Art of Noël Coward*. The Hand and Flower Press, 1953.

Grenfell, Joyce. *Darling Ma: Letters to her Mother, 1932–44*. Hodder and Stoughton, 1988.

Guerrier, Jenny and Tim. *Family Memories*. Privately printed, 2017, Guerrier collection.

Guinness, Alec. *Blessings in Disguise*. Hamish Hamilton, 1985.

Hackforth, Norman. *"And the next object. . ."* Angus and Robertson, 1975.

Hall, Peter. *Diaries: The Story of a Dramatic Battle*, second edition, ed. John Goodwin. Oberon Books, 2000.

Hand, Richard J., and Michael Wilson. *London's Grand Guignol and the Theatre of Horror.* Exeter: University of Exeter Press, 2007.

Hanson, Bruce K. *Peter Pan on Stage and Screen, 1904–2010.* Jefferson, NC: McFarland, 2011.

Harding, James. *Cochran: A Biography.* Methuen, 1988.

———— *Gerald Du Maurier: The Last Actor-Manager.* Hodder and Stoughton, 1989.

Hare, David. *Obedience, Struggle and Revolt.* Faber and Faber, 2005.

Hastings, Selina. *The Secret Lives of Somerset Maugham.* John Murray, 2009.

Hawtrey, Charles. *The Truth at Last*, ed. W. Somerset Maugham. Thornton Butterworth, 1924.

Heilpern, John. *John Osborne.* Vintage, 2008.

Hibberd, Dominic. *Wilfred Owen: A New Biography.* Weidenfeld and Nicolson, 2019.

Hoare, Philip. *Noël Coward: A Biography.* Sinclair-Stevenson, 1995.

———— *Serious Pleasures: The Life of Stephen Tennant.* Penguin, 1992.

———— "Tyson, (Dorothy Estelle) Esmé Wynne (1898-1972)", *Oxford Dictionary of National Biography*, 23 September 2004. Oxford: Oxford University Press, online edition (accessed April 2020).

———— *Wilde's Last Stand: Decadence, Conspiracy and the First World War.* Duckworth, 1998.

Holroyd, Michael. *Bernard Shaw*, 4 vols. Chatto and Windus, 1988–92.

Huggett, Richard. *Binkie Beaumont: Eminence Grise of the West End Theatre, 1933–1973.* Hodder and Stoughton, 1989.

Hunting, Guy. *Adventures of a Gentleman's Gentleman.* John Blake, 2003.

Hyde, H. Montgomery. *The Quiet Canadian: The Secret Service Story of Sir William Stephenson.* Constable, 1962.

———— *Secret Intelligence Agent.* Constable, 1982.

Isherwood, Christopher. *Diaries: Volume One, 1939–1960*, ed. Katherine Bucknell. Vintage, 1997.

Israel, Lee. *Miss Tallulah Bankhead.* W. H. Allen, 1972.

James, Elliot. *The Importance of Happiness: Noël Coward and the Actors' Orphanage.* Leicester: Matador, 2020.

Jeffery, Keith. *MI6: The History of the Secret Intelligence Service, 1909–1949.* Bloomsbury, 2010.

Joseph, Charles M. *Stravinsky Inside Out*. New Haven: Yale University Press, 2001.

June [Tripp]. *The Glass Ladder*. Heinemann, 1960.

Kaplan, Joel, and Sheila Stowell (eds). *Look Back in Pleasure: Noël Coward Reconsidered*. Methuen, 2000.

Kempson, Rachel. *A Family & its Fortunes*. Duckworth, 1986.

Kiernan, Robert F. *Noël Coward*. New York: The Ungar Publishing Company, 1986.

Lahr, John. *Coward the Playwright*. Methuen, 1982, second edition, 1999.

———— "Introduction" (pp. vii–xi), *The Noël Coward Diaries*. Second American edition. New York: Da Capo Press, 2000.

Laffey, Bruce. *Beatrice Lillie: The Funniest Woman in the World*. Robson Books, 1990.

Langguth, A. J. *Saki: A Life of Hector Hugh Monro*. Hamish Hamilton, 1981.

Lathom, Ned. *The Plays of Edward Bootle-Wilbraham and Letters Sent To His Publisher*, ed. John Hunter Knowles. Privately printed, 2002.

Lawrence, Gertrude. *A Star Danced*. W. H. Allen, 1945.

Laye, Evelyn. *Boo, To My Friends*. Hurst and Blackett, 1958.

Lesley, Cole. *The Life of Noël Coward*. Jonathan Cape, 1976.

Lesley, Cole, with Sheridan Morley and Graham Payn. *Noël Coward and His Friends*. Weidenfeld and Nicolson, 1979.

Levin, Milton. *Noël Coward*. New York: Twayne Publishers, 1968.

Lownie, Andrew. *The Mountbattens: Their Lives and Loves*. Blink Publishing, 2019.

———— *Traitor King: The Scandalous Exile of the Duke and Duchess of Windsor*. Blink Publishing, 2021.

Lycett, Andrew. *Ian Fleming*. Weidenfeld and Nicolson, 1995.

MacDermott, Norman. *Everymania: The History of the Everyman Theatre, Hampstead, 1920–1926*. The Society of Theatre Research, 1975.

Macdonald, Bill. *Intrepid's Last Secrets: Then and Now*. Manitoba: Freisen Press, 2019.

———— *The True Intrepid: Sir William Stephenson and the Unknown Agents*. British Columbia: Timberholme Books, 1998.

MacLiammóir, Micheál. *All for Hecuba: An Irish Theatrical Autobiography*. Methuen, 1947.

———— *Enter a Goldfish: Memoirs of an Irish Actor, Young and Old*. Thames and Hudson, 1977.

McGilligan, Patrick. *Alfred Hitchcock: A Life in Darkness and Light*. John Wiley, 2003.

McIntyre, Ian. *The Expense of Glory: A Life of John Reith*. Harper Collins, 1993.

Mander, Raymond, and Joe Mitchenson. *Theatrical Companion to Coward: A Pictorial Record of the Theatrical Works of Noël Coward*, 1957, second edition, ed. Barry Day and Sheridan Morley. Oberon Books, 2000.

Mannin, Ethel. *Confessions and Impressions*. Jarrolds, 1930.

———— *Young in the Twenties*. Hutchinson, 1971.

Marchant, William. *The Privilege of His Company: Noël Coward Remembered*. Weidenfeld and Nicolson, 1975.

Marsh, Edward. *A Number of People*. William Heinemann, 1939.

Massey, Anna. *Telling Some Tales*. Hutchinson, 2006.

Massey, Raymond. *A Hundred Different Lives*. Robson Books, 1979.

Massine, Léonide. *My Life in Ballet*, ed. Phyllis Hartnoll and Robert Rubens. Macmillan, 1968.

Maurois, André. *Call No Man Happy*. Jonathan Cape, 1943.

———— *Memoirs, 1885–1967*, trans. Denver Lindley. New York: Harper and Row, 1970.

Maxwell, Elsa. *R.S.V.P.: Elsa Maxwell's Own Story*. Boston: Little, Brown, 1954.

Merriman, Andy. *Greasepaint and Cordite*. Aurum, 2014.

Miles, Jonathan. *The Nine Lives of Otto Katz*. Bantam, 2010.

Mills, Clifford, and John Ramsay. *Where The Rainbow Ends*. Samuel French, 1951.

Mills, John. *Up in the Clouds, Gentlemen Please*. Weidenfeld and Nicolson, 1980.

Moorcroft Wilson, Jean. *Siegfried Sassoon: Soldier, Poet, Lover, Friend*. Duckworth Overlook, 2013.

Morley, Sheridan. *Gertrude Lawrence*. New York: McGraw-Hill Book Company, 1981.

———— *John G: The Authorised Biography of John Gielgud*. Hodder and Stoughton, 2001.

———— *A Talent to Amuse: A Life of Noël Coward*, 1969, revised edition. Dean Street Press, 2016.

Morris, Sylvia Jukes. *Rage for Fame: The Ascent of Clare Boothe Luce*. New York: Random House, 1997.

Morton, H. V. *Atlantic Meeting*. Methuen, 1942.

Munro, H. H. *see* Saki.

Murray, Nicholas. *Aldous Huxley: An English Intellectual*. Little Brown, 2002.

Neame, Ronald. *Straight From the Horse's Mouth: An Autobiography*. Lanham: The Scarecrow Press, 2003.

Nevinson, C. R. W. *Paint and Prejudice − The Life of an Artist*. New York: Harcourt, Brace & Co, 1938.

Nichols, Beverley. *Are They The Same At Home?* Jonathan Cape, 1929.

——— *The Sweet and Twenties*. Weidenfeld and Nicolson, 1958.

——— *Twenty-Five*. Jonathan Cape, 1926.

Nicholson, Virginia. *Singled Out*. Penguin, 2007.

Nicolson, Harold. *Diaries and Letters, 1939–1945*. Collins, 1967.

Noble, Peter. *Ivor Novello: Man of the Theatre*. White Lion, 1975.

Ogilvy, Ian. *Once a Saint: An Actor's Memoir*. Constable, 2016.

Olivier, Laurence. *Confessions of an Actor*. Weidenfeld and Nicolson, 1982.

Owen, Harold. *A Little Fowl Play: A Farcical Comedy in One Act*. Samuel French, 1913.

Palmer, Lilli. *Change Lobsters and Dance*. Warner Books, 1976.

Parker, Matthew. *Where Bond Was Born: Ian Fleming's Jamaica*. Hutchinson, 2014.

Payn, Graham. *My Life with Noël Coward*, with Barry Day. New York and Tonbridge, Kent: Applause Books, 1994.

Pearson, John. *The Sitwells: A Family's Biography*. New York: Harcourt Brace Jovanovich, 1980.

Peters, Margot. *Design for Living: Alfred Lunt and Lynn Fontanne, A Biography*. New York: Alfred A. Knopf, 2003.

——— *Mrs Pat: The Life of Mrs Patrick Campbell*. The Bodley Head, 1984.

Phipps, Sally. *Molly Keane*. Virago, 2017.

Pollack, Howard. *George Gershwin: His Life and Work*. Berkeley: University of California Press, 2006.

Rankin, Nicholas. *Churchill's Wizards: The British Genius for Deception, 1914–45*. Faber and Faber, 2009.

Rattigan, Terence. "Noël Coward: An Appreciation", in Raymond Mander and Joe Mitchenson, *Theatrical Companion to Coward* (Rockcliff, 1957), pp. 1–6.

Read, Anthony and David Fisher. *Colonel Z: The Secret Life of a Master of Spies*. New York: Viking, 1985.

Redgrave, Michael. *In My Mind's Eye*. Weidenfeld and Nicolson, 1983.

Rhodes James, Robert. *Bob Boothby: A Portrait*. Headline, 1992.

Riley, Kathleen. *The Astaires: Fred and Adele*. Oxford: Oxford University Press, 2012.

Robinson, John Martin. *The Country House at War*. Bodley Head, 1989.

Rorem, Ned. *The Later Diaries*. San Francisco: North Point Press, 1983.

———— *The Nantucket Diary*. San Francisco: North Point Press, 1987.

Ross Moore, James. *André Charlot: The Genius of Intimate Musical Revue*. Jefferson: McFarland, 2005.

Saki [H. H. Munro]. *The Complete Works*, introduced by Noël Coward. Doubleday, 1976.

Salewicz, Chris. *Firefly: Noël Coward in Jamaica*. Victor Gollancz, 1999.

Salter, Elizabeth. *The Last Years of a Rebel: A Memoir of Edith Sitwell*. The Bodley Head, 1967.

Sassoon, Siegfried. *Siegfried's Journey, 1916–1920*. Faber and Faber, 1945.

Schanke, Robert A. *That Furious Lesbian: The Story of Mercedes de Acosta*. Carbondale: Southern Illinois University Press, 2003.

Shepard, E.H. *Drawn From Life*. Methuen, 1961.

Sitwell, Edith. *Selected Letters*. ed. John Lehmann and Derek Parker. Macmillan, 1970.

———— *Taken Care Of: An Autobiography*. Hutchinson, 1965.

Slide, Anthony. *Lost Gay Novels: A Reference Guide to Fifty Works from the First Half of the Twentieth Century*. Routledge, 2013.

Souhami, Diana. *Gluck, 1895–1978: Her Biography*. Pandora, 1988.

Stephenson, William (ed). *British Security Coordination: The Secret History of British Intelligence in the Americas, 1940–45*. New York: Fromm International, 1999.

Stevenson, William. *A Man Called Intrepid: The Secret War*. New York and Harcourt Brace Jovanovich, 1976.

———— *Spymistress: The Life of Vera Atkins*. New York: Arcade Publishing, 2007.

Strachan, Alan. *Secret Dreams: A Biography of Michael Redgrave*. Weidenfeld and Nicolson, 2004.

Sturrock, Donald. *Storyteller: The Life of Roald Dahl*. William Collins, 2010.

Thornton, Michael. *Royal Feud: The Queen Mother and the Duchess of Windsor*. Pan, 1986.

Tippett, Michael. *Those Twentieth Century Blues: An Autobiography*. Hutchinson, 1991.

Tripp, *see* June.

Tuchman, Barbara W. *Sand Against the Wind: Stilwell and the American Experience in China, 1911–1945*. Papermac, 1991.

Tynan, Kenneth. *The Diaries of Kenneth Tynan*, ed. John Lahr. Bloomsbury, 2001.

———— *Tynan on Theatre*. Penguin Books, 1964.

Van Vechten, Carl. *The Splendid Drunken Twenties: Selections from the Daybooks, 1922–30*, ed. Bruce Kellner. Urbana and Chicago: University of Illinois Press, 2003.

Vansittart, Robert. *The Mist Procession: The Autobiography of Lord Vansittart*. Hutchinson, 1958.

Vickers, Hugo. *Cecil Beaton: A Biography*. Weidenfeld and Nicolson, 1985.
———— *Vivien Leigh*. Little, Brown, 1988.

Walpole, Hugh. *Extracts from a Diary*. Glasgow: Robert Maclehose, 1934.

Wansell, Geoffrey. *Terence Rattigan: A Biography*. Fourth Estate, 1995.

Watts, Marjorie. *Mrs Sappho: The Life of C. A. Dawson Scott, Mother of International P.E.N.* Duckworth 1987.

Webster, Margaret. *Don't Put Your Daughter on the Stage*. New York: Alfred A Knopf, 1972.

Wilson, John C. *Noël, Tallulah, Cole and Me: A Memoir of Broadway's Golden Age*, ed. Thomas S. Hischak and Jack Macauley. Lanham: Rowman and Littlefield, 2015.

Winter, Keith. *Impassioned Pygmies*. William Heinemann, 1936.

Woolf, Virginia. *The Diary of Virginia Woolf*, ed. Anne Olivier Bell, 5 vols. The Hogarth Press, 1979–85.
———— *The Letters of Virginia Woolf*, ed. Nigel Nicolson and Joanne Trautmann, 6 vols. The Hogarth Press, 1975–80.

Wynne-Tyson, Jon. *Finding the Words: A Publishing Life*. Norwich: Michael Russell, 2014.

Ziegler, Philip. *Mountbatten*. HarperCollins, 1985.
———— *Olivier*. MacLehose Press, 2013.

MANUSCRIPT SOURCES

The location is the United Kingdom unless otherwise specified.

NOËL COWARD COLLECTIONS

Cadbury Research Library, University of Birmingham
    Works (COW/1/A-C and Q)
    Published material and recordings (COW/2/D-G, P, R)
    Business records (COW/3/L-O)
    Personal papers, diaries and correspondence (COW/4/H-K)

Frederick R. Koch Collection, Beinecke Rare Book and Manuscript Library, Yale, USA
  Coward, Noël, diaries, holograph and typescript (GEN MSS 601, Boxes 358-62)

New York Public Library, USA
  Noël Coward Collection of Papers, 1919–72, Henry W. and Albert A. Berg Collection of English and American Literature (Berg Coll. MSS Coward)

Noël Coward Archive, London [privately held and catalogued]
  Coward, Violet. *Reminiscences of Noël*. Manuscript, 1933–4 (uncatalogued)
  Diaries and appointment books of NC (Section A)
  Family, inc. correspondence (Section B)
  Friends, inc. correspondence (Section C)
  Notebooks of NC (Section D)
  Estate of Cole Lesley (Section N)
  Estate of Graham Payn (Section O)

OTHER COLLECTIONS

Beaton, Cecil, papers. St John's College Archives, Cambridge.
Burckhardt, Carl, archive. University of Basel, Switzerland.
Calthrop, Gladys, papers. Cadbury Research Library, University of Birmingham.
Churchill, Winston, papers. Churchill Archives Centre, Churchill College, Cambridge.
Colefax, Sibyl, archive. Oxford Bodleian Libraries.
Cooper, Duff, papers. Churchill Archives Centre, Churchill College, Cambridge.
Dalton, Hugh, papers. The British Library of Political and Economic Science, London.
Dane, Clemence, letters from Noël Coward. Beinecke Rare Book and Manuscript Library, Yale University, USA.
Dane, Clemence, papers. Department of Theatre and Performance, Victoria and Albert Museum.
DeAcosta, Mercedes, papers. The Rosenbach, Philadelphia, USA.
Dean, Basil, papers. John Rylands Research Institute and Library, University of Manchester.

Eden, Anthony. Cadbury Research Library, University of Birmingham.

Ervine, St. John, papers. Harry Ransom Center, University of Texas at Austin, USA.

Hyde, Harford Montgomery, papers. Churchill Archives Centre, Churchill College, Cambridge.

John Lane Company Records. Harry Ransom Center, University of Texas at Austin, USA.

Kennedy, Margaret, collection. Archives and Special Collections, Somerville College, Oxford.

Lawrence, Gertrude, papers. Butler Library, University of Columbia, New York, USA.

Lillie, Beatrice, papers. New York Public Library, USA.

Lloyd, George, papers. Churchill Archives Centre, Churchill College, Cambridge.

Lord Chamberlains Plays. British Library, London.

Lunt, Alfred, and Lynn Fontanne, papers. Wisconsin Historical Society Archives, USA.

Maugham, William Somerset, papers. Howard Gotlieb Archival Research Center, Boston University, USA.

Mountbatten, Louis and Edwina, papers. Hartley Library, Archives and Manuscripts, University of Southampton.

National Archives, Kew.

Nichols, Beverley, papers. University of Delaware Library.

Olivier, Laurence, archive. British Library, London.

Pepper, Claude, papers. Florida State University Libraries, USA.

Shaw, George Bernard, papers. Harry Ransom Center, University of Texas at Austin, USA.

Stern, G. B, collection, Howard Gotlieb Archival Research Center, Boston University, USA.

Stuart, Campbell, The Private Papers. Imperial War Museum Collections, London.

Vansittart, Robert, papers. Churchill Archives Centre, Churchill College, Cambridge.

West, Rebecca, collection. McFarlin Library, University of Tulsa, Oklahoma, USA.

West, Rebecca, papers. Beinecke Rare Book and Manuscript Library, Yale University, USA.

Willert, Gp Capt Paul Odo, collection. Hart Liddell Military Archives,

King's College London.

Wilson, John C., papers. Beinecke Rare Book and Manuscript Library, Yale University, USA.

Woollcott, Alexander, correspondence. Houghton Library, Harvard University, USA.

Wynne, Esmé, and Noël Coward collection. Department of Theatre and Performance, Victoria and Albert Museum, London.

Wynne-Tyson, Esmé, collection. Sussex Records Centre, Chichester.

Changes in money value calculated by www.measuringworth.com

Much use has been made of www.findmypast.co.uk: England, Wales & Scotland Census, 1901, 1911, 1921; Passenger Lists leaving the UK, 1890-1960

INDEX